Acclaim for **Richard's Russo's**

NOBODY'S FOOL

"The fun of this novel is in hearing these guys (and women) talk...they're funny, quick and inventive. The novel's tone has the same...intelligence as its characters." —*The New York Times Book Review*

"Reading this large, comfortable, good-natured novel...feels great....[It] teems with local characters...richly conceived and drawn so lovingly that you can't help but like them." —*Philadelphia Inquirer*

"[Sully is] reminiscent, in a way, of Bellow's old men....One never tires of watching him, because he has the capacity to make everyone around him feel better, including the reader." —*The New Yorker*

"Few novelists plow this soil with more even-handed ease and naturalness than Russo....He demonstrates a rare ability to find affection for even his most empty [characters] while questioning the choices of those he most values....His success in keeping us involved is especially impressive." —*Chicago Sun-Times*

"*Nobody's Fool* is a giant hard-edged comedy, a Flannery O'Connor story taken north and gone ballistic....Russo's smart prose gives Sully's, and everyone else's, dim propsects a witty, allegorical weight." —*Mirabella*

"Richard Russo [is] a masterful storyteller with a mission: to chronicle with insight and compassion the day-to-day life of small town America....He is compulsively readable....Alternating episodes of boisterous humor with moments of heart-wrenching pathos, he captures with perfection the pulse of small-town life and the rhythm of dramatically changing seasons....His characters are wholly sympathetic, but they also are human." —*Houston Chronicle*

"An intelligently drawn portrait...What has made Russo's work so consistently compelling is the depth of character, the richness of life." —*Minneapolis Star Tribune*

Richard Russo

NOBODY'S FOOL

Richard Russo lives in coastal Maine with his wife and their two daughters. He has written five novels: *Mohawk, The Risk Pool, Nobody's Fool, Straight Man,* and *Empire Falls,* and a collection of stories, *The Whore's Child.*

NOBODY'S FOOL

WIDDOM'S FOOL

NOBODY'S
FOOL

Richard Russo

VINTAGE CONTEMPORARIES

Vintage Books

A Division of Random House, Inc.

New York

FOR JEAN LEVARN FINDLAY

FIRST VINTAGE CONTEMPORARIES EDITION, MAY 1994

Copyright © 1993 by Richard Russo

Library of Congress Cataloging-in-Publication Data
Russo, Richard, 1949–
Nobody's fool / Richard Russo. — 1st Vintage Contemporaries ed.
p. cm.
Reprint. Previously published: New York: Random House, ©1993.
ISBN 0-679-75333-8
1. City and town life—New York (State)—Fiction.   I. Title.
[PS3568.U812N6   1994]
813'.54— dc20   93-42193
CIP

Author photograph © Jere DeWaters

ACKNOWLEDGMENTS

The author gratefully acknowledges generous support from the John Simon Guggenheim Foundation and Southern Illinois University in Carbondale. Thanks also to Linda Stuart and Alan Rancourt for advice on technical matters. Gratitude as well for coffee and understanding to the staffs of Cristaudos and Denny's in Carbondale and The Open Hearth in Waterville. And, for priceless faith and encouragement, my dearest thanks to Nat Sobel, Judith Weber, Craig Holden, David Rosenthal and, always, my wife, Barbara.

PART ONE

WEDNESDAY

Upper Main Street in the village of North Bath, just above the town's two-block-long business district, was quietly residential for three more blocks, then became even more quietly rural along old Route 27A, a serpentine two-lane blacktop that snaked its way through the Adirondacks of northern New York, with their tiny, down-at-the-heels resort towns, all the way to Montreal and prosperity. The houses that bordered Upper Main, as the locals referred to it—although Main, from its "lower" end by the IGA and Tastee Freez through its upper end at the Sans Souci, was less than a quarter mile—were mostly dinosaurs, big, aging clapboard Victorians and sprawling Greek Revivals that would have been worth some money if they were across the border in Vermont and if they had not been built as, or converted into, two- and occasionally three-family dwellings and rented out, over several decades, as slowly deteriorating flats. The most impressive feature of Upper Main was not its houses, however, but the regiment of ancient elms, whose upper limbs arched over the steeply pitched roofs of these elderly houses, as well as the street below, to green cathedral effect, bathing the street in breeze-blown shadows that masked the peeling paint and rendered the sloping porches and crooked eaves of the houses quaint in their decay. City people on their way north, getting off the interstate in search of food and fuel, often slowed as they drove through the village and peered nostalgically out their windows at the old houses, wondering idly what they cost and what they must be like inside and what it would be like to live in them and walk to the village in the shade. Surely this would be a better life. On their way back to the city after the long weekend, some of the most powerfully affected briefly considered getting off the interstate again to repeat the experience, perhaps even look into the real estate market. But then they remembered how the exit had been tricky, how North Bath hadn't been all that close to the highway, how they were getting back to the city later than they planned as it was, and how difficult it would be to articulate to the kids in the backseat why they would even want to make such a detour for the privilege of driving up a tree-lined street for all of three blocks, before turning around and heading back to the interstate. Such towns were pretty, green graves, they knew, and so the impulse to take a second look died unarticulated and the cars flew by the North Bath exit without slowing down.

Perhaps they were wise, for what attracted them most about the three-block stretch of Upper Main, the long arch of giant elms, was largely a deceit, as those who lived beneath them could testify. For a long time the trees had been the pride of the neighborhood, having miraculously escaped the blight of Dutch elm disease. Only recently, without warning, the elms had turned sinister. The winter of 1979 brought a terrible ice storm, and the following summer the leaves on almost half of the elms strangled on their branches, turning sickly yellow and falling during the dog days of August instead of mid-October. Experts were summoned, and they arrived in three separate vans, each of which sported a happy tree logo, and the young men who climbed out of these vans wore white coats, as if they imagined themselves doctors. They sauntered in circles around each tree, picked at its bark, tapped its trunk with hammers as if the trees were suspected of harboring secret chambers, picked up swatches of decomposing leaves from the gutters and held them up to the fading afternoon light.

One white-coated man drilled a hole into the elm on Beryl Peoples' front terrace, stuck his gloved index finger into the tree, then tasted, making a face. Mrs. Peoples, a retired eighth-grade teacher who had been watching the man from behind the blinds of her front room since the vans arrived, snorted. "What did he expect it to taste like?" she said out loud. "Strawberry shortcake?" Beryl Peoples, "Miss Beryl" as she was known to nearly everyone in North Bath, had been living alone long enough to have grown accustomed to the sound of her own voice and did not always distinguish between the voice she heard in her ears when she spoke and the one she heard in her mind when she thought. It was the same person, to her way of thinking, and she was no more embarrassed to talk to herself than she was to think to herself. She was pretty sure she couldn't stifle one voice without stifling the other, something she had no intention of doing while she still had so much to say, even if she was the only one listening.

For instance, she would have liked to tell the young man who tasted his glove and made a face that she considered him to be entirely typical of this deluded era. If there was a recurring motif in today's world, a world Miss Beryl, at age eighty, was no longer sure she was in perfect step with, it was cavalier open-mindedness. "How do you know what it's like if you don't try it?" was the way so many young people put it. To Miss Beryl's way of thinking—and she prided herself on being something of a free-thinker—you often *could* tell, at least if you were paying attention, and the man who'd just tasted the inside of the tree and made a face had no more reason to be disappointed than her friend Mrs. Gruber, who'd announced in a loud voice in the main dining room of the Northwoods Motor Inn that she didn't care very much for either the taste or the texture of the snail she'd just spit into her napkin. Miss Beryl had been unmoved by her friend's grimace. "What was there about the way it looked that made you think it *would* be good?"

Mrs. Gruber had not responded to this question. Having spit the snail into the napkin, she'd become deeply involved with the problem of what to do with the napkin.

"It was gray and slimy and nasty looking," Miss Beryl reminded her friend.

Mrs. Gruber admitted this was true, but went on to explain that it wasn't so much the snail itself that had attracted her as the name. "They got their own name in French," she reminded Miss Beryl, stealthily exchanging her soiled cloth napkin for a fresh one at an adjacent table. *"Escargot."*

There's also a word in English, Miss Beryl had pointed out. Snail. Probably horse doo had a name in French also, but that didn't mean God intended for you to eat it.

Still, she was privately proud of her friend for trying the snail, and she had to acknowledge that Mrs. Gruber was more adventurous than most people, including two named Clive, one of whom she'd been married to, the other of whom she'd brought into the world. Where was the middle ground between a sense of adventure and just plain sense? Now there was a human question.

The man who tasted the inside of the elm must have been an even bigger fool than Mrs. Gruber, Miss Beryl decided, for he'd no sooner made the face than he took off his work glove, put his finger back into the hole and tasted again, probably to ascertain whether the foul flavor had its origin in the tree or the glove. To judge from his expression, it must have been the tree.

After a few minutes the white-coated men collected their tools and reloaded the happy tree vans. Miss Beryl, curious, went out onto the porch and stared at them maliciously until one of the men came over and said, "Howdy."

"Doody," Miss Beryl said.

The young man looked blank.

"What's the verdict?" she asked.

The young man shrugged, bent back at the waist and looked up into the grid of black branches. "They're just old, is all," he explained, returning his attention to Miss Beryl, with whom he was approximately eye level, despite the fact that he was standing on the bottom step of her front porch while she stood at the top. "Hell, this one here"—he pointed at Miss Beryl's elm—"if it was a person, would *be* about eighty."

The young man made this observation without apparent misgiving, though the tiny woman to whom he imparted the information, whose back was shaped like an elbow, was clearly the tree's contemporary in terms of his own analogy. "We could maybe juice her up a little with some vitamins," he went on, "but—" He let the sentence dangle meaningfully, apparently confident that Miss Beryl possessed sufficient intellect to follow his drift. "You have a nice day," he said, before returning to his happy tree van and driving away.

If the "juicing up" had any effect, so far as Miss Beryl could tell, it was deleterious. That same winter a huge limb off Mrs. Boddicker's elm, under the weight of accumulated snow and sleet, had snapped like a brittle bone and come crashing down, not onto Mrs. Boddicker's roof but onto the roof of her neighbor, Mrs. Merriweather, swatting the Merriweather brick chimney clean off. When the chimney descended, it reduced to rubble the stone birdbath of Mrs. Gruber, the same Mrs. Gruber who had been disappointed by the snail. Since that first incident, each winter had yielded some calamity, and lately, when the residents of Upper Main peered up into the canopy of overarching limbs, they did so with fear instead of their customary religious affection, as if God Himself had turned on them. Scanning the maze of black limbs, the residents of Upper Main identified particularly dangerous-looking branches in their neighbors' trees and recommended costly pruning. In truth, the trees were so mature, their upper branches so high, so distant from the elderly eyes that peered up at them, that it was anybody's guess as to which tree a given limb belonged, whose fault it would be if it descended.

The business with the trees was just more bad luck, and, as the residents of North Bath were fond of saying, if it weren't for bad luck they wouldn't have any at all. This was not strictly true, for the community owed its very existence to geological good fortune in the form of several excellent mineral springs, and in colonial days the village had been a summer resort, perhaps the first in North America, and had attracted visitors from as far away as Europe. By the year 1800 an enterprising businessman named Jedediah Halsey had built a huge resort hotel with nearly three hundred guest rooms and named it the Sans Souci, though the locals had referred to it as Jedediah's Folly, since everyone knew you couldn't fill three hundred guest rooms in the middle of what had so recently been wilderness. But fill them Jedediah Halsey did, and by the 1820s several other lesser hostelries had sprung up to deal with the overflow, and the dirt roads of the village were gridlocked with the fancy carriages of people come to take the waters of Bath (for that was the village's name then, just Bath, the "North" having been added a century later to distinguish it from another larger town of the same name in the western part of the state though the residents of North Bath had stubbornly refused the prefix). And it was not just the healing mineral waters that people came to take, either, for when Jedediah Halsey, a religious man, sold the Sans Souci, the new owner cornered the market in distilled waters as well, and during long summer evenings the ballroom and drawing rooms of the Sans Souci were full of revelers. Bath had become so prosperous that no one noticed when several other excellent mineral springs were discovered a few miles north near a tiny community that would become Schuyler Springs, Bath's eventual rival for healing waters. The owners of the Sans Souci and the residents of Bath remained literally without care until 1868, when the unthinkable began to happen and the various mineral springs, one by one, without warning or apparent reason, began, like luck, to dry up, and with them the town's wealth and future.

As luck (what else would you call it?) would have it, the upstart Schuyler Springs was the immediate beneficiary of Bath's demise. Even though their origin was the same fault line as the Bath mineral springs', the Schuyler springs continued to flow merrily, and so the visitors whose fancy carriages had for so long pulled into the long circular drive before the front entrance of the Sans Souci now stayed on the road another few miles and pulled into the even larger and more elegant hotel in Schuyler Springs that had been completed (talk about luck!) the very year that the springs in Bath ran dry. Well, maybe it wasn't exactly luck. For years the town of Schuyler Springs had been making inroads, its downstate investors and local businessmen promoting other attractions than those offered by the Sans Souci. In Schuyler Springs there were prizefights held throughout the summer season, as well as gambling, and, most exciting of all, a track was under construction for racing Thoroughbred horses. The citizens of Bath had been aware of these enterprises, of course, and had been watching, gleefully at first, and waiting for them to fail, for the schemes of the Schuyler Springs group struck them as even more foolish than the Sans Souci with its three hundred rooms had been. There was certainly no need for *two* resorts, two grand hotels, within so small a geographical context. Which meant that Schuyler Springs was doomed. There were limits to folly. True, Jedediah Halsey's Sans Souci hadn't been so much foolish as "visionary," which, as everyone knew, was what you called a foolish idea that worked anyway. And, people were quick to point out after the springs ran dry and the visitors moved on, the Sans Souci hadn't so much worked as it had enjoyed temporary success. The vast majority of its nearly five hundred rooms (for the hotel had expanded on a very grand scale, not three years before the springs went dry) were now empty, just as everyone had originally predicted they would be. And so people began to congratulate themselves on their original wisdom, and the residents of the once lucky, now tragically unlucky, community of Bath sat back and waited for their luck to change again. It did not.

By 1900 Schuyler Springs had swept the field of its competitors. The Sans Souci fire of 1903 was the symbolic finish, but of course the battle had long been lost, and most everyone agreed that you couldn't really count the Sans Souci fire as bad luck, since the blaze had almost certainly been started by the hotel's owner in order to collect the insurance. The man had died in the blaze, apparently trying to get it started again after it became clear that the wind had shifted and that only the old original wooden structure, not the newer, grander addition, was going to burn unless he did something creative. There is always the problem of *defining* luck as it applies to humans and human endeavors. The wind changing when you don't want it to could be construed as bad luck, but what of a man frantically rolling a drum of fuel too close to the flames he himself has set? Is he unlucky when a spark sends him to eternity?

In any case, the town of North Bath, now, in the late autumn of 1984, was still waiting for its luck to change. There were encouraging signs. A restored Sans Souci, what was left of it, was scheduled to reopen in the summer, and a new spring had been successfully drilled on the hotel's extensive grounds. And luck, so the conventional wisdom went, ran in cycles.

The morning of the day before Thanksgiving, five winters after that first elm turned on the residents of Upper Main, cleaving old Mrs. Merriweather's roof and reducing Mrs. Gruber's birdbath to rubble, Miss Beryl, always an early riser, awoke even earlier than usual, with a vague sense of unease. As she sat at the edge of her bed trying to trace its source, she had a nosebleed, a real gusher. It came upon her quickly and was just as quickly finished. She caught most of the blood with a swatch of tissue from the box she kept on her bedstand, and as soon as her nose stopped bleeding she flushed the tissue emphatically down the toilet. Was it the quick disappearance of the evidence or the nosebleed itself that left her feeling refreshed? She wasn't sure, but she felt even better after she'd bathed and dressed, and when she went into her front room to drink her tea, she was surprised and delighted to discover that it had snowed during the night. Nobody had predicted snow, but there it was anyway, the kind of heavy wet snow that sits up tall on railings and tree branches, the whole street white. In the gray predawn, everything outside looked otherworldly, and she watched the dark street and sipped her tea until a car slalomed silently by, leaving its track in the fresh snow, and the vague sense of unease she'd felt upon waking returned, though not as urgently. Who will it be this winter? she wondered, parting the blinds so she could see up into the trees.

Though Miss Beryl was far too close an observer of reality to credit the idea of divine justice in this world, there were times when she could almost see God's design hovering just out of sight. So far, she'd been lucky. God had permitted tree limbs to fall on her neighbors, not herself. But she doubted He would continue to ignore her in this business of falling limbs. This winter He'd probably lower the boom.

"This'll be my year," she said out loud, addressing her husband, Clive Sr., who sat on the television, smiling at her wisely. Dead now for twenty years, Clive Sr. could boast an even temperament. From his vantage point behind glass, nothing much got to him, and if he worried that this might be his wife's winter, he didn't show it. "You hear me, star of my firmament?" Miss Beryl prodded. When Clive Sr. had nothing to offer on this score, Miss Beryl frowned at him. "I might as well talk to Ed," she told her husband. "Go ahead, then," Clive Sr. seemed to say, safe behind his glass.

"What do you think, Ed?" Miss Beryl asked. "Is this my year?"

Driver Ed, Miss Beryl's Zamble mask, stared down at her from his perch on the wall. Ed had a dour human face modified by antelope horns and a toothed beak, all of which added up, to Miss Beryl's way of thinking, to a mortified expression. He looked, Miss Beryl had insisted when she purchased Ed over twenty years ago, like Clive Sr. had looked when he discovered he was going to be required to teach driver education at the high school. Clive Sr. had been the football coach, and his later years had not gone the way he'd planned. First, when the football team had begun to lose, he'd been required to teach civics, and when it continued to lose, he'd been required to teach driver education. Eventually, football had been dropped, a victim of declining postwar enrollments, demographic shifts, and continued humiliation at the hands of archrival Schuyler Springs, leaving Miss Beryl's husband bewildered and adrift. Driver ed turned out to be the death of him when a girl named Audrey Peach, without warning or reason, braked Clive Sr. through the front windshield of a brand-new driver ed car early one morning before he was entirely awake. Clive Sr. never wore a seat belt. He made sure his student drivers and passengers wore them, but he himself disliked the sensation of restraint. The way Clive Sr. looked at it, once he got wedged into a compact car, there was no place for him to go. A big man, he required a big car, and he suspected that the little piece of shit driver ed car the school board had purchased was a punishment for the losing seasons he was now suffering in basketball, a sport he didn't even like. Once inside the compact car, he felt so claustrophobic it was hard to concentrate on his teaching. The low roof required him to hunch forward to see where young Audrey Peach was pointed. When she hit the new brakes, the little car stopped impressively, but Clive Sr. kept going, his bullet-shaped skull punching right through the windshield, where he lodged, briefly, like a sinner in the stocks, until the car rocked and flung him back into his seat, neck broken, a bloody object lesson and the only driver ed teacher in upstate New York ever to be killed in the line of duty.

"See?" Miss Beryl addressed her husband's photograph. "Ed thinks so too."

At least, she comforted herself, when the divine boom got lowered she'd be in better financial condition to receive it than many of her neighbors. She could congratulate herself that she was not only well insured but reasonably secure. Miss Beryl, like so many of the owners of the houses along Upper Main, was a widow, technically not "Miss" Beryl at all, and her husband had left her in possession of both his VA pension and retirement, which, together with her own retirement and Social Security, added up, and she knew herself to be far better off than Mrs. Gruber and the others. Life, which in Miss Beryl's considered opinion tilted in the direction of cruelty, had at least spared her financial hardship, and she was grateful.

In other respects life had been less kind. Her being known in North Bath as "Miss" Beryl derived from the fact that the militantly unteachable eighth-grade schoolchildren she'd instructed for forty years considered her far too odd looking and misshapen to have a husband. They refused to believe it, in fact, even when confronted with irrefutable evidence. They instinctively called her Miss Peoples or Miss Beryl on the first day of class and paid no attention when she corrected them. Clive Sr. was of the opinion that kids just naturally thought of their teachers as spinsters, and he had found the whole thing amusing, often referring to her as "Miss Beryl" himself. Clive Sr. had not been a profoundly stupid man, but he missed his fair share of what Miss Beryl referred to as life's nuances, and one of the nuances he missed was the hurt he thoughtlessly inflicted on his wife when he called her by that name, a name that suggested he saw her the same way other people did. Clive Sr. was the only man who'd ever treated Miss Beryl as desirable, and it seemed to her almost unforgivable that he should, without thinking, take back the gift of his love for her in this one small way, take it back repeatedly, always with a big grin.

But he *had* loved her. This she knew, and the knowledge was another of the ways she was better off than most of her neighbors, whose husbands, when they died, left their widows alone and largely unprepared for another decade or two of solitary existence. Mrs. Gruber, for instance, had never worked outside the home and had little notion how the world operated beyond the obvious fact that it was getting more expensive. Indeed, Miss Beryl was the only professional woman among these frightened Upper Main Street widows. Alive, their husbands had protected them from life's falling limbs, but now their veteran's benefits and meager Social Security did not stretch very far, and so they rented their second-floor flats out of necessity, though the rents they received often did little more than cover the repairs necessitated by the disintegration of hundred-year-old pipes, the overloading of antiquated electrical circuits, the falling of tree limbs. To make matters worse, taxes were skyrocketing, pressured upward by down-state speculators in real estate, many of whom seemed convinced that Bath and every other small town in the corridor between New York City and Montreal would appreciate dramatically during the eighties and nineties. It might not look it, but Bath had much to recommend it. Not only was the old Sans Souci, grandly restored, scheduled to reopen next summer, but a huge tract of boggy land between the village and the interstate was being considered for development of a theme park called The Ultimate Escape. Miss Beryl's son, Clive Jr., for the last decade the president of the North Bath Savings and Loan, was leading a group of local investors to ensure that the theme park became a reality, and he subscribed enthusiastically to the view that because land was limited, the future was limitless. "In twenty years," he was fond of saying, "there's going to be no such thing as a bad location."

Miss Beryl did not argue, but neither did she share her son's opti-mism. To her way of thinking there would always be bad locations, and unless she was gravely mistaken Clive Jr. would discover this by investing in them. Clive Jr. was a cynical optimist. He believed that people went broke for two reasons: stupidity and small thinking. Stupidity in others was a good thing, according to Clive Jr., because there was money to be made by it. Other people's financial failures were opportunities, not cause for alarm. He liked to analyze failure after the fact, discover its source in small thinking, limited ambition, penny antes. He prided himself on having rescued the North Bath Savings and Loan from just such unhealthy no-tions. For years that institution had been edging by slender centimeters toward insolvency, the result of Clive Jr.'s predecessor, a deeply suspicious and pessimistic man from Maine who hated to loan people money. The fact that people came to him asking for money and often truly needing it suggested to him the likelihood of their not being able to repay it. He could see the need in their eyes, and he couldn't imagine such need going away. He thought the institution's money was safer in the vault than in their pockets. The man had actually died *in* the bank, on a Sunday, seated in his leather chair, his office door closed, as it always was, as if he suspected he might be petitioned even on a weekend night with the doors to the bank locked. He was discovered on Monday morning in a state of advanced rigor mortis not unlike, it was later remarked, the condition of the institution he oversaw.

When Clive Jr. took over, things loosened up right away. The first thing he did was put down a new carpet in the lobby, the old one having evolved several stages beyond threadbare except in the passageway that led to the CEO's office, where there'd been little traffic. His goal for the decade was to increase tenfold the savings and loan's assets, and he made known his intention to invest what money was left aggressively and even, when the situation seemed to call for it, to loan money out. After so many years of pessimism, Clive Jr. maintained, it was time for a little optimism. Furthermore, that was the mood of the nation.

The only policy Clive Jr. shared with his late predecessor was his deep distrust of the residents of North Bath, whom both men considered shiftless. That's the way his high school classmates had been, and they'd grown up shiftless, in Clive Jr.'s view. He preferred to deal with investors and borrowers from downstate, indeed from out of state, indeed from as far away as Texas, convinced that these were the future of Bath, just as they had been the salvation of Clifton Park and the other recently affluent Albany suburbs. "Downstate money is creeping up the Northway," Clive Jr. told his mother, a remark that always caused her to peer at him over the rims of her reading glasses. To Miss Beryl, the idea of money creeping up the interstate was sinister. "Ma," he insisted, "take it from me. When the time comes to sell the house, you're going to make a bundle."

It was phrases like "when the time comes" that worried Miss Beryl. They had a menacing resonance when Clive Jr. delivered them. She wondered what he had in mind. Would she be the judge of "when the time came," or would he? When he visited her, he looked the house over with a realtor's eye, found excuses to go down into the basement and up into the attic, as if he wanted to make sure that "when the time came" for him to inherit his mother's property it would be in good condition. He objected to her renting the upstairs flat to Donald Sullivan, against whom Clive Jr. harbored some ancient animosity, and no visit from Clive Jr., no matter how brief, passed without a renewed plea for her to throw Sully out before he fell asleep in bed with a lighted cigarette. Something about the way Clive Jr. voiced this concern convinced Miss Beryl that her son's anxiety had less to do with the possibility that his elderly mother might go up in flames than that the house would.

Miss Beryl was not proud of entertaining such unkind thoughts about her only child, and at times she even tried to reason herself out of them and into more natural maternal affection. The only difficulty was that natural maternal affection did not come naturally where Clive Jr. was concerned. The Clive Jr. who sat on the television opposite his father seemed pleasant enough, and the face the camera caught did not seem to be that of an unhappy, insecure, middle-aged banker. In fact, Clive Jr.'s face, still boyish in some ways, seemed full of possibility at an age where the countenances of most men were etched indelibly by the certainties of their existences. Clive Jr., at least the Clive Jr. who sat on the television, still struck Miss Beryl as unresolved, even though he would be fifty-six on his next birthday. Clive Jr. in real life was a different story. Whenever he appeared for one of his visits and gave Miss Beryl a dry, unpleasant peck on the forehead before scanning the living room ceiling for water damage, his character, if character was the right word, seemed as fixed and settled as a fifth-term conservative politician's. She endured his visits, his endless financial advice, with as much good cheer as she could muster. He would tell her what to do and why, and she would listen politely for as long as it took before declining to follow his advice. In her opinion Clive Jr. was full of cockamamie schemes, and he treated each as if its origin were the burning bush and not his own fevered brain. "Ma," he often said, on those occasions when she emphatically declined to follow his advice, "it's *almost* as if you didn't trust me."

"I *don't* trust you," Miss Beryl said aloud, addressing her son's photo on the television, then adding, to her husband, "I'm sorry, but I can't help it. I don't trust him. Ed understands, don't you, Ed."

Clive Sr. just smiled back, a tad ruefully, it seemed to her. Since his death he'd increasingly taken their son's side in matters of conflict. "Trust him, Beryl," he whispered to her now, his voice confidential, as if he feared that Driver Ed might overhear. "He's our son. *He's* the star of your firmament now."

"I'm working on it," Miss Beryl assured her husband, and in fact, she was. She'd loaned Clive Jr. money twice during the last five years and not even asked him what he intended to do with it. Five thousand dollars the first time. Ten thousand the second. Amounts she would not be pleased to lose but which, truth be told, she could afford to lose. But both times Clive Jr. had paid her back when he said he would, and Miss Beryl, on the lookout for a reason *not* to trust her son, discovered that she was mildly disappointed to have the money back in her own possession. In fact, she was unable to fend off a particularly shameful suspicion—that Clive Jr. had not needed the money at all, that he'd borrowed it to demonstrate to her that he was trustworthy. She even began to suspect that what he must be after was not part of what would be his soon enough, but rather control of the whole. But to what end? Miss Beryl had to admit that the logic of her suspicions was flawed. After all, her money, the house on Upper Main and its considerable contents, everything would belong to Clive Jr. eventually, when, as he put it, "the time came."

One of the things that drove her son to distraction, Miss Beryl suspected, was not knowing how much "everything" amounted to. There was the house, of course, and the ten thousand dollars he knew his mother had because she'd loaned it to him. But how much more? It was this information about her finances that Miss Beryl did not trust her son with. She had an accountant in Schuyler Springs do her taxes each year, and she instructed him to surrender no information about her affairs to Clive Jr. For legal advice, she dealt with a local attorney named Abraham Wirfly, whom her son continued to warn her against as an incompetent and a drunkard. Miss Beryl was not unaware of Mr. Wirfly's shortcomings, but she steadfastly maintained that he was not so much incompetent as unambitious, a character trait almost impossible to find in a lawyer. More important, she considered the man to be absolutely loyal, and when he promised to divulge nothing of her financial and legal affairs to Clive Jr., she believed him. Without ever saying so, Abraham Wirfly seemed also to entertain reservations about Clive Jr., and so Miss Beryl continued to trust him. Clive Jr.'s growing exasperation was testimony to her excellent judgment. "Ma," he pleaded pitifully, pacing up and down the length of her front room, "how can I help you protect your assets if you won't let me? What's going to happen if you get sick? Do you want the hospital to take everything? Is that your plan? To have a stroke and let some hospital take their thousand a day until it's all gone and you're destitute?"

The logic of her son's concern was inescapable, his argument consistent, yet despite this, Miss Beryl could not shed the feeling that Clive Jr. had a hidden agenda. She knew no more about his personal finances than he knew about hers, but she suspected that he was well on his way to becoming a wealthy man. She knew too that despite his realtor's eye, he had no interest in the house, that if he were to inherit it tomorrow, he'd sell it the day after. He'd recently purchased a luxury town home at the new Schuyler Springs Country Club between North Bath and Schuyler Springs. The house on Upper Main might bring a hundred and fifty thousand dollars, maybe more, and this was nothing to sneeze at, even if Clive Jr. didn't "need" the money. Yet she was unable to accept at face value that this was her son's design. There was something about the way his eye roved uncomfortably from corner to corner of each room, as if in search of spirit trails, that convinced Miss Beryl he was seeing something she couldn't see, and until she discovered what it was, she had no intention of trusting him fully.

Outside Miss Beryl's front window a thick clump of snow fell noiselessly from an unseen branch. There was a lot of it, but the snow wouldn't stay. Despite appearances, this wasn't real winter. Not yet. Still, Miss Beryl went out into the back hall and located the snow shovel where she had stored it beneath the stairs last April and leaned it up against the door where even Sully couldn't fail to see it when he left. Back inside, she became aware of a distant buzzing which meant that her tenant's alarm had gone off. Since injuring his knee, Sully slept even less than Miss Beryl, who got by on five hours a night, along with the three or four fifteen-minute naps she adamantly refused to admit taking throughout the day. Sully woke up several times each night. Miss Beryl heard him pad across his bedroom floor above her own and into the bathroom, where he would patiently wait to urinate. Old houses surrendered a great many auditory secrets, and Miss Beryl knew, for instance, that Sully had recently taken to sitting on the commode, which creaked beneath him, to await his water. Sometimes, to judge from the time it took him to return to bed, he fell asleep there. Either that or he was having prostate problems. Miss Beryl made a mental note to share with Sully one of the ditties of her childhood:

> Old Mrs. Jones had diabetes
> Not a drop she couldn't pee
> She took two bottles
> Of Lydia Pinkham's
> And they piped her to the sea.

Miss Beryl wondered if Sully would be amused. That probably depended on whether he knew what Lydia Pinkham's was. One of the problems of being eighty was that you built up a pretty impressive store of allusions. Other people didn't follow them, and they made it clear that this was *your* fault. Somewhere along the line, about the time America was being colonized, Miss Beryl suspected, the knowledge of old people had gotten discounted until now it was worth what the little boy shot at. Had Miss Beryl been a younger woman, it might have made an interesting project to trace the evolution of conventional wisdom on this point. Somehow old people, once the revered repositories of the culture's history and values, had become dusty museums of arcane and worthless information. No matter. She'd share the jingle with Sully anyway. He could stand a little poetry in his life.

Upstairs, the alarm clock continued to buzz. According to Sully, the only deep sleep he got any more was during the hour or so before his alarm went off. He'd recently purchased a new alarm clock because he kept sleeping through the old one. Also the new one. The first time Mrs. Beryl had heard that strange, faraway buzzing, she'd mistakenly concluded that the end was near. She'd read somewhere that the human brain was little more than a maze of electrical impulses, firing dutifully inside the skull, and the buzzing, she concluded, must be some sort of malfunction. The fact that the buzzing occurred at the same time every morning did not immediately tip her off, as it should have, that it was external to herself. She'd assumed that the time Clive Jr. was always alluding to had indeed come. It was the abrupt cessation of the buzzing, always followed immediately by the thud of Sully's heavy feet hitting the bedroom floor, that finally allowed Miss Beryl to solve the mystery, for which she was grateful, because, having solved it, she could stop worrying and shaking her head in search of the electrical short and giving herself headaches.

Perhaps because of her original misdiagnosis, the distant buzzing of Sully's alarm was still mildly disconcerting, so she did this morning what she did most mornings. She went first to the kitchen for the broom, then to her bedroom, where she gave the ceiling a good sharp thump or two with the broom handle, stopping when she heard her tenant grunt awake, snorting loudly and confused. She doubted Sully was aware of what really woke him so many mornings, that it was not the new alarm.

Perhaps, Miss Beryl conceded, her son was right about giving Sully the boot. He *was* a careless man, there was no denying it. He was careless with cigarettes, careless, without ever meaning to be, about people and circumstances. And therefore dangerous. Maybe, it occurred to Miss Beryl as she returned to her front window and stared up into the network of black limbs, Sully was the metaphorical branch that would fall on her from above. Part of getting old, she knew, was becoming unsure. For longer than any of her widowed neighbors, Miss Beryl had staved off the ravages of uncertainty by remaining intellectually challenged and alert. So far she'd been able to keep faith in her own judgment, in part by rigorously questioning the judgment of others. Having Clive Jr. around helped in this regard, and Miss Beryl had always told herself that when her son's advice started making sense to her, then she'd know she was slipping. Perhaps her fearing Clive Jr.'s wisdom on the subject of Sully was the beginning.

But she'd not concede quite yet, she decided. In several important respects Sully was an important ally, just as he had been a month ago when she'd taken a tumble and sprained her wrist painfully. Fearing it might be broken, she'd had Sully drive her to the hospital in Schuyler Springs, where the wrist had been X-rayed and taped. The whole episode had taken no more than two hours, and she'd been sent home with a prescription for Tylenol 3 painkillers. She'd taken only two of the pills because they made her drowsy and she didn't mind the pain once she knew what it was. As soon as she'd learned the wrist wasn't fractured, she felt better, and the next day she made a gift of the remaining Tylenols to Sully, who since his injury was always in the market for pain pills.

Sully could be trusted, she knew, to keep her secret. She wished the same could be said for Mrs. Gruber, whom Clive Jr. used, Miss Beryl suspected, to check up on her. Mrs. Gruber denied this, of course, but then she would, having been forbidden by her friend to communicate any information of a personal nature to Clive Jr. But Miss Beryl was pretty sure Mrs. Gruber was a snitch just the same. Clive Jr. could be ingratiating, and one of Mrs. Gruber's chief enjoyments in life was discussing other people's illnesses and accidents. Miss Beryl doubted that her friend could resist an insidious sweet-talker like Clive Jr.

Still at the front window, Miss Beryl peered for a long time through the blinds and up the street in the direction of Mrs. Gruber's house. Quarter to seven. The street was still silent, the new blanket of snow spoiled by just the one set of dark tire tracks. Miss Beryl sighed and stared up into the web of tree limbs, starkly black against the white morning sky. "Fall," she said, pleased and heartened as she always was by the sound of her own decisive voice. "See if I care."

"You probably *wouldn't* care if I fell," said a voice behind her. "I bet you'd laugh, in fact."

Miss Beryl had been so preoccupied with her thoughts, she had not heard her living room door open or her tenant enter. It seemed only a few seconds before that she'd heard him snort awake in the upstairs bedroom, surely not enough time to rise, dress, do all the early morning things a civilized person had to do. But of course men were strange creatures and not, strictly speaking, civilized at all, most of them. The one she saw standing before her in his stocking feet, work boots dangling from their leather laces, had no doubt simply rolled out of bed and into his clothes. She doubted he wore pajamas, probably slept in his shorts the way Clive Sr. had, then grabbed the first pair of trousers he saw, the ones draped across a chair or over the bottom of the bed. Knowing Sully, he probably slept in his socks to save time.

Not that her tenant was much worse than most men. He had the laborer's habit of bathing after his day's work was done instead of in the morning, which meant that when he awoke he had only two immediate needs—to relieve himself and to locate a cup of coffee. In Sully's case the coffee was two blocks away at Hattie's Lunch, and he often arrived there before he was completely awake. He left his work boots downstairs in the hall by the back door. For some reason he liked to put them on in Miss Beryl's downstairs flat rather than his own. The boots always left a dirty trail, in winter a muddy print on the hardwood floor, in summer a dry cluster of tiny pebbles which Miss Beryl would sweep into a dustpan when he'd left. Men in general, Miss Beryl had observed, seldom took note of what they trailed behind them, but Sully was particularly oblivious, his wake particularly messy. Still, Miss Beryl wouldn't have given a nickel for a fastidious man, and she didn't mind cleaning up after Sully each morning. He provided her a small task, and her days had few enough of these.

"Lordy," Miss Beryl said. "Sneak up on an old woman."

"I thought you were talking to me, Mrs. Peoples," Sully told her. He was the only person she knew who called her "missus," and the gesture reserved for him a special place in Miss Beryl's heart. "I just thought I'd stop in to make sure you didn't die in your sleep."

"Not yet," she told him.

"You're talking to yourself, though," he pointed out, "so it can't be long."

"I wasn't talking to myself. I was talking to Ed," Miss Beryl informed her tenant, indicating Ed on the wall.

"Oh," Sully said, feigning relief. "And here I thought you were going batty."

He sat down heavily on Miss Beryl's Queen Anne chair, causing her to wince. The chair was delicate, a gift from Clive Sr., who had bought it for her at an antique shop in Schuyler Springs. She had talked him into buying it, actually. Clive Sr. had thought it too fragile, with its slender curved legs and arms. A large man, he'd pointed out that if he ever sat in it, "the damn thing" would probably collapse and run him through. "It wasn't my intention for you to sit in it, ever," Miss Beryl had informed him. "In fact, it wasn't my intention for anyone to sit in it." Clive Sr. had frowned at this intelligence and opened his mouth to say the obvious—that it didn't make a lot of sense to buy a chair nobody was going to sit in—when he noticed the expression on his beloved's face and shut his mouth. Like many men addicted to sports, Clive Sr. was also a religious man and one who'd been raised to accept life's mysteries—the Blessed

Trinity, for one instance, a woman's reasoning, for another. Also, he remembered just in time that Miss Beryl had made him a present, just that winter, of what she referred to as the world's ugliest corduroy recliner, the very one he had his heart set on. To Clive Sr.'s way of thinking, there was nothing ugly about the chair, and it was certainly more substantial, with its solid construction and foam padding and sturdy fabric, than this pile of skinny mahogany sticks, but he guessed that he was had, and he wrote out the check.

Both had been correct, Miss Beryl now reflected. The corduroy recliner, safely out of sight in the spare bedroom, *was* the ugliest chair in the world, and the Queen Anne *was* fragile. She hated for anyone, much less Sully, to sit in it. There were many rudimentary concepts that eluded her tenant, and pride of ownership was among these. Sully himself owned nothing that he placed any value on, and it always seemed inexplicable to him that people worried about harm coming to their possessions. His existence had always been so full of breakage that he viewed it as one of life's constants and no more worth worrying about than the weather. Once, years ago, Miss Beryl had broached this touchy subject with Sully, tried to indicate those special things among her possessions that she would hate to see broken, but the discussion appeared to either bore or annoy him, so she'd given up. She could, of course, ask him not to sit in this one particular chair, but the request would just irritate him and he wouldn't stop in for a while until he forgot what she'd done to irritate him, and when he returned he'd go right back to the same chair.

So Miss Beryl decided to risk the chair. She enjoyed her tenant's stopping by in the morning "to see if she was dead yet" because she'd always been fond of Sully and understood his fondness for her as well. Affection wasn't the sort of thing men like Sully easily admitted to, and of course he'd never told her he was fond of her, but she knew he was, just the same. In some respects he was the opposite of Clive Jr., who steadfastly maintained that he visited her out of affection and concern but who was visibly impatient from the moment he lumbered up her porch steps. He was always on his way somewhere else, and the mere sight of his mother seemed to satisfy him, as did the sound of her voice on the telephone, and so Miss Beryl was unable to fend off the suspicion whenever the phone rang and the caller hung up without speaking that it was Clive Jr. calling to ascertain the fact of his mother's continued existence.

"Could I interest you in a nice hot cup of tea?" Miss Beryl said, watching apprehensively as the Queen Anne protested under Sully's squirming weight.

"Not now, not ever," Sully told her, his forehead perspiring. Getting into and out of his boots was one of the day's more arduous tasks. The good leg wasn't that difficult, but the other, since fracturing the kneecap, remained stiff and painful until midmorning. This early, about all he could do was loosen the laces all the way and work his foot into the opening as best he could. He'd locate the shoe's tongue and laces later. "I'll take my usual cup of coffee, though."

He was having such a terrible time with the boot, she said, "I suppose I *could* make a pot of coffee."

He rested a moment, grinned at her. "No thanks, Beryl."

"How come you're wearing your clodhoppers?" Miss Beryl wondered. In fact, Sully was dressed in preaccident attire—worn gray work pants, faded denim shirt over thermal underwear, a quilted, sleeveless vest, a bill cap. Since September he'd dressed differently to attend the classes in refrigeration and air-conditioning repair he took at the nearby community college as part of the retraining program that was a stipulation of his partial disability payments.

Sully stood—Miss Beryl wincing again as he placed his full weight on the arms of the Queen Anne—and, having inserted his toes into the unlaced work boot, scuffed it along the hardwood floor until he managed to pin it against the wall and force the entire foot in. "About time I went back to work, don't you think?" he said.

"What if they find out?"

He grinned at her. "You aren't going to squeal on me, are you?"

"I should," she said. "There's probably a reward for turning people like you in. I could use the money."

Sully studied her, nodding. "Good thing Coach kicked off before he found out how mean you'd get in your old age."

Miss Beryl sighed. "I can't suppose it would do any good to point out the obvious."

Sully shook his head. "Probably not. What's the obvious?"

"That you're going to hurt yourself. They'll stop paying for your schooling, and you'll be even worse off."

Sully shrugged. "You could be right, Beryl, but I think I'll try. Anymore my leg hurts just as bad when I sit around as when I stand, so I might as well stand. I've pretty much decided I don't want to fix air conditioners for the rest of my life."

He stomped his boot a couple times to make sure his foot was all the way in, rattling the knickknacks. "I swear to Christ, though. If you could learn to put this shoe on for me mornings, I'd marry you and learn to drink tea."

When Sully collapsed, exhausted, back into the Queen Anne and took out his cigarettes, Miss Beryl headed for the kitchen, where she kept her lone ashtray. Sully was the only person she allowed to smoke in her house, this exception granted on the grounds that he honestly couldn't remember that she didn't want him to. He never took note of the fact that there were no ashtrays. Indeed, it never occurred to him even to look for one until the long gray ash at the end of his cigarette was ready to fall. Even then Sully was not the sort of man to panic. He simply held the cigarette upright, as if its vertical position removed the threat of gravity. When the ash eventually fell anyway, he was sometimes quick enough to catch it in his lap, where the ash would stay until, having forgotten about it again, he stood up.

By the time Miss Beryl arrived back with the crystal ashtray she'd bought in London five years before, Sully already had a pretty impressive ash working. "So," Sully said, "you decide where you're going this year?"

Every winter for the past twenty, Miss Beryl had sallied forth, as she called it, around the first of the year, returning sometime in March when winter's back was broken. Her flat was crowded with the souvenirs from these excursions—her walls adorned with an Egyptian spear, a Roman breastplate, a bronze dragon, tiki torches, her flat table surfaces crowded with Wedgwood, an Etruscan spirit boat, a two-headed Foo dog, the floor with wicker elephants, terra-cotta pots, a wooden sea chest. In the months preceding her safaris, she read travel books on her destination. This year she'd checked out books on Africa, where she hoped to find a companion for Driver Ed, who had been purchased in Vermont, actually, and might or might not have been authentic Zamble. Vermont had been about as far as she'd ever been able to convince Clive Sr. to sally forth. He didn't like to go anywhere people wouldn't recognize him as the North Bath football coach, which put them on a pretty short leash.

"I'm staying put this winter," she told Sully, surprised to discover that she'd come to this decision just a few minutes before while looking up into the trees.

"That must mean you've been everywhere," Sully said.

"The early snow convinced me that this is our winter. God's going to lower the boom. One of those limbs is going to come crashing down on us."

"Sounds like a good reason to head for the Congo," Sully offered.

"There's no such place as the Congo anymore."

"No?"

"No. And besides," Miss Beryl reminded him, "God finds Jonah even in the belly of a whale."

Sully nodded. "God and the cops. That's how come I stay close to home. So they know where to find me. Maybe that way they'll go easy."

Miss Beryl frowned at him. "You're not in Dutch with the police again, are you, Donald?" Her tenant did wind up in jail occasionally, usually for public intoxication, though when he was younger he'd been a brawler.

Sully grinned at her. "Not to my knowledge, Mrs. Peoples. These days I try to be good. I'm not a young man anymore."

"Well," she said, "you were a bad boy far longer than most."

"I know it," he said, taking another drag on his cigarette and noticing for the first time how hazardously long the gray ash had become. "You going out for Thanksgiving, at least?"

Miss Beryl took the cigarette from him, put it into the ashtray, and then put the ashtray on the side table. With Sully, you didn't just set the ashtray down nearby and expect him to recognize its function. "Mrs. Gruber and I are going to the Northwoods Motor Inn. They're having a buffet. All the turkey and trimmings you can eat for ten dollars."

Sully exhaled smoke through his nose. "Sounds like a hell of a good deal for the Northwoods. You and Alice couldn't eat ten dollars' worth of turkey if they gave you the whole weekend."

Miss Beryl had to admit this was true. "Mrs. Gruber likes it there. It's all old fogies like us, and they don't play loud music. They have a big salad bar, and Mrs. Gruber likes to try everything on it. Snails even."

"Snails are good, actually," Sully said, surprising her.

"When did you ever eat a snail?"

Sully scratched his unshaven chin thoughtfully at the recollection. "I liberated France, if you recall. I wish snails were the worst thing I ate between Normandy and Berlin, too."

"It must be true what they say, then," Miss Beryl observed. "War is heck. If you ate anything worse than a snail, don't tell me about it."

"Okay," Sully said agreeably.

"I just eat a couple of those carrot curls and save myself for the dinner. Otherwise, I get full, and if I eat too much I get gas."

Sully stubbed out his cigarette. "Well, in that case, go slow," he said, laboring to his feet again. "Remember, you got somebody living above you. It's too cold to open all the windows."

Miss Beryl followed him out into the hall, his untied shoelaces clicking along the floor.

"I'll shovel you out after I've had my coffee," he said, noticing the shovel she'd leaned against the wall. "You got anywhere to go right away?"

Miss Beryl admitted she didn't.

Until he hurt his knee, Sully had been much envied as a tenant by the other widows along Upper Main. Many of them tried to work out reduced rent arrangements with single men, who then shoveled the sidewalk, mowed the lawn and raked leaves in return. But finding the right single man was not easy. The younger ones were forgetful and threw parties and brought young women home with them. The older men were given to illnesses and complications of the lower back. Single, able-bodied men between the ages of forty-five and sixty were so scarce in Bath that Miss Beryl had been envied Sully for over a decade, and she suspected some of her neighbors were privately rejoicing now that Sully was hobbled. Soon he would be useless, and Miss Beryl would be paid back for years of good fortune by having to carry a renter who couldn't perform. Indeed, it seemed to Miss Beryl, who saw Sully every day, that he had failed considerably since his accident, and she feared that some morning he wasn't going to stick his head in to find out if she was dead and the reason was going to be that *he* was dead. Miss Beryl had already outlived a lot of people she hadn't planned to outlive, and Sully, tough and stubborn though he was, had a ghostly look about him lately.

"Just don't forget me," she told him, recollecting that she would need to go to the market later that morning.

"Do I ever?"

"Yes," she said, though he didn't often.

"Well, I won't today," he assured her. "How come you aren't going out to dinner with The Bank?"

Miss Beryl smiled, as she always did when Sully referred to Clive Jr. this way, and it occurred to her, not for the first time, that those who thought of stupid people as literal were dead wrong. Some of the least gifted of her eighth-graders had always had a gift for colorful metaphor. It was literal truth they couldn't grasp, and so it was with Sully. He had been among the first students she'd ever taught in North Bath, and his IQ tests had revealed a host of aptitudes that the boy himself appeared bent on contradicting. Throughout his life a case study underachiever, Sully— people still remarked—was nobody's fool, a phrase that Sully no doubt appreciated without ever sensing its literal application—that at sixty, he was divorced from his own wife, carrying on halfheartedly with another man's, estranged from his son, devoid of self-knowledge, badly crippled and virtually unemployable—all of which he stubbornly confused with independence.

"I was invited by The Bank, but I prefer to pay my way," Miss Beryl told him, a small lie. Clive Jr. had called last week to tell her he'd be out of town for the holiday, alluding to his planned absence cryptically, hoping, perhaps, to pique Miss Beryl's curiosity, a tactic he might have known was doomed to failure. Miss Beryl had her share of natural curiosity, but she resented having it manipulated so transparently. The mere fact that Clive Jr. solicited her interest suggested to her the opposite response was called for. "It's no fun eating with a financial institution," she added.

Sully grinned down at her. "We wear the chains we forge in life, old girl."

Miss Beryl blinked. "Who'd have thunk it? A literary allusion from the lips of Donald Sullivan. I don't suppose you remember who said that."

"You did," Sully reminded her. "All through eighth grade."

The first thing Sully saw when he stepped outside onto the large porch he shared with his landlady was Rub Squeers tramping up the street through the snow. At just over five feet tall, Rub was powerfully built, and at the moment he was staring at his feet as he walked, trying, Sully suspected, to pretend that this meeting was a coincidence. Sully had known Rub too long to believe in this particular coincidence. He could tell by the way the young man was carrying his large head, like a medicine ball precariously balanced on his thick shoulders, that he was coming to see Sully and that he wanted to borrow money. In fact, Sully could tell just by looking at him how much Rub wanted (twenty dollars), how much he'd settle for (ten), and how long it would take for them to arrive at this figure (thirty minutes).

"Hello, dumbbell," Sully called. "Don't you own any boots?"

Rub looked up and feigned surprise. "Somewheres," he said, looking down at his ruined black shoes. "How was I supposed to know it'd snow the day before Thanksgiving?"

"You're supposed to be prepared," Sully said, though he himself had led a life of studied unpreparedness. He put a work-booted foot up on the porch railing, tied its laces. "You're just in time, actually," he added. "Do this one for me."

Rub climbed the steps, kneeled in the snow, tied the laces on Sully's left boot.

"Leave some circulation," Sully suggested. "My knee's about the size of two already."

Rub untied the boot, started over. "You look like you're dressed for work, not school," he observed. "You going back to work?"

"That's the plan," Sully said.

"You gonna hire me again?"

"Would you stop borrowing money if I did?"

"Sure," Rub said, though he looked disappointed to have the subject of borrowing come up so negatively. His knees now sported large wet patches. "I miss us working," Rub said. "I wisht we'd just start up again like before."

"I'll see if I can find us something," Sully told him.

Rub was frowning now. "Old Lady Peoples is spying on us again," he said, having noticed the front room curtains twitch. Rub was normally even-tempered, but he harbored a deep animosity toward Miss Beryl as a result of her attempts to educate him back in the eighth grade, some dozen years ago, the year before she'd retired. Whenever Rub saw her, his eyes got small and hard, his voice edgy and scared, as if he imagined that Miss Beryl were still capable of wielding absolute power over him. She was still paying attention to him, and he didn't like people who paid attention. Rub himself seldom paid attention, and he considered inattention normal human behavior. Back in eighth grade Miss Beryl was always cracking her ruler on the edge of the desk in her English class, right after lunch when he was about to doze off, and barking, "Pay attention!" Sometimes she stared right at Rub and added, "You might learn something." Rub still considered attentiveness hateful and exhausting and perverse. And since he knew no one in Bath more alert than Miss Beryl, there was no one he disliked more.

Sully couldn't help grinning. "Let's go have a cup of coffee before she comes out and warns me against bad companions."

As they crossed the street where the snow had already begun to turn to slush and headed toward Hattie's Lunch, Sully was surprised by an unexpected feeling of well-being he could find no rational justification for. The feeling was far too strong to ignore, though, so he decided to be grateful and enjoy it and not be troubled by the fact that throughout his life, such sudden sensations of well-being were often harbingers of impending catastrophe. They were, in fact, leading indicators of the approach of a condition that Sully had come to think of as a stupid streak, where everything he did would turn out wrong, where each wrong turn would be compounded by the next, where even smart moves would prove dumb in the particular circumstance, where thoughtlessness and careful consideration were guaranteed to arrive at the same end—disaster.

He generally suffered through about one stupid streak a year and was under the impression that this year's was already in the books. But then again, maybe not. Or maybe this year he'd be awarded two. Maybe going back to work on an injured knee was the beginning of the granddaddy of all stupid streaks. He already knew that one of the things he had to look forward to today was everybody telling him he was stupid, he'd be better off to stay in school, collect his partial disability, let his knee heal completely and, since it wasn't likely to heal completely, let Wirf, his lawyer, work on getting him his full disability. What kind of sense could it possibly make for him to go back to work on a busted, arthritic knee?

Some sort of sense, obviously, Sully concluded, or he wouldn't be feeling so good about doing it. Of course, he might feel differently later, *after* a day's hard work, but right this minute, as he limped down Upper Main in the direction of Hattie's and coffee, half listening to Rub complain about Miss Beryl, going back to work made more sense to him than driving over to the community college north of Schuyler Springs, where he had, for the last few months, been taking classes with teenagers and feeling foolish. The only class he enjoyed was philosophy, the course he'd been forced to sign up for when one of the classes he needed was full, and the philosophy class, ironically, was the one that made him feel the most foolish. It was taught by a young professor with a small body and a massive head who would have looked like Rub except for a crop of unruly black hair. The young professor seemed bent on disproving everything in the world, one thing at a time. First he disproved things like chairs and trees that fell in the forest, and then he moved on to concepts like cause and effect and, most recently, free will. Sully'd gotten a kick out of it, watching everything disappear but the bad grades he got along with all the other students. If going back to work turned out okay, philosophy was the only class he'd miss. In fact, he already felt bad about quitting with only three weeks left in the term and a few things left, like God and love, to be disproved. He wasn't sure how the young professor meant to make these disappear with the rest, but Sully was sure he'd find a way.

What was disappearing even faster than trees in his philosophy class was Sully's small reserve of money, and besides, he was curious to know if work was something he could still do. The fact that he could barely get his shoes on did not bode well. But lately the knee hurt worse when he sat there in the classroom than when he walked around on it. The classroom desks were anchored to the floor and placed too close together, and he couldn't seem to get comfortable. If he straightened the leg out in the aisle, he ran the risk of somebody bumping it. If he tucked it beneath him, out of harm's way, it throbbed mercilessly to the drone of his professors' voices.

Fuck it. He was better off going back to work and turning the kind of slender profit that was his life. If he was careful he'd be okay, for a while anyhow. Right now, a while seemed enough. It was enough to be sauntering down the Main Street of his life toward the warmth of Hattie's, where there'd be people he knew and knew how to talk to.

"I couldn't live with fuckin' Old Lady Peoples spying on me," Rub was saying, still angry. "You couldn't even have a good piece of ass."

Sully shook his head in wonderment, as he often did around Rub, who couldn't get laid in a whorehouse wearing a thousand-dollar bill for a rubber. Rub had once confessed to Sully that even his wife, Bootsie, had stopped extending him conjugal privileges. "Well, Rub," Sully told him, "I don't get laid that much any more anyhow. I wish Beryl Peoples was the reason, too."

Rub apparently accepted this and calmed down a little. "You got Ruth, anyways," he observed before thinking.

Sully considered how to answer this. Ruth was one of the people he was going to have to explain himself to today. Maybe if he was lucky he'd run into all the people who were going to tell him how stupid he was today and be done with it. "Ruth is another man's wife, actually. He's the one that's got Ruth, not me."

Rub took this in slowly, perhaps even believing it, which, if true, would have made him and Ruth's husband the only believers in Bath, though not many people knew for sure. "It's just that people keep saying—" Rub explained.

"I don't care what people say," Sully interrupted. "I just know what I'm telling you."

"Even Bootsie says—" Rub began, then stopped, sensing he was about to get cuffed. "I just wisht you could get a piece of ass without Old Lady Peoples spying on you," he insisted.

"Good. I thought that's all you meant," Sully said, adding, "Ruth is going to be kind of upset when she hears you called her a piece of ass, though."

That Ruth might somehow hear of this clearly frightened Rub, who was scared of women in general and Ruth in particular. His wife, Bootsie, was a genuine horror, but Ruth struck him as even scarier, and he admired Sully for having the courage to involve himself with a woman like Ruth who had such a tongue on her and wasn't afraid to use it on anybody. "I never called her that," he said quickly.

"Oh," Sully said, "I thought I just heard you."

Rub frowned, tried to scroll back through the conversation, finally gave up. "I never meant to," he said weakly, hoping this explanation might suffice. It did with Sully sometimes, even if it never had with Old Lady Peoples, not even once.

Hattie's Lunch, one of North Bath's oldest businesses, was now run by Hattie's daughter, Cassandra, who saw the business as operating strictly according to the law of diminishing returns. She planned to sell it and move out west as soon as her mother died, which the old woman, now pushing ninety pretty hard, was bound to do eventually, despite her clear intention to live forever. Cass had thought her mother's stroke would be the beginning of the end, but that was nearly five years ago, and the old woman had recovered miraculously. "Miraculously" was the doctor's term, and not one Cass herself would have thought to apply to her mother's recovery, however surprising. The physicians had been astonished to see a woman of Hattie's years rebound so fiercely, and they were full of admiration for her tenacious grip on life, her stern refusal to surrender it. Testimony to the human spirit, they'd called it.

Cass called it bullheadedness. She loved her mother but was less effusive on the subject of her longevity than the old woman's physicians. "Basically she's just used to having her own way," she told them. But except for her old friend Sully, to whom she could tell things, confident he'd forget them before he walked out the door, Cass kept her resentment to herself, knowing that it would be neither understood nor tolerated. Hattie was an institution in Bath, and besides, everybody romanticized old people, seeing in them their own lost parents and grandparents, most of whom had bequeathed to their children the usual legacy of guilt, along with the gift of selective recollection. Most fathers and mothers did their children the great favor of dying before they began fouling themselves, before their children learned to equate them with urine-soaked undergarments and other grim realities of age and infirmity. Cass knew better than to expect understanding, and she understood how profound was the human need to see old people as innocent, all evidence to the contrary notwithstanding. Some days, like today, she would have liked to tell everybody in the diner a few things about both her mother and herself. Mostly herself. She'd have liked to tell somebody that every time she changed Old Hattie's stockings, she felt her own life slipping away, that when the old woman made one unreasonable demand after another her hand actually itched to slap her mother into reality. Or Cass might confess her fear that her mother's death might just coincide with her own need of assistance, since she didn't share her mother's ferocious will to keep breathing at all costs. Indeed, she was grimly pleased that she was childless, which meant that when her own time came there'd be no one upon whom she'd be an unwanted burden. Whoever got the job would be paid for doing it.

This morning Hattie's was busy as usual. Between 6:30 and 9:30 on weekdays, Roof, the black cook, could not fry eggs fast enough to fill all the Hattie's Specials—two eggs, toast, home fries and coffee for a dollar forty-nine. When Sully and Rub arrived, there was no place for them to sit, either at the short, six-stool counter or among the dozen square formica booths, though a foursome of construction workers was stirring in the farthest. Old Hattie herself occupied the tiny booth, half the size of the others, nearest the door, and Sully, to Rub's dismay, slid gingerly into the booth across from the old lady, leaving Rub in the crowded doorway. "How are you, old woman?" Sully said. Hattie's milky eyes located him by sound. "Still keeping an eye on business, I see."

"Still keeping an eye on business," Hattie repeated, nodding vigorously. "Still keeping . . ." Her attention was diverted, as it was during all conversations, by the ringing of the cash register, the old woman's favorite sound. She had manned the register for nearly sixty years and imagined herself there still, each time she heard it clang. "Ah!" she said. "Ah . . ."

"There's a booth," Rub said when the road crew got up with their checks and started for the register.

"Good," Sully said. "Go sit in it, why don't you."

Rub hated being dismissed this way, but he did as he was told for fear of losing the booth. It was the perfect booth, in fact, the last in the row, away from traffic, where he could beg a loan from Sully in relative privacy, the threat of interruption greatly reduced.

"What do you say we go dancing some night?" Sully suggested to Hattie in a loud voice, partly because the old woman was hard of hearing, partly because their conversations were much enjoyed by the regulars at the lunch counter, several of whom rotated on their stools to watch.

"Dancing?" Hattie said, then bellowed, "Dancing!"

Now everyone turned and looked.

"Why not?" Sully said. "Just you and me. First dancing, then we'll go over to my place."

A sly grin crossed the old woman's face. "Let's just go to your place. Nuts to the dancing."

"Okay," Sully said, winking at Cass, who was watching now also, with solemn disapproval, as usual.

"Just tell me one thing!" Hattie shouted. When she got revved up, her voice always reminded Sully of walruses at the zoo. "Who are you?"

"What do you mean, who am I?" Sully said in mock outrage. "What are you, blind?"

"You *sound* like that darn Sully."

"That's who I am, too," Sully told her.

"Well, I'm too old to dance," Hattie said. "I'm too old for your place too. You live on the second floor."

"I know it," Sully said, massaging his knee. "I can hardly get up and down those stairs myself."

"How old are you?" Hattie said.

"Sixty," Sully said. "Except I feel older."

"I'm eighty-nine." Hattie cackled proudly.

"I know it. Aren't you ever going to go meet St. Peter? Make room for somebody else?"

"No!"

Sully slid back out of the booth, his leg straight out in front until he could get it safely under him and put some weight on it. "Take it slow, old girl," he said, patting one of her spotted hands. "Can you still hear the cash register?"

"You bet I can," Hattie assured him.

"Good," Sully said. "You wake up some morning and you can't hear it, you'll know you died in your sleep."

In fact, the old cash register's ringing did have a soothing effect on Hattie. Together with the sound of dishes being bussed and the loud rasp of male laughter, the rattle and clang of the ancient register opened the doorway of Hattie's memory wide enough for the old woman to slip through and spend a pleasant morning in the company of people dead for twenty years. And when her daughter closed the restaurant behind the last of the lunch customers and ushered Hattie out back to the small apartment they shared, the old woman was exhausted and under the impression that the reason she was so tired was that she'd worked all day.

A stool had been vacated at the end of the counter, so Sully slid onto it and accepted one of Cass's dark looks. "How will you know when *you've* died?" Cass wanted to know.

"I guess everything will stop being so goddamn much fun," Sully told her.

"Those don't look like your school duds," she observed. "No classes today?"

"None for me."

She studied him. "So. You're giving up."

"I don't think I'll be going back, if that's what you mean."

"What have you got, three more weeks till the end of the term?"

Sully admitted this was true. "You know how it is," he said.

Cass made a face. "No idea. Tell me how it is, Sully."

Sully had no intention of explaining how it was to Cass. One of the few benefits of being sixty and single and without the enforceable obligations to other human beings was that you weren't required to explain how it was. "I don't see why it should frost your window, in any case."

Cass held up both hands in mock surrender. "It doesn't frost my window. In fact, I may have won the pool. You lasted three months, and all those squares were vacant. Either Ruth or I must've won."

Sully couldn't help grinning at her, because she *was* upset. "I hope it was you, then."

"You and Ruth still on the outs?"

"Not that I know of. I try not to have that much to do with married women, Cassandra."

"Sometimes you don't try very hard, the way I hear it."

"I've been trying pretty hard lately, not that it's anyone's business but mine."

Cass let it go, and after a moment she nodded in Rub's direction. "Somebody's about to hemorrhage, in case you haven't noticed."

Sully smiled. "There's the real reason I gotta go back to work. Rub's going to hell without my good example to live by."

Ever since Sully had slid onto the stool at the counter Rub had been waving, trying to catch Sully's attention. Sully waved back now and called, "Hi, Rub."

Rub frowned, confused, unable to figure out whether to leave the booth or not. He'd been under the distinct impression that when Sully told him to go grab a booth, he himself had intended to join him there when he finished with the old woman. Except that now Sully was seated at the counter talking to Cass as if he'd forgotten all about Rub and the booth. To make matters worse, several people had come in and were waiting near the door for a booth to be vacated. They kept looking at Rub, all alone in his big one. Had the stool next to Sully been empty Rub would have made for it, but that stool was occupied, which meant he had to choose between sitting alone at a booth for six and not having a place to sit at all. His deeply furrowed expression suggested that the conundrum might be causing a cranial blood clot.

"He *has* been even more pathetic than usual this fall," Cass had to admit. "He was in here earlier looking for you."

"I figured."

"He ask you yet?"

Sully shook his head. "He keeps getting interrupted. In another minute or two he'll cry."

Indeed, Rub looked to be on the verge of tears when Sully finally relented and waved him over. Jumping up quickly, he came toward them at a trot, like a dog released from a difficult command.

"There's no stool," he said as soon as he arrived.

Sully swiveled on his, a complete circle. "You know what? You're right."

The people waiting by the door made for the booth Rub had vacated. Rub sighed deeply as he watched them take possession. "What was wrong with the booth?"

"Nothing," Sully told him. "Not a goddamn thing. Booths are great, in fact."

Rub threw up his hands. The look on his face was pure exasperation.

"Think a minute," Sully reminded him. "What'd you just do for me over at the house?"

Rub thought. "Tied your shoe," he suddenly remembered.

"Which means?" Sully prompted.

Cass set a steaming cup of coffee in front of Sully and asked Rub if he wanted any.

"Don't interrupt," Sully told her. "He's deep in thought."

"I never minded tying your shoe," Rub said. "I know your knee's hurt. I didn't forget." This last was delivered so unconvincingly that Sully and Cass exchanged glances.

"You want some coffee?" Sully said.

"Okay," Rub said sadly. "I just don't see how come you can sit in her booth and not in the one down there." His face was flushed with the effort to understand. "And how come you can sit on a stool, but not in a booth?"

Sully couldn't help grinning at him. "I wish I could give you this knee for about fifteen minutes," he said.

"Hell, I'd take it," Rub said earnestly, shaming Sully with his customary sincerity. "I just wisht there was someplace for me to sit here at the counter, is all. We could have both sat over there in that booth."

Both Sully and Cass were grinning at him now, and after a few seconds of being grinned at, Rub had to look at the floor. He was devoted to Sully and just regretted that, with Sully, whenever there were three people, it ended up two against one, and Rub was always the one. Sully could stare and grin at you forever, too, and when he did this Rub got so self-conscious he had to look down at the floor. "We going back to work?" he said finally, for something to say.

Sully shrugged. "You think we should?"

Rub nodded enthusiastically.

"Okay," Sully said. "As long as you're not too worried."

Rub frowned. "About what?"

"About my bad knee. The one you never forget about. I thought you might be worried I'd hurt it again."

Rub wasn't at all sure how to respond to this. He could think of only two responses—no, he wasn't too worried, and yes, he was worried. Neither seemed quite right. He knew he was supposed to be worried. If true, this meant he was expected to hope they *didn't* go back to work, something Rub couldn't really hope, because he'd missed working with Sully a great deal this fall and hated working with his cousins collecting trash, almost as much as they hated letting him. North Bath had recently suspended trash collection as a city service, leading to entrepreneurial daring on the part of Rub's relatives, who had for generations worked for the sanitation department. Last year they'd purchased the oldest and most broken down of the town's aging fleet of three garbage trucks, had SQUEERS REFUSE REMOVAL stenciled on the door, and prepared to compete on the free market. In addition to the driver, there were always at least two Squeers boys hanging on to the back of the truck as it careened through the streets of Bath, and when the vehicle came to a halt they leapt off the truck like spiders and scurried for curbside trash cans. There were only so many places you could safely stand on the back of a garbage truck, and the Squeers boys owned and occupied these, so that when Rub was permitted to tag along he had to latch onto the side as best he could. The turns could be treacherous, and Rub sometimes had the impression that his cousins were waiting for him to be thrown from the truck so they wouldn't have to stretch their already thin profits with an extra worker. Being family, they couldn't deny him the work, but if Rub let himself get tossed on some sharp turn it'd be his own fault.

"I could do all the hard jobs," Rub offered.

"You might have to," Sully told him.

"I don't mind," Rub said, which was true.

"I'll see if I can find us something for tomorrow," Sully told him.

"Tomorrow's Thanksgiving," Rub reminded him.

"So be thankful."

"Bootsie'll shoot me if I have to work on Thanksgiving."

"She probably will shoot you one of these days," Sully conceded, "but it won't be for working."

"I was wondering . . ." Rub began.

"Really?" Sully said. "What about?"

Rub had to look at the floor again. "If you could loan me twenty dollars. Since we're going back to work."

Sully finished his coffee, pushed the cup toward the back of the counter where it might attract a free refill. "I worry about you, Rub," he said. "You know that?"

Rub looked up hopefully.

"Because if you think I've got twenty dollars to loan you right now, you haven't been paying attention."

Down at the floor again. Sometimes Sully was just like Miss Beryl, who'd also specialized in making Rub stare at the floor. He hadn't had the courage to look up more than half a dozen times in the whole of eighth grade. He could still see the geometric pattern of the classroom floor in his mind's eye. "I been paying attention," he said in the same voice he always used with Miss Beryl when she cornered him about his homework. "It's just that tomorrow's Thanksgiving and—"

Sully held up his hand. "Stop a minute. Before we get to tomorrow, let's talk about yesterday. You remember yesterday?"

"Sure," Rub said, though it sounded a little like one of Sully's trick questions.

"Where was I yesterday?"

Rub's spirits plunged. He remembered yesterday. "Albany."

"How come I was in Albany?"

"For your disability."

"And what did they tell me?"

Rub fell silent.

"Come on, Rub. This was only yesterday, and I told you at The Horse as soon as I got back."

"I know they turned you down, Sully. Hell, I remember."

"So what do you do first thing this morning?"

"How come you can't just say no?" Rub said, summoning the courage to look up. The conversation had attracted exactly the sort of interest Rub had hoped to avoid over in the far booth, and everybody at the counter seemed interested in watching him squirm. "I wasn't the one busted up your knee."

Sully took out his wallet, handed Rub a ten-dollar bill. "I know you didn't," Sully said, gently now. "I just can't help worrying about you."

"Bootsie told me to buy a turkey is all," he explained.

Cass came by then and refilled Sully's cup, topped Rub's off. "I don't think you heard her right. She probably said you *were* a turkey."

Rub put the ten into his pocket. Everybody in the place was grinning at him, enjoying how hard it was for him to get ten dollars out of his best friend. He recognized in one or two of the faces the same people who, as eighth-graders, had always enjoyed the fact that he couldn't produce his homework for Old Lady Peoples. "You're all in cahoots against me," he grinned sheepishly, relieved that at last the ordeal was over and he could leave. "It's less work to go out and earn money than it is to borrow it in here."

"Did they even look at your knee yesterday?" Cass wanted to know. In the five minutes since Rub had left, the diner had emptied out. Sully was the only customer seated at the counter now, which allowed him to flex his knee. It was hard to tell, but the swelling seemed to have gone down a little. Mornings were the worst, until he got going. He didn't really blame Rub for not understanding why he could neither sit nor stand for very long, or how if he happened to be seated the knee throbbed until he stood up, giving him only a few moments' peace before throbbing again until he sat down, back and forth, every few minutes until he loosened up and the knee settled into ambient soreness, like background music, for the rest of the day, sending only the occasional current of scalding pain, a rim shot off the snare drum, down to his foot and up into his groin, time to rock and roll.

"They don't look at knees," Sully told her, finishing his second cup of coffee and waving off another free refill. "They look at reports. X rays. Knees they don't bother with."

In fact, Sully had suggested showing the judge his knee, just approaching the bench, dropping his pants and showing the judge his red, ripe softball of a knee. But Wirf, his one-legged sot of a lawyer, had convinced him this tactic wouldn't work. Judges, pretty much across the board, Wirf said, took a dim view of guys dropping their pants in the courtroom, regardless of the purpose. "Besides," Wirf explained, "what the knee looks like is irrelevant. They got stuff that'd make even my prosthesis swell up like a balloon. One little injection and they could make you look like gangrene had set in, then twenty-four hours later the swelling goes down again. Insurance companies aren't big believers in swelling."

"Hell," Sully said. "They can keep me overnight. Keep me all week. If the swelling goes down, the drinks are on me."

"Nobody wants you overnight, including the court," Wirf assured him. "And these guys can all afford to buy their own drinks. Let me handle this. When it's our turn, don't say a fuckin' word."

So Sully had kept his mouth shut, and after they waited all morning, the hearing had taken no more than five minutes. "I don't want to see this claim again," the judge told Wirf. "Your client's got partial disability, and the cost of his retraining is covered. That's all he's entitled to. How many times are we going to go through this?"

"In our view, the condition of my client's knee is deteriorating—" Wirf began.

"We know your view, Mr. Wirfly," the judge said, holding up his hand like a traffic cop. "How's school going, Mr. Sullivan?"

"Great," Sully said. "Terrific, in fact. The classes I needed were full, so I'm taking philosophy. The hundred bucks I spent on textbooks in September I haven't been reimbursed for yet. They don't like to pay for my pain pills either."

The judge took all this in and processed it quickly. "Register early next term," he advised. "Don't blame other people for the way things are. Keep that up and you'll end up a lawyer like Mr. Wirfly here. Then where will you be?"

Where indeed? Sully had wondered. In truth, he wouldn't trade places with Wirf.

"So, are you going to keep after them?" Cass wanted to know.

Sully stood up, tested his knee with some weight, rocked on it. "Wirf wants to."

"What do you want?"

Sully thought about it. "A night's sleep'd be good."

When he started for the door, Cass motioned him back with a secretive index finger and they moved farther down the counter. "Why don't you come to work here at the restaurant?" she said, her voice lowered.

"I don't think so," Sully said. "Thanks, though."

"Why not?" she insisted. "It's warm and safe and you're in here half the time anyway."

This was true, and even though Sully had half a dozen reasons for not wanting to work at Hattie's, he wasn't sure any of them would make sense to Cass. For one thing, if he worked at Hattie's he wouldn't be able to wander in off the street when he felt like it because he'd already be there. And he much preferred the side of the counter he was on to the side Cass was on. "You don't need me, for one thing," he pointed out.

"Roof's talking about moving back to North Carolina," she said without looking at the cook, who had taken a stool around the other side of the counter to enjoy the lull and was studying them.

"And has been for twenty years," Sully reminded her.

"I think he means it."

"He's meant it all along. Half the town's been meaning to leave. They don't, though, most of them."

"I know one person who's going to," Cass said, and she sounded like she meant it. "The day after the funeral."

They both glanced at old Hattie, who was leaning forward intently and grinning, as if she were in an arm-wrestling match with Death himself, an opponent she was confident of whipping. "Maybe the day before."

Something of the desperation in her voice got through to Sully, who said, "Listen. You want to get out some night, let me know. I'll baby-sit."

Cass smiled dubiously. "And where would I go?"

Sully shrugged. "How the hell should I know? A movie? I can't figure out everything for you."

Cass smiled, didn't say anything immediately. "I should take you up on it. Just to find out what you'd do when she wet her pants and asked you to change her."

Sully tried to suppress a shudder and failed.

"Right." Cass nodded knowingly.

"I better go shovel my landlady out," he said. "How'd this town get so full of old women, is what I'd like to know."

"We're closed tomorrow, remember."

"How come?" Sully said.

"Thanksgiving, Sully."

"Oh, yeah."

At the door Sully noticed Hattie was beginning to list slightly to starboard, so he took her by the shoulders and righted her. "Sit straight," he said. "Bad posture, you'll grow up crooked."

Hattie nodded and nodded at no external referent. Sully made a mental note to shoot himself before he got like that.

A block down the street from Hattie's, two city workers were taking down the banner that had been strung across Main Street since September, where it had become the object of much discussion and derision. THINGS ARE LOOKING ↑ IN BATH, it said. Some of the town's residents claimed that the banner made no sense because of the arrow. Had a word been left out? Was the missing word hovering in midair above the arrow? Clive Peoples, whose idea the slogan had been, was deeply offended by these criticisms and remarked publicly that this had to be the dumbest town in the world if the people who lived there couldn't figure out that the arrow was a symbol for the word "up." It worked, he explained, on the same principle as I ♥ NEW YORK, which everybody knew was the cleverest promotional campaign in the entire history of promotional campaigns, turning a place nobody even wanted to hear about into a place everybody wanted to visit. Anybody could see that the slogan was supposed to read "I Love New York," not "I Heart New York." The heart was a symbol, a shortcut.

The citizenry of Bath were not fetched by this argument. To most people it didn't seem that the word "up" needed to be symbolically abbreviated, brevity being the word's most obvious characteristic to begin with. After all, the banner stretched all the way across the street, and there was plenty of room for a two-letter word in the center of it. In fact, many of Clive Jr.'s opponents on the banner issue confessed to being less than taken with the "I Heart New York" campaign as well. They remained to be convinced that upstate was much better off for it, and now, after three months of this new banner, the local merchants along Main still remained to be convinced that things were looking ↑ in Bath either. They were waiting for something tangible, like the reopening of the Sans Souci, or groundbreaking on The Ultimate Escape Fun Park.

The new banner (GO SABERTOOTHS! TROUNCE SCHUYLER SPRINGS!) was even more optimistic. The choice of the word "trounce" was more indicative of the town's mounting frustration with the basketball team's losing streak to Schuyler Springs than of a realistic goal. The more traditional "beat" had been rejected as mundane and unsatisfying. The real debate had been between "trounce" and "annihilate." The proponents of "annihilate" had surrendered the field when they were reminded that it was a ten-letter word, and Bath was a town that had recently established a precedent when it abbreviated the word "up."

The banner also promised to revive another controversy, this one turning on a point of grammar. Nearly three decades earlier, when football had to be dropped due to the postwar decline in the region's population and the high school's other sports began to show signs that they could no longer compete successfully against archrival Schuyler Springs, the high school's principal had decided it was time to change the school's nickname (the Antelopes) to something more ferocious in the hopes of spurring Bath's young athletes to greater ferocity. After all, there weren't any antelope within fifteen hundred miles of Bath, and all those animals were famous for was running anyway. So there had been a Name the Team contest and the Sabertooth Tigers were born, all the antelope logos repainted at town expense. Predictably, the whole thing had not turned out well. The fans had immediately shortened the name to the Tigers, which the high school principal thought common and uninspiring and a violation of the contest rules. The best thing about the sabertooth tiger was its saber teeth, which ordinary tigers didn't have, and the principal insisted that the name not be corrupted, even in casual conversation. He'd spent good money repainting all the logos, even if the saber teeth had turned out looking like walrus tusks.

If all this weren't enough, a controversy had erupted on the editorial page of the *North Bath Weekly Journal* over whether the plural of Sabertooth should be Sabertooths or Saberteeth. When the cheerleaders led the spell cheer, how should it go? The principal said Saberteeth sounded elitist and silly and dental. The chair of the high school's English department disagreed, claiming this latest outrage was yet another symptom of the erosion of the English language, and he threatened to resign if he and his staff were expected to sanction tooths as the plural of tooth. Why not? the public librarian had asked in the next letter to the editor. Wasn't this, after all, the same English department that had sanctioned "antelopes" as the plural of "antelope"? The letters continued to pour in for weeks. Beryl Peoples, who'd nursed a twenty-year grudge against the principal for caving in and allowing history courses in the junior and senior high school to be redesignated "'social studies," had the last editorial word, reminding her fellow citizens that the sabertooth tiger was an extinct animal. Food, she suggested, for thought.

Nevertheless, this new banner read GO SABERTOOTHS! TROUNCE SCHUYLER SPRINGS! and the men whose job it was to string the banner across the street were more concerned with it than with the old banner, which had become gray and tattered in the wind and would not be restrung after the weekend's big game. On the Monday following Thanksgiving the Christmas lights always got strung. And so, as the new banner was being attended to—the workers and onlookers shouting instructions to one another to make sure the new banner was centered and straight, as if a botched job might affect the outcome of the game—the old banner was allowed to lie stretched across the street in the slush. When the workers were satisfied that the new banner was secure and had climbed down from their ladders, one of them picked up one end of the old banner just as a car drove by and hooked the cord with one of its rear wheels, dragging the banner all the way up Main and finally out of sight. Sully, shoveling Miss Beryl's driveway as promised, looked up and saw the banner trail by, though he had no idea what it was.

As much as Sully hated the idea, he was going to have to go find Carl Roebuck, who owed him money and refused to pay it. Sully was pretty sure what the result of this visit would be, too. He'd end up going back to work for Carl, something he'd sworn back in August he'd never do. Even worse, he'd sworn it to Carl, who'd looked smug and said, "We'll see."

Carl Roebuck was all of thirty-five and, the way Sully saw it, was threatening to use up, singlehandedly, all the luck there was left in an unlucky town. Just this year he'd won two church raffles and the daily number (on three separate occasions). Five years before that, just as Bath real estate had begun to appreciate, Carl, using part of the money he'd inherited when his father keeled over, bought an old three-story Victorian house on Glendale, getting it for back taxes and the resumption of a tiny 1940 mortgage when the elderly owner died intestate and without relatives. That wasn't enough. The first thing Carl did was to go up into the attic, where he'd found a box of old coins worth forty thousand dollars. The man could shit in a swinging bucket.

Carl's red Camaro was parked at the curb below his third-floor downtown office, right in front of the company El Camino. Sully double-parked his pickup so that both of Carl's vehicles were effectively hemmed in. Carl was not above going down the back way when somebody he didn't want to see was coming up the front. "When are you going to spring for an elevator, you cheap bastard?" Sully called when he got to the top of the stairs and opened the door that read TIP TOP CONSTRUCTION: C. I. ROE-BUCK.

Carl's new secretary, hired during the summer, was a pretty girl, though not as pretty as the one she replaced. She made a face at Sully, whom she hadn't seen in three months and hadn't missed. "He called in sick, he's on the phone, he's in the Bahamas. Take your pick. He doesn't want to talk to you."

Sully pulled up a chair, sat and massaged his knee, which was pulsing from the climb. He could hear Carl Roebuck on the phone in the inner office.

"The Bahamas sound all right, Ruby," he said. "Get his checkbook and we'll go."

"There's about a thousand guys I'd take with me before you," Ruby informed him.

"Don't be mean," Sully said. "This is a small town. There can't be more than a couple hundred guys you'd prefer to me."

"As long as there's one, you're shit out of luck," she smiled unpleasantly.

Sully shrugged. "Okay, except the one you're after's no good for you."

Ruby's unpleasant smile vanished, replaced by an expression even more unpleasant. "And who'm I after, in your opinion?"

Sully realized he'd messed up. That she and Carl, a married man, had something going was common knowledge. The look on Ruby's face suggested she didn't know this.

Luckily, before Sully could make matters worse, Carl Roebuck was heard to hang up the phone in the inner office. "If those are the dulcet tones of the long-lost and unlamented Donald Sullivan," he called, "send him in. Tell him I've got a job for him that even he can't fuck up."

Ruby relocated her unpleasant smile. "Go right in," she purred. "Mr. Roebuck will see you now."

Carl Roebuck was leaning back in his swivel chair when Sully opened the door, and the smug expression on his face was identical to the one he'd worn back in August when Sully swore he'd never work for him again. "How's my favorite cripple?" he wanted to know.

Sully plopped down in one of the room's fake leather chairs. "In the world's worst fucking mood," he said. "I'd like to toss you right out that window just to see what you'd land on."

Carl smiled. "I'd land on my feet."

Sully had to admit this was exactly the way it would probably go. "We may have to try it some time, so we know for sure."

Carl swiveled lazily, grinning. "Sully, Sully, Sully."

Bad mood or no bad mood, Sully couldn't help grinning back. Carl Roebuck was one of those people you just couldn't stay mad at. His father, Kenny Roebuck, hadn't been able to, and neither, apparently, could Carl's wife, Toby, who had a world of reason to. The fact that nobody could stay mad at him was, perhaps, the source of Carl Roebuck's luck. No wonder he had his way with people, especially women. What he managed to convey to all of them was that they were just what he needed to fill his life with meaning.

"What am I going to do with you?" Carl wondered out loud, as if it really were his decision.

"Pay me the money you owe, and I'll let you alone," Sully offered.

Carl ignored this. "Is your truck running?"

"At the moment."

"Then I got a job for you."

"Not till you pay me for the last one."

Carl stood up. "We've been through this. I'm not paying you and that moron Rub Squeers for that half-ass job. You dug a goddamn hole, stood around in it all afternoon, drank a case of beer, filled the hole, and left my lawn all tore up. And we don't have an ounce more water pressure now than we did before."

"I never said you would," Sully reminded him. Carl became instantly red-faced, and this pleased Sully. "Don't get all bent out of whack, now," he added, knowing full well that nothing was more likely to bend Carl Roebuck out of whack than to be instructed by Sully to calm down. Along with Tip Top Construction, Carl had inherited from his father a heart condition that had already required bypass surgery.

"You know the trouble with guys like you?" Carl stood, glowing red now, even though he hadn't raised his voice. "You figure you got a right to steal from anybody that's got a few bucks. I'm supposed to assume the position because you got a busted knee and no prospects, like this is some kind of Feel-Sorry-for-Sully Week. Well, it ain't, my friend. This is Fuck-You Week."

Carl was pacing back and forth behind his desk as he spoke, and for some reason his speech had a soothing effect on Sully, who put his feet up on Carl's desk. "That was last week, actually. And the week before."

"Then go away. You did shoddy work, and I'm not paying you for it. You think I got where I am doing shoddy work?"

Sully couldn't help but smile at this. Maybe later in the day when he remembered it, this line of bullshit would piss him off, but right now, watching Carl Roebuck, beet red with trumped-up self-righteousness, constituted something like partial payment for the debt. And when Sully finally spoke, his voice was even lower than Carl's.

"No, Carl," he admitted. "You didn't get where you are by doing shoddy work. You didn't get where you are by doing any work. You got where you are because your father worked himself into an early grave so you could piss away everything he worked for on ski trips and sports cars."

Sully let this much sink in before continuing. "Now personally, I don't care about the ski trips and the sports cars. I don't even care if you wind up broke, which you probably will. But before you do, you're going to pay me the three hundred bucks you owe me, because I dug a fifty-foot trench under your terrace in ninety-degree heat and busted my balls tugging on hundred-year-old pipes that snapped off in my hands every two feet. That's why you're going to pay me."

He got to his feet then, facing Carl Roebuck across his big desk. "I'll tell you another thing. You're going to pay for the beer. I just decided. It was only a six-pack, but since you think it was a case, you can pay for a case. Call it a tax on being a prick."

That seemed like a pretty good exit line to Sully, and he slammed the door on the way out. The glass hadn't stopped reverberating, however, before he thought of an even better way to leave, so he went back in. Carl was still standing there behind the desk, so Sully picked up right where he left off. "The other reason you're going to pay me is that someday you're going to catch me in a *really* bad mood. My knee's going to be throbbing so bad that even Feel-Sorry-for-Sully Week won't make any difference. The only thing that'll make it feel better will be seeing your sorry ass go flying out that window. About two seconds before you hit the bricks, it'll dawn on you that I wasn't kidding."

Instead of slamming the door again, Sully stood in the open doorway to witness the full effect of his verbal assault. Almost immediately he wished he had slammed the door. Carl's color, instead of deepening, actually began to return to its normal shade, and with its return came the grin that made it impossible for people to stay mad at Carl Roebuck. Instead of storming out from behind the desk and taking a swing at Sully, as Sully half hoped he would, Carl returned to his swivel chair, sat down and put his own soft-loafered feet up. "Sully," he said finally. "You're right. I'm not going to pay you, but you're right. I *am* lucky. Most of the time I remember, but sometimes I forget. Anyway, since we're friends, I'll give you a tip. When you leave, stop outside there on the landing for about five minutes before you go down. That'll save you having to walk back up here when it occurs to you."

"When what occurs to me?"

Carl Roebuck wagged an index finger maddeningly. "If I told you, it would ruin the surprise, schmucko."

Ruby was also grinning at Sully when he left, which probably meant that whatever the surprise was, she'd already figured it out. Outside on the landing, where he'd been told to wait, where the cold air of reality tunneled up from the street, Sully still couldn't think what the surprise was, but he stood there buttoning his coat and pondering his visible breath in the hallway. Things had gone pretty much the way Sully had envisioned. Naturally, they'd argue over the money Carl refused to pay, and naturally he'd tell Carl where to get off and storm out of his office. Then later Carl would come looking for him at The Horse and offer some shitty job as a peace offering, which Sully would tell him he could stuff, and then Carl would offer him something else, probably just as shitty, but Sully would accept this offer because at least he'd gotten some satisfaction out of telling Carl off, not once but twice. By the end of the week he and Rub would be back on the Tip Top payroll.

Except that Carl had thrown him a curve by offering him work right away, which meant that Sully was not only storming out on Carl but the work he'd really come for. On the other hand, Carl hadn't crowed. That was what Sully had dreaded most, Carl smiling smugly and saying, I told you you'd be back. Sully knew from experience that "I told you so" were the four most satisfying words in the English language. He couldn't remember ever passing up the opportunity to say them, and he had to admit it was pretty decent of Carl not to gloat. And he was definitely right about the stairs.

Carl Roebuck was swiveling and grinning when Sully came back in.

"I'll take the money up front," Sully said. "Since I'm working for a man who can't be trusted."

"Half now, half when I've inspected the job," Carl insisted, their standard arrangement. "Since I'm employing Don Sullivan."

Sully took the money, counted it while Carl explained the job. As he listened, it occurred to Sully that he was relieved, glad to be back working for a man he wanted to kill half the time, glad he wasn't driving every day to the community college where he didn't belong, glad to be taking the judge's advice about not blaming people for the way things were, glad not to be placing his trust in lawyers and courts. He'd been afraid that a job working for Carl might be one of the real things that had disappeared while he was taking philosophy.

"I should let one of my regular guys do this," Carl was saying. "But I know you need the money, and besides, we're friends, right?"

"You're lucky I need the money, friend," Sully said.

"You always need the money," Carl pointed out. "Which is why I always have you by the balls."

That smile again. How could you hate the man?

"Does this mean you're through with higher education?" Carl wondered as Sully prepared to leave.

Sully said he supposed it did.

"I wonder who won the pool," Carl said absently.

"Ruby," Sully said, without looking at Carl's secretary on his way through the outer office.

"What?" the girl wanted to know in her best bored-to-death voice.

"Don't take your love to town."

One thing was for sure: compared to some of the other guys Carl Roebuck hired, Sully himself was a genius. Apparently one of Carl's regulars had loaded up about ten tons of concrete basement blocks on the company flatbed and dropped them off at the wrong site. Sully found them in a sloppy pyramid next to a small, two-bedroom ranch home that was already half built. The unexpected snow, together with the fact that tomorrow was a holiday, had apparently sent the guys working on the house back home. In fact, they'd probably never left their homes this morning. Carl didn't hire union men when he could help it, but even the guys who worked for Tip Top Construction didn't work in the snow.

Most of the overnight snow had already melted, and the uneven ground was a quagmire of patchy brown slush. The bank sign had said forty-two degrees when Sully drove by. It felt colder now.

There was only one sensible way to approach this, and that was to go fetch Rub, who was surefooted and didn't mind working in slop of any description. Something was terribly wrong with Rub's nose, Sully was certain. Rub could stand hip deep in the overflow of a ruptured septic tank as pleasantly as if he were in the middle of a field of daisies. This made him invaluable to Sully who, while not overly fastidious, could distinguish between the smell of shit and that of daisies. The downside was that Rub couldn't smell himself either, and when he was ripe his own personal odor greatly resembled what he stood in. Still, the smart thing to do would be to go get Rub, station him in the muck. That way Sully could stay up in the dry bed of the pickup and stack the blocks as Rub handed them up to him. He guessed four or five loads would do the trick, and with Rub's help they could be finished by early afternoon.

Since this was the only sensible way to proceed, Sully decided against it. Rub wasn't expecting work so soon, and it might take Sully an hour to find him if he wasn't home or at Hattie's or the donut shop or the OTB. Then he'd have to listen to Rub chatter all day, and later they'd split the money. Sully didn't mind splitting the money, but he hadn't worked in three months, and he wanted to see how things went. Alone, he could work at his own pace, and if his knee couldn't take it, he could just quit and not owe anybody any explanations. Next week he'd just go back to school.

So he backed the truck up close to the pile of concrete blocks, got out, lowered the tailgate and tested the footing, which wasn't good. I should definitely go get Rub, he thought. Instead he planted half a dozen blocks in the mud for a makeshift walkway between the pyramid and the truck. Then he began, carrying blocks in each hand at first, then a stack of four balanced against his chest, piling them in rows on the truck bed. The hard part was climbing up onto the truck. The only way was to sit on the tailgate, swing his legs aboard, get his good leg under him, then the bad one. Surprisingly, his knee didn't feel too bad. In fact, it felt pretty good. If it held up, maybe he'd use the money he earned today to buy a couple new radials for the truck, whose tires were bald from running back and forth to Schuyler Springs every day to study philosophy. It was as if the young professor had disproved the tread on Sully's tires along with everything else.

It was when he thought of all the things the truck was going to need that he got mad about the money Carl Roebuck wouldn't pay him. The pickup had been pretty long in the tooth when Sully bought it. It had needed new tires a month ago, along with a rebuilt carburetor. The valves needed grinding too. In another month the truck would need all of these repairs even worse, and the month after that it would need them so bad he'd have to make them. And pay for them. New shocks, too, Sully thought, as the truck groaned beneath the weight of the concrete. The three hundred Carl Roebuck owed him would have paid for the tires or the valves or the shocks, whichever Sully decided to fix first. Not that he would necessarily have used the money on the truck if he had it in his pocket that very minute. Sometimes when he got money ahead he gave some to Miss Beryl as advance rent, a hedge against the scarcity of winter work. Sometimes he'd give Cass a hundred so that if things got skinny he'd be able to eat on account for a while. Other times he gave money to Ruth to hold on to for him, which was one way of ensuring that the OTB or the poker table wouldn't get it. The trouble with Ruth was that once he instructed her not to give it back to him unless he really needed it, then it was up to her to decide his need, and sometimes her judgment was a little too refined. And one time her no-good husband Zack had stumbled onto her stash and spent Sully's money, thinking it was his wife's. The more Sully thought about it, the more it didn't seem like such a bad idea to be owed the three hundred. Letting Carl hang on to the money for a while might actually be the safest thing. When Sully needed it most, money had a way of first liquefying, then evaporating, and finally leaving just a filmy residue of vague memory.

And so, as Sully fell deeply into the rhythm of his work, he had the luxury of knowing that his money was safe without in any way diminishing his righteous anger at Carl Roebuck for refusing to pay up, anger that swelled like music in his chest to the distant beat of his throbbing knee. Smiling, he imagined Carl Roebuck tossed out his office window, his arms flapping frantically, his legs wildly pedaling an invisible bicycle as he fell. Sully didn't allow him to hit the ground. He just tossed Carl from the window again and again, so that the other man tumbled and pedaled and screamed.

It was so much fun tossing Carl Roebuck out of his office window that Sully had the truck over half loaded before he noticed it was starting to tilt slightly, like old Hattie in her booth. At first he thought it might be an optical illusion, so he stood back away from the truck and looked at it. There was no reason the truck should be tipping. Off to the side Sully noticed some sheets of plywood, and he wished he'd seen them before so he could have lined the bed of the truck and cushioned the load. Probably it wouldn't have been a bad idea to separate every other layer too, not that the plywood would have distributed the weight differently. It was too late now, in any case. That was the bad news. The good news was he'd worked hard for an hour and his knee didn't feel any worse. In fact, by working and contemplating Carl Roebuck tumbling from his office window, he'd forgotten all about his knee. It wasn't strictly logical, but maybe his injured knee actually was encouraging him to work. Either that or it was telling him to murder Carl Roebuck.

He knew one thing for sure. It was more satisfying to be mad at Carl than to be mad at the courts. Over the last nine months that Wirf had been trying to get him total disability, Sully'd come to understand that all his trips to Albany, even the hearings themselves, were only tangentially related to his deteriorating knee. Maybe the knee wasn't quite as bad as Wirf portrayed it. Maybe. But Sully's growing sense of these legal proceedings was that they were taking place independent of reality. The question wasn't his injury, or whether or not it allowed him to work, or how an injured man might fairly be compensated. At issue was whether the insurance company and the state could be forced to pay. Sully hadn't seen the same insurance company lawyer twice, but they were all sharp and their sheer numbers suggested that he and Wirf, who referred to them as "the Windmills" and insisted that you just had to keep tilting at them, were fighting a losing battle. You couldn't even get good and angry and entertain yourself by imagining that the next time you saw that smug son of a bitch of a lawyer you'd throw him out the window, because the next time there'd be a different guy altogether. You didn't even get the same judge all the time, though all the judges seemed to have pretty much the same attitude toward Sully's claim. They all lectured Wirf and, when the hearing was over, kidded cozily with the insurance company lawyers. Sully himself was generally ignored, and lately he'd come to suspect that if his leg just went ahead and fell off, this (to him) significant event probably wouldn't change anything. Nobody would admit they'd been wrong. They'd use the old X rays to prove he still had a leg. It'd be a philosophical argument.

Sully knew all this was worth getting angry about, and sometimes he did get mad when he thought about it, but there in court he merely felt intimidated, and he was glad to be represented by a lawyer, even one as bad as Wirf, who looked almost as lost and out of place in court as Sully himself. Probably, it occurred to Sully, this was why you paid an attorney to represent you. If it weren't for Wirf, the judge would talk down to you personally and not to Wirf, whose single professional skill seemed to be his ability to eat shit and not mind. Wirf didn't even dress like the lawyers for the insurance company, nor did he appear to notice the way the other lawyers regarded him. Sully felt bad for him, because he and Wirf went way back, but he knew it was better for Wirf to eat shit than for Sully to eat it, because Sully would eat only so much before he'd decide it was somebody else's turn, whereas Wirf seemed to understand that it was always his turn. Since they were friends, Wirf was representing Sully on contingency. If they ended up winning any of the half-dozen concurrent litigations Wirf had filed on Sully's behalf, they would share the booty. Lately, though, it had become obvious to Sully that they weren't going to collect a dime, and he'd begun to feel guilty about letting Wirf file appeal after appeal. To win, you'd have to throw every one of the bastards out the window, and there were more lawyers and judges than windows.

When the pickup was three-quarters loaded and listing even more dangerously, Sully roped off the load and surveyed it dubiously. There was no reason the blocks on the right side of the truck should be heavier than the ones on the left, but they must have been, because the truck was tilting right. As Sully stood there, ankle deep in muck, he realized that he was faced with an honest-to-God decision. He could, against his better judgment, take the unbalanced load out onto the highway and hope for the best, or he could unload it partway, make the first load a small one, drop it off and go find Rub to help him finish.

Free will. An issue much discussed in his philosophy class, and one of the first things to disappear. His professor, a very young man it seemed to Sully, had surprised him by taking the position that there was no such thing as choice, that free will was merely an illusion. Sully had been one of the few older students in the large class and had never said much, but he wished he had the professor here now so he could explain why this wasn't really a choice. He'd probably go about it by disproving the truck. To Sully it looked for all the world like a choice. His. Fuck it, he decided.

Climbing into the cab, Sully turned the ignition, ground the truck into gear, released the brake, paused and stepped on the accelerator. He might have stopped when he heard and felt the tires spinning in the mud, but he didn't, even though he knew what that meant. Instead, he gunned the engine, put the accelerator to the floor, months of submerged fury suddenly at the surface, the high-pitched unrelenting scream of the truck's engine almost his own, the truck's rear wheels shooting mud all the way up the side of Carl Roebuck's half-built house. Then, without moving either forward or back, the truck began to shake so violently that Sully was barely able to keep his hands on the wheel until the engine finally hiccuped twice, shuddered and died. Just as well, too. The rear wheels' lug nuts were already below ground. Stupid, he thought. Just an hour ago he'd been wondering if a second stupid streak in the same year was a possibility, and now here he was right in the middle of one before he'd even had a chance to contemplate the odds. Sully got out and surveyed the situation. The wind had picked up, and whistling through the pines nearby it sounded like laughter.

Mrs. Gruber, who had been disappointed by the snail, phoned midmorning, wondering if Miss Beryl's mail had been delivered and if she'd looked over the circular that announced the grand opening of the new supermarket out by the interstate exit. Miss Beryl, as Mrs. Gruber feared, had tossed the circular into the trash without so much as a glance.

"They have some wonderful bargains," said Mrs. Gruber, who hated to miss a grand opening of anything. She had pored over the circular with mounting excitement and regret, the latter caused by the fact that she did not drive and that the supermarket was five miles away. The circular had been six full pages, and each page was in full color, picturing deep red cuts of beef, Kelly green vegetables. Even the most mundane items, like toilet paper and laundry detergent, looked exotic and thrilling. And all at incredible savings. Mrs. Gruber wanted to go to the supermarket and find out for herself if the circular truly represented the wonders of the new store. She knew it was against the law for advertisers to say things that weren't true, so she was hopeful. Wasn't it just like Miss Beryl to toss the circular, she thought, genuinely irked by her friend's perverse refusal to be excited by anything exciting. "Go find it," she urged Miss Beryl. "Take a look at it."

"It's in the trash," Miss Beryl told her. "Under my wet tea bag."

"You won't believe the bargains," Mrs. Gruber said, quoting almost directly from the circular itself.

Miss Beryl glanced out the front room window, hoping the snow might be pretext for refusal. She did need to go to the store today, though the North Bath IGA would do her fine. It was close, and she didn't mind that there weren't any bargains. It was Miss Beryl's view that anything involving crowds of jostling bargain seekers wouldn't be a bargain. But most of the snow had melted, and the street was actually dry in a few spots.

"It'll be good to get out," Mrs. Gruber said. "Let's go. Let's sally forth," she said, purposely using one of her friend's favorite phrases.

"I'll pick you up in half an hour," Miss Beryl told her.

"I'll be outside," Mrs. Gruber said. To her mind, being on the porch and saving her friend the necessity of pulling into the driveway was a way of paying Miss Beryl back for agreeing to go to the new supermarket.

"Stay inside," Miss Beryl said. "I'll toot."

"I don't mind," Mrs. Gruber insisted. "I'll be on the porch."

"Half an hour," Miss Beryl said.

"Goody," Mrs. Gruber said, hanging up.

Miss Beryl had half a page remaining in the chapter of her Trollope, so she finished it, then stood up. From the side windows of her front room she could see up and down Main Street, and when she set her book down and looked up Main in the direction of Mrs. Gruber's house she could see that Mrs. Gruber was already standing on her porch and peering down the street at Miss Beryl's house, fully expecting, no doubt, Miss Beryl's car to be backing out of the drive. All of two minutes had elapsed since they'd hung up.

Miss Beryl rose and sighed. She was just about to fetch her overcoat when a big, noisy car she'd never seen before pulled up at the curb outside her front window and a young woman who looked to be in her early twenties got out and checked something written on a slip of paper. She was wearing a sweater and no overcoat, and Miss Beryl could not help but notice, even at that distance, that the young woman had an absolutely huge bosom.

"Who the heck are you?" the old woman said out loud. "Look at those bazooms," she added to Clive Sr., on the TV, who smiled back at her appreciatively, though he was facing the wrong direction to see. "You too, Ed. Take a gander at those," she instructed Driver Ed.

Before closing the car door, the young woman leaned back inside. At first, she appeared to be looking for something on the seat, but then Miss Beryl saw a small head move inside the vehicle on the passenger side of the front seat.

When the young woman started across the snowy terrace and up the walk toward the porch, the car door opened and a very small child clambered out. Apparently, the young woman (the child's mother?) heard the door open, because she spun and almost flew back to the curb, shoving the child back inside roughly, punching the door lock down and slamming the door shut. Even from inside, Miss Beryl could hear the young woman shouting. "Sit, goddamn it!" she was instructing the child. "I'm coming right back. You hear me? Just sit in the goddamn car and look at your goddamn magazine. You hear me? If you get out of this car again, I'm going to knock your block off, you hear?"

"Someone ought to knock *your* block off," Miss Beryl said as the young woman turned on her heel and started back across the terrace. She wasn't quite to the porch when the door opened again, and the child climbed back out. This time the young woman stayed where she was, looked up into the web of black elm branches as if some answer, in the form of a chattering squirrel perhaps, might be offering advice. "You could close the goddamn door, at least," she yelled at the child, who had begun to follow and now stopped. Miss Beryl couldn't tell if the child was a boy or a girl, but whichever it was turned, put a small shoulder to the heavy door and pushed. When the door swung shut, the child lost its footing and slipped to its knees. Again the young woman looked to the sky for answers. "Come on, then, if you're coming," she shouted, and the child, wet kneed now but surprisingly dry eyed, did as it was told. There was something frighteningly robotlike about the child's movements, and Miss Beryl was reminded of a movie she'd started to watch on television years ago about zombie children, a movie she'd quickly turned off.

"What's wrong with that child?" she asked Clive Sr. as she moved from the front to the side window so she could watch the young woman and the child climb the porch steps. It was a little girl, Miss Beryl decided, and all she was wearing from the waist up was a thin T-shirt.

When Miss Beryl heard the outside door grunt open, she opened the door to her own flat to confront the young woman, who apparently intended to head upstairs to Sully's apartment. "Move it, Birdbrain," she said, apparently to the child, though she was looking directly at Miss Beryl when she spoke.

"May I help you?" Miss Beryl said, not particularly trying to convey any real desire to be helpful.

"He up there?" the young woman wanted to know. Up close, she looked vaguely familiar, like she might once have been one of Miss Beryl's eighth-graders.

"Who?" Miss Beryl said. Sully had few visitors, and Miss Beryl knew most of them by sight, if not by name.

"The guy who *lives* up there," said the young woman with undisguised irritation.

"He's not in," Miss Beryl said.

"Good," said the young woman. "Something was bound to go right today if I waited long enough."

Miss Beryl paid no attention to this. She was looking at the child, who stood motionless at her mother's side, staring at Miss Beryl. Or she would have been staring, if something hadn't been wrong with one of her eyes, which looked off at a tragic angle, at nothing at all. Miss Beryl felt her heart quake but was only able to say, "This child should be wearing a coat. She's shivering."

"Yeah, well, I told her to stay in the car," the young woman said, "so whose fault is it?"

"Yours," Miss Beryl said without hesitation.

"Right, mine," the young woman said, as if she'd heard this before. "Listen. Do me a megafavor and mind your own business, okay?"

The sheer outrageousness of this suggestion left Miss Beryl momentarily speechless. She hadn't been sassed since she retired from teaching, and she'd forgotten what she used to do about it. The moment of stunned silence was apparently enough for the young woman to reconsider her tactics.

"Listen," she said, her shoulders slumping. "Don't mind me, okay? Everything is mega–screwed up right now. I don't usually yell at old ladies."

Just children, Miss Beryl almost said, but held her tongue. That was how she'd always handled sassing, she remembered. She'd said nothing and glared at the miscreant until it dawned on him or her that a serious mistake had been made and that Miss Beryl hadn't been the one who'd made it.

"It's just Birdbrain here," she explained. "I'd like to give her to you for about an hour, just for laughs."

They were both studying the silent child now. The little girl, for her part, might as well have been standing all alone in the hallway for all the sense she conveyed of being in the proximity of other human beings.

"Hello, sweetheart," Miss Beryl said, and hoped that she wasn't glowering at the child as she had been at her mother. She'd more than once been accused of frightening small children, though no one had ever explained to her precisely what she was doing to frighten them.

"That's a good idea," the young woman said. "Make friends with this nice old lady while Mommy makes a phone call." Then, to Miss Beryl, "He got a phone up there?"

"Use mine," Miss Beryl said, still not sure she should be allowing the young woman into her tenant's flat. Not that Sully probably would have minded or had any cause to object, since he never locked up when he left.

"Suit yourself," the young woman said, slipping her shoes off. "I wasn't planning on stealing anything. Take your shoes off, Birdbrain. We're going in here for a minute, I guess."

The child was wearing cheap blue canvas tennis shoes, and Miss Beryl could tell that they were wet, as were the child's socks.

"Don't touch nothing in here," the young woman warned the child. "These aren't our things, and Mommy doesn't have money to pay for what you bust."

Miss Beryl showed the young woman where the telephone was in the front room. The young woman picked up the receiver and looked at Miss Beryl. "Thanks," she said. "Been awhile since I've seen one of these," she added in reference to its rotary dial. In fact, the phone did go back about thirty years. "Regular museum you got in here," she said, looking around the room.

Before Miss Beryl could respond to this observation, the young woman was talking into the phone. "Ma. He there yet?" A brief pause. "No, I'm at the old lady's downstairs. I don't think she's too thrilled about us going up there."

Miss Beryl could hear the tinny voice of whoever she was talking to, but not clearly enough to make out any words. She still couldn't take her eyes off the child, who stood patiently at her mother's side, facing Miss Beryl. The child's good eye was taking her in, Miss Beryl decided.

"The more I think about it, the more I doubt he's even coming, Ma. He's just pulling your chain. How the hell should I know? He probably guessed. He's probably threatening everybody. That's the way he does things. Threaten everybody. That way you're sure. You want to know how I know? Because if he was coming here like he said, he'd have to give up a day of deer hunting. No, he won't. You don't know him like I do. Besides, if he was coming, he wouldn't call to warn us, he'd just be here." Another pause. "No, you're wrong. He's out in the woods, is where he is. He's out there laughing at you for believing him. Believe me, he's out in the middle of the woods. Maybe I'll get lucky and he'll get lost and freeze to death out there. That'd be a break, huh?"

To Miss Beryl's way of thinking, the most objectionable thing about this objectionable conversation was the fact that the child was listening to it. Since the little girl was still staring at her, Miss Beryl picked up her red, two-headed Foo dog from the coffee table and showed it to the little girl. The dog had the same grinning head on both ends of its body.

"See my Foo dog?" she said, offering the stuffed animal to the child, who made no move to take it. Miss Beryl rotated the dog so that the child could see its two heads, that it was the same at both ends. If the little girl noticed this unusual feature, she gave no sign, though she studied the animal dully.

"You know what a Foo dog says?" Miss Beryl asked.

The child's good eye found her again.

"Foo on you," Miss Beryl said, hoping for a smile.

The little girl's eye again found the animal, again studied it seriously, as if to determine whether the dog in question would say such a thing.

"I call him Sully," Miss Beryl said, "because he doesn't know whether he's coming or going."

This time when she offered the animal, the child took it, without enthusiasm, almost as if she were doing Miss Beryl a favor.

"Yeah . . . yeah . . . yeah," the child's mother was saying. "Okay, I'll go upstairs if I can talk her into letting me. Call me up there in half an hour. You should see the phone I'm talking into. It must've been made during the Civil War. . . . Okay. . . . Go back to work. . . . Yeah, okay."

When she hung up the phone, the young woman picked the little girl up and rubbed noses with her. "False alarm, Birdbrain. Daddy pulled a fast one on Grandma. He's probably real proud of himself too. Daddy doesn't get to outsmart people very often." Then, to Miss Beryl, "You gonna let us go upstairs, or what?"

"I guess if you know Mr. Sullivan, he won't mind," Miss Beryl said.

"Yeah, well, I don't know him," said the young woman on her way to the door. "He's been balling my mother for about twenty years, though. She's the one who knows him."

Once again, Miss Beryl was speechless. She watched her visitors go, watched the door close behind them, watched it open again. "Here's your dog back," the young woman said, setting the Foo dog back on the table. "And thanks again for the phone." She cast a half-amused, half-contemptuous glance around Miss Beryl's flat. "You're missing the boat. You should charge admission to see this place."

When she was gone again and the child's and the mother's footsteps had climbed the stairs and entered the room above, Miss Beryl found her voice again. "Well," she said to Clive Sr. "What do you think of that?"

Before her dead husband could answer, the phone rang. "Now what?" Miss Beryl said.

It was Mrs. Gruber, whom Miss Beryl had forgotten completely.

"I'm coming," Miss Beryl told her. "Keep your girdle on."

■ ■ ■

There were only half a dozen paved roads into and out of North Bath. In addition to Route 27A, the two-lane blacktop that became Main (Upper and Lower) within the city limits, there were five other narrow two-lanes linking Bath to its neighbors: Schuyler Springs to the north and smaller communities like Shaker Heights, Dollsville, Wapford, Glen. And there was the new four-lane spur that linked Bath to the interstate that ran between Albany and Montreal. The new spur was just three miles long, traversing the large tract of marshy land that separated Bath from the interstate, the future site, according to a large billboard planted just off the roadway, of the five-hundred-acre "Ultimate Escape Fun Park," an "extravaganza of water slides, roller coasters, a Wild West town and a fantasy village where fairy-tale characters spring to life." The majority of the huge billboard was a garish clown's face, and there was something about this face, about its lewd grin perhaps, that suggested more malice than fun, and small children who had the sign pointed out to them by their mothers as they sped by had been known to burst into tears of fright. Adults were disconcerted also to notice that within sight of the billboard, just before you entered the village of North Bath, was the new cemetery, a stark, treeless place of, for the most part, horizontal gravestones. There was considerable speculation that the cemetery would have to be relocated once construction on the fun park got under way. Already the juxtaposition of the two "ultimate escapes" had become a dark local joke.

This midmorning, thanks to the grand opening of the new supermarket at the interstate exit, there was more traffic than usual speeding down the spur toward the demonic clown billboard. For the most part, the motorists were housewives hurrying back toward town, the back of their vans and station wagons loaded down with groceries. They'd gotten carried away in the festive new store and bought twice as much as they normally would, purchasing items not available at the North Bath IGA. As they flew home, feet bearing down a little more heavily on the accelerator than was their custom, contemplating their greater-than-anticipated expenditure of time and money, they were greeted by an unsettling apparition in the form of a hitchhiker attempting to thumb a ride into town. These housewives, many of whom had small, fussy children with them, were not the sort to pick up even decent-looking hitchhikers, and so they were not even fleetingly tempted to stop for this one, who was so besotted with mud that the speeding housewives concluded, despite the fact that there was no prison within a hundred-mile radius, that the man must be an escaped convict, a murderer surely, who had spent the night in the marsh to escape the dogs. Either that or he was a premature burial from the nearby cemetery who had clawed his way out of his casket and up through the black earth and into the air. Where most hitchhikers at least attempted to look friendly or, failing that, pitiful, this one looked just plain dangerous. Something about the way he held out his thumb suggested that the fist attached to it might contain a live grenade. One young woman driving a station wagon full of groceries actually swerved into the left lane when she drew near him, as if she feared he might lunge at the car and grab the door handle as she hurtled by.

Nothing could have been further from Sully's intention. If he was dangerous, he certainly wasn't dangerous in the way the young woman feared. His murderous expression was simply the result of spending the morning doing a thankless job on a bum knee, getting his truck stuck in the mud, spending half an hour of fruitless exertion trying to get unstuck, during which time it had occurred to him what Carl Roebuck, the man he'd sworn he'd never go back to work for, would say when he found out what Sully'd done. Carl Roebuck would say he'd been wrong—that the job *had* been one Sully could fuck up after all, a remark Sully did not want to hear uttered outside the precincts of his own thoughts. Every time Carl said it, even within those precincts, Sully threw him out the window. To make matters worse, he could hear his young philosophy professor snickering an I-told-you-so about free will.

Also his father, who lay buried in the cemetery another half mile up the highway, a man with whom Sully had not yet made peace. In fact, on the way out to Carl Roebuck's development, he'd done what he always did when he drove by the cemetery. He'd rolled down the window, cold be damned, and given Big Jim Sullivan the finger as he flew by. Unlike most of the residents of Bath, Sully didn't care much whether The Ultimate Escape Fun Park got built or not, except that if it did, they'd probably relocate the cemetery, which meant they'd have to disturb his father's eternal rest. Sully hated to think of his father at rest, and had there been a way, and if Sully'd had the money, he'd have left instructions to have Big Jim dug up every decade or so, just to make sure he didn't get comfortable. And so, right now, he was hoping to get a lift past the cemetery so his father wouldn't have a chance to get a close-up look at him in his present condition. Whenever he was on a stupid streak he was conscious of the faraway sound of his father's laughter. His next-to-last stupid streak, a little over a year ago, had begun when he fell off a ladder and injured his knee.

Anybody could fall off a ladder, of course. That hadn't been the stupid part. The stupid part had been the reason he'd fallen. Halfway up the ladder, he'd heard a man laughing raucously, and off across the job site, on the other side of the chain-link fence, Sully'd spotted a big man who, from a distance, was a dead ringer for his father. Dead ringer he would indeed have been, since Big Jim had himself been dead for several years. Whoever the man with the horselaugh was, Sully was paying attention to him and not to his footing. He'd fallen twenty feet and then listened to the distant sound of his father's laughter all the way to the hospital. Right now, so close to the cemetery, the sound of laughter was nearer, was ringing, in fact, in Sully's ears.

When he saw the expression on the face of the young woman who swerved, Sully made a conscious effort to look less like a serial killer. After a while he gave up, both the hitching and the trying to look harmless. It was only a mile back to town, and he'd already walked nearly that far backward. He even began to look on the bright side. As long as the truck was buried in the mud, he couldn't capsize the load. The other good thing was that Rub, whose assistance he would now seek, was blessedly devoid of a sense of humor and therefore never derived much benefit from other people's stupidity. If Rub himself had backed a truck into a mud hole and then loaded on a ton of concrete blocks and couldn't drive out again, his stupidity would have been the first thing Sully noticed. But other people's stupidity elicited only sympathy in Rub, who identified so strongly and immediately with dumbness that he lost all advantage. All Rub would want to know, Sully realized, was how come Sully hadn't come to get him in the first place, since this was obviously a job for two men, a job that even two men would be hard pressed to finish by dark, now that the morning had been wasted.

Lost in the soothing contemplation of Rub's intellectual limitations and having given up on the idea of anybody stopping, Sully did not immediately notice when a small olive green Gremlin pulled over to the shoulder of the road some fifty yards ahead, its turn signal blinking. That it had stopped for him occurred to Sully only when it tooted. The Gremlin was old and banged up, and he half recognized the car as belonging to someone he knew, but couldn't think who. Sully didn't know anybody in Bath who drove a Gremlin, which deepened the mystery, because he didn't know that many people outside of Bath. When the Gremlin tooted a second time, Sully realized that he had stopped walking, that he was stalled right there along the shoulder, as if solving the riddle of who owned the

Gremlin were prerequisite to accepting a ride in it. Somebody had rolled down the passenger side window and was waving impatiently. Sully started walking.

The Gremlin had an out-of-state license, though it was too dirty for Sully to guess which state. The little car's slanting rear window was piled high with clothes and blankets and toys, making it impossible to see inside, and Sully approached the car with serious misgivings, which only increased when a familiar-looking young woman poked her head out the passenger side window and glared at him. Her expression bespoke considerable irritation, as if one look at Sully had reminded her of half a dozen unpleasant things she'd forgotten about him. Without knowing exactly why, Sully felt a sudden urge to flee, as if the woman hailed from some amnesiac past and had returned bent on slapping him with a patrimony suit.

"Hi, dolly," he said when he was close enough to be heard, having decided to brazen it out. In his sixty years he'd forgotten enough people to know that the best way to handle such situations was to pretend you knew who they were until they gave you a clue. Whoever this unpleasant-looking young woman was, he'd remember eventually. All his adult life he'd called young women "dolly," so if this one knew him, she wouldn't be surprised. When he got alongside the car, he saw there were three children crowded into the cramped backseat among pillows and stuffed animals, slightly older versions of children he knew from somewhere. The young woman got out and pulled one of the bucket seats forward so Sully could crawl in back, and as he leaned forward and caught a glimpse of the driver it dawned on him who the hell these people were.

"Shove over, you runts," he said, making a face at the children. "Make room for Grandpa."

"Give me Andy," said Charlotte, his son's wife. "That way you'll have a *little* room anyway," she let her voice trail off.

Sully would have liked to give her Andy, but he was momentarily confused. He was half in the Gremlin's backseat and half out of it, and pretty sure which of his grandsons was Andy but unable to commit fully. He was almost positive Andy was the baby, but if he was, then Charlotte's request made no sense. The child was strapped into a car seat, and even if Sully were able to unbuckle him—and this looked doubtful, given the contraption's complexity—the only result would have been an empty car seat, not more room for an adult.

"Unstrap your brother, Will," said Peter, Sully's son. "Don't just sit there like this is TV."

The oldest boy, who looked amazingly like his father at the same age, did as he was told, but he wore a brooding expression, as if he'd been asked to bear too much responsibility. If the oldest was Will and the youngest was Andy, that left only the middle boy, who was staring at Sully in unself-conscious bewilderment, a bubble of snot at one nostril pulsing to the beat of his respiration. Sully conceded that, to the boy, he must look strange, caked with mud.

When Andy was passed into the front, Charlotte turned her weary attention to the middle boy. "Get in your brother's seat, Wacker. You expect Grandpa to sit in it?"

"That's a *baby* seat," the boy frowned.

"I'll sit in it," the oldest boy sighed, unhooking his seat belt.

This put the middle boy into motion. "Mom said me! Mom said me!" he cried and let his big brother have one as Will attempted to climb into the seat he clearly would not fit into. The smaller boy's fist caught the larger boy right on the bridge of the nose, and for a second Will's eyes welled up, allowing his little brother to scramble into the baby's car seat, from which he grinned malevolently at his injured brother. To Sully's surprise, the older boy made no move to retaliate.

Now that there was a free crevice, Sully let himself slide into it, gingerly maneuvering his leg into the restricted space, bending it slowly at the knee. What was Wacker's real name? he wondered. Something that sounded like Wacker, maybe. He searched his memory for a boy's name that sounded like Wacker.

"Wacker punched me again," Will said to no one in particular. He was inspecting his nose for blood, seemingly disappointed there was none. Had there been blood, somebody might have believed him. Wacker showed his big brother a small, bony fist, and his eyes narrowed, as if to imply that a second assault might just provide the evidence.

"Punch him back," Sully's son suggested, pulling the Gremlin back onto the road. He had not turned around in the seat or offered to shake hands or given any sign that he was happy to see Sully. But then that's the way it had been between them since Peter had gone off to college—what? fifteen? twenty years ago? Probably Peter considered such treatment pay-back, simple karmic justice, and if true, Sully did not object. When the boy was growing up, Sully had never willfully ignored him, certainly wouldn't have passed him on life's highway if the boy had needed a lift. It was just that his mother had seen to it that the boy never needed a lift. She and Ralph, the man she'd married a year or so after divorcing Sully, had done such a good job raising Peter that the boy never needed anything, and Sully knew Ralph was doing a better job as a father than he himself could have managed. By staying out of his son's life, he was doing the boy a favor, or that had been his reasoning. Not an unwise decision, it seemed to Sully even now. True, Peter had grown up laconic and without much apparent ambition of his own, but he had Vera's considerable ambitions on his behalf to draw from, tempered by his stepfather's easy good nature, and somehow Peter had made himself a college professor of something or other, Sully couldn't remember what.

"Clobber him, in fact," Peter said without much conviction. "People hit you, hit 'em back."

"This from a former conscientious objector," Charlotte snorted, as if her husband's remark were final proof, were any needed, of his fundamental hypocrisy. Sully, who seldom registered such things, couldn't help noticing the tension in the front seat and wonder as to its cause. Had one of them not wanted to stop and give him a lift? If so, it probably would have been Charlotte, not Peter, who insisted on stopping. He seldom saw his daughter-in-law, but he'd always been fond of her. She was a big, awkward girl with an open face who didn't as a rule mind being kidded, and kidding was one of the relatively few things Sully had to offer, that and the unspoken camaraderie that had naturally evolved as a result of Vera's disapproval of both of them. Vera had never made much of an attempt to disguise her opinion that Peter had not married well, that Charlotte was not the kind of woman who was likely to advance his career. They had lived together before marrying, and Vera hadn't approved of that either. That they'd married only when Charlotte became pregnant with Will proved, to Vera's way of thinking, that her son had been trapped. Charlotte had explained all this to Sully once, and he'd felt bad for her. What little he knew about his son's life he got from Charlotte's chatty Christmas cards.

"What are you doing out here?" Peter wanted to know. He adjusted his rearview mirror so he could see Sully in the backseat.

"I was about to ask you the same thing," Sully said, not anxious to explain.

"We've been summoned to Thanksgiving dinner," Charlotte said. "And of course we dare not offend royalty."

This was clearly a reference to Vera, who would run things if allowed to. In the end she had failed to run Sully, but not for lack of effort. Her second husband she'd chosen more carefully. "I don't think I've seen Vera since the last time you were here," Sully said, taking a neutral position on the subject of Vera. "How long ago was that?" he wondered, realizing as he gave this question voice that it was not a simple one. Often when his son and family visited Vera and Ralph they snuck into and out of town without seeing him.

"How can you live in a town the size of Bath and not see everybody all the time?" Charlotte wondered.

"Well, dolly, Vera and I don't travel in the same circles," Sully explained. "In fact, Vera doesn't travel in circles at all. She goes pretty much straight forward."

"Does she ever," Charlotte agreed unpleasantly.

"*Some*body had to," Peter offered.

Sully glanced at the rearview mirror, but Peter's eyes were straight ahead on the road. Out the passenger side window, Sully noticed that they'd just passed the cemetery where Big Jim Sullivan lay buried, and Sully resisted the urge to give his father the finger, a gesture he would then have had to explain to his grandsons. He wondered if, when Peter saw him alongside the road, there'd been a moment when the boy considered rolling down the window, tooting, and flipping Sully the bird. Speaking of karma.

"I'd let you hold your grandson," Charlotte said, "except he's busy pooping at the moment." Andy was on her shoulder, staring at Sully over the back of the seat. The child's face was intense, but focused on a vacant spot between the end of his nose and his grandfather. A gaze full of rectal purpose.

"Thanks," Sully said. "I'd hate like hell to get it all over my good clothes."

This remark startled Will, who stopped fingering his nose and looked over at Sully, clearly wondering if these could be his grandfather's good clothes. His eyes widened with fear and sympathy.

"Hello, Mordecai," Sully said to Wacker, who had not stopped staring at him even for a second, though he did not seem to share his older brother's fear that these might be Sully's good clothes.

"My name's not Mordecai!" the boy said angrily. "It's Wacker!"

"How come they call you Wacker?" Sully said, winking across Wacker at Will.

Wacker's face brightened instantly, and before Sully could prevent it, the little boy located a long hardback Dr. Seuss and brought it down with a crash on Sully's knee, resulting in an explosion of sincere expletives that Sully hadn't had the least intention of using in the company of his son's family. Will, who had bravely held back the tears occasioned by Wacker's attack on himself, now burst into tears of genuine terror and sympathy.

As soon as Sully could catch his breath, he told his son to pull over, which Peter did reluctantly, into the parking lot of the IGA supermarket. Once out of the Gremlin, Sully headed straight across the lot toward the abandoned photo shack some hundred yards away. For some reason, the faster he limped, the less the knee hurt. In about fifty yards, Peter caught up to him.

"Jesus, Dad," he said, his face a study in annoyance, pretty much devoid of concern, it seemed to Sully, who was surprised to discover that a little concern from his son might have been a comfort. "What'd the little bastard do?"

Sully slowed, the waves of pain and nausea subsiding a little. He took a deep breath and said, "Wow."

"He's just a kid, for heaven's sake," Peter said. Apparently this was intended to be a comment on Wacker's strength, his inability to inflict significant pain. What he wanted to know was why his father, lifelong tough guy, was carrying on like this.

Since it was the simplest way to explain, Sully pulled up his pant leg to show him. When he saw his father's knee, Peter's eyes went so round with fear that he looked like Will. "Wacker did that?" he said, incredulous. "With Dr. Seuss?"

"Don't be an idiot," Sully told him, satisfied with his son's reaction. "I fell off a ladder. A year ago."

Peter looked greatly relieved to learn this. "Jesus," he repeated. "You should see a doctor."

Sully snorted. "I've seen about twenty so far."

When he lowered his pant leg, Peter still stared at the spot, as if he could see the grotesque, purple swelling right through the fabric. They turned back toward the Gremlin. "What do they say?" Peter wanted to know.

"Twenty different things," Sully said, though this was not precisely true. "They wanted to give me a new knee, back when it happened. I should have let them, too."

At the time, it hadn't seemed like a good idea. After the injury, the pain had been intense but manageable, and Sully had thought that given time the pain would gradually ebb, the way hurt always did. Had he agreed to the operation, he'd have been out of commission even longer, and he told himself he couldn't afford that, which was pretty close to true. But the real reason he hadn't let them operate was that the whole idea of a new knee had seemed foolish. In fact, Sully had laughed when the doctor first suggested it, thinking he was joking. The idea of getting a new anything ran contrary to Sully's upbringing. "Don't come crying to me and wanting a new one if you can't take care of the one you got," his father had been fond of saying. In his father's house, if you spilled your milk at the supper table, you didn't drink milk that night. If your ball got stuck up on the roof, too bad. You shouldn't have thrown it up there. If you took your watch off and left it someplace and you wanted to know the time, you could always walk downtown and see what it said on the First National Bank clock. They put that there, according to Sully's father, specifically for people too dumb to hang on to their watches.

As a boy Sully had hated his father's intolerance of human error, especially since that intolerance was chiefly reserved for others. But the attitude took, and Sully, as an adult, had come to think of making do without things you'd broken as the price you paid for having your own way.

"Why not let them do the operation now?" Peter wanted to know.

"Listen," Sully said, "don't worry about it." He'd wanted Peter to know about the injury, but he had little desire to go into details or offer explanations. In the year since he'd fallen, the knee had become arthritic, which according to the insurance company physicians was the reason the pain was getting worse. It was their contention that Sully had fucked up by not letting them operate when they wanted to. This was Wirf's paraphrase of their position, actually.

"The swelling's mostly fluid," Sully told him. "I should probably get it drained again. Except it's expensive and hurts like hell and it doesn't feel that much better when they're done."

Slowly, they made their way back to the car. Andy, Sully noticed, had been returned to his car seat. Will had stopped crying and was now studying his grandfather fearfully through the side window. Wacker was examining Dr. Seuss with what looked to Sully like newfound respect for the written word. Charlotte, who had not gotten out, was staring straight ahead, massaging her temples.

"I haven't done something to offend your wife, have I?" it occurred to Sully to ask. He often did offend women without meaning to or even knowing how he'd managed. Maybe she didn't want someone as filthy as he was in her car. Maybe he'd been wrong before. Perhaps it was Peter who'd insisted on pulling over, Charlotte who hadn't wanted to.

But Peter shook his head. "It's me, not you," he admitted.

Sully waited for him to elaborate, and when he didn't, said, "I'm sorry to hear it."

"She's got cause, I guess."

Sully studied his son, who was in turn studying his family as if they belonged to somebody else. His remark had been delivered in an offhanded way, but Sully thought for a second that he recognized it as a confidence of sorts. If so, it was a first, and before Sully could decide whether or not he liked the idea of being confided in, Peter followed the first confidence with another.

"I don't suppose Mom told you I was turned down for tenure."

This pretty much decided the issue of confidences. Sully already knew he was no happier for this knowledge. "No," Sully said. "I wasn't kidding. I haven't seen your mother, even to say hello to."

"This happened last spring, actually," Peter said. "They give you a year to find something else."

Sully nodded. "Any luck?"

"Yup," Peter said. "All bad."

"I'm sorry to hear it, son," Sully told him, which was true, though not much to offer.

Peter had still not looked at him, was still studying his family, wedged so tightly into the battered Gremlin. "Sometimes I think you did the smart thing. Just run away."

The usual bitterness was there, of course, but Peter's observation seemed more melancholy than angry, and the only thing to do was to let it go, so Sully did. "I only made it about five blocks, if you recall."

Peter nodded. "You might as well have gone to California."

"You trying to get me to say I'm sorry?" Sully said.

"Nope," Peter said. "Not unless you are."

Sully nodded. "Say hello to your mother for me. And thanks for the lift."

Peter studied his shoes. He looked suddenly ashamed, something Sully hadn't intended. "Why don't you stop by tomorrow?"

Sully grinned at him. "You better clear the invitation with your mother."

"I don't have to ask permission to invite my own father to stop by on Thanksgiving," he said.

Sully didn't contradict him. "She's changed, then."

"Will you be okay here?"

Sully said he would. There was a pay phone outside the IGA, and Sully promised he'd call Rub to come get him. He also promised to think about stopping by Vera's the next day. According to Peter, his stepfather, Ralph, whose health had been poor for some time, had just gotten out of the hospital and things hadn't been going too well. Sully said he'd try to stop by and cheer everybody up. One look at him should do it, he told Peter, who misunderstood and concluded it was Sully's intention to come by in something like his present condition, which Peter counseled against. They managed to shake hands successfully then, all of this accomplished a few feet from the Gremlin, the windows of which remained tightly rolled up.

Sully knocked on the side window, startling Charlotte, who looked like she'd been somewhere else, as if she'd genuinely forgotten his existence. When she rolled down the window, he saw that her eyes were red and puffy. "Nice to see you're still so good looking, dolly," he offered, though in fact she'd put on weight, he could tell. The compliment failed to cheer her up.

"That's a minority view," she said.

"My views usually are," Sully admitted, realizing as he did so that he'd just taken the compliment back. To get out of the awkward moment, he rapped on the window Wacker was seated next to. "Next time you whack me, whack my right leg," he told his grandson. "That's the good one. You ever whack the left one again, I'm going to chase you all the way back home to West Virginia."

Wacker did not look impressed by this threat. In fact, he raised the Dr. Seuss over his head by way of invitation. The tiny white bubble of snot still pulsed calmly in one nostril. Will, by contrast, looked like he was about to wet his pants in sheer terror. When Sully flashed him a grin to show that it was all in fun, the boy was visibly relieved, and as the Gremlin pulled away, he offered his grandfather a shy smile.

Carl Roebuck's house, the one where he'd found the coins in the attic, was about a block away on Glendale, and since this was more or less on his way downtown, Sully decided what the hell. Most of the morning was already lost and besides, it'd be nice to see Toby, Carl's wife, again.

Toby Roebuck was, to Sully's mind, the best-looking woman in Bath by no small margin. She had the kind of looks he associated with television.

She was perfectly formed, confident, sassy, soap-commercial pure. The sort of girl he'd have fallen for hard had he been thirty years younger. He was sure of this because he'd fallen for her hard just last year at age fifty-nine and old enough to know better. He hadn't seen her to talk to since he quit working for Carl back in August, when his swelling infatuation was yet another reason—along with his swollen knee—to give up manual labor for a while.

Who but Carl Roebuck, the little twerp, wouldn't be satisfied with such a woman, Sully wondered as he limped up the driveway of the Roebuck house. Well, most men wouldn't be, he had to admit, because most men were never satisfied. Still, he couldn't help thinking *he'd* be satisfied, now, at age sixty. Of course, he was nearly twice Carl's age and over the years he'd grown sentimental where women were concerned and had gradually developed the older man's confidence that he'd know how to treat a woman like Toby, confidence born of the fact that there was now no chance he'd ever have one.

Toby Roebuck's Bronco, a vehicle Sully had long coveted along with its owner, was in one of the open stalls of the Roebuck garage. The bay where Carl's red Camaro usually sat when he was at home stood empty, which was good. Sometimes Carl came home for the lunch hour for a little afternoon delight. Most days, though, he went someplace else for the same thing. Sully had been hoping that would be the case today, because he didn't want to run into Carl just yet. Alongside the back porch a shiny new snowblower was parked. The machine looked like it probably cost about what Carl Roebuck owed him. Maybe more. Probably more. Sully made a mental note to price them.

Since the back door was unlocked, he knocked on his way in, calling, "Hi, dolly. You aren't naked or anything, are you?" Once last summer he'd come upon Toby Roebuck sunbathing topless in the back yard, a happenstance that had apparently embarrassed him far more than her. She'd hooked her bikini top quickly, chortling at his stunned confusion, his having flushed crimson.

"No, but I can be in about two minutes," her voice, light and girlish, came down from somewhere upstairs.

"Take your time," Sully called, pulling out a chair at the kitchen table and collapsing into it, his knee still humming from Wacker's assault. This was one of the things he'd missed during these last four months, he realized. There were few places he enjoyed more than Toby Roebuck's kitchen, where, miraculously, a pot of drip coffee, which Sully located by smell, was now brewing on the counter. "I need a cup of coffee first, as soon as I can find the energy to get up and get it."

It was at this point that Sully noticed a man in gray work clothes on one knee at the front door, two rooms away. "That you, Horace?" Sully squinted, recalling now that he'd seen Horace Yancy's green van parked at the curb outside, without drawing any inferences.

"Hi, Sully," Horace said over his shoulder. "I ain't naked either."

"Thank God for that," Sully said. "What are you up to?"

"I'm tightening these screws," Horace grunted, twisting his screwdriver. "Then I'm all done."

Since the coffeepot had gurgled twice and stopped dripping, Sully got up, found his favorite mug in the cupboard, the one bearing a poetic inscription on its side:

> *Here's to you, as good as you are,*
> *And here's to me, as bad as I am,*
> *But as good as you are,*
> *And as bad as I am,*
> *I'm as good as you are,*
> *As bad as I am.*

Sully was not a man who cared much for material possessions, nor was he particularly envious of what other people had. How odd, Sully thought, that so many of the things he coveted were Carl Roebuck's. For starters there were Carl's wife and Carl's wife's Bronco. Big-ticket items, these. And now there was the new snowblower. But there were little things too. One day he'd come in when Toby was doing laundry, stacking Carl's underwear and socks on the kitchen table. Sully had counted over twenty-five pairs of underwear and an equal number of socks. To Sully, a man who did his wash in laundromats and who was forced to go more often than he would have liked when he ran out of socks and shorts, the idea of having twenty-five pairs of underwear seemed a very great luxury. That Carl Roebuck should have so many pairs didn't seem quite fair. The fact that he also had the prettiest girl in the county to wash them for him didn't seem even remotely fair. Sully tried his best not to think about these things. He was pretty sure coveting was wrong in general, and he was certain it was not a good thing to covet another man's undershorts. And of course there was the specific injunction, etched in stone, against coveting another man's wife. But what about his favorite mug? Toby Roebuck probably would have made him a present of it if she'd known how fond he was of it. Then again, he wasn't sure he wanted it, exactly. If he brought it home with him, he'd never use it, would probably forget all about it. Here, in Toby's cupboard, he got to use it occasionally and regret that he didn't have one like it.

By the time he sat back down, Horace was snapping his toolbox shut and struggling to his feet. He was a few years older than Sully and had about as much trouble getting up and down. Toby Roebuck skipped down the stairs then, dressed in her usual getup: tight, faded jeans, a sweatshirt, running shoes. She'd been a two- or three-sport athlete in college, and she still jogged, every day in warm weather, her blond ponytail bouncing youthfully down the tree-lined streets of Bath. Sully noticed she'd cut her hair short since he'd last seen her, though. It was styled rather mannishly, he thought, and he regretted there'd be no more bouncing ponytail come spring. Fortunately, other things still bounced delightfully, Sully noted when Toby Roebuck reached the bottom step.

"All done, Mr. Yancy?" she sang.

"All done, Mrs. Roebuck." Horace sighed, presenting her the bill. "I wish I hadn't let you talk me into it."

"I'll write you a check," she said, taking the bill and disappearing into the den.

"I'm the one he's going to be mad at, not you," Horace said, setting his toolbox down to wait, glancing at Sully as if to suggest that Sully at least would understand his position, even if this crazy, beautiful young woman didn't.

"Men are *such* cowards," came Toby Roebuck's voice from the den. A minute later she emerged with a check and handed it to the sad-faced locksmith, who studied it with the expression of a man who's just realized he's going broke by centimeters, having made a wrong career move thirty years ago. Sully knew the feeling.

"I wouldn't wait to cash that, though," Toby advised.

"Okay," Horace stuffed the check into his shirt pocket. "Here's the extra keys."

She took these and slid them into her jeans. Sully could see the perfect outline they made.

When Horace was gone, Toby Roebuck turned to face Sully, who, until that moment, she'd not looked at. "Tell me," she said, "how does a man—even a man like you—get *that* dirty?"

"Working for your husband," Sully informed her, since it was true.

"Ah," she nodded, as if it all made perfect sense now. "He makes you look like he makes me feel."

"He's a beaut'," Sully conceded. "Listen. While you got your check-book handy, how about writing me a check for the work I did this summer? Dummy and I have ironed things out, but all he had down at the office was the company checkbook."

Toby Roebuck grinned at him. "Nice try, Sully."

"What?"

"He called this morning and warned me you'd probably be by. He told me what you'd say almost word for word."

Sully grinned sheepishly. "He does owe me, you know."

"Get in line," she advised. "He owes everybody."

"Good thing he's got all that money," Sully observed.

"All what money?"

"Don't kid a kidder," Sully said.

"I tell you what, Sully. You take a big pile of money and then go have quadruple-bypass surgery and see how much money is left by the time you get back to the pile."

Sully decided he wouldn't argue the point, but he didn't buy what Toby Roebuck was telling him either. In his experience, people who had Carl's kind of money had few real duties, and about the only one they took seriously was convincing other people they didn't have all that money you knew they had. Toby Roebuck seemed sincere enough, and Sully didn't doubt the hospital had been expensive, but he doubted she knew much about her husband's finances. Carl was shifty and probably had money stashed in places nobody knew about. It was probably hid so well it would stay hid when Carl finally keeled over in the middle of some nooner. "So . . . you going to tell me what's going on with the new locks?"

"I thought you'd never ask," she said. "I decided just this morning that my husband no longer lives here. In fact, I don't see him living here in the immediate future."

Sully nodded. "Well, it's a bold move. It won't work, but it might get his attention."

"We'll see," Toby Roebuck sang. She didn't sound that worried. "So . . . you're no longer a college student. The old dog couldn't learn the new tricks."

"I wish there were some new tricks for an old dog to learn, dolly."

"And you're back working for Carl?"

"For a while," Sully admitted, unwilling to concede a permanent arrangement. "We'll see."

Neither said anything for a moment, neither wanting, apparently, to admit that their lives were in any meaningful way tied to a man like Carl

Roebuck. "You want to see our new hot tub?" Toby Roebuck finally said.

"Where is it?"

"Upstairs."

"Then I don't want to see it," Sully said, not wanting to add another item to the growing list of things to covet.

Toby poured herself a cup of coffee, doctored it over at the counter. "Is it the knee still, or have you done something else to yourself since I saw you last."

"Nope. Same old thing, dolly," he said, staring at her close-cropped hair. "While we're on the subject of doing things to ourselves . . ."

"I got a part in this play in Schuyler," she explained happily. "Shakespeare, only modernized. I'm disguised as a boy."

Sully leered at her appreciatively. "Good luck."

Toby Roebuck ignored this. She joined him at the table, sitting in one chair, putting her feet up on another. "So you're going back to work. You and Carl deserve each other. You're both self-destructive. He just has more fun. You come home with broken knees, he comes home with the clap."

Sully flexed his knee. "I have to admit, I wouldn't mind trading places for a while."

Toby grinned at him. "I wish you would. Broken knees aren't contagious."

Sully frowned and considered this, unsure whether Toby Roebuck was issuing him an invitation or wishing her husband a painfully broken knee. The latter, he decided, since it made more sense. "He's given you the clap?"

"Only three times," she said.

"Jesus," Sully said, genuinely surprised. He'd always been amazed that Toby Roebuck managed to take her husband's myriad infidelities in stride. Even this latest outrage she reported matter-of-factly, as if venereal disease were part of an equation she understood, or should have understood, when she married Carl Roebuck. As if this third dose of the clap was beginning to strain her tolerance. To Sully it was spooky. Tolerance of male misbehavior had not been prominently in evidence with any of the women Sully'd ever found himself involved. In fact, they identified, judged and exacted punishment for his misdeeds in one swift, efficient motion. It didn't make any kind of sense, Sully recognized, that this young woman, who could have any man in the county for the asking, would stick with one who kept giving her the clap.

"I warned him last week to fire that little tramp at the office. She's a walking incubator."

"Thanks for the tip," Sully said, though there was nothing to worry about. The only thing Ruby had ever offered him was her contempt.

"You tell me, Sully," she said, studying him seriously. "What does it mean that he won't fire her?"

Sully shrugged. "I don't think he's in love with her, if that's what you mean."

Toby considered this, as if she wasn't sure what she'd meant.

"To be honest," Sully admitted, "I have no idea why he does what he does. Most of the time I don't even know why I do what I do, much less anybody else." He'd finished his cup of coffee, pushed it toward the center of the table. "Thanks for the coffee. Hang in there."

"That's the sum of your wisdom on the subject?" she said, pretending outrage. "Hang in there?"

"I hate to tell you, dolly, but that's the sum of my wisdom on all subjects. You sure you don't want to write me that check while you're feeling rebellious?"

"That he'd never forgive me for."

Sully got to his feet, flexed at the knee. "Okay," he said. "I guess I'll settle for a lift downtown."

"Where's your sad-ass truck?"

"Stuck in the mud," he admitted reluctantly.

"Old stick-in-the-mud Sully," she grinned at him in a way that made him wonder if he *had* been given an invitation earlier. "That's one thing I have to say about Carl"—pulling her parka off the hook by the door—"he never settles."

The "even for me" she left unspoken.

Sully had Toby Roebuck drop him off in front of the OTB, which was a good place to look for somebody who probably wasn't there. "You didn't see me today, in case anybody asks," he reminded her as he got out.

"See who?" Toby said.

Sully started to answer, then realized she was making a joke.

"Come see me in my play," she suggested.

"You got any nude scenes?"

"Tell me something," she said, before he closed the door. "What were you like when you were young?"

"Just like this," he said. "Only more."

The OTB was busy as usual, though a quick scan of the premises did not turn up Rub among the crowd. Between eleven and twelve on weekdays the North Bath OTB was always occupied by a small army of retired men in pale yellow and powder blue windbreakers who would disappear by noon, heading home to lunches of tuna-fish sandwiches on white bread and steaming bowls of Campbell's tomato soup, surrendering the field to the poorer, more desperate, more compulsive types who turned the state's profit. This late in the year, the well-scrubbed, well-mannered windbreaker men all wore sweaters beneath their jackets, and many wore scarves at the insistence of their wives, who, since their husbands' retirement, had come to treat them like school-bound children, making sure their scarves were wrapped high and snug about their wattled throats, jackets zipped up as far as they would go. Toasty was the word these wives used. Toasty warm. In response to being treated like children, these husbands retaliated by behaving like children, unzipping and unwrapping as soon as they were safely out of sight. They shared the child's natural aversion to heavy winter wear and could not be induced to don bulky overcoats until it snowed and the snow stayed. It had snowed today, but the snow was melting.

"Sully!" they cheered when he came in, all doffing their baseball caps. Sully knew most of these men and liked them well enough, their comparative good fortune notwithstanding. Why shouldn't they wear thin windbreakers in late November? They left warm houses at midmorning, got into cars with good heaters that had been sitting in warm, if not toasty warm, garages overnight, drove five minutes to the donut shop, dashed inside where it was warm, and there they stayed, gossiping over hot coffee refills, until it was time to visit the OTB and play their daily double. Then home again. When they wanted a change of pace, they visited the insurance office or the hardware store or the post office or the drugstore where they'd worked for thirty years before retiring. They were never outside long enough to find out what the temperature was, much less catch a cold, and so they all looked hale and hearty and weather resistant even in their out-of-season clothing.

They were insulated against cold economic weather too. Having spent their working lives in North Bath, they were not rich, but they were comfortable, and they congratulated themselves that they'd be more comfortable still if Bath real estate would just go ahead and boom like everybody was predicting. Or like everybody in Bath was predicting. Albany had already spilled northward, and realtors were predicting excitedly that the entire interstate corridor would share in the boom. The best of the shabby old Victorian houses along Glendale, like the Roebucks', had already been bought up and restored by young men and women, most of whom worked in Albany. They hopped on the interstate in the morning and returned in the evening, a twenty-five-minute drive. These OTB men were angry with themselves for having once considered the old Victorians mere dinosaurs. Thirty years ago such houses could have been bought for a song, but instead they had built well-insulated, new, split-level ranches with picture windows. These were also beginning to creep up in assessed value and taxes, but much more slowly. They all knew now they could have made their killing in the Victorians if they'd guessed that an entire generation of Vietnam draft protesters in torn, faded jeans would end up with money and spend it resuscitating decrepit old houses. Now all they could do was watch the value of their split-levels inch up and worry about timing. Higher taxes were eating into their pensions and Social Security and savings. They didn't want to sell their split-levels too early, only to discover that the real boom in the market hadn't come yet. The conventional wisdom seemed to be that things were just beginning to pick up momentum, what with the Sans Souci scheduled to reopen in the summer and the groundbreaking on the amusement park imminent.

But, of course, waiting was risky, too. What if the Ultimate Escape deal collapsed at the last minute? They didn't want to wait too long and find themselves stuck with their dream homes of thirty years ago. They had new dream homes now—condos in warmer climes—and they spent the long mornings discussing these. Most favored condos on the Florida gulf, except these were getting expensive and there were disturbing reports of alligators lumbering out of the glades and devouring small children. The windbreaker men didn't have any small children, but the alligator stories haunted them anyway, a single incident circulating so many times that you'd have thought there was an army of Florida alligators advancing against a defenseless line of condos all the way from the Everglades to St. Petersburg. Even the golf courses were rumored to be full of alligators. Talk about your hazards. For this reason an increasing number of these morning OTB men favored Arizona, where the condos were rumored to be cheaper and where there weren't any alligators. There were rattlesnakes and scorpions and tarantulas and spiders and Gila monsters, but none of these were big enough to glom onto a man and drag him back into the swamp to eat. In the desert there weren't even any swamps to drag you into.

Sully had been overhearing parts of this serial conversation for years but doubted he'd ever engage in it even if he made it to retirement. He had no house to contemplate the increasing value of, unless he counted his father's place on Bowdon Street, at the edge of the Sans Souci property, the legal status of which was no longer clear, at least to Sully. Wirf had informed him when his father died that he'd inherited the house, but Sully had told Wirf he not only didn't want it, he wouldn't take it. When Sully had been seventeen and enlisted in the army he'd promised his father he'd have nothing further to do with him, in life or in death, and except for one afternoon shortly before the old man died when Ruth had talked him into visiting the nursing home, he'd kept his pledge. His father's long-neglected house was falling down, its windows boarded up, the grounds overrun with tall weeds. Unless Sully missed his guess, the accumulated back taxes were probably more than the house would bring on the market. Definitely not the sort of house that would gain Sully entry into the Florida/Arizona condo conversation, even if he had wanted to be included, which he didn't.

The only thing Sully envied these men was that they were finished, like ballplayers in an old-timers game who could look back on an episode in their lives that had a particular shape. Having completed it, they could move on to something else. Their lives were full of dates. They could tell you when they married, when their children were born, the date they retired from their jobs. In Sully's life the years (never mind days) elided gracefully without dividers, and he was always surprised by the endings and new beginnings other people saw, or thought they saw, in their existences. One day thirty-odd years before, he'd run into Vera on the street, and she'd smiled sadly and said, well, at least it was finally over, a chapter of their lives behind them. Sully had looked at her blankly, wondering what she was talking about. It turned out her reference was to their divorce, which had become final a few days before, the fact of which he had not been notified. Either that or he'd trashed the notification along with the other mail he wasn't interested in. He'd known Vera was relieved not to be married to him anymore (she would marry her second husband, Ralph, within the year), but the finality of the divorce had impressed her, and Sully could tell she was feeling a little melancholy about the failure of their marriage. For her, the divorce had drawn a line that Sully had missed altogether.

The graceful merging of his days was either depressing or reassuring, depending upon his mood. Even now, at age sixty, he couldn't imagine feeling finished in the way that the OTB men were, or of being on the brink of anything new. Maybe that's what had gotten to him about taking classes at the community college, about talk of a new career. That was the point of the philosophy class, he'd come to understand. It was the young professor's intention to make everything disappear, one thing at a time, and then replace all of it with something new, a new kind of thought or existence maybe. Out with the old, in with the new. And maybe this wasn't such a bad idea if you were talking to twenty-year-olds. Hell, at twenty, he'd been ready to junk everything and start over too. But now, at sixty, he was less willing to throw things away that could be patched together and kept running for a few more months. He wanted to keep going forward, not stop and turn around and analyze the validity of decisions made and courses charted long ago. He wasn't even sure he wanted Wirf, his lawyer, to succeed in the various litigations he was pursuing in Sully's behalf. If Wirf got Sully his total disability, that would be the end of life as he knew it, the beginning of something new, not necessarily good news to a man who didn't believe in new beginnings any more than he believed in new knees.

"You're looking especially well this morning," Otis Wilson observed, in reference, no doubt, to Sully's crust of mud. Otis claimed every summer that come winter he was Florida bound.

Sully turned a circle so all the windbreaker men could see. "Somebody's got to work in this country," he said. "Wasn't for guys like me, guys like you'd have to get your hands dirty occasionally."

"We been meaning to say thank you," Otis said.

"I heard on the news an alligator made off with another one," Sully said. Otis, a big, soft man with a florid face, was particularly susceptible to alligator stories, and Sully, as part of a running gag, had been for years warning Otis not to go to a wild place like Florida without a tough, experienced guide, someone not afraid to wrestle gators. Someone like Sully. To Sully's delight, at the mention of alligators Otis's face drained. "If I was you I'd get a second-floor condo. Alligators hate stairs."

"Get away from me," Otis said when Sully joined his elbows together to make alligator jaws. "Go on now, git!" Otis parried Sully's thrusts nervously. "Go play your damn sucker triple and leave smart people alone."

"There are no smart people within a block of here," Sully told him. "The OTB is a tax on stupidity."

"How many stupid people you paying taxes for beside yourself?" somebody wanted to know.

"I'm smart enough not to move someplace where I'm going to get eaten by an alligator," Sully said.

"Go bet that fool's triple," Otis said.

"All right, I will," Sully said, heading for the window. For the last year or so he'd been playing 1-2-3 trifectas regardless of the horses or jockeys involved. Never much of a handicapper, he'd given up on trying to figure triples, which, he'd concluded, were invented to drive you crazy. Anymore he bet 1-2-3 and explained, when people wanted to know why, that the horses running around the inside of the track didn't have as far to go as those running around the outside, which would have been true if there were lanes. "If my triple runs I'll buy Hilda one of those video cameras to take with you to Florida," he called back to Otis. "That way she can get it on film. We can show it over at The Horse. Charge admission to see Otis get dragged off into the swamp."

Sully bet his triple and was about to leave when through the front window he saw Carl Roebuck round the corner a block away and head up the other side of the street in Sully's direction. Sully couldn't help but smile at Carl's jaunty stride, which wouldn't have been so jaunty had he known that his wife had changed the locks.

In front of the savings and loan, Clive Peoples, who'd just come out, was studying with satisfaction the new banner recently hung across Main Street. Clive Jr., a study in self-importance, was one of the few apples Sully knew that had fallen miles from the tree. True, his father, whom Clive Jr. had grown to greatly resemble, had been proud of his local celebrity as the football coach, but he'd been good-natured too, and Miss Beryl's gentle mockery shamed him when he got too puffed up. Not so Clive Jr., who lacked, among other things, a sense of humor. That he took himself seriously was proof positive, in Sully's view. In fact, Sully had little use for his landlady's son and would have actively disliked him were it not for Miss Beryl, who, Sully sensed, was disappointed in her son, his having become a big shot in town notwithstanding.

Before Clive Jr. could get into his car, a long, sleek black affair that he always parked out front of the savings and loan, Carl Roebuck collared him for one of their thirty-second conversations. Sully didn't have to be there to know how it would go. "Tell me we're still in business," Carl Roebuck would urge, conspiratorially. Clive Jr. would assure him that they were, and then Carl would say, "If this thing ever goes south, don't tell me. Just come out to the house and shoot me in the head." Talk that made Clive Jr., a nervous-looking man, even more nervous looking. Clive couldn't get into his car and away from Carl Roebuck fast enough.

When Carl crossed the street and headed right for the OTB, Sully got ready to slip out the back, but Carl continued right on by, heading Sully couldn't imagine where. A heavy gambler, Carl seldom bet at the OTB, preferring bookies who didn't siphon the state's percentage and who took action all day and most of the night over the phone. Actually, Carl preferred betting sporting events to betting horses. Sully watched Carl out of sight and was about to venture back into the street when he noticed the man at his elbow was Rub.

"I was just looking for you," Sully said.

"You wasn't looking very hard," Rub pointed out. "I been standing right next to you for five minutes."

"You get your turkey?"

Rub looked blank.

"I thought maybe you were shopping for a turkey here at the OTB," Sully said.

Still blank.

"Let's go," Sully said. "I got us some work."

"Who for?"

"Carl Roebuck."

"Wasn't that Carl you was just hiding from?"

Sully admitted this was true, without offering explanation.

"You said you was never going to work for him again."

"You want to work or not?"

"I hate that Carl."

"You hate his money?"

"No," Rub admitted. "Just Carl."

Out in the street it felt colder, and Sully noticed that the temperature on the bank clock had fallen several degrees since morning.

"That wife of his I like, though," Rub said after they'd walked a block. "I wisht she'd take an interest in me. I'd let her be on top."

Where women were concerned, Rub knew no higher compliment.

"How come women like her are never interested in guys like us?" Rub asked seriously. His innocence regarding women was comprehensive. Rub honestly saw no reason why Toby Roebuck would not be interested in any man who'd let her be on top.

"I only know why they don't like you," Sully said. "Why they don't like me is a mystery."

"How come they don't like me?"

"They just don't."

Rub accepted this. "Where's your truck?"

"Out at the job," Sully told him. Partial explanations always satisfied Rub. It would not occur to him to wonder how Sully and his truck had come to be separated. "Where's your car?"

"Bootsie's got it," Rub said. "She always parks out back of Woolworth's."

They turned down the narrow alley that led to the Woolworth's lot, walking single file. The morning's snow remained untrampled there in the dark, narrow alley, and Rub walked backward so he could watch the footprints he left.

"I hope she won't be too bent out of shape when she finds the car's gone," Sully said. He made a mental note to return Bootsie's car once they got the truck unstuck. That way Rub wouldn't take a beating.

"She's been bent out of shape for ten years," observed Rub, who was generally brave in his wife's absence.

"How long you been married?"

"Ten years."

Sully nodded. "See any connection?"

"Shit," Rub said, turning and surveying the parking lot. "It ain't here."

"Let's take this one then," Sully suggested, since they happened to be standing right next to Rub's and Bootsie's old Pontiac. "You don't even recognize your own car?"

Rub unlocked the Pontiac and got in, leaning over to unlock the passenger side door for Sully. "At least I recognize my own best friend when he's standing right next to me," he said, pulling out of the lot.

It only took them about ten minutes to drive back out to the site. Sully used the time to consider how Rub ever got the idea they were best friends.

"You know what I wisht?" Rub said.

Since he and Sully left the OTB, Rub had already wished for a new car, a raise for himself and a raise for Bootsie, who worked as a cashier at Woolworth's and hadn't had a raise in over a year. He'd also wished some big ole company would build a big ole plant right in Bath and make him a foreman at about fifteen dollars an hour. He'd wished it was spring already and not Thanksgiving, that California would just go ahead and fall into the ocean if it was going to, that the climate in upstate New York was more tropical, that someone would die and leave him a big ole boat he could sail down to Mexico, that the Royal Palm Company would start making that red cream soda again. And he'd wished ole Toby Roebuck would sit on his face, just once.

Rub had wished all of this in the space of roughly an hour, one wish gliding naturally into the next, unimpeded by plausibility. Since September, Sully had forgotten how full of wishes Rub's life was. As fast as Sully's professor explained things out of existence, Rub wished other things into being. It was not unusual for him to say, "You know what I wisht?" fifty times a day, and the worst part of it was he'd just keep repeating the question until Sully acknowledged it with a "What? What for sweet Jesus' sake do you wish now?" The thing that always amazed Sully about Rub's wishes was that most of them were so modest. After wishing a whole company into existence, Rub would settle for a forty-hour-a-week job at union scale, as if he feared some sort of cosmic retaliation for an arrogant imagination. Sully tried to explain from time to time that if he was going to wish an entire corporation into existence, he might as well wish he owned it and had somebody else to do the actual work. But Rub didn't see it this way. He liked the smaller wishes and he liked to wish them one at a time. Out loud.

"I wisht we were all through with this job and sitting in The Horse eating a big ole cheeseburger" was what Rub would have liked at this instant. He was as covered with mud as Sully, and his wish for warmth and a cheeseburger probably seemed as remote to him as the possibility that somebody would die and leave him a big ole boat. "Next time you find us work, I wisht you'd let me eat lunch first," he added.

They were now on their second load, and this time they were loading the blocks right, cushioning the bed of the truck with plywood. Half of the bottom two layers of the first load hadn't made it. Having located Rub with so little trouble, Sully'd made up his mind to reload the truck, but fate had conspired against them. By the time they got back to the site the temperature had dropped and the sloppy ground had firmed up, and the truck, hopelessly mired an hour before, drove right out on the first try. This had looked to Sully like a sign, so he'd said screw the reloading, let's go. His thinking was that even with the two of them working, they'd be lucky to finish before seven o'clock, which meant they'd have to do the last couple of loads in the dark. He was having all he could do to avoid disaster when he could see the ground.

They'd just left the blocks that broke when Sully hit a pothole right there in the truck. The others they'd piled with extra care out at the new site, next to the shallow hole out of which one of Carl Roebuck's no-frills government-subsidy two-bedroom ranches would grow in about a week, weather permitting. Carl was behind on the contract, just like he was behind on every contract, and his guys would have to work right through Christmas, probably, or until the ground froze. On the way back for the next load, they'd stopped and tossed the broken blocks behind the clown billboard. "What if somebody finds them?" Rub had wanted to know.

"You didn't write your name on them, did you?" Sully said.

They were nearly finished with the second load when they heard a car coming and Carl Roebuck's El Camino, with its TIP TOP CONSTRUCTION COMPANY: C. I. ROEBUCK logo on the door, careened into view. It bore down on them at such an unsafe speed that it could mean only one thing—that Carl Roebuck himself was at the wheel. Carl was careful never to take his Camaro onto a job site, but he considered it executive privilege to wreck at least one company car a year by bouncing it over rutted, unpaved roads at fifty miles an hour.

"Uh-oh," Rub said. "I bet he found them blocks already."

Sully just looked at him. "Pay attention a minute," he said.

Rub was paying attention, all right, but not to Sully. He was watching the approaching El Camino and looking scared.

Sully reached down from the truck bed where he was standing and cuffed Rub, who was stationed in the mud below. "I don't want you to say a word, understand? If you so much as open your mouth I'm going to brain you with one of these blocks and bury you in the woods. And I'm going to pile all those broken blocks on top of you."

"I wisht you wouldn't say things like that," Rub said. "You always sound like you mean it."

"Mean what?" Carl Roebuck said, getting out of the El Camino.

Rub started to answer and Sully cuffed him again. Rub's mouth closed with an audible click of his teeth.

Carl surveyed the mound of remaining blocks, which had not diminished perceptibly. "I should apply for a federal grant," he said, shaking his head. "When you hire the handicapped, you're supposed to qualify."

Sully sat down on the tailgate of the pickup, took off his work gloves, lit a cigarette. "You could help. That way things'd go faster. Except then you'd break a sweat and your girlfriends'd all wrinkle their noses."

"Let's not even talk about women," Carl suggested. Indeed, the mere mention of the subject made him look even more morose. "You know what the C. I. in my name stands for?"

"What?" Rub said, genuinely interested.

"Coitus Interruptus," Carl said sadly.

"What?" Rub frowned.

"That's Latin, Rub," Carl reassured him. "Don't worry about it. Learn English first."

"If you'd use your lunch hour to eat lunch this wouldn't happen," Sully observed. "This used to be a nice, peaceful town. Now everybody has to go home between twelve and one to make sure your car isn't in their driveway."

"I wish it was just between twelve and one that they checked," Carl said. "I can take my lunch break whenever I want."

"Go home and see Toby," Sully suggested, wondering if Carl knew yet about the locks. "You're married to the best-looking woman in town, you jerk."

Carl rubbed his chin thoughtfully. "A man's reach should exceed his grasp," he said. "You remember who said that?"

Sully didn't remember.

"Where do they talk Latin?" Rub wanted to know.

Nobody said anything for a moment, but Carl was grinning now. Talking to Rub seemed to have cheered him. Sully knew the feeling. It was hard to feel sorry for yourself when Rub was around.

"I'm thinking of establishing a college scholarship," Carl told him. "You should apply."

"I never graduated from goddamn high school," Rub said, halfway between recollected anger and regret.

"Then what makes you think you're eligible for a college scholarship?" Carl asked him.

This question so confused Rub that he looked to Sully for help. "Just don't listen to him," Sully advised.

"I can't believe this is as far as you've got," Carl said, surveying the huge pyramid of blocks that remained.

"I can't believe anybody set them down here in the first place," Sully remarked. "Right next to a basement that's already built."

Carl Roebuck, more interested in today's lunacy than yesterday's, did not appear to have heard this. "At this rate you'll still be here Christmas."

"You'll know right where to bring my Christmas present then," Sully said. "Don't go to a lot of trouble. The money you owe me will be fine."

Carl appeared not to hear this, his attention having been captured by a detail at his feet. There in the mud were the two blocks Sully had placed in front of the truck's rear wheels three hours earlier. They looked like they were just sitting there, like a man might be able to bend over and just pick them up, except that when Carl Roebuck tried, he discovered they were frozen in place, as immovable as the blocks cemented the day before into the basement foundation a few feet away. Carl looked at Sully, who was grinning at him.

"Go ahead," Sully invited. "Pick 'em up."

"You'd like to see me have another heart attack, wouldn't you?"

Sully snorted at the suggestion. "Don't worry. It's not your destiny to die working."

Carl apparently agreed with this assessment, or was insufficiently motivated to argue the point, though he continued to try to budge the frozen blocks with the heel of his loafer, as he leaned back against the El Camino for leverage. From where they were standing, they could just see the top of the Ultimate Escape billboard across the highway and a quarter mile in toward town. "I'm going to feel a lot better when they get started on that son of a bitch," Carl reflected.

Sully followed his gaze across Carl's tract of housing development land, across the four-lane spur, all the way to the clown's head. "Tell me something," Sully said. "Who the hell's going to buy these houses with an amusement park across the street? You should be praying they never start."

"Sully, Sully, Sully," Carl said. "You just don't understand the world."

Sully had to admit this was probably true.

"As soon as they break ground over there, they're going to need everything on this side of the road for a parking lot. For which they will pay dearly."

"Then why are you building houses?"

"So they will pay *more* dearly."

Sully considered this. The reasoning was vintage Carl Roebuck, of course, and Sully could feel Carl's father roll over in his grave. Kenny Roebuck had built the company on eighteen-hour days of hard, honest work, only to surrender what he'd built to a high roller, a rogue. "What happens if they don't build the park?"

"Bite your tongue," Carl said.

"Well," Sully said, "I'm sure you'll be lucky as usual."

Carl looked as if he'd have given a good deal to be that certain. "Clive Peoples swears it's going through," he said with the air of a man comforted by the sound of his own voice.

"And you trust Clive Peoples?"

"He's in deeper than anybody. He's got investors lined up all the way to Texas," Carl said. "What's in trouble is the Sans Souci. That spring they drilled last summer's going dry already. They should call that place the Sans Brains."

Rub was frowning.

"That's French, Rub," Carl explained. "You can learn it right after English and Latin." Then to Sully, "You want to sheetrock the house on Nelson tomorrow? I can have Randy drop all the shit off in the morning if you want the job."

"Tomorrow's Thanksgiving," Rub said.

"Nobody's talking to you," Sully told him. Actually, he was of two minds about working tomorrow. If he did, he'd have an excuse not to go to Vera's, where he wouldn't be welcome. And he could use the money. And the holiday would go faster if he worked. On the other hand, he hated sheetrocking, and he didn't know yet how his knee was going to react to today's labors.

"I ain't working on Thanksgiving, is all I'm saying," Rub insisted.

"Nobody asked you to," Sully reminded him. "When somebody asks you, you can say no." He turned to Carl. "Double time?"

"In your dreams."

"Go away and leave us alone then," Sully said. "Sheetrock the fucker yourself."

Carl massaged his temples. "Why do you have to hold every simple negotiation hostage? Why should I pay you double time?"

"What's tomorrow, Rub?" Sully said.

Rub looked even more confused. In his opinion, they'd already been over this. "It's fuckin' Thanksgiving," he said.

"Shut up, Rub," Carl said. "Nobody's talking to you."

"Sully was."

"When?" Carl said.

"Just now."

"Just when?"

Rub looked like he might cry.

"What burns my ass, Sully," Carl said, "is that you wouldn't even know it was Thanksgiving. You don't even have a family, for Christ sake. I'm offering to keep you out of trouble for twenty-four hours, and all you can think about is extortion."

Sully briefly considered telling Carl a couple of things. That his son was in town, for instance, and that strangely enough, he did have an invitation for tomorrow, even if all parties concerned were hoping it would not be accepted. He also considered telling Carl Roebuck what he didn't know yet—that *he* was the one who'd probably not have a place to go on this particular Thanksgiving, that none of the keys dangling from the ring in the El Camino's ignition fit the doors to his house anymore.

Carl got back into the El Camino and started the engine. "Shit," he said. "All right, time and a half. Call it a Christmas bonus."

"Pay me what you owe and call it honesty," Sully suggested.

Carl chose not to hear this. "Time and a half?"

"I'll consider it," Sully said, though he knew he'd take it, and knew Carl knew he'd take it.

"It's a two-man job," Carl said, nodding imperceptibly in Rub's direction.

"I ain't working Thanksgiving," Rub said stubbornly, and to look at him an objective observer would have concluded that it'd be a waste of time to try to change his mind.

"He will if I ask him," Sully assured Carl Roebuck. "Won't you, Rub."

"Okay," Rub said.

Carl shook his head sadly, as if to suggest it was a constant trial, this living in an imperfect world. "I see you're using the plywood, anyway," he said, shifting the El Camino into gear. "Knowing you two, I'd have sworn it wouldn't have occurred to you. I figured you'd bust up the whole first load for sure. I just came out to see if I could save the rest."

Sully didn't look at Rub. He didn't have to, having too often seen Rub's expression when he was about to wet his pants. Fortunately, Carl Roebuck wasn't paying attention. Sully and Rub watched the El Camino turn and bang its way back out toward the blacktop, where a dark sedan was sitting. For some time Sully had been vaguely aware of the sedan's presence, but wasn't sure exactly how long it'd been sitting there. When the El Camino bounced onto the blacktop and headed toward town, the sedan started up and followed.

"Who do you figure was in that other car?" Rub wondered.

"Somebody's husband, probably."

They went back to work, silently for a while, until the pickup was all loaded and ready to go. Cold or no cold, Sully rolled down a window in the cab when Rub got in beside him. Rub was as gamy as he ever got in cold weather. "I wisht he'd *give* me that scholarship," Rub said.

It was nearly seven when they finally finished. They'd done the last two loads in the dark, with just the quarter moon, darting in and out of high clouds, for light and company. For entertainment Rub continued to wish. Since five o'clock he'd wished it wasn't dark. He wished they'd stopped for dinner, especially since they didn't get any lunch. He wished he had one of those big ole double cheeseburgers they served at The Horse, the kind with lots of onions and a big ole slice of cheese and some lettuce and tomato, so big you had to open your mouth as far as you could just to get a bite. He wished he had some of that coleslaw they serve too, and some fries, right out of the grease, so the salt stuck real good. And he wished he'd never said yes to working on Thanksgiving. Only his final wish was really worth wishing. He wished they'd thought to return Bootsie's car to the Woolworth's lot before his wife got off work and had to walk home, which always made her mad enough to whack his peenie.

"Let's stop at The Horse," Rub said when they'd dropped off the last load of blocks and Sully'd paid him. Rub didn't like to keep money lying around. He liked it to get up and work. To buy big ole double cheeseburgers and draft beers. He liked to spend it before his wife discovered he had it.

"Not me, Rub," Sully said. "I'm tired and filthy and I stink almost as bad as you."

"So?" Rub said. It was impossible to insult him with references to the way he smelled. "It's just The Horse. Ain't you hungry?"

"Too tired to chew, actually." All of Sully's earlier enthusiasm for going back to work had fallen victim to fatigue. He couldn't imagine the optimism that had led him to believe he'd be able to do the job without Rub's help.

"Anybody's got enough strength to chew," Rub said.

"Maybe later I'll feel like it," Sully said. "Say hi to Bootsie for me. Tell her I'm sorry she married such a dummy."

"I wisht I didn't have to go home and see her," Rub admitted, getting into his wife's Pontiac. "She's gonna whack my peenie."

"Bob and weave," Sully advised. "It's a small target."

Sully's flat was identical in floor plan to Miss Beryl's below. The floor plan was the only similarity. Where the downstairs flat was crowded with Miss Beryl's heavy oak furniture, terra-cotta pots and wicker elephants, its walls freshly papered and hung with framed prints and museum posters under glass, its tables covered with ghostly spirit boats and ornate vases, the various mementoes of her travels, Sully's flat was wide open, pastoral. In fact, it didn't look dramatically different from the way it had looked before he moved in with his furniture so many years ago. That morning, it had taken him just under an hour to complete the move, and the few things he brought with him only served to emphasize the flat's high ceilings, its terrible spaciousness, the echoing sounds he made moving from room to room over the hardwood floors. He'd been forty-eight then and had lived almost his entire adult life in dark, cramped, furnished quarters, which he'd found pretty much to his liking. Ruth had been urging him for a long time to find a decent place to live, claiming that what ailed Sully was his morbid surroundings. He hadn't argued with her, but he hadn't moved, either. He hadn't had any idea, then or now, what ailed him, but he suspected it wasn't his surroundings. In fact, about the only thing that could have induced him to move was the thing that had happened. He'd left the old flat one afternoon to go buy a pack of cigarettes. The last cigarette of his last pack he left half smoked in an ashtray perched on the arm of his battered sofa.

The corner grocery was only two blocks away, so Sully had walked. He was between jobs and in no particular hurry. When he ran into a couple of guys he knew, he stopped to shoot the breeze. At the store he bought cigarettes and talked with a cop who was loitering near the register. When a fire alarm sounded, the cop left, so Sully took the opportunity to bet a daily double with Ray, the sad, fatalistic store owner who was in his last year of competition with the IGA supermarket. The OTB would open the following year, officially burying Bath's three neighborhood groceries. "Looks like we got us some midday excitement," Ray said when the fire engine roared by.

"We could probably stand a little," Sully'd said absently, lighting a cigarette and trying to account for the vague, distant unease, a sense of menace almost, that he'd become aware of at the edge of his consciousness. He said good-bye to Ray and started home. The fire engine had careened around the corner onto Sully's street and for some reason turned its siren off. People were running through the intersection, and Sully saw there was a black plume of smoke ascending into the sky above the rooftops. There were more sirens in the distance. A police car flew by.

By the time Sully arrived a large crowd had gathered to watch the house burn. Flames were shooting out of the windows and into the low gray sky. The firemen had already given up combating the blaze and were using their hoses to wet down the houses on either side, trying to prevent them from bursting into sympathetic flame. Losing a house was one thing, but they didn't want to lose the whole block. There didn't seem to be anything to do but join the crowd and watch, so Sully did.

After he'd been there awhile, a man he knew noticed him and said hello. "You live around here somewheres, don't you?" the man added. "I live right there," Sully pointed at the inferno. "Or I used to." This admission attracted considerable attention. "Hey!" somebody yelled. "There's Sully. He's not dead, he's right here." Everybody looked at Sully suspiciously. A rumor that he had burned up in the blaze had been circulating, and people had quickly adjusted to the idea of profound human tragedy. They were reluctant to give it up, Sully could tell. He smiled apologetically at the crowd.

Kenny Roebuck, Carl's father, who owned the building, arrived finally and came over to where Sully was standing. "I heard you were dead," he said. "Burned alive."

"I hope they don't put it in the paper," Sully said.

Kenny Roebuck agreed. "I wonder how the hell it started."

"The rumor or the fire?"

"The fire."

"That would be me, probably," Sully admitted. He told his landlord and sometime employer about the cigarette he vaguely remembered leaving when he went out to buy more cigarettes. "I hope to Christ there *wasn't* anybody inside," he added. The house had been divided into three flats. In the middle of the afternoon there was probably nobody home, but he wasn't sure.

"I don't think there was," Kenny said, adding, "according to a cop I just talked to, you were the only one killed."

The roof fell then, shooting red embers high into the afternoon sky and down into the crowd.

"You're taking this well," Sully observed.

Kenny Roebuck leaned toward him confidentially and lowered his voice. "Just between us, I've been thinking about burning the son of a bitch down myself. Costs me more to fix what goes wrong every month than I collect in rent. I guess I wasn't cut out to be a slumlord."

The two men watched until the fire burned itself out.

"Well," Kenny Roebuck said. "That's about it, and I should get back to work. I don't know how to thank you."

Sully was still mulling over what his landlord had said before in light of Ruth's constant pestering him to find a decent place to live. "I never thought of it as a slum," he admitted.

"You're the only one that didn't, then," Kenny Roebuck said. "Somebody said old Beryl Peoples has a flat for rent on Upper Main."

This rumor turned out to be true. Kenny Roebuck also wasn't kidding about being grateful. The next day he gave Sully five hundred dollars for new clothes and some furniture, since Miss Beryl's flat wasn't furnished. That made the whole episode pretty much of a bonanza as far as Sully was concerned. He spent two hundred on underwear, socks, shirts, pants and shoes. Two hundred went a considerable distance at the Army-Navy store, which had a used clothing outlet around back. He spent another two hundred on some well-broken-in furniture—a double bed and rickety nightstand, a lamp in the shape of a naked woman, a small chest of drawers, a metal dinette and chairs with plastic seats, a huge sofa for the living room and a coffee table that came with only three legs. The other leg was around somewhere, the man at the used furniture store said. To show his appreciation for Sully's business he threw in a used toaster. When Sully got all these new worldly goods set up in Miss Beryl's flat, he plugged in the toaster to see if it worked, without much in the way of expectation. The inner coils glowed angry red though, so he unplugged it again. Since then he hadn't found an occasion to use the toaster. The only place he ever ate toast was at Hattie's, as part of the breakfast special.

It was ironic that in a flat so remarkable for its wide-open spaces Sully should be cramped in the kitchen, but he was. The room was tiny, like kitchens in most old houses that had formal dining rooms, so there wasn't much room for the dinette. Sully finally wedged it into the corner anyway so he'd have something to bang into and swear at. He'd originally set it up in the dining room, but it looked like a joke there, so small and bent and metallic in the middle of such a large room. He couldn't imagine sitting down and eating anything in there, not even a bowl of cereal. So he ended up shutting the floor register to save on heat and closed the room. He did the same with the second bedroom, which also stood empty.

He was glad the sofa he bought was huge because it at least displaced some air in the cavernous living room. He set it and the tippy, three-legged coffee table against the long wall facing the television he planned to get as soon as he could afford one. He made a mental note that the television had better be a good-size one if he was going to be able to see it from all the way across the room. He made another mental note to do something about the floral pink wallpaper. And he'd need a rug or two to cut down on the constant reminders of his own presence as he tapped across the hardwood floors. He still had a hundred dollars of Kenny Roebuck's money, so he went out in search of bargain rugs.

As luck would have it, he found Kenny Roebuck instead, and Kenny was on his way to the track. He forced Sully into accompanying him there by asking him if he wanted to. On the way back Sully decided he hadn't needed the rugs anyway. They stopped at Ray's corner market for a six-pack of beer and from there went to the new flat so Kenny could see how Sully was making out. Sully took the six-pack and put it in the refrigerator while Kenny Roebuck laughed. In fact, Kenny stood in the middle of the living room and howled. He couldn't stop. He went from room to room, each room striking him as funnier than the last. In the two empty, closed-off rooms he laughed until tears rolled down his cheeks. Finally he joined Sully in the tiny kitchen and collapsed into one of the plastic dinette chairs, his face beet red with exertion. "How long do you figure before you'll fill it up?"

Sully took two beers out of the refrigerator. He felt the metal shelf before handing one to Kenny Roebuck. "I'm not sure the refrigerator works too well," he said, which started Kenny in all over again.

It didn't seem possible to Sully that Kenny Roebuck had been dead for most of the dozen years since he got that first look at Sully's new flat. One thing was certain. If Kenny were there now he'd get just as good a laugh. Except for a throw rug and a big white-cabineted television with a small screen, the flat looked pretty much as it had the day he moved in. What he'd decided to do about the floral wallpaper was to let it peel off.

Tonight, like most nights, he was too tired to care. Regulating the water as hot as he could stand it, Sully stripped, climbed into the shower and let the water beat down on his shoulders and lower back. In a few minutes the rising steam brought with it a childhood memory he'd not thought of in forty years. It was a Saturday afternoon, and his father had taken Sully and his older brother, Patrick, to the new YMCA in Schuyler Springs for the free swim, a monthly event intended to drum up membership. Sully's father had no intention of letting his sons join, but as long as it was free, well. . . . Also, he'd discovered there was a Saturday afternoon poker game in back. When Sully and his brother were buzzed downstairs, his father remained above to play cards. The locker room was cold and uncarpeted, and the pool lifeguards had made all the boys shower and then stand, shivering, at the side of the pool while each boy was inspected for head lice and read the rules about no running, no pushing, no diving in the shallow end. Several boys were found to be dirty and required to go take another shower. The clean ones, including Sully and his brother, had to wait for them.

Sully, who had been eight at the time, couldn't stop shivering, even when they were finally allowed to jump into the pool. The water felt cold, and he was one of the youngest boys there. All the rules frightened him, and he was afraid he'd violate one unintentionally and be expelled while his brother, four years older, was allowed to stay. The building's subterranean corridors were confusing, and Sully wasn't sure he could find his locker again, much less his father. Also permitted to join the boys' free swim were two old men who lived at the Y, and they swam without bathing suits, which also frightened Sully, even after his brother explained that it was okay since they were all men and there weren't any girls around to see your equipment. Sully's own equipment had withdrawn almost into his body cavity. He tried to have a good time, but his lips were blue and he couldn't stop shivering. One of the lifeguards noticed and ordered him back into the showers until he warmed up.

In the tiled shower room he'd stood beneath the powerful spray, the hot water beating down on him until it began to cool, whereupon he moved to another on the opposite side of the room. Every time the hot water ran out, he moved. Soon the room was thick and comfortable with steam, and Sully had allowed himself to drift into its moist warmth, mindless of the passage of time, coming out of his reverie only when the hot water ran cool, necessitating another change. He spent the entire two-hour free swim in the showers, listening to the distant shrieks of the other boys in the pool, not wanting to get out of the steam, or to return to the cold pool water, or to venture back into the locker room on the cold concrete floor to search for the locker where he and his brother had put their clothes.

"See if I ever take you again," his father said later, his breath boozy in the front seat of the car he had borrowed to make the trip, when Patrick told on him. Sully was shivering in the backseat of the car as they returned to Bath. He was sick the entire week that followed. "Just see if I do."

It didn't take nearly as long to run out of hot water in Sully's flat, and when he stepped out of the shower, he wondered if he was going to be sick, if that was why he'd suddenly remembered the YMCA episode after so many years in the limbo of his memory. He doubted it could be that he needed another reason to bear a grudge against his father, whose ghost, for some reason, seemed to be visiting him more often and vividly of late, starting right around the time he'd fallen from the ladder.

The good news was that his knee didn't feel too bad, and Sully considered for the umpteenth time the illogic of his own body. Immediately after hard work, the knee felt pretty good. Tomorrow morning, he knew from experience, he would pay.

Which meant that he would have to go see Jocko first thing. He was almost out of Tylenol 3s, or whatever it was he was taking. Jocko did not always dispense his relief in labeled bottles. At least not to Sully. When Sully needed something for pain, Jocko didn't stand on formalities like a physician's prescription. When he got samples he thought Sully might be interested in, he slipped a bright plastic tube full of pills into Sully's coat pocket and whispered verbal instructions for their use: "Here. Eat these."

Downstairs, Miss Beryl was waiting for him in the hall, dressed in her robe and slippers. She always looked tinier and even more gnomelike when she stood in the large doorway to her flat. She was holding a fistful of mail, most of it, Sully could tell at a glance, junk. He often went weeks at a time without checking his mailbox and then, after a cursory glance, tossed whatever had accumulated there in the trash. People who wanted to contact him left messages for him at The Horse. People who didn't know him well enough to do that were probably people he didn't want to hear from anyway. Sully had no credit cards, and since his utilities were included in the rent he paid Miss Beryl, he didn't have to worry about bills. To his way of thinking, he had no real relationship with the postal service. He didn't even have his name on the mailbox, refused to put it there, in fact, not wanting to encourage the mailman. Now and then Miss Beryl would gather what collected there and thrust it at him, as she was doing now, with communications she judged to be of possible importance on top. The envelope on top of this particular fistful of mail looked to be a tax document from the Town of North Bath, no doubt reminding him of his obligations on the property his father left him when he died. Sully did not bother to open it to be sure. He leafed through the rest to make sure his disability check was not in the stash. He'd already thrown that away once in his rush to dispose of all the junk.

"You got a pen handy, Mrs. Peoples?" he asked, knowing full well she kept half a dozen in a glass by the door. In fact, she had anticipated his need and was holding a pen out to him disapprovingly. On the tax envelope he wrote in bold letters RETURN TO SENDER and deposited the junk mail in the small decorative trash can just inside his landlady's door.

"You're the most incurious man in the universe," Miss Beryl remarked, as she often did on these occasions. "Hasn't anyone ever told you that inquiring minds want to know?"

"Maybe you just have better luck with the post office than I've had," he suggested. "So far the mail has brought me my draft notice, my divorce papers, jury duty, half a dozen different threats that I can think of. And not a single piece of good news I didn't already know about because somebody told me."

Miss Beryl shook her head, studied her tenant. "You look better, anyhow," she said.

"Than what?"

"Than you did when you came in," said Miss Beryl, who had been watching at the window.

"Long day, Beryl," Sully admitted.

"They get longer," she warned. "I read about five books a week to pass the time. Of course, I read only half of some of them. I always stop when I realize I've read a book before."

"Who said 'A man's reach should exceed his grasp'?" Sully suddenly remembered Carl's quotation.

"I did," she said. "All through eighth grade. Before me, it was Robert Browning. He said it only once, but he had a better audience."

"What grade did he teach?" Sully grinned.

"I bet you can't finish the quotation, smarty."

"I thought it was finished," Sully said truthfully.

"You had visitors this afternoon," Miss Beryl said.

"Really?" Sully said. He had few visitors. People who knew him knew they had a better chance of running into him at Hattie's or The Horse or the OTB.

"A young woman with a huge bosom and a tiny little girl."

Sully was about to say he had no idea who this could be when it occurred to him. "Did the little girl have a bad eye?"

"Yes, poor little soul," Miss Beryl confirmed. "The mother was all mouth and chest."

This did not strike Sully as a fair assessment of Ruth's daughter, Jane, though it was an accurate enough first impression.

"I must be losing patience with my fellow humans," Miss Beryl went on. "Anymore I'm all for executing people who are mean to children. I used to favor just cutting off their feet. Now I want to rid the world of them completely. If this keeps up I'll be voting Republican soon."

"You're definitely getting mean in your old age, Mrs. Peoples," Sully said, trying to match her joking tone, though he could sense that the encounter had upset her. "She didn't say what she wanted?" he asked, half fearfully, though he doubted Ruth's daughter would have revealed much to Miss Beryl.

"I think she was just as glad you weren't here," Miss Beryl told him. "I got the impression she was on the lam from a no-good husband."

"That would fit," Sully admitted, recalling now that back in the summer, when Jane had run away from her husband the first time, Sully had told Ruth to send her and the little girl over to his flat if they needed a place her husband wasn't likely to look. "She married some stiff from Schuyler Springs who's in and out of jail."

"Well," Miss Beryl said. "I'm relieved that's the explanation. I thought at first you'd gone and got that young thing pregnant."

"The young ones won't have me anymore, Beryl," Sully told her, Toby Roebuck flashing into his consciousness unbidden, as she'd been doing all afternoon. "I wish one or two would."

"You're a cur, sir," Miss Beryl told him. "I've always wanted to say that to a man."

Sully nodded, accepted the indictment. "I thought you *were* a Republican," he said.

"No," Miss Beryl told him. "Clive Jr. is. His father was too. Clive Sr. was a hardheaded man in many respects."

"Not a bad one, though," Sully remembered.

"No," Miss Beryl admitted thoughtfully. "I miss arguing with him. It would have taken a lifetime to win him over to my way of thinking. There are times I think he died so he wouldn't have to admit I was right."

When Sully was gone, Miss Beryl returned to her chair in the front room where she had been reading. The chair was placed directly in front of the television she seldom turned on. On top of it were Clives Jr. and Sr., stars present and past of her firmament. "You *were* hardheaded," she informed her husband. Never an articulate man, Clive Sr. had lost every argument he ever got into with Miss Beryl, who possessed sufficient intellect and verbal dexterity to corner and dispatch him, and so he learned early on in their marriage not to detail his logic to a woman who was not above explaining where it was flawed. "I have my reasons," he'd learned to say, and to accompany this statement with an expression he deemed enigmatic.

He died wearing that very expression, and he was still wearing it when Miss Beryl arrived at the scene of the accident. After young Audrey Peach had braked him into the windshield, Clive Sr. had rocked back into the car's bucket seat, his head angled oddly because of his broken neck. He appeared to be thinking. I have my reasons, he seemed to say, and for the past twenty-five years he'd left her alone to ponder them.

"And *you* . . ." she told her son, but she let the sentence trail off.

Miss Beryl was still holding the letter that Sully had marked RETURN TO SENDER. She did not need to open it to know what was inside. In the metal box in her bedroom she had an entire manila folder marked "Sully," and she would add this letter to the others when she retired for the night. "I'm doing the right thing," she said aloud to the two Clives. "So just pipe down."

One of the things Sully appreciated about the White Horse Tavern was that it had a window out front with a Black Label Beer sign that hadn't worked in years. That allowed Sully to peek in and see who was inside before committing himself. There were nights—and this was one of them—when he didn't want to get involved. What he wanted was supper and bed. One beer might not be bad, but one had a way of leading directly to half a case. Tonight, a quick glance inside was enough to convince Sully. Wirf, predictably, was there, no doubt preparing his lecture about why Sully should stay in school, about how his going back to work would fuck everything up. Carl Roebuck, less predictably, was anchoring the near corner of the bar, a bad sign. Carl usually did his drinking and carousing in Schuyler Springs and came into The Horse only when he was looking for somebody. Usually Sully. And Sully knew that if Carl was trying to find him, he'd just as soon stay lost. True, Carl owed him for the other half of his day's work, but that couldn't be why he was there. Kenny, Carl's father, had been the kind of man who went looking for people he owed, but Carl just looked for people who owed him. Maybe he was just there because he was locked out of his house, but Sully decided not to take a chance.

When Carl slid off his stool and headed for the men's room, Sully ducked back from the window, peering in again in time to see Carl disappear into the head. Though Sully'd never noticed it before, it occurred to him now how much Carl reminded him of his father, even though he was about half Kenny's size and Kenny had been far too homely to be much of a ladies' man. Sully found himself wishing it was Kenny, not his son, who was peeing in the men's room trough. Had it been Kenny, Sully wouldn't have minded getting involved. There was much to be said for a man who wouldn't hold it against you when you burned down his house.

The only other place that might be open at this time of night was Jerry's Pizza a few doors down, where all the kids hung out. Normally a greasy burger at The Horse would have been preferable, but there weren't any kids hanging around Jerry's entrance, so Sully decided to take a chance. It was Thanksgiving Eve, after all, and maybe the kids were all home and the jukebox that blared heavy metal would be silent for once. Besides, Ruth would be working, and he was going to have to face her eventually anyway. Maybe he'd find her in a holiday mood. Maybe if he saw her he'd quit thinking about Toby Roebuck. It could happen. And it might be a good idea to find out why Jane had come over to the flat that afternoon.

Blessedly, the place was empty. Sully selected a booth out of sight from the street and far from the jukebox which, though silent, glowed red and angry, as if gathering energy and venom from the unaccustomed quiet. "Sully!" a voice boomed from the kitchen. "Thank God we stayed open!"

The voice belonged to Vince, who owned Jerry's. Jerry, Vince's brother, ran another pizza place just like it, called Vince's, in Schuyler Springs. The Schuyler Springs restaurant did a better business, and whoever won the wager on the Bath-Schuyler basketball game got to run the Schuyler Springs place for the following year. By betting on his alma mater, Bath, Vince had lost the better business the last ten years in a row. Jerry always gave his brother points, but never enough of them. Both brothers were huge, burly men with more hair on their chests than their heads. They looked so much alike that over the years people had begun to confuse them, thanks to their physical resemblance and the fact that for the last ten years each had been managing the other's restaurant. Vince minded losing his identity a lot more than losing his restaurant to basketball wagers, and so, sensing this, Sully had taken to calling him by his brother's name.

"How about a little service?" Sully called, rapping the back of the booth with his pepper shaker.

The door to the kitchen swung open and Ruth appeared. She did not look to be in a holiday mood. It took her a minute to locate Sully at the far end of the room. "I don't know what good it does to send a man to college who can't even read," she said, in reference to the THIS SECTION CLOSED sign in the center of the floor.

In fact, Sully had not noticed it. He'd just found a spot where nobody would notice him from the street and feel compelled to keep him company. "Sorry," he said. "I just wanted to get as far from the jukebox as I could. Besides," he added when Ruth came over, "I don't go to college any more."

"So I heard," Ruth said. "Wirf was in looking for you earlier." She was making rather a point of just standing there over him instead of slipping into the booth like she would have done if they were still friends. Eventually, Sully knew, they would quarrel over his going back to work, but not now. That was one of the things Sully'd always liked about Ruth. She knew when not to say what she was thinking. What he didn't like about her was her ability to make clear what she was thinking without saying anything. Right now, for instance, she was thinking his going back to work was not smart, which it probably wasn't. You'll be sorry, she was thinking, which he probably would.

"You smell good, anyway," Ruth said, finally sliding into the booth.

"So do you," Sully said, grinning at her. "I've always liked the smell of pizza."

Ruth just sat there, nodding and smiling at him, that rather knowing, unpleasant smile she had, the one that never boded well. Still, she looked good to Sully, and he found himself hoping they'd quarrel sooner rather than later, get it over with quickly, because he had missed her company.

"Youth," she told him now, "is what you like the smell of."

This was a strange remark, even by Ruth's standards, and Sully found himself squinting at it, trying to get a handle. True, Ruth *was* twelve years younger than Sully, but he had a pretty good idea from her tone of voice that Ruth was not referring to herself.

"So," she continued after a moment's awkward silence. "How was work?"

"Hard."

"It got hard today, did it?" Ruth's knowing smile had become a malicious grin now. She was enjoying herself, watching him squirm and squint at her.

"Is there any way I can get in on this conversation?" Sully asked. "The one you're having without me?"

"Hey," Ruth said. "I just wondered how your day went. I thought maybe you struck up an old acquaintance. I take that back. A young acquaintance."

Now it all fell into place. Someone had seen Toby Roebuck give him a lift downtown and reported it to Ruth, who, just before he'd quit working for Carl in August and enrolled at the college, had accused him of having a crush on Carl's wife. It had been true, of course, but that hadn't made the accusation any less surprising, and Sully had wondered, as he sometimes did, if Ruth might be gifted with ESP. He'd even accused her of prescience once or twice, though Ruth had replied that nobody needed any extra senses to figure Sully out.

"Do you realize," Sully said, "that you and I have been together so long the town gossips treat us like we're married. They used to talk about you and me to Zack. Now they report my activities to you. Just out of curiosity, what were you told?"

"It's a kinky relationship, apparently," she went on. "Involving mud wrestling by way of foreplay."

Sully smiled at her. "I'm too goddamned tired even for foreplay, Ruth."

"I'm glad," Ruth said seriously. "I don't think I'd take it very well if you threw me over for a cheerleader. You want something to eat?"

"Linguine," Vince's voice sang out from the kitchen. Vince's hearing was legend. He'd been known to come out of the steamy kitchen, stalk across the floor of his raucous restaurant, elbowing among his clientele of screaming teens, and break up a fight before the first punch was thrown, explaining afterward that he'd been listening to the conversation. "He wants linguine and clams. I throw away two goddamn dozen cherrystones a week so he can have linguine the once a month he comes in."

"Did it ever occur to you that I might want something else once?" Sully shouted at the kitchen door. "Just because I let you sell me half a dozen spoiled clams five years ago doesn't mean I have to keep ordering linguine forever."

"Wasn't for you, I'd never have to order a single goddamn clam, you ingrate," Vince bellowed. "Order whatever you want. Less work for me. I was going to have to pick through the trash for the clams anyhow."

"Then that's what I'll have," Sully said. "If it'll cause you extra work, I'll eat poison."

"The life of Don Sullivan in a nutshell. Don't run off when you finish," Ruth said, looking serious again.

"Everything all right?"

"Not really." Ruth nodded in the direction of the closed kitchen door, which meant that whatever this was about, she didn't want to discuss it in the field of Vince's radar. Which worried Sully, since there wasn't much Ruth wouldn't discuss in front of Vince.

Sully'd eaten about half his linguine when Wirf came in, stood in the center of the room, pivoted on his prosthetic limb, and was about to leave when he spotted Sully off by himself in the dark, closed section of the restaurant. "What the hell are you doing back here?" he wanted to know as he slid uncertainly onto the bench, red-eyed. Wirf was about half in the bag, from the look of him.

"Trying to eat my dinner in peace for once," Sully said.

Wirf nodded sympathetically, secure in his apparent belief that Sully's observation in no way pertained to himself. He took off his gloves and scarf, put them next to the rubber plant on the ledge. "I saw you peek in at The

Horse, but then you disappeared. I bet I been up and down this street half a dozen times trying to figure where you went."

Sully twirled a forkful of linguine. "You should have given up, Wirf."

"I was afraid you might be thinking black thoughts, after yesterday," Wirf said. He was watching like an expectant dog as Sully raised the pasta to his mouth. Wirf, his brain permanently fogged by alcohol, forgot all sorts of things. Often he forgot to eat. Food seldom appealed to him except when he saw it actually being consumed. Then longing entered his expression, as if he'd suddenly recollected a lost love.

"Help me eat some of this," Sully told him. The booth was set up for two and Ruth hadn't bothered to clear away the other silver, so all Wirf needed was a plate. Since Sully had finished his salad, he pushed the bowl toward Wirf, who emptied the dregs of the oil and vinegar into the nearby rubber plant. With fork and spoon he transferred exactly half the remaining linguine into the bowl. "You ate all the clams?" he said, peering at the stack Sully'd made of the empty shells.

"I wasn't expecting you, Wirf," Sully said.

"All I wanted was one," Wirf said. "I hate the slimy bastards, but I keep thinking I'll be surprised someday and like them."

"I'm glad there aren't any left then. I like them every time I eat them," Sully said, pushing the breadbasket toward Wirf.

"Don't be stingy," Wirf said, pointing his fork at Sully. "Don't go through life stingy."

"Okay," Sully said.

"A clam's a small thing," Wirf explained. "But there's a principle."

"I could order you some clams," Sully offered. He had no intention of doing that, but Wirf was easy to shame with gestures.

"This goddamn kitchen is closed!" Vince bellowed.

"Old radar ears," Wirf said. "The government should put him on top of a mountain and make him listen to sounds from deep space."

"That would be the place for him, all right," Sully agreed.

Nothing from the kitchen. In a minute Ruth came by and set a clam in front of Wirf. It was uncooked and clamped tight.

"How can you put up with this untrustworthy son of a bitch?" Wirf asked her.

"Easy," Ruth said. "I never see him."

"So," Wirf said when she was gone, "I'm hearing you went back to work."

Sully pushed his plate toward the center of the table. "I didn't do too bad either, you'll be pleased to know. I enjoy it more than talking to judges."

Wirf made a face. "Yesterday was no good," he admitted, in reference to their most recent day in court, "but we'll wear the bastards down. There's a zillion things we haven't even tried yet, and one of these days we're going to get a judge who's actually done an honest day's work at some point in his worthless life. Then we're home free."

"By then I'll be seventy and already dead for five years."

"See," Wirf pointed the fork again. "These are black thoughts. I thought we'd agreed you'd stay in school and wait this out. Be smart for once. Bide your time. They ever find out you're working, and we're *really* fucked."

"That's a black thought, Wirf," Sully pointed out.

Wirf sighed, shook his head. "Why do I even try with you?"

"Now *there's* a question. Go home and think about that."

They were grinning at each other now. "Jesus," Wirf said.

"Right," Sully agreed.

"Carl paying you under the table?"

"You have to ask?"

"Just don't go on the fucking books. Anywhere," Wirf advised solemnly.

"Listen. You don't have to tell me to work under the table," Sully reminded him. "The only time I ever worked on the up and up I got hurt."

This was not literally true, but pretty near. One of Sully's myriad financial headaches was that he'd done so little work on the books and paid so little FICA that his Social Security at retirement was going to be a drop in the bucket. His service pension was going to be the other drop. Which meant he'd be eligible for welfare and food stamps. The trouble with that was that he knew too many people on the public dole and he didn't want to be one of them. You had to stand in too many lines and fill out too many forms, and Sully had a low opinion of both. He'd made up his mind in the army that if he ever lived through the war he'd never stand in another line. That was one of the reasons he'd returned to Bath, a town pretty much devoid of queues. Besides, welfare was begging, and he'd been saying for years that when the time came that he couldn't be useful enough to earn what little he needed to live on he'd shoot himself, a promise two or three people he could think of would hold him to if they could.

"Work a little if you gotta, but remember our strategy," Wirf was saying. "Keep 'em busy with paperwork, keep documenting the deterioration of that knee. Sooner or later they'll see it's costing them by not settling one or two of these claims. The court's already starting to get pissed. You hear the judge yesterday?"

"He sounded pissed at *you*, Wirf."

"Only 'cause he knows I won't go away," Wirf explained.

"I know how he feels," Sully said.

Wirf didn't rise to the bait. He pushed his salad bowl to the center of the table. "When they start getting bent out of shape, then you know you're getting somewhere. Intro Law 101."

"You ever take 102?"

Wirf dropped his fork, looked hurt.

"I just wondered," Sully grinned.

"I can't do this without you," Wirf implored. "I'm way the fuck out on a limb here, and all I can hear is you sawing away."

"I been telling you to quit for months," Sully reminded him. "I'm tired of watching you get beat up. I can't pay you what I owe you now."

"Have I asked you for anything?"

"Yes. Just now. You ate half my linguine."

"I never asked for that. You offered."

"I can't stand to see you look starved. I wish you'd go away and do something profitable. If guys like you and me could beat insurance companies there wouldn't be any insurance companies. Common Sense 101."

Wirf waved his hand at Sully in disgust, then picked up the clam in the center of the table and made a pretense of braining Sully with it. "I guess it's true," he said. "A little knowledge is a dangerous fucking thing. Who'd have guessed you could learn anything at Schuyler Springs Community College? I liked you better when you were completely stupid."

Ruth reappeared and began to bus their dishes. "Vince says to take this discussion upstreet to The Horse. It's almost Thanksgiving, and if you leave he'll have the one thing to be thankful for." She balanced the stack of dishes against her chest. "He also wants to know what makes you think Sully isn't completely stupid."

"Call it a hunch," Wirf told her, then to Sully, "Come have a beer with me."

"There's no such thing as one beer with you," Sully said.

"That's true," Wirf admitted. "So what?"

"So I'm working tomorrow."

"Tomorrow's Thanksgiving."

"I heard that somewhere."

Wirf gave up, slid out of the booth, located his scarf and gloves. "Listen to me. Don't drop your classes officially. That would fuck us. Take incompletes. That gives us until spring, maybe fall. With any luck by then we'll be able to prove you're a complete cripple. It's time for another X ray, too, and photos of that knee, so get in and get that done."

Sully agreed to all this so Wirf would go away. X rays were not cheap, but if he mentioned this, Wirf would start pushing money at him.

"Come have a beer with me," Wirf said.

"No. Don't you understand no?"

"And next time save me a clam," Wirf called over his shoulder.

"You didn't eat the one you got," Sully reminded him. It was still sitting in the middle of the table.

When Wirf was gone, Ruth returned and slid quietly into the booth behind Sully. Kneeling there, she gave his shoulders a rub over the back of the booth. "How's Peter?" she wondered.

Sully relaxed into the massage, too tired to try to figure out how she knew his son was in town. "Is there anything about my day you don't know?"

"Yup," she said cheerfully. "I don't know why you jumped out of his car and ran across the parking lot of the IGA."

"I thought Wednesday was your day off," he said. Her day job was as a cashier at the IGA, which meant she must have seen him out the window.

"Not since the end of September," she told him. "You used to keep better track of my days off."

"Well, I know my memory stinks, but I do seem to recall you were the one who wanted to cool it for a while."

They'd agreed to this back in August when Gregory, Ruth's youngest, now a senior at Bath High, had seen them together coming out of The Horse late one night. Having lied about his own plans for the evening, the boy was in no position to accuse his mother, and in fact he'd said nothing about seeing her with Sully, but their eyes had met across the nearly deserted street, and Ruth had seen the look on his face when the realization dawned on him. She'd told Sully right then that they were going to have to be good for a while.

And so, since August, they'd been good, Ruth working her two jobs, Sully going to school and spending his evenings at The Horse with Wirf and the other regulars, often until closing. In truth, their being good every now and then had always been part of the rhythm of their relationship, and

Sully sometimes thought that had they been able to marry, as they'd once wanted to, by now they'd have succeeded in making each other miserable. Being good was often just what they needed, provided they weren't good too long.

Because their sporadic abstinence was imposed upon them by periods of heightened suspicion in Ruth's husband, they'd never had to face the possibility that they enjoyed being good nearly as much as being bad. Lately their periodic seasons of virtue had grown gradually longer, and this, though Sully didn't dare admit it to Ruth, suited him fine. Adultery, like full-court basketball, was a younger man's sport, and engaging in it these last few years had made Sully feel a little foolish and undignified. Over twenty years now he and Ruth had been lovers, and they were unable to decide, together or separately, whether to be proud or ashamed of their relationship, just as they had been unable to explain the ebb and flow of their need for each other. It was far easier to acknowledge the need when it was upon them than to admit its absence later, and their bitterest arguments tended to be over who it was that decided to be good for a while, who was responsible for their lapse into virtue, who had been avoiding and ignoring whom. Sully could feel one of these arguments coming on now, and he also sensed that he was going to lose it.

"So you're saying that when I said 'a while,' you thought I meant three months," Ruth said, her thumbs digging deeper now between Sully's shoulder blades, skillfully crossing the boundary between pleasure and pain.

"No," Sully countered. "I thought you meant seven. I thought you wanted Gregory graduated and away at college."

An indirect hit, apparently, since Ruth's thumbs returned a little closer to affection mode. "Well, you didn't have to go along so agreeably."

"I'm not a mind reader," he said, deciding to press his luck a little further, a tactic that seldom reaped dividends with Ruth. "You have to let me know what you want."

Ruth stopped the massage and did not answer immediately. "What I want," she finally said, "is for *you* to want. I think I could be reasonably content if I were sure you couldn't get through the day without thinking about me. If I knew you picked up the phone half a dozen times just to tell me different things. That's what I'd like, Sully."

"You'd be happy if you knew I was miserable?" Sully paraphrased her position.

"You got it."

"How about if I just tell you I've missed you?"

Ruth resumed the massage. "I guess I'd settle for that and an explanation of why your son was chasing you across the IGA parking lot."

So Sully explained how his grandson had cracked his bad knee with Dr. Seuss, mentioning also that he'd received an invitation to stop by Vera's tomorrow. Ruth always felt bad about the holidays Sully spent alone, but she also harbored a deep distrust of Sully's ex-wife that he'd never been able to account for until Ruth confessed to him one day that she always feared they'd end up remarried, an irrational fear that persisted even though Vera was already remarried to someone else. "Are you going to go?"

"I may drop by when I finish up work," Sully said without much enthusiasm. "I promised Dummy I'd sheetrock a house for him tomorrow."

"On Thanksgiving?"

Sully shrugged. "Why not?"

There were so many reasons why a sane man would not want to sheetrock a house in the freezing cold on Thanksgiving that Ruth declined to select among them. When Sully asked why not, he didn't mean that he couldn't think of any reasons. He meant that he'd decided in advance not to accept their validity. Ruth quit the massage for good and slid into the booth facing him. "Will it take all day?"

"Might," Sully admitted. "I had a half-day job today and it took all day and half the night. Rub did most of it."

"Your first day back. What'd you expect?"

"More."

"Maybe tomorrow will be better."

"Tomorrow will be worse," he told her honestly. "That much I'm sure of. The day after that might be better. I can't work at the old pace, that much I know already. I might not be able to manage at all."

"Want some advice?"

"Not really."

"Go back to school."

Sully didn't respond immediately, hoping to create through silence the impression that he was actually considering her wisdom. "I can't make any money at school, Ruth," he said finally.

"You need some money?"

He shook his head. "Not right this very minute. I might someday, though. I'm for sure going to need a new truck, probably by the first of the year. The back and forth to school has just about finished mine. I've half planned for that, but if there are any surprises . . ."

"Rolling with the punches is what you're good at," Ruth reminded him. "It's what we're both good at."

Sully nodded, because he knew it was true and because it heartened him to have Ruth say so. Sitting across the table from her this way brought home to him how much he had indeed missed her. There were times when he wondered if perhaps they couldn't continue in just this way, content with each other's companionship, with the memory of shared intimacy, the assurance of continued friendship. He knew better than to suggest this to Ruth, though. She was twelve years younger than he, and their lovemaking, however infrequent, was more important to her than to him. "I don't know about you, but I wouldn't mind slipping a few punches this round."

He was trying to find a way to bring up the subject of Jane and her visit, which Ruth might or might not know about, when they heard a throaty rumble outside. Ruth stood quickly to peer out the window. "Well, I'm glad you're in a peaceful mood because Guess Who just pulled up. It's a good thing he's too cheap to fix that muffler."

"Go. I can handle Zack," Sully said without much confidence, but Ruth had already disappeared into the kitchen. A second later, when the front door to the restaurant swung open, Sully didn't turn around.

It took Ruth's husband, Zack, a minute to realize who it was sitting down there in the closed section of the restaurant and another minute to decide what to do about it. What he'd come in for was to borrow some money from Ruth, since Wednesday was the night Vince paid her. Any public altercation with Sully would compromise this modest plan, and so Zack gave deep and careful consideration to just turning around and slipping outside again and waiting for Ruth to come out, which she'd have to do eventually. And he might have adopted this strategy if he could have been sure that nobody would see him slinking away. Zack was frequently accused of cowardice. People kept telling him they couldn't understand why Zack didn't just shoot Sully or at least club him a good one with a baseball bat. He disliked being called a coward, so he took a deep breath and attempted to summon an indignation he didn't really feel at Sully's presence.

"What do you know?" Zack said when he arrived at Sully's booth, Sully still seated, his back to Zack. "Look who's here. Sully, of all people."

"Zachary," Sully said, motioning to the empty bench opposite.

Zack considered this genial offer. Except for the rumors that persisted about his wife and Sully, Zack didn't object to Sully personally. He had no hard evidence that Sully and Ruth were lovers (he himself did not love Ruth and couldn't see why anyone would), and this lack of evidence prevented him from building up a good head of righteous steam. Every time he tried, usually at someone else's instigation, he ended up being made a fool. Sully had a way of besting him at prefight verbal sparring, and when Sully landed a good one, Zack took the mandatory eight count, trying to think of a retort. Sometimes, failing to think of one, he just threw in the towel right there.

The last time, this summer, had been the worst, and the confrontation was still fresh in Zack's mind. He and his cousin Paulie had gone to find Sully at The Horse. Somebody had called to say he was there with Ruth, but when they arrived it was just Sully seated at the bar. At Paulie's insistence they'd slid onto the two vacant stools next to him. "See this guy here?" Zack had announced in a stage whisper to his cousin. "He thinks he's a real ladies' man."

Sully'd swiveled on his stool then and examined Zack so patiently and with so little concern that Zack's confidence first eroded, then crumbled. "I am, too, compared to some people," Sully finally said, a remark that struck Zack as neither confirmation nor denial and therefore impossible to act upon.

"A real ladies' man," Zack had repeated lamely. Then he decided on a veiled accusation. "Some people says he likes my wife, but Sully says no."

Sully, who had swung back around on his stool, rotated again. He ran his fingers through the stubble on his chin thoughtfully. "I never said I didn't like your wife, Zack," he said. "I think she's terrific, in fact. I probably like her better than you do."

And Sully'd paused there, apparently confident that it would be a while before Zack would be able to take this in, analyze the data, arrive at a conclusion. Zack too was aware that he was slow, which was why he sometimes practiced verbal sparring with Sully when he was alone, trying to anticipate how the conversation might go, preparing a snappy rejoinder or two. Except that the conversation never did go that way, and it wasn't going that way this time, either. In fact, Zack could feel desperation already seeping in. He was about to say, for the third time, "Some ladies' man," when Sully lowered the boom.

"I never said I didn't like your wife, Zack. I just said I wasn't screwing your wife."

"That makes two of you," somebody piped in from down the bar, and Zack had felt the whole room go out of focus. He had to be led out of The Horse by his cousin Paulie, who, out in the bright sunlight of the street, finally got him to quit muttering "Some ladies' man." When he was finally able to shake the cobwebs, he'd made a resolution. There'd be no more talk. Next time he'd either leave Sully alone or sucker-punch him as a solution to prefight jitters.

Unfortunately, the present circumstance conspired against him. He couldn't very well sucker-punch Sully in his wife's place of employment. Truth be told, he was a little afraid to, anyway. Sully might be an old fart, but he'd been a tough customer when he was younger, and Zack, who had never been a tough customer, was afraid that at sixty, Sully might still have a few tricks up his sleeve, and Zack did not want to get beat up by an old cripple. On the other hand, he couldn't very well ignore Sully's presence here in the restaurant, especially seated down here in the dark part, which seemed significant somehow. As usual, Zack found himself kind of in between. He had to engage Sully in another conversation. "What're you up to, need I ask?"

With his dishes all bussed, the only evidence of Sully's having eaten dinner was his coffee cup and a tiny dice of Bermuda onion on the formica tabletop. And the cherrystone clam, still clamped tightly shut. Sully hoped Ruth's husband would notice these and draw the correct inference, but he wasn't optimistic. Zack had already drawn one inference in the last minute or so, and that would be it for a while. "I was just sitting here wondering how things could get worse," Sully told him.

"Oh," Zack said, feeling the jab land. As usual, he hadn't seen it coming.

"I must have been thinking out loud," Sully went on, "because here you are." He didn't much care for the idea of being wedged into a tight booth when the man blocking his exit might summon the necessary conviction to punch him. Zack would probably get in a half-dozen good licks before Sully could get to his feet. And if Zack ever kicked Sully in the knee there'd be nothing to do but just sit back down in the booth and cry. The good news was that if Zack was going to start a fight, he probably would have by now. In fact, he had the look of a man who'd already decided to cut his losses. "Take a load off your feet, why don't you?" Sully suggested again. "Your wife'll be out in a minute. You can give her a lift home. She looks beat."

Zack wasn't ready to sit down. "I'm not sure I like walking in here and finding you," he complained.

Sully shrugged. "I don't know what to tell you. It's one of three restaurants in town." He thumbed the sliver of Bermuda onion and flicked it into the rubber plant with his forefinger.

"How come you're sitting way down here in the dark?"

"I don't know, Zachary." Sully sighed. "Do I need a reason? Do I follow you around and ask you how come you sit in one chair and not another one?"

Zack didn't have an answer.

"Pretty funny, you sitting here in the dark," Zack managed, though he'd clearly lost the edge, somehow. He couldn't help thinking he should have had Sully in some kind of corner, that the other man had a hell of a lot of explaining to do. But here they were arguing pleasantly over whether Sully had a right to sit in here by himself in the dark if he felt like it. Which he did, Zack had to admit.

Ruth emerged from the kitchen drying her hands on a rag. She glared at Zack, who immediately fidgeted guiltily. "What's the matter?" she said. "Can't start a fight?"

"What's he doing here?"

"Let's you and me go home, sport," Ruth said. "*I'll* fight with you."

Zack looked like he'd rather fight with Sully and was sorry now to have missed the opportunity.

Ruth turned to Sully. "I'd like to go home tonight," she said. "Are you going to leave me a tip or what?"

"I'm half afraid to," Sully said. "Some not-too-bright person might get the wrong idea."

"Let him," Ruth said. "Somebody's got to make a living in this family."

Zack watched his wife pick up the dollar and change Sully put on the table.

"Not the sort of tip that would make anybody suspicious, is it?" she said, stuffing the money into her husband's shirt pocket. "Can I trust you to act like a grown-up for about two minutes while I get my coat?"

"Sure." Zack shrugged, not looking up from the floor.

When Ruth was gone, Sully again motioned to the bench across from him, and this time Zack sighed and sat down. He looked so pitiful and unhappy that Sully had half a mind to tell him the truth and promise to reform. "I don't know, Zachary," he admitted instead.

Zack was studying his fingernails now. "Me neither, I guess," he said.

Which made Sully laugh.

Which made Zack grin sheepishly. "I don't know what I'm worried about even," he admitted. "Hell, I'm a grandpa and she's a grandma."

"Me, too," Sully said, his knee humming to the tune his grandson Wacker had taught it that morning. "A grandfather, that is."

Zack shrugged. "We're too old to get ourselves arrested for fighting in public, I guess."

"That's assuming that people would recognize it as fighting."

Ruth came out with her coat on, stood by the door. "Well," she barked. "Come on, dumbbell."

Sully and Zack exchanged glances. "I think she means you," Sully said.

Zack got up slowly. He knew who she meant without having to be told. "You drive," Ruth told him as they headed out the door. "I want both my hands free."

When the door swung shut behind them, Vince came out of the kitchen and started switching off the restaurant's remaining lights and singing, "Hello, young lovers, wherever you are." When he pulled the plug on the jukebox, it made a resentful sound before the light went out. "Tell the truth and shame the Devil," he said. "Are you doing the two-step with young Mrs. Roebuck? Don't tell me you're too tired, either."

Sully slid out of the booth. "I suppose I could find the energy if she'd have me," he admitted. It was a question he had never seriously considered. "My guess is she loves her husband. Why is a mystery, but apparently she does."

"What makes you think so?"

Sully didn't know why he thought so exactly, but he did. Maybe because she was supposed to. Maybe because every other young woman in Bath seemed to.

"The reason I ask," Vince said, "is that I keep hearing she's involved with somebody in Schuyler."

"I doubt it," Sully said, perhaps too quickly.

"You do?" Vince grinned.

"I do."

"I don't." Vince said. "Know why?"

"No, why."

"Because I don't want to go through life like that dumb bastard Zack. Twenty years you and Ruth have been giving him horns, and he still can't make up his feeble mind if it's true. I'd rather be suspicious than a damn fool."

"He's not too bright, is he?" Sully conceded.

"Not too."

Feeling around in the dark for his keys, Sully located the clam and put it into his coat pocket. A clam, as Wirf pointed out, was a small thing, but you never knew when you might need one.

"Where the hell's the door?" he said.

Vince lit his cigarette lighter up next to his face to show where he was. His huge good-natured face reminded Sully of the demonic clown on the billboard outside of town.

"If I bang my knee between here and there," Sully warned, "your brother's going to own two restaurants."

The White Horse Tavern had gone, in Sully's lifetime, from a classy watering hole for the Albany young and well-to-do, a summer haunt of well-dressed New Yorkers upstate for the August Thoroughbred meet at Schuyler Springs, to a shabby local restaurant/pub. The completion of the interstate, which allowed New York and Albany direct access to Schuyler Springs, Lake George, Lake Placid and Montreal did the deed, effectively isolating Bath, Schuyler Springs' onetime rival for healing waters. The old, winding, two-lane blacktop once invited half a dozen drunken stops and supported twice that many roadhouses. In the forties and fifties, on an average Saturday night, there were numerous accidents along the twenty-five-mile stretch of road between Albany and Schuyler Springs, though fatalities, even serious injuries, were relatively rare. On the dark, tree-lined curves it was difficult to generate deadly speed, and the roadhouse taverns were close together and enough alike when you got there to make speed unnecessary. It wasn't unusual for drivers involved in head-on collisions to get out of their cars and fight drunkenly in the middle of the road over whose fault the accident had been. The occasional hot-rodding teen would kill himself, as Sully's older brother, Patrick, had done, but everyone knew teenagers were going to kill themselves. You couldn't blame the road or the roadhouses, really.

On the new interstate there were no head-on collisions. Most places, the median dividing north- and southbound traffic was fifty yards or more across. Drivers simply fell asleep on its straight, smooth surface, then left the pavement, flew through the air at eighty miles an hour and located the nearest tree. The drivers didn't pick fights over whose fault it was. They were taken to the hospital as a formality, to be pronounced dead.

Of the two dozen taverns that once had flourished in the corridor before the interstate was completed, only a handful were still in existence, and of these only The Horse and one or two others weren't seasonal. Most reopened, often under new ownership, during the summer, doing real business only during August, when the Schuyler Springs flat track opened and downstate headed north for the meet. Then every restaurant and bar within a twenty-mile radius of the track made a killing by raising its prices. Or as much of a killing as they could hope to make, knowing it'd have to last them the year. The owners of these local spots owed their marginal existence to the downstaters, who were used to being stolen from and who admired upstaters' limited imaginations when it came to thievery.

The Horse, because it was located in the village of North Bath and was not technically a roadhouse at all, stayed open year round, though its character was dramatically different during racing season. In June, the whole place got a facelift. Stools and tables got repaired, the bar got varnished, the large back room was opened and cleaned, the light bulbs in its chandeliers replaced. A whole new staff, mostly college students imported from the Albany area, arrived wearing tennis shorts and polo shirts and began their drills ("Hi, I'm Todd, and I'll be your server tonight"), and this was the sign for the locals to slink off into their seasonal exile. The new drink prices told them they weren't welcome in July and August. So did the new bartenders, ponytailed girls in some instances, who didn't have much to say to the likes of Sully and Wirf. Rub Squeers wasn't even allowed in the door.

Come September, after the snotty New Yorkers went home, taking with them their insults and their downstate accents and what remained of their cash, the roadhouses closed up one by one. The air was again cool at night, and familiar faces began to reappear at The Horse to compare notes and assess the damages of the season. Tiny Duncan, who owned The Horse, often thought about trying to keep the big dining room open, then thought again and closed it. Business was always so good in August that he never quite believed it would shut off, like water from a new tap, after Labor Day. Intellectually he knew it would, because it always did, every year, without exception. But in August, when he surveyed the crowded dining room, the line at the door that snaked down the street, he simply was unable to credit what he knew to be true. He began to contemplate the laws of cause and effect, wondering if maybe, just maybe, he didn't have things backwards. What if it was closing the dining room after Labor Day that caused the crowds to disappear, and not the disappearing crowds that caused him to close the dining room? But when the college-student waiters and bartenders said good-bye and returned to Albany and another semester at SUNY and RPI and Russell Sage, taking their bizarre, cheery optimism with them, Tiny knew that the gig was again up, and he allowed the establishment to slide again into gentle decline. For Tiny, the worst day of each year was the one when he let the regulars talk him into lugging the pool table back into the bar, where it stayed until the following July, when he would again need the space. The big round table in the dining room, the one he reserved for parties of eight to ten, got centered under a chandelier and became a poker table. It was all very depressing. For the winter holidays Tiny ran a single string of festive lights along the back bar, and each year the string contained fewer lights that worked. After New Year's, nobody was able to summon the energy to take them down.

Tonight, despite his steadfast intention, Sully had gone to The Horse and gotten involved. Tiny had given his regular bartender, a man he suspected of stealing and giving away too many free drinks, the night off and was being a pain in the ass as usual. He didn't know why he bothered to stay open in the winter, when he lost money. As soon as The Ultimate Escape opened, he was going to sell out and take his money and go live in Florida. If there was any money left after so many winters of bad business. For the past two hours Sully had half listened to Tiny bellyache, and he was now tired of it. Wirf had been listening to the same shit, but Wirf was impossible to bend out of shape, this night or any other. The more Wirf drank the drunker he got, and the drunker he got the more tolerant he became, and by this time of night he wouldn't have said shit if he had a mouthful.

"You know what," Sully told him, not bothering to conceal his irritation. "You wouldn't say shit if you had a mouthful."

"Wouldn't be much point," Wirf observed. He was wearing his postmidnight grin, and this grin had been known to get Sully worked up. It wasn't really a grin at all. Past a certain point of intoxication, Wirf had imperfect control of his facial muscles, and this was just his rictus face. A big shit-eating grin.

"When was the last time you won a case?" Sully asked him.

The question surprised Wirf without, apparently, angering him. "What's that got to do with anything?"

"You let everybody piss on your shoes is what it's got to do with," Sully explained. "They walk right up, unzip and pee. And what do you do? Stand there and grin at them."

Wirf chuckled good-naturedly now. "Who pisses on my shoes, Sully? Besides you, I mean."

"Exactly," Tiny said from down the bar, where he'd retreated to avoid Sully. Tiny, at nearly seventy, was huge, and when he sat on the stool he kept behind the bar on slow nights like this the stool disappeared, creating the illusion that Tiny was being magically supported on a pillow of air, like the puck in a game of air hockey. Tiny's obesity was another thing that irritated Sully after his fifth or sixth bottle of beer. That and the fact that Tiny kept reminding him of the fact that he'd run his father, Big Jim, out of The Horse when Sully was a boy, thrown him out bodily into the street more than once, and was publicly on record as saying that one asshole Sullivan was pretty much the same as the next.

"Come here a minute," Sully suggested.

There were only a half-dozen customers in the bar. Carl Roebuck had left before Sully and Vince came in. Vince had drunk one beer, handed Sully, like a baton, over to Wirf and then left. Tiny was comfortable right where he was. "What for?"

"Just come here," Sully explained.

Tiny hated this shit. He hated having his chain yanked, especially by Sully. On the other hand, he was tending bar and Sully was with Wirf and Wirf was Tiny's best customer. He climbed off his stool. "What do you want?"

Sully waited for him to come all the way down the bar, then said, "How are you?"

"What do you want?" Tiny repeated.

"I was just wondering how you are," Sully said. "Doing well, I hope?"

Wirf gave Tiny a don't-blame-me look.

"I don't get a chance to talk to you that much," Sully explained. "I wanted to make sure you were okay. You need any money or anything?"

When Tiny turned and headed back down the bar, Sully said, "I also thought you might let us in on how you got to be such a cheap son of a bitch."

"Don't start this again," Tiny warned.

In fact, Sully's complaint *was* an old one. He just couldn't get over how cheap Tiny was, especially with regard to Wirf, who dropped a lot of money in The Horse every night. The regular bartender would buy every fifth round or so, but Tiny never sprung. He couldn't even be shamed into buying a round by Sully, who was a past master at shaming bartenders.

"Look at those fucking lights," Sully said, pointing to the string of Christmas lights Tiny had just put up that afternoon. Nearly half were fluttering or dead out. "What would it cost you to put some new lights on that string. A buck?"

"Anymore you can't buy a candy bar for a buck," Tiny said, and this observation produced general agreement, despite its being obviously and demonstrably false. Tiny himself sold Snickers bars for seventy-five cents.

Tiny's bellyaching was also an old song, and tonight's lyric had been about how expensive utilities were anymore and how it didn't pay to keep the place open on slow nights in winter.

"I got an idea," Sully said. "Let's take up a collection and help Tiny out. He's beginning to look thin. I don't think he's got enough money for food."

"Go home, Sully," Tiny advised.

Sully returned to Wirf. "I just don't see how you can let guys like him piss on your shoes. How much money have you spent in here tonight?"

"Not a dime," Wirf said. "I haven't paid my tab yet. Besides, I don't expect people to buy me drinks. I can buy my own drinks."

"That's not the point."

"What *is* the point, then?"

Sully wasn't sure, but he knew there was one. He wasn't really angry with Tiny or Wirf, though he'd been bickering with both of them. The one he was really angry at, somewhat belatedly, was Ruth's husband, Zack, whom he now realized he should have punched. And for reasons that made less than perfect sense to him he was also mad at Ruth, whom he'd never treated as well as she deserved. And he was angry over the general state of things. He'd allowed himself to start working for Carl Roebuck again after swearing he wouldn't. And he was angry at himself for slipping back into his old infatuation with Carl's wife. He was even mad and drunk enough to fight about all of this if he could find somebody to fight with.

"I tell you what," Wirf said. "Let's call it a night before you get us eighty-sixed from the only bar in the county that doesn't play rock-and-roll music."

"Hell, yes," Sully agreed. "I never wanted to come in here in the first place, if you recall."

They left money on the bar. "You must've," Wirf pointed out. "Otherwise you'd have gone home."

On the way out Sully stopped at the end of the bar where Tiny had returned to his stool. "Let me have one of those Snickers bars if it's not too much trouble," he said.

Tiny got up and handed Sully the candy bar suspiciously. Sully handed him two one-dollar bills. Tiny shoved one of the bills back at him, growling, "Seventy-five."

"Nah," Sully said, pushing it back. "You can't get a candy bar for a buck anymore. You said so yourself."

"Take your fucking dollar, Sully. Don't be a pain in the ass."

Sully put his hands up, as if he were under arrest. "Uh-uh," he said. "That's *your* dollar."

Tiny put it into his pocket. "That make you happy, you mallet head?"

"Yes," Sully told him. "I've never been happier."

"You remain the uncontested master of the futile gesture," Wirf observed as they struggled drunkenly on with their winter coats by the door. "Give me half of that, will you?"

"Sure," Sully said, breaking the candy bar in two. "You owe me a dollar. I'll let it go, since I owe you about two thousand."

"Why don't you go back to school?" Wirf wanted to know. "You're just going to get hurt."

"It's out of my hands," Sully said before shoving his half of the candy bar in his mouth. Wirf waited for him to chew and swallow. "My philosophy professor doesn't believe there's any such thing as free will."

"What *does* he believe in?" Wirf wanted to know.

Sully shrugged. "He's a Jew. He probably believes in all sorts of screwball things."

"Not necessarily," Wirf said, pushing the door open and holding it for Sully. "I'm a Jew, and I don't believe in much of anything."

Outside, the two men stopped on the top step and stared out into the street in disbelief. They'd been vaguely aware that it had started snowing again. Sully had seen the flakes coming down through the Black Label sign in the tavern's window. But neither man had expected this. Beneath the lamps that lined Main the whole street was ghostly white.

"I believe it snowed," Sully said. "That's what I believe."

They stepped down into it. "About a foot, I believe," Wirf said, staring at where his scuffed brown wingtips had disappeared. "I believe I need some boots."

Sully was wearing his work boots, but the snow was over these too, and it was still snowing. "I didn't know you were a Jew," Sully said truthfully. "I thought Jews were supposed to be sharp lawyers."

"Sully," Wirf said, whipping his scarf over his shoulder so that it swatted Sully in the face. "You're a prince. Remember. No black thoughts."

Sully watched Wirf inch his way across the street warily to where his Regal was parked before heading upstreet toward his flat. In a minute the Regal slalomed by. Wirf had his window rolled down so he could chant "Goodnight, sweet prince."

The thick blanket of snow was a silencer on the land, and by the time Sully got home the street was utterly still. It was after one o'clock, and the curb-parked cars along the street looked like white hills, and Sully would not have been surprised to see a horse-drawn carriage turn down the street, its harness bells all astir.

All this peace on earth could mean only one thing. Tomorrow would not be peaceful. So much unseasonal snow would slow the work on Carl Roebuck's unbuilt houses and make him doubly anxious to finish them before the ground froze and things got really impossible. Unless the weather warmed up some, he and Rub would freeze their asses tomorrow. Sheetrocking was a job you couldn't do with gloves on, and by midmorning their hands would be so cold they'd feel their fingers only when they hit them with hammers. And Carl would probably visit half a dozen times to badger them and tell them about the next shitty job he had planned for them on Friday, one, he'd claim, even they couldn't fuck up. And before they could even get started working for Carl, he'd have to shovel the sidewalk and driveway so his landlady could get out. All on a knee that by morning would be a symphony of pain.

It would have been discouraging if he hadn't gotten an idea.

It took him a minute to find the long-handled brush in the back of his pickup, but when he did he was in business. In thirty seconds he'd brushed the snow off the pickup's front window and hood, and two minutes after that he was backing the truck into Carl Roebuck's driveway, right up to where the snowblower sat, itself covered with snow. There were still three sheets of plywood on the floor of the pickup, and these Sully used to form a makeshift ramp. They buckled but did not break under the weight of the snowblower. When Sully popped the tailgate back up with a bang, a light came on upstairs and Toby Roebuck appeared, a dark silhouette in the window, which she slid up so she could poke her head out. "That you, Sully?" she wanted to know.

"Yup," Sully admitted. "I may deny it tomorrow, though."

"You come to steal our brand-new snowblower?"

"I've done it already, just about."

"I could legally shoot you and get away with it," Toby informed him.

"Not really. Not unless I was trying to break into the house."

"Are you going to break into my house?"

"Not tonight, dolly," Sully said. The conversation, even with their voices lowered, was a bit unnerving at this hour. Quiet as it was, the whole neighborhood could be listening. "Where's Dummy, by the way?"

"Who knows?" Toby Roebuck said. "He tried to get in earlier, then gave up. He took my threat to shoot him a lot more seriously than you just did, Sully."

"I don't blame him," Sully said. "You got more reason to shoot him."

"Do I now," she said, then after a minute added, "You ever get so mad you just wanted to shoot somebody and didn't care who?"

"Sure," Sully admitted, without feeling much urge to tell her that was how he'd been feeling about fifteen minutes ago at The Horse. "It's the reason I don't own a gun."

"You should get one," she suggested. "I've got Carl's. The two of us could go on a rampage. Rob banks. Go out in a blaze of glory. Bonnie and Clyde."

"You'd have to be Clyde," Sully told her. "I couldn't do much more than drive the getaway car."

"Men have no imagination," Toby said, reminding Sully of what Vince had told him at the restaurant, that Toby Roebuck might be involved with someone from Schuyler Springs. Apparently not, to judge from this remark, unless the man in question didn't have any imagination either.

"Well," Sully said, surprised to discover that he was about to stand up for Carl Roebuck, of all people, "don't be too hard on him. The heart bypass is still on his mind. He's probably just trying to do everything in six months. When it dawns on him he's going to live to be seventy, he'll slow down."

"He pretty nearly didn't live till Thanksgiving," she said with what sounded to Sully like genuine conviction. Then, after a long moment of silence, she said, "Well, go ahead and steal our snowblower. You're the slowest thief I ever saw. I don't think you'd even be a decent wheel man."

Back at his flat Sully was suddenly exhausted again, having burned off the energy he'd derived from the half Snickers bar, and he was tempted to leave the snowblower right there in the back of the pickup, except he was afraid he might oversleep in the morning. When Carl Roebuck came over to find out where he was, he'd be just as liable to steal the snowblower back again before Sully had a chance to use it. So he unloaded the machine and hid it safely out of sight in the corner of Miss Beryl's garage under a tarp.

It turned out to be a good decision, because the first thing Sully noticed when he got upstairs was Carl Roebuck asleep on the couch, his mouth wide open, an empty pint of Canadian whiskey on the floor below his outstretched hand. For a brief moment, Sully wasn't sure Carl was alive, thought perhaps he'd had his final heart attack right there on the couch. But then Carl snorted loudly and rearranged himself, and Sully was relieved that it was a living man asleep on the sofa and not a dead one, even if that man happened to be Carl Roebuck.

Sully had an extra blanket around somewhere, but he was too tired to think where, so he covered Carl with the blanket off his own bed. His bedroom was often too warm anyway, and the sheet would be plenty. He was asleep before he could doubt it.

THURSDAY

Carl Roebuck woke early. Sully heard him turn the TV on low, to an exercise show. The clock on Sully's dresser said six-thirty, which meant that Carl was watching *Wake Up, America*, whose aerobic hostess, to judge from her face, had to be in her forties. Her body was pretty remarkable, toned and athletic, but it wasn't a young body, Sully had noticed. When she danced next to her youthful assistants, she looked merely heroic. Maybe that was what made Sully sad when he watched her. The woman seemed to be dancing for her very life, and Sully would have liked to tell her to go slow.

Carl Roebuck was watching her absently, half asleep, hand in the open fly of his boxers, when Sully looked in.

"Lose something?" Sully said. "Or have you just worn it down to a nub?"

Carl betrayed not the slightest embarrassment. "This is the worst couch I ever slept on," he observed sleepily without looking up at Sully.

"How old are you?" Sully asked, genuinely curious. Sitting there with his hand in his shorts, Carl Roebuck looked, despite his paunch, like a kid.

Carl gave no evidence of having heard this question. In a minute he said, "You ever wake up horny anymore?"

"No," Sully told him. In truth, he'd seldom woken up horny as a younger man, and morning lovemaking, back when he was married, had never been terribly successful. Before noon his orgasms were always vague, like the distant rumblings of a train half a mile away and headed in the other direction. It was one of the things wrong with his marriage. Vera had often awakened feeling frisky, an enthusiasm that had seldom survived breakfast. Sully attributed this to her Puritan upbringing. Some girls you just had to catch before they woke up enough to remember who they were.

"Tell me you don't want to get it on with this broad right now," Carl challenged. He still hadn't taken his eyes off the TV, though he'd finally removed his hand from his shorts.

"What's wrong with you, anyway?" Sully said.

Carl Roebuck sighed. "I have no idea. Honest to God," he confessed. "Lately I want to fuck 'em all. Even the ugly ones. You ever want to fuck the ugly ones?"

"This conversation's getting kind of personal," Sully told him.

Carl looked hurt. "Okay. Ignore me in my moment of pain and crisis. I reach out to you as a friend, and what do I get? Heartache."

Sully grinned at him. This "What do I get? Heartache" line was one of Carl's favorites and was impossible to take seriously, though it occurred to Sully that there just might be an element of seriousness now. "Just because I don't lock my front door doesn't make us friends. What're you doing here, anyhow?"

Carl stood up, pretended to do jumping jacks, his feet firmly planted on the floor, only his arms in motion. "I wanted to make sure you got an early start. You have a lot of work to do," he observed. "You and your smelly dwarf finish with those blocks yesterday?"

Sully told him they had.

"I missed you at The Horse last night," Carl said. "Rub was there. He said you finished."

"Then why'd you ask me?"

" 'Cause Rub had that scared look he gets when he lies," Carl said and stopped with the jumping jacks to study Sully.

Sully had to smile at the idea of Rub trying not to blurt out that they had broken a load of blocks. "He's always nervous around his betters," Sully explained. "I've told him you aren't one of them, but Rub's a slow learner."

"I don't see how you can work with somebody who smells like a pussy finger."

"I keep him downwind when I can."

"Wouldn't it be simpler to tell the little fuck he stinks?"

"I have," Sully said. "He thinks I'm kidding. He says if he stunk that bad Bootsie would mention it."

Carl shuddered. "That's what I should do when I get horny. Think of Bootsie."

"I thought you wanted to fuck the ugly ones," Sully reminded him.

"Not that ugly," Carl conceded.

Sully went back into the bedroom to dress. He could hear Carl poking around the tiny kitchen.

"You got any coffee?" he called.

"No," Sully said. "Hattie's does though, just down the street."

Sully was seated on the edge of the bed, flexing his knee, when Carl poked his head in. "Mind if I grab a quick shower?" he said. Then, catching sight of Sully's knee, he added, "Jesus."

Anymore, that's the effect Sully's knee had on people, which was one reason he didn't like to let people see it. The sight of the grotesque swelling, the deep discoloration, the skin stretched so tightly that it glistened, was something Sully himself had grown accustomed to. It was the look on other people's faces that scared him.

He pulled on a fresh pair of work pants, stood to zip and buckle. "Yesterday was a long one," he explained.

Carl was still looking at the knee, as Peter had done yesterday, through the fabric.

"I got a hell of an idea," Sully said. "Why don't you pay me for yesterday. My knee always feels better when I take money from you."

"You should have that operation," Carl said. "If they can fix my heart, they can fix your knee."

"I got news for you," Sully said. "They didn't fix your heart. They just made it so it wouldn't stop beating for a while. If they'd fixed it, you'd be faithful to your wife and pay your employees what you owe them."

"I've thought about paying you for last August," Carl admitted. "But if I did that you'd have nothing to bitch about. You're better off thinking you've been cheated. This way you've got somebody to blame. You can tell yourself if it wasn't for C. I. Roebuck, you'd have the world by the short hairs."

When Carl hit the shower, Sully went downstairs and outside. It was only quarter to seven, but Miss Beryl had already leaned the shovel against the porch post. The sun was out, but the early morning air was bitter, and the sun's reflection off the new powder contained little warmth. What did warm Sully was the sight of Carl Roebuck's snowblower sitting snugly under the tarp in the corner of the garage where he'd left it. The motor started on the first pull.

Sully had finished the sidewalk and half the drive by the time Carl Roebuck, freshly showered but in yesterday's clothes, appeared on the porch.

"Meet me at the donut shop," he called. "I'll pay you for yesterday."

Sully turned the snowblower off. "You should go home and tell Toby you love her before somebody else does. Say it like you mean it," he suggested, suddenly feeling something like affection for his dead friend's son. He remembered the dark sedan at the job site yesterday—that it had followed Carl back to town. Maybe he was wrong about Toby's devotion to him. Maybe she was considering a divorce and had hired someone to follow him. Sully considered mentioning the sedan to Carl, then decided not to. "Say Happy Thanksgiving to her for me," he said instead.

Carl was looking at the snowblower. "I've got one just like that," he said. "Identical."

By the time Sully finished with the driveway, he knew that his first order of business was to find Jocko and some prescription painkillers. Just as he'd predicted to Ruth, his knee, which always hummed dully, was singing full throat this morning. Naturally, the drugstore would be closed on Thanksgiving, which meant that Jocko, who lived alone and wasn't in the book, would not be easy to locate. Actually, Jocko had given Sully his phone number half a dozen times, but Sully'd always managed to lose it.

The first place to check was Hattie's because Hattie's was only half a block away and if he didn't find Jocko, he'd at least find coffee. And besides, Rub was supposed to meet him there. The trouble was that when Sully arrived the CLOSED sign was hanging in the window. He had a vague recollection of Cass warning him of this yesterday. The rest of Bath looked closed too, and Sully wondered if he might be better off to go home and wait for the town to wake up, even if that meant waiting until tomorrow. It wouldn't kill Carl Roebuck if his two-bedroom ranch didn't get sheet-rocked until Friday. Except that on Friday, Carl might hire the guy who regularly did the sheetrocking and line up an even shittier job for himself and Rub. In a few weeks there'd be nothing but indoor work, up and down stairs, and precious little of that. Today might be his last chance for a while to do a job he hated in the freezing cold.

Normally, the best place to look for Jocko was the OTB, except the

OTB wouldn't be open on Thanksgiving either. Since it wasn't, Sully decided to stop by the Rexall where Jocko worked just in case. As he expected, the interior of the store was dark, its rows of shelves disappearing into deepening shadow as they receded from the street. The donut shop, at least, would be open.

There, Sully found Rub sitting at the counter, and since Rub didn't see him coming, Sully cuffed Rub's wool hat halfway down the counter, where it landed on top of a sugar dispenser. "I thought I told you to meet me at Hattie's," he said, sliding onto the stool next to Rub. Except for a sullen teenage waitress and a foursome of sleepy-looking truckers in a booth, they had the place to themselves.

Rub didn't appear to miss his hat, nor did he make any attempt to smooth the cowlick Sully'd created. "Hattie's was closed," he observed. "I wisht we didn't have to work on Thanksgiving."

"You don't *have* to," Sully assured him. The young woman behind the counter intuited that Sully would want coffee and that he'd want nothing else. She put a steaming cup in front of him and walked away without inquiring. On her way past the sugar dispenser she delicately removed Rub's hat by making forceps of her thumb and forefinger.

"If I don't work, you'll be mad at me," Rub said sadly.

"Well, that's true," Sully admitted.

"And Bootsie's still mad at me about the car," Rub told him. "Everybody's mad at me."

"See?" Sully said. "You're better off working."

"I just wisht I had money for a donut."

"What happened to your pay from yesterday?"

"Bootsie took it."

Sully got the waitress's attention, ordered Rub a donut.

"One of them big ole cream-filled deals," Rub explained to her, pointing to the ones he meant. When the girl put one in front of him, he waited for her to go away and then said, "She gave me the smallest one."

"They're all the same size," the girl said, as if to no one in particular. She was standing by her post at the register. She looked at neither Rub nor Sully.

"Are not," Rub whispered, staring at the donut.

"Eat the fucking thing," Sully said.

Rub did as he was told. When he bit the donut, cream filling bulged out the anus-shaped opening at the other end. Sully had to look away. "Carl been by?" he said.

Rub was intent on the donut and didn't hear. His first bite made a large opening, leaving wings on either side of the puncture. No matter which wing he bit into now, the cream filling was going to escape.

"I'm going to knock you right off that stool in a minute," Sully said.

Rub looked over at him to see if this threat was genuine. Apparently it was. "What?" he said.

"I asked you if Carl was here."

"When?"

"Before I came in, Rub."

"Only for a minute. He came over and told me I smelled like a pussy finger. I wisht we didn't have to work for him on Thanksgiving."

Sully took out two dollars, enough to cover the coffees, Rub's donut and the tip their sullen waitress hadn't earned. "Did he give you any money?"

"He said come by the office when we're finished."

Than which there was no more typical Carl Roebuck maneuver.

"Meet me at Hattie's in ten minutes," he said. "Maybe we can get this job done by midafternoon."

"Hattie's is closed," Rub reminded him.

"Outside," Sully said.

Rub looked dubious.

"Don't try to figure this out, Rub," Sully told him. "Just do it."

"You don't have to get mad," Rub said. "You get mad as easy as Bootsie."

"We keep the same company," Sully said.

Sully left. From outside the donut shop he could see Rub poised over the donut, and for some reason Sully stopped, curious to see how Rub would resolve the problem. Instead of biting either wing of the donut, Rub inserted his open mouth into the hole his first bite had created. Naturally, this was a perfect fit. When Rub sucked, the cream bubble forced out through the anal aperture was drawn back into the donut. This was an oddly cheering solution, and Sully wondered briefly if people underestimated Rub. Briefly.

When there was only one person in the world you really wanted to see, what were the odds you'd run into him outside a closed OTB in North Bath at 7:30 on Thanksgiving morning? Better than you might imagine, it occurred to Sully, because on the way over to Carl Roebuck's office he spotted Jocko's silver Marquis parked in the empty lot, Jocko at the wheel, reading the newspaper. When Sully sneaked up and banged on the window about two inches from Jocko's ear, he jumped about a foot, pleasing Sully, a man for whom sneaking up on people and scaring the shit out of them had always been a profoundly satisfying activity. Jocko too seemed pretty well satisfied when he recognized Sully, who was often his own explanation, grinning in at him. Jocko flipped him off, then used the same middle finger to direct Sully around to the other side of the Marquis. Sully got in gingerly, left the door open and his leg mostly outside. "Howdy, Chester," Jocko said, studying Sully over his glasses. Jocko was dressed conservatively as always. Light blue shirt, fat tie, sans-a-belt slacks. In his late thirties, his hair was short, graying at the temples, and he was about fifty pounds overweight. There was nothing about his appearance to suggest his radical, long-haired student days, during which, he'd admitted to Sully, he also majored in pharmaceuticals.

"You plan to sit here until they open tomorrow?" Sully asked.

"Churches and OTBs should never close," Jocko said. "There should be a law."

"There is," Sully reminded him. "It closes OTBs on Christmas and Thanksgiving. I know of a couple churches that are open if you're interested."

Jocko waved this suggestion away. "I try to stay away from long shots."

"Can't be much worse than betting trifectas."

"I don't bet them either," Jocko said. "Triples are for lost, desperate souls like you." His face brightened suddenly. "I like the idea, though. Special trifecta wagers on Christmas and Easter. I can see the promotion. Trinity wagers. Christianity finally pays off."

"That solves Christmas and Easter. It still leaves Thanksgiving."

"No problem," Jocko shrugged. "Most people think Thanksgiving *is* a Christian holiday. This is a mighty confused nation we live in."

They were grinning at each other now.

"I was hoping I'd run into you . . ." Sully said.

Jocko folded his newspaper, tossed it into the backseat. "Step into my office," he suggested, leaning past Sully to open the glove box. "And close that goddamn door before we both freeze, will you?"

"I'm not sure this knee will bend so early in the morning," Sully said.

"Try," Jocko suggested as he rummaged in the glove compartment.

Sully winced, finally got his whole leg inside and closed the door. "You must have the shortest legs of any grown man in town."

Jocko's glove compartment resembled a small pharmacy, or candy store, full of small, bright plastic bottles. Jocko yanked out several of these, held them up to the light, said "Nah" and tossed them back. After a minute he found a tube that met his approval. "Here," he said, handing it to Sully. "Eat these." His standard line.

There was no label on the tube, but Sully accepted it gratefully.

"Don't operate any heavy machinery," Jocko advised.

"Just a hammer today," Sully promised. "I'll probably pound my thumb all morning."

"Go ahead. You won't feel it," Jocko said. "Somebody told me you'd gone back to work. I figured that was so dumb it had to be true."

"Just for a while, probably," Sully said. "I'd like to get a little ahead for the winter. Then I'll go slow for a while. Maybe I'll feel better in the spring."

Jocko looked at him over the rims of his glasses. "Arthritis doesn't get better," he said. "It gets worse. Every time."

"Two more years and I can take early retirement," Sully said. "After that, fuck 'em."

This came out sounding like the bravado it was. Sully knew that the only reason Jocko didn't argue was kindness. They both knew his knee wasn't going to give him two more years of hard labor.

"What's the line on the game Saturday?" Sully wondered. He was both genuinely interested and anxious to change the subject.

"You can get Bath and twenty points is what I'm hearing."

Sully raised his eyebrows. "That's tempting." Like Vince, Sully had lost on Bath against Schuyler Springs every year for the last dozen. And like Vince, he always got points, just never enough of them.

"I know what you mean," Jocko commiserated. "I'd love to see the kids win one. Your paramour's kid is a pretty good little guard. He doesn't get much help, though."

Sully ignored the fact that Jocko, like so many people in town, knew of his relationship with Ruth. "A win would be a lot to ask," Sully admitted. Recent Bath–Schuyler Springs contests had become so lopsided that Schuyler was threatening to drop the smaller school from its schedule on humanitarian grounds. The preservation of "the game" was a hot political issue, and the man who'd won the most recent Bath mayoral election had made the continuation of the game his only campaign promise. "I'd personally be thrilled if they beat the spread. Who's giving twenty, by the way?" Bath would probably lose by more than twenty, but so far twenty was the most Sully'd heard anybody giving.

"You know Jerry's brother Vince?" Jocko said.

"You mean Vince's brother Jerry?"

"The one that has the Schuyler restaurant," Jocko clarified.

"Right. Jerry."

"How can you tell them apart?"

"Apparently Jerry will give you Bath and twenty points. That's one way," Sully said. "Listen, what do I owe you here?"

"Nada. They're samples. Let me know if they make you sick," Jocko suggested when Sully opened the door and began the slow process of getting out. When this was finally accomplished and Sully'd limped back around to the driver's side, Jocko was shaking his head. "You know what you should do?" he said.

"No, what?" Sully said.

"You should go back into the arson business."

Sully pretended to consider this. "It's a thought," he said, since Jocko was probably joking. Ever since he'd burned down Kenny Roebuck's house, people kidded him about being an arsonist. Some of them, he'd learned over the years, really thought he was, thanks to Kenny's publicly treating the fire as good fortune.

"Hell," Jocko snorted, "if that theme park ever falls through, you'd have clients up and down Main Street. I might hire you myself."

"Keep the faith," Sully suggested. "They'll run again tomorrow."

Carl's red Camaro was parked out front of the third-floor office and so was the El Camino, which meant that Carl was probably inside. Still, that was three flights up, so Sully made a snowball, went out into the middle of the empty street and tossed it at the row of windows that said TIP TOP CONSTRUCTION: C. I. ROEBUCK. The sound the snowball made on the windowpane was louder than Sully expected, and Carl's face quickly appeared at the window behind the snowball's powdery smudge. Also his shoulders, which were inexplicably bare. There was movement behind him too, a white, frightened face darting away. Carl raised the window. "I ever tell you what the C.I. in my name is for?"

"Yesterday," Sully grinned up at him. A curtain in the next-door window that represented the outer office drew stealthily back. "Hi, Ruby," Sully waved. "Happy Thanksgiving." The curtain fell back into place.

"What the hell do you want, Sully?" Carl said. "You're supposed to be sheetrocking."

And you're supposed to be home, Sully considered reminding him. Instead he said, "I missed you at the donut shop. You probably don't remember saying you'd meet me there because that was where you were going to pay me."

"And when I'm not there that means you come here and give me a heart attack by throwing snowballs at my office window."

"It's a good thing I did, too," Sully said. "It'd be just like you to let me walk up three flights of stairs and then not answer the door."

"Why don't I follow you out to the site in half an hour?" Carl said. On his face was a pleading, man-to-man, I'm-in-the-middle-of-something-here, have-a-fucking-heart sort of expression.

Sully wanted no part of it. "Put the money in an envelope and drop it. It'll take you two seconds. Even you can't lose a hard-on that fast."

"It must be a long time since you've had one," Carl said. "You've forgotten." He disappeared.

In a minute he was back again with an envelope. "This is going to land on the ledge, you know."

"I'll take my chances," Sully said. "The money you owe me usually ends up stuck in your pocket, not on window ledges."

"This is no way to do business," Carl said, but he let go of the envelope, which cleared the second-story ledge and Frisbeed out into the street. Sully fielded it cleanly, opened the envelope, extracted the bills. "Before you go I got something else for you," Carl called down, and when Sully looked up he saw he was being mooned. Carl's white ass was sticking out the window, and there was the sound of female laughter inside. The ass disappeared before Sully could pack and deliver a new snowball. The window slammed shut.

Sully was about to leave when he noticed that the dark sedan that had been parked along the road by the job site yesterday was parked a ways down the street. There was a man at the wheel who appeared to be closely inspecting some sort of black box. Sully waved. The man did not wave back. Only when the snowball exploded on his windshield did he lower the electric window and poke his head partially out.

"You get a good shot of all that?" Sully said, indicating the window above.

"I don't follow you," the man said evenly.

"I thought that's all you guys did."

"I think you have an imperfect understanding of the situation," the man said in the kind of voice that Sully despised. It reminded him of the way the insurance company lawyers talked at his disability hearings.

"I'd be careful just the same," Sully said. Carl, he knew, owned a handgun.

"Are you threatening me?" the man wanted to know.

"Not unless you're afraid of snowballs."

"Good," the man said, and the window hummed up.

Rub was dancing back and forth on the balls of his feet when Sully arrived at Hattie's.

"I wisht Hattie's was open," he said. He had dried donut cream in both corners of his mouth.

"How come, Rub?"

"So I could've gone inside and waited for you where it was warm," he explained seriously.

Sully just stood there and grinned at him until Rub got embarrassed and studied his shoes. "You're going to rag me all day, aren't you," he said sadly.

They walked up the street to where Sully's pickup was parked. Miss Beryl, clutching her thick robe to her throat, was standing on the side porch, peering down at the snowblower. Which gave Sully an idea. Taking the chain he always kept in the toolbox and the Yale lock he used to secure the box, he limped up the drive to where his landlady was standing. "That's so you can start doing the driveway yourself when you feel like it," Sully told her.

"I couldn't, even with that," Miss Beryl said. She was staring at the machine suspiciously. "It'd probably get going along and just drag me down the street. The neighbors would look out their windows and say, 'There goes old Beryl.' "

"Don't be silly," Sully kidded her. "It'd be good exercise."

"I don't want exercise. These are my golden years. What are you going to do with that chain?"

Sully already had the snowblower secured to the railing. He could have just hidden the machine in the garage, but he liked the idea of showing Carl right where it was. "Keeping the man I stole this from stealing it back. If he comes by, call the cops."

It took Miss Beryl a minute to digest this. She was an old woman who'd lived a schoolteacher's life, but she was also a good sport, Sully knew. "As I said, you're a cur, sir."

Then she grew serious. "Tell me something, Donald," she said. "Does it ever bother you that you haven't done more with the life God gave you?"

Sully had decided years ago not to take offense at Miss Beryl's more personal observations. "Not often," he admitted, rattling the chain to make sure it was secure. "Now and then."

Maybe sheetrocking wasn't one of Sully's favorite jobs, but like most physical labor, there was a rhythm to it that you could find if you cared to look, and once you found this rhythm it'd get you through a morning. Rhythm was what Sully had counted on over the long years—that and the wisdom to understand that no job, no matter how thankless or stupid or backbreaking, could not be gotten through. The clock moved if you let it. This morning, in fact, it moved right along. The temperature rose steadily, and Sully and Rub, who had figured to be frozen by midmorning, still had feeling in their fingers. The two men fell naturally into a smooth, moderate pace that would probably get them finished more quickly than hurrying.

Carl Roebuck wondered how Sully could stand to work with Rub, but in truth, Rub was one of the few people he'd ever been able to work with. Rub was the perfect dance partner, always content to let Sully, or whoever he was working with, lead. The beauty of Rub was that he had no agenda of his own. If Sully was in a hurry or had somewhere to go, another job to do when this one was finished, hauling ass was fine with Rub. If for some reason—like they were being paid by the hour—they needed to go slow, then Rub was even more of a marvel the way he was able to stay in motion without accomplishing anything. Rub was a perfect laborer, born to follow orders, not minding in the least when he was told to do things wrong, able to convey the impression of progress even as he ensured that the job wouldn't get done today. If need be, you could rest easy that the job wouldn't get done until there was another one to replace it. All of this without ever appearing to stall or even rest. Sully always maintained that if you had ten guys working on a rock pile, Rub would be the last you'd fire for laziness. Only when you'd fired all the others would you realize that Rub had not yet addressed his first rock.

Truth be told, Sully and Rub had gone slow the day they dug up Carl Roebuck's terrace and laid the new water pipe. It'd been a hot August day, and somehow they'd managed to talk Carl into an hourly wage arrangement, which meant there was no reason to bust their balls, especially with Toby Roebuck coming out every now and then to ask how it was coming and wonder how they could actually work in such heat. She gave them tall, cold glasses of lemonade to drink. Dressed in a thin, loose-fitting blouse, she'd bent over to hand the lemonade down into the trench they'd dug, and every time she did this Rub stared deep into her blouse, as if it afforded a glimpse of the promised land. Even when she went back into the house Rub continued to stare, slack-jawed, at the place in the air where Toby Roebuck's full naked breasts had been, as if he could still see them there, like an afterimage burned in the dark. "They're tan all over," he kept saying, half admiring, half angry, perhaps at the fact that these breasts had so little to do with himself.

Sully'd been guilty of five errors in judgment that day. Five that he knew of. There might have been more. First, he'd overestimated the amount of time the first part of the job would take. It had been raining all week and the ground was unexpectedly soft, and they dug most of the trench so quickly he feared they'd be finished by noon with a job they'd hoped to stretch into a full day. So they'd slowed down but good. If Rub was a master at looking busy above ground, he was an absolute artist in a ditch.

Sully's second error was in assuming that the last third of the job would go along at the same pace as the first two thirds. He knew better than to assume this, just as Carl Roebuck knew better than to hire him and Rub by the hour, but knowledge, as Sully's young philosophy professor was fond of observing, often bore little relation to behavior. By the time he and Rub got up close to the house and encountered the roots of the old oak that had provided them with shade to drink their lemonade in during the long, pleasant afternoon, they'd slowed down so completely that it was hard to get started again. By then it was the hottest part of the day and they'd drunk too much sweet lemonade. Stirred by lust for Toby Roebuck, the lemonade had begun to churn in their stomachs. And so around four in the afternoon they talked her into going over to the IGA and getting them a six-pack of beer (Sully's third error in judgment), which arrived ice cold. That first can, in conjunction with the terrific heat, pole-axed them. To make matters worse, Toby Roebuck drank one with them, and then another, and they all began to enjoy the heat. Toby sat at the edge of the ditch and dangled her long creamy legs down into the hole like the schoolgirl she so resembled.

She'd finally gone inside, to draw a cool bath, she said, before they had to turn the water off, when Carl came home to a sight he found difficult to credit. He'd hoped, if not expected, that the job would be finished, the new pipe laid, the trench filled in, water pressure restored. Instead he found a trench extending from the street all the way up the lawn to the house, a trench that was about twice as wide and ugly as it needed to be, beer cans strewn along its edge, and Sully, half in the bag with heat and beer, flailing maniacally with his pickax at the stubborn tough roots of the recently encountered oak.

Sully's fourth error in judgment had been fated when he looked up and saw that what Carl Roebuck had slung over his shoulder was his golf clubs. At that moment, for Sully, the whole world took on the aspect of feces. Golf was not a game he'd ever particularly wanted to take up. Nobody he liked had ever played golf, and a lot of the people he disliked intensely played all the time. But the moment he looked up and saw that Carl Roebuck had been playing golf while he and Rub were busting their balls in the heat (it seemed to him at that moment that they *had* been busting their balls all day), it occurred to Sully that golf was one of a great number of fine things in life that had been denied him. And he could have listed all the others, had anyone asked him what they were. No one did.

So, before Carl Roebuck could say a word, Sully had held up a grimy index finger in warning and told his employer that if he said one word he was going to take one of those golf clubs and shove it up Carl Roebuck's ass until he could hit high "C."

Then Carl Roebuck made an error in judgment. He set his golf bag down on the lawn, sat down on top of it and laughed. By laughing, of course, he was doing as he was told. He was not saying a word, and this fact kept Sully in the trench, from which he'd been prepared, bum leg or no bum leg, to climb out and make good on his threat. Instead, he stayed where he was and waited for Carl to stop laughing, which, eventually, he did.

"You think this is funny?" Sully had said weakly.

Carl nodded, still not saying a word.

"Well, wait till you get the bill."

Carl grunted to his feet, shouldered the golf bag. "Sully, Sully, Sully," he said. "You're right. That will be funny too. Not as funny as the look on your face when you try to cash the check I'm going to pay you with, but definitely funny."

Sully hadn't thought Carl Roebuck would follow through on his threat, and that had been his fifth mistake. He and Rub had run into more trouble, all of it legitimate, and he'd thought Carl understood this. The pipes they'd exposed were old, as old as the house probably, and they disintegrated like papyrus to the touch, which was fine until Sully managed to break the last section off at the elbow joint where the pipe connected to the main line under the street. The old pipe was rusted and frozen there, impossible to remove, impossible to install the new plastic pipe around. It was terrible luck, but the only decent piece of metal in the whole line was the six-inch joint, frozen there at the elbow. If it could have been removed by banging on or swearing at, Sully would have managed it, because he swore at the pipe and banged on it until it was too dark to see anymore. Then Carl Roebuck called the County Water and Sewer and was told they'd send a man out in the morning. Which meant that the Roebucks would have to spend the night without water. Fortunately, Toby had already taken her cool bath, and when she came out to say an embarrassed good-bye she looked fresh and cool in a thin blouse that was even looser than the one she'd been wearing earlier. Sully had to lead Rub back to the truck.

Today, months later, as they sheetrocked, the only breasts around were those in the obscene jingle Sully was trying to teach Rub, who always worked happily when he had something to distract him. Almost anything distracted Rub. Several times, after he'd recited it perfectly, they'd congratulated themselves that Rub had mastered its intricacies:

> *I like Carnation best of all.*
> *No tits to pull*
> *No shit to haul.*
>
> *No shit to haul,*
> *No hay to pitch.*
> *Just pop a hole in that son of a bitch.*

But ten minutes later Rub would forget how it began. He kept wanting to start it "I like tits best of all." Which rendered the second line inaccessible. "It's because I *do* like tits best of all," Rub explained. "I like pussy too, as long as I don't have to look at it. It kind of scares me to look at."

What scared Sully was the pain in his knee. It'd been growing steadily worse all morning, pain shooting all the way down into his ankle and up almost to his groin. Until a few weeks ago he'd been able to ignore it. He'd always prided himself on a high threshold of pain. Pain, he'd learned as a kid, would peak, and from that point forward it would get no worse. What you looked for was the moment when the pain peaked and you realized you could stand it, that it wouldn't kill you. As a boy, Sully had learned to accommodate his father's drunken whuppings by waiting for Big Jim's fury to hit its apex, then slide away, spent, leaving Sully full of pride and, yes, love. You could feel good in pain, and that was something not everybody knew. One of his father's favorite jokes had been the one that went "Why did the moron beat his head against the wall? Because it felt so good when he stopped." Sully understood that the reason his father liked the joke was not so much that it was funny as because it was literally true. There was pleasure to be taken from the diminishment of pain. It *did* feel good when you stopped.

What frightened Sully about this new, more intense pain in his knee was its relentlessness. As a boy, he had not realized what his father must have known, that pain could have a cumulative effect. Your ability to withstand it had much to do with your ability to catch your breath between its assaults. The pain in Sully's knee had not truly worried him as long as bad days alternated with good ones. But now he was beginning to suspect that the periods of respite, the troughs in the wave that had so far allowed him to prepare for the peaks, were beginning to disappear. Anymore, it was rare for him to sleep more than four hours a night, and even these hours were tinged with dream pain. Even the self of his dreams was hobbled now, and when he awoke it was with the sensation that he hadn't really been asleep.

If this weren't enough, Jocko's pills made him feel dreamy even when he was awake, and Sully'd begun to fear that he was slowly migrating toward a state that was somewhere in between sleep and consciousness where the only constant was pain, and this to Sully was more frightening than the specific shooting pains he felt on bad days like today. Shooting pains were human, like the whuppings he got from his father. He'd endured such pain by remembering that his father had only so much strength, so much meanness, in him. At some point Big Jim always saw what he was doing and would be satisfied and the pain would stop. What Sully feared now was that he was facing a new kind of pain, one that wouldn't know or care when he'd had all he could take. It might never be satisfied.

This morning Sully'd resisted taking one of Jocko's pills, fearing that it would render him useless. It didn't take a lot of mental agility to sheetrock, but it did take some. You couldn't do it and sleep too, and some of Jocko's better painkillers worked like Mickey Finns, with about as much warning. And Rub required supervision at all tasks. Rub's cousins, none of whom would themselves be mistaken for theoretical mathematicians, complained that he couldn't even collect garbage right, and Sully didn't want to be doped up and in the immediate vicinity of a grown man who couldn't learn a short bawdy jingle after three hours of practice. No pills until they finished.

"Doesn't pussy kind of scare you to look at?" Rub wanted to know.

"I don't remember," Sully told him.

"How can you forget pussy?" Rub said.

"How can you forget the Carnation jingle?"

"Well," Rub said, ignoring this. "I don't like how it looks."

It was nearly two in the afternoon when they finished. Rub was disappointed at not mastering the jingle but able to console himself that at least they were done working on Thanksgiving and therefore no longer in need of the jingle's distraction. He was also pleased to contemplate the big ole turkey Bootsie had browning in the oven, getting all crispy. "I like that big ole flap of skin over the turkey's asshole," he told Sully as they stashed their hammers and belts in Sully's toolbox.

Sully suspected that Rub's understanding of a turkey's anatomy was imperfect. The "asshole" he was referring to was probably the turkey's neck cavity, which Rub couldn't visualize with the head missing, the neck detached. "I don't know, Rub," Sully said as they climbed into the pickup. "The sight of pussy scares you, but you can't wait to eat the asshole out of a turkey." He extracted one of Jocko's pills from its bright pink tube, made the sign of the cross, and swallowed it dry.

"Say la vee," Rub said.

Sully, who had been half listening to Rub and half to the singing of his own knee, blinked and looked over at his friend, who was patiently waiting for him to turn the key in the ignition so they could go home to the big ole turkey. Rub was only vaguely aware of having spoken in a foreign language, and when he saw Sully staring at him, he concluded that for once he knew something somebody else didn't. "To each his fuckin' own," he translated for Sully's benefit.

Sully was still laughing ten minutes later when he dropped Rub off in front of his house. "Uh-oh," Rub said, and Sully saw why.

Rub's wife, Bootsie, was coming down the walk from their apartment, and she had a pretty good head of steam up, given her size. As Wirf was fond of observing, there was enough of Bootsie to make two perfectly ugly grown women and enough left over to make the ugliest baby you ever saw. When angered, as she apparently was now, she was a fearful sight.

Sully rolled down his window anyhow. He'd managed to avoid hostilities with Zack last night by remaining seated and being friendly, and he wondered if the same tactic might work again. He had his doubts. Unlike

Zack, Bootsie liked to fight. "Happy Thanksgiving, dolly," he called. "How are you?" What she looked like was a complete list of a man's past sins come to life, bent on retribution.

"My Thanksgiving turkey's burnt to shit, is how I am," she said. "You don't have no work for him all fall and then you make him work Thanksgiving and ruin the damn holiday is how I am."

One of the things Sully was never able to get Rub's wife to understand was that he himself wasn't an employer, that Rub didn't really work for him, that he wasn't Rub's boss. Her difficulty in grasping the situation may have been in part due to the fact that Sully seemed to be the one who provided the work (since there wasn't any when Sully *didn't* provide it) and because Sully was the one who paid Rub for his services and because Sully told him what to do and when, which made Sully look enough like a boss to Bootsie that she was disinclined to draw the crucial distinction. Sully guessed this wasn't the proper time or place to press for clarification.

"Well," he said. "I am sorry. It's the way these things go sometimes. The job took us a little longer than we figured."

"Ruined the whole holiday is all," Bootsie said, though Sully thought he detected a slight softening in her tone. Rub wasn't taking any chances. He'd made no move to get out of the truck, and it was clear to Sully that he had no intention of entering into the conversation. Sully was on his own for the moment. Later, Rub knew, he'd be on *his* own, so for now he'd let Sully fend for himself.

"I suppose we could have just turned our noses up at the money," Sully admitted. "Thanksgiving or no Thanksgiving."

Bootsie mellowed another degree in volume without giving in. "The dime store only gives me three goddamn paid holidays a year, and you have to go and ruin one of them."

"Well, we'll leave Christmas alone," Sully assured her. "I promise."

Bootsie leaned forward so she could glare at her husband. "You gonna get out of there, or do I have to come around and drag you out?"

Rub reached for the door handle. "I was just saying good-bye to Sully," he explained lamely.

"You had the whole damn time my turkey was burning up to say good-bye. Get out of the damn truck."

Rub did as he was told without exactly hurrying. Bootsie watched him, relenting a little more. "You might as well come in and help us eat the fucker," she told Sully. "He started out weighing twenty pounds and he still must weigh about eight."

"I'd love to, dolly," Sully told her, "but I've got a previous engagement."

Bootsie snorted. "In other words, you ruined two damn turkeys. Mine and somebody else's."

In fact, Sully hadn't considered this, and he didn't like to now. However unlikely, it was possible that Vera was holding the Thanksgiving meal for him, growing more and more homicidal as the bird dried out.

At home, Sully drew a hot bath and climbed in. He was too tired and he hurt too bad to stand in the shower. He didn't remember falling asleep, but he must have because the telephone woke him up and the water in the tub that had been as hot as he could stand it when he climbed in was now cool.

"I just wanted to say I was proud of you last night," Ruth said, skipping the preliminaries, as was her custom when she called Sully. "The old Sully would have started a fight."

Part of their relationship over the long years, part of the way Ruth dealt with the guilt of cheating on her husband, was by reminding both herself and Sully that she'd been a good influence on him, which in fact she had been. Still, he found her references to "the old Sully" mildly irritating. That as a younger man he'd been prone to barroom brawls, that he'd been in need of reform might be true. Still, this old Sully/new Sully stuff was predicated on her assumption that she'd performed this needed service, a point he'd never officially conceded. "The old Sully could have won it, too," he pointed out.

"So could the new one," Ruth said. "The new one's mature enough to walk away."

"I didn't walk away," Sully reminded her. "Zack walked away. I couldn't even get out of the booth."

"You know what I mean."

"Like hell. I never know what you mean."

There was a momentary silence. "All right, have it your way," Ruth finally said. "Screw me for bothering you on Thanksgiving."

"I'm glad you did," Sully relented, because he was glad, profoundly glad, to hear her voice. "I'm just standing here dripping, is all." After a moment's silence, he said, "Why don't you and I get married?"

"Because."

"Oh," Sully said. "I've always wondered what the reason was."

"There's a different reason every time you ask me. They're all good ones, though."

"Where are you calling from?" it occurred to him to ask.

"Home. Guess Who is fast asleep on the couch. You know how food affects him. He'll wake up in time to make a turkey sandwich and then go to bed."

"He's got a good life. You work two jobs, cook his meals. In his shoes I'd do the same thing."

"No, you wouldn't."

"Why don't you come over for a while? My landlady's out having Thanksgiving dinner someplace. You could bring me a drumstick."

"Zack ate both drumsticks," Ruth said. "Also a thigh."

"You're ignoring my invitation."

"I don't think so, babe."

Sully flexed his knee. Jocko's pill had still not kicked in, which made Sully wonder if Jocko was experimenting with placebos. "Well, I guess I'll have to go over and see Vera, then," Sully said, in the hopes of getting Ruth to change her mind. The mere mention of his ex-wife had been known to do this. "She'll feed me, at least."

When Ruth didn't respond, Sully realized she was crying, though he hadn't any idea why. "Why don't you come over?" he said. "We could go someplace, if you want. Have Thanksgiving dinner out. Drive into Schuyler."

"I've already eaten, Sully," she reminded him. "Besides. I don't really want to see you. Desperate as I'm feeling right now, I might agree to marry you, and then where the hell would I be?"

"Happy?"

"*You'd* be happy, you mean."

In truth, Sully doubted either of them would be happy, though he would have married Ruth if she'd consent. "At least one of us would be better off," he said.

"Right," she agreed, her voice steadier now. "Zack would be better off."

"Then I withdraw my proposal," Sully said. "I'd hate to think Zack was better off because of me."

He heard Ruth blow her nose. "Have a nice dinner at Vera's."

"They've probably eaten already. What time is it?"

Ruth told him almost four.

"I'll probably end up at The Horse later. Stop in if you feel like it."

"I need to talk to you, Sully," she said.

"Aren't we talking right now?"

"Not on the phone."

Sully suddenly had a bad feeling. "Are you okay?" Had she been to the doctor and been told something? "You aren't sick?"

"No."

"What then?"

"Tomorrow's plenty of time," she insisted. "Or the next day. You were saying you wouldn't mind slipping a few punches this round, right?"

"Not if you have to take them."

"I'm fine. Really," she said, and in fact she sounded a little better. Maybe whatever it was wasn't so bad, Sully thought. "Happy Thanksgiving."

"Right."

Before leaving the flat, Sully swallowed another of Jocko's pills. They were pain pills, after all, and an afternoon at his ex-wife's promised to be painful.

Outside on the back porch, something looked different, missing. Sully just stood there until he realized what it was. The snowblower was gone. When he touched the railing, it moved. The large Phillips-head screws that had anchored it to the bottom step had been removed. All Sully could do was smile at this, which meant Jocko's pills were kicking in.

Miss Beryl and her friend Mrs. Gruber had decided to eat their Thanksgiving dinner midday at the Northwoods Motor Inn on the outskirts of Albany. After suggesting half a dozen other places she would have preferred, Miss Beryl agreed to the Northwoods, Mrs. Gruber's favorite. Miss Beryl drove, while Mrs. Gruber chattered happily about the unseasonable snow and other weighty topics the whole way to the restaurant. Miss Beryl knew that her friend's buoyant good spirits were attributable to Miss Beryl's decision not to travel this year. Winters were long, and when Miss Beryl departed in mid-January she knew that Mrs. Gruber became a virtual shut-in until she returned. Ten years Miss Beryl's junior, Mrs. Gruber was far less self-sufficient. She'd not been prepared for widowhood when her husband died seven years before, and she still wasn't prepared for it. "We'll have fun right here," she'd said when Miss Beryl informed her of her decision not to try Morocco this winter. "On nice days we'll just sally forth. See things." In Mrs. Gruber's opinion there was plenty to do right in the county. All you had to do was open the newspaper and look at the ads. You didn't have to go to Morocco to see new things. Mrs. Gruber, Miss Beryl often reflected, would have been the perfect mate for Clive Sr., who'd felt

NOBODY'S FOOL ■ 141

the same way about Schuyler County. He'd waxed downright philosophical about it. In his opinion everything in the world was represented, somehow, right where they lived. It was just a matter of how you looked at things. Miss Beryl always looked at her husband cross-eyed when he arrived at this predictable conclusion and then told him he was probably right.

Mrs. Gruber had lived in North Bath all her life and had been to Albany countless times, but still had no idea how to get there or, having got there, how to return. She had never in her life driven an automobile. Driving she'd left to her husband, and since his death she'd left it to Miss Beryl. It did not occur to Mrs. Gruber to wonder whether her friend minded driving, any more than it ever crossed her mind that she herself ought to learn. She considered the fact that she did not drive to be an inconvenience similar to being born left-handed, and no remedy for either suggested itself.

Increasingly, Miss Beryl *did* mind driving, especially in less than ideal weather, especially on the busy interstate, especially when their destination was a restaurant that was not among her favorites. Miss Beryl never drove over forty-five miles an hour, and on the interstate cars swerved around her Ford and raced by, horns blaring to full Doppler effect, causing Miss Beryl to slow and brace for impact. The blaring horns had no discernible effect upon Mrs. Gruber, whose hearing had begun to fail and who seldom, at least in a car, roused to external stimuli. As far as Miss Beryl could tell, her companion, while possessed of normal eyesight, never saw anything she was looking at while riding in a car. The view through the front windshield of Miss Beryl's Ford was to Mrs. Gruber a television screen upon which a program she wasn't interested in was playing. She'd have turned it off if she could.

Invariably the first thing to register upon Mrs. Gruber's senses was the sight of the Northwoods Motor Inn itself, a low-lying structure that was, to Miss Beryl's mind, the most nondescript building in the city of Albany. Then Mrs. Gruber would point to it and exclaim "There!" a particularly annoying gesture, especially after Miss Beryl had already pulled into the left-turn lane and hit her blinker. She understood, of course, that left-turn lanes, turn signals and traffic lights bore no particular significance to her companion, but nonetheless it was annoying to navigate solo the ten miles of pulsing interstate traffic, find the correct exit and make the necessary turns through busy city traffic amid honking horns, only to have her destination pointed out to her at the end of Mrs. Gruber's bony finger.

Miss Beryl, who did not this day share her friend's buoyant good spirits, did her best to shut out Mrs. Gruber's chatter and stave off regret at having so hastily decided not to travel. Midmorning, Clive Jr. had called to wish her a happy Thanksgiving and wondered, near the end of their conversation, what time she and Mrs. Gruber would be getting back from Albany. Miss Beryl knew her son too well to believe that this was a casual inquiry. The very fact that Clive Jr. had stressed the "oh-by-the-way" nature of the query suggested to her that finding out what time she'd be returning from Albany was the real purpose of the call. Also, she was pretty sure she hadn't mentioned that she and Mrs. Gruber were going to Albany for dinner.

Miss Beryl saw her exit coming up, turned on her blinker and began to edge the Ford to the right in anticipation of the off-ramp lane. When that finally arrived, she slid the car even farther right and finally stopped at the traffic signal and used the opportunity to glance at her friend, whom she suspected of being Clive Jr.'s snitch. If Mrs. Gruber knew she was being examined suspiciously, she gave no sign, but rather continued to chatter aimlessly, joyously. Whatever Clive Jr. was up to, Miss Beryl decided, Mrs. Gruber already knew about it. Or knew more about it than Miss Beryl did. Which left Miss Beryl to speculate. He'd seemed disappointed, almost alarmed, to learn that she'd not be traveling this year. Knowing Clive Jr., who was full of schemes, this latest could be just about anything. He might be looking into retirement communities for her again, though he'd promised to give that up. Clive Jr. himself lived in a luxury town house in a community of town homes built along the edge of the new Schuyler Springs Country Club. He'd had Miss Beryl out to visit one afternoon last summer shortly after he'd moved in. The same builder, he told her, was starting a new community designed specifically for the elderly on the other side of town. They'd eaten lunch outdoors on the enclosed patio while Clive Jr. showed her a brochure and explained the advantages of community living while golfers on the nearby fourteenth tee sliced balls off the side of the town house to gunshot effect. One ball even made it into the enclosed patio where they sat and rattled around the perimeter angrily. "We seem to be under siege here, son," Miss Beryl observed when Clive Jr. bent to pick up the smiling Titleist that finally came to rest at his feet. His expression at that moment was like the one so often captured in photographs of Clive Jr. as a boy showing off a Christmas or birthday present. The idea of these photos was always to capture the boy in a moment of happiness, but Clive Jr., more often than not, wore an expression that suggested he'd already discovered what was wrong with the gift and why it couldn't possibly perform the feats illustrated on the package it came in.

When the light turned, Miss Beryl pulled through the intersection and considered what Clive Jr. was up to now, whether it had anything to do with her leaving her home. She was still contemplating this possibility when she heard Mrs. Gruber ask, "Wasn't that it, dear?" and noticed that her friend's bony finger was indeed pointed at the one building in Albany that she recognized, the Northwoods Motor Inn, their destination, already overshot.

"Oh dear," said Mrs. Gruber sadly, watching the Northwoods Motor Inn recede behind them, as if her friend's mistake might well be too severe to admit correction. "Can we turn around, do you suppose?"

In fact, they could not, at least for a quarter mile. The street they were on was divided by an island, the existence of which escaped Mrs. Gruber's notice. When the Northwoods Motor Inn disappeared from sight in the rear window, Mrs. Gruber let out a loud sigh. Several blocks farther on, when they stopped at a traffic light, Mrs. Gruber spied an alternative. "That might be nice," she offered. "It certainly *looks* nice."

"That's a bank," Miss Beryl said, though she had to admit that except for the huge sign identifying it as a bank, it did look more like a restaurant.

Mrs. Gruber sighed again.

Miss Beryl turned, looped through the bank's empty lot, and headed back the way they had come, a maneuver that befuddled Mrs. Gruber, who expressed both surprise and excitement when the Northwoods Motor Inn came into view a second time, now on the other side of the street. "There!" Mrs. Gruber pointed. She also directed Miss Beryl to a parking space. "There!" she pointed again after her friend had slowed, signaled and begun to turn into the space. Things were going to work out after all. Things had a *way* of working out, even when they looked the darkest, Mrs. Gruber mused. It was a lesson in life that she'd learned again and again, and she made a mental note right there in the front seat of Miss Beryl's Ford to quit being an old Gloomy Gus.

The Northwoods Motor Inn catered, especially on Sundays and holidays, to old people. The dining room was large and all on one level, and there was plenty of room between the white-clothed tables for wheelchairs. The young waitresses, attired in friendly Tyrolean costume, were all strapping girls, sturdy enough to support an elderly diner on each arm when it came time to sidle down the soup-and-salad buffet. These girls knew from experience that their clientele were enthusiastically committed to the buffet concept in direct proportion to their physical inability to negotiate it. The more compromised by arthritis, ruptured discs, poor eyesight, dubious equilibrium and tiny appetite, the more the Northwoods' diners were enamored of the long buffet tables with their sweeping vistas of carrot and celery sticks, cottage cheese, applesauce and cheese cubes speared with fancy cellophaned toothpicks, as well as the exotica, pea and three-bean and macaroni-vinaigrette salads, many of which required explanation. The buffet tables had a way of backing up as these explanations were made and choices narrowed, until the line snaked halfway around the room.

This was the state of affairs when Miss Beryl and Mrs. Gruber were seated at a table far too large for the two of them in the very center of the room. Miss Beryl was still unnerved at having driven right past the restaurant, and she was far too peeved at her companion to think seriously of food. Mrs. Gruber was all for joining the buffet line immediately, before it got any longer. Miss Beryl refused, ordering a Manhattan. "It's not going to get longer," she explained. "Except for us, everyone in the room is already *in* it."

"If you say so, dear," said Mrs. Gruber, who deferred to Miss Beryl, albeit reluctantly, in most worldly matters. "What's that tasty highball I always like?"

"An old-fashioned," Miss Beryl reminded her.

Mrs. Gruber ordered an old-fashioned.

The menu was a special Thanksgiving issue scripted onto an onionskin page with scalloped edges, and Mrs. Gruber studied this as if it were the Rosetta Stone. They had a choice among roast turkey, glazed ham, and Yankee pot roast. Mrs. Gruber's lips moved as she read each description and broadened into a smile as she arrived at her decision, which Miss Beryl could have predicted at the outset. "I'm going to eat Old Tom," Mrs. Gruber announced, much too loudly. Several people nearby looked up, startled. "Old Tom Turkey will be just the thing," Mrs. Gruber said. She was reading the menu a second time, just to make sure. "Succulent, it says."

What Mrs. Gruber liked about the food at the Northwoods Motor Inn was precisely what Miss Beryl disliked about it—everything came overcooked. Vegetables were recognizable only by their color, or a bleached version of it, the original shapes and textures lost to the puree process. Meats too were always on the verge of losing their natural composition, so broken down by heat and steam that Mrs. Gruber was always prompted to remark that you could cut it with a fork.

"Succulent is the wrong word to describe turkey," Miss Beryl said.

Mrs. Gruber put down her menu. "What?" she said.

Miss Beryl repeated her observation.

"You always get angry about words when you're in a bad mood," Mrs. Gruber said, apparently having decided to acknowledge her friend's offishness. "There's nothing wrong with the word 'succulent.' It's a perfectly lovely word. You can see it, almost."

Miss Beryl conceded that you could almost see the word 'succulent,' but she doubted that what she almost saw was what Mrs. Gruber almost saw. It was entirely true, however, that she found fault with words when it was really something else that troubled her. Perhaps she was even guilty of being in a bad mood. Clive Jr.'s call and her suspicions concerning Mrs. Gruber were only part of it. She'd been feeling vaguely annoyed with everything since the morning when she'd conversed with Sully on the back porch and Sully had unexpectedly admitted to having misspent his life. Miss Beryl had always admired in Sully his fierce loyalty to the myriad mistakes that constituted his odd, lonely existence. She'd expected his usual defiance, and his sad, uncharacteristic admission had made him seem even more ghostlike than usual. The whole town of Bath, it sometimes seemed to Miss Beryl, was becoming ghostlike, especially Upper Main Street with its elms, the tangle of their black branches overhead, the old houses, most of which were haunted by a single surviving member of a once-flourishing family, and that member conversing more regularly with the dead than the living. Maybe she would be better off living next to a golf course. Maybe it was better to act as a magnet for slicing Titleists than sit beneath limbs that were bound eventually to fall. That morning after Sully had left and before Clive Jr. called, Miss Beryl had a long and not terribly satisfying discussion with Clive Sr., whom she always missed most urgently on holidays. She'd tuned in the Macy's parade, but her attention was drawn to the photograph of her husband, whose round face hovered above the Snoopy balloon. Was there something in his expression this morning suggestive of mild disapproval? "If you don't like the way I'm handling things, you can just butt out," Miss Beryl told him. "You too," she told Driver Ed, who looked like he was about to whisper more subversive Zamble advice from his perch on the wall.

Until recently, Miss Beryl had lived a more or less contented existence on Upper Main, and she didn't understand why she shouldn't be contented now, since the circumstances of her existence had changed so little. True, death was nearer, but she didn't fear death, or didn't fear it any more than she had twenty-five years ago. What she suffered from now, it seemed, was an indefinite sense of misgiving, as if she'd forgotten something important she'd meant to do. Seeing that wretched little girl and her mother yesterday had focused and intensified the feeling, though Miss Beryl was at a loss to account for why this child, however pitiful, should heighten her own personal regret. Regret, when you thought about it, was an absurd emotion for an eighty-year-old woman to indulge on a snowy Thanksgiving, when she had, Miss Beryl was compelled to admit, a great deal to be thankful for. All of this staring up into trees and waiting for God to lower the cosmic boom was nonsense, evidence no doubt that her mind was becoming as arthritic as her toes and fingers. It would have to stop. All of it. Sully wasn't a ghost, he was a man. And Clive Jr. was her son, her own flesh and blood, and there was no reason to believe that his protestations of concern for her well-being were other than genuine. Her suspicions were paranoia, pure and simple. Clive Jr. had nothing conceivable to gain by scheming against her independence, and if he had no reason to do it, then he wasn't doing it. And if he wasn't scheming against her, then Mrs. Gruber couldn't be his accomplice.

There, Miss Beryl said to herself, glad to have reasoned this through so she could enjoy her dinner and be thankful. She once again studied Mrs. Gruber, who'd gone back to her menu and was examining that document as if it contained a plot. Probably, Miss Beryl conceded, she owed Mrs. Gruber an apology. And she was about to offer one, when she heard herself say something entirely unexpected. "Tell the truth," she said, as if she meant it. "Does my son call you to check up on me?"

Mrs. Gruber started to put her menu down, then did not. "Whatever do you mean?"

"I mean, does he call you and check up on me?"

"Of course not, dear," Mrs. Gruber said to her menu. "Why ever would he call me?"

Miss Beryl smiled, her spirits lifted by her friend's feeble lie and her own ability to detect it. "I didn't tell him we were coming here for dinner today," Miss Beryl said, suddenly certain that this was true. "But this morning when I talked to him, he knew."

"You must have told him before," Mrs. Gruber told her menu. "You just forgot."

"Look at me, Alice," Miss Beryl said.

Mrs. Gruber lowered her menu fearfully.

"Clive Jr. isn't really my son," she told her friend. "The bassinets were exchanged in the hospital."

Mrs. Gruber's stricken look was testimony to the fact that she believed this for a full five seconds. "That's a terrible thing to say."

"It was a joke," Miss Beryl said, though it hadn't been. It was a wish, was what it was.

When Miss Beryl finished her Manhattan, she noted that the line at the salad bar had begun to dwindle. "Well," she said, rising. "Let's establish a beachhead at that buffet."

Mrs. Gruber, still looking guilty, received this suggestion gratefully. "Beachhead," she repeated, pushing back her chair. "You and your words."

At the salad bar Mrs. Gruber filled two plates, which she allowed one of the Tyrolean waitresses to deliver to their table.

"I like words," Miss Beryl said when they were seated again and Mrs. Gruber had begun eating, with great solemnity, her cottage cheese. "I like choosing the right ones."

An hour later, on their way back to Bath, Mrs. Gruber got the hiccups. Miss Beryl remembered one of her mother's favorite quips, which she now shared with her companion. "Well," she told Mrs. Gruber. "Either you told a lie or you 'et' something."

Mrs. Gruber looked guilty and hiccuped again. When they arrived back at Upper Main, Clive Jr.'s car was parked at the curb.

Sully's ex-wife, Vera, stood at the sink in the kitchen of her house on Silver Street, feeling, for the umpteenth time today, liquid emotion climb in her throat like illness. From the kitchen window in the gathering dusk she was able to make out a ramshackle pickup truck idling at the curb, its blue exhaust creating a cloud that threatened to take over the entire block. Apparently whoever owned it had gone into the house across the street, leaving the truck running, its viral pollution not so much dissipating as enshrouding. Vera imagined the cloud of noxious fumes growing until it covered not only the block but the entire town of her childhood, her life, leaving a greasy film on everything.

For nearly sixty years she'd lived on Silver Street in the town of North Bath, for the last thirty in this modest, well-tended house with Ralph Mott, the man she'd married soon after divorcing Sully. For the first twenty years of her life she'd lived down the block in a house that, until a decade ago when her father took up residence in the veterans' home, had been as pretty and well-tended as any on the street. Since then the whole neighborhood had slipped into unmistakable decline. Her father's house, the house of her happy girlhood, was now rented to its third grubby, loutish welfare family. The current owner was a man Vera had known and disliked when they were in the same high school class. At the time he bought her father's house everyone had assumed he'd move in, but instead he rented it, along with the one his parents had lived in around the corner, and he himself moved to Schuyler Springs. He'd bought her father's house for a song when Robert Halsey, who was in slowly declining health, sensed that it would not be long before he would be in need of constant care. He'd sold the house well below market, without consulting his daughter or anyone else, perhaps without suspecting what the house was worth, perhaps fearing that if he waited too long, the house could conceivably be lost to illness. He'd sold it in the summer, when Vera and Ralph and Peter were away for their week's vacation, and had moved into the veterans' home in Schuyler Springs before she returned. He knew that she would try to dissuade him, and perhaps succeed in doing so, knew that it was her intention to tend to his needs for as long as he allowed her. He was unsentimental where his daughter was concerned, knew all too well the preternatural strength of her devotion to him, knew that she would put his needs, his well-being, before her own, and maybe even before her family's. When she'd been a younger woman, away at her first year at the state teachers' college at Oneonta and he'd taken ill, she'd simply dropped all her classes and come home to tend to him. When he got well again, at least for a time, she never went back, instead allowing herself to slip into a doomed marriage with Sully (so she could be close by, he suspected) and then, after the divorce, into a more satisfactory but—her father suspected—equally unhappy marriage to Ralph Mott.

Robert Halsey had been concerned, though not terribly surprised, when his daughter talked her second husband into buying a house down the street. He understood that the proximity made Vera feel safe and good, and he was never able to find a way to tell her that it was time for her to give him up, just as he was never able to tell her when she exercised bad judgment in other respects, despite the numerous opportunities she provided. Her love for him was the most terrible thing he'd ever witnessed, and he could think of no way to combat it, no way to prevent her from injuring herself further. By selling the house and giving her and Ralph the money, by moving to Schuyler Springs and into the VA home, he had fled her devotion and helped his daughter and her second husband get out from under the burden of debt brought on by her earlier lapses in judgment.

Though he had never found a way to tell her, Vera knew that she was a disappointment to her father. He had worked hard and sacrificed much on his small-town teacher's salary to provide her with an opportunity to attend college. Instead of going to the university as he'd urged her, she'd insisted on the state teachers' college because it was closer, and then had walked away from even that. She'd known that returning home to tend him would not please her father, that doing it was some sort of deep-down lie. She had not liked the college or her life there, had not made friends, had not been able to focus on her studies. Her father's illness had been an excuse to return home and share his life. She loved him that much and found it impossible to question her unflagging devotion to him, even though she understood, at least in moments of brutal clarity, that it was this devotion, as much as Sully's myriad shortcomings, that was responsible for the failure of her first marriage, just as it was responsible for the continued unhappiness of her second. The simple fact was that no man measured up to Robert Halsey, her father, a man of noble bearing, directly descended from Jedediah Halsey, the man who first envisioned, then made a reality of, the Sans Souci.

The only person who came close to measuring up was her son, Peter, in whom Vera had a great deal invested. In Peter she saw a boy destined to redeem her father's faith and sacrifice. He was bright, a far better student than she had ever been, and he did very well in school despite the fact that his teachers seemed not to like him. His achievements always seemed to fall just short of brilliance, a fact for which his mother was never able to account. He was an exceedingly nervous child, but she did not suspect that he studied out of fear, propelled forward only as far as fear could push him, which was a goodly distance. When she finally began to recognize her son's terrors for what they were, it did not take her long to isolate their source, which could only be Sully, the man who both was and was not his father, who was lurking in the back of her son's consciousness.

Vera was able to identify this fear because she shared it. She had always carried with her the knowledge that Sully possessed the power to destroy them all, possibly through carelessness, perhaps even through misguided good intentions. Her most nagging fear when Peter was growing up was that Sully might one day wake up and take an interest in their son. This turned out to be an unwarranted concern, but Vera spent many a sleepless night developing strategies for coping with Sully in the unlikely event that he should become an issue, and each time he turned up at her door, usually at her foolish husband Ralph's instigation, with plans to take Peter somewhere, Vera was terrified that he would suddenly love the boy. What would she do then? What *could* she do?

It was this irrational concern that had so often led Vera's judgment to falter. Recalling how homesick she'd been in college at Oneonta, how out of place she had felt, how hard it had been to focus on her studies, she decided to spare Peter North Bath's suspect high school by sending him to an all-boy prep school in New Hampshire. The decision had been an agonizing one because she'd known that even as the strategy protected Peter from his father, it also separated the boy from herself. In the end she decided the risk was worth it, telling herself that the better educated and more refined he became, the less appealing he would be to his father, the less likely Sully would be to come to his senses and love his own son.

Some would call it justice, she supposed, the way things had turned out—file under "Be careful what you wish for." As she had hoped, Sully showed even less interest in their son after he went away to prep school. It occurred to Vera too late that this would have happened in any case. The responsibility and burden of affection had always weighed heavily on her ex-husband. Given half a chance, he gravitated naturally to the easy camaraderie of the lunchroom, the barroom, the company of men, of another man's wife. By sending her son away, Vera had prevented something that did not need preventing, and at a cost to herself. Her attempts to protect Peter, her devotion to him, had once again, just as it had with her father, set into motion the law of unintended consequences, along with the cruel laws of irony and paradox. For Peter, in becoming a son to be proud of—an educator like her father, a college professor at home in the very environment that had intimidated Vera—had learned to lose his interest in and affection for her, coolly dismissing the books she recommended to him, smiling his ironic smile at her political views as if to suggest that she was incapable of any opinion or observation that wasn't entirely typical or predictable. There was so much she would have liked to tell him, now that they were both adults, and he wasn't interested in any of it. He seemed more pleased to spend time with Ralph, her husband, who had no views at all, than with herself. That her son remained capable of affection but could spare so little for herself was the cruelest twist of all.

Today, at their Thanksgiving dinner together, Vera had seen more clearly than ever before what a terrible thing love was, or at least the kind of love that had rooted most deeply in her own anxious heart. Knowing how difficult it would be, she had planned the day carefully. Yesterday she'd baked the pies and then had risen early this morning to stuff the turkey and prepare her father's favorite squash. Then, midmorning, she'd driven to Schuyler Springs with Ralph to gather Robert Halsey from the dreadful veterans' home, not an easy task because they had to transport not only the fragile man but also his breathing apparatus—the portable oxygen tank and mask—which they could not just put in the trunk, since her father might need it on the drive back to Bath.

For a while it had seemed the day would work. Back on Silver Street they'd been able to get her father, who was having one of his better days breathing and required the oxygen only sporadically, installed in the living room. Peter, who had always been fond of his grandfather, had drawn up a chair, and the two had swapped teaching stories, Peter suppressing for once his cynicism, along with, at Vera's insistence, the fact that he'd been denied tenure at the university. Ralph had turned the football game low, and horsey Charlotte had managed to keep the horrid little Wacker, a truly monstrous child, from tormenting his brother and everyone else. Vera had stayed in the warm kitchen, humming over the final dinner preparations and allowing herself to become intoxicated by the smells and sounds of food and family and terrible, terrible love and longing. If she felt a fear, it was the distant one that Sully might show up and spoil everything, since Peter had informed her that he'd issued the invitation, surely to vex her. But she told herself that God would not be so cruel to her as to allow this, at least not today.

Half an hour before dinner, she got Ralph to help her slip the leaf into the dining room table, and together they covered it with the white linen tablecloth she saved for holidays. She set the table with the family silver she had inherited from her mother, who had died when Vera was a child. At each end of the table she set two candles, which she lit, then dimmed the lights before calling the family to the table. She instructed each person where to sit, an annoyance, she could tell, Peter and Charlotte exchanging glances, Wacker refusing to vacate a chair at the head of the table until horsey Charlotte physically removed him. She could tell that Peter disapproved not only of the concept of a seating plan in general but of her seating plan in particular, which called for her father to take the head and Peter the foot, and leaving Ralph, whose table it was, somewhere in the middle, though Ralph could have cared less, provided he was close to the platter of turkey.

And so, when the table was full of food and Vera's family had come together, and Vera herself had the satisfaction of knowing that she'd skillfully accomplished a difficult task, when the image she'd borne in her imagination had been replicated as faithfully as possible in her dining room, her father, looking healthier than she'd seen him in months and having left his oxygen set up in the next room, anchoring one end of the table and Peter, looking handsome and only a little imperious at the other, when the family had begun to pass in the candlelight the food she'd prepared, only then when the doorbell did not ring and Sully did not show up at this perfect moment and spoil everything, only then did Vera have the leisure to note that the perfect moment, so long awaited and planned for, was a lie. As the platters of food got passed, Vera felt the truth rise in her throat, and she knew she would not be able to swallow so much as a mouthful. Only Ralph, who never noticed anything, seemed oblivious to this truth as he ladled gravy over everything on his plate, including the cranberries. Her father, she suddenly realized, had left his oxygen behind not because he didn't need it but because he thought it would spoil everyone's dinner. She could hear him wheezing, gasping really, as he awaited the turkey, and when it came, his hand shook so that he was unable to spear a slice and had to be meted a portion by horsey Charlotte, who gave him dark meat, not knowing his preference for white, and he was too tired to say anything. "Everything is delicious, Mom," Peter said, looking down at his plate. Twice that day he and Charlotte had gone into the bedroom they used during these visits, and Vera had heard their angry, lowered voices and understood fully what she'd suspected for some time, that theirs was a worse-than-loveless marriage and that it would not hold together another year, maybe not even another month. "Yes . . . Vera," her father managed. "Very . . . fine." But he hadn't the strength to say more, and she felt powerfully that he would not last the year, either. Neither of the men in her life had looked at her when he spoke, and she understood that neither was able to face her, or wanted to face her. What they needed from her was for this to be over, and neither looked up even when she did not respond to their compliments, her throat constricting with bitter truth, rising dangerously. Only Will, her grandson, seemed aware of her distress, and he watched her so fearfully that she wished there was a way to reassure him that this feeling would pass, that truth was something she'd always been able to swallow and keep down.

She was not surprised when her father pushed back his chair and rose unsteadily. "I'm . . . so . . . sorry . . . Vera," he said, turning away from the table and heading for the living room.

She rose quickly to help him, but with the leaf in the table the room was crowded and horsey Charlotte and the horrid little Wacker were between them, and anyway, he didn't need her. What he needed was oxygen. Air.

Outside Vera's kitchen window the pickup truck at the curb continued to belch thick fumes, though it had grown dark enough now that the pollution was not clearly defined. Dark had overtaken dark, it occurred to her. As she watched, the street lamp kicked on, to little effect. She became aware of Peter then, and when she turned he was studying her from the doorway. He was carrying the cutting board that contained the turkey carcass. She'd bought a larger bird than necessary, and Peter had carved only half of it. Now, the way he held the cutting board, the uncarved portion facing her, the golden brown bird appeared intact, as if no one had eaten, as if her offering were being returned to her untouched, spurned. Peter, seeing there was no room on the counter around the sink, set the board and carcass down on the dinette table. "I told the boys to get started on their baths, if that's okay," he told her.

"Why wouldn't it be okay?" Vera said, though she knew why. The single bathroom in Ralph and Vera's house was always a bone of contention when they visited. Always occupied, never adequate to the traffic, impossible to keep stocked with clean towels, impossible to keep fresh with so much use. Foul humans walking in on each other in their foulest moments.

"Would you like me to dry?" Peter said, joining her tentatively at the sink. "I'm not doing anything."

"I do better alone," she said. Peter was rarely kind, it seemed to her, and he seemed to offer kindness only at times she was unable to accept it, when she was beyond kindness. "It's an *awfully* small kitchen."

"There's nothing wrong with the kitchen, Mom," Peter said, his voice laden with significance, an attitude of her son's that she found almost impossible to bear. If anything was wrong, it was with her; that's what he was saying.

"Why don't you keep your grandfather company?" she suggested. "I'm fine. Really."

Peter had taken a dish towel from the drawer. "He's dozing," he said. "He ate pretty well."

After hooking him back up to his tank, Vera had brought her father a plate of food and set it up for him on a TV tray while he sucked hard at his oxygen.

"You've tried to do too much," Peter said, adding, just as she knew he would, "as usual."

"Yes, no doubt," she agreed. "I should have let him spend Thanksgiving in the VA home."

"I didn't mean that," Peter sighed. "We're the ones you shouldn't have invited." When she said nothing to this, he added, "Charlotte wants to leave in the morning."

Vera looked at him now, stunned.

"It's just—" Peter began.

"What a hateful woman she is," Vera interrupted. When dinner was barely over, Charlotte had left, claiming there were some things she had to get at the store, but Vera had overheard part of yet another angry conversation that had taken place behind the closed door of the spare bedroom. "That old man isn't the only one strangling in this house," she'd heard Charlotte say. "It's like living inside a can of deodorant here. She's got two air fresheners in every room. She runs in and sprays every time somebody uses the bathroom. No wonder you hate women." Apparently Peter had found this amusing, because Charlotte had added, after a pause, "Don't laugh. Fucking them isn't the same as liking them."

Peter looked down at the dish towel now. "We're not doing all that well, Charlotte and I," he conceded. "Being here just makes everything worse."

"I make everything worse, you mean," she said, scraping food from the side of the sink into the garbage disposal.

Peter said nothing.

"Go then," she said. "By all means."

"I had a feeling you wouldn't take this well," Peter told her. "You always make it seem like people do things just to disappoint you. You should have seen yourself in the other room. As if Grandpa's not being able to eat with us was just him being mean to you, messing up your plans."

"I'd be grateful if you didn't analyze me," she said, scraping the last of the plates into the sink. That done, she grabbed the bowl that contained the turkey stuffing and scraped it into the sink, then the remaining squash. "Especially about your grandfather. I know you're educated and I'm not, but there are some things in this world that you don't understand and never will."

Peter was staring at her now. "That's good food," he pointed out.

She followed the squash with the potatoes and the green beans. "Why save them?" she said. "Who's going to be here to eat leftovers?"

"What about Ralph?"

"What about him," Vera said, turning on the disposal, which thundered into operation, shaking the sink. Apparently a bone had found its way in with the rest of the scrapings, and it rattled around the disposal like a stone. When Peter reached for the switch above the sink to turn it off, she grabbed his wrist, clutching it fiercely, refusing to let go, even when he tried to pull away. She surrendered him only when she'd regained a tenuous grip on herself and turned off the disposal. "You treat him as if he didn't exist," Peter said quietly.

For a moment Vera was unable to respond. "I don't mean to," she finally managed. "I mean, I do mean to, but I don't know why."

Neither said anything for some time.

"Everything's coming apart, isn't it," she said when she could finally locate her voice.

"What, Mom?" Peter said, not bothering to disguise the frustration in his voice. "What's coming apart?"

"Me," she told him, grinning now. "Can't you tell?"

She stared out the kitchen window into the street of her life. The street lamp was doing a better job now. It had to get really dark before such man-made illumination did any good. "Remember what a pretty street this used to be?" she asked her son. "Remember how it was when you were a boy growing up, how we could let you wander the neighborhood and be completely safe? Remember how it was before the invasion?"

Peter was frowning at her. She didn't even have to look at him to know that. "What invasion, Mom?"

She made a sweeping gesture at the street, the world outside her kitchen. "The barbarians," she explained. "Open your eyes."

Peter looked out the window, noticing the pickup truck at the curb for the first time. "Huh," he said, puzzled, as if he might actually see her point. "That's Dad, isn't it?"

That possibility had not occurred to her, and Vera was about to say no, it couldn't be, when that certainty was replaced by its opposite. Of course, she thought, as her son pulled on his coat and started down the driveway to investigate. She watched Peter as he went around the truck to the driver's side and peered in. She saw him knock on the window, then try the door, saw the truck rock gently in response to his efforts. Of course, she thought to herself. With the whole wide world to die in, and the days lined up all the way to eternity, wasn't it just like Sully to die on Thanksgiving in the very shadow of the home she'd managed to build in his absence?

This was a bitter, vengeful thought, and so the tears that welled up in her eyes took her by surprise.

In Sully's dream he and Rub and Carl Roebuck and a famous television judge were sitting naked in a tiny sauna, arguing. Sully explained all about the job he and Rub had done for Carl Roebuck last August, and also Carl's steadfast refusal to pay them for it. When called upon, Carl admitted to nonpayment, but explained that Sully had hooked up the pipes all wrong. Anymore when they flushed the toilet, shit came out the water faucets. "It's put a terrible strain on my marriage," he added by way of explaining his countersuit. When the judge asked Rub what light he could throw upon the affair, Rub recited the Carnation Milk jingle flawlessly and challenged Sully to do the same. During the entire testimony, Sully had been distracted by someone banging for admittance at the sauna door, and, when challenged to repeat the jingle, Sully found himself unable to. He couldn't remember how it went, despite the fact that Rub had just recited it. "I'm going to find for the defendant," said the judge, who brought his gavel down hard on Sully's knee. At this moment the sauna door flew open and Toby Roebuck appeared, also naked. Rub focused first on her breasts, then on her loins. He screamed. A gun materialized in Toby's hand, and she pointed it at her husband. "Don't take the law into your own hands," the judge advised. "Take him to court." Toby Roebuck, her face hard and unforgiving, her feet planted wide apart in a man's stance, fired anyway, and it was Sully's turn to scream.

These screams had a strange sense of reality to them, perhaps because they were real. The first scream was not Rub's. It belonged to Peter, Sully's son, who was peering into the pickup's window at his father. The second scream was Sully's, starting awake. He was parked at the curb, in front of his ex-wife's house, where he'd fallen asleep. It had been his intention merely to close his eyes for a minute, to gather himself and take a deep breath before going up the walk and knocking at the door of the house, where he expected a mixed reception. It was not immediately apparent how long he'd actually slept, but he suspected the sauna might have been only the last of a series of dreams. Also, it appeared that dusk was falling.

"Jesus Christ, Dad," Peter kept saying. He was now walking up and down alongside the pickup, shaking his head, holding one hand over his heart. "You realize you sleep with your eyes open?"

Sully understood this to be true, though it was a fairly recent phenomenon. Ruth had witnessed and reported it with considerable irritation. It couldn't have been the case when he was married to Vera, because his wife had kept a careful, detailed list of the things he did of which she disapproved, and she was not the sort of woman to hold anything back. She surely would have mentioned it if he'd slept with his eyes open.

Sully tried to shake off some of the deep grogginess. "I must have dozed off," he said.

"With the motor running and door locked?"

The motor *was* running. Sully turned it off. The door was not locked, but it was tricky. From the outside you had to pull up and out at the same time. Sully demonstrated for his son's benefit. Way off he heard a siren, and, as he always did when he heard a siren, he tried to remember if he'd left a cigarette burning somewhere.

Both men listened to the approach of the ambulance. "I knocked on the window, but I couldn't get you to wake up," Peter explained guiltily.

Sully tried to make all this add up, but he still was too groggy from Jocko's pills and the truck's heater, and from breathing the pickup's gasoline fumes. When the ambulance turned down their street and Peter flagged it, Sully looked at his ex-wife's house and said, "Is somebody sick?"

"You," Peter explained, looking embarrassed now. "We thought you were dead."

Sully just sat with the door open and let the cold air bring him back while Peter explained as best he could to the ambulance crew, who were reluctant to believe that this could be an honest mistake. They kept looking over at Sully suspiciously, as if the verdict was still out on whether or not he'd died, as originally reported. In their expression they reminded him of the people who'd been told he died in the fire he'd started twenty years ago. This was twice now he'd cheated people out of a tragedy, and even his own son looked conflicted on the point of his continued existence, though this was probably due to the fact that his not being dead after all made Peter, who'd called for the ambulance, look like a fool.

When Ralph came out, Sully was delighted to see him. "You ain't dead after all," Ralph said, beaming at him. Sully and Vera's second husband had always gotten on fine and would have gotten along even better had they not both understood that Vera considered their inclination to like each other a betrayal. It seemed not to bother Ralph in the least that his wife had been intimate with Sully, had borne him a son. Worse, it seemed not to bother Sully that what had once been his now belonged to another man. It was as if they'd agreed she wasn't worth fighting over. Indeed, it was more like they considered themselves fellow sufferers.

"No, not yet, Ralph," Sully said. "You wouldn't mind too much if I threw up here in your gutter, would you?"

Ralph shrugged. "I'd offer you the bathroom, except the boys are in there to take a bath."

"I wouldn't make it anyhow," Sully said, feeling the vomit rise in his throat. "Besides, I may not have learned much married to Vera, but I know better than to throw up in her bathroom. Unless she's changed, she doesn't even like people to shit in it."

"She hasn't changed," Ralph admitted sadly. "She's got about a dozen air fresheners opened up all over the house. We couldn't even smell the turkey."

Just hearing about the smell of air fresheners did the trick, and Sully leaned forward and threw up into the street. Ralph looked away. Not having eaten all day, there wasn't much, and Sully, who had been sweating in anticipation, immediately felt better. He thought he recognized the decomposed remains of the second of Jocko's yellow pills.

Seeing what he'd done, the two men from the ambulance, who'd given a form to Peter to sign, came over to where he sat. "You all right, pal?" the smaller man wanted to know. "You want us to take you back to the hospital?"

"Nope, I sure don't," Sully told them. "I feel much better."

The man glanced at the vomit and looked away.

"Sorry you had to come out here," Sully said. "My son can't tell dead people from sleeping ones. I guess that's why they made him a doctor of history and not medicine."

Peter had come over in time to hear this.

"If you'd breathed much more exhaust, you might *be* dead," the ambulance driver said. "You should get checked out."

Sully stood to show that he was okay. "I'm fine," he said. "I promise."

"Okay," the man said, handing Sully a form. "Sign this. It proves we were here."

When Sully signed, the two men got back into the ambulance, burped their siren once and drove off. Sully, Peter and Ralph watched them go, and when the ambulance disappeared around the corner, all three men turned reluctantly to face house and home and family and explanation.

"Well, son," Sully addressed Peter, though it was Ralph he winked at. "Let's go inside before our courage fails completely."

■ ■ ■

If it was women these three grown men feared—and it was—they needn't have worried, because when they entered, the kitchen was empty, not a woman in sight, though this struck all three as perhaps even more ominous. The sink was still piled high with scraped dinner plates and casserole dishes plus assorted pots and pans, including the roasting pan in which Vera had made the gravy. In the sink she'd drawn a yellow tubful of water that wore a round hat of suds. The house was preternaturally still except for the sound of the television on low in the living room. From where they stood, Sully could see Vera's father asleep in his chair two rooms away. "Where'd your mother go?" Ralph wondered, surprised by her sudden disappearance.

Peter was not. "I'd be careful in here today," he warned Sully. "Mom's all upset."

"What about?" Ralph said, since this was news to him.

"Let me guess," Sully said. "Nobody loves her."

"Close," Peter admitted. "Nobody loves her enough."

"I'll go talk to her," Ralph said like a man volunteering for hazardous duty.

"How long have you and Vera been married?" Sully said significantly. Ralph thought. "Thirty years. More."

"And you still don't know any better than that?"

"She probably still thinks you're dead," Ralph said.

"Then don't disappoint her," Sully advised.

From the direction of the bathroom came the sound of running water and Will's whining voice. "Wacker. Quit."

Peter rolled his eyes. "I'll be right back."

Since no one had told him not to, Sully sauntered into the living room, where Robert Halsey slept fitfully, hooked up to his oxygen, green plastic tubing forming a childish mustache on his upper lip. A plastic mask dangled from the portable oxygen rig. The football game was on, and Sully sat down at the end of the sofa just in time to see somebody kick a field goal and the score come up across the bottom of the screen before going to a commercial.

"Hey," Sully said to Vera's father, who opened his eyes in response to this sound that was not television. "Wake up. You've got company."

The old man blinked, focused. "Sully," he said, sitting up straighter, having slumped down during his nap.

"How are you, Mr. Mayor?" Sully said. Vera's father had run for mayor as a Democrat forty-some years ago and suffered the fate of all

Democrats seeking elected office in Bath, only worse, suffering the worst defeat in memory. In Bath, where mayor was a part-time office and mayoral candidates tended to be the owners of automobile dealerships, the real contest was always the Republican primary. Once that was settled, the actual election was pretty much a foregone conclusion, the Democratic candidates leaning decidedly in the direction of masochism or, in Robert Halsey's case, fatalism. He had run on an educational platform and had been rejected so overwhelmingly that no one had dared bring up the subject of education in a local campaign ever since.

"What's the score here?" Sully asked.

"I don't know," Robert Halsey confessed.

"They told me you were in charge here," Sully said.

"I am," the old man admitted. "Dallas was ahead when I fell asleep."

"They still are," Sully said. "Twenty to fourteen in case anybody asks you."

"Where are they?" Vera's father wondered, looking around the room.

"I think they saw me coming and ran for it," Sully said.

Mr. Halsey smiled. "And left me behind."

"It's the law of the jungle, Mr. Mayor," Sully said. "You feeling pretty well these days?"

"Not too bad," the old man wheezed. "It's a struggle I won't be sad to give up."

"Not much fun anymore?"

"It's *no* fun anymore."

"Well," Sully said. "Just don't let your daughter hear you say that. You may think things can't get any worse, but they can."

"How's my old friend Mrs. Peoples?" Robert Halsey wondered. Miss Beryl had been one of the few ardent supporters of his doomed mayoral campaign.

"Just the same," Sully assured him. "She hasn't changed in twenty years."

"What makes people unhappy, do you suppose?" Robert Halsey wondered out loud, confusing Sully, who thought at first that they were still on the subject of his landlady, then realized that the old man was thinking about his daughter, who hadn't changed in twenty years either.

"I don't know," Sully confessed.

"It's either their own fault or it's ours," Robert Halsey said, as if he were a long way from deciding. They watched the game for a while. "It's the trouble with getting old and sick," he said when Sully'd just about concluded their conversation was over. "There isn't much to do but think."

Since there didn't seem to be much to say in response to this, Sully didn't offer anything, and the next time he looked over at Robert Halsey, the old man was asleep again.

In the bathroom the boys were fighting as they undressed to prepare for their baths. When Peter opened the door to check on them, he caught Wacker, hand raised ready to do something, and Will, the older and larger boy, flinching and pulling away. Wacker looked more inconvenienced than embarrassed to be caught in an act of aggression, Will only temporarily relieved. "Cut it out, Wacker," Peter told the younger boy. "You aren't funny."

Will studied his brother to see if these instructions would take. He didn't look too hopeful.

"Get undressed. Get in the bathtub. And don't let it overflow or Grandma will skin you," Peter said, another ineffectual warning, he realized. In fact, he thought he detected a sly smile cross Wacker's lips.

"Where's Mom?" Will said, looking worried. It was usually their mother who supervised baths.

Peter was studying the bathtub with dismay. The water had been on forever and it was only half full. The water pressure was bad almost everywhere in Bath but ridiculous in Ralph and Vera's house, where you couldn't even take a shower. You had to start the tub ten minutes before you planned to get in, and the temperature was almost impossible to gauge. Peter felt the water in the tub and turned on more hot on the theory that it would cool down before the boys got in. Bath. What a ridiculous name, Charlotte always maintained, for a town where you couldn't take a decent one.

"Where's Mom?" Will repeated. He would repeat questions patiently until you answered them.

"At the store," Peter told him impatiently, wondering as he did so if the boys had overheard his and Charlotte's quarrel before dinner. "She'll be back in a few minutes. You'd better be finished with your baths too."

Another sly smile from Wacker. Or what? he seemed to be saying.

Closing the door on them, Peter went quietly into the downstairs bedroom, the den really, that he and Charlotte used when they visited, while the boys were given the room upstairs that had been his when he was a boy. The bed had been folded back into the couch, which meant that his mother had been in and done it. Kicking his shoes off, he lay down on the sofa and stared at the ceiling. In truth, he had no idea where Charlotte had gone.

When Andy snorted loudly in his playpen, Peter raised up on one elbow to study him, but the baby had not woken up and so Peter lay back down. Before making the trip, he and Charlotte had agreed to separate after the holidays, an eventuality he was looking forward to with mixed feelings. Liberation was what he'd expected to feel, but having reached this agreement with Charlotte, his spirits had declined. The fact that Charlotte was leaving him and not the other way around was not the comfort he'd imagined it would be, and as he lay in the den of the house he'd grown up in, he wondered whether it was a husband he wasn't cut out to be, or a father. Or both. He wasn't, in all honesty, much good at either. In the living room last week Will, who was prone to introspection, had been watching TV and picking his nose thoughtfully when he extracted a booger, the size of which had amazed and startled him. Since it was not, however, the sort of thing he could share with his parents, he simply sat there in the middle of the floor and stared at his finger, full of pride, unaware that Wacker was sneaking up behind him. When Wacker snatched the booger and ran off with it, Will, outraged, gave chase, screaming, "Mine! Mine!"

When the dispute erupted, Peter had been working in his cramped study, the utility room actually, which he shared with Charlotte's washer and dryer, trying to finish an article he already knew no one would publish. Even when he finally discovered that this particular dispute was over ownership of a booger, his parental options seemed equally absurd. Possible responses ran through his mind, one after the other. He might, for instance, address the fairness principle. ("Wacker, give your brother back his booger. Get your own booger from your own nose.") Or he could ignore the booger entirely. ("I thought I told you boys to be quiet so Daddy could work.") Or even appeal to the older boy's reason. ("Will, for heaven's sake, you can't really *want* that. Let the little jerk *have* it.") In the end he'd said nothing, opting instead to collect his materials and retreat to the university library where there'd be peace and quiet. On the way out the door, he told Charlotte it was no great surprise he hadn't gotten his tenure and promotion. People who lived in insane asylums never got tenure.

And then after dropping this guilt bomb, he hadn't even gone to the library, but rather to the house of a young woman colleague whose lover he'd been since September. Her tiny house was in a rundown section of town consisting of, for the most part, large old houses subdivided by their slumlord owners into rental units. It was as if, Peter sometimes thought, someone had announced a contest to see how many Malaysian students could be crammed into a five-bedroom house. Deirdre's place was actually a guesthouse out back of one of these Malaysian dorms, and each time Peter made his way along the narrow, roller-coaster sidewalk, he took a deep breath, as if to acknowledge that it would be the last pure air he'd breathe for a while.

Deirdre liked heat, and she especially liked wandering around the house in her underthings, a habit that had excited Peter at first, like everything about Deirdre. In the beginning he'd thought it was just the September weather and the fact that the cottage wasn't air-conditioned, until later in the month the temperatures began to fall everywhere except at Deirdre's place. One night after making sticky love he'd searched for another explanation and found it. She had her thermometer set at eighty. Her office at the college was the same. Mechanically gifted, Deirdre had managed to disassemble the thermostat, disengage the device that prevented individual tampering, and boost the temperature there too, although she did not, so far as Peter knew, run around the office in her bra and panties. "I like it hot," she explained the night he discovered that she had the heat set at eighty. "I like to *be* hot," she purred, taking his hand and slipping it into her panties by way of illustration.

It had taken Peter nearly three months to discover he could do with a little less heat. What had been exciting back in September—stopping by Deirdre's little cottage on his way home from the library and finding her seated on her broken-down sofa, cross-legged in nothing but her bikini panties, sucking noisily on a peach and watching television in the dark— now seemed to Peter just a little unhealthy. In September he'd felt his dick rise in anticipation of this heartwarming spectacle as he hurried up the crooked little walkway, dodging the low-hanging tree branches. Now, in mid-November, it was his stomach that threatened to rise when he visited Deirdre and inhaled that first breath of fetid, tropical air. Both the atmosphere of the cottage and Deirdre herself seemed to be deep in the process of fermentation.

Also, her behavior seemed to be getting progressively more decadent, a circumstance that no longer thrilled him. Her eating habits in particular revolted him. She liked to share food with him while she was eating it. Overly ripe peaches were her favorite, and she liked to masticate a mouthful of peach partway, then kiss Peter, so that he got to share. "I want us to have identical sensations," she explained. Peter doubted they were having identical sensations. The fact that Deirdre was apparently enjoying herself in all of this suggested to him that they couldn't be.

Deirdre was, in fact, the reason he had insisted on visiting Bath over Thanksgiving, a trip they could not afford and which was certain to infuriate Charlotte, who dreaded such visits and who made clear that she considered it cruel and unfair to expect her to make the journey at Thanksgiving and then again at Christmas. Deirdre too had pouted, pleading with him not to go, not to leave her alone for the long, four-day weekend. In fact, she'd made him several explicit erotic promises if he'd agree to stay in town, promises that made him all the more determined to get away from her long enough to clear his head. He wondered if it was clear enough to call her now and found he was dialing the phone on the end table before he could decide.

"Hi," he said softly when she'd answered the phone and accepted the charges. "Sorry to have to call collect. I don't want this to appear on my mother's bill."

"I knew you'd call," she said, as if she'd just been arguing the matter with someone and was saying I told you so. In fact, it occurred to him that she might have someone with her. He wasn't sure someone as constantly horny as Deirdre would be able to go the distance of a long, chaste holiday weekend. Maybe she'd invited half a dozen little Malaysian neighbors over to take turns until he got back. They'd discovered that she seldom wore clothes when she walked around the cottage, and they'd taken to hanging around on their back patio, grinning and clucking and waiting for a glimpse.

"How could you know I'd call when I told you I wouldn't?" Peter said.

"I know *you*," she said. "I know what a dirty little boy you are, and I knew you wouldn't get laid in your mommy's nice clean house."

"Clean doesn't begin to describe it," Peter told her.

"I said you should have stayed with me."

"According to Charlotte, my mother's the reason I hate women."

"The cow had an idea?"

Peter let this go. He didn't like for Deirdre to say nasty things about Charlotte, but in this business of infidelity it wasn't easy to draw lines. He wasn't sure he was in any position to criticize his lover for being unkind to the wife he was cheating on. "Do you think I hate women?"

"As long as you love me, I don't care."

Peter considered this. "Don't they make you surrender your membership in NOW when you say things like that? How can you write a dissertation on Virginia Woolf and say such things?"

"I bet she didn't give great head like I do."

"Lord," Peter said, hoping his mother wasn't listening on the extension. He was pretty sure she wasn't. He'd heard what sounded like two people—his mother and Ralph—coming down the stairs, and now there were the sounds of voices coming from the kitchen, which meant that his mother had pulled herself together enough to come down and offer Sully a cup of coffee.

Across the room Andy rolled over in his playpen, snorted again, momentarily opened his eyes, then closed them again. "Didi," Peter said, after a moment.

"I'm here."

"You need to start preparing for the end. Of us, I mean."

"I'm not listening," she said.

"I have children. I'm a father."

"So?"

"So I need to be a better one."

"You need me."

"I know," he admitted. Outside, he thought he heard a car pull up. "But I can't keep on like this. We'll talk when I get back. Finish your dissertation chapter. I'll proof it for you."

"You're so full of bullshit, Peter."

"I'm going to have to hang up now," he said, and he did, but not before he heard her say, "You're mine, buddy boy."

He stood then and looked out the window. The Gremlin was again parked at the curb, behind his father's truck. Charlotte, empty handed, was halfway up the walk. Peter watched her from behind the curtain. Since he'd admitted there was someone else, Charlotte had rediscovered her interest in him. She'd known for several weeks, and they'd made angry love every night, the unhappy sex punctuating their discussions about the logistics of their separation, planned now for the first of the year, after the holidays.

In the bathroom next door Peter could hear the water still running, and he felt his anger rise at his sons, who were still squabbling, probably not even in the tub yet. But before he could move, he heard a loud bang, followed almost immediately by a startled cry, and he stopped where he was in the middle of the den, counting five in his head, allowing Charlotte enough time to arrive at the back door, share the responsibility of this most recent crisis, whatever it turned out to be, in this wreck of their married lives.

Robert Halsey, who had been dozing in the living room, pure oxygen tunneling up his nostrils and down the back of his throat and into what remained of his lungs, also heard the loud bang and cry in the bathroom, and he started awake, faced as he always was when suddenly awakened from one of his naps with determining how long he'd been asleep. Anymore, it was hard to tell. Sometimes a five-minute nap felt like hours, whereas hours of sleep sometimes felt like minutes. At least a little time had elapsed, because when he'd dozed off, he'd been talking to Sully, who'd been seated at the end of the sofa. Now Sully was in the kitchen with Vera and Ralph, neither of whom had been around when he'd fallen asleep.

This was how far Robert Halsey had gotten in solving the riddle of how long he'd been asleep when he was presented with another riddle. Down the hall, the bathroom door was flung open so hard that it banged against the wall like a gunshot. A small naked boy, Robert Halsey's great-grandson, the one they called Wacker, the one he'd caught earlier that afternoon turning off the valve on his oxygen tank, bolted from the bathroom and ran hooting down the hall and clutching his tiny penis as if it were an emergency brake. In the kitchen doorway the boy skidded on the slick linoleum, where he paused, appearing to count the stunned house, taking in who was present, who absent, as well as the implications of these. Then he flung himself into the air, crashed down hard on his back and bounced along the floor like a tiny beached whale, his little stem spraying small blasts of urine into the air. Vera, who had been on her way over to the table with a pot of coffee, went into retreat, as if the spray her grandson were emitting might be sulfuric acid. "Ooooh!" she cried. "The little—" she searched here for the correct word, "—beast!"

It was then that the kitchen door opened and the boy's mother appeared, took in the situation at a glance and smiled unpleasantly at her husband, Peter, who had that moment emerged from the den, where the baby started to cry. Now ringed by speechless adults, Wacker continued to bump and hoot and squirt along the floor, impossible to ignore, impossible to take seriously.

Robert Halsey took all this in from the living room and made no attempt to get up from his chair. By his own calculations, seconded by numerous physicians, he had no more than three months to live, and he studied the cluster of humans in the next room with detached, almost clinical interest. Both sexes and the spectrum of ages were represented, and the old man managed to take in each person efficiently—his unhappy daughter, Vera, and her long-suffering husband, his crippled ex-son-in-law, Sully, the little boy's father, Peter, and his large, graceless, sad wife, and the boy himself, his great-grandson, little dick in hand, so full of life and energy. Robert Halsey took them all in, felt affection for one and all, but concluded then and there that even if his next breath of pure oxygen proved to be his last, he wouldn't trade places with any of these people, and so he closed his eyes and drifted back to sleep, riddles still unanswered, mysteries still unsolved.

When Wacker bolted from the bathroom, his brother Will closed the door behind him and locked it. He wasn't afraid of getting spanked. His father never spanked him hard. Nor was he afraid of the humiliation attendant upon what he'd done. His young life was full of embarrassment, all of which he shouldered with adult resignation. What he was afraid of was his little brother, who had made no promises of amnesty and who would not honor them if he had. Wacker was a boy without honor, a boy born to terrorize other boys, even bigger ones. Will was deeply afraid of Wacker's fearlessness, which, combined with the little boy's long memory, made him a formidable adversary. His parents understood none of this, Will knew. They were simply disgusted with Will's cowardice. "You're bigger than he is, for Christ sake," his father always said. "He's a half-pint. You're a full pint. Are you going to go through life tattling and running to Mommy and Daddy? It's"—his father took a while to locate the right word—"unnatural," he finally said.

In Will's opinion it was Wacker who was unnatural. It was unnatural the way his brother's eyes narrowed when he contemplated a new act of terror, the way those narrowed eyes focused on Will to let him know that once he'd perfected whatever he was concocting, Will would derive its full benefit. Also, Wacker's lack of fear was unnatural. He wasn't afraid of anything, even Grandpa Sully, who looked like a murderer on TV, all limping and grinning and covered with dirt. Will himself liked his grandfather, even though he knew he wasn't supposed to. Grandpa Sully had at least *tried* to scare Wacker yesterday, warning him not to whack his bad knee again. How was he to know that nothing scared Wacker, whose attack on Grandpa yesterday signaled to Will that his little brother had reached a new plateau of courage and malice? He had actually attacked and hurt a grown-up. That Wacker truly inflicted pain was one of the things Will had never been able to convince his father, who seemed to think Wacker was too small to really hurt anyone. Will knew better. Pain was Wacker's business. He gave it to you like a present. You'll like this, the expression on his face always said.

Until recently Wacker's favorite act of terror had been the twisting pinch, administered from behind. Wacker had learned somehow that the loose skin on the underside of the arm, just above the elbow, was especially tender, and he always waited until Will's back was turned before sneaking up and locking on with thumb and forefinger. Wacker was still perfecting the twist-pinch maneuver that sent Will high onto his tiptoes, howling in pain. The injuries that Wacker inflicted never had a chance to heal either, because he always returned to the same spot, where the broken blood vessels and flesh were still tender. And lately Wacker had shown indications of branching out. At the dinner table he'd catch Will's eye and show him the sharp tines of his fork.

Anymore, Will thought of little except keeping Wacker in front of him and in full view. He relaxed only when his brother was asleep. Each night Will remained awake in their room until he was sure Wacker was sleeping soundly, and his last waking thought was to remind himself that he must wake up before his brother. Wacker seemed aware of how much he occupied his older brother's thoughts and was proud to be his waking nightmare.

And so today Will had finally retaliated. Neither forgiveness nor negotiation nor sweeping policies of appeasement had the least effect on Wacker, and Will had come to suspect that his brother was permanently stuck in attack mode. Until recently Will had tried to do anything he could to avoid even greater cruelty. He now understood that there was no need to fear greater cruelty. If Wacker were capable of greater cruelty, he'd already be engaging in it. And so, this afternoon, when Will saw his opportunity, he'd seized it.

He'd been awaiting his turn at the commode, and Wacker was stalling as usual. The water running in the tub made Will have to go bad, and Wacker would not share Grandma Vera's tall, old-fashioned commode, which Wacker was just tall enough to pee over if he stood on his toes and rested his little penis on the cold porcelain. His trickle had stopped minutes before, but he refused to budge.

"Come *on*, Wacker," Will had whined. "I gotta *go*."

Wacker responded by grinning and releasing another spurt of urine into the commode to prove he wasn't done.

Will clutched himself. He knew from experience that this could go on a long time. His brother liked to "save it." He'd stop peeing, then start again, half a dozen times.

The toilet seat, Will noticed, was raised. Will stared at the seat, then at his brother, who emitted two short blasts of urine, like a signal in Morse code. It acted like a signal for Will, who, before he allowed himself to consider the consequences, let go of his penis, stepped around his brother, grabbed the upraised toilet seat and slammed it, hard.

Wacker had not been badly hurt. The bottom of the toilet seat was prevented from lying flat against the porcelain by four small rubber knobs that were of approximately the same thickness as Wacker's penis and which protected him from the full impact. He'd been startled mostly, and the tip of his penis tingled from the concussion. In the split second before he cried out, Wacker formulated a plan, and his eyes narrowed in that way that terrified his brother, and he'd bolted, bare-assed, from the bathroom to play the scene out, a strictly over-the-top performance, for the adults in the kitchen. Will watched through the keyhole while his father and Grandpa Ralph took turns examining Wacker's penis. Their evident concern for his brother's well-being caused Will's heart to sink. Didn't they understand anything? Didn't they know that Wacker couldn't *be* hurt?

When he couldn't stand to watch anymore, Will backed away from the door, realizing as he did so that he was standing in warm water. Grandma Vera's tub was finally full, the water a level sheet right at the top, like glass. He turned off the faucets then, understanding as he did so the full consequences of his rash act. By trying and failing to inflict pain upon Wacker, he had succeeded only in losing the sympathy and slender protection of the adults, all of whom now sided with Wacker. Neither his father nor his mother would protect Will now. By flooding the bathroom, he'd even lost the protection of Grandma Vera, who, he suspected, had been on his side. She alone had seemed to understand that Wacker was cruel and unnatural. Now even she would be on Wacker's side.

The way Will saw it, he had two options. One was to stay locked in Grandma Vera's bathroom for the rest of his life, the other to make a break for it. Maybe Grandpa Sully would take him. He recalled with fondness Grandpa Sully's fearlessness yesterday, and remembered how his grandfather had winked at him as they drove off, a wink that had conveyed an understanding.

When the bathroom door rattled and his father's angry voice ordered him to unlock the door, Will was already half dressed and fully resolved. Thankfully, he'd piled his clothes on top of the bathroom sink, and they were dry, whereas Wacker's were a soggy lump on the floor. His sneakers were a little wet, but he didn't care. By standing on the commode he was able to reach the lock on the small bathroom window. The screen was loose, the air outside cold, the ground a long way down, but Will's decision was made. He would find a new life.

The confusion reigning in his ex-wife's house reminded Sully of the confusion of war, the principal difference being that at Vera's it seemed no terribly dishonorable thing to slip out the back, which was what he did when the others converged on the bathroom door to cajole Will into opening it. Peter was the only one who'd noticed him go, and Sully had thought he saw his son smirk. Was it that knowing smirk or the chaos of Vera's family that he was fleeing? he wondered, turning his key in the ignition. Whichever. When he pulled away from the curb, he stomped the gas pedal hard and the truck roared up the quiet street at unsafe speed, taking the corner as if he feared pursuit. Only when he turned onto Main and stopped at the traffic light in front of the OTB did he feel relatively safe. At The Horse, in the company of relatively sane men, he'd feel even safer, and since this could not be brought about soon enough, he considered just driving on through the long red light he was sitting beneath. His was the only moving vehicle on the whole dark deserted street, which made obedience to the traffic signal seem even more ridiculous than usual, so he revved the engine, inched forward, did a quick scan of the street and checked the rearview for cops.

What he saw in the mirror so startled him that his foot slipped off the clutch, causing the truck to lurch forward and die beneath the traffic light. There in the mirror, for just a moment, like an ancient accusation, were the frightened eyes of his son. Not Peter the adult, whom he'd left at Vera's talking to the bathroom door, twisting the doorknob back and forth, but the boy he'd been so long ago. The plea in those eyes in the mirror had been so urgent, so real that Sully thought for a second that this must be another dream, like the sauna one, that he'd again fallen asleep in the truck. The light turned green, but Sully sat, stalled, the need to flee suddenly gone out of him. And then the eyes were there again, along with the apologetic smile of a stowaway.

"Hi, Grandpa," Will said when Sully got out of the truck, his voice as thin with fear as a voice could be.

Sully searched for his grandson's name, locating it finally. "You okay?" Sully said, lifting the boy out of the pickup's bed.

He'd hidden beneath an old swatch of burlap, daring to come out from under it only when the truck stopped at the traffic light. Then when it lurched, he'd lost his balance and hit his forehead against the cab.

Will seemed not to hear his grandfather's question. What had captured his attention was the lump magically growing on his forehead, just below the hairline. The lump didn't hurt, at least not like the hurts his brother inflicted, but it made him feel woozy and he was impressed by the way the lump had sprung magically into being, how it was still growing. He could tell it was growing as he fingered it. "I'm not going back," he finally told his grandfather. "Ever."

Sully nodded. "Who are you going to live with?"

Will sighed. "You, I guess." It seemed the only sensible thing, and he tried to conceal from his grandfather that he'd have preferred some other arrangement.

A car pulled up behind them at the traffic light, which had turned green for the second time. "Okay, get in then," Sully suggested, picking the boy up again, placing him inside the cab. "Slide over," he said when it became clear that the boy wouldn't do it unless specifically instructed. Peter had been the same way, an almost comatose kid, it had seemed to Sully. If you didn't tell him to open a door, he'd just stand in front of it. At the time it had not occurred to Sully that the reason might be fear. The fear of doing the wrong thing. It seemed obvious now.

When his grandson had made room, Sully climbed in after him, banging the door shut behind him, causing the boy to jump. How did he get to be such a bundle of nerves? Sully wondered.

"So," Sully said. "You got back at your brother, huh?"

Will shrugged, again reminding Sully of Peter, who as a boy had been almost impossible to engage in conversation.

When the driver behind Sully made the mistake of tooting, Sully got out of the truck and stared at him until the man shrugged sheepishly, backed up and pulled around, giving Sully wide berth. "Two cars in the whole street, and you've got to toot at me," Sully called as the man slid by into the intersection.

Will was studying him nervously when Sully got back in. "Dad does that too," he observed sadly, as if he'd discovered a genetic flaw.

"Does what?"

"Gets mad at people in cars," Will explained. "He doesn't get out, though."

Sully nodded. That sounded about right. His son seemed exactly this sort of man. Angry enough to yell, not angry enough to get out.

At a pretty nearly complete loss about what to do with his grandson, he said, "How about some ice cream?"

"We had dessert already," Will said.

Sully sighed. Vera did raise good citizens. Another boy who could not tell a lie. It was discouraging. "You had ice cream?"

"Pumpkin pie."

"With ice cream?"

"No."

"Then you can have the ice cream now. We'll pretend it was on top of the pie."

Will thought about this. He'd been warned about Grandpa Sully, who was irresponsible. Still, if he was going to live with his grandfather, he was going to have to get used to such things. He sighed. "Okay."

"Good," Sully said, turning the key in the ignition. Thank God, in fact.

They headed out of town, Will silently fingering the lump on his forehead. Almost as interesting as the lump was the fact that his grandfather's truck had a hole the size of a basketball in the floor beneath the passenger's seat.

"Don't fall through," Sully warned when he saw his grandson peering down through the hole at the racing pavement below.

When they got to the new spur and had it pretty much to themselves, Sully said, "You want to drive?"

Will looked at him fearfully.

"Slide over," Sully said, adding, "be careful of my bum knee."

Will settled carefully onto Sully's right leg, allowing his own small legs to dangle in the direction of the gas pedal and brake, careful not to let them bump his grandfather's left knee. Together they held the steering wheel.

"It's jiggling," Will observed, clearly unsure whether this vibration was natural.

"Trucks do," Sully explained. "Especially broken-down old trucks like Grandpa's."

"It's a nice truck," Will said, his voice vibrating from holding the wheel.

"I'm glad you like it," Sully said, taken aback by the little boy's compliment, and without planning to, he kissed his grandson on the top of his head. "Now you've driven a car. I bet you didn't know you could," he said, adding, "don't tell your mother."

Some phrases were truly magical in their ability to dredge up the past from the bottom of life's lake, and for Sully, like all errant fathers, "Don't tell your mother" was such a phrase. He hadn't used it in about thirty years. But the words were right there, anxious to be spoken again after so long, a holy incantation. It was the phrase he'd been born to speak, having learned the words from his own father, who, if they hadn't already existed, would have had to invent them. "We'll stop in here for just a minute," Big Jim had been fond of saying outside his favorite tavern, and Sully and his brother, Patrick, would wait a beat or two until his father pulled the heavy door toward them and pushed them gently into the cool darkness, warning as he did so, "Don't tell your mother." Inside, Sully and his brother were always bribed with nickels to play shuffleboard and pinball while Big Jim located a spot at the bar and ordered the first of many boilermakers, paid for with money he withheld from Sully's mother, whom he kept on a strict allowance, money Big Jim now kept in a careless pile on the bar to ensure his welcome. Sometimes, when Sully got tired of pinball (he had to stand on a wooden stool and even then couldn't reach the buttons comfortably) or ran out of nickels and joined his father at the bar, he'd stare at the pile of bills, aware that this was the same money his mother talked about so bitterly when his father wasn't around, money she'd have spent on food and clothes if she had it, so they could have decent things, she said. His father, already on his third boilermaker and getting mean, would see Sully staring at the money and cuff him a good one to get his attention. "Don't tell your mother," he'd say. "She don't have to have every last nickel I earn, does she?" And so Sully would promise, not wanting to get cuffed again because subsequent cuffs always got harder, not softer. Then Big Jim would order another boilermaker or toss a dollar off the top of the now diminishing pile at the bartender, who doubled as a bookie. "On his goddamn nose," Big Jim always instructed, having decided on a horse. To him, place and show bets were cowardly and he wanted no part of their measly payoff. "You hear me? Right on his goddamn nose."

Most of these afternoons had ended the same way, with Big Jim being told he'd have to leave, because the more he drank, the meaner he got, and it was only a matter of time before he'd start a fight. Sometimes one of the men in the bar would try to reason with him and head off hostilities. What did he want to go and behave like this for, in front of his boys? the man would ask. This tactic, which should have worked, was always a mistake. Big Jim Sullivan was not a man tortured by self-doubt, and of all the things he was certain of, he was most certain of his skill as a parent. When anyone offered even the slightest hint that he might be less than a model father, that person did well to duck, because Big Jim always defended himself in this matter with all of his pugilistic skills.

Unfortunately, after so many boilermakers, pugilistic skills were not Big Jim's strong suit. A lifelong believer in getting in the first punch, he never hesitated to throw it, or at least he never meant to hesitate. The trouble was that the roundhouse he always had in mind got telegraphed so far in advance of its arrival that Big Jim's adversary usually had ample opportunity to avoid the blow, and when the force of the big man's swing spun him around Big Jim usually found himself in a full Nelson and heading for the door someone was usually holding open for him. Finding himself seated outside, he always picked himself up with great dignity, got his bearings and lurched in the direction of home, having forgotten entirely that his sons had been with him when he entered the tavern.

One afternoon, still vivid in Sully's recollection, his father had tried to start a fight with a man who was not a regular and did not know the drill, that Sully's father was to be ejected without being injured. Perhaps, not being a regular, the man didn't know that Big Jim, drunk, wasn't nearly as dangerous as he looked, unless you happened to be married to him or were one of his children. Big Jim had focused on the man for some reason and had been insulting him for about half an hour, and when the man finally had enough and said so and Big Jim had taken his inevitable wild swing, the man had slipped the punch gracefully. As Big Jim stumbled forward under the impetus of his miss, instead of letting him go down, the man had caught him with a short, compact uppercut that not only broke Big Jim's nose but repositioned it on the side of his face. The force of the blow had the effect of righting Sully's father, restoring his magical drunk's equilibrium, and he didn't lose that equilibrium again until the man had hit him half a dozen more times, each blow more savage than the last. No one, not even the men who had been merciful to Sully's father in the past, intervened. Perhaps they too had had enough.

Finally, his face a mask of blood, Sully's father, reeling from the last of the blows that had been rained upon him, had simply let the last punch spin him toward the door and he stumbled on outside, as if he'd been meaning to leave for some time. He waited until the door closed behind him before going to his knees, vomiting onto the sidewalk and passing out. He lay where he fell for about ten minutes, time enough for a small crowd to gather and for someone to send for a doctor. Despite his brother's assurances that Big Jim was simply unconscious, Sully had thought his father was dead, didn't see how he could be anything but dead the way his one eye was swollen shut and his nose no longer occupied the center of his face. But before the doctor arrived, Big Jim snorted awake and got to his feet, to all appearances refreshed by his nap. And when he lurched in the direction of home, nobody tried to stop him. Sully and his brother, Patrick, had followed at what they considered a safe distance, but when they were a block from home Big Jim had sensed their presence, turned and grabbed his sons roughly by the collar and drew them up close to his ruined face, so close Sully could smell his father's blood and vomit. "Don't tell your mother," he warned.

Even after his divorce from Vera, Sully had remained convinced that he'd been a better father to Peter than Big Jim had been to him, though this, he had to admit, was not a lofty goal. It saddened him to realize he'd accomplished this intention by such a slender margin. Instead of abusing Peter, he'd ignored the boy, forgotten him for months at a stretch, a simple truth he now found difficult to credit though impossible to deny. The years had simply flown by, and Vera, with Ralph's help, had seemed more than competent in the business of providing whatever it was their son might need. Without ever saying so, Vera had often managed to convey to Sully that they were doing fine without him, which indeed they seemed to be. Ralph, she assured him, was a natural father, even if he wasn't *the* natural father, and Peter didn't lack for love or anything else. They were a family, she told him in a way that suggested to Sully that if he were to intrude upon them with his presence he would be endangering that family. And so he had found the excuse he needed to stay away, grateful, truth be told, for his freedom.

It had been Ralph, not Vera, who'd sought him out occasionally, told him he should stop by some time, see the boy, see how big he'd gotten since the last time, so big Sully'd hardly recognize him. Which was not true. Sully always recognized Peter by the odd, worried expression he had about the eyes, an expression he'd passed on to Will, who wore it, Sully thought, with more grace than Peter ever had. His few outings with his son had always been strained affairs, since Sully couldn't imagine what to say to a kid with a perpetual frown who always watched the speedometer and reported back to his mother how fast Sully had driven. They usually went somewhere where there'd be a crowd—a movie or an amusement park—so they'd seem less alone.

And, it was true, Sully was a menace as a parent. He never saw that it was a bad idea to feed the kid a corn dog and then take him on the Tilt-a-Whirl until the corn dog came back up and Sully was faced with the necessity of cleaning the boy up so he could be brought home. Sooner or later on each of their outings they ended up in some grungy men's room with Sully, wet paper towels in hand, trying to sponge the boy's sour vomit off the front of his shirt and pants and listening to himself say, in Big Jim Sullivan's voice, "Don't tell your mother, okay, sport?" Then they'd get back into the car and Sully would roll down all the windows and drive like hell in the hope that the wind would dry Peter's clothes by the time they got home.

Sometimes Peter had fallen asleep against him on the way home, and when they arrived back at Vera's, Sully would carry his son up the walk. The little boy's hair always smelled sweet and clean, the way Will's smelled now. It smelled, Sully had realized, like a good home, like cleanliness and decency and safety. Like the things Vera and Ralph had provided for Peter. And it was the reason he never went back to Vera's until the next time Ralph came looking for him.

At a twenty-four-hour restaurant just off the interstate ramp Sully ordered Will a dish of ice cream with a cherry on top. His own stomach was rumbling ominously, so he ordered just coffee for himself. "Extra caffeine," he told the waitress.

The girl who took the order was apparently too unhappy to be working on Thanksgiving to respond to humor. When the ice cream came, Sully used the pay phone at the front of the restaurant. Vera answered on the first ring.

"Hi," he said. "You missing anybody?"

"I knew it," his ex-wife said. "Where are you?"

"None of your business," he said. "And you couldn't have known it, because I just found out myself. He hid in the back of the truck."

From where he was standing in the phone booth, he could see his grandson fidgeting nervously. Finally, he got up on his knees so he could see over the back of the booth. When Sully waved, the boy smiled, clearly relieved to have located his grandfather.

"They're all out combing the neighborhood, Sully," she said, her voice still rich with accusation.

"Well, now they can stop," he said. "I'll have him home in half an hour."

The line was quiet for so long that Sully wondered if Vera had hung up and he'd missed the click. "You still there?"

"I don't know."

"You don't know if you're there?"

"Haven't you ever felt like that?"

"Like what?"

"Like you don't even exist?"

This was not the kind of conversation Sully wanted to be having with his ex-wife, whose capacity for self-pity was without limitation, in Sully's view. "Never," he said. "Not even once." He said this because it was true and because he wanted to make his lack of sympathy for her position clear.

"Lucky you," Vera told him and hung up.

When Will finished his ice cream, Sully showed him the cherrystone clam he'd discovered was still in his pocket while he was on the phone.

"It's a seashell," Will said, touching the clam where it lay in the center of the table.

"Right," Sully said. "Except there's something inside."

Will drew back his hand, reevaluated the clam.

Sully tapped it with the butt of his knife. The clam made a fizzing sound.

"Can it get out?"

"It's attached to the inside of the shell," Sully explained. "It doesn't want to get out."

"I would," Will said.

"Not if you were a clam. It's safe in there," Sully said. "You and your brother fight all the time?"

Will wasn't sure how to answer this question. In fact, they never fought, unless Wacker's terrorist attacks on himself constituted fighting. If those attacks were what Grandpa Sully meant by fighting, then they fought all the time. Will decided to split the difference. "Sometimes," he said.

"I used to fight with my brother, too," Sully told him.

"Not anymore?"

"He died in a car accident," Sully told him.

This information startled Will, who had stopped just short of wishing his brother dead for fear that it might come true and somebody would later find out about the wish.

"I'm going to live with Dad," Will blurted out his own wish and surprised himself in the process. What a strange day it had been. So far he'd retaliated against Wacker and driven a car, and now he'd told his grandfather a whopper. For about the last month, Will had begun to imagine a new and better life. His parents would divorce and he would live with his father. At first the idea had frightened him. He knew divorce was a terrible thing to hope for, but it wasn't as bad as wishing Wacker dead, which he was afraid he might do if he couldn't think of an alternative. So he'd settled on the divorce. He hated to lose his mother in the bargain, but there was no help for it. She had to go.

The best part of the divorce idea was that Will felt sure that with Wacker out of the picture he'd be able to demonstrate to his father that he was really a good boy, a boy worthy of great love, a boy who would never—or seldom—cause trouble. And once the family separated, his mother would soon realize that it had been Wacker who'd caused all the adversity all along. At present she seemed pretty confused. No matter what happened or who was to blame, she meted out equal punishment. She yelled at both boys, spanked both boys, sent both boys to their room. After the divorce, when Will was gone and trouble persisted, she'd call his father and the two would compare notes. She'd tell his father what a bad boy Wacker had been all week, and his father would say, "That's too bad. Will's been just perfect." Then it would dawn on them both.

Eventually they would get back together, Will always thought happily. Except everything would be different. They'd get a house, not an apartment. Each boy would have his own room, and his parents would take Will's advice and lock Wacker in his and slide all his meals under the door. They wouldn't let him out until Will was grown up and moved away. He'd make his parents promise not to tell Wacker where he lived. This was important, because when Wacker finally got out of that locked room he was going to be mad.

Will told Sully all of this. Once he started, it all came out, and the new fantasy life seemed even more real for having been voiced. If his grandfather saw any flaw in the plan, he didn't say so. Grandpa Sully just listened, for which Will was grateful. In his entire life no adult had ever just listened to him without offering all sorts of objections, all sorts of reasons why things weren't the way Will thought they were or thought they could be. As Will talked, uninterrupted, he gathered confidence and momentum. He described the house he and his father would live in, as well as the terrible punishments Wacker would have to endure once the jig was up. His grandfather's stunned silence was just the sort of validation he'd been hoping for. He'd never been happier. Ice cream had never tasted better. Usually, Will didn't care for the taste of food. Fear made it rise, sour, in his throat. But this ice cream tasted so good he licked the dish.

"You could come visit whenever you want," he told Sully, as if Wacker might be the reason his grandfather had, until now, stayed away.

"I will, too," Sully assured him, consulting his watch. The boy had been talking for half an hour, which made them overdue back at the house. "We better head back, don't you think?"

Will's face fell. "I'd rather live with you."

"If you lived with me, then I couldn't come visit," Sully pointed out. "Besides, if I stole you away from Mommy and Daddy, they'd put me in jail. Grandma Vera would see to it."

Will knew this was true. He didn't want to head back, but he didn't want Grandpa Sully to go to jail, either. Somehow, just talking with Grandpa Sully had made him feel braver. He wasn't quite so afraid of Wacker anymore. True, Wacker would get back at him for the toilet seat, but when it happened, Will would just think of all those years his brother would have to spend locked in his room.

At the register, Sully paid for the coffee and his grandson's ice cream. In the nearest booth somebody was eating a chicken-fried steak, which looked and smelled good. Sully's stomach had settled a little and he remembered he hadn't eaten all day. On the way out of the restaurant he considered calling Vera and telling them they were on their way, then decided not to. In ten minutes they'd be there in person.

And they would have been, too, if there'd been any gas in Sully's truck. There'd been over a quarter of a tank this morning, but most of that had idled away at the curb outside his ex-wife's house, and now the truck was bone dry, which Sully would have seen if he'd thought to look at the gas gauge on the way to the restaurant.

Fortunately, this time it was Ralph who answered the phone when Sully called, and fifteen minutes later when the Buick pulled into the restaurant parking lot, it was Ralph at the wheel. "Grandpa to the rescue," he chortled when Will ran to him. Ralph flushed then, realizing. "I kinda think of myself as their grandpa," he admitted to Sully.

"That's okay," Sully said. "It's the way I think of you, too."

"You better get in the car," Ralph told the boy. "You don't have no coat on."

This was true, though Sully hadn't noticed it. Will scrambled into the front seat and behind the wheel of Ralph's Buick. Ralph handed Sully the five-gallon gas can he was carrying. "How'd he get the bump on his head?" he asked somewhat conspiratorially, as if he knew he'd be required to explain when he got home.

Sully explained guiltily. Vera had always maintained that he was a dangerous man, and he knew what she'd say when the boy came home damaged. Ralph, on the other hand, seemed to understand that these things could happen.

"Hell," he said. "We didn't even know he was gone there for a while. Then we thought he'd run clean away. I was glad to hear he was with you."

"Vera wasn't."

"Well, you know her."

"Yes, I do. She's still convinced nobody loves her, I gather."

"She's having a rough day. Her dad being so sick and having all the company. She gets all twisted up inside."

"I should've known better than to come over," Sully said, affected by Ralph's generosity. "I did know better."

"Don't feel that way," Ralph said, genuinely hurt. "You're always welcome."

"Well, I sure appreciate your coming out," Sully said. "I must have idled away five gallons right outside your house."

Sully unscrewed the gas cap and inserted the can's retractable spout.

"Go ahead and put it all in," Ralph suggested. "I won't be mowing no more lawns for a while."

"You don't have a snowblower?"

Ralph shook his head sadly. "I gotta get one, though. I can't shovel since my colon. Damn near killed me this morning, and I waited until half of it melted. It's hell getting old, ain't it?"

When Sully was sure he'd put in enough gas to get back to town, he removed the spout and screwed the gas cap back on.

"Go ahead and use it all," Ralph said.

"This'll do fine," Sully said. "Thanks again."

"You want to come back to the house?" Ralph asked. "Things have settled down. You never even got no turkey."

"That's all right, I didn't come for turkey," Sully said. "What's the story with Peter and Charlotte?"

Ralph shrugged. "I never understand things," he admitted. "I don't know why people can't just get along."

"You don't?" Sully said. "How old are you?"

"It ain't that hard to get along," Ralph insisted. "Just treat people good and they treat you good, most of 'em, anyhow."

Sully nodded. "Except for the ones who don't. And except for the times you don't feel like treating other people good."

"I never mind treating people good," Ralph said.

"I know it," Sully conceded, "but you're the exception." He took out his cigarettes, offered one to Ralph, who, he sensed, was in no hurry to return. The air was mild and "God Rest Ye Merry, Gentlemen" was being piped into the parking lot.

Ralph refused the offered cigarette. "Vera made me give them up," he said. "Beer too, except when I sneak."

Sully lit a cigarette. "I won't tell."

Ralph grinned, shook his head. "I gotta admit I feel better," he said. "It was the doctor made me quit, actually. Vera just makes sure."

"She's a natural."

Ralph studied his shoes. "You really missed out, not spending your life with her," he said, much to his own and Sully's surprise.

"You could be right," Sully agreed, not so much because he thought so as because it was an oddly touching thing for Ralph to say, for one man to say to another about a woman they'd both been married to.

"I know she's bossy," Ralph admitted. "And she's not happy unless she's trying to change people. She's not mean, though."

"Vera was never mean," Sully agreed. "Just frustrated about not getting her own way."

"I guess they all want their own way."

"So do we," Sully pointed out.

Ralph thought about it. "Not me," he said finally. "I just like for people to all get along. I don't care whose way. What difference does it make, whose way?" Ralph wanted to know. Having admitted to letting Vera have hers, he would have liked to get Sully to agree about the wisdom of his practice.

Sully shrugged. "All day long people have been trying to get me to eat turkey. What I really feel like eating is a chicken-fried steak. Why shouldn't I eat one?"

Sully had chosen the example at random and unknowingly struck a nerve. Ralph was inordinately fond of fried foods and was no longer allowed to eat them. "They're bad for you," he pointed out weakly, aware that this particular argument wasn't likely to succeed with Sully.

"Suppose I want one anyhow?"

"Why would you want something you know's bad for you?"

"Good question," Sully admitted. "I always do, though." He put his cigarette out with his shoe by way of punctuation. "By the way," he added when they'd shaken hands. "I know a guy who might be getting rid of a snowblower cheap."

"How come?" Ralph wondered. After all, winter was about to descend on them in earnest.

"Moving to Florida," Sully lied.

"Won't need it there, will he?" Ralph said.

"If you're interested . . ." Sully said. "It's practically brand-new. I've used it myself."

"I don't know," Ralph said, looking away. "How much does he want for it?"

"I think I might end up with it for free," Sully said. "You could keep it over at your place and I could borrow it."

Clearly this made no sense at all to Ralph. Snowblowers cost a lot of money, and it wasn't like you couldn't sell a used one, especially this time of year. Ralph himself was always inclined to trust Sully, but this was by no means his wife's inclination. Vera would smell something wrong with this arrangement immediately and probably find a way to insult Sully for making the offer. "Sounds awful good," Ralph admitted sadly, like a little boy imparting bad news to a friend—my mom won't let me.

"I'll let you know how it works out," Sully promised, then nodded in the direction of the boy. "Don't be too surprised if he wants to drive home."

Ralph studied the boy, smiled. "I kinda wish I could be around to see him and his brothers grown up safe. I'd feel a lot better knowing they were okay."

"What makes you think you won't be?" Sully said.

Ralph apparently found encouragement in this question. "Maybe I will," he shrugged, his face brightening. "Hell, maybe we both will."

"Hold that thought," Sully suggested by way of good-bye, and the two men shook hands again before Sully went back inside. At the cigarette machine by the door Sully was able to watch Ralph back out cautiously and point the car back toward Bath, driving like a man who didn't intend to die in an accident. Sully caught just a glimpse of his grandson snuggled into Ralph's big body for safety.

The same girl who had waited on Sully and his grandson came over when he went back into the restaurant. "More coffee?" she said. She actually smiled.

"Okay," Sully agreed. "And a chicken-fried steak on the side."

She blinked. "You want a chicken-fried steak?"

"Right," he said.

"We got a special on turkey and stuffing," she said. "All the trimmings for six ninety-five."

"Terrific," Sully said. "I'll see if I'm still hungry after my chicken-fried steak."

The girl's smile disappeared. In her opinion there should have been a law against wise-asses on Thanksgiving.

Carl Roebuck's car was in the driveway, so Sully pulled in behind it. He looked around for the snowblower, but it wasn't in sight. Carl himself was seated at the kitchen table staring at a half-empty bottle of Jack Daniel's when Sully knocked and went in.

"You know," Carl looked up. "When we bought this house, the realtor swore people like you weren't even allowed in the neighborhood."

Sully pulled up a chair. "You must have misunderstood her," he said. "She probably said there were no niggers allowed."

"I've always considered you a nigger," Carl said. "You do nigger work for nigger wages. Niggers have higher aspirations, of course."

Sully lit a cigarette and blew smoke in Carl's direction by way of response. "I'd be happy if I could just get you to pay me my nigger wages. That's my only aspiration, in fact."

Carl inhaled Sully's smoke deeply. "Can I have one of those?"

Sully tossed him the pack. Carl pushed the bottle in Sully's direction.

"We'll drink right out of the bottle, like men," Carl said. "This'll be men's night here at Casa Roebuck. Glasses? We don't need no fucking glasses." He inhaled his own cigarette deeply. "You never go to the movies, do you?"

"Never," Sully said.

"You don't even own a VCR, I bet."

"Not even," Sully admitted.

Carl shook his head. "Sully, Sully, Sully. You're not an eighties guy."

"If I had a VCR, would I be happy like you?" Sully said.

"Not *as* happy, probably," Carl said. He took a swig from the bottle Sully hadn't touched, then set it back down. He laughed suddenly and let his head loll back so he could look at the ceiling and ran his fingers through his hair. "Fuck me," he said. He sounded absolutely exhausted.

"Exactly which of your doctor's instructions are you following these days," Sully inquired.

"All of them," Carl said to the ceiling. "Every one."

"He advised you to drink and smoke and screw your brains loose?"

"Except those," Carl grinned drunkenly. "Those were unreasonable requests. He wouldn't have made them in the first place had he known me."

"If he knew you, he wouldn't have resuscitated you. Where's Toby?"

"Toby who?"

Sully let the question hang.

"Around someplace. She wouldn't want to join us for men's night." Carl Roebuck studied him drunkenly. "God, I hope I don't end up like you."

Sully nodded. "I hope you don't either," he said agreeably.

Carl shook his head. "Sixty years old and still getting schoolboy crushes. By the time I'm your age, I hope to be smart."

"Well, it can't hurt to hope," Sully said. "You're off to a slow start, though, if getting smart is your goal."

Carl ran his hands through his hair. "That's my wife's position," he admitted. "She's displeased with me at the moment, even though I took your advice this morning and went home. Problem was, I got laid twice on the way. Then I made the mistake of telling her about it and asking her forgiveness. I think I may have ruined her Thanksgiving."

"You can sleep on the couch again if you want," Sully said. He got up, stubbed his cigarette out in the sink, washed the ashes down the drain.

"That's the worst couch in Bath," Carl said. "I had nightmares on that couch." He took out his wallet, extracted a wad of bills and tossed them in front of Sully. "Buy yourself a new fucking couch. You can't expect houseguests to sleep on a couch that gives them nightmares."

Sully fanned the notes with his pinky. There looked to be roughly a thousand dollars. "I'll come by tomorrow," he said. "You can pay me then."

"Take it now," Carl advised. "When my wife divorces me I won't be able to pay attention. This is your chance. Take whatever the fuck you think I owe you."

"Don't worry," Sully said. "I'll get what you owe me. I'll get it when you're sober, too. That way you'll be good and pissed off."

Carl shook his head. "You do nigger work for nigger wages, but you got a white man's scruples. No wonder you don't have a VCR."

"Or a snowblower."

Carl howled, his face turning beet red with delight. "I'll tell you the God's honest truth. The only fun I had all day today was stealing back my own fucking snowblower."

"Well," Sully got up. "You go ahead and keep it till it snows again. Next time screw the railing back down, at least. My landlady falls, and she'll own C. I. Roebuck."

"She can have it," he said. "If they don't start on that fun park, I won't be able to give it away." Then he thought of something. "I didn't tell that nosy fucker anything, by the way."

Sully stopped at the door. "Who?"

"That guy this morning."

"What guy, for Christ sake?"

"The guy who came into the office right after you left."

Sully remembered the man in the dark sedan who'd said he had an imperfect understanding of the situation. "Little guy?" Sully said. "All dressed up?"

"The very one."

"He was parked down front," Sully told him. "I threw a snowball at him. He seemed unhappy I noticed he was there. I figured some angry husband hired him."

"He wanted to know if you worked for me. I told him no. Which reminds me. I might have something for you and your dwarf tomorrow," he said. "Stop by the office."

"Okay," Sully agreed. "Why don't you go to bed?"

"Because I'm not tired."

"You're exhausted. You should see yourself."

"I may be exhausted," Carl conceded. "But I'm not tired."

Toby Roebuck was sitting quietly in the truck when Sully got in. The truck's dome light didn't work, and the glowing tip of her cigarette was the only testimony to her presence.

"God, you're a jumpy man," she said.

She had, in fact, startled him. "I wasn't expecting you," he said.

She looked at him. "There must be a lot of surprises in your life, Sully."

This was true, and Sully didn't deny it. Today had been a pretty surprising day, start to finish. "How come you let him back in?"

"I didn't," she said. "I think Horace gave him a key, the dirty, double-crossing snake. Carl was there when I got back from Schuyler."

This reference jogged Sully's memory. "I hate to be the one to tell you this, but there's a rumor circulating about you."

"Really!" Toby clapped her hands in mock excitement. "How exciting! Do tell."

"You've got a boyfriend in Schuyler."

Toby studied him seriously for long enough to make him squirm, then broke into laughter. "Poor Sully," she said when she was finished. "You are a hoot."

As was almost always the case with women, Sully suddenly felt himself to be on the fringes of the conversation. "Hey, I didn't make it up," he insisted. "In fact, I told the guy I didn't believe it."

This set Toby Roebuck off again, though she stifled her hilarity more quickly this time. "You really are a sweet man," she said, striving for seriousness.

"It's true," Sully grinned at her. "I just wish more women realized it."

Inside the house, Carl had come over to the window and was peering out, scout fashion, into the drive where they sat. Sully doubted he could see anything but his own reflection. He started the truck, realizing that not hearing it might have been what had brought Carl to the window. "Maybe you shouldn't stay here tonight," he said. "He's in pretty rough shape."

She noticed his glance and followed it. "I can't take much more of this," she admitted. "Look at him."

Carl, still shading his eyes, was right up against the window. He looked unsteady, like he might tumble through the glass.

"Go away for a while," he suggested. "I'll keep an eye on him."

The suggestion brought a smile. "That's a funny idea. You looking after anybody."

"Why?"

"Oh, Sully, don't go getting your feelings hurt. I know you'd mean to. After about two minutes you'd get sidetracked and forget, and you wouldn't think of him again until about two weeks after the funeral. You'd be walking down the street and wondering why you hadn't seen him around."

Carl had stepped back and gone to the foot of the stairs, his back to the window.

"By the way, where'd he hide the snowblower?"

"Out at the yard," she confided. "In the shed."

"All right," he said. "I'll steal it back tomorrow or the next day."

"Careful of that mean-ass dog."

"I'm not worried about the dog," Sully said. "I'm trying to figure how I'm going to scale the fence."

"You're a man among men, Sully."

"Thanks," he said.

"It wasn't a compliment," she assured him.

"You don't have to get all dressed up to come in here," Tiny said when Sully, clean-shaven and dressed as he'd been for his visit to Vera's, came in and took a seat at the end of the bar. The shirt was a gift from Ruth, given to him months earlier, and this was the first time he'd worn it. He'd put it on right out of its plastic wrapping. The shirt's creases still conformed more to its cardboard packaging than to Sully's torso. The pinholes had still not closed, in fact.

A college football game on the television above the bar occupied the attention of the dozen or so men who'd escaped their families late on Thanksgiving afternoon. The holiday had begun too early with the Macy's parade, and they hadn't been able to enjoy the afternoon football with all the holiday commotion. At The Horse they hoped to watch the second game in peace.

"I always like to look spiffy when I know you're tending bar," Sully said. Tiny appeared to be in a better mood, and Sully knew they would not renew last night's quarrel until later in the evening. For the next few hours both would pretend they were not going to renew it at all, a notion they would surrender only when the quarrel was actually under way. "Where's your best customer?"

Tiny consulted his watch. "Should be along any minute," he said. "You're popular today. I been open all of an hour and already you've had a phone call and a delivery." Tiny produced a foil-covered plate from underneath the bar. "Smells like turkey."

Sully peered beneath the foil. Turkey, stuffing, squash, cranberry sauce. Still warm. He examined both sides of the foil. "No return address."

"Your ex," Tiny said. "What's-his-face brought it. The mailman."

"Ralph?"

"He said you missed dinner."

"I just finished eating, actually. Who phoned?" he asked, expecting it to be Ruth, who wouldn't leave her name, of course.

"Somebody about a job." Tiny had scribbled a note, which he handed to Sully. The note contained a phone number and a man's name: Miles Anderson.

Sully frowned. "Who the fuck is Miles Anderson?"

"Never heard of him," Tiny admitted. "Said he just bought a house here in town. Needs some work done on it. Another asshole yuppie, probably."

"The woods are full of them, all right," Sully admitted. "At least they've got money."

"That's what makes them yuppies," Tiny said. "Otherwise they'd just be assholes."

"I wish I could stay busy just working for people I admire," Sully said.

He was on his second beer and still chatting amiably with Tiny when Wirf slid stiff-legged onto the stool next to him. "Nice to see all my loved ones are on speaking terms again," he observed. "What's that?" he said, pointing at the foil-covered dish at Sully's elbow. "It smells like food."

"No dinner, huh?" Sully said.

"I had dinner with you," Wirf reminded him. "Remember?"

"That was yesterday," Sully pointed out.

"Oh." Wirf grinned. "You meant today?"

"Stick this in the microwave, will you?" Sully said, pushing the plate in Tiny's direction.

Tiny did as he was told, a shade unhappily, it seemed to Sully.

"He'll be bellyaching about that before the night's over," Sully predicted.

"He'd rather sell me half a dozen pickled eggs over the course of the evening," Wirf said. "And who can blame him?"

"I'll be able to after another beer or two."

The microwave chirped and Tiny returned with the plate of turkey and stuffing, steaming now. Several men watching the football game placed orders for the same.

"See the trouble you cause?" Tiny said.

Wirf dove into the food hungrily.

"I don't think I can watch this," Sully said, wondering how a man could get a degree in law without picking up some rudimentary table manners. Wirf forked with his left, knifed with his right, put neither utensil down until they were no longer of practical use.

Sully went across the room and dialed the number on the slip of paper Tiny had given him.

"Adirondack."

"What?"

"Adirondack Motel."

"You got a Miles Anderson staying there?"

"Why don't I check."

"Why don't you."

After a moment: "Miles Anderson."

"This is Don Sullivan."

"Who?"

"Okay, good-bye."

"Oh . . . right . . . Mr. Sullivan. Sorry. Listen. I just purchased a house here in town. On Upper Main. You know where that is?"

"I've heard of it," Sully said.

"Ah." Miles Anderson hesitated. "That's a joke, I'll bet."

"I live on Upper Main," Sully confessed.

"You do?" Incredulity.

"Which house did you buy?"

"The one across the street from the Sans Merci."

"Souci."

"Right," Miles Anderson said. "I knew it was without something. I must have been thinking of Keats."

"Must have been," Sully said. "That's a big house, Mr. Anderson." He'd located the house, the largest on Upper Main, in his mind.

"The plan is to convert it into a B-and-B," Miles Anderson confided.

"Okay, I'll bite," Sully said. "What's a B-and-B, besides brandy?"

"Bed-and-breakfast," Anderson explained. "Surely you've heard of bed-and-breakfasts?"

"Never."

"They're the rage."

"Okay," Sully said agreeably.

A good pause. "Anyway, the place is in, shall we say, imperfect condition. In fact, the whole place needs sprucing up."

"Sprucing?" Sully said.

"A little of everything, I fear. Painting. Lots of painting. Plumbing. Electrical. Insulation. Also yard work. Two tree stumps that need digging up and carting off. There's time, though. I won't actually need to take possession until spring. Mid-May, in all likelihood. The plan is to open in August for the racing season."

"I don't do electrical work," Sully said. "I can recommend someone though."

"Yes . . . well . . . that might work, mightn't it?"

"It might," Sully said. In fact, he was calculating in his head just how well. A winter's worth of work, done at his own pace, when his knee permitted. Good timing, too. After the ground froze, Carl Roebuck would have little for him until late April.

"I understand you own a truck?" Miles Anderson said.

"Most days."

"You own it most days?"

"I own it every day. It runs most days."

"I see. Yes. Well, what else can I tell you? It's going to be strenuous work, I fear."

Since Miles Anderson made that sound like a question, Sully answered it. "I'm used to strenuous work."

"Hmmm. Yes. Well. All right then. Listen, I hope you don't mind my asking how old you are?"

"I'm sixty," Sully told him. "How old are you?"

"Touché. I wonder. Would you be willing to drop by sometime tomorrow morning and see the place? Give me an estimate? I have to be back to the city in the afternoon."

"Which city?"

"New York City. I wonder. Did your hourly rate just go up?"

"No," Sully said. His hourly rate had gone up when Miles Anderson had used the phrase "mightn't it."

They agreed that Sully would meet him at the house at eleven. Sully took down the address. "I live about two blocks from there," he said.

"Indeed," Miles Anderson said, his voice rich with indifference.

"Who recommended me, by the way?" Sully thought to ask before hanging up.

"Several people," Miles Anderson said. "You have an excellent local reputation."

Sully hung up. He'd considered asking Miles Anderson if he had any objection to paying him under the table, but decided that part of the negotiation could wait. Miles Anderson didn't sound like a man who'd be hung up on an ethical matter.

Wirf was nearly finished with Sully's dinner when he returned. "I just talked to a man who said I had an excellent reputation," he told Wirf.

Wirf wiped a patch of glistening gravy from his chin with a cocktail napkin. "Out-of-towner, huh?"

"New York," Sully said.

"Big job?"

"All winter, sounds like."

"He'll pay you under the table?"

"I didn't mention it yet, but I will."

"Good, no records. They catch you working, we're kaput." Wirf said, then added, "Hey, I got a hell of an idea. Let's you and me sit right here and drink beer all night."

"Okay," Sully agreed, deciding not to mention the man in the dark sedan or the fact that he might already have been caught. In fact, he half hoped he had been caught. Then the die would be cast. Right this minute, he felt good. His knee was murmuring but not singing. Could it be things were looking up? Had he yanked himself out of his stupid streak in record time? It was a possibility worth contemplating. "Maybe if we stay right here long enough that deadbeat bartender will buy a round."

FRIDAY

C live Jr. sat across the breakfast table from his mother, trying to match the splinters of the demolished Queen Anne chair, which sat in an impressive pile at his feet. His mother was fully dressed and so utterly alert that Clive Jr. understood her to be furious. Still furious. Her lips were drawn into the same thin white scar that had frightened him as a boy and, truth be told, frightened him still. The irony of his being frightened of his mother was not lost on Clive Jr., who weighed, the last time he checked, just over two hundred and twenty pounds—too much, he admitted, for a man five-ten, but easily dismissable as genetic. These last ten years, he had come to bear an uncanny resemblance to his father, Clive Sr. Miss Beryl, all four foot ten of her, Clive Jr. estimated to weigh in at about ninety pounds fully dressed, as she was now, at six-thirty in the morning the day after Thanksgiving, the morning after he'd made what Clive Jr. now understood to have been a tactical error of sizable dimension. "Ma," he said, setting down the two splintered pieces of wood that didn't want to match. He kept his voice low, so as not to awaken his fiancée. "I'm sorry."

Miss Beryl glanced up from the teabag she was dunking angrily in her cup of steaming water. "Why?" she said, purposely misunderstanding, he was certain. "You're not the one who broke it."

"I'm not talking about the chair," he said, though he again picked up and examined the larger of the two pieces of fractured wood. "I thought you'd be thrilled," he explained, though this was not true. "I guess I shouldn't have surprised you."

Miss Beryl studied her son and relented a little, he looked so miserable. He was sleepy-eyed and unshaven and he'd rushed over first thing in the morning, displaying more courage than she was accustomed to expect. He'd even brought with him a copy of *The Torch,* his high school yearbook, which contained a picture of the Joyce woman, as if to prove that she was who he said she was. "I used to enjoy surprises more, back when nothing surprised me," she admitted.

Indeed, Miss Beryl had spent the majority of her sleepless night trying to decide whom she was most furious with—Clive, Jr. (the obvious choice) or the dreadful Joyce woman now asleep in the guest bedroom, or herself. In retrospect, Miss Beryl was deeply ashamed of yesterday's disorientation, of the way she'd allowed a simple situation to throw her. Her son had explained twice who the woman squirming uncomfortably in Miss Beryl's Queen Anne chair was, but Miss Beryl's confusion had been a black hole, dense and resistant to illumination.

A little over a year ago she'd reluctantly agreed to let him have a key to the back door. "If there was ever an emergency . . . ," he'd explained, allowing his voice to trail off meaningfully. And so, when his car had been parked at the curb yesterday afternoon, she'd been prepared to find Clive Jr. himself pacing in her living room, going over everything in the house with his appraiser's eye, something he could do openly only when she was gone. Either that or snooping around Sully's flat upstairs, assessing the damages.

But who was this too carefully dressed, bosomy woman, her hands nervously aflutter as she sat, her thick knees and anklebones touching, as she waited to be introduced? Miss Beryl immediately pegged her as some kind of social worker, or perhaps the proprietress of a nursing home. Clive Jr. had more than once alluded to the eventual necessity of her moving into "a nice safe environment when the time came," and even offered to "screen some of the literature" for her, an offer Miss Beryl had emphatically declined. She'd been indulging a great many suspicions about Clive Jr. of late, and so, when she saw that Clive Jr. was accompanied by a nervous, rather prim-looking woman of advanced middle age, she concluded that, in her son's view at least, the time had come.

This erroneous conclusion, having gotten lodged in Miss Beryl's brain, she'd been unable to *dis*lodge, despite her son's careful, labored introduction. Much to her eventual embarrassment, Miss Beryl had continued to glare menacingly at the increasingly agitated woman. "My *fian-cée*, Ma," Clive Jr. kept repeating, but the word refused to compute. Why would Clive Jr. be engaged to a social worker? Miss Beryl had given up on her son marrying years ago, and now she was being asked to believe this absurd coincidence—that he was going to marry some nursing-home proprietress. Only later was she able to sort it out, that this woman's connection to social work and nursing homes had existed only in her own imagination.

And so, this morning, Miss Beryl was still furious with Clive Jr., and with the dreadful Joyce woman, but during the long sleepless night she'd also begun to entertain again the terrible possibility that the time *had* come, that she no longer had any business living alone. She was no longer safe on the interstate. She got confused going places she'd been to a hundred times before. She was becoming suspicious and paranoid. Miss Beryl had always believed that she herself would know "when the time came" for her to give up her independence. But what if she didn't? What if everybody else knew already? Miss Beryl, who had always suffered the cruelty of her eighth-graders' jokes, had no desire to become a legitimate figure of fun for these same children, now age forty.

And so, just before dawn she'd made up her mind to apologize to both her son and his fiancée, a resolution she began to entertain second thoughts about at first light. These seconds thoughts had evolved into reluctance by the time the sky outside her bedroom window had become white. Clive Jr.'s appearance, before she'd even made her tea, put the resolution to rout. Now, watching him ineffectually trying to match the splintered pieces of the Queen Anne had the effect of causing her to wonder what had possessed her to even consider yielding territory to her son.

"Joyce feels terrible about the chair, Ma," Clive Jr. said, as if he suspected her decision to tough things out.

Actually, Miss Beryl had mixed feelings about the Queen Anne. The chair's destruction afforded her the opportunity to continue her instinctive dislike for Clive's fiancée, who was mouthy and full of silly opinions about subjects of which she was wholly ignorant, the length and breadth of which had been discussed during the course of what had been for Miss Beryl one of the longest evenings of her life. Among the dreadful Joyce woman's devotions was the president, newly elected to a second term. Having *lived* in California, the Joyce woman said, of course she *knew* Mr. Reagan far better than non-Californians. She had cam*paigned* for him there and, of course, again here in New York when he ran for president. Fixing Miss Beryl rather unpleasantly with her doughy eyes, the Joyce woman had stated, without apparent irony, that the *only* thing that concerned her was the president's age, a man that old, doing a job which *aged* you so. "He seems so *tired*," the Joyce woman said seriously, as if she had a personal relationship with the president, feared not just for the office, but for the man, "but I truly think he's sharp as ever."

"So do I." Miss Beryl had fixed her savagely and excused herself from the room under the pretext of scrounging up a plate of cookies and some coffee.

"Decaf?" the Joyce woman had pealed. "Oh, I'd *love* some decaf."

Clive Jr., who'd lapsed into comatose silence during the Joyce woman's soliloquy, followed Miss Beryl into the kitchen. "I wish you'd quit glaring as if you meant to murder her," he complained.

"I can't help it," she told him. "I have what's called an open face."

Handing her son the plate of cookies, Miss Beryl shooed him out of the kitchen, then searched out the instant coffee in a remote cupboard. It took her a few minutes to boil the water, arrange the coffee cups on a tray, compose herself and return to the living room, where the Joyce woman was brushing cookie crumbs from her ample bosom. The plate was empty.

"Mmmm," the woman cooed when she sipped her coffee. "I'm sorry to be such trouble, but *honestly*, if I have caffeinated after five, I'm up *all night long*!"

And then she was off again, explaining how she had always *adored* coffee, had always drunk twenty cups a day and never had problems until recently. But now, *lord*, it was simply *tragic* what coffee did to her. There was no other *word* for it besides tragic, but wasn't that the way with all the good things, the things you *really loved*. Everything good was either immoral or fattening, she added, apropos of nothing, and then cackled as if the cleverness of this observation were attributable to herself.

While the woman talked, Miss Beryl sank comfortably into her seat and tried not to glare, taking what solace there was in the fact that the coffee she'd given her guest was not decaf. Slender consolation, since the fool woman was probably as wrong about caffeine as she was about everything else. Thinking she'd drunk decaf, she'd sleep like the dead, like the president she admired, all three of their shared ideas rattling around in their otherwise empty heads, unassailed by doubt or caffeine.

In this, it turned out, Miss Beryl had been wrong. She'd heard the dreadful Joyce woman get up to use the bathroom at midnight, then again at two, and finally at four-thirty. Each time, Miss Beryl had muttered "Good!" in the dark.

One of the other things she'd been slow on the uptake about was that Clive Jr. had planned for the Joyce woman to spend the night in the spare bedroom rather than return to Lake George, where she lived. Even after she caught her son's drift, she wasn't sure what his intention meant, or was supposed to mean. Was it simply Clive Jr.'s plan for the two women to get to know each other? Or were Clive Jr. and his fiancée trying to reassure her that they were not sleeping together? Was this propriety for show or for real? Poor Clive Jr., either way, Miss Beryl thought.

When the Queen Anne buckled, the two brittle back legs had splintered lengthwise and it was a matter of great good fortune, Miss Beryl supposed, that the Joyce woman had not been impaled. As it was, she'd hit the floor hard enough to shake the walls. Driver Ed had come crashing down from his wall, denting his chin, which made him look even more dour and disapproving. Also a little like Kirk Douglas. The look that had come over the Joyce woman's face, more of mortification than pain, had been horrible. She'd looked at Clive Jr. as if he'd played a practical joke on her by seating her, or allowing her to be seated, on a trick chair. Her bottom lip had begun to quiver and then her whole face came apart in the kind of grief that Miss Beryl associated with the sudden, violent loss of a loved one, not a momentary loss of dignity. Clive Jr. had ushered her, choking and sobbing, into the bathroom, where she stayed for nearly half an hour. In the living room, Clive Jr. and Miss Beryl had spoken in whispers, each pretending to ignore the ebb and flow of sorrow on the other side of the bathroom door.

"Joyce's emotions are very near the surface," Clive Jr. had explained as he gathered up the pieces of the Queen Anne. "Menopause devastated her."

Miss Beryl had narrowed her eyes at this observation, so clearly out of character for Clive Jr., whom she'd never known to see anything from a woman's point of view. No doubt he was repeating the Joyce woman's own explanation for her emotional instability. Miss Beryl herself was not particularly sympathetic to the "devastations" supposedly wrought by menopause, a condition she herself had weathered with good grace. She'd observed that women who were "devastated by menopause" were often vain creatures to begin with. They'd spent their young lives trading on their looks, knowing, in fact, no other currency.

This Joyce woman had been attractive all right, at least to judge from her yearbook photo. It had occurred to Miss Beryl this morning when she'd studied the pretty girl in *The Torch,* that in a way the Joyce woman who had whimpered for half an hour in the bathroom *was* grieving the loss of a loved one—the self she had been when she was flush with the currency of youth. And Miss Beryl was unable to decide whether it was appropriate to sympathize with such a person. She was inclined not to. It had been within her power to comfort the Joyce woman by telling her, once she returned from the bathroom, that the chair's destruction was not so much her fault as Sully's, whose squirming into his work boots every morning had no doubt readied the chair for its final collapse. But every time Miss Beryl had been about to make this gesture, the Joyce woman had said something disagreeable, and finally Miss Beryl had decided to let her suffer.

When she'd finally returned to their company in the living room, the Joyce woman's mood had swung dramatically. She'd become heroically yakky, as if only a steady stream of pointless, breathless, one-sided conversation could ensure that Clive Jr. and Miss Beryl would be prevented from inquiring after her health, physical and emotional. Miss Beryl wondered if she'd popped a pill. The Joyce woman made no mention of the broken chair, refused, in fact, to glance in its direction.

"She's really a wonderful girl, Ma," Clive Jr. now insisted with uncharacteristic sincerity. "She wasn't herself yesterday."

"Who was she?" Miss Beryl said, an unkind question perhaps, though not as unkind as the other that occurred to her: "What girl?" The woman had to be in her late fifties.

Clive Jr. looked at his hands. "You're always hard on people, Ma."

Miss Beryl had to concede that this was probably true. Clive Sr. had pointed it out to her more than once, and Mrs. Gruber was of the same opinion. So had been her legion of eighth-graders, whose mediocre efforts she'd rewarded with mediocre grades. "I wasn't aware of being mean to her," she told Clive Jr., "but if I was, I'm sorry. It's not my opinion of her that matters anyway. I'm not the one who's going to marry her. You're the one that's got to like her."

"Well, I do," Clive Jr. insisted, that same stubborn quality to his voice that he'd had as a child. "I love her," he added. He'd set the splintered sticks he'd been trying to match on the floor with the remains of the crippled chair and taken back from her the yearbook, the ribbed surface of which he massaged affectionately with his pink thumb, a gesture so pathetic that Miss Beryl felt herself soften toward him.

Getting up from the table, she gathered her teacup and saucer. "I'm glad for you," she said. "There are worse things than love. Give me a minute and I'll think of one."

She'd meant this remark as a joke, but it had come out with such conviction it had startled her. Why had she said such a thing? She had no doubt that if Audrey Peach had not put Clive Sr. through the windshield of the driver ed car, they'd still be happily married, that Clive Sr.'s surprising love for her would still be the centerpiece of her life, even as its memory was now. She could think of no reason for this sudden regret about having loved and been loved.

Clive Jr. cocked his head. "I think I hear her," he said.

Miss Beryl shook her head and pointed at the ceiling with her thumb. What Clive Jr. had heard was the thud of Sully's heavy feet hitting the floor upstairs. For the last ten minutes she'd been vaguely aware of the buzzing of Sully's alarm, not quite so audible to her in the kitchen as it was in her front room. On Clive Jr. the sound had apparently not registered at all, which allowed Miss Beryl to indulge an inward smile. Her faculties, or at least one of them, were intact.

When Clive Jr. looked at the ceiling, his face clouded over, and together they listened to Sully's footfalls traverse the ceiling and into the upstairs bathroom. Which meant they were about to resume an old discussion.

"Have you given anymore thought to . . . things?" Clive Jr. said. "I know you don't like the idea, but you should sell me the house while you still can."

"You're right," she told him. "I don't like the idea."

"Ma," he said. "Let me explain something. If you got sick tomorrow and you had to go into the hospital, they wouldn't *let* you sell it. The law wouldn't allow it. You have to sell before you get sick. They don't let you sell to avoid loss."

"What happens if I sell it to you and *you* get sick tomorrow?"

Clive Jr. massaged his temples. "Ma," he said. "You have to play the odds."

Miss Beryl sighed. She knew the odds. She didn't need to be lectured about the odds. She just hated conceding arguments to Clive Jr., who was, as a general rule, easily vanquished in debate. "I'll take the matter under advisement," she promised, hoping this would satisfy her son for the moment.

"What about upstairs, at least?" he said, his voice confidential now, as if he suspected that Sully might somehow be eavesdropping on their conversation, ear to the radiator. Clive Jr. always referred to Sully as "upstairs," just as Sully always referred to Clive Jr. as "The Bank." "The first of the year would be a perfect opportunity for a new arrangement."

"I'm content with the old arrangement," Miss Beryl said.

"You promised—"

"I promised to think about it," Miss Beryl reminded him.

"Ma," Clive Jr. said. "Keeping the house is dangerous enough, but Sully has to go."

Right on cue, the upstairs toilet flushed. Miss Beryl smiled, grudgingly, and was ashamed of herself again.

"You need another sign?" Clive Jr. was also smiling, smug again. "Even God agrees."

"That wasn't God on the commode," Miss Beryl reminded him. "Just a lonely, stubborn, unlucky man."

"Whose bad luck is going to rub off on you someday," Clive Jr. insisted.

Miss Beryl sighed. Like most discussions with her son, this one always went exactly the same way. Next Clive Jr. would remind her that Sully had once burned down another house he was living in.

"He's already burned down one house in Bath," Clive Jr. recalled innocently. "You should see it upstairs. There are cigarette burns everywhere. Fresh ones, Ma."

Here, so soon after the last, was another point Miss Beryl had to concede. Sully did smoke, did forget lighted cigarettes, letting them tip off ashtrays onto the floor and roll under the sofa, probably even smoked himself to sleep. Clive Jr. swore he'd seen brown cigarette holes in Sully's pillowcases.

"Don't believe me, Ma," Clive Jr. insisted. "See for yourself. Go up and see the condition of that flat. Count the cigarette burns. See for yourself how many bullets you've dodged."

The last thing Miss Beryl wanted to do was visit Sully's flat. No doubt what Clive Jr. was reporting would be true. Perhaps not even exaggerated. Sully *was* negligent and therefore dangerous. She wasn't sure there was any way to explain to Clive Jr. that having Sully upstairs was simply a risk she was willing to take. Maybe she couldn't even explain to herself why she was willing to take it. Part of it was that she'd always viewed Sully as an ally, someone whose loyalty, at least, could always be depended upon. She still thought of him this way, even now that he was getting older and more banged up and forgetful. Even now that he reminded her more of a ghost every day, he struck her as a dependable spirit, despite the conventional wisdom that what he could be depended upon to do most was to bollix things up. Resisting Clive Jr. on this issue, Miss Beryl had to admit, was surely bad judgment on her part, yet she couldn't banish the notion that evicting Sully would constitute a great treachery, a violation that would both surprise and wound him. And, irrational or not, she couldn't help feeling that her own death, which could not be *that* far off, would not be the result of Sully's bollixing.

"I could do the whole thing if you don't want to," Clive Jr. offered, adding weakly, "I can handle Sully."

Miss Beryl couldn't help smiling at this assertion, and her son's face darkened, registering the insult.

"He's got you snookered, Ma," Clive Jr. said angrily. "He always did. Even Dad saw that by the end."

"Let's leave your father out of it," Miss Beryl suggested.

Clive Jr. smiled, apparently aware that this missile had located its target. He'd successfully invoked his father before, knew his mother could be approached through Clive Sr.'s memory.

"I just wish you'd trust me," he continued after a long silence, his eyes no longer focused on her, but on something else, close enough, almost, to touch. "This time next year, Ma, you aren't even going to believe this town. The Gold Coast is what it's going to be. Once they break ground on The Escape . . ." he allowed his voice to drift off into a pleasant trance, then, as if he understood that his mother was blind to what he was seeing so clearly, quickly came out of it. "Even Joyce is excited," he said, as if to suggest that getting the woman he planned to marry excited was no easy task, and he looked around, as if in the hope that she'd materialize beside him and verify that, yes, she was excited.

"And you plan to wed this Joyce person?" Miss Beryl said.

"Yes, Ma, I do. I'm sorry you don't approve."

"If she makes you happy, Clive, then I approve. I just thought I'd point out for the record that I'm not the only one in this kitchen who can be snookered."

Clive Jr. seemed to honestly consider this sad possibility, shaming Miss Beryl, who seldom gave much real consideration to her son's views and advice.

"You always see things going wrong, Ma," her son said. "I see them going right."

Miss Beryl decided not to argue the point. It was true that they saw things differently and always had. She could tell by the way her son massaged the yearbook that when he looked at the dreadful Joyce woman, he saw the eighteen-year-old of the photograph. And he wasn't kidding when he said he could see the Gold Coast from her front window. He seemed to see that past and the future with stunning clarity. The present just wasn't there for him somehow.

"I wonder if I should look in on her?" he said, pushing back his chair. He seemed so desperately unsure of whether this would be the right thing to do that Miss Beryl, having deposited the last of their dishes in the sink, felt less like being mean. "Let her sleep," she suggested. "I'll have her call you at the bank later."

"I should go on in, I guess," Clive Jr. admitted, looking at his watch. "It's only seven, but if I'm going to take the afternoon . . ." His voice trailed off as he stood and hitched his pants, preparatory to visiting the bathroom. Clive Jr.'s last official act before leaving was always to relieve himself.

Miss Beryl thought about doing up the few dishes now, then decided to just let them soak. The Joyce woman would probably have something when she finally roused herself, and Miss Beryl decided she'd do them all together. At the sink she caught a glimpse through the kitchen doorway of Clive Jr. standing outside the spare bedroom, listening, no doubt, for some auditory signal that his fiancée was awake. And perhaps because Clive Jr. so resembled his father in outward appearance, and also because he looked so pitiful standing there, Miss Beryl thought her heart would break at the sight. When Clive Jr. noticed her observing him, he straightened guiltily and shrugged, then disappeared into the bathroom, shutting the door quietly behind him.

Since he'd left the yearbook in the center of the kitchen table, Miss Beryl opened it again with the intention of having another look at the Joyce woman, this time out from under her son's needy, watchful gaze. Instead, the book fell open naturally to a page that had been mutilated with a ballpoint pen that had been pressed into the glossy paper with such force that it had come through the other side, leaving an inky blotch on the page beneath. It took Miss Beryl a moment to realize that the defaced picture was of Sully. She was still staring at it when the toilet flushed in the next room.

Shutting the book and pushing it away before Clive Jr. emerged was easy, but what to do about the tears that had filled her eyes? How could she banish these when she didn't even know who they were for? What did it mean that at age eighty she suddenly seemed unable to decide who she was angry at, who was deserving of pity and understanding?

In the living room, waiting for her son to emerge from the bathroom, Miss Beryl avoided entering into imaginary conversations with either of her advisers, unwilling to listen to her husband's pleading on behalf of their son, the natural consequence of their love for each other, or Driver Ed's subversive whispers from the opposite wall. "Pipe down, both of you," she warned softly. In the lonely silence that ensued, the old woman peered out her front window at the street where she had lived all her mature life, the street where Clive Sr. had brought her to spend her days, a pretty street really, a comfortable street, the kind of street where she and her husband should have been able to raise a son less profoundly unhappy than she had always suspected Clive Jr. to be. She looked up into the black tangle of branches of the elms and then down the street in the direction of Mrs. Gruber's house. It didn't look like the Gold Coast, but no branches had fallen during the night, and Miss Beryl was about to conclude that God had lowered the boom on no one when a small movement caught her attention. Making her way up the very center of the street, dressed in a thin housecoat and fuzzy slippers, was an old woman whom Miss Beryl immediately recognized as Hattie. She was bent forward as if into a gale, her housecoat billowing out behind her in the breeze. "Oh dear," Miss Beryl said to herself. "Dear, dear God in Heaven."

Sully was outside in the hallway, struggling on with his boots as quietly as he could. He'd looked out the window and seen Clive Jr.'s car at the curb below. The last thing he needed in his present hungover condition was to encounter Clive Jr. True, if he ran into Clive now, it'd save him a trip later in the day, but right now, the way his head felt, he didn't want to raise his voice. Also, he preferred to spare Miss Beryl. Just before falling asleep last night Sully'd caught a whiff of Clive Jr.'s perfumy after-shave lingering in the apartment, which meant that he'd been up there snooping around. Clive Jr. had been warned about this before, and now he'd have to be warned again. Later in the day Sully might even enjoy warning him. Clive Jr.'s fear of Sully was always rewarding. But Sully wanted to be fully awake and not hungover to appreciate it. And so, when his landlady's door opened, Sully was relieved to see Miss Beryl emerge and not her son. "Good morning, Mrs. Peoples," he said, struggling to his feet with the help of the banister. "You aren't going to slam that door, are you?"

"Thank heaven you're still here," Miss Beryl said. "Hattie's escaped again."

"Uh-oh," Sully said, not terribly alarmed. This would make the fourth time the old woman had flown the coop this year. She never got more than a block or two. He flexed his knee, just to see if it would. "You remember what we did with the net?"

"Hurry," Miss Beryl insisted. "She's in the middle of the street."

"Hurrying isn't what I do best, at least first thing in the morning," Sully reminded her, putting some weight on the knee, which belted out a hearty hello. "Isn't that The Bank's car I saw outside?"

Miss Beryl's own coat was hanging just inside the door. When she started to put it on, Sully saw that his landlady was genuinely distressed.

"Stay put. I'll get her," he assured Miss Beryl, zipping his overcoat and locating his gloves.

"Hurry," Miss Beryl said again.

"I am hurrying. It just looks like slow motion."

"Should I call the daughter?"

Sully was half out the door. "No," he said. "I'll just take her back. I was headed there for coffee anyhow, since I can see you don't have mine ready again."

"Hurry!"

"Tell The Bank I'll be by to see him later. Tell him he's in trouble again," Sully said, and closed the door before Miss Beryl could tell him to hurry again. He consulted his watch. Not quite seven o'clock. Way too early for this shit.

Hattie was only vaguely aware that she was in the middle of the deserted street. Her vision was dim at the edges of her milky cataracts, and anyway she was looking down at her slippered feet and watching them go. The sight impressed her, suggesting, wrongly, rapid flight. She'd made her break a full fifteen minutes ago and in that time had traveled a block and a half. The wind billowed her thin housecoat behind her like a sail. She was unaware of the cold or the fact that the slush had begun to seep through her slippers. She was bound for freedom.

Sully, who didn't feel like chasing anybody first thing in the morning, was grateful to be chasing Hattie, perhaps the one person in Bath he could catch before his knee loosened up. Since Miss Beryl had spied her coming up the middle of the street, Hattie'd traversed another twenty feet and was now directly in front of the house. Her stride, Sully calculated, was about six inches, but her feet churned dutifully, and she darted furtive glances over each shoulder to check for pursuit. She did not notice when Sully fell into step alongside of her.

"Hello, old girl," he said.

Hattie let out a little cry and ran faster, as if on an exercise treadmill.

"You running away from home?"

"Who are you?" the old woman wanted to know. "You sound like that darn Sully."

"Right on the first guess," Sully told her. A car turned onto Main and headed toward them. Sully got the driver's attention, directed him around them.

"No driving on the sidewalk," Hattie yelled when she heard the car go by, close.

"Where you headed?" Sully said.

"To live with my sister in Albany," Hattie answered truthfully, because this was indeed her plan, the most obvious flaw of which was the fact that her sister had been dead for twenty years. Also, Albany lay in the other direction.

"How about I give you a lift," Sully suggested. "We'll get there a lot faster."

"Let's."

Sully steered the old woman back toward Miss Beryl's driveway, where they arrived a few minutes later. Clive Jr. had come out onto the porch and was watching. Before he could say anything, Sully held up a finger to his lips, then pointed at Clive Jr.'s car, which was nearest. Clive nodded, went back inside for his keys. Sully got the old woman into the backseat on the passenger side, then went around and slipped in beside her. Clive Jr. got in and started the engine.

"Who's driving?" Hattie said, squinting in the direction of the front seat.

"Me," Sully assured her.

Hattie located his voice beside her. "Who's up there?"

"Me," Sully insisted. "Who'd you think?"

"My feet are cold," Hattie said, noticing for the first time. She began to cry.

Sully took her slippers off. Her feet were wet and ice cold. One of Clive Jr.'s sweaters was in the backseat, so Sully used this to dry and massage the old woman's bony toes.

"Who's driving?" Hattie said.

"Me," Sully said. "How many times do I have to tell you? We're almost there, too."

Sully had Clive Jr. pull in behind the diner and motioned for him to stay put while he went to fetch Cass. Miss Beryl's son wasn't happy to be left alone in the car with Hattie, partly because his continued nonexistence would be harder to prove with Sully gone.

"I gotta get some gas, old girl," Sully explained before he left them. "You wait here."

"Here," Hattie repeated, wriggling her toes in the warmth of Clive Jr.'s cashmere sweater.

Inside, Cass was taking the orders of two men Sully didn't know who were seated at the counter. Sully waited for them to finish. "What kind of mood are you in?" Sully said when she put his usual coffee in front of him.

"Rotten," Cass said. "Like always."

"Good," he said. "I'd hate to ruin your day."

"Impossible," Cass told him, then frowned suspiciously, as if she knew it were all too possible. Instinctively, she glanced toward the rear of the diner and the attached apartment where she and her mother lived. "God, what?" she said, stepping back quickly.

"She's fine." Sully held up a cautioning hand. "Clive Peoples has her out back in his car."

"I'll wring her neck," Cass said, her panic turning quickly to anger, and she bolted from behind the counter. "So help me."

Sully decided not to follow. Old Hattie was going to be furious, and he didn't like to watch. The last time he'd brought her back, she'd called him a fart blossom and tried to kick him. Of the four times the old woman had tried to escape her daughter's care, she'd been returned three of them by Sully. Luckily she never remembered his past treacheries. Only her distant memories were vivid and distinct. More recent perfidy she forgot almost immediately.

Sully went behind the counter and put on an apron, nodding at Roof, the cook. "Looks like you and me, Rufus," he said.

Roof flipped two eggs onto a platter with his long spatula by way of reply. The platter already contained hash browns and toast triangles at the edges. Two more smooth movements and three more platters were complete, and all four checks came down from the circular spindle. "Ding dong," he said. "Order up."

"You're not even going to let me drink my coffee, are you," Sully said, grabbing a platter in each hand. Cass could balance them up and down her arm, but Sully didn't think he'd try. Roof was even-tempered until you dropped his eggs.

Working behind the counter, Sully forgot all about Clive Jr., who remained in the car with Hattie until her daughter came flying out the back to fetch her. Then he gave Cass a hand as far as the door, for which Clive Jr. was rewarded by a torrent of abuse from the old woman, who thought he was Sully and who called him, among other things, a fart blossom. Then he went back to the car and waited, glancing at his watch every thirty seconds or so with increasing irritation. He didn't mind being pressed into service, but it was just like Sully to disappear, to leave him sitting next to the foul-smelling Dumpster in the alley behind Hattie's Lunch. Also, he'd discovered the use to which his cashmere sweater had been put.

Now that he had the leisure to consider it, he was also miffed at his mother, who had instinctively summoned Sully when she saw the old woman in distress, as if Clive Jr. himself were not to be trusted with so delicate a task. Secretly, he doubted he would have performed as well as Sully. He had little experience in trying to talk ninety-year-old runaways into returning home, and he probably would have messed everything up. In his mind's eye he could see himself struggling with the old woman in the middle of the street like a mugger or purse snatcher, being clawed and cursed at until he finally gave up. What annoyed him was that his mother apparently had imagined a similar outcome and had turned to Sully, a man who would know what to do.

Was it his mother's implied opinion of him or Sully's ability to assume command that made a boy of Clive Jr. again? He couldn't be sure, but as he sat in the car, obediently following Sully's instructions, the irony of the situation did not escape him. After all, he, Clive Jr., was arguably the most important man in Bath, and once when they broke ground on The Ultimate Escape, there'd be no arguing the issue. Then everyone would be forced to admit that Bath's renaissance was attributable to Clive Jr., who'd made it happen by bringing in the big boys from downstate, from as far away as Texas, making them see the area's potential through Clive Jr.'s own eyes, making them all believers.

Well, almost all. For Clive Jr. had come to realize that there would always be at least two skeptics in Bath, at least as long as his mother and Sully were on the scene. The two of them seemed not to notice that it was a new Clive Jr. who'd returned to Bath to rescue the savings and loan and give the town a future. They seemed to see the boy he had once been, not the man he'd made of himself. How odd that these two skeptics lived in the same house, *his* house, the house of his childhood on Upper Main. His own mother and Sully, who'd been an intruder in that house for almost as long as Clive Jr. could remember. Living there together in the house that Clive Jr. had come to think of as his opponents' campaign headquarters.

Clive Jr. knew he was lucky to have two such opponents, neither of whom would act against him, both of whom would be surprised to discover he considered them in this role. Especially his mother, whom he'd work so hard to convert. He'd done everything he could think of to earn her trust. He'd borrowed large sums of money he didn't need and paid her back when he said he would, even offering interest. He'd given her excellent investment advice that would have made her money, advice that to his knowledge she had never, not one single time, followed. Any more than she had even once in the last twenty years asked his advice on any subject. Most of the time he was able to console himself that his mother just happened to be the most independent, free-thinking woman in all of Schuyler County. Maybe she didn't require his counsel, but then she didn't require anyone else's either. She jokingly claimed to get all the advice she needed from Clive Sr., long dead, and, even more spookily, from the African spirit mask hanging on the living room wall. Which would have been tolerable, except for those rare occasions like this morning, when she discovered there were limits to her self-sufficiency and then turned not to Clive Jr., but rather to Sully, arguably the least trustworthy man in Bath. And even that, which would have been bad enough, wasn't the worst of it. No sooner did his mother turn to Sully than Sully enlisted Clive Jr. in a subordinate role. It was worse than ridiculous. The most important man in Bath taking orders from the least important man in Bath, Donald Sullivan, a man essentially forgotten while he was still breathing, a man who'd peaked at age eighteen and who'd been sliding toward a just oblivion ever since.

Sully and Clive Jr. went way back. In fact, though it would have surprised Sully to know it, Clive Jr. considered Sully an integral part of his prolonged and painful adolescence. As a boy Clive Jr. had feared for his masculinity. In fact, he'd pretty much concluded he was destined to be a homosexual—a homo, as they were called in Bath back then. Oh, he got hard-ons, like other boys his age, looking at pictures of naked girls in the magazines he stole from the drugstore and stashed in the upper reaches of his closet, where his tiny mother wasn't likely to run across them by accident. But Clive Jr. had discounted these erections as irrelevant, certain that the day would come (next year? next month? tomorrow?) when he would wake up and the naked women would no longer stir him. There were a few that didn't stir him already, and he stole more magazines in the hopes that a variety of new naked women would forestall his inevitable homodom.

The cause of Clive Jr.'s fear was that he seemed to harbor deeper, more intense feelings for boys than for girls, in much the same fashion he craved the affection and love of his father far more urgently than that of his mother, whose diminutive stature had always seemed to Clive Jr. emblematic of her insignificance. He couldn't imagine what had possessed his father to marry her or what had attracted him to her in the first place. No teacher in the entire junior high school was the butt of more cruel jokes than Beryl Peoples, whose round-shouldered, gnomelike appearance and correct speech were mimicked to devastating effect, especially in Clive Jr.'s presence. He hated to think what his life would have been like had his father not been the football coach.

Clive Jr. had loved his father, and as a boy he'd loved all the boys his father loved. He himself had never excelled in sports. He'd inherited his father's size (he'd nearly killed Miss Beryl in being born) but was blessed with neither speed nor balance nor eye-hand coordination. Clive Sr. was too kind a man to express his disappointment in his son's inability to catch, throw or dribble a ball of any size or description, but Clive Jr. sensed it, in part, from his father's enthusiasm for the boys he coached. At dinner Clive Sr. was often unable to restrain himself from recounting tales of their athletic prowess. The coach himself had been an indifferent athlete, but he possessed a pure love of sport and had gone into coaching because he believed that sport was the truest and best metaphor for life. He remained unshakable in this conviction, despite Miss Beryl's gentle ridicule of the clichés that lay imbedded so deeply in his soul.

And of all the boys he had coached, Clive Sr. had seemed fondest of Sully, and it was Sully's praises that were sung the loudest at the dinner table. He was a varsity starter as a sophomore, and it was Clive Sr.'s contention that if he had a dozen Sullys he could take his team to state every year, this despite the fact that Sully himself was gifted with neither extraordinary size nor speed. Nor was he coachable. He was lazy in practice, resentful of constructive criticism, and he could not be made to understand the concept of team play. At times he seemed not to care whether the team won or lost. He refused to quit smoking, even when threatened with suspension, and he provided about the worst possible example to the other players, most of whom naturally gravitated to bad example.

But come game day, Sully was a wrecker. He chased down boys who were faster than he was and ran through others twice his size. He sometimes cost the team by not being where he was supposed to be, but just as often where he was turned out to be even better. After Sully botched a play, Clive Sr., livid, would call him over to the sideline to read him the riot act. Sometimes Sully came, sometimes he didn't. Often, before Clive Sr. could substitute for him, Sully'd recover a fumble or intercept a pass, and he'd bring the ball with him so the coach could see the wisdom of doing things his way. "If I only had a dozen more just like him," Clive Sr. would shake his head. "What a team I'd have." He was wrong about that, of course. A dozen more like Sully, and he wouldn't have had a team at all.

Clive Jr., as the son of the coach, was always allowed to hover around the bench as long as he didn't get in the way. And it was there along the sideline that he'd fallen in some kind of love with Sully and began to doubt his masculinity. Sully, even as a sophomore, was everything Clive Jr., an eighth-grader, aspired to be—reckless, imaginative, contemptuous of authority and, above all, indifferent to pain. Sully, it seemed, scarcely got interested in the contest until someone on the other team landed a good shot or offered an insult, after which something changed in Sully's eyes. If Sully couldn't win the game, he'd start a fight and win that. If he couldn't win the fight he'd started, he'd continue to hurl himself at whatever he couldn't beat with increased fury, as if the knowledge that the battle was unwinnable heightened its importance. What Sully did better than anybody else was pick himself up off the ground, and when he returned to the huddle, bruised, nose-bloodied, limping, he'd still be hurling insults over his shoulder at whoever had put him on the ground. Seeing this, Clive Jr. had filled with terrible admiration and longing.

And awful as that was, it would have remained longing and admiration, except that in August of what would be Sully's senior year, Sully's older brother had gotten drunk and killed himself in a head-on collision late one Saturday night on the way home from Schuyler Springs. Clive Sr. had felt bad for Sully, who took it hard, and he also felt bad for his football team, which needed a focused Sully. Everyone knew what the boy's home life was like, his father a drunken barroom brawler, his mother a cowed little mouse of a woman whose slender comfort derived from the Catholic church where she confessed her husband's sins in the cool darkness of the confessional where you couldn't see her black eyes. So Clive Sr. had invited Sully over to dinner one evening and later that night told him he was welcome anytime, an invitation Sully took literally. He became, for the rest of the football season, a fixture in their dining room. The first few nights Miss Beryl set an extra place for him when he arrived. Then, after a week, she decided it was easier to just set Sully's place in the beginning. The boy clearly preferred the Peoples family, their table, their food, to that of his own now diminished family.

Actually, it was Clive Jr.'s job to set the table, and in this way he was made an unwilling accomplice, forced to welcome the intruder into their home. By the time Sully was a senior, Clive Jr. was himself in high school and the ambiguous longing he'd felt when he looked at Sully two years before had mutated into an equally impossible longing to be more like Sully, who was dating the new object of his desire, Joyce Freeman, a junior who was far too good-looking and popular to talk to. And so Clive Jr. hadn't the slightest desire for Sully to join their family, where Clive Jr.'s own light already shown dimly enough under the bushel of his parents' disappointment in him. And so Clive Jr. did everything he could think of to suggest to Sully that he was not welcome. If there was a chipped plate, Clive Jr. set it where Sully would be seated. If there was a fork with a bent tine, Sully got that too, along with the glass that hadn't come quite clean the night before. The inference should have been clear to anyone, but Sully seemed oblivious, incapable of registering any slight. If the bent tine of the fork jabbed him in the lip, he simply straightened the offending prong between his grubby thumb and forefinger, held it up to the light to make sure all the tines were lined up and said, "There, you little rat." Since Clive Jr. had been the one who bent the tine dangerously to begin with, Sully, speaking to the fork, seemed to be speaking to him.

Midway through football season Clive Sr. seemed to understand that he'd made a mistake inviting Sully into their home. He didn't say anything, but Clive Jr. could tell his father knew he'd goofed. The idea had been to make Sully a better citizen, a better team player. Clive Sr. had seen an opportunity to take one of his pivotal players home with him and extend practice sessions over the dinner table, get the boy *thinking* straight, to understand he was part of something bigger than himself, that the team came first. That, Clive Sr. was confident, would also stand Sully in good stead in the larger context of life. "The larger context of life" was one of Clive Sr.'s favorite phrases. Everything that took place on a football field was applicable to The Larger Context of Life in Clive Sr.'s view, and this was what he wanted Sully to grasp.

What Clive Sr. hadn't anticipated was that Sully would find a natural subversive ally in Miss Beryl. True, his wife had always made gentle fun of Clive Sr.'s most serious themes, but he hadn't imagined she'd thwart his design to educate Sully. If that's what she was doing. Which Clive Sr. couldn't be sure. It seemed to him that his wife must be up to something subversive, even though he couldn't put his finger on any single thing she was doing that warranted specific reprimand. Mostly, it was little things, like calling Sully "Donald" instead of "Don" or "Sully," the names— men's names—that everyone else called him. Clive Sr. didn't like his heaviest hitter thinking of himself as "Donald," though he wasn't sure he wanted to raise this issue with Miss Beryl because he could hear her snort in his mind and knew how he'd feel when he heard it for real in his ears. There were some things women just didn't understand and you couldn't teach them and were better off not trying.

But it wasn't just the business of calling Sully "Donald." What he'd had in mind was a dinner table at which two sportsmen—himself and Sully—would talk strategy about their next opponent in such a way that his own son, who would never be an athlete, might become more educated and aware of, albeit vicariously, the sporting life and the lessons of sport. What he had not anticipated was that every night Sully would become involved in conversations not with himself, but rather with Miss Beryl, conversations about books and politics and the war America wasn't going to be able to stay out of much longer, subjects that somehow diminished football and therefore its lessons about The Larger Context of Life.

It was as if his wife were bent on undermining every lesson in citizenship that Clive Sr. was trying to impart. Gertrude Wynoski had been a case in point. For many years the junior high school social studies teacher, Mrs. Wynoski was, to Miss Beryl's mind, a crackpot. Her particular area of interest was local history, and until her forced retirement she'd drawn for every seventh-grade student at Bath Junior High a parallel between Schuyler Springs and Babylon, claiming that the latter's prosperity was built on a precarious foundation of moral corruption. After her retirement, feeling the loss of her captive audience, she commenced to share her views with the citizens of Bath in a series of jeremiads published in the Letters to the Editor section of the *North Bath Weekly Journal,* reminding all and sundry that Schuyler Springs' good fortune had its roots in immorality. That community had always condoned every form of gambling, legal and illegal, from horseraces to cockfights to savage prizefights and for decades had even tolerated the existence of a particularly infamous whorehouse. "House of ill repute" was actually the term she used, much to the confusion of her seventh-graders, for whom the phrase remained opaque, Mrs. Wynoski demurring exegesis. Her readers at the *North Bath Weekly Journal* followed her drift, and she concluded all of her epistles with strong hints that it was only a matter of time before Schuyler Springs was visited by some form of retribution, possibly biblical in nature.

Clive Sr., who loved Bath and felt out of place in Schuyler Springs, especially during the tourist season, privately inclined toward Mrs. Wynoski's view. As football coach, he felt an obligation to take the moral view, and he wanted badly to believe in a moral world. What he wished for more than anything was that the comeuppance Mrs. Wynoski predicted for Schuyler Springs would come, if God willed, at the hands of his football team. The Schuyler team was always rumored to have players who did not actually reside in the city, and Clive Sr. didn't mind sharing these rumors with his student athletes in the hope of spurring them to moral outrage. They were cheaters, he said, and cheaters never prospered. This was the point he'd been trying to make one night at the dinner table, the subject of cheating having been raised by the publication of another Wynoski letter. He'd hoped Miss Beryl might champion this view.

"Cheaters *always* prosper, you mean," his wife had corrected him before his voice had even dropped. Moreover, she continued, if Schuyler Springs was built on a foundation of gambling and sin, there was no reason to expect the edifice to crumble anytime soon. There was nothing in the least shaky about such foundations, she said. If anything was shaky, it was Gert Wynoski's intellectual dexterity. Finally, there was no reason to wait for God to speak on the subject of Schuyler Springs. The evidence rather suggested he had already spoken, and it was Bath's springs that had run dry.

How, in such an atmosphere, Clive Sr. despaired, could you teach football, much less The Larger Context of Life? He would have liked to put his foot down, but every time he tried, Miss Beryl made short work of him. Had she been mean-spirited in demolishing the moral positions he'd staked out so carefully, he might have known how to proceed, but she was always so gentle and loving when she crushed his arguments that anger seemed unbecoming. But as his arguments were systematically ground to dust he became increasingly exasperated, as if civilization were crumbling as well, which at times he suspected it was. Miss Beryl, with Clive Sr.'s star athlete for an audience, seemed actually to be arguing that government, law, even God's own church were not always worthy of respect. In Clive Sr.'s view, if these were seriously questioned, how long would it be before football coaches came under attack as well?

Not that Miss Beryl had found a convert in Sully. In fact, the two argued all the time, and Miss Beryl gently chided Sully in much the same way she chided Clive Sr. Nor did Sully ever take Miss Beryl's side in discussions that involved Clive Sr. In fact, Sully seemed unaware that there was a conflict, a tug-of-war for his attention. He seemed unaware of Clive Sr.'s mounting irritation at how his subjects kept getting derailed in favor of hers. He hadn't invited Sully to their table to talk about poetry. He'd brought him there to talk about football. He'd hoped to convince Sully that football *was* poetry.

Clive Jr. had watched his father's frustration grow, and he waited until he sensed the right time. It came one night when Sully volunteered to help Miss Beryl with the dishes—imagine, Clive Sr.'s all-conference halfback/linebacker doing dishes—and Clive Sr., unable to watch, had retreated to the living room to listen to the radio, or pretend to. Clive Jr. had followed him in there and sat frowning in a chair across the room until their eyes met, and then Clive Jr. had spoken. "I liked it better," he told his father, "when it was just us. When it was just our own family." His father had started to say something, then stopped, his dark gaze finding the kitchen door and the sound of raised, argumentative, joyful voices. "And that's the way it's going to be again," his father had said, his voice never more purposeful, even on the football field.

After dinner the next evening, when Sully had left to go out some-where with his friends, Clives Sr. and Jr. had taken a walk up Main in the direction of the Sans Souci. It was early November, but the weather had already turned bitter and the elms were bare overhead, a network of black branches, impossibly high and distant. At the corner of Main and Bowdon, they had turned left, as Clive Jr. had known they would. At the tiny Sullivan house, they had knocked and waited for a long time until Sully's mother, dressed in a robe, had finally answered the door. She seemed to know why they'd come, though she'd waited patiently in their shabby living room for Clive Sr. to express his sympathy for the loss of their eldest son, to explain how proud he was of Donald (he used his wife's nomenclature in this instance), how he was the backbone of the team, how the team was really a family in the larger context and how the season had only another week to go before that family split up. They'd enjoyed having Sully over at their house so much during the season, and he hoped Mrs. Sullivan hadn't thought they were trying to steal him away from them and her home, from his own mother and father. Clive Jr. had watched as the meaning trailing his father's words gradually came clear to the woman.

"I'll keep him home," she promised when Clive Sr.'s voice finally dropped.

The two Clives got to their feet then, and Clive Sr. said again that Sully was a fine young man, that he'd be a fine citizen, that if sports taught anything, they taught citizenship. This last point elicited a peal of unexpected, thunderous laughter from Big Jim Sullivan, who'd appeared in the doorway behind them noiselessly, filling that doorway really, dwarfing Clive Sr., himself a sizable man. "You all got tired of him is what you're saying," he snorted.

Before Clive Sr. could protest, Big Jim had turned his back on them, and when he spoke again, it was over his massive shoulder. "You just send him on home, coach," he said. "I'll straighten him right out."

He kept his word, too. Sully had not appeared at their table again.

Had it been wrong, what he and his father had done? The twinge of guilt Clive Jr. felt when he recalled the episode was suggestive, though not conclusive. When he thought it through objectively, Clive Jr. didn't see what was so wrong about a young boy wanting to keep his own family intact. Yet he and his father made no mention of their visit to Miss Beryl. It remained their unspoken secret, and yet instead of drawing father and son closer together, it had driven a further wedge between them. Clive Sr. seemed to enjoy his son's company even less after their visit to the Sullivans', and in truth Clive Jr. was never able to look at his father in exactly the same way.

Which was a shame, because time had vindicated them. After all, the intruder had not been expelled. After Clive Sr.'s death, while Clive Jr. was away, Sully had again taken up residence in his mother's home and in her heart, it seemed to Clive Jr., and now he could be budged from neither her house nor her affection. His mother could not be made to see that he was dangerous, and her stubbornness had put Clive Jr. into the unfortunate position of having to finish, as an adult, the job that he and his father had begun when he was a teenager. Expelling Sully, once and for all, seemed the sort of task that the most important man in Bath ought to be able to accomplish, and it galled Clive Jr. to be so impotent in this regard. A man governed more by the commonsense laws of commerce than by emotion, Clive Jr. was unable to explain, even to himself, why his own sense of well-being was increasingly tied to the imperative of Sully's banishment, but there it was. Even the validity of his most compelling public reason—to remove the very real threat of danger to his mother that a careless man like Sully represented—could not expel or diminish his more private and personal motives.

It was irrational, Clive Jr. had to admit, as he sat beside the Dumpster in back of Hattie's, studying his visible breath, to feel that Sully would have to go before Clive Jr. would be able to accomplish his other goals. And surely it was irrational to feel, to *know*, that as long as that coalition on Upper Main existed, he would always see himself as the boy he'd been and not the man he'd become. Unless he could rid himself of Sully, he'd always be right where he was now, out in the cold, in a dark, narrow alley, the odor of the town's refuse assailing his nostrils. It was intolerable, was what it was. And so Clive Jr. got out of the car.

"Hello, Clive," Sully said, clearly surprised to see Clive Jr. when he materialized before the register, looking homicidal. "You want some breakfast?"

Since he'd been left in charge, Sully was conducting the diner's business his way. For one thing, it was easier to leave the register's drawer open. He wasn't ringing anything up, either. He rounded off the checks, too, sometimes in the customer's favor, sometimes to the advantage of the establishment, making change from the open drawer. Today, the dollar-forty-nine special cost a buck and a half, screw the tax. For the two-seventy-nine breakfast of eggs, bacon, toast and hash browns, Sully was getting three dollars. So far everyone had paid up cheerfully, understanding the unusual dynamics of the situation and Sully's adamant refusal to deal with legal tender smaller than quarters. Clive Jr. pointed at his watch. "You know where I've been?" he asked Sully.

"No clue," Sully said.

"Sitting out back, waiting for you."

"I've been a little busy," Sully pointed out with a sweeping gesture that took in the whole diner. It wasn't as busy now as it had been when he'd gone behind the counter, but the point was still valid. "I figured you'd know enough to go home."

Clive Jr. bristled. "You're the one who said to wait."

"I didn't mean forever," Sully said.

Clive Jr. thought he heard someone snicker. This was not the place to confront Sully, it occurred to him.

"Have a cup of coffee," Sully suggested, pouring him one. "Tell me about your Thanksgiving. You had a pleasant one, I hope?"

"Actually, I had dinner with my fiancée," Clive Jr. informed him. He was about to hint that his fiancée was someone of Sully's acquaintance when he was interrupted.

"Yeah?" Sully said, apparently uninterested in Clive Jr.'s matrimonial plans. "What else did you do?"

Clive Jr. narrowed his eyes, guessing now where this conversation was heading. Yesterday, while they were waiting for his mother's return from her Thanksgiving, he and Joyce had gone upstairs to Sully's flat to see how much damage Sully'd done since the last time he'd checked. "Nothing much," he said weakly.

"Nothing much," Sully repeated. "I thought maybe you went someplace you weren't supposed to go."

Clive Jr. could feel the other men at the counter tuning in, with undisguised interest, to this conversation. He could also feel whose side they were on. Not his.

"We've been through this before," Clive Jr. ventured. "A landlord has the right—"

"You aren't my landlord," Sully interrupted.

"My mother—"

"Is the only reason I don't kick your ass," Sully finished for him. "Next time you go in my apartment without my permission even she won't save you."

Clive Jr. could feel himself begin to shake with rage. And, as always happened in moments of high drama, he found himself outside his own person, one step back, a critical observer of his own weak performance. From this vantage point he saw himself stand with badly feigned dignity, take a dollar out of his wallet, put it wordlessly onto the counter, saw himself pivot like a comic German soldier on television, march ludicrously to the door past the row of silent men at the lunch counter. Maybe they weren't silent. Maybe silence was what happened when the separation occurred and he found himself outside his own person. Be that as it may, the only thing Clive Jr. heard as he strode out of Hattie's was the sound of his own voice telling his mother, that very morning, "I can handle Sully."

And, as always, it took him a while to reintegrate. The next thing he was aware of was sitting at his oak desk in the savings and loan, which meant that he'd either walked or driven there and let himself in by the side door. Also, he must have drawn back the front curtain that opened onto the street. Through the dark, tinted glass he could see all the way up Main to Hattie's, where the door of the diner opened and two laughing men emerged. How many times over the years had he looked out this window just in time to see Sully coming up the street, looking for all the world like a man limping away from an accident, too dazed and stupid to assess the extent of his own injuries? Sully's only design was to keep going, in defiance of reason.

To Clive Jr. he sometimes seemed immortal, indestructible. He'd sensed Sully's immortality forty years ago, late that spring afternoon of Sully's senior year when he'd returned to their house one last time to tell Miss Beryl he was going to enlist in the army. Miss Beryl, to Clive Jr.'s great embarrassment, had tried to talk him out of it. When she was unsuccessful, she had pleaded with Clive Sr. to talk with him. But Clive Sr., as the football coach and a man with a moral duty to the community, took a dim view of draft dodging and applauded Sully's patriotism. "You fool," Miss Beryl had said, shocking Clive Jr., who could not recall her ever being contemptuous of his father's views, though she often made gentle fun of them. "It has nothing to do with patriotism," she told her husband, who looked a little frightened by her vehemence. "That boy is already at war. He's just like his brother was. He's looking for a car to hit head on."

Clive Jr., young though he was at the time, had known his mother was wrong. Not in her analysis of Sully's motives, which, he supposed, might be true. What she was mistaken about was Sully's ability to wreck himself in a collision. It was the guys in the oncoming vehicle who were not long for this world, in Clive Jr.'s view. Sully might even manage to kill everybody else, but it would be his own personal destiny to be thrown clear of one head-on collision after another, always the worse for the experience but never dead of it.

And his prediction had come true. It was not Sully who had died going ninety miles an hour but rather Clive Sr., going all of twenty.

Still, Sully wasn't immortal, Clive Jr. knew. He was just a man. A dinosaur of a man, marking time patiently toward extinction. Quite possibly he was dead already and was just too dumb to know it. Clive Jr. would have liked to explain this to Sully, and he imagined an exchange he hadn't quite the courage to make real. "You know how the dinosaurs figured out they were extinct?" he'd have liked to ask. And Sully would have to admit he didn't have a clue. "They never did," Clive Jr. would tell him. "They just were."

By the time Cass returned with Hattie on her arm and deposited the old woman, bathed and warmly dressed, in her booth, Sully's generous impulse had about run its course. He was a man capable of sporadic generous impulses, which he enjoyed while they lasted without regretting their absence once they played themselves out.

"Next time let her go," Cass said when she joined Sully behind the counter. Sully had already taken off his apron.

"What gets into her?" he said, sliding onto the stool that had been occupied until recently by Clive Peoples.

"She was still mad from yesterday," Cass told him, her voice low and confidential. "She wanted me to open on Thanksgiving so she could sit in her booth. I told her she could go out and sit in it if she wanted to, and I'll be damned if she didn't. Sat right there for three hours and then came back and told me I was ruining the business."

"She does seem happy in that booth," Sully admitted. The old woman was smiling broadly now, her misguided flight forgotten.

"No 'seem' about it. If I kept the place open twenty-four hours a day and let her sit there the whole time, she'd be the happiest woman alive."

"So let her sit," Sully suggested. "What's it hurt?"

"Right." Cass glared at him. "Why should I have a life?"

Sully shrugged. "Then put her in a nursing home. Who's going to blame you?"

"Everyone, including you," Cass said with conviction. "Including me." She looked past Sully at her mother. "They'd strap her in a wheelchair and forget all about her, Sully," she said, her voice even quieter now.

Sully was spared from having to comment by the arrival of Rub, who trotted up outside, put his face to the window and peered in with a worried expression.

"Somebody told me you were working here now," he said, as if the rumor were too terrible to contemplate.

"Who, me?" Sully said.

Cass brought Rub a coffee.

"I never should have believed it," he said seriously.

"Why not?" Sully wondered, always curious about Rub's logic.

"Because it wasn't true," Rub explained.

"There you go." Cass nodded at Sully, as if in perfect comprehension.

"Could I borrow a dollar?" Rub said.

Sully gave him a dollar. Rub put it into his pocket.

Sully stared at him, shook his head.

"What?" Rub said.

"Nothing," Sully told him.

"Then how come you're looking at me?"

Sully didn't answer.

"You're both looking at me," Rub observed, since Cass was also watching the two of them with her usual quiet astonishment.

"You're a good-looking man, Rub," Sully told him. "Handsome." Rub looked at Cass, hoping for a clue as to how to take this remark.

"Am not," Rub said.

"Sure you are," Sully said. Pushing his empty coffee cup away, he stood and planted a kiss on Rub's bristly cranium.

Rub flushed bright red. "You're going to make people think I'm queer," he said sadly.

"That ship has sailed, Rub," Sully said. "Let's go to work."

Rub stood, gulped his coffee down. "I didn't know we had work."

"There's always work," Sully told him. "Today some of it's ours."

Cass wouldn't take money for the coffees. "Thanks," she said to Sully. "I'm grateful, even if I don't act like it."

"So long, old girl," Sully said loudly to Hattie on their way out.

"Who is it?" the old woman grinned maniacally. "It sounds like that darn Sully."

Perfect silence. This in response to Sully's key being turned in the ignition of the pickup. It was as if the ignition were connected to nothing but the cold November air on the other side of the dash. Sully tried it several more times, trying to elicit some sort of sound, even a bad one. A bad sound—a grating, a straining, a scraping—might have suggested some diagnosis, and a diagnosis might have had some tentative price tag affixed to it. Sully wasn't sure what the sound of perfect silence meant, pricewise. What it suggested was finality, a vehicle beyond resuscitation. Sully leaned back, left the key in the ignition, ran his fingers through his hair. Rub stared at his knees, afraid. This was a hell of a time to be seated next to Sully, who was not above flying into rages at inanimate objects. In such a confined space there was the danger of ricochet.

Rub didn't want to be the first to speak, but the unbroken silence took a greater toll on him than on Sully, who looked to Rub like he might sit there all winter. When he couldn't stand it anymore, Rub said, "Won't it start?"

Sully just looked at him. Ricochet was the least of his worries, Rub realized.

"Let's take a walk," Sully suggested, getting out.

Rub got out too. "Don't you want to take your keys?" he said.
"What for?"
"Somebody might steal your truck," Rub said.
"Think about it," Sully advised.
Rub thought about it. "Somebody might steal your keys."
"There's only three on the ring," Sully said. "One's for the truck. I don't remember what the other two are for, even."
"Old Lady Peoples is spying on us again," Rub noticed, grateful for the change of subject. The curtain in the front room had twitched. "I wisht she'd just go ahead and die instead of spying on people."
"That's kind of mean, don't you think?" Sully said, as they headed back downtown on foot.
"She started it," Rub said. "She was mean to me all during eighth grade. I'm just being mean back."
"She probably just wanted you to learn something," Sully suggested.
"She wanted me to learn everything," Rub recalled angrily. "I wisht she'd just die so I could forget her."
Jocko was at the OTB, holding up one section of wall. "Those were some pills," Sully told him. "I slept like a baby."
"Good," Jocko said, suspicious of something in Sully's voice.
"Only trouble was, I happened to be at the wheel of my truck at the time."
Jocko nodded. "I warned you, if you recall. I see you're in one piece, anyhow."
"Mmmmm," Sully said. "What was Wednesday's triple?"
"Three-one-seven," Jocko told him. "The reason I remember is that's what I bet."
"Good for you," Sully told him. "The rich get richer. Do me a favor and don't spend it all. I may need a loan."
"I just signed it over to my wife. Brought me almost up to speed, alimonywise. I'm still on the same rung of the ladder, affectionwise."
"I like a woman whose love can't be bought. What was that triple again?" Sully wanted to know.
"Three-one-seven. Pay attention, for Christ sake."
Sully had located the stub and stared at it to make sure he hadn't been given the winner by mistake. "I had two thirds of it myself," he said.
"Good," Jocko congratulated him. "How many of those pills did you take yesterday?"
"Two."

Jocko nodded. "They're not aspirin."

"The first one didn't seem to have much effect."

"How about the second one?" Jocko said.

"That was a doozy," Sully admitted.

"Next time wait for the first one to kick in."

"I will."

Sully bet his 1-2-3 triple and collected Rub, who'd used the dollar Sully had given him earlier to bet a daily double.

"What'd you bet?" Sully said when they were back on the street.

"I forgot," Rub admitted.

"Naturally," Sully said. "You bet it almost a minute ago."

"I like Carnation best of all," Rub said, and he recited the rest of the Carnation Milk jingle as flawlessly as he'd done yesterday in Sully's dream.

"Well, what do you know," Sully said, stopping dead in the middle of the sidewalk. He'd have bet Jocko's winnings that Rub wouldn't be able to remember yesterday's jingle.

"Old Lady Peoples always tried to get me to memorize poetry back in eighth grade," Rub told him. "Back then I never could."

The same girl was behind the counter at the donut shop, and she looked less than thrilled to see Sully and Rub. Carl Roebuck was sitting at one of the tables in back, and that thrilled Sully, who, since hearing the deathly silence of his pickup truck, had been wishing fervently that he'd taken a fistful of Carl's money the night before when he had a chance. The woman with Carl in the booth was a blonde, and Sully thought for a minute it was Toby until he saw it wasn't.

"Can I borrow another dollar?" Rub said.

"If you'll sit here at the counter and not bother me while I'm over there," Sully said, indicating Carl's table.

"I hate Carl," Rub reminded him.

Sully handed him a dollar. "There are women in this town I could associate with who'd be cheaper than you," he said.

"They wouldn't be your real friend," Rub reminded him seriously.

"Well, I see you've recovered," Sully said when Carl looked up and saw him approaching.

"Two hours' sleep," Carl said proudly. "And I'm fresh as a fucking daisy."

Carl did look amazingly well, Sully had to admit. "If you were a daisy, that'd be the kind, all right," he said. He put a hand on the shoulder of the woman sitting across from Carl, who, now that Sully looked at her, was about the plainest-looking woman he'd ever seen, her age indeterminate, her gender less obvious from the front than the rear. "Would you give us about two minutes, dolly?" he said.

The woman looked at Carl, who shrugged a yes.

"Go keep that fellow at the counter company," Sully suggested, indicating Rub, who'd ordered a big ole cream-filled donut. "He'll recite you a poem if you ask him nice."

The woman went over to the counter but settled on a stool far from Rub, perhaps because his donut had already erupted obscenely.

"You have to be the dumbest man in Bath," Sully told Carl Roebuck.

"That wouldn't be such an insult if you hadn't just walked in here with the dumbest man in Bath," Carl said. "You never count yourself, either."

"Speaking of counting," Sully said. "Count out what you owe me for yesterday."

"I haven't even been out to check on your work," Carl said.

"This is the wrong fucking day to start that," Sully said. "Last night you shoved about a thousand dollars at me. Told me to take what I wanted."

Carl nodded, recalling it. "What a day that'd been," he sang. "What a rare mood I was in."

Sully nodded impatiently. "Well, fork it over if you want to be around for your next mood swing."

Carl counted out the money he owed Sully for the sheetrocking, pushed it across the formica tabletop. "What?" he said when Sully put the money in his pocket. "You aren't going to bust my balls about the other?"

"I don't want to think about it," Sully told him. "My truck died this morning, and if I start thinking about all the money you owe me I might kill you before you kill yourself."

"Who will you blame for your sad pitiful state of affairs when I'm gone?" Carl wondered.

Sully got up. "I'll still blame you," he said.

Neither man spoke for a second. Sully didn't think he'd ever seen a sadder-looking man than Carl Roebuck at that moment. "How about letting me take the El Camino for a day or two," Sully said.

"Why not? It's about shot anyhow," Carl said, fishing in his pocket for the keys. "Somebody said you were working at Hattie's," he added.

Sully shook his head, amazed as always about the speed with which inconsequential news traveled in Bath. "I better go see if Harold's got another beater to sell me. And I'm supposed to meet a guy named Miles Anderson who wants me to renovate some house on Main for him."

"You should have some business cards printed up," Carl suggested. "Don Sullivan: Jack-Off. All Trades."

"Thanks for the car." Sully jiggled the keys.

"I was under the impression you were going to do a job for *me* today," Carl said.

"I'll see if I can work you in this afternoon when I'm done jacking off," Sully said, sliding out of the booth again.

"Send that girl back over on your way out," Carl told him. "She was just offering to give me a header under the table."

Rub was wiping cream off his face with a paper napkin when Sully returned. "That girl kept looking at me," he said, indicating the woman who'd been sitting in Carl's booth and who now returned to it. "Now Carl's got her," he added unhappily.

Proxmire Motors was located a mile out of town, just off the blacktop, sandwiched in between Harold's Junkyard and Harold's Auto Parts, all three establishments owned and operated by Harold Proxmire. A tow truck with PROXMIRE WRECKING stenciled on the doors also sat in the yard. The sign out front, atop a bent pole, said HAROLD'S AUTOMOTIVE WORLD. Harold's had five full-time employees—Harold Proxmire; Harold's wife, Gloria; his chief and only mechanic, a sour-dispositioned man Harold had instructed never, under any circumstances, to speak to the public; a tiny, elderly man who wandered up and down the aisles of the auto parts store, squinting up into the dark upper reaches of the metal shelving stacked with remaindered auto parts; and a teenager, usually a dropout from the high school, whom the Proxmires took under their wing. Harold and Mrs. Proxmire were both Christians, and they hired only troubled Christian teens to fill the teenager slot in their employment scheme. Harold always tried to find a boy who'd been to jail or reform school at least once, somebody no one else would hire. He paid this boy minimum wage, and Mrs. Harold tutored him in Christian precepts for free from her seat at the cash register. Harold usually hired three of these boys a year. Four months was their average tenure, after which some were lured away by Mammon, in the form of a quarter-an-hour raise. Others just cleaned out the till and bolted. The last had left Mrs. Harold a note in the big bill slot of the cash register that said: "Jesus was a stupid fuck. And so are you."

Harold's current teenager, Dwayne, was lanky and red-haired and sullen, and so far he hadn't stolen anything from Harold's Automotive World, though he was beginning to wilt under the weight of daily moral instruction. Mrs. Harold's lectures about honesty, her constant reminders to be on the alert for Satan in his many guises, worried him some. Dwayne was never tempted to steal anything from Harold, whom he was fond of and grateful to, or even from Mrs. Harold, whom he could tolerate in small doses, and he wondered what was wrong with him that Satan should pay him so little attention. What annoyed him even more than the fact that Satan ignored him was the fact that Harold's customers did too. Every one of them wanted to deal with Harold only, and Dwayne's principal duty was to locate his boss, who divided himself among the lot, the garage, the junkyard and the parts store, supervising the operation of all of these at once, abandoning one to wait on an impatient customer in the other.

When the C. I. Roebuck El Camino pulled in, therefore, Dwayne did not expect to be accorded much respect, and he wasn't disappointed when Sully got out and said, "Where's Harold?" Dwayne had lost track. Weekday mornings there were so few customers at Harold's that Dwayne spent most of his time daydreaming and trying to steer clear of Mrs. Harold, who that day happened to be in an Old Testament mood.

Harold Proxmire himself was tall and lean and sallow-skinned and always clad in gray, and on a day as gray as this one he moved about the lot like a phantom on quiet, thick-soled shoes. "Somewheres," Dwayne said with a sweeping gesture that included all three businesses.

While her husband might be anywhere, Mrs. Harold, a tiny, round woman with a beehive hairdo that appeared to nearly double her height, could always be found at the cash register, and so this was where Sully sought her out. Mrs. Harold was the immediate source of her husband's Christianity, which had burrowed deep into his bones, an inner presence to counterbalance Mrs. Harold's brand of devotion, which was right out there in the open. In between sales she read scripture on her stool at the cash register, surrounded by Disney souvenirs. Disney World was Mrs. Harold's favorite place, and every year in February she dragged her husband to Orlando and rode every ride in the Magic Kingdom, where everything was clean and sunny and the lines moved. There was probably dirty, smelly, greasy machinery somewhere that ran the whole Kingdom, but the Disney people knew enough to keep it out of sight. Underground, probably. There was supposed to be a tour you could take where they'd show you how everything ran, but it was the one thing in Disney World Mrs. Harold wasn't interested in. It'd spoil the magic, was the way she looked at it. She wouldn't let Harold go see it either for fear he'd explain everything to her, which would be even worse.

Each year before they returned home, Mrs. Harold bought about two thousand dollars' worth of Disney paraphernalia, and she ran a small Disney concession, without authorization or permission, in the office of Harold's Automotive World. For most of the spring the walls would be covered with Disney movie posters and T-shirts, the cash register surrounded by water-skiing Goofys and rubber Plutos and a stack of big-eared mouse hats. Now, in late November, most of the merchandise had been sold off and the drab walls were again bare, except for a tall Cinderella poster that depicted, among other things, three plump Disney fairies, one of which reminded Sully of Mrs. Harold herself. Next to the cash register was a small box of cheap plastic Disney figurines and a half-dozen rubber alligators.

Invoices and purchases at all three businesses were rung through her register, and when she looked up from that register at her customers, her suspicious expression conveyed something of her inner fear that any one of them might be Satan in disguise. She was certain that Sully, for instance, was in league with the Devil somehow, though she doubted he was very far up in the satanic hierarchy. In a deep, secluded part of her heart to which Mrs. Harold no longer had immediate access, she was very fond of Sully, who always kidded with her, something nobody else had the courage to do, even her husband. Whenever Sully appeared, something of the girl she had once been always slipped out of the fortress she'd been imprisoned in, though that girl was easily recaptured, having forgotten how or where or even why to flee many long years ago.

"Hello, Esmerelda," Sully said when the door had swung closed behind him and Rub.

Esmerelda was not Mrs. Harold's name, of course, but it was the name Sully, who couldn't remember names, had been calling her for years and years. Was it the name of the imprisoned girl?

Mrs. Harold set her Bible down and refused Sully the smile she knew he was after. "Harold!" she barked into the intercom, which crackled to life over the bullhorns mounted on wooden poles in the yard outside. "Customer!"

Sully picked up and examined one of the rubber alligators from the box beside the cash register. "What extortionary price are you asking for these?" Sully asked Mrs. Harold.

Mrs. Harold had been charging three dollars for them and was about to tell Sully this when, to her surprise, Esmerelda spoke up and said, "One dollar."

"Okay," Sully said, slipping one of the alligators into his coat pocket and handing Mrs. Harold a dollar. "I'll take one. I know somebody who likes alligators. But tell me something before your husband gets here." Sully lowered his voice confidentially and leaned forward toward her, elbows planted on the countertop. "Don't lie to me, either," he warned. "Lying is a sin."

"Christians don't lie, Mr. Sullivan," Mrs. Harold said, her eyes narrowing. She leaned back on her stool to preserve the distance between them, even as the young girl imprisoned in Mrs. Harold's heart leaned forward.

Sully shrugged, as if to suggest that such statements were not worth arguing about. He'd let her skate if she wanted to. "Tell me the truth, then," he said. "You getting any?"

"Harold!" Mrs. Harold barked into the intercom.

Sully held up his hands as if she'd pointed a gun at him. "What'd I say?" He appealed to Rub, who was standing just inside the door looking like he might wet his pants. "Listen, Esmerelda. Correct me if I'm wrong, but there's nothing wrong with getting a little if you're married. Jesus doesn't mind as long as it's with Harold, right?"

"Harold!" Mrs. Harold's voice rocked the bullhorns.

Sully still had his hands raised in surrender. "I understand you gotta slow down a little at our age, but you don't have to stop completely. Every couple weeks, you should close up for the lunch hour, send the help home, lock the register, take Harold out back where there's nobody around . . . Be good for you. Be good for Harold too."

Harold rushed in then, wheezing and gray-faced, followed by Dwayne. "Oh," he said immediately, relieved once he'd taken in the situation. "It's you. I thought we were being robbed."

"You should hear the things he says when you're not around," Mrs. Harold reported, calmly now. With Harold on the scene, she was able to capture the girl, corral her, herd her back inside her heart's fortress.

"Esmerelda," Sully said, causing that girl to look back over her shoulder one last time. "Someday you're going to hurt my feelings." He pointed at the Bible. "Show me where it says in there that you're supposed to be mean to people."

The very worst thing about Sully, to Mrs. Harold's way of thinking, was that he had a way of routing scripture with sheer outrageousness. As a rule she could locate and quote a scriptural passage for almost any occasion. The moment he was gone, she'd think of dozens of passages that pertained, but never in Sully's presence. Right now, for instance, she found it impossible to take up his challenge to show him where in the Bible it said you were supposed to be mean to people, though she was sure it was there.

Before Mrs. Harold could think how to respond, Sully had turned away from her to talk to Harold, and both she and Esmerelda were sad.

"You got anything on the lot I might be interested in?" Sully asked.

"Truck give out?" Harold said, feeling guilty. He hated repeat automobile customers. That meant that the car or truck he'd sold them hadn't lasted forever, as he'd hoped. He knew that anything mechanical, like anything human, had a finite life, but he wished for a better world, one where the vehicles he sold people would run and run. Sully was particularly embarrassing as a repeat customer because the trucks he bought from Harold were always pretty well used up when he bought them. Harold had never sold Sully anything with fewer than eighty thousand miles on it. In fact, he always tried to talk Sully out of his purchases. "You'll just be back in six months," he'd warn. But six months always seemed a long way off to Sully, who was by and large an optimist and who always concluded that in six months he'd be better off than he was now for the simple reason that he couldn't be any worse off. He was almost always wrong, of course, in both the result and the reasoning. The truck Harold sold Sully today would be more dubious than the last, which would make Harold feel guiltier still, and in another year it would happen all over again. Harold wasn't sure capitalism and Christianity were compatible, even when the capitalism involved was as modest as Harold's Automotive World, which barely provided a living for Harold and Mrs. Harold, a surly mechanic, a half-blind clerk and a delinquent teenager.

Sully told Harold that the pickup had died this morning, describing its condition for Harold, who listened hopefully. "Could just be corrosion on your battery cables," he offered.

"Could be," Sully agreed. "But it isn't."

They had strolled outside, Rub tagging along a respectful stride behind, Dwayne lurking even farther in the background. "How do you know?" Harold said.

Sully thought about it. He didn't know for sure, of course, but it just made fatalistic sense the truck would die today. Yesterday he'd had a job offer that was contingent upon having a truck, which meant the truck had to die. Mired as he was in a stupid streak, Sully credited the perversity of cosmic law that governed such things. "Call it a hunch," he told Harold.

"Why don't you let me have a look," Harold said. He didn't discredit hunches exactly, but he liked to check them out just in case. "We'll send Dwayne out and have him tow it back."

"That'd be good," Sully admitted, momentarily buoyed by Harold's common sense.

"You met Dwayne?" Harold said, catching the boy, who wasn't expecting to be introduced, with his finger in his nose. "Go get Sully's truck and bring it here," Harold told him. Dwayne nodded, headed for the wrecker.

"Dwayne?" Harold called after him. "Don't you want to know where it is?"

Dwayne returned.

Sully gave him his address on Upper Main, told him the truck was parked at the curb.

"What color is it?" Dwayne asked.

Sully told him green. "It'll be the one that looks like it's not worth towing," he added.

Harold smiled as Dwayne retreated again. "Minute ago he was going to get a truck he didn't know the location of. Then after you tell him right where it is, he wants a full description."

Rub was wiping his palms on his shirt. "He picked his nose and then shook my hand," he said angrily.

"Here's what you should buy," Harold said on the way past the junkyard, indicating a snowplow blade that was leaning up against the chain-link fence. "Guy that owned it made good money doing driveways."

"How come he sold it?" Sully said.

"He didn't," Harold said. "His widow sold it. I picked it up at an auction."

"I don't seem to have a truck to attach it to, is the problem," Sully pointed out, although he was intrigued with the idea. With the town of Bath always cutting back on services and snow already in November, a plow might not be a bad idea. "I don't think I have the strength to push it myself."

"I'll make you a deal if you decide you want it," Harold said and quoted Sully a price that wasn't much more than what he'd paid for it at the auction. "Don't wait too long."

"I'd have to rob a bank if I'm going to buy a truck and the plow rig both," Sully said.

"Some people borrow from banks," Harold pointed out.

"Not people like me," Sully said. "Banks like you to own something of equal value they can take from you in case you run into some bad luck."

Harold had only two trucks at the moment. One was in pretty good shape. Sully took the other one for a test drive. It was marginally better than the truck he already owned, which was dead.

"I wouldn't charge you much for it," Harold said when Sully returned and looked at the vehicle skeptically. "But then it's not worth much. I bought it for parts myself. You'd be money ahead to buy the other one."

"I know it," Sully said. "But the money I'd be ahead is money I don't have."

"Well," Harold said. "Who knows. Maybe I can fix the one you got."

At that moment they heard the wrecker returning and watched Dwayne pull into the yard towing a truck that was not Sully's. Neither was it green.

Harold sighed mightily. "I'll be darned," he said quietly. He'd almost said he'd be damned, but he caught himself at the last second.

The house Miles Anderson had bought occupied the southwest corner of the intersection. It was the largest of the big houses on Upper Main, a three-level brick affair with two small widow's walks on the upper story and a huge wraparound porch that looked out upon both Main and Bowdon streets. The previous owner had been an elderly widow frightened into a nursing home two years before when a huge limb from one of Upper Main's ancient elms had fallen on her roof during the famous ice storm. Since then the house had sat empty. Sully could not recall ever seeing a For Sale sign in front of the house, but he seldom ventured up this way, so there might have been one.

"I wisht I could afford a big ole house like this," Rub said as he and Sully sat at the curb in the El Camino waiting for Miles Anderson to show up. So far Anderson was fifteen minutes late, and Rub was no good at loitering he wasn't paid for.

"Be a little big for just you and Bootsie, wouldn't it?" said Sully, who'd been sitting there wondering what anybody would do with a house that big, how you'd go about filling it up. Actually, Bootsie might be one of the few people he knew equal to the task. She swiped something from the Woolworth's she worked at every day and brought it home with her, and their apartment was about to burst under the strain. The easiest thing to steal at Woolworth's was goldfish, and Rub and Bootsie had an aquarium so full of them that the fish barely had room to turn around without knocking into one another. The murky water they swam in was permanently brown from processed fish food. In such conditions the fish died about as fast as Bootsie could slip them in their water-filled baggies into her spacious pockets. She also took things that didn't fit into her pockets. Somehow she'd managed to swipe a sofa-sized painting of the Atlantic Ocean at sunset, its crashing waves bright orange and blue. Neither Bootsie nor Rub had ever seen the Atlantic and so could not judge the painting's realism.

"I'd have my room way up there." Rub pointed to the room under the eave where the larger of the two widow's walks was located. "I could just walk out there on that little porch and stand there."

"I suppose you could, Rub," Sully said, trying to picture Rub on the widow's walk.

"I wisht we'd stopped for lunch," Rub added.

Sully consulted his watch for the umpteenth time. "Go eat," he said. His meeting with Miles Anderson would probably go better without Rub anyway. The only reason he'd wanted Rub along was to reassure Miles Anderson he had an able-bodied helper. Time enough for that later.

"Where?" Rub said.

"Hattie's is just down the street."

Rub turned and looked out the rear window, as if to verify this information. "What about you?"

"Bring me a hamburger."

"Could I borrow five dollars?"

"No," Sully said. "But I'll pay you for yesterday."

"Okay." Rub shrugged.

Sully gave him the money.

"What do you want on yours?"

"A bun."

"That's all?" Rub frowned.

"And ketchup."

"Okay." Rub started to get out.

"And cheese."

"Okay."

"And a pickle. And a slice of onion."

"Okay."

"And some relish."

"That's a hamburger with everything." Rub frowned.

"Okay. A hamburger with everything." Sully grinned.

"How come you didn't just say that?"

"And some fries," Sully told him. "And some ketchup for the fries."

Rub sighed, thought about it, waited for the information to sift down. "Okay," he said finally.

Sully gave him another three dollars.

"Why don't you come with me," Rub suggested.

"Because if I do, Miles Anderson will turn up here."

"How do you know?"

"Because that's the way it works."

When Rub was gone, Sully lit a cigarette and started making a list in his head. The porches were all sagging and the wood trim around the windows needed sanding and repainting and the odd board needed replacing. The roof didn't look too bad except where the limb had fallen, causing the chimney to tilt. On the ground there was a huge stump that Sully would have just left there but which Miles Anderson apparently wanted removed. Brown tangles of weeds festered everywhere. Indoors? Miles Anderson had mentioned half a dozen time-consuming tasks, which was fine with Sully, because most of the outdoor stuff would have to wait for spring anyway. If the weather turned mild, he might prune some bushes, rake up the two years' worth of sticks and leaves that had accumulated on the lawn, cart everything off. There looked to be enough work to keep him and Rub occupied, if not busy, all winter and most of the spring. Since Miles Anderson would be in New York, they could putter around at their own pace. On days when he felt up to it, Sully could do little jobs in the evening, which would actually save some money by keeping him out of The Horse and away from Wirf and out of conflict with Tiny. And on days when his knee wouldn't let him work, he could say screw it and Miles Anderson would never know.

Stubbing out his cigarette, he got out of the El Camino, went up the front walk, climbed the front porch. Through the large, uncurtained front window Sully could see a huge staircase leading upstairs, and along one wall was a fireplace big enough for a grown man to sit in the center of. In fact, the empty rooms were about twice as cavernous looking as his own, and he remembered how empty the rooms in Carl and Toby's house had looked before they started filling them up with possessions. This house was bigger than the Roebucks'. Whoever Miles Anderson was, Sully thought again, he must have a lot of shit if he expected to fill so many rooms. In two and a half decades he hadn't been able to fill his own flat, half the rooms of which he'd closed off. Other people seemed to have the opposite problem, he knew. Ruth was always complaining that she couldn't turn around in her house without bumping into something that wasn't there yesterday. And Miss Beryl's flat, the same size as Sully's own, was full of stuff she'd brought back from her travels. Sully was sure his inability to attract clutter meant something, but he wasn't sure what. He sat on the front porch steps and thought about it.

When it got to be eleven-thirty and Miles Anderson was half an hour late, Sully pulled out the slip of paper on which he'd written the address and checked it again, not that there was much chance of having made a mistake. This was the only vacant house on the street, and he had repeated what Anderson said on the phone. No, Miles Anderson was just late, and Sully was not surprised. He'd had the kind of voice Sully hated, the kind that suggested whatever time he arrived at a place was "on time" by definition. The good news was that if he hired Sully they wouldn't have to see each other much. That wouldn't be a bad arrangement if Sully could keep from getting bent out of shape here at the start. To avoid that, he stood, flexed his knees, strolled to the corner.

A block and a half down Bowdon, just before the street dead-ended, was the house where Sully had grown up. Until the Sans Souci went under and the baths were closed to the public, the house had been the caretaker's. For years Sully's father himself had been employed there, his job being to enforce the NO TRESPASSING signs posted every few feet along the eight-foot-high, rusting, cast-iron fence that ringed the estate. Basically the job was keeping kids out and making sure that no one got into the old hotel and stole its fixtures, its marble tiles and stained glass. Big Jim Sullivan was the perfect man for a job with few defined duties besides being mean to other people's kids. He was mean to his own for free, and it suited him fine to be paid for being mean to other people's. One boy he'd sent to the hospital, where he nearly died. Sully's father had caught him inside the fence and given chase, catching the boy perched delicately atop the fence where he was attempting to negotiate its jagged iron spikes.

Big Jim had been a slow, powerfully built man, proud of his bulk when bulk was called for and easily infuriated when faced with any situation, like chasing kids, that called not for bulk but for speed. And so it had enraged him to be first outrun, then made fun of (his father had claimed the boy was taunting him from atop the tall fence). And so Big Jim shook the fence, "to get him on down from there before he hurt himself," he later told the police. When the boy slipped, Big Jim had returned to the house, his face pale, to tell Sully's mother to call the fire department to come get the boy down. Also to call for a doctor. Both Sully and his brother had run outside to see. What they found had looked, at first, unreal, as if something from a strange dream had invaded the real world. From a distance the boy, his arms straight down at his sides, appeared to be standing up next to the fence and peering up into the sky. Except that his feet were dangling four feet off the ground. The boy had looked like he was standing on air.

The iron spike had entered the soft cavity under the boy's chin and now protruded from his open mouth like a black tongue. The kid's eye reminded Sully of the terrified eye of a fish, darting around in confusion at first, though, by the time the help finally arrived, the eye was still and glazed, staring disinterestedly into the blue sky. Years later, in France and Germany, Sully had seen men die in every manner imaginable, but he'd never seen anything to equal the sight of that boy hanging from the fence. Recollecting it, even now, was still powerful, and Sully suddenly realized that he had walked the block and a half to the house of his childhood and stopped right in front of the spot where the boy had hung. The spikes had been removed from atop the fence not long after the accident, as if to prevent a repetition of the freak tragedy, or perhaps to help people forget so ghastly a sight.

As Sully stood there, clutching the rusting fence, he became aware of a distant rumbling, and the ground beneath his feet began to shake, as if the past he'd been contemplating were trying to punch a hole through to the present, and he half expected to see his father appear, grinning, at one of the dark, vacant windows. Instead, a huge dump truck, its enormous bed full of dirt, emerged from the trees that surrounded the Sans Souci and bore down on the crooked house at unsafe speed, turning at the last moment and blowing on by, its thunder shaking the ground. Sully's first thought was that the driver had lost control, for while the truck was slowing, he could tell that it wouldn't be able to stop before it reached the wrought-iron fence Sully was still clutching with both hands. As he braced for impact, the truck drove right through where a section of fence had been cut away, turned left onto Bowdon and proceeded up the street toward Sully's position. When the truck rumbled by, the grinning driver saluted Sully with the tip of his billcap, one of his father's favorite drunken gestures, and it was only when the truck had turned onto Upper Main and disappeared in the direction of Schuyler Springs that Sully, still gripping the fence, was able to dispel the sense of disorientation that had washed over him like a wave. It was the pain shooting through his knee that located him again, though even this did not entirely dispel the feeling that Big Jim had paid him a visit.

As vivid to Sully as the horror of the hanging boy was the memory of his father, who'd worked the crowd that gathered to gawk at the boy and await help. "You just wait and see . . . this goddamn country anymore. I bet a hundred dollars they fire me for doing my job," his father had whispered conspiratorially to anyone who would listen. "You just wait and see if they don't." By the time the ambulance arrived, Sully's father had persuaded half the onlookers to feel sorry for *him,* even though the boy, deep in shock, still hung quietly from the spike a few feet away.

This gift of persuasion had been, Sully would come to realize, what his father had always been best at. The power to elicit sympathy was not a bad talent for a lazy, mean-spirited man to possess. If you could hang a twelve-year-old boy on a spike by his jaw and convince people who might more reasonably be expected to lynch you that they should be concerned for your job security, what couldn't you get away with? Certainly you could knock the hell out of your wife and kids and still be thought a regular guy by your neighbors, a guy who maybe had one too many now and then and got a little carried away, but an okay Joe. If you were persuasive enough, the only ones who knew for sure that you were a monster were your wife and kids, and probably you could convince even them that it was love that caused this pain, that the pain had its source in duty, not meanness and frustration. Sully's brother, Patrick, had never stopped loving the old man. Their mother? Who knew? Maybe even she, the most frequent victim of their father's cruelty, had remained perplexed to the end, waiting for her husband to change back into the man she'd fallen in love with.

Ruth had not understood Sully's refusal to make amends with his father. She'd thought she was making headway when Sully agreed to visit the old man at the VA nursing home in Schuyler Springs. That had been almost five years ago, a year before Big Jim Sullivan died, as it turned out. It was clear to Sully right from the start that his father had not lost his gift. It took the old man about three minutes to charm Ruth, a woman not easily fooled, into easy affection. Big Jim's act had changed a little, Sully observed, to take full advantage of the wheelchair he was now confined to after his stroke, but it was basically the same sly appeal. The nurses scurried around him, ignoring the urgent appeals of the other residents to attend to his father's needs in much the same fashion as his mother had attended to them, though she had done it out of fear. "I've made a man's mistakes," Big Jim, seemingly on the verge of tears, had told Ruth with that same mixture of humility and arrogance that Sully recalled from his childhood. He still slipped quite naturally into obsequious charm and sentimentality around those whose favor he wished to curry—professional men whose skills he feared or attractive young women whom he occasionally invited out to see the old hotel. Indeed, when Big Jim Sullivan was finally fired from his caretaker's job, it was for sneaking young women onto the property, not hanging the boy on the fence by his chin. "Yes, I've lived a man's life and made a man's mistakes," he told Ruth sadly, "and I'm plenty sorry for them, but they tell me God forgives all sinners, so I guess he'll forgive me too.

"Not that my own son ever will," he added when Sully snorted.

In fact, Sully's heart had hardened as soon as he saw his father, upon whom he had not laid eyes in years. He nodded agreement with his father's assessment of the situation. "You may fool God, Pop," he told the old man. "But you ain't shittin' me even for a minute."

"So," Ruth had said on the way home. "I always said you were nobody's fool. But I wouldn't have guessed you were smarter than God if you hadn't told me."

"Just on this one subject," said Sully, who could tell Ruth was ready to start a fight he'd just as soon have avoided.

They'd driven the rest of the way in silence, though Ruth had tried once more when they got back to town. "What does it say about a grown man who won't forgive his father?" she wanted to know.

"I have this feeling you're going to tell me," Sully sighed.

"You're just like him, you know," Ruth offered.

"No, I don't know that."

"It's true. I look at him and see you."

"I can't help what you see, Ruth," Sully told her when she pulled over to the curb to let him out. "But you can be thankful you aren't married to him."

"I'm thankful I'm not married to either of you," she said, pulling away from the curb.

They'd "been good" for quite a while after that.

His father's house was in far worse condition than Miles Anderson's. Sully could tell that even from outside the gate. The whole structure seemed to tilt, and the wood had gone gray with weather. Black tar paper was visible in patches where the shingles had come free and slid off the pitched roof and into a disintegrating heap on the ground below. Which meant that the weather had probably penetrated the interior, though without going inside it was hard to tell how badly. There was an attic to act as buffer between the roof and the two floors below. But there were probably other problems. Nobody had lived in the house in a long time. For all Sully knew, the cellar might be flooding every time it rained. The house might be rotting from the ground up even as it ruptured from the top down. Probably there were termites, maybe even rats. Ruth had been after him for years to fix up and sell the property, not understanding that he got more pleasure out of its gradual decay than he would out of the money from its sale, which would disappear so completely that a year later he wouldn't be able to remember what he'd spend it on. Whereas if he held onto the property it was always right there, visibly worse than the last time he'd looked. He didn't even want to think about changing his mind or to contemplate what it would cost to reverse the long process of decomposition. There were piles of dog shit everywhere, and the first thing he'd have to do was shovel all that into a wheelbarrow and cart it off. A job for Rub, actually.

Speaking of whom. From where he stood he could see that Rub had returned from Hattie's and discovered Sully missing. The El Camino was still there, though, presenting Rub with a puzzle he wasn't likely to solve on his own. He was peeking into the windows of Miles Anderson's house when Sully returned to the intersection and called to him. "What're you looking for?"

Rub stood, looking relieved. "You."

"You know what I'm looking for?" Sully wondered. "My hamburger."

Rub looked stricken. "I forgot."

Sully motioned for Rub to get into the car. "Good," he said. "The whole time you were gone I was wondering whether you'd forget the ketchup or the pickle or the relish or the fries. Instead you just forgot the whole thing."

"I told you you should have come with me," Rub said, playing the only card in his hand. "That guy never showed up, did he."

"He never did," Sully admitted, turning the key in the ignition. He didn't pull away from the curb, though.

"Where we going now?" Rub asked, hoping he'd deflected the razzing.

"No place," Sully told him. "You're still forgetting something."

"What?"

"The three dollars I gave you for the hamburger you didn't get me."

Rub found the money, handed it over, settled in for more razzing, probably an afternoon's worth.

"You want to know the good news?" Sully asked him.

Rub didn't but said yes anyway.

"I wasn't hungry," Sully told him, making a U-turn.

Ruby's mascara was on the move again. It had been running all morning. Every time she quit crying, she went into the tiny bathroom, washed her face with the gradually graying yellow washcloth and reapplied the eye shadow. No sooner was this accomplished than she started crying again, thinking about what a rat Carl Roebuck was and how desperately she loved him anyway. It had not occurred to her until this morning that a man who would cheat on his wife would also cheat on his secretary, and the realization made her bitter. More than bitter. Angry. In the bathroom mirror she'd just noticed that her mascara had stained the neckline of her favorite blouse, the expensive one, the pearl white, semitransparent one she liked to wear under her scarlet bolero. The bolero was made of thick wool, and with it on you couldn't tell that she was wearing no brassiere beneath the pearl white blouse. Ruby was light skinned, and she possessed a perfectly matched set of small dark nipples that showed through the semitransparent blouse to intoxicating effect. Naturally, she kept the bolero buttoned when Carl's construction workers were in the office, but when she and Carl were alone she let the bolero swing open.

Now the collar of this prized blouse was ruined with mascara, and Ruby was ruined too, right back where she'd been throughout her entire life, crying her eyes out about yet another man who wasn't even worth it. A man who'd make all kinds of promises and then not deliver. Ruby had never known a man who'd ever told her the truth about anything, and the ones she gravitated to, like a moth to a flame, were the biggest liars of all.

And if all this wasn't rotten enough, if her day wasn't as completely ruined as her pearl white, semitransparent blouse, now she was going to have to deal with Sully. She could hear him stumping slowly up the three flights of stairs, grumbling every step of the way. It wasn't bad enough that Carl Roebuck, who'd told her once that his only desire was to spend the rest of his mortal life—no, of all eternity, he'd said—in Ruby's arms, was the biggest rat of all; now she was going to have to listen to Sully's I-told-you-so.

"Ruby," he said from the doorway where he'd stopped to catch his breath, "are those your nobs staring at me or what?"

Ruby quickly threw on the bolero, having forgotten, in her distress, that she'd taken it off to examine the extent of the damage to her blouse. The last person on earth she wanted to show her nipples to was Sully.

"He's not in," she sneered.

"That's what you always say," Sully pointed out, plopping down in one of the outer-office chairs and taking a deep drag on his cigarette.

"Sometimes it's true," Ruby told him.

"Did he leave a message?"

"Why would he leave you a message?"

"Because he had a job for me, which I could do, maybe, if he'd tell me what it is and where."

"Your ash is going to fall on the carpet," Ruby observed.

Since this was true, Sully stubbed out the cigarette in a tiny ashtray on the magazine-strewn coffee table. "He's not worth crying over, you know."

"How do you know who I'm crying over?" Ruby said.

"I know Carl has half the female population of Bath in tears at any given moment," Sully said. "Why is a mystery, I admit."

"He understands women, is why," Ruby said defiantly.

"Well," Sully said, "if that's true, he deserves them all. Any idea where he's at?"

"Probably with his perfect wife that he won't divorce," Ruby guessed bitterly. "The one he buys brand-new cars for. The one who lives in the mansion on Glendale while I live in a studio apartment and drive an eight-year-old car I bought secondhand."

"Life's unfair," Sully said to keep from smiling.

"It's a blow job is what it is," Ruby agreed seriously. "I always get the slimy end of the dick, too."

"The other end's attached," Sully pointed out.

"Oh, buzz off, Sully. Can't you see I'm all upset?"

"Okay, dolly," Sully said, getting to his feet again. "Tell him I was here and I'll be at The Horse if he wants me to do that job. And Ruby—"

"What?"

"Don't take your love to town."

∎ ∎ ∎

Sully parked Carl's El Camino outside the OTB in the middle of the diagonally striped no-parking zone. A young cop named Officer Raymer, whom Sully'd had run-ins with before, was bending at the knees in the doorway. "You got two minutes to move that," he told Sully, not unreasonably. "Or you get a ticket."

"Go ahead," Sully said. "It's not my car."

Inside, Otis was among the other yellow windbreaker men, several of whom called out, "Sully!"

"Get away from me, you," Otis warned. "You gave me a nightmare."

"Good," Sully said.

"I dreamed an alligator crawled up the stairs and got in bed with me. Woke up kicking and screaming. My wife's got a big bruise on her thigh."

"And you believe that's how she got the bruise, Otis?" Sully said. He considered giving Otis the rubber alligator he'd bought from Mrs. Harold, but decided the occasion was not right.

Except for Otis, this remark struck the windbreaker men as pretty funny. Several offered other explanations for the bruise. Sully watched Officer Raymer grow impatient through the OTB's front window.

"I'll have you know my wife's been faithful to me for forty years," Otis said indignantly.

Sully nodded. "That's pretty near the whole time you've been married, isn't it?"

"Go bet your sucker triple," Otis advised. "Before you give me another nightmare."

Sully held up his hands in self-defense. "I never meant to give you bad dreams, Otis. In fact, I think Florida's a good place for you. I just wanted you to be careful of alligators, is all."

"Get away," Otis said, swatting at him. "Just get away from me."

"I think you *should* move to Florida," Sully went on. "If you're careful, you'll probably be safe."

"Go. Get lost."

"Just one little word of advice," Sully insisted. "When you wake up in the morning?"

"He won't go away," Otis said, appealing to the others.

"Just peek under the bed," Sully said, demonstrating. "A quick peek. If you see teeth, stay in bed."

"I'll dream about this all night now," Otis said miserably.

Sully bet his triple, shot the breeze for a minute with the ticket seller and sauntered out just as Officer Raymer finished writing the ticket.

Sully took it with good grace, opened the passenger side door and tossed it into the glove box. "Who do you like in the game Saturday?" he said genially.

The policeman looked suspicious, but this particular topic was too tempting, Sully too convincingly interested in his opinion. "Ah, Schuyler," he said sadly. "They're too damn big."

Sully nodded. "You played for Bath, didn't you?"

"Varsity, three years," Office Raymer said proudly.

"I'd sure like to see our kids win one," Sully said, starting around the El Camino. "Maybe then they'd go out into the world and make something of their lives."

Officer Raymer started to agree, then caught a whiff of something. His nose actually wrinkled.

"The losers all stay around here and become cops." Sully grinned, opening the door of the El Camino.

When the policeman actually rested his hand on the butt of his revolver, Sully laughed out loud.

"I heard a great joke," Wirf said, pivoting on his bar stool when Sully came in off the street, having given up entirely on work for the day. There was a certain degree of aggravation beyond which Sully would not go, and today he'd reached it. There were days when the world set up more than its usual phalanx of obstacles, and when Sully sensed this principle in action he hung it up. "You'll appreciate it, too, since it's the story of your life," Wirf said.

"I bet I don't laugh," Sully said, winking up at Birdie, the day bartender, who had climbed up onto a stool to adjust the focus on her soap channel. The picture came in fine as long as she stood there.

"This guy wants to get on the freeway," Wirf began.

"Stop a minute," Sully told him. "I like to concentrate when I look up Birdie's skirt."

Birdie fiddled with the fine tuning, unconcerned. "There's nothing up there anymore," she said. "How come the only channel we don't get worth a sour old dog turd is the channel my soaps are on?"

"I see something up there," Sully said, leaning forward. "But I'm not sure what."

"This guy's heading up an off ramp by mistake," Wirf said. "Off to the side there's this sign that says 'Wrong Way.' "

"I swear to God I'm going to quit if Tiny doesn't spring for cable,"

Birdie said, finally climbing down. "Look at that. You can't tell who's in bed with who."

"They all look alike to me anyhow," Sully said, craning his neck to see the TV. "And I don't think that's a bed."

"You gotta watch every day," Birdie said. "Otherwise soaps don't make sense."

"So the guy keeps going anyway," Wirf continued. "And pretty soon there's another sign. This one's all in capital letters. It says 'YOU'RE GOING THE WRONG WAY.' "

"You had a call about half an hour ago," Birdie said.

"Miles Anderson?" Sully guessed.

"Woman," Birdie said. "Said she'd reach you at home tomorrow morning."

"So the guy keeps going up the off ramp," Wirf continued. "Now there's a great big sign with huge red letters that says 'DANGER! TURN AROUND!' "

Sully fished around in his pocket for change that wasn't there. He handed Birdie a dollar bill. "How about some quarters?" he said. Birdie was squinting at the set intently.

"Anyway," Wirf said. "The guy ignores the sign and keeps going the wrong way, and just before he hits the oncoming traffic there's a tiny sign on the shoulder that says 'What the hell, you've come this far.' "

Birdie slapped four quarters onto the bar in front of Sully.

Wirf picked his money off the bar and stood up. "I don't know why I even come in here," he said.

"To be among friends?" Sully guessed.

"That must be it." Wirf nodded. *"Vaya con huevos, amigos."*

"That was a pretty terrific joke, Wirf," Sully called to Wirf's retreating figure. "Laugh, I thought I'd die."

"All you people should treat me better," Wirf said over his shoulder. "When I'm gone, you'll discover how hard it is to find another one-legged attorney who's always in a good mood."

"He's right, too," Birdie said seriously when the door closed behind Wirf. "I don't know how we'll replace him."

Sully frowned. "Why would we want to? He's right there on that bar stool about eight hours a day."

"I hear he's a sick man," Birdie said.

Sully considered this possibility. "I don't think so," he said. "He just drinks too much."

"My cousin works up at the hospital," Birdie said ominously. "According to her, his liver's about gone. He's been peeing blood for months."

"Wirf?" Sully said. Hell, he started to say, they'd been standing together side by side peeing into the trough in The Horse's men's room every night for the past ten years. Except that this wasn't true, Sully realized. Lately, though he couldn't recall when it had started, Wirf had been peeing in the single-stall commode. "He doesn't look sick," Sully said weakly.

Birdie shook her head. "He looks sick as hell. When was the last time you really looked at him?"

"He'd have said something," Sully said.

"No," Birdie said. "He wouldn't."

She was right, too, Sully was suddenly sure. Wirf wouldn't have said shit if he had a mouthful. "I hope you're wrong, Birdie."

"Me too," she said. "Go make your phone call."

Ruth picked up on the first ring. "Hi," Sully said. "That you that called The Horse?"

"It was," she said. "I've got exactly an hour and a half if you feel up to some love in the afternoon."

"There is nothing in this wide world I'd like more," Sully said quite honestly. "Except a new truck." More honestly still. A new truck and an assurance that what he'd just heard about Wirf wasn't true.

"Did he say, 'Go with eggs'?" Birdie wondered when Sully returned.

"Who?" Sully said.

"Wirf," Birdie said. "He said, *Vaya con huevos.*' "

"I wasn't paying any attention," Sully admitted.

"No kidding," Birdie said.

"You're just all discombobulated," Mrs. Gruber explained in response to Miss Beryl's announcement that she was not in the best of spirits. Discombobulated was one of Mrs. Gruber's favorite terms, and when she used it over the phone, she did so unself-consciously, as if it were common, a word you'd hear half a dozen times in conversations everywhere, regardless of demographics. "I'm all discombobulated myself," she told Miss Beryl. "I just can't help thinking it's Monday." She went on to explain why. Yesterday, Thanksgiving Day, they'd gone out for dinner at the Northwoods Inn, a place they seldom visited except for Sunday dinner. So yesterday had become Sunday in Mrs. Gruber's mind, which meant that today had to be Monday.

"I don't see what difference it makes," Miss Beryl told her friend irritably. It wasn't as if Mrs. Gruber now had to look forward to a work-week instead of a weekend. "Let it be Monday if it wants to."

Mrs. Gruber considered this lunatic advice. "Well," she said after a brief pause. "I see somebody's grumpy today."

This was true enough. The dreadful Joyce woman was gone at last. She'd finally emerged groggily from the guest bedroom at eleven o'clock in the morning, having finally been awakened by the telephone. Clive Jr. had called three times between nine and eleven to check on her. It was his plan to finish up at the bank and take her to lunch in Schuyler Springs, there being no suitable place in Bath. Proximity to Schuyler was a good way to sell Bath, Clive Jr. had long ago discovered. His usual strategy was to put visitors up in a plush Schuyler Springs hotel, wine and dine them there, take them to the races or to a concert in the summer and thereby impress them that all this was only ten minutes from where the money'd be spent. When he could avoid it, he never took potential investors to Bath at all.

"Do you think she's all right?" he asked Miss Beryl the last time he called. "I can't believe she's still asleep."

"You would if you could hear the way she's snoring," Miss Beryl had told him.

Normally, getting this dreadful Joyce woman out of her house would have improved Miss Beryl's spirits enormously, but all morning she had remained haunted by the sight of old Hattie in grim flight, her flimsy housecoat trailing behind her like a cape in the wind. Miss Beryl had never much cared for the old woman, whom she'd always considered grasping and crude, but the indignity of her flight and capture had brought Miss Beryl to the edge of tears. Worse, she'd seen herself in the old woman and recognized that it was this very eventuality that her son was attempting to guard against. The day would come when they'd need a net for her too. Clive Jr. just wanted to make sure that "when the time came" at least her financial affairs would be in order. Maybe that's all he wanted. She would just have to face reality and do as Clive Jr. asked. Sell him the house as a hedge against the boom getting lowered. Do it now rather than later. Come to terms instead of stubbornly putting it off until it was too late.

Having reached this sensible conclusion, her spirits plummeted precipitously the rest of the morning. Midmorning, she'd had a nosebleed, then, just when she thought they couldn't get any lower, the *North Bath*

Weekly Journal arrived, as it always did on Friday, midmorning. Today, as usual, two of its eight pages were devoted exclusively to local opinion. Those voiced in the "Sound Off!" section collectively represented the rhetorical sophistication of a Bronx cheer played through a bullhorn. Since the authors were allowed to use aliases, there were no discernible rules. One letter was a character assassination of the high school marching band leader, another a fundamentalist Christian credo of sorts, the point of which, if one existed, was lost to faulty grammar and syntax, while yet another letter was an inflammatory attack on homosexuals in particular and perverts in general, a letter which stopped just short of advocating their summary extermination. The reason for the author's reticence on this last ethical point was that extermination was thankfully not needed now that God had sent His very own virus to do the job. Yet another writer urged every resident of Bath to turn out for the long-awaited Big Game this Saturday, thus proclaiming to the whole world that their community was second to none when it came to school spirit. This last was the sort of letter that would have warmed the cockles of Clive Sr.'s heart. School spirit had been one of his most deeply held tenets until his school did away with football and gave him driver education by way of compensation.

Miss Beryl read each of these letters in its entirety, searching among them for some even accidental lapse into good sense, true feeling, even rudimentary decency or goodwill and wishing that the thoughts therein expressed by her neighbors could be explained as simple discombobulation. The best she was able to do was to reflect that people invariably exhibited the very worst side of their flawed natures when invited to put their thoughts into writing, especially when the invitation was sanctioned hit-and-run posing as democracy in action.

Here was the rub, Miss Beryl knew. If she was going to surrender her affairs and thus her freedom, one had better trust the wisdom of so doing. Admittedly, Clive Jr. was not one of the letter writers in the *Bath Weekly*, and turning over her affairs, her leverage, to him was not the same as signing over her assets to eighth-graders, past or present. Still, Miss Beryl could not help suspecting that even if she was slipping, even if she was not the woman she had been a decade ago, her health, like her equilibrium, more precarious, even if she was more given to momentary confusions and disorientations, she was still sharper than most of the people she knew, including the people who wrote letters to the *Bath Weekly*, including her friend Mrs. Gruber, who wanted today to be Monday, perhaps even including her son, who looked out her front window and saw the Gold

Coast. Miss Beryl was not old Hattie and never had been. More to the point, there was a good chance she never would be.

"This is your fault," she'd been telling Clive Sr. when Mrs. Gruber called to explain her present discombobulation. The last time Miss Beryl had willingly surrendered her future to another human being had been when she'd allowed Clive Sr. to talk her into marrying him and living out their lives in Bath. How had he ever managed that? she wondered. Love, dern it, was how. He had loved her, and in return for this great gift she had allowed him to bring her to Bath, where he had then promptly abandoned her to a life of fighting with eighth-graders. Then he'd gone and let himself be killed and left her to live out the rest of her many years with "Finally Fed Up" and "A True Christian" for company. Now here she was contemplating mortgaging her independence to this same man's son, a man who'd grown to resemble his father so minutely that he might have been Clive Sr.'s clone.

"I'm sorry if I sound grumpy," Miss Beryl told Mrs. Gruber. "I was just sitting here wishing I had somebody to fight with when you called."

Mrs. Gruber ignored this explanation. "I saw Clive Jr. drive by," she said. "Was that a woman with him in the car?" Mrs. Gruber knew perfectly well it was.

"Clive Jr., star of my firmament, is to wed," Miss Beryl said. "I only just learned of it myself."

"And that's made you grumpy."

"Hardly," Miss Beryl objected. "I'm perfectly happy to turn Clive Jr. over to any woman who will have him, and this one apparently will."

"Well, I'm eating like a bird today," said Mrs. Gruber, who had little use for transitions. "Prune juice. Later a little dry toast and tea."

Dry toast, tea and prune juice was Mrs. Gruber's way of warding off the constipation that tormented her after a heavy meal at the Northwoods Inn. Yesterday she had eaten a green salad, ambrosia salad, carrot-raisin salad, pea-cheese salad and macaroni salad from the buffet. Then Old Tom, stuffing, cranberries and a candied yam. Then pumpkin pie and whipped cream. There wasn't room for all of this on Mrs. Gruber's ninety-five-pound frame, and today it all weighed on her rather heavily.

The other thing that weighed her down was guilt. For more than a year, as Miss Beryl suspected, she had been secretly feeding information concerning her friend to Clive Jr., who called her at least once a week to make sure that his mother was okay. She wasn't spying for Clive Jr. exactly, just passing along information. For Miss Beryl's own good, as Clive Jr.

himself insisted. His mother was too stubborn for her own safety. Hadn't she tried to keep a secret of her fall last summer, along with the badly sprained wrist that resulted? Mrs. Gruber understood Clive Jr.'s concern for his mother, and so she told him little things. In return, he told her things, too. She already knew, for instance, that Clive Jr. was getting married, and she now made a mental note to pretend she hadn't known.

The only misgiving that Mrs. Gruber had about her arrangement with her best friend's son was that sometimes she ended up telling Clive Jr. things she never intended to. This morning, for instance, when Clive Jr. called from the bank to inquire whether they'd had a pleasant Thanksgiving dinner at the Northwoods Motor Inn, Mrs. Gruber hadn't the slightest intention of telling him how Miss Beryl had gotten lost in Albany and how they'd nearly not found the restaurant at all.

"Tell me about her," Mrs. Gruber said.

"About whom?"

"Clive Jr.'s young woman."

"She's not young," Miss Beryl said. "She's late fifties, if she's the girl in the yearbook."

"Is she nice?"

"She talks a lot," Miss Beryl said. "She's a fan of the president's."

"She sounds nice," said Mrs. Gruber, who also liked the president and didn't mind talk nearly so much as the silence of her big house. "When will the wedding be?" she asked, anxious to find out how much Clive Jr. had told his mother. Early spring was what he'd told Mrs. Gruber. Around Easter.

"I neglected to ask," Miss Beryl admitted. "I don't believe there's any hurry. I'm sure the bride's not pregnant."

"Will Joyce work at the bank?" This was actually a question she'd been meaning and kept forgetting to ask Clive Jr., who had mentioned that his wife-to-be was an accountant.

Miss Beryl was about to confess that she didn't know the answer to this question either when something occurred to her. "How did you know her name was Joyce?"

Mrs. Gruber froze. Despite her intention to be careful, she'd spilled the beans. "I have to go," she said. "My telephone's ringing."

"You're *on* the telephone," Miss Beryl pointed out. "It can't be ringing."

"The doorbell, I meant," Mrs. Gruber said. And hung up.

Miss Beryl hung up too but let her hand rest on the phone while she thought. At least now she was sure who the snitch was. Lately she'd begun to fear it might be Sully. Her advisers had been divided on this issue, just as they were on all issues. Clive Sr. subscribed to his son's view that Sully had had her snookered for years, while Driver Ed assured her that Sully was loyal and even whispered suspicions about Clive Jr., suspicions Miss Beryl felt guilty about listening to. Now that she was sure, Miss Beryl couldn't help smiling. "How do you like them apples?" she asked Clive Sr.

Clive Sr. looked sheepish behind glass.

Miss Beryl's hand was still on the phone in its cradle when it rang again.

"There wasn't a soul at the door," Mrs. Gruber said, as if this were a great mystery. "I can't understand it. I heard the bell."

"You know what you are?" Miss Beryl said ominously, winking at Driver Ed across the room.

Mrs. Gruber gulped. "What?" she asked a little fearfully.

"You're all discombobulated."

Ruth was in a good mood and at a loss to explain why. Just yesterday, Thanksgiving, of all days, she'd hit some sort of new low. Things had been so rotten she'd telephoned Sully, hoping he'd cheer her up. Talk about desperation. After so many years the one thing she should have known about Sully was that he was better at prolonging the good mood you happened already to be in than getting you out of the doldrums. He was far too honest to cause anybody to feel better than they were inclined to feel on their own.

And so, not surprisingly, Sully, who had failed dismally to cheer Ruth up yesterday, had been just the thing she needed today, when her own inclination was toward high spirits. Today Ruth felt fine, despite the tawdriness of the motel room, the grunginess of its shower and the fact that Sully had fallen dead asleep no more than a minute after they'd finished making love for the first time in many months. When she emerged from the shower, wrapped in a motel towel, he was snoring peacefully, his eyes half open but showing nothing but the whites. Though it was late November, he still hadn't entirely lost his summer coloration, which always made Ruth smile, the way his face and neck and forearms were brown, almost gray, from exposure to sun and wind while the rest of him remained pale, almost translucent. Always a strangely shy man, he'd taken the trouble of pulling the sheet up to his waist before falling asleep. His head lay tilted up against the bed's headboard, his hands locked behind his neck, a posture designed, in all probability, to ward off the sleep that had overtaken him anyway. That he should try to stay awake when he was so tired struck Ruth as sweet, the sort of small gesture Sully was capable of at times. She knew he needed the sleep a lot more than he had needed to make love.

Ruth, on the other hand, had needed to make love. She no longer granted her husband conjugal privileges, a fact he seemed barely to have noticed. It was possible he had another woman, but Ruth doubted this. As far as she could tell, Zack was just one of those men who gravitated naturally toward abstinence, as if celibacy were an old La-Z-Boy recliner, comfortable and molded and requiring more effort to get out of than into. She doubted he cared much about her affair with Sully. He was capable of jealousy when properly instigated, but she understood that what really bothered him was being made a fool of. And Ruth suspected that what Zack really would have liked was for people to quit telling him about her and Sully so he could pretend ignorance. He pretended ignorance as convincingly as laziness, and his pretense of laziness was indistinguishable from the real thing.

Nearly two and a half months of "being good" had left Ruth needy, and making love with Sully this afternoon had made her happy without, unfortunately, diminishing her need. What she hoped was that the pendulum of their affair was swinging back again, that their being good for a while would have the salutary effect of rekindling both their passions. She felt such tenderness for Sully as he lay before her now, asleep, that she indulged for a moment the idea of accepting his proposal of marriage, contemplating what their life together would be like. That, however, was an excellent way to spoil a good mood, something Ruth adamantly refused to do. Instead she let the towel fall to the floor, carefully drew back the sheet and began to stroke Sully, whose eyelids fluttered by way of response, though for a few seconds he continued to snore. When he finally opened the eyes that never entirely closed, even in sleep, he grinned at her. "Oh," he said. "It's you."

"Yes, it's me," Ruth said. "And watch yourself. You see what I've got here, don't you?"

Sully closed his eyes again, inhaling deeply. "I just hope you don't have any further plans for it. I'm sixty, remember. And in no shape for double-headers."

"Too bad," Ruth said. "And here I was actually considering your proposal."

"Which?"

"Yesterday's. You asked me to marry you."

Sully thought about it. "No, I didn't," he said finally. "I asked you why we didn't get married. I knew there was a good reason. I'd just forgotten what it was."

Ruth continued stroking. "That's not how I remember the conversation."

"I guess if you insisted," Sully said, wide awake now. "I would marry you. You're one of the better-looking older women in Bath. Ow!"

"Take that back."

"You're *not* one of the better-looking older women in Bath? Ow again."

"You know what?" Ruth said. "I think you *like* pain."

"Just don't lean on my bad knee," he warned. "I've enjoyed about as much of that pain as I can stand."

"I didn't hurt before, did I?" she said, recalling their lovemaking.

"No," Sully assured her, feeling a little guilty about his own greatly reduced abilities as a lover. "It couldn't have been much good for you."

"It was grand," she told him dreamily. "I like being on top."

Sully grinned at her. "You and every other woman."

Ruth ignored this. "I like being on the bottom, too."

"Well, I'm glad you're flexible," he told her. "But I think you're going to be on top from now on."

She was tracing a line down the inside of his thigh with her fingernail, stopping just short of the swelling, as if she knew precisely where the pain began. "It's gotten worse, hasn't it?" she said. The sight of his knee had surprised her when he slipped out of his pants. He'd done this with his back to her so she couldn't get a good look, but she'd seen enough.

"It's just fluids, probably," Sully told her. "I'll go in to the VA one of these weeks and let the bastards drain it. I've got even bigger headaches right now, if you can believe it. You wouldn't happen to have a spare two grand on you?"

Ruth propped herself up on one elbow. "On me?"

"I didn't think so." He explained to her about the truck, about the one Harold wanted him to buy, about the snowplow blade.

"Sounds perfect," Ruth said. "Therefore, you won't do it, right?"

"I don't see how I can," Sully said. "Even if I could find somebody dumb enough to lend me that kind of money. I'm getting too old to owe people more than I can make in a month or two."

"Will you get mad if I remind you that you own property?"

Sully shook his head. "Not if you don't object to me reminding you that I don't. At least not really."

"Then who does, Sully?" Ruth wanted to know. "If you don't own your father's property, who does?"

"I have no idea," Sully told her. "The town of Bath, probably. My father hadn't paid his taxes in years, and I sure haven't paid any. They keep telling me they're going to sell it at auction. They may have already, for all I know."

"They'd notify you first, Sully."

"They may have. I throw all that shit out unopened along with the sweepstakes entries."

"Would you like me to find out for you?"

"No. I don't want anything of his, Ruth," he told her for the umpteenth time. "You know I don't."

"It's not a question of want anymore, Sully. It's need. You need transportation. Sell the place and use the money for what you need. Forget your father."

"That would be the sensible thing," he admitted, hoping that this would end the discussion. Sometimes admitting that Ruth was right satisfied her.

"Which is your way of saying you won't, right?"

Sully sat up, found his cigarettes, lit one and shared it with Ruth. "I drove by there today, oddly enough," Sully admitted. Even this much, acknowledging the existence of the house and his possible interest in it, was hard. So hard he'd been guilty of a half truth by suggesting that all he'd done was drive by, that he hadn't stopped, hadn't looked the house over from outside the gate, thought about what the land it was sitting on might bring. "Back taxes would probably be more than it's worth. Not that it matters, since I don't have the back taxes."

"Suppose you sell the property and it only brings ten thousand, which is nothing. And suppose there's seven thousand in back taxes. That'd be a lot. That's still three grand left. But you don't need three grand, is that what you're telling me?"

"What I was thinking about was giving it to Peter," he said, wondering what Ruth's reaction to this idea would be. She was alternately solicitous and resentful of Sully's son, whom she had never met.

"That doesn't solve *your* problem," Ruth pointed out.

"I'd give it to you if there was a way," he smiled. "It might make

Zack suspicious if I gave you a house, though. People have been telling him about us for twenty years, and that might just convince him they weren't all lying."

"Thanks anyway," Ruth smiled, "but I've already got a decrepit house."

"What about if I sold it and slipped you the money somehow? You could use it for Gregory's college. Zack wouldn't have to know."

"It's a sweet offer, but Gregory's my responsibility," Ruth said.

The way she emphasized her son's name made clear that they were going to talk about her daughter—their daughter, Ruth liked to think—which meant they were destined to enter the old argument. The girl had Zack's features written all over her, though Ruth wouldn't admit it. "I'm sure," she kept telling Sully. Most of the time Sully was just as sure of the opposite. Ruth just had some woman's need for Janey to be theirs, not hers and Zack's.

There'd only been one time Sully had seriously doubted his conclusion, and that had been a year ago spring, a few months after his accident. He'd gone to the IGA and stood in Ruth's checkout line as the shifts were changing. When she finished ringing up Sully's purchases—a tube of toothpaste, a pack of cigarettes—she rang out her register and they walked out together. "Here's somebody I want you to meet," Ruth said when a loud rusty old Cadillac pulled up alongside and tooted.

Ruth towed him over and was about to introduce him to Janey when she noticed the small child sitting next to her mother in the front seat. "Where the hell's the car seat I bought you?" Ruth said, immediately angry.

"I figured you'd notice that, first goddamn thing, before hello even," Janey said.

"It cost sixty bucks," Ruth told her. "You're damn right I noticed."

"Guess Who sold it," Janey informed her. Sully couldn't help smiling to himself at the fact that Ruth's daughter had picked up her mother's terminology for referring to her husband.

"I buy her a car seat and he sells it?"

"Well, it's not like I didn't warn you," the girl said, without apparent sympathy for her mother's position. "Buy another one and see if the same thing doesn't happen, you idiot."

Ruth was glaring at her daughter now.

"Don't look at me like that," Janey told her mother. "Wasn't me that sold it. All I did was inherit my mother's bad judgment in men." She eyed

Sully suspiciously as she said this, as if to suggest he'd been put there in her field of vision at that moment to illustrate her point.

Which did not escape her mother. "Say hi to Sully," Ruth told her. "Don Sullivan, actually."

The girl shook Sully's hand like a man would. "Hi," she said, adding, to Ruth's apparent surprise, "Heard a lot about you."

"Yeah," her mother said. "Well, small towns . . ."

"Right." Janey grinned. Then to her mother, "You want a ride home or not?"

Ruth, peering inside the car again, ignored this. "You want to come see Grandma?" she said.

"Go ahead," Janey told the child, who climbed over her mother's lap, then to the open window and Ruth's waiting arms. Only then did Sully see the child's eye and feel something inside him lurch.

"Listen, I've got to run," he'd told Ruth.

"Yeah, I know," Ruth said. "I'll see you sometime."

Later that night she'd called him at The Horse. By then he'd had time to consider why he'd seen himself in the child's deformity, why his heart had leapt to responsibility even as it counseled flight.

"I didn't mean to embarrass you this afternoon," she'd told him.

"You didn't," he lied.

"Like hell."

"I have a son, Ruth," he told her. "No daughters. No granddaughters." Then he hung up on her.

He and Ruth had "been good" for a long while after that.

"My landlady tells me I had visitors yesterday," he ventured now, since the subject was going to come up anyway.

Ruth nodded. "Crisis situation. You *did* offer, as I recall."

Sully nodded. "They kind of threw old Beryl for a loop, is all," he explained.

"Why?" Ruth frowned, instantly annoyed to learn this.

Sully shrugged, unsure how best to explain to Ruth that her daughter was a raucous, often crude young woman, something Ruth, who could also be raucous and crude, never seemed to notice. In truth, it wasn't something Sully would have taken much notice of had it not been in connection with his landlady. "It doesn't take much. She's an old woman."

Ruth seemed satisfied with this explanation. "Well, I wouldn't have sent them over there if I could have thought of someplace else. I thought Roy was here in town."

She explained then that Janey had finally decided to leave her husband. She'd snuck out when he was deer hunting. She had a job lined up in Albany. Also an apartment, as of the first of the month. Roy had discovered her gone and threatened to come get her, beat the shit out of her and bring her back home just as soon as he got his deer, which they were hoping would take a few more days. Once Janey got moved into her place in Albany, she was confident Roy would never find her.

A dime-store hood from Mohawk, Roy had spent his youth in and out of reform schools and jail. According to rumors Sully'd heard, he'd beaten a bartender half to death in the empty parking lot in back of a Schuyler Springs bar he'd been tossed out of earlier in the evening. Since there were no witnesses, Janey's husband had walked. "Of course everybody told her he was no good when she married him, if I remember."

"Right, Sully," Ruth said. "*You've* never made a mistake. Is that what I'm hearing? That you've never ignored good advice? That you've never been stubborn and done something just because everybody told you not to? If anybody in this world ought to understand her behavior, it's the man who won't admit he owns the house he owns."

"Here we are back at the house," Sully observed.

"We're not talking houses," Ruth insisted. "We're talking bullheadedness and who inherited it from whom."

"You're sure she got it from me," Sully said. "Not from you, for instance. Or Zack."

"Nope." Ruth smiled. "This kind of stubbornness is so dumb it's got your name on it. Who do we know that had a chance to be partners in Tip Top Construction and said no? Who could be sitting pretty now if he didn't have rocks in his head? Who all these years later won't admit what a dope he was?"

They'd been down this road too, of course. It was one of Ruth's favorite arguments against him. It was true, of course, that Kenny Roebuck had offered him a sweat equity partnership in Tip Top Construction when they were both younger men. And it was also true that Sully probably should have said yes. Still, Sully didn't see much margin in regret. If he allowed himself the luxury of lamenting that he hadn't become a partner in Tip Top Construction, he'd just start regretting other things, and once he started in that direction there'd be no stopping. He'd end up a maudlin old fraud like his father, telling his nurses and anyone else who would listen that he'd lived a man's life and made a man's mistakes. No, Sully'd decided long ago to abstain from all but the most general forms of regret. He allowed himself the vague wish that things had turned out differently, without blaming himself that they hadn't, any more than he'd blamed himself when his 1-2-3 triple never ran like it should at least once. It didn't pay to second-guess every one of life's decisions, to pretend to wisdom about the past from the safety of the present, the way so many people did when they got older. As if, given a second chance to live their lives, they'd be smarter. Sully didn't know too many people who got noticeably smarter over the course of a lifetime. Some made fewer mistakes, but in Sully's opinion that was because they couldn't go quite so fast. They had less energy, not more virtue; fewer opportunities to screw up, not more wisdom. It was Sully's policy to stick by his mistakes, which was what he did now. "I was pretty smart to say no, as it turned out," he told Ruth. "If I owned half of Tip Top Construction and saw Carl pissing it away, I'd have to shoot the son of a bitch. Then I'd end up in jail. As it is, I'm walking around a free man and I don't care what he does."

"Walking is right," Ruth reminded him, "which brings us back to your needing a car."

"I've got the El Camino right outside," Sully reminded her.

"Terrific," Ruth said. "So instead of owning the company car, you get to borrow it."

"I'd rather borrow it," Sully told her truthfully, explaining that he'd already gotten a ticket in the El Camino this morning. "I put it in the glove compartment for Carl. Be a nice little surprise for him."

"And what do you call that?" Ruth shook her head in disbelief. It was amazing how quickly Sully could exasperate her. "Having other people pay your tickets."

"With Carl Roebuck I call it justice," Sully grinned.

Ruth got angrily to her feet, started dressing. As she feared, her good mood had not survived a serious discussion with Sully. "I'll tell Janey that's what you call it."

Sully blinked. "Were we talking about Janey just now?"

"One of us was."

Sully sighed, swung his legs out of bed, searched for his shorts, which were somewhere in the tangle of bedding. "Well, as usual, you lost me," he admitted.

"It's never hard, once the subject of responsibility comes up," Ruth told him, hooking her bra angrily.

Sully threw up his hands. "All I'd like to know is what you want, Ruth. One second we're talking about traffic tickets, the next we're talking about Janey. Is there something you want me to do for her? Is there something *she* wants me to do? I need a clue here, Ruth."

"You might think about her, Sully," Ruth explained, furious now. Maybe she wasn't always clear in her expression, but she suspected there was something wrong with this man that he couldn't follow connections that struck her as obvious. She suspected his blindness was intentional, that always making her explain was merely a delaying tactic. Probably he was hoping she'd be unable to put her feelings into words, a failure that would allow him to continue drifting. Trying to get Sully to see things her way was like trying to put a cat into a bag—there was always a leg left over. "You might even worry about her. That's normal for people who care about each other."

He was standing now with his back to her, but she could still see the swelling of his knee. "It's the reason I worry about you, for all the good it does me."

Sully stepped into his shorts before turning around to face her. "I never asked you to worry about me," he said. "In fact, I'd prefer you didn't."

Ruth fought the tears she felt coming, finished dressing as quickly as she could, while Sully searched for his undershirt. "It's really your plan to end up alone, isn't it?" she said.

"It might be best," Sully admitted.

At the motel room door, she turned back to him. "You should have forgiven your father," she told him. "And I should have known what it meant when you didn't."

When she was gone, Sully studied the slammed door curiously. Somehow his father had sneaked back into the conversation. Even dead he was a crafty son of a bitch.

"You again," Sully said, sliding onto the bar stool next to Rub, who was nursing a beer.

"Where'd you go?" Rub wondered. "I went over to Carl's but you weren't there."

"I must've already left," Sully explained.

"Where?"

"None of your business, Rub," Sully told him. "There's no law says I've got to spend every hour of every day with you, is there?"

Rub shrugged.

"Is there?" Sully said.

"You get mad when you want me and I'm not around," he reminded Sully.

This was true. "Anyhow, here you are."

"We got work?"

"Carl wasn't there."

"He's in back, playing cards." Rub nodded, indicating the big dining room, the one Tiny closed during the off-season.

"That explains it," Sully said.

Birdie came over. "You had a call right after you left," she said.

"Miles Anderson?"

"Miles Anderson. He wants you to call him back 'at your very first convenience.'" Birdie imitated Miles Anderson's speech. "Here's his number."

Sully took the slip of paper Birdie handed him and stuffed it into his pocket.

"Aren't you going to call him?" Rub wanted to know.

"Not right now," he said, though he knew that was exactly what he should do. That was the trouble with stupid streaks. You often knew the right thing to do, you just couldn't locate the will.

"How come?"

"Because right now it's not convenient," Sully told him, confusing Rub, to whom the empty moment looked as convenient as could be. "Because I waited an hour for the bastard and now he can wait for me. Because right now I'd rather play poker. How about you?"

Rub studied the dregs of his beer sadly. "Bootsie took my money," he confessed. "I never should have gone by the dime store," he admitted.

"How does she always know when I've paid you?" Sully marveled.

"She always guesses, somehow," Rub said, himself mystified. "Don't do no good to lie to her, either."

"I thought you were working this afternoon," Carl Roebuck said when he looked up and saw Sully. There were four players in the game seated at a round table directly beneath a chandelier. In addition to Carl, the others were all men Sully knew. They could all afford to lose, too, which was good, provided they could be coerced to do it.

"I thought I was too," Sully said, pulling up a free chair. "Just as well, though. This looks like a better career move."

"I wouldn't be too sure," one of the other men said. "This son of a bitch is winning every other hand."

Everyone looked at Carl Roebuck, who did not look like a man ashamed of winning.

"Mr. Lucky," one of the men said.

Sully took out some money in order to make himself truly welcome. "His secret is, he cheats," Sully said. "Luckily I know all his tricks, which means he's done cheating for today."

Carl sold Sully some chips. "You could be roofing the house on Belvedere, you know."

Sully nodded. "Just like you to send a one-legged man up on a roof. I fall off on my head and then you don't have to pay me all the money you owe me."

"Have it your way." Carl dealt cards around the table. "Even with one leg you'd be safer up there on the roof than you are here, though."

"Can I play?" Rub said. He'd been standing just inside the doorway since they came in, eyeing the one remaining free chair. These were not men Rub presumed in the presence of.

"No, Rub," Carl said.

"Nope," the others agreed.

Rub looked at the floor.

"Sure, Rub," Carl said. "Jesus. Can't you tell when people are pulling your chain?"

In fact, Rub couldn't. Sometimes these same men refused to let him play, claiming he stank. He wasn't sure how he was supposed to tell it was a joke now, when most of the time it wasn't. "You didn't deal me in," Rub noted when he'd taken the chair next to Sully.

"You weren't playing when the hand started," Carl explained.

"I was standing right there," Rub said, pointing at the air he had so recently displaced.

"How can I deal you in when you're standing over there?" Carl said. To illustrate, he sent a card whistling through the air toward the doorway. "That what you wanted me to do?"

"Misdeal," somebody said.

"I had a pair of wired sevens," one man complained angrily. "That was a deliberate misdeal."

Carl turned over his own hole cards, revealing a pair of tens.

"Mr. Lucky," the man who had said this before repeated, then whistled the theme song.

Rub went and fetched the card Carl had tossed across the room, then sat back down. Carl reshuffled. Sully cut. Carl dealt, skipping Rub again.

"What about me?" Rub said.

"Sorry, Rub," Carl said. "Did you want to play?"

Everybody tossed their cards back in, groaned.

"Make up your mind," Carl said. "You want to play or not?"

"In about one minute I'm going to rip your head off," Sully said.

Carl shuffled, dealt again. "I told you you'd be happier roofing. Some people don't know what's good for them."

The man to Rub's left opened. Rub, who was a surprisingly good poker player, raised.

"Did it ever occur to you that you might be one of them?" Sully asked, calling Rub's bet.

"I know exactly what's good for me," Carl said, tossing his cards into the center of the table. Two others followed, leaving just the man who had opened, Rub and Sully. Sully consulted his hole cards, which made, together with his first two up cards, a Sausalito straight—two, four, six, eight.

Tiny had set up an old space heater near the table. Its whirring reminded Sully of the sound of approaching traffic. No doubt about it, the smart thing to do would be to fold. On the other hand, Sully considered, he'd come this far.

Miles Anderson called back three times during the afternoon. The last time Sully, an even hundred dollars down in the game, took the call.

"I thought we were going to meet today," Miles Anderson said, his voice a study in impatience.

"Me too," Sully said. "In fact, I was so sure of it I actually went over there and waited for you for about an hour."

"We must have just missed each other," Anderson said, backing off a little in his tone of voice. He was apparently willing to share responsibility. "I was delayed at the bank." When Sully didn't say anything, Anderson added, "Do I understand this silence to mean that you're no longer interested in the job we discussed?"

"No," Sully said. "I didn't know it was my turn to talk."

"Then I'm to understand that you *do* want the job?"

Sully said he did.

"Because, frankly, I don't sense much enthusiasm at this moment," Miles Anderson said, his former impatience returning. "And if you aren't sure, I'd rather you said so. A man I talked to at the bank this morning intimated you were less than reliable."

"Look, Mr. Anderson," Sully said. "I need the work. I'm just too old to jump up and down, okay? Inside, I'm all aflutter. Trust me."

"Hmmm," Miles Anderson mused. "Well, I was also told you were insolent, though I suppose that's to be expected. The gruff, frontier independence of the American blue-collar worker and all that."

Who *was* this guy? "I'm dropping out of college to fix your house, actually," Sully informed him, since this was almost true. "Listen, Mr. Anderson. What do you say we start all over? You could begin by saying you're sorry for standing me up, and then I could say I'm sorry for being insolent, and then we could set up another time to meet at the house, and you could promise to be there this time, and we could just go from there."

"How's ten in the morning?" Miles Anderson suggested.

"We skipped a few things there, didn't we?" Sully observed. "Okay, ten. I'll be the one wearing a carnation in my lapel."

"I wonder. Might I ask you a question?"

"Sure."

"Have you been drinking?"

"Only a little. Can I ask you one? What do you do for a living?"

"I'm a university professor."

"So is my son."

Incredulity. "Indeed?"

"He was just denied tenure."

"These are dark times. Where?"

"West Virginia."

"Oh, my," Miles Anderson said. "Where *does* one go from there?"

When Sully returned to the game, Carl Roebuck was selling chips to Wirf, who had come in while Sully was on the phone. Sully could tell at a glance that Wirf was drunk. When the transaction was complete, Carl Roebuck still had about ninety percent of the chips stacked in front of himself. Still, Sully was optimistic. The winter's worth of work he'd counted on had returned, and having Wirf in the game meant he didn't have to worry about going bust right away. Sully sat, then stood again and walked around his chair, clockwise first, then counterclockwise, to dispel the afternoon's bad luck. "Red River round a green monkey's asshole," he added, making a complicated sign in the air over the deck of cards.

"You through?" Carl said, picking up the deck.

"Yes, I am."

"Want to cut?"

"No, they're fine now."

Actually, the cards were fine for Carl Roebuck. Before Sully could get adjusted again, the pot was up to forty dollars and Sully realized he'd have been wise to drop two cards ago. To make matters worse, Wirf was beaming at him so benevolently that Sully half expected him to make the sort of maudlin declaration of friendship Wirf was capable of when his blood alcohol level achieved a certain balance.

"What?" Sully finally said.

"I'm trying to communicate with you telepathically." Wirf grinned drunkenly.

"Well, quit it," Sully said.

"Don't waste your time," Carl Roebuck agreed, tossing chips into the center of the table. "The only way to communicate with Sully is to hit him in the head with a shovel."

"Screw you both," Sully said, raising the bet.

By the time they finished, it was a seventy-dollar pot. Carl won it with a full house and pulled the money toward him sadly.

"I was telepathically advising you to drop," Wirf explained, tossing in his three deuces faceup.

Sully tossed his own cards in facedown. He didn't want anyone to know what he'd stayed in with.

The game broke up at five when three of the players said they'd better go home and eat some leftover turkey while they were still welcome. "I'm going to have to bring my wife in for testing," a man named Herbert remarked, pushing his chair back from the table, pocketing what money Carl Roebuck hadn't won. "Just her and me anymore, and every year she buys the biggest turkey in the store. We eat off the son of a bitch all the way to Christmas, and then she buys another one even bigger."

"I like turkey," Rub said.

"I used to myself," Herbert said, "before I had to eat fifty pounds of it every year."

"Should we wake him up?" somebody wondered in reference to Wirf, who had fallen asleep with his mouth open midway through the last hand. Wirf, playing drunk and unpredictably, had been the final nail in Sully's coffin.

"Let him sleep," said Sully, who had come to view sleep as a precious commodity since his knee.

In the bar it was warmer than in the back room, and Sully realized he'd been cold and achy for about two hours and wondered if he was coming down with something. Maybe it would be quick and painless and fatal.

Carl Roebuck, having stuffed his winnings into his pockets, slid onto the bar stool next to Sully. "Well, smart guy, how bad was the damage?"

Sully ran his fingers through his hair. "Bad enough," he said. Three hundred and fifty or four hundred dollars was what he figured. Maybe more.

"I told you you'd be safer on the roof," Carl reminded him.

"How did you know that I-told-you-so was just what I wanted to hear?"

"To know you is to need to say it. Ask anybody," Carl observed.

"Somehow I always mind it more coming from you," Sully observed. Actually, he minded it more or less universally. He'd minded it earlier when Ruth had either said or suggested it half a dozen times in the hour they'd been together. He minded it when Wirf said it. He minded it even when people didn't say it but were thinking it.

"I gotta go pee," Carl said. "You want anything while I'm in there?"

Rub was coming out of the men's room when Carl went in. He joined Sully at the bar but didn't sit down. "I gotta go home," he said. "Bootsie's gonna whack my peenie for sure."

"Aren't you going to drink your beer at least?" Sully said, indicating Carl Roebuck's long-neck bottle.

"I thought that was Carl's," Rub said.

"I bought it for you," Sully assured him.

Rub looked at it suspiciously. "It looks like somebody already took a drink out of it," he said.

"Nah," Sully told him. "I've been sitting right here."

"How come it's not full, then?"

"Sometimes they aren't," Sully told him. "No one knows why."

Rub took a swig. "It feels like somebody's lips have been on it," he said.

Sully grinned at him. "How'd you end up?"

Rub took out his money and counted it. "I won twenty dollars," he said happily.

"Good," Sully said. "Terrific, in fact. Just as long as you didn't forget anything."

Rub frowned.

"Like the twenty I loaned you to get into the game, for instance," Sully told him.

Rub handed Sully the money, then shoved his hands into his pockets. "I had fun anyhow," he said.

"Me too," Sully assured him. "That's the main thing."

"You lost, and now you're going to rag me, huh," Rub said.

Carl returned from the men's room, slid onto the stool Rub was blocking and took a long swig from the bottle Sully had told Rub was his. Rub started to open his mouth, then closed it, blood draining from his face.

"I gotta go," Rub said and went.

Carl Roebuck was staring at the lip of his bottle. "Did he drink out of this?" he said.

"Nah," Sully said.

Carl took another swig, more tentatively this time, then frowned over at Sully, who was grinning. "Maybe just a little," Sully admitted.

Carl stood, leaned over the bar, poured the remainder of the beer into the sink. "Sully, Sully, Sully," he said.

"What, what, what?"

"I wish you were rich."

"Me, too," Sully said.

"If you were, I'd chain you in my basement and play you for a living."

"Bad cards," Sully said. "It happens. Not to you, but to other people."

Carl waved Birdie away. "I leave you alone to consider that pathetic explanation. I'm overdue somewhere. You all right?"

Sully assured Carl Roebuck he was fine, but the truth was he was far from it. As he often did at such moments to stave off regret, he was trying to remember what he'd been thinking about when he sat down at a poker game with money he couldn't afford to lose, as if recollecting his reasoning and discovering it to be valid, or partly valid, would restore the money. Unfortunately, his reasoning had vanished as completely as the money. Even had he won four hundred dollars instead of losing it, he still wouldn't have been able to afford the truck he needed to buy from Harold, and it was crystal clear to him now that he'd lost the money that the truck was his first order of business. He couldn't shake the irrational conclusion that four hundred dollars in the debit column right now loomed far larger than the same four hundred in the credit. The desperate situation that had induced him to play poker with money he couldn't afford to lose was now the precise situation to which he aspired. He would have to work for several more days to climb back to the financial plateau that had had him feeling so rotten to begin with. The more he thought about it, the closer he came to feeling the kind of specific regret to which he had always been opposed.

The good news was that the Miles Anderson deal had not gone south as he'd feared. The scary part was that he'd very nearly let it go south by being a smart-ass on the phone. Giving guys like Miles Anderson shit was something he'd been doing all his adult life, though he'd not become the richer for it even once. It was his father again, sneaking into his life, Sully suspected. When sober, Big Jim was meek and groveling, almost doglike, in the presence of the educated, the well-dressed, the well-spoken. Later, drunk, he'd vilify these absent doctors, lawyers and professional men and take out his resentment of them on whoever was handy. Sully, even as a boy, had understood that such men held great power over his father. Without knowing exactly how, Big Jim had guessed that men who dressed this way and spoke this way were capable of doing him harm if they chose, and whenever he saw such a man on the street, his eyes narrowed in suspicion and, yes, fear. A bully himself, Big Jim knew what it felt like to be bullied by money and privilege. Sully suspected his father saw such men in his mind's eye all the time. Like the men who gave him his orders at the Sans Souci. It was probably them he imagined himself fighting with in the taverns. It was always somebody that Big Jim thought was putting on airs that he made trouble for. Somebody who made a little more money at his job or was dressed a little better. Somebody who could serve as a stand-in for the ones he really hated. And so Sully, as a younger man, had decided not to be cowed by the sort of men who made his father feel small. Giving the Miles Andersons of the world their share of shit had gotten him no further than obsequiousness had gotten his father, of course, but Sully considered his way more satisfying, and he hated to think he might have to give up such small satisfactions. But the truth was that he was in pretty deep, a lot deeper than he could ever remember being, and almost losing the work that would help him climb out would have been the species of stubborn stupidity that Ruth always claimed was uniquely Sully.

But somehow he'd gotten away with it, which meant he wasn't done quite yet. Tomorrow he'd be more agreeable, tell Miles Anderson he hadn't meant to be such a prick. Even losing all this money to Carl Roebuck might not be totally bad, since Carl would now feel guilty enough to let him keep the El Camino for a few days until he could solve the problem of how to buy a new truck. If Sully could come up with a decent down payment, Harold might be convinced to let him take the truck and the snowplow blade and make monthly payments until the balance was paid off. If it snowed like hell all winter, as it looked like it might, he might be able to pay Harold off by spring, assuming he didn't get into any more poker games, didn't do anything else equally deficient in judgment.

Sometime soon, he feared, he was going to have to swallow hard and ask to borrow money from somebody. Ruth would give it to him if she had it, but she didn't have it. Wirf probably did, and probably would give it to him, but Sully owed him far too much already. On principle he refused to borrow money from old women, which left Miss Beryl out. Carl Roebuck might give him some money if Sully could catch him drunk again, but he disliked the idea of taking money from Carl, whom he preferred to resent. He could go see Clive Jr. at the savings and loan, but Sully's stomach curdled at the thought, and it occurred to him, now that he thought about it, that it was probably Clive Jr. who had warned Miles Anderson against him.

Finally, there was Ruth's solution: sell his father's property and use the money. He wondered how much more desperate he'd have to get before that became a real possibility. Quite a bit more, he suspected.

"Well," Carl said, breaking into Sully's reverie, "the time has come for me to see if I have a home to go home to this evening."

"I wouldn't suggest going to visit Ruby right away," Sully advised.

"Still worked up, huh?"

"I don't know about now. She was pretty bent out of shape early this afternoon."

Carl looked genuinely sad to hear it. "I should never have mentioned marriage," he conceded.

"That's right," Sully said, recalling that he himself had proposed marriage within the last twenty-four hours. "Women tend to take that kind of talk seriously, even when they know better."

Carl sighed. "Ruby deserves marriage," he reflected. "That's the trouble, though. They all do. They spread their beautiful legs, and I hear myself saying why don't you and I get married, and right then I mean it, too. Every time."

Sully couldn't help grinning, Carl looked so genuinely lost. "You're a piece of work."

"It seems wrong not to offer them something," Carl said. "I'd marry them all if I could."

"I believe it," Sully assured him. "You wouldn't leave a single one for the rest of us, either."

"I'd leave Bootsie for Rub," Carl said, then nodded in the direction of the big dining room where they'd been playing poker. "I see Ahab woke up."

Wirf was standing in the doorway, trying to shake the cobwebs. "What happened to the game?" he wondered, stumping over to the bar.

"The white whale went that way," Carl Roebuck said, pointing up Main Street.

Wirf slid onto the stool Carl had vacated. "Good," he said. "Let him. Why should I chase whales?"

"Beats me," Carl said on his way to the door.

"I woke up in there and couldn't remember where I was. It felt like New York City in the forties, staring up into that chandelier. I thought I'd died and gone to the Waldorf-Astoria."

"You aren't going to believe this," Carl called from across the room. He was out through the beer sign in the window. "But it's snowing again."

"I believe it," Sully said. In fact, it was perfect.

"Something stinks over here," Carl said, then went outside and the door swung shut behind him.

Sully and Wirf considered Carl Roebuck's departing statement. It was Wirf who came up with the solution. "Let's stay over here, then," he said.

Fish, Miss Beryl decided.

She'd been trying to place the odor that permeated Sully's entire flat. It was a mystery. How did a man who never cooked, who didn't even keep food in his refrigerator, manage to have an apartment that smelled like fish? By not opening his windows was one way, she speculated. Granted, he couldn't very well open them now in the late November subfreezing weather, but she doubted Sully ever aired the place, even in summer. In fact, now that she thought about it, she knew he hadn't done so for the simple reason that he never bothered to remove his storm windows. He'd dutifully replaced hers with screens every spring for the last twenty years, but he always maintained it was too much trouble to do his own.

"You'll swelter," Miss Beryl always warned, to which Sully responded with his usual shrug, as if to suggest that she was probably right, he *would* suffer. "Don't worry, Mrs. Peoples," he always added. "If it gets too hot up there I'll come down and sleep with you."

Miss Beryl wondered how oppressive it would have to get before the heat would register on Sully as discomfort. At the moment the flat was insufferable, as if all the heat it had stored up in August had not yet escaped the sealed rooms. The thermostat provided the explanation. Seventy-five degrees. No wonder the wallpaper was peeling.

Miss Beryl set the thermostat back to seventy and thought, as she often did whenever she considered her tenant's odd existence, that Sully should have found a way to stay married. He needed a keeper. Somebody to take charge of the thermostat and rescue the lighted cigarettes (Clive Jr. was right; there were brown burns everywhere) he left burning on tables and counters. Also to flush the toilet, Miss Beryl noted when she peered into the bathroom and was greeted by the solemn pool of urine he'd left in the toilet that morning when he left for work.

Miss Beryl flushed and watched the bright yellow water become diluted until finally, with a gurgle, it was clear again. The cycle of the flush was the exact amount of time she needed to solve the riddle posed by Sully's urine, for Miss Beryl remembered the timing of this morning's dramatic flush that had coincided with Clive Jr.'s insistence that Sully be evicted. Was it possible that after that dramatic flush Sully had been able to dye the water in the bowl so deeply yellow with a second release of urine so soon after the first? Possible, she supposed, if he'd spent the evening drinking beer with his cronies at The Horse. A second, more satisfying explanation occurred to her though, and this was that Sully was the sort of man whose flushing was preparatory to elimination rather than its natural conclusion. His morning flush removed the previous evening's offering. His morning release would be noticed for the first time this evening when he returned from work. Miss Beryl couldn't help wondering whether discovering clear water in the commode when he returned would alert Sully to the fact that he'd had a visitor.

Men, she thought. Surely they were a different species. Only their essentially alien nature could account for any sane woman's attraction to and affection for a male. Had any woman ever looked at a man and felt kinship? Miss Beryl doubted it. Ironically, though, only an alien would be so understandable. Compared to women's, men's needs were so simple. What's more, men seemed unable to conceal them. Sully was an exaggeration, of course—a man with even fewer needs than most men, the male principle taken to some outlandish extreme—but Clive Sr. had not been so different. He'd liked thick, fleece-lined sweatshirts and soft chinos, considering these the greatest perk of his position as football coach since he was allowed to wander around the high school dressed pretty much the same way he dressed at home (except that at school he wore a whistle around his neck), while his colleagues suffered (he imagined, since *he* would have suffered) in jackets and ties and sharply creased dress pants. Keeping Clive Sr.'s sweatshirts soft and fluffy, replacing them when they got thin and scratchy, had been one of the few demands her husband had ever made upon her. When his sweatshirts felt good, so did he, and whenever Miss Beryl bought him a new one and slipped it into his dresser drawer, she could count upon his coming up behind her in the kitchen and giving her a big, affectionate hug. When she asked him what it was for, he'd always reply "Nothing," and in fact she was never able to tell for sure whether Clive Sr. was able to trace his sudden affection to her love—the source of these simple gifts—or whether the fleecy sweatshirt itself fulfilled a basic need in him, his affection for her the mere by-product of his satisfaction. She was never quite sure how she was to feel about a man whose affection, whose inner contentment, could be purchased for the price of a sweatshirt and then maintained with fabric softener. What she felt for her husband was love, then and now, but she had her doubts she'd be able to justify this reaction to another woman. Or at least to another woman who'd known Clive Sr.

And it was even harder to imagine any woman being able to justify love for Sully, Miss Beryl had to admit as she returned to her tenant's front room. He had, according to gossip, a longtime paramour, a married woman who apparently sustained her affection by never visiting his flat. Standing in the middle of Sully's front room, Miss Beryl tried to think of what these surroundings reminded her of, and finally it dawned on her. Sully's rooms looked like those of a man who had just gone through a ruinous divorce, whose wife had taken everything of value, leaving her ex-husband to furnish the place with the furniture they had long ago consigned to their damp cellar and forgotten. Maybe it was his sofa that was responsible for the fishy odor. Miss Beryl went over and sniffed a cushion tentatively. It was redolent of old, slept-in clothing, but not fish.

Maybe, Miss Beryl considered, what she was sniffing was the odor of her own perfidy. Driver Ed had advised her not to betray Sully with this sneak inspection. And it did no good to rationalize that Sully would not mind, that he trusted her with his affairs. He knew that she screened his mail, thrusting at him items she felt he should open. He probably was even aware that she retrieved and opened envelopes he'd consigned to her trash can that had contained disability checks and reimbursements for medication. He probably did not suspect that she kept a large manila envelope marked "SULLY" that contained important documents he might someday need, but she doubted he'd mind if he did, and besides, Miss Beryl never felt guilty about surreptitiously guarding her tenant's interests. But this was a different kind of intrusion, and she knew it. She had not intended to follow up on Clive Jr.'s suggestion to inspect Sully's flat for herself until she was actually on the stairs, and now that she was here, she wished that she had followed her usual rule of thumb and dismissed Clive Jr.'s advice on general principle. How had he managed to convince her to invade her longtime tenant's privacy? Was Clive Jr. becoming more persuasive? Or was she becoming, in her advancing age, more uncertain and susceptible to persuasion? She feared it could well be the latter and wondered if it might be a good idea to make, for future reference, a list of things she should never agree to do at her son's urging. That way, if she became more uncertain or weak-willed, if she woke up some morning and discovered that Clive Jr.'s advice suddenly made sense, she could consult her list, made when she was still in command of her faculties. Everything would be right there on paper:

1. Don't invest in any of Clive Jr.'s sure things.
2. Don't tell him how much money you have. It would not be good for him to know this until you are dead and it's his.
3. Don't sell Clive Jr. your house, because then it will be his house. Don't listen to his reasons, because they're good ones.
4. Don't let him convince you to vote Republican. This would not be in your spiritual best interest.

The question was whether to add number five:

5. Don't let Clive Jr. talk you into evicting Sully, who is fond of you, just as you are fond of him. If Sully burns your house down with you in it, he will not have meant to.

Miss Beryl frowned at her mental list. Each item on it struck her as dubious, and number five was especially unconvincing. At bottom, the other four represented a failure of generosity to Clive Jr., not to mention a near total collapse of any natural maternal instinct to accord one's children more credit than they are due. They were Driver Ed speaking, not herself.

So deeply was Miss Beryl plunged into these interior considerations that she did not hear footsteps on the stair outside or notice that she was no longer alone. And when the intruder spoke, the old woman nearly jumped out of her skin, not so much out of surprise to discover that she was not alone as because for a split second it seemed to her that the new voice, one she recognized vaguely, was in her head. What this new voice said was: "Six. Quit talking to yourself. Everybody will think you're nuts."

Miss Beryl could not take her eyes off the little girl, who sat perfectly still, staring without apparent comprehension at Miss Beryl, her tiny legs hanging over the cushion, not quite touching the floor. Another child would have swung her legs, banged the backs of her shoes against the sofa. But this child's legs remained preternaturally still. Which wasn't even the most amazing part. Her mother had declined to be seated on the sofa next to her daughter, planting herself on the floor, back braced against the sofa arm, as if in sad acknowledgment of unworthiness. But once she got situated, Miss Beryl learned why the child's mother had settled herself at her daughter's feet, for, without actually looking at her mother, the girl's small right hand found her mother's upper arm, then the fingers traveled lightly along the shoulder and up the young woman's neck until they located her ear. Miss Beryl watched, fascinated, as the child gently caressed her mother's earlobe between her thumb and forefinger. The young woman even helped the little girl locate it by brushing back her hair with her opposite hand and holding it until the tiny fingers had located the lobe, explaining, "Birdbrain here likes to keep in touch, don't you, Birdbrain?"

The child did not react to this observation, though, Miss Beryl noticed, she now looked more relaxed and tranquil as she caressed the lobe of her mother's ear. Miss Beryl also saw once again that the little girl had a migrating eye, and since she had located her mother's earlobe, the bad eye had wandered more noticeably, glancing off at the ceiling while the good eye continued to fix Miss Beryl, who suspected the little girl might literally be blind in the wandering eye. Perhaps she was blind in both, Miss Beryl considered, there was so little recognition or expression in either. The way she sat there, so still, gently massaging her mother's earlobe, as if she could only ascertain her mother's presence by touch, she might have been both blind and deaf.

"Anyhow," the young woman continued, "I'm sorry about the other day. I was just pissed at the world. You ever have days where you don't know whether to shit or go blind?"

Miss Beryl chose to ignore this question, guessing that it must be rhetorical.

"What's your name?" Miss Beryl said, looking first at the girl, then at her mother. "I assume 'Birdbrain' is a term of endearment?"

"It's a perfect description, is what it is," the young woman said matter-of-factly, cocking her head just slightly to wink up at her daughter. "Tina's her real name, isn't it, Birdbrain? Tiny Tina Two Shoes."

Tina kept after the earlobe. Otherwise, nothing.

"We've been doing this ever since we finally stopped breastfeeding, haven't we," the young woman explained. "I hope it don't go on too much longer, either. It's like wearing a forty-pound, vibrating earring."

Miss Beryl focused on the little girl's good eye and addressed the child slowly. "Would you like a cookie, Tina?"

"She'd probably eat about twelve if we were home. I doubt she'd eat one of yours, though."

The little girl was silent.

"She's not much of a talker, as you probably guessed. Some days there's just nobody home, is there, Birdbrain?"

Miss Beryl rose, too angry with the young woman to stay in the room. "Let's see about a cookie anyway. I had a houseguest last night who ate a whole plateful, so I know they're good."

In the kitchen Miss Beryl could hear the little girl's mother, her voice lowered only slightly, talking to the little girl. "This here is some place, huh, Birdbrain? You ever see so much shit in one place? It's kind of like that museum I took you to in Albany, isn't it? Look at that big old Victrola over there. Music used to play out of that. How about that guy on the wall with the horns and the beak?"

There was a pause. Had the little girl spoken?

"You remember the big museum? Remember how we saw the Indians? How they all sat around the fire? You remember the fire? That was your favorite. Remember the big dinosaur? All those bones standing up so tall?"

"Dear God," Miss Beryl whispered to herself in much the same fashion as she had that morning when she saw old Hattie heading up Main into the wind, her housecoat billowing out behind her. What a crazy thing life was. Returning to the living room with the plate of cookies, she set them on the coffee table. Neither of the child's eyes located them.

The young woman took one. "Sometimes if I go first," she explained, taking a bite, chewing and finally swallowing thoughtfully. "Some guy ate a whole plate of these?" Incredulity.

"A woman," Miss Beryl said. "I'm sorry you don't like them."

"No, they're okay," the young woman said. "I'd puke if I ate a whole plateful of them, though."

"Now there's an expression I haven't heard in about twenty years," Miss Beryl said.

The young woman grinned mischievously. "Yeah, I remember you weren't too fond of it." Then, "You don't remember me at all, do you."

In fact, now that she thought about it, the young woman did look vaguely familiar to Miss Beryl. But so did nearly everyone in Bath between the ages of twenty and sixty, which represented the span of her tenure as the eighth-grade English teacher.

"Don't worry, I looked like a boy then," the girl explained. "These came in ninth grade," she added, indicating her enormous breasts with her two index fingers.

"Donnelly," Miss Beryl said, the girl's family name taxiing back to her suddenly. "I also attempted to teach your father, Zachary. I see the resemblance now."

Janey Donnelly's eyes narrowed. "You're sure."

Miss Beryl was reasonably sure. Having taught several generations of many North Bath families, she considered herself something of a reluctant expert on the local gene pool and its predictable eddies. "The mouth and chin mostly," Miss Beryl said. It had occurred to her that she might have insulted the girl by recognizing Zachary Donnelly in her features. "And I'm relieved to learn that I didn't allow you to use the term 'puke' in my classroom."

"You wished you had at the time," the girl recalled. "I said I was sick and needed to go to the can so I could puke. You didn't think much of the word 'can' either. You said I could just stand there until I came up with 'synonyms suitable for a decent audience.' " She mimicked Miss Beryl rather effectively here, without malice.

Miss Beryl vaguely remembered the incident now. And Janey Donnelly *had* looked like a boy, her hair chopped severely, her features and carriage and language all distressingly masculine. Where the other eighth-grade girls had all been experimenting with makeup to vulgar excess, Janey's pale features were sadly unhighlighted.

"I got 'bathroom' right away," Janey recollected, "but I puked before I could come up with "regurgitate.' "

The young woman was clearly enjoying herself, and for some reason Miss Beryl was less angry with her. "Regurgi*tate*," she corrected.

"Whatever," the girl said, having turned her attention to her daughter. "How about it, Birdbrain? You want some cookie or not?"

No response.

"Just the ear, huh? How about we take a couple for later?"

Janey Donnelly took two of the cookies, wrapped them in a napkin and deposited them in her purse. "This okay?"

"I insist," Miss Beryl said.

"I guess they probably miss you over at the junior high," the girl continued. "I don't know who they got to be the hard-ass after you quit."

Miss Beryl couldn't help but smile. "It's my understanding that they decided to do without one."

Janey Donnelly shrugged. "Too bad," she said. "I still like to read stories, in case you're interested. I never get the chance, but I like to. I bet Birdbrain here will like it too if she ever learns. She's nuts about anything she can do on her own, aren't you, Two Shoes?"

"How old are you, Tina?" Miss Beryl said to the child, who was still staring at her with one eye.

"She just turned five," her mother answered. "Kindergarten in the fall, though I have my doubts. School in the fall, right, Birdbrain? No more Mommy's earlobe then. We'll have to sit you next to somebody with big ears, huh. Put the desks right together." Then, to Miss Beryl, "If life ain't an adventure, what the hell is it?"

The young woman consulted her watch. "Would it be okay if I used your phone? It'd just be local."

Miss Beryl gestured to the phone, the same one the girl had previously insulted. "Sorry there's no place to sit. I used to have a chair over there," she told the young woman. "Something happened to it."

"That's okay," Janey assured her, turning to face her daughter and gently removing the little girl's thumb and forefinger from her earlobe. "Why don't you just sit here and look at these magazines, okay? You listenin' to me, Two Shoes? See all the pretty magazines the old lady's got here? Look at all the pictures. You look 'em all over and when I come back you can tell me which one's your favorite. How'd that be? Maybe we could find you a pair of scissors so you could cut out pictures like you do at home. How'd that be?"

She opened one of Miss Beryl's magazines to a two-page insert of holiday pastries and set it on the little girl's lap. "Oh boy," she said. "Those there look yummy, don't they? We could eat all of them, just the two of us, huh? You look at all these pictures for a minute while Mommy makes a phone call, okay? I'm just gonna be right over there by the door, okay? Right where you can see me, okay? That okay with you?"

During this entire performance the little girl's expression never changed, though she did finally consent to look at the picture before her. "You let Mommy make her phone call, then we'll go back to Grandma's."

The Donnelly girl was on her knees facing her daughter as she pleaded, unnecessarily, it seemed to Miss Beryl, since the child now seemed lost in contemplation of the pastries. Why didn't the young woman just get up and go make her call?

"Mommy's only gonna be gone a minute. You look at this picture, and before you're done I'll be back, okay, Tina? I'll be right over there. See where the phone is? I'm gonna call Grandpa, and then I'll be right back, okay? You stay right here and look at the pictures, and maybe we can find you some scissors." Here she looked pleadingly at Miss Beryl, who was less than thrilled with the idea of the child cutting up her magazines.

When the Donnelly girl got to her feet, she just stood there a moment, staring down at her daughter, then turned and made for the phone across the long room. As soon as she was out of the little girl's peripheral vision, the magazine slid from the child's knees and she stood up, clearly intending to follow her mother, who spun around angrily.

"Tina, you sit your ass right back down there this minute!" she shouted, stopping the little girl in her tracks. The child did not sit back down, though. Her mother was halfway across the room, and it was as if, somewhere in the little girl's brain, she was measuring the distance between them and gauging that she could not sit down without risking her mother's loss. There was nothing Miss Beryl could do but watch, fascinated and horrified.

"This here's the shit that drives me stark raving," the young woman said to Miss Beryl, as if she were glad to have a witness. "You ever see anything like it? Watch this."

She turned and took a step toward the phone, stopped and spun around again. The little girl, without actually looking up at her mother, had also taken a step, then stopped when her mother turned.

"How'd you like to deal with this for about a week?" the young woman asked Miss Beryl angrily. "How about for a day? After twenty-four hours you wouldn't know whether to eat shit, chase rabbits or bark at the moon."

"I'll get scissors," Miss Beryl offered weakly.

"Yeah. And stab me with them, would you? Put me out of my

misery." Then she addressed the little girl again. "How the hell am I gonna be able to go back to work with you like this? Tell me that. How can I waitress at the Denny's with you? I'm gonna carry you up and down the goddamn restaurant all day so you can feel my ear? I can just explain it to the customers, right? Here's your eggs. This here's my daughter. She's five years old but she goes ape-shit if she can't feel my earlobe every minute of the goddamn day. I'm sure everybody'll understand that, right?"

If the little girl heard or comprehended a word of this, she gave no sign. To Miss Beryl, she appeared oblivious to the sound of her mother's voice. She was simply waiting for the next signal she understood. If her mother moved away from her, she'd follow. If not, she looked prepared to stand right where she was for all eternity.

Oddly, having shouted at the little girl, her mother's anger seemed to have leaked away. Or perhaps she was just resigned. "Just what the hell we gonna do, Birdbrain? That's what I'd like to know, and I'll listen to any advice on the subject. You got the answer rattling around inside that head of yours? If so, let me in on it, okay?"

The little girl stood.

"All right, come on over here," her mother finally gave in. "We'll call Grandpa together. That suit you? We'll call Grandpa and see if your daddy's been and gone. Then we'll leave this poor old lady alone before she calls the cops and reports us crazy."

The little girl still had not moved, and she didn't until her mother got down on her knees and extended her arms. Then she went to her mother slowly, almost cautiously, and they hugged there in the middle of Miss Beryl's living room, an embrace that lasted almost long enough to break an old woman's fragile heart. The hug ended with a loud slap and the little girl's hand shooting down to her side.

"Don't start with the goddamn ear again," her mother said, getting back to her feet. "I need the ear for the telephone. Jesus."

Then she took her daughter by the hand she'd slapped and led her across the room to the phone, picking up the receiver and staring at the phone critically. "I bet you've had this since Christ was a corporal," she hollered to Miss Beryl, who had gone into the kitchen to look for the scissors because she could think of nothing else to do.

If there was anything more obscene than Rub eating a cream-filled donut, it was Wirf eating one of The Horse's pickled eggs. To Sully, just the sight of the eggs floating in their salty brine was unsettling enough. He always positioned himself in such a way that he didn't have to look at them or at Wirf eating them.

Wirf was on his third and, sensing Sully's discomfort, was taking his time, sucking off the brine from both ends of the soft egg before puncturing its flesh with his front teeth. The sound Wirf made eating an egg was not unlike the sound of a tennis shoe being extracted from mud. "Want one?" Wirf grinned. "I'll buy."

Sully was green and sweating. "You should hire yourself out to people who want to lose weight. After watching you, my appetite's always gone for about a week."

Or what was left of his appetite. Anymore Sully had to be reminded. Left to himself, he'd eat no more than a single meal a day. The only reason he ate more regularly was Rub, who was always hungry and served as a reminder to eat, even as his personal aroma ruined Sully's appetite.

"You've got the stomach of a thirteen-year-old girl," Wirf said. "How the hell did you survive the army?"

"I never stepped on anything that exploded, was one way," Sully told him, deflecting the conversation. For reasons Sully had never understood, he'd eaten with more genuine appetite when he was in the army than at any other time in his life, this despite the fact that he'd never eaten worse-tasting food. The other times in his life he'd eaten with genuine appetite were few. In high school he'd eaten pizza ravenously with his teammates after football games. But it was true what Wirf said. He'd always been a nervous, fastidious eater, and getting older had only made him worse. He'd get the occasional craving, as for the chicken-fried steak he'd eaten to celebrate Thanksgiving, but these were infrequent. One reason was probably that he had never entirely disassociated food from fear.

As a boy, at his father's table, Sully had frequently, though unintentionally, enraged his father, a man of prodigious appetites who had known hunger and viewed Sully's fastidiousness as an affront both to the food and to its provider. On such occasions the dinner table became a battleground. Big Jim could not comprehend that certain foods Sully found offensive were capable of inducing the gag reflex, which the boy had learned to control by taking very small bites and chewing until there was virtually nothing left, at which point it became possible, with great effort of will, for him to swallow. But this process took forever, and as he chewed and chewed the odd morsel, his father's rage smoldered. Sully always sensed this without having to look up from his plate, and the knowledge that his father was about to combust did not make the job of chewing any easier. He would try to hurry the reluctant piece of mutton gristle along, swallowing before it was possible to do so, and then the piece of meat would get caught there in the back of his throat until Sully gagged and coughed it up into his napkin. Whereupon his father would take the napkin, open it, and force Sully to examine what had refused to go down. Seen in the harsh yellow light of the kitchen, Sully had always been surprised to see how tiny the morsel was as it sat there in his napkin in a puddle of mucus. It had felt ten times that size in his throat. "*This* is what you're telling me you can't swallow?" his father would say, his hands shaking with anger. He'd show it to Sully's mother then, and sometimes her refusal to look would transfer some of his rage to herself, for which Sully was always grateful.

There had always been something about his father—and Sully had intuited this even as a boy—that made him do things wrong. "Leave him alone," Sully's mother always counseled wisely. "You only make things worse by scaring him."

"Scaring him!" Big Jim always bellowed. "Jesus Christ, everything scares him. A piece of goddamn carrot scares him. What happens when he runs up against something *really* scary? What then?"

"All I'm saying," his mother said quietly, knowing better than to raise her voice when her husband was in such a state, "is that he does better when you leave him alone. Yelling at him guarantees he *won't* eat. You know that."

"I'll *tell* you what I know," his father said, turning to Sully. "He's going to eat this stew. Every bite. If we have to sit here till Tuesday, it's going down. If he throws up, he gets another bowl, and that one'll have more stew in it. Every time he throws up, he gets more stew, until it stays down."

And so they'd sat there in the tiny kitchen, always the hottest room in the house, all the other dishes cleared away from the table except for Sully's small bowl of mutton stew, Sully choking back tears and choking down stew for what seemed to him like hours, his mother and brother exiled to the porch by his father's order. It was just the two of them, alone with their thoughts and the food, which disappeared a grain at a time, Sully swallowing sobs of fear with every mouthful. He paused when he felt his stomach rise until he was sure it would accept his next mouthful, all under his father's unwavering gaze. He believed his father's threat to keep feeding him more stew, and so he did not dare throw up what he'd already forced down. He'd have died rather than start over.

"There," his father said when Sully had swallowed the last of it, and Sully hung his head, which was pounding now with his effort. When it was over, he felt exhausted, as if he could have slept right there, sitting upright in the kitchen chair, for days. Depositing the bowl in the sink, Big Jim returned to Sully. "You ate it, didn't you," he said, and Sully realized that his father was still furious, his rage undiminished by Sully's accomplishment. He even suspected that his father was secretly disappointed that the ordeal was over. He'd expected the food to rise in his son's throat and had looked forward to making good on his threat to force-feed Sully another bowl. This realization, harder to swallow than the mutton had been, almost brought it all back up, but somehow Sully had willed the food to stay where it was.

"You learn anything tonight?" his father wanted to know. What he was getting at, Sully guessed, was who the boss was at 12 Bowdon Street. Sully nodded.

"Because we can do this every night until you do learn who the boss is around here." His father stood then, glaring down at Sully. "You can fight me all you want, but you aren't going to win."

As it turned out, though, his father was wrong. The very next night, Sully, in a state of even greater nervous excitement and fear, had to be led to the table by his mother when his father refused to accept the boy's claim of being sick. He'd have been wiser to accept it. Sully took one bite of his mother's steaming hot macaroni casserole, which she had made precisely because everything in it was soft and did not require chewing, and Sully tossed his school lunch the length of the table. For some reason this had not angered his father as much as the previous night's chewing, the boy's inability to swallow. And Sully realized, to both his surprise and relief, that his father *had* been bluffing the night before. He had no intention of engaging in lengthy combat every night. That night, for instance, his father felt a particularly strong urge to leave their house in favor of the corner tavern, and so when he saw the mess Sully had made of the dinner table, he calmly stood, shot his wife a look of contempt and strode out the door. He didn't return home until late, after the tavern closed, and then he'd taken it out on Sully's mother, not him. Sully, who'd been unable to fall asleep, heard it all, first his father shouting at her, then the slap that resounded throughout the house, his mother's cry of surprise, then silence. Sully remembered smiling to himself in the dark. He'd won after all.

"You can look now," Wirf grinned. "I'm all done."

Sully had been feigning interest in the college football game above the bar and wondering what the reason might be for all these recent visitations from his father. Now he looked Wirf over, shaking his head. Since there was no one close enough to overhear, he decided what the hell, he'd ask. "What's this I hear about you being sick?"

"Who, me?" Wirf said, not very convincingly. It occurred to Sully, now that he looked Wirf over, that Birdie was right. Wirf didn't look so hot. His skin looked yellow, something Sully probably hadn't noticed because he so seldom saw Wirf in natural light.

"No, the pope."

"The pope's sick?"

"Have it your way," Sully said. "It's none of my business."

"Sure it is." Wirf grinned. "Anything happens to me and you don't get your disability."

Sully nodded. "Same result if you live to be a hundred, though."

Wirf contemplated his beer. "Apparently I'm not going to live to be a hundred," he conceded.

"Is this a medical opinion or just you guessing?"

"This is a medical opinion with which I happen to concur," Wirf said, then added, "It's also just between us."

"Okay," Sully said.

Neither of them said anything for a moment then.

"They tell me I eat too many pickled eggs," Wirf finally continued. "The stuff they pickle the eggs with is dangerous. Eats away at your liver."

Sully nodded. "Especially if you wash each one down with about a gallon of beer."

"Especially," Wirf said.

"Well," Sully said. "You could cut back on your pickled eggs."

Wirf shrugged, then shook his head sadly. "The time to cut down on the pickled eggs was about five years ago. Ten, maybe. They tell me that my liver is irreversibly pickled. They don't like to say it right out, but I gather that it doesn't make much difference anymore whether I zig or zag."

Sully shook his head, feeling much of the same frustration he'd felt two days ago listening to Cass, who'd explained to him her lack of options with regard to her mother. Here was Wirf telling him the same thing, that he was damned if he did, damned if he didn't. Maybe Sully's young philosophy professor at the college had been right. Maybe free will was just something you thought you had. Maybe Sully's sitting there trying to figure out what he should do next was silly. Maybe there was no way out of this latest fix he'd gotten himself into. Maybe even the trump card he'd been saving, or imagined he was saving, wasn't in his hand at all. Maybe his father's house already belonged to the town of Bath or the state of New York. Maybe Carl Roebuck had bought it at auction for back taxes.

There was a certain symmetry to this possibility. Maybe Carl had used the money he refused to pay him and Rub as the down payment. Who knew? Maybe even Carl Roebuck didn't have any choices. Maybe it just wasn't in him to be thankful for having money and a big house and the prettiest woman in town for his very own. Maybe he was just programmed to wander around with a perpetual hard-on, oozing charm and winning lotteries. Maybe. Still, Sully felt the theory to be wrong. It made everything slack. He'd never considered life to be as tight as some people (Vera came to mind for one, Mrs. Harold for another) made it out to be, but it wasn't that loose either.

"So what's your plan?" he asked Wirf.

Wirf shrugged. "I don't know," he admitted. To Sully's surprise, Wirf didn't sound all that discouraged. "Maybe I'll just keep zigging til I can't zig any more. I can't even imagine zagging at this late date."

Sully nodded. "How many more years of zigging do they figure?"

"Months," Wirf said. "If I continue to zig. If I zag, I might get a year or two. A little more. We all end up in the Waldorf-Astoria, Sully. Zigging or zagging. I'm not that afraid. At least not yet," he added. "In fact, I wasn't afraid at all until we started this conversation."

Sully stood, said he was sorry for bringing it up, which he was.

"That's all right," Wirf said. "I've been wondering when you'd say something."

Sully suddenly felt awash in guilt for not having seen it earlier, for not paying attention, or the right kind of attention.

"Where you off to?" Wirf wanted to know.

"Home, for once," Sully said. The idea of spending another long night at The Horse was suddenly insupportable. He'd been hoping to find someone to help him steal Carl Roebuck's snowblower, but it was just himself and Wirf, and he didn't see how enlisting another one-legged man would improve his chances. "See if I can plan my next move."

"I hope this doesn't mean you won't be zigging with me anymore."

Sully assured him this was not the case. "Maybe we should cut back, though," he said. "Without giving it up entirely."

"Hmmm." Wirf nodded thoughtfully. "Zigging in moderation. An interesting concept. I like it as an alternative to cowardly zagging. Speaking of common sense, is this Miles Anderson going to let you work under the table?"

"I forgot to ask," Sully said, heading for the door.

"Insist," Wirf called to him. "Otherwise you're in trouble."

Given his present circumstances, the idea of future trouble struck Sully as pretty funny. At the coatrack he chortled, his knee throbbing to the beat. As he put on his overcoat, he realized that Carl Roebuck was right. Something by the front door *did* smell foul. Or were they both imagining the stench, each of them realizing, as they were about to step out into the world, the deep shit they were in?

This latter interpretation was one that his young philosophy professor at the community college would have favored. He liked screwball theories, the wackier the better, in fact. Sully was just the opposite, and he wrinkled his nose. Something stank, but it wasn't destiny.

Opening the door, Sully nearly ran into his son coming in, and it took Sully a moment to realize who it was. Beyond Peter the street was white again and the snow was falling heavily in the fading late-afternoon light. For dramatic effect the street lamps kicked on.

"Son," Sully said, offering Peter his hand. "What's up?"

For some reason this question struck Peter as funny. "How long do you have?" he said, shaking his father's hand with weary resignation.

"You're just in time," Sully told him, studying the snow. "I got a job for you."

Miss Beryl pointed up the street in the direction of Mrs. Gruber's house. It had begun snowing again. Mrs. Gruber, three houses up Main, had turned on her porch light and was attacking the fresh snow on her steps with a broom.

"That's my buddy Mrs. Gruber," Miss Beryl informed the little girl, Tina. "She ate a snail once, if you can believe it."

The old woman and the little girl had been standing at Miss Beryl's front window for about five minutes, ever since the Donnelly girl had gotten off the phone and said she'd better move the car just in case. "Just let Birdbrain see me out this window and she'll stay right there till I get back. She won't be no trouble unless you try to move her. She'll just stand there."

There didn't seem to be much Miss Beryl could do but agree, though she made a mental note that all of this was what came of poking around upstairs in Sully's flat, which she shouldn't have done. The present situation was God's punishment for following Clive Jr.'s advice.

When the Donnelly girl slipped out the front door, the child tried to follow, but when Miss Beryl said, "Here's your Mommy," Tina had returned to the window, watched her mother get into the car and drive off. She'd been standing there since, just as her mother had predicted. Miss Beryl had been afraid the little girl would start crying, but she didn't. She just stood, watching the exact place she'd last seen her mother, apparently expecting her to materialize again in the same spot. She did, however, briefly follow Miss Beryl's bony finger when she pointed out Mrs. Gruber.

"She chewed on it for about half an hour and then spit it into her napkin," Miss Beryl told the child. "She's a real corker about keeping her front steps clean. If it keeps snowing, she'll probably sweep them two or three more times tonight before she goes to bed, and then she'll do it again in the morning."

Without trying, Miss Beryl had listened to most of the Donnelly girl's telephone conversation. She'd tried to take the old phone she'd insulted out into the hall, but the cord wasn't long enough, so she'd set it down in the doorway and stretched the cord out as far as it would go so she could sit on the stairs that led up to Sully's flat. She wasn't able to manage all that and still close the door, so Miss Beryl overheard most of the one-sided conversation. Apparently, things had not gone well right from the start. Miss Beryl gathered that the young woman was calling her father to ascertain whether it was safe for her and the little girl to come out of hiding. Instead, it was her husband, a man named Roy, who had answered the phone.

"Put Daddy on the phone, Roy," Miss Beryl heard the young woman say. "Because I don't want to talk to you, is why. If I'd wanted to talk to you, I'd have called you."

Silence, a minute, from the hall.

"Well, I'm tickled you got your buck, Roy," the young woman said when it was her turn again. "I hope you'll be content with it, 'cause there's no way I'm coming home. You can cart him back home and eat the son of a bitch all by yourself. I got a job all lined up and an apartment too. . . . Don't tell me you'll find me, Roy. Get you out of Schuyler and turn you around once and you couldn't find south. You couldn't find Albany with a map, much less me in it. I'm amazed you found Bath without me to tell you where to turn. You only been here a couple dozen times. . . . Don't threaten me, Roy, you're all done threatening me. You're just going to have to find yourself another dumb teenage girl to bully, is all. Be a whole lot easier than you trying to find me once I'm gone. . . . Yeah, well, you let me worry about Tina, okay? And don't tell me you're going to change. You don't change your underwear but once a week, and you haven't changed your mind once since we been married. Change is a subject you should steer clear of. . . . Yeah, well, Daddy doesn't even know where the hell I am, which means he can't tell you. And you aren't either smart or tough enough to get it out of Mom. . . . Yeah, well, don't go threatening, Roy. Remember what the judge told you. Next person you go and beat the shit out of and you go to jail. . . . Yeah, well, go ahead and risk it, then. I wouldn't mind seeing you in jail. Anyhow, I'm going to hang up on you now. This is the longest conversation we've had in about a year. The part I like best is I can end it without getting punched. . . . Just go on home, Roy. Go home and eat your deer. Start at the end with the asshole and just keep going. . . . No, you don't know where I am, either. If you did, you'd be over here making everybody's life misery. You don't have no idea where I am, and you can just file that with all the other things you don't know. There's probably room for one more. . . . Bye, Roy. . . . Yeah, yeah, yeah. . . . I'll look forward to it, okay? . . . Go on back to Schuyler, Roy. Go on back and eat your deer."

Hang up the phone, Miss Beryl thought, but the conversation went on in this manner for another five minutes, escalating without moving, and when it did finally end and the young woman came back in and set the phone back on the end table, Miss Beryl had the strong impression that it was her husband who had finally hung up.

"I better go move the car," she said, her facial expression a curious mix of annoyance and misgiving. "He's just dumb enough to find me by pure luck. When I get back, me and Birdbrain'll go upstairs and wait. You don't want to get in the middle of this."

Outside Miss Beryl's front window the street lamps made halos of the falling snow. Up the street Mrs. Gruber had finished her sweeping and was vigorously banging her broom against her porch pillar to get the snow off. She broke two or three brooms this way each winter and complained bitterly about how brooms weren't built to last.

Miss Beryl heard the low, throaty throb of a car engine coming up the street from the other direction. It belonged to a huge, rusted-out old Cadillac the color of dirty snow. Miss Beryl simply could not believe what was riding on the car's hood. She was unable to convince herself, in fact, until the big car lurched over to the curb directly beneath the street lamp, coming to a rocking rest in the spot where the Donnelly girl's car had been until she moved it.

The deer was secured by ropes that snaked under the car's hood and through the grille and front windows in a pattern that could only have been improvised on the spot. The animal's head swayed on its slender neck, tongue lolling out, its entire body sliding dangerously. A large man wearing an orange plaid jacket and cap with earflaps got out of the car then, and when he slammed the door the deer slid further among the straining web of rope. The man seemed to be surveying not Miss Beryl's house but that of her next-door neighbor.

"Daddy," the little girl said, her voice, so unexpected, startling Miss Beryl, who had momentarily forgotten she was there despite the fact that she had both hands on the child's shoulders. When she tried to draw the little girl back from the window, she discovered, as the young woman had predicted, that Tina would not budge. Since that was the case, Miss Beryl drew the sheer that she pulled back each morning to let light into her front room, and she turned off the nearby floor lamp as well. Through the sheer's gauzy material, she and the child were still able to make out the man's movements, saw him open the Cadillac's rear door and take out a rifle. When he slammed this door also, the deer slid again, its antlers forming a tripod on the snowy curb. The man with the rifle came around the car then, looked at the animal, shook his head, turned back to the house, shouldered the rifle and fired. The explosion of the gun was immediately mixed with the sound of shattering glass.

Miss Beryl did not wait for a second shot. Before that came, she had dialed the phone for the police. Her conversation with the officer at the desk was punctuated by further explosions as the Donnelly girl's husband systematically shot out every window on the second floor of both the front and side of Miss Beryl's neighbor's house, shouting, indistinctly, in between volleys, for his wife to get her ass outside and not make him go up after her.

"I'll be damned," said the policeman on the telephone. "That does sound like somebody shooting. You sure it's not the television?"

By the time Miss Beryl got back to the window, the man had stopped shooting, and Miss Beryl saw why. The Donnelly girl was standing there with him beneath the street lamp, apparently furious and unafraid. He wasn't holding the rifle at his shoulder anymore, but rather across his body with both hands, one on the stock, the other on the barrel. He appeared to be listening intently to his wife and trying to comprehend, among other things, that he was shooting out the windows of the wrong house. He must also have been listening to his wife's low opinion of him.

In the distance Miss Beryl heard a siren. The patrol car pulled up just as the man with the rifle had apparently heard enough. Miss Beryl saw the butt of the rifle come up and the Donnelly girl's head snap back. As she crumpled to the sidewalk, Miss Beryl cried out and reached down to cover the little girl's eyes, only to discover that the child was no longer there. In fact, when Miss Beryl turned to look, she discovered that the little girl was no longer in the room. Both the door to Miss Beryl's flat and the outer door stood open.

Their first stop was the IGA, where Sully bought the smallest package of ground beef he could find.

"How about buns?" Peter said, abstractedly, picking up a package. It was one of the things Sully liked least about his son, the fact that he seldom seemed to focus. No matter where he was, he was half somewhere else. Right at the moment he had an excuse, though. Yesterday, when Ralph went to pick Will up at the restaurant where Sully had taken him for ice cream, and while Vera and Peter were returning Robert Halsey to the VA home in Schuyler, Charlotte had packed Wacker and Andy into the Gremlin, along with their clothes and toys, and left. She had warned Peter of her intention to leave, even offered him the opportunity to come with her. He could go pick up Will, and when they returned, they'd be off. They could return to Morgantown, at least, as a family. But Peter had refused, telling her to calm down, they'd discuss everything when he and Vera returned from Schuyler Springs. Charlotte had warned him again that there'd be nobody to discuss anything with, but he had not taken this threat seriously. He knew that she was furious and that she had reason to be. He just couldn't imagine her doing it. Packing everything up and driving back to West Virginia by herself, at night.

Vera, at the end of her short rope, had precipitated this confrontation by blaming Charlotte for her ruined bathroom. She'd insisted that it was ruined, that the overflow from the boys' tub had gotten beneath the tiles, which would now have to be torn up, which would cost thousands of dollars. This seemed to Charlotte demonstrably untrue. After all, they were standing in an inch of water, which meant it wasn't beneath the tiles but rather on top of them. The bathroom floor wasn't ruined, it was wet. The floor needed to be mopped up, not pulled up, and she made the mistake of saying so, of refusing her mother-in-law the gravity she felt the situation deserved. Which allowed Vera the opportunity to tell Charlotte about all the other things her daughter-in-law was responsible for. It was Charlotte's fault that Peter had been denied the tenure he'd earned, Vera said. Maybe that wasn't the reason the university gave, but everyone knew that men were often held back in their careers because of their wives' deficiencies. Charlotte was also to blame not only for the fact that their children didn't know how to behave but for the dreadful state of their unhappy marriage. "*You*'re what's wrong with my son," Vera had hissed at Charlotte before dropping tragically to her knees on the wet tiles and starting to mop up the flooded bathroom floor with her brand-new bath towels, which now, she sobbed, would have to be replaced, along with the floor. Everything, just everything, was ruined.

Charlotte had been struck dumb by her mother-in-law's litany of accusation, but the sheer outrageousness of it finally allowed her to locate her voice, and she had just expressed her heartfelt belief that Vera was full of more shit than the Thanksgiving turkey when Robert Halsey, looking pale and feeble, appeared behind them in the bathroom doorway, gasping for breath from his journey from the living room. "Would some- one . . ." he said in his thin, high voice, "be so kind . . . as to take . . . me . . . home."

Vera gasped, struggled to her feet. "Now look what you've done," she sobbed, glaring not only at Charlotte, but at Peter, who had. been trying ineffectually to calm his mother down. "Look at him!" she de- manded. "You're all trying to *kill* him!"

Peter confided very few of the details of these events to his father, telling Sully only that Charlotte had left with the two boys, that her leaving was the immediate result of hostilities with Vera that had been brewing for a long time and finally boiled over. And he hinted again that there were other causes which had nothing to do with his mother.

Sully was surprised that his son was confiding even this much. After all, it wasn't likely Sully would find out on his own. And, as was usually the case with confidences, the knowledge did not sit well. Something about the way Peter chose to relate what had transpired, or the broad outlines of what had transpired, suggested that he was not fully committed to or engaged by these events, even in the telling. He was indeed the sort of man to express outrage in a car without ever being motivated to get out with a clenched fist. He'd told Sully about Charlotte's leaving matter-of-factly, almost abstractly, staring into the meat case, as if what it all meant might be explained on the labels of packaged hamburger. He'd actually picked up several packages to inspect them.

"Dogs don't eat buns," Sully assured him in answer to Peter's question about whether they'd need any.

"You're buying ground beef for your dog?" Peter said absently, without real curiosity.

Sully decided not to explain until Peter showed some genuine interest. "I don't own a dog," he said. "This is for someone else's."

When they got to the checkout, Sully paid the girl and grabbed the hamburger before she could bag it. "This is fine as it is, dolly," he assured her.

"Want your receipt?" she called to him urgently.

"What for?" Sully said.

Outside, he tossed Peter the keys to the El Camino. "You drive," he said.

"What's wrong with Alpo?" Peter wondered as he backed the El Camino out of the parking space and headed for the street.

"I want to be sure," Sully said, tearing the cellophane off the package. "This particular dog might not like Alpo."

Following Sully's instructions, Peter headed out of town. Sully found the vial of Jocko's pills in his pants pocket. From the plastic tube he extracted two capsules and buried them in the mound of hamburger. "That oughta do it," he said, "don't you think?"

Peter looked at the meat blankly.

Sully couldn't help grinning. There was something about educated people that made it impossible for them to admit when they didn't understand something. His young philosophy professor at the college was that way, pretending he understood the sports talk that was always under way when he entered the classroom. "Maybe you're right," Sully said, extracting a third pill. Two had done the trick for him, but he wanted to be safe. He added the third pill to the hamburger. "Pull in here," he said, pointing to the yard where Carl Roebuck kept his heavy equipment. "Go around by the back gate."

Peter did as he was told, still not comprehending.

"Stay here," Sully said, and he got out.

Rasputin, Carl Roebuck's Doberman, was already snarling and leaping at the fence. Sully checked along the bottom, looking for a gap big enough to slide the hamburger through, while Rasputin, foaming at the mouth, lunged at the fence with undiminished fury. Finding a space, Sully set the package down and pushed it under with a stick. Rasputin stopped barking for about two seconds, long enough to inhale the package of hamburger in one impressive gulp, then resumed his attack on the fence.

"I hope you have better dreams than I did," Sully said, recalling the one Peter had awakened him from the day before.

"I can't believe it," Peter said when Sully climbed back into the El Camino. "I just helped you poison a dog, didn't I?"

"Nope," Sully said. "For one thing, it wasn't poison. For another, you were no help. Your part comes later. We got time for one beer though."

"Why not?" Peter said, with the air of a man whose day couldn't get much worse.

"You had dinner?"

Peter admitted he hadn't.

"Good," Sully said, suddenly feeling hungry. "I'll buy you a hamburger."

"I'm not sure I want to eat one of your hamburgers," Peter said, pulling back onto the blacktop.

Back at The Horse Wirf was right where Sully had left him. There was an episode of *The People's Court* on the television above the bar, and Wirf and half a dozen other regulars were trying to predict how the judge would rule. This was an evening ritual. The regulars had a running contest to see who guessed the most correct decisions. Wirf was currently in fourth place behind Jeff, the night bartender, Birdie, the day bartender, who sometimes stuck around after her shift ended, and Sully, who wasn't a big believer in justice and usually just flipped a mental coin between the defendant and the plaintiff.

"The defendant's an asshole," Jeff was saying. Jeff was opinionated and pretty good at predicting how things would go in the court. "The judge will never rule for him."

Birdie shook her head. "This is a court of law," she said. "Being an asshole is beside the point."

"That's where you're wrong," Wirf said. "Judges don't like assholes any better than you do."

Since Wirf hadn't seen them come in, Sully nudged Peter to keep still while he snuck up behind his lawyer and kicked him hard in the calf of his prosthetic leg, so hard the leg flew off the rung of the bar stool and ricocheted off the front of the bar. "Jesus Christ!" Peter gasped, the same look of horror on his face as when he had realized his father's intention to poison the dog at the yard. He couldn't decide which was more bizarre, that his father would sneak up behind a man and kick him or that the kicked man registered no pain.

"Move," Sully said, sliding onto the stool next to the man he'd just kicked. "How come you always gotta take up two stools?"

"I was saving that one for you," Wirf said.

"Why?" Sully said. "I told you I was going home."

"I never believe anything you say," Wirf explained. "And I certainly don't believe it when you say you're going home at six-thirty on Friday night. Someday," he added, "you're going to forget which is my fake leg."

Sully nodded. "I've already forgot," he said. "I was just guessing. You ever met my son?"

Wirf rotated on his stool, offered his hand to Peter. "I don't get it," Wirf frowned. "He looks intelligent."

"He is," Sully said, feeling an unexpected surge of pride. He tried to remember the last time he'd introduced his son to anyone. Many years ago, he decided. "He's a college professor."

Peter shook Wirf's hand. "Your old man was a college student up until a couple days ago," Wirf said. "He must've been on the verge of learning something, though, because he quit." To Sully he added, "You missed all the excitement, as usual."

"Good," Sully said. "I've had enough excitement today. What excitement?"

"Some guy shot a deer right in the middle of Main Street."

Sully frowned, considered this. A deer in the middle of Main Street was possible. When he was growing up, deer used to graze on the grounds of Sans Souci. Even now, at first light and after a fresh snow, people on Upper Main sometimes claimed to see deer tracks across their lawns, though Sully had never seen any himself.

"Guy must have thought it was his lucky day," Wirf went on. "Spent all day out in the woods till he froze his nuts off, finally drove home, parked his car, took his gun out of the backseat and shot a deer dead on his own front lawn. Next year he'll probably just sit by his front window and wait where it's warm."

"I take it you didn't witness this shooting yourself," Sully said. In Bath news traveled two ways. Fast and wrong.

"Nope," Wirf said. "I sat right here. Heard all about it, though."

"You have any doubts about the testimony?"

"A few," Wirf admitted. "But I'm fond of the story. And the guy who told it swore he saw the deer."

Sully grinned at him. "He was probably drunk, like you. Some guy ran over a dog and left it there. What do you want to bet?"

"What'd I tell you!" Jeff, the bartender, bellowed. The judge had just found for the plaintiff, as he'd predicted.

Birdie threw up her hands. "That does it," she said. "I'm going home."

"How about making us a couple hamburgers before you go?" Sully suggested.

"The kitchen closes at seven," Birdie said, pointing at the beer sign clock on the wall, which said seven-fifteen.

"Okay," Sully said. "I'll go make them myself."

Jeff shook his head. "Tiny doesn't want you back there. You always leave the grill a mess."

"What do you want on them?" Birdie sighed, sliding off her stool.

"A bun'd be nice," Sully said, "and whatever else looks good." These were pretty much the same instructions he'd given Rub at noon for the hamburger he never got.

"How about you, handsome?" Birdie said.

"Everything," Peter said.

Sully noted with some interest that Peter seemed used to being called handsome. As a boy he'd been easy to embarrass, but no more.

"Thanks," Peter added.

"Now there's a word you never learned from your father," Birdie said as she disappeared into the kitchen.

On television the judge was explaining the principle of shared culpability, which allowed him to assign percentages of blame. The explanation wasn't as impressive as the ones Sully's young philosophy professor came up with in class. By the time he got finished explaining something like free will it had disappeared without a trace, disproved. Dividing up things like responsibility, as this judge was doing, wasn't a bad trick either, but it wasn't as clean as philosophy. A good philosopher could just make the thing in question disappear. One minute it was there, the next that son of a bitch was gone and there wasn't anything to divide up either.

"He ruled for the defendant?" Wirf said, surprised, glaring at the TV judge with the same perplexed expression he always wore at Sully's disability hearings.

"Same as he did last week," Sully said. "This is a rerun, you jerk."

Wirf nodded. "I thought it looked familiar."

"Every time we go to Albany it's a rerun too," Sully pointed out. "Which is why we're about to quit."

Wirf had taken a five-dollar bill out of his wallet. He'd been about to hand it over to Jeff, who'd narrowly won the week's wager. "Had you seen that one before?"

Jeff had shifty eyes, and they shifted now. "Sully's full of shit as usual. That wasn't no rerun."

"I thought I remembered it too," Wirf said.

"Then you should pay double," Jeff pointed out. "If you guess wrong on reruns."

Wirf must have considered this a valid point, because he shoved the five across the bar. When Jeff drew two beers, Sully took them and headed down to the other end of the bar where he and Peter could talk.

"What?" Wirf said when he noticed Sully and Peter had moved down to the vacant end of the bar. "You don't want to talk to me?"

"Not right this minute," Sully admitted.

"I didn't finish telling you about the guy that shot the deer."

"There's more?"

"They arrested that son of a bitch," Jeff bellowed from down the bar. He was standing on a stool, switching stations to yet another holiday football game. When somebody wanted to know how come he was arrested, Jeff explained, "You can't discharge a firearm inside the city. It's against the law."

Wirf sighed. "Everybody's a lawyer."

"Except you," Sully agreed.

Wirf ignored this, turning his attention back to the television. "Are they playing this game now?" he asked Jeff suspiciously. A man who wasn't above getting his friends to bet on reruns of *The People's Court* wouldn't balk at betting on tape-delayed sporting events he already knew the outcome of.

"So," Sully said. "What're you going to do?"

Peter stared into his beer, bubbles rising from nowhere in the bottom of the glass, ascending into foam.

"Head back tomorrow, I guess," he said. "I don't suppose you'd be able to give me a lift to Albany? I can rent a car there."

"Sure," Sully said. "I could have taken you today. I wish you'd come around, in fact. You could have saved me some money."

"I wish I could have gotten away sooner," Peter said.

Sully nodded, understanding, he thought. "Your mother?"

"She's getting worse," Peter said, surprising Sully, who couldn't remember ever having confided in Peter his strong conviction that Vera was nuts.

"She seemed about the same to me," he said, though he'd been surprised when he saw his ex-wife. Vera had aged a good deal since he'd seen her last. She seemed smaller, too, than he remembered her. Or more tightly wound. Or something.

"I think she's on the verge of a nervous breakdown, and she's liable to give Ralph one too."

"Ralph didn't look too good," Sully admitted. "What was he in the hospital about?"

"Prostate," Peter said. "Colon."

Sully nodded. "What'd they say?"

"They're saying he's going to be okay," Peter said. "I don't think he believes them. They want to do radiation. He doesn't understand why, if they got the cancer like they said."

"He should do what they say, though," Sully said, even though he reserved the right to arrive at the opposite conclusion if the situation were ever his own. "That's why she's all bent out of shape?"

"I wish it were," Peter said. "That would make sense."

Sully discovered he didn't care for Peter's tone that much. Maybe it was true that Sully considered Vera nuts, but it didn't seem right for his son to share such a low opinion of his own mother. "Don't be too hard on her," he advised. "Most of what she does is for you."

Peter smiled at that. "You think so?"

"You don't?"

He seemed to think about it. "I think most of what she does, she does for herself," Peter said. "Especially her suffering."

"You think she likes to suffer?"

"That's what I think."

"I think you're wrong," Sully said, though he didn't, at least not exactly.

"You should have seen the look on her face tonight when I told her I was coming to see you. As if I'd killed her. I think it was the happiest moment of her life."

Sully studied his son, aware that his momentary pride in Peter's accomplishments had leaked away into serious misgivings about his character. It was Peter who seemed to be enjoying the recollection of his mother's suffering.

When their hamburgers came, Sully, feeling his stomach shrink as it frequently did at the sight of food, cut his in half, placed the larger half and some fries on a napkin. "Give this to Long John Silver," he instructed Jeff.

Wirf, down the bar, had smelled the food, then seen it and was now watching Peter eat with his customary longing.

Peter devoured his burger with excellent appetite, the result, no doubt, of having escaped the atmosphere of Vera's air fresheners. He regarded his father half humorously as Sully struggled with the last of his half hamburger before giving up. "Speaking of doctors," Peter said, "when was the last time you saw one?"

"A couple months?"

"For your knee."

"Right," Sully said.

"I meant for a checkup. You've lost weight."

Sully knew that this was true, though it didn't concern him. "You look like you've gained a little, if you don't mind my saying so," he observed, having noticed that his son, for all his good looks, had the beginning of a paunch, rather like Carl Roebuck's.

"The sedentary life," Peter explained, adding, when Sully didn't reply, "Sitting on your ass."

"I know what it means," Sully said. "You forget I was a college student until a couple days ago. It was the sitting on my ass that I objected to most."

Peter was grinning. "It's hard to imagine you in class," he said.

"It's hard to imagine you climbing a fence." Sully stood up, flexed. "But we're going to find out if you can." He threw a ten-dollar bill onto the bar to cover the burgers and beer. His last ten dollars, it occurred to him vaguely. "Let's go see if that mutt's asleep."

"Where you going this time?" Wirf wondered when they headed for the door. "Drink one beer with me."

Sully noticed that Wirf had picked the cheese off his burger. "What's the matter with the cheese?" he said.

"Makes me constipated," Wirf confessed. "Next time ask them to hold the cheese on my half."

"Next time I'll eat the whole thing myself."

"Sit down. Drink a beer with me."

Sully shook his head sadly, looked at his son. "You ever meet a man with only one speed before?"

"Yes," Peter said. "You."

Wirf clearly enjoyed this rejoinder. "I like him," he told Sully.

"That's understandable," Sully said. "I helped make him."

"That's not the part I like, though," Wirf said.

At the door, as Sully struggled into his coat, he again noticed the strange odor that lingered there, a smell he'd been aware of off and on all day, except it was stronger now.

"Do I want to know why I'm going to have to climb that fence?" Peter said.

"Easy." Sully opened the door so Peter could precede him. "You're going to steal me a snowblower."

"I don't know about this," Peter said for the third time. His father was running a stick along the chain-link fence, making a hell of a racket, calling to the dog. The big yard on the other side of the fence was dark, full of heavy machinery. The dog could be anywhere. "He could be waiting to pounce," Peter said.

Sully looked at him. "Remember when we drove up the last time? He wasn't waiting to pounce. He was pouncing."

This was true. The dog had been foaming at the mouth and lunging at the fence before his father had been able to get out of the car. Still, the dog's absence seemed significant. And scary. Had they found him, drugged and dreaming peacefully up against the chain-link fence as they'd expected, Peter wouldn't have hesitated. But there was no sign of Rasputin. Even the styrofoam packaging for the ground beef had disappeared. "Where's the styrofoam package?" Peter wondered out loud.

Again Sully directed the beam of the flashlight along the ground inside the fence. No package. "He probably ate it," Sully said. "This isn't the world's smartest dog we're talking about here. Just the world's meanest."

"That's the part that worries me," Peter admitted. "The way the last few days have gone, it'd follow that I'd end up getting my throat ripped out by a junkyard dog."

"Are you going to climb over or what?" Sully said. "I should have asked Wirf. Even a one-legged drunk could have climbed this fence by now."

"Tell me again how this is your own snowblower we're stealing," Peter said. Sully had explained to him on the way that "in a sense" the snowblower was really his, because the man who owned it also owed Sully some money and wouldn't pay. Sully'd already stolen the snowblower once, and this Carl Roebuck guy had stolen it back. This was kind of a game, apparently. Still, the whole thing gave Peter pause. What they were up to resembled burglary so closely that the law might not be able to tell the difference.

"I had a feeling your mother was raising you this way," Sully said, a more potent criticism than he could have guessed.

Peter grabbed the chain-link fence and tested it by shaking.

"Climb," his father said. "We're getting old."

It was not easy climbing the fence. The bottoms of Peter's tennis shoes were wet from standing in the slush, and they kept slipping. Also, he hadn't climbed anything since he was a kid, and his clumsiness embarrassed him mightily. When he finally got the side of one foot planted on top of the fence, wedged in between two twists of the chain link, he discovered he hadn't the necessary strength to hoist himself over.

"What's the matter?" his father wanted to know. A fair question.

"Nothing," Peter lied, his arms trembling. "I'm just catching my breath."

"Don't get stuck."

Don't get stuck. Words to live by.

Then suddenly Peter was over and standing on the other side, facing Sully, who was barely visible in the dark, though only a foot away, separated by just the chain-link fence. Feeling his hand burn, Peter examined his palm and discovered he'd raked it along the top of the fence. His father aimed the flashlight beam on the injury. It was only a scratch, but small beads of blood were forming along its length. Peter felt an odd exhilaration at the wound and the sight of his own blood, drawn in the dubious service of a dangerous man. Who happened to be his father.

"Here's the hacksaw," Sully said, slipping the blade under the fence. "It's just a padlock."

Peter took the blade and followed along the fence a few feet until he felt the gate. Sure enough, there was a padlock dangling on the inside. Sully illuminated it with the flashlight as best he could. "Try not to saw your thumb off," he advised.

Peter gripped the hacksaw's handle, which was smooth and fit perfectly over the fresh scratch on his palm. For some reason it was satisfying to return his father's saw with his own blood on the smooth grip. Sully, Peter knew, was suspicious of intellectuals and therefore suspicious of himself and his education, especially the private schools he had attended until the money had run out. According to his mother, when Peter had been sent off to prep school, Sully had accused her of trying to raise him above his station. Vera had replied that this was not true, that she was just trying to raise their son above Sully's station. It was one of his mother's favorite anecdotes, though Peter suspected the conversation had probably not gone that way.

"You want a glove?" his father offered.

Peter declined the offer and began to saw. In the night's stillness, the rasping sound was louder than he'd expected, and Peter imagined it waking his mother back in town, imagined her understanding intuitively that it was the sound of her thirty-five-year-old son, the college professor, helping his father, whose influence she had long warned him against, to burglarize Tip Top Construction. It was a pleasant feeling, this father-son complicity against a long-suffering woman, and its thirty-five-year absence welled up in Peter powerfully. With it came the less pleasant possibility that he was not so different from his natural father as he'd always liked to think. True, he wasn't the sort of man who'd leave his wife and family. Rather, he was the kind who'd drive that wife and family away, so it'd be their decision, not his.

As Peter worked at the padlock and considered all of this, he became gradually aware of a silent, motionless presence in the darkness on his side of the fence. Peter did not immediately look, conditioned as he was *not* to look by his son Will, who had a habit of coming noiselessly into Peter's study, the utility room, actually. Peter always left the door open for air, which allowed Will to come up behind him and stand silently at his father's elbow, where he quietly watched Peter work and patiently waited for him to look up and discover him there so he could tell his father about Wacker's latest atrocity. Peter often became aware of his son's presence gradually, and he was aware that the boy, through some intuited adult sympathy, was allowing Peter to complete the paragraph he was reading or the thought he was committing to a note card. This kindness was a small gift that Peter always accepted solemnly before swiveling slowly in his desk chair so as not to startle Will, the jumpiest of little boys, and taking him onto his lap.

This was the sort of presence Peter now felt at his elbow, a presence so still and considerate that it might have been nothing at all, or a small boy awaiting permission to speak, and so Peter did not turn to investigate until he'd succeeded in cutting through the first prong of the padlock. Irrationally or not, he half expected to see Will standing there in the dark at his elbow.

It was not Will, but rather Rasputin.

The Doberman stood there, perfectly motionless, even when Peter jumped and backed into the fence in terror. The beam of Sully's flashlight, which had been angled sideways to fix the padlock, did not immediately locate the dog, but when it did, Peter nearly passed out from fright. The Doberman appeared to be grinning, its teeth bared, lips pulled back from the gums hideously. The perfect absence of sound—of even the low growl that Peter expected from an animal prepared to pounce—made the sight that much more terrifying. The dog's hind legs were planted wide apart.

And so Peter, before he could even begin to decide whether he was a man like or unlike his natural father, prepared to die. There was no question of climbing the fence. The dog would be on him as soon as he moved. No question of anyone coming to his rescue. The fence separated him from his father, and Sully lacked a weapon anyway. To judge from the fact that the beam of the flashlight stayed fixed on Rasputin's face, Sully was frozen too, in surprise if not fear. At least, Peter thought, it would be over in a second. When the dog leapt, it would tear out his throat quickly and, he prayed, painlessly, as it had no doubt been trained to do. It was his father who would have to watch in horror as the dreadful scene played itself out, helpless on the other side of the fence. Peter didn't envy his father or mourn the loss of his own life. In a way it would free him. Of Charlotte, of whom he'd long wished to be free. Of hothouse Didi and her shared peaches. Of the profession he had failed at and that had failed him. Of his mother's merciless, unrelenting expectation. All of it gone, mercifully, in a moment. And then blessed oblivion.

If only the dog would just spring and tear out his throat and be done with it. Rasputin continued to grin, but that was all, at least at first. As the eternal microseconds elapsed, Peter noted a subtle tremor in the Doberman's front legs, like a cold shiver. Gradually the trembling became more violent until the dog's front legs gave way and he collapsed, snout in a puddle, haunches still in the air. The dog remained that way, balanced for a moment, then either sighed or farted, Peter couldn't tell which, and tipped over onto a patch of brown snow.

Peter nearly followed the dog's example, saved from collapse by the sound of his father's voice at his ear. "That third pill was the winner," Sully said in that maddening way he had of congratulating himself on his own sound judgment in situations that were hardly conducive. "Hurry and finish before he wakes up."

Unfortunately, Peter was now shaking too badly to make much of a job of it. The blade didn't want to stay in the track he was cutting, and his father's hand on the flashlight didn't seem as steady now. Peter had nearly cut through three separate places on the remaining prong when the hacksaw blade broke.

"Never mind," his father said, getting into the El Camino.

"What do you mean, never mind?" Peter wanted to know.

His father rolled down the window and leaned out. "Step back from that gate a minute."

Peter did as he was told. As things got crazier, he was actually getting the hang of coexisting with his father. Following orders was pretty much essential, far more important than understanding them. Different rules entirely from those that governed his life as an educator. Out on the blacktop the El Camino did a three-point turn and backed into the drive, right up to the gate. "How am I lined up?" his father called.

"For what?"

"Never mind," Sully said. Then he backed the car into the gate, which strained inward until the padlock stood straight out for a split second, then popped clean, the gate swinging slowly open, stopping only when it came into contact with the inert Rasputin, who didn't so much as twitch.

The rest of the job took them no more than five minutes. Two minutes to locate the snowblower where Carl Roebuck had hidden it under a tarp, three more to load it into the El Camino. When Sully drove through the gate, Peter started to swing it shut until his father stopped him. "What now?" Peter asked. To his way of thinking, he'd been more than patient.

As usual his father offered no explanation. He was rooting around in the big toolbox in the bed of the truck until his fingers located what they were searching out. Another padlock, as it turned out, which Sully tossed to Peter. "We better lock up. Somebody might come by and steal something."

At the traffic light by the IGA, Sully switched on the dome light. "Let's see that hand."

Peter showed him, proudly, the long, jagged scratch on his palm. It had bled considerably and dried brown and crusty.

Sully nodded and turned off the dome light. "Good," he said, pulling into the intersection, the light having turned green. "I was afraid you'd gone and hurt yourself."

Peter stared at the tilting structure. "You're going to turn *this* into a bed-and-breakfast?"

Sully couldn't help smiling. He'd told Peter about the job he'd been hired to do and, when Peter surprised him by exhibiting interest, offered to show Peter the house in question. But then instead of stopping at Miles Anderson's place, he'd gotten another idea and turned the corner onto

Bowdon, parking at the curb in front of Big Jim's house. "Let's get out for a minute," he suggested.

Peter did as he was told, a bit reluctantly, it seemed to Sully, who couldn't blame him. When they stopped at the black iron fence that surrounded the property, indeed most of the perimeter of the Sans Souci, Peter gave the fence a dubious shake, sending a chill through his father. "You aren't going to ask me to climb this, are you?"

"Not unless you want to," Sully said. "In fact, there's an opening farther down." He pointed to where the earth mover had passed magically through the fence the day before.

In fact, the last thing Sully wanted was for Peter to climb this fence, even though the spikes that had once run along its top had long since been removed. Half an hour ago, though, out at the Tip Top Construction yard, when Peter had looked like he might lose his balance atop the chain-link fence and impale himself there, the symmetry between this imagined event and the one fifty years ago when Big Jim Sullivan had shook the fence and impaled the boy perched on top was so powerful that in the moment Sully recognized the parallel he had known that the second awful event was fated to happen. It suddenly seemed perfectly natural that he should cause what his father had caused, only more terribly. Afterward, he'd probably act the same way his father did, and during the few seconds that Peter was stalled atop the fence, Sully had imagined not only that his son would be impaled but his own attempt to explain to Vera what had happened to their son, the son she had tried to protect by steering him clear of his father, the son he'd tried to protect by helping her do it, only to be his destroyer in the end. This was what he had caught a whiff of at the door of the White Horse Tavern.

"You got any idea what this place is?" he asked Peter now.

Peter examined the structure in the faint glow of the distant street lamp. "Should I?"

Sully shrugged. "I guess not. I thought maybe your mother might have pointed it out to you. It belonged to your grandfather. It's the house I grew up in."

The significance of this, if indeed there were any, seemed lost on Peter, who kept looking at the scratch on his palm, a gesture that caused Sully to realize how different, as father and son, they were, how much Sully had surrendered by allowing Peter to be raised by his mother. He couldn't very well start lecturing the boy now. There was every reason to believe that the first thirty-five years of Peter's life had been the formative ones. Still, it was tempting to tell him to quit looking at the scratch. It hadn't changed or gotten worse since the last time he'd examined it. The thing to do with wounds was ignore them, like your hole cards in a game of stud poker, which also never changed, no matter how many times you looked at them. Like Sully's knee, which he allowed himself to examine once, first thing in the morning, and which he then ignored the rest of the day. Like all the mistakes a man made in his life, which could be worried and picked at like scabs but were better left alone. It would have been good to say all this to his son, but age thirty-five was an awkward time to begin parental advice.

"I don't suppose you could make any use of this property?" Sully suggested.

Peter looked at his father, then at the sagging house, then back at his father. Sully knew what his son must be thinking. It was hard to see where the worth might be. Intellectually he knew Ruth was right, that the land the house was sitting on was probably worth something, especially the way it abutted the property of the Sans Souci, but looking at the graying, weathered structure, you had a hard time imagining anybody being interested enough for money to change hands.

"Sure," Peter said. "We could use it as a summer home."

"I know," Sully admitted. "It doesn't look like it's worth much, but I apparently own it, and I'd just as soon somebody else did."

Peter was still looking at the house. "I don't blame you," he said.

Sully didn't want to be angry with Peter, but he could feel his exasperation growing. What he especially hated was being reduced to using someone else's logic, which was what he knew he'd have to do now. He'd have to say what Ruth would say if she were here. "You're looking at the wrong thing," he told his son without much conviction. "If you owned it, the first thing you'd probably want to do is knock the house down, sell it for scrap. It's the ground that might be worth a few thousand. You'd pay the back taxes, sell it, put the profit in your pocket."

"You could do the same thing," Peter pointed out, not unreasonably.

Sully decided not to go into the real reason, his refusal to have anything to do with Big Jim Sullivan, alive or dead, which had never convinced anybody yet and wouldn't convince Peter either. In fact, it occurred to Sully that Peter could well have made just such an oath at some point in his own life. Perhaps it was still in force. "I might, if I had the back taxes, but I don't."

"Well," Peter said. "Neither do I. In fact, I'm not sure I can afford to rent a car in Albany tomorrow. If they don't take my credit card, I'm going to have to ask you for a loan."

Sully thought about this, about where he might be able to get the money. "I thought you were doing okay," he frowned. "You're a college professor, right?"

Peter chuckled unpleasantly, as if to suggest unworldliness in his father. "You have any idea what an assistant professor makes, Dad?"

In truth, Sully did not. "As high up as you are, I figured quite a bit."

"High up?" Peter repeated, as if Sully'd said a stupid thing.

"I don't know the term for it," Sully said, "but you got your doctorate, right?"

"Low down is the term for it," Peter explained. "Everybody has a doctorate. If you'd stayed in school another month or two they'd have probably given *you* one."

Sully let the implied insult pass. "Then why'd you want to be a professor?"

"So I wouldn't be you," Peter said so quickly that Sully wondered if he'd imagined this conversation in advance and had an answer all prepared. As usual, Sully was surprised at how quickly Peter's resentment surfaced. It wasn't that he didn't have reason, just that they'd be going along fine and then, without immediate cause, there it would be. "Actually, that was Mom's reason. She was the one that wanted it."

"Well, you can both stop worrying about you ever being me," Sully told him.

Peter offered his most annoying smirk. "I'm not as tough as you, right?"

"Not nearly," Sully told him, since it was true and since Peter's smirk had pushed him beyond his threshold of annoyance. "You're smarter, though, so that's something."

"But not much, in your opinion," Peter said. "I can tell."

Sully didn't reply immediately, and when he did, he chose his words carefully. "I've never wanted you to be more like me," he said. "There've been times I wished you were less like your mother, but that's a different issue."

Peter's smirk was less contemptuous now. "Terrific," he said. "She's afraid I'll end up like you, you're afraid I'll end up like her."

When they arrived, Sully pointed out the Miles Anderson property. "This is it."

"What's the inside like?" Peter wondered.

"I don't know," Sully said. "I'll see it tomorrow. Apparently it needs a lot of work. Which is good, because I do too. Assuming my knee can stand it."

Peter nodded, studying the house thoughtfully. "What would you say to my helping you out for a month?" he said, surprising Sully completely.

"You mean it?"

"My last class is December thirteenth. I don't go back until mid-January."

"I don't know how much I could pay you," Sully said.

"Minimum wage?"

"Maybe a little better than that," Sully said, calculating. Unless he let Rub go, which he couldn't, he wasn't sure he'd have enough for three men, not if it was going to last. "It'd all be under the table, though."

"Okay," Peter agreed.

"You're not just doing this to piss your mother off, are you?"

"No, I need the money."

"Because it's sure to," Sully said.

"Too bad," Peter said, as if it weren't.

Again Sully felt what must surely be an irrational urge to defend his ex-wife, a woman for whom he had little use and, he thought, less affection. Instead he said, "You can stay with me if you like. I've got room."

Peter grinned. "Now that *would* piss her off."

Sully turned up the collar of his coat against the wind, which was tunneling up Main the way it always did in winter, the way it had when Sully himself was a boy and had to trek uptown to school.

"Bring Will with you," he suggested.

Peter grinned. "Not Wacker?"

Sully shrugged, not wanting to express a clear preference for one of his grandsons, though clear preference was what he felt. "He told me yesterday that you and Charlotte were going to split up."

This clearly surprised Peter. "Will did?"

"He must have overheard a conversation," Sully suggested. He recalled himself and his brother, Patrick, listening in the dark of their small bedroom to his parents, waiting for the sound of fist or open hand on flesh. At first it had scared them both, but Sully had noticed a gradual change in his brother, whom he sometimes caught smiling darkly at the sounds of violence. Sully hoped his grandsons hadn't had to listen to anything like that.

"I doubt it," Peter said. "Talk is one of the things Charlotte and I almost never do. If one of us walks into the room, the other generally gets up and leaves."

Sully tried to imagine this and couldn't. The only two women he'd ever had much to do with—Vera and Ruth—were both fighters. Their styles differed: Vera always jabbing, nicking you, two steps forward, one step back, relentless, tap-tap-tapping, right between the eyes; Ruth lunging at you, bullying, enjoying the clinches, not above throwing low blows. He guessed he preferred either to silence.

"She blames you for everything, you know?"

Sully found this hard to believe. He'd always been under the impression that Charlotte liked him. "Charlotte does?"

"No, Mom."

"Oh," Sully said, relieved. He thrust his hands deeper into his coat pockets, one of which, he noticed, had a hole. Rooting around in the lining and feeling something foreign there, he extracted the rubber alligator he had bought from Mrs. Harold and then forgotten about. Peter studied the alligator without surprise or interest. Strangenesswise, the evening had already been too rich. Why shouldn't his father have an alligator in his pocket?

Sully sniffed the alligator, which reeked powerfully of the same foul stench that had been pursuing him all night. "I think this son of a bitch shit in my pocket," he said.

Peter wrinkled his nose and stepped back.

Sully returned the alligator to his pocket. "I don't hate your mother," he said for the record.

"That's good of you," said Peter.

They drove back to Vera's house, parked at the curb right where Sully had fallen asleep. Neither man made a quick move to get out of the car. "You want to hear a good one," Peter finally said.

Sully wasn't sure, but he said yes.

"I had fun tonight," Peter told him, adding, "Poor Mom. It's her worst fear. That your life has been fun."

"Tell her not to worry."

The garage door opened then and Ralph emerged slowly, peering into the street at the strange car. Peter rolled down the window and called to him quietly, "It's just me, Pop."

"That your dad with you?" Ralph wondered.

Sully got out, waved.

Ralph sauntered down the drive to where they were parked. "What's that?" he wanted to know, pointing at the snowblower in back of the El

Camino. Having successfully swiped it back from Carl Roebuck, Sully had all but forgotten the snowblower. Which fit in with one of his theories about life, that you missed what you didn't have far more than you appreciated what you did have. It was for this reason he'd always felt that owning things was overrated. All you were doing was alleviating the disappointment of not owning them.

"It's the snowblower I promised you," Sully said. "Come have a look."

Ralph approached dubiously. "It's a beauty," he said when he'd had a chance to examine it under the street lamp. "I can't afford it, though, Sully."

"Sure, you can," Sully told him. "I got it for nothing."

"It's true," Peter said, surprising Sully, who hadn't expected such easy complicity. He'd half expected Vera's stern moral training to reassert itself, for Peter to confess to Ralph that the snowblower was stolen. Instead, there he was, grinning mischievously beneath the halo of lamplight.

"I might want to borrow it sometimes," Sully warned. "Like every time it snows real hard."

"Sure," Ralph said.

Together the three men unloaded the snowblower, put it safely into Ralph's garage, where, unless Carl Roebuck conducted a house-to-house search, it would be safe for a while. The three men stood in the dark garage, staring at the stolen snowblower.

"Awful good of you, Sully," Ralph said. "I'm sure Vera'd want me to thank you for her too."

"If you're sure." Sully grinned. "Tell her she's welcome."

"Where is she?" Peter said, his voice confidential, as if a normal tone of voice might possess the power to conjure her into their midst.

"Asleep, finally," Ralph said, as if he shared his stepson's fear.

"Some day, huh?" Sully said.

They all agreed it had been a humdinger.

"Charlotte didn't call, did she?" Peter said.

Ralph shook his head. "I still can't believe she went off and left you here." Clearly, he'd never heard of a woman doing anything like this to her husband before, and even after a lifetime of women doing things that surprised him, he'd been unprepared for this one.

"Dad's going to give me a lift to Albany in the morning, so you can stay here with Mom," Peter told him.

Ralph didn't look like he was one hundred percent behind this plan. "What if Charlotte comes back for you?"

"Dad," Peter said with exaggerated kindness, as if to cushion a blow. "She's gone. When they leave like that, they don't come back and say they're sorry."

Ralph sighed and looked like he might cry. "I can take him to Albany if you can't," he told Sully.

"I can," Sully said.

"It's the first favor I've asked him in about twenty years," Peter said, his edgy resentment surfacing again, though clothed in humor this time.

Which gave Sully an idea. "Come back to my place a minute," he suggested.

"Now?" Peter said, exhausted. He'd had his wife leave him and he'd stolen a snowblower and he'd nearly been killed by a Doberman. It was already a full day.

"Just for a minute," Sully insisted. Then, to Ralph, "I'll bring him right back."

A minute later they pulled up in front of his own flat, and Sully took the El Camino's keys out of the ignition and handed them to Peter. "Take this," he said. "You'll be coming back in three weeks, right?"

"Yeah, but—"

"Take it." Sully dropped the keys in his son's lap.

"First you want me to take your house, now your car. Next you'll be offering me your woman."

"I don't have one of those. Actually, I don't have a car. This one belongs to the same guy we stole the snowblower from. He'll understand."

"He'll understand," Peter repeated.

"Right. I'll make him."

"What'll you drive?"

"I'm getting a new truck tomorrow," Sully assured him. "This was just a loaner. Normally, it just sits in the yard," he lied.

Peter picked up the keys and studied them dubiously. "I'm going to get arrested before I cross the state line, aren't I," he sighed.

"Not if you leave tonight," Sully told him. "He might be mad for a day or two. That's all."

"I wasn't going to leave until morning," Peter reminded him.

Sully read his son's mind. "Go now. Ralph will take care of your mother. You'll just make things worse. That's one way you are like me."

Peter studied him for a moment before putting his key into the ignition. "I think Mom's right," he said. "You *do* have fun. You've enjoyed your life."

"When I could," Sully admitted. In fact, giving his son a car he didn't own had buoyed his spirits considerably. For much of the evening he had considered that in his son's hour of need Sully had nothing to give him, and it was good to realize now that he hadn't been thinking clearly.

They shook hands on it more or less successfully, since irony and resentment were difficult to convey through the medium of palms.

When Peter swung the El Camino around and headed back down Main, the sweep of its headlights caught something on the terrace next door that stopped Sully, causing him to squint into the darkness. His first thought was that a cat was crouching low to the ground, that its eyes had been caught in the indirect light and glowed momentarily. But when he got closer Sully saw that it was no cat but rather a deer lying perfectly motionless in the snow. The very deer Wirf had told him about, apparently, which meant that the story had been true. Even stranger than finding a dead deer on the terrace was the fact that this one was tangled in a veritable web of rope, as if the man who'd shot it had tied the animal up first. Either that or he'd tied a dead deer up to protect against the possibility of reanimation. Whosever job it was to remove the animal, assuming that had been determined, had apparently felt it could wait until morning. A tag fluttered from the animal's rack, and since there was writing scrawled on it, Sully bent down to see. DON'T REMOVE THIS DEAR, it said, and down in the corner, POLICE DEPT. The note had been scrawled in pen, and someone had inserted, in pencil, a comma between the words "this" and "dear." Sully considered the various riddles presented by both the dead animal and the note for about thirty seconds before giving up, glad that there were some riddles in this always strange life that had nothing to do with himself, a conclusion that was probably valid in general, if not in this instance.

Upstairs, he tossed his winter coat onto the arm of the sofa and collapsed there, exhausted but feeling better, he knew, than he had a strict right to feel. The situation he would awaken to in the morning was dramatically and demonstrably worse than it had been in recent memory. His magnanimous gifts to Ralph and Peter represented not solutions but the deepening of his personal dilemma. Still, he felt an unreasonable surge of sleepy confidence that he would figure something out. There *were* solutions. Some you discovered, some you made, some you willed, some you forced.

Of life's mysteries, the one Sully fell asleep, sitting up on the sofa, trying to solve, was the smell that had been following him around all night. Carl Roebuck had noticed it first near the front door of The Horse, but when Sully'd left the bar the stench had followed him. In the car, on the way out to the IGA, Peter had noticed it, remarked that the smell reminded him of the place near Boca Raton where he and Charlotte had honeymooned. Later, the odor had been so powerful in the El Camino that Sully'd had to roll down a window despite the cold.

He slept only a few minutes before awakening violently from a dream in which the smell was his leg rotting off. Oddly, he awoke with the answer. Picking up his overcoat, he fished around in the pocket until he located the tear in the lining, then finally the putrefying cherrystone clam, which had opened and trailed slime all the way to the other pocket, where it had come to rest beneath the wad of Sully's gloves. The clam, as Wirf had observed, was a small thing, but Sully was unable to restrain his jubilation at having found a solution.

Downstairs in her dark bedroom, Miss Beryl could hear her tenant laughing. In fact, she'd heard the car pull up outside and considered getting up and meeting him at the door, but decided not to. Morning was a few short hours away, plenty of time for bad news. In truth, she did not want to see Sully tonight or be charmed by him or be reminded of the boy she and Clive Sr. had been so fond of so long ago. Nor would she listen to Driver Ed anymore. If she'd been able to, she'd have turned a deaf ear to the sound of Sully's defiant laughter filtering down through the ceiling, as if to lift her deadened spirits, as if, after the events that had taken place outside her front window, anything were capable of lifting them. Still, what a fine sound that laughter was compared to Clive Jr.'s humorless, professionally modulated banker's voice, his "Haven't I been warning you all along" that she'd been forced to listen to tonight. He had come by with the dreadful Joyce woman, claiming to have seen the police cars, but Miss Beryl suspected her friend Mrs. Gruber had called him. And at the time she was still badly shaken by everything that had happened and not unhappy to see Clive Jr., who was, after all, her son, who bore the name of the man who'd loved her, who'd been the star of her firmament. No, she was grateful to see Clive Jr., who'd spoken to the policemen outside with the calm assurance of a man who paid their salaries, and they had nodded at him in perfect agreement. Later, she had told him her fear that this was the year God intended to lower the boom, and then she'd let him convince her that Sully, as he had so long warned her, was the symbolic branch poised to fall upon her from above. How disappointing to have to admit that her son was right, to see the sense of accomplishment in his face when he realized that at last she intended to follow his advice. What a shame to lose Sully as an ally after so many years. How dreadful to see clearly, finally, what she had no choice but to do.

PART TWO

TUESDAY

Outside Hattie's in the dark mid-December gray of first light, a new banner was being strung, and Cass, behind the lunch counter, paused to see what this new one would say. Recent banners had not brought much luck. Bath had not trounced Schuyler Springs. They had not beaten Schuyler Springs. Indeed, Bath had not been in the game, and the *Schuyler Springs Sentinel* had again run an editorial suggesting that Bath be dropped from the Schuyler schedule on humanitarian grounds. People were none too sure things were looking ↑ in Bath, either. A rumor had recently begun to circulate that the Sans Souci would not reopen in the summer as planned, and there was new trouble with The Ultimate Escape. Opposition had arisen in the form of a group concerned that the new Bath cemetery on the outskirts of town would be uprooted, the eternal rest of its inhabitants disturbed. So far the group consisted of no more than a handful of residents whose attempts to draw attention to its cause had been unsuccessful in their own community. The *North Bath Weekly Journal* had failed to cover their maiden protest in front of the demonic clown billboard. Predictably, the *Schuyler Sentinel*, ever alert to the possibility of humiliating its onetime rival and current straw opponent, had covered the protest in a small article in the back section of the weekend edition and since then had run three more articles on the ensuing "controversy," each longer than the previous, each inching closer to section A. The interest raised by the *Sentinel* articles had forced the

North Bath Weekly Journal to run a stern editorial suggesting that Schuyler Springs, which had its racetrack and its baths and its summer theater and concert series, should stay out of its less fortunate sister city's affairs, quit trying to torpedo its long-awaited and much-deserved good fortune. The living residents of Bath needed this economic shot in the arm, the *Journal* said, so let the dead bury the dead. More important, the land designated for the new cemetery had never been suitable for a burial site, the ground being far too boggy. Last spring, after several days of heavy rain, a plot had been backhoed only to discover that the ground beneath already contained an occupant. The casket had migrated several feet from where it was supposed to be located and was no longer precisely beneath the gravestone that marked it, though another casket was. It was feared that the entire regiment of caskets planted since the new cemetery opened ten years earlier, row upon row of them, was slowly marching toward the freeway at the rate of an inch or two a month. Face it, the editorial said, all these dead people were already on the move. Better to dig them up now while they were still more or less where they were supposed to be, before they reached the sea. The *Journal* urged the establishment of a commission to find another cemetery site.

At the front door of the diner, after letting himself in, Sully stared at the new banner, trying to draw the words into focus. NEW ENGLAND HOLY DAYS, it seemed to say.

"Holy Days?"

Sully looked again. "Holly Days," he corrected.

"Neither one makes much sense, does it," Cass said, "since this isn't New England."

"Well, we're only thirty miles from Vermont," Sully reminded her, closing the door behind him and locking it again.

"Seems like more, doesn't it," she said. "How come their towns look like postcards?"

"Want me to get the old girl?" Sully said, seeing that Hattie was not in her booth.

When Cass did not answer, Sully took this for a yes. It was becoming clear to him that gathering the old woman from the apartment in the rear of the diner and getting her settled in her booth for the long morning was one of his duties. Otherwise, Cass was perversely content to let her mother pound on the apartment door with her bony fists. Hattie had been instructed not to try to come into the diner by herself because the passageway between the apartment and the diner had a step and she needed help to negotiate this, but if the old woman felt that she was being left alone too long in the apartment she felt no compunction about bellowing at the top of her voice and banging on the door until her arthritic hands swelled grotesquely. Then she sat in her booth and chewed Anacin tablets all morning for the pain. "Let her bang," Cass always advised, but Sully knew it was better to fetch the old woman, make her happy and comfortable in her booth. He also suspected that Cass appreciated his accomplishing this task, that it was a small vacation from the larger burden of her constant responsibility. Cass also enjoyed the few minutes she had in the dark diner by herself before her early morning customers arrived when she opened at six-thirty.

Old Hattie, who couldn't hear much of anything else, always heard Sully when he came to get her. Either that or she felt the vibration of his heavy footfalls in the passageway, because when Sully poked his head into the dark living room of the apartment, the old woman was always in the process of struggling to her feet. "Hello, old woman," he said this morning. "I see you're still kickin'."

"Still kickin'." Hattie grinned fiercely, righting herself with the aid of the sofa arm and extending a bony elbow to him.

"Ready for another hard day's work?" He took her arm and steadied himself for her added weight. Hattie couldn't weigh more than eighty-five pounds, but he'd learned quickly that eighty-five pounds was enough to cause him to lose his own balance, especially this early, before his knee loosened up.

"Hard day's work!" Hattie echoed, latching onto him with her claws.

"Wait a second," Sully said, trying to unfasten her talons. "Get on my good side. Every morning we go through this. Pay attention, will you?"

"Attention!" Hattie bellowed.

It took a minute, but he finally got her situated and they headed for the door. "I know you love to bang my bad knee, but I'm not going to let you do it today, all right?"

"Right!"

"Here comes the step."

"Up?"

"Down, dumbbell, same as yesterday. You think somebody built a new step going the other way just to confuse you?"

"Down," Hattie said, and together they took the step.

"There," Sully said. "We made it again."

"Made it!"

"Now," he said. "When you go back tonight, which way will the step be?"

"Down!"

"Down?" Sully said. "You just went down. They can't all be down. Sooner or later you got to go up, don't you?"

"Up!"

"Here you are, old girl," Sully said when they'd traveled the length of the diner under Cass's watchful eye. "You want anything?"

The old woman slid in, smoothed her hands over the cool formica tabletop as if there might be a message for her there in Braille. "Who are you?" she said finally. "You sound like that darn Sully."

"She's losing ground," Sully said when he joined Cass behind the counter and tied on an apron.

Cass looked at him over the tops of her glasses. "Don't try to cheer me up," she said.

Sully had been working at Hattie's for over two weeks now, since Roof quit and went back home to North Carolina, leaving the village of Bath temporarily without a black man and thus a convenient external referent for the word "nigger." It was not a much-used word anyway, and the residents of Bath, at least those who frequented Hattie's, discovered that its rare use was now tied to muscle memory. For years whenever they'd used the word they'd looked around to locate Roof and make sure he hadn't overheard them or to apologize if he had. Now that he was gone they still looked around and felt a little foolish when they remembered he was gone. For a day or two the regulars at Hattie's had joked that a delegation would have to be sent over to Schuyler Springs, which had plenty of blacks, as evidenced by their football and basketball teams, and borrow a nigger until a permanent replacement for Roof could be found. When Sully decided to help Cass in the mornings, he'd had to take a lot of ribbing from those (it was Carl Roebuck's line) who said they were relieved to discover how easy it was to find another nigger when you lost one.

Helping Cass out was Sully's official reason for doing the breakfast shift, but there were other reasons, all of them money. Since borrowing a small down payment from Wirf and getting Harold Proxmire to let him make payments on the truck and borrow the snowplow blade when it snowed, it hadn't snowed once, which meant that Sully wouldn't be able to make his first payment next week. Harold wouldn't be expecting it, given the fact that it hadn't snowed, but the continued blue skies made

Sully nervous. Last winter there'd been virtually no snow, and if this winter was another one like it, he'd be going into spring buried under the kind of debt he'd have had a hard time paying off even on two good legs. His knee didn't seem to be any worse since going back to work, but it wasn't any better either, and he dreaded another accident on it, knowing that would finish him for good.

Working behind the lunch counter at Hattie's had its advantages. Standing next to the warm grill gradually loosened his knee, which always felt its worst early in the morning. The two or three steps he had to take between the grill and the fridge was just the right amount of exercise for the first three hours of his day, between six-thirty and nine-thirty, after which he'd be limber enough to join Rub and Peter out at the Anderson house or go out on a job for Carl Roebuck if Carl happened to have one of those small, scum-sucking, nasty jobs he delighted in giving to Sully. He preferred to work for Carl when he could, because there wasn't really enough work at the house to keep three men busy for an entire winter, even when one was a cripple, another a born sandbagger and the third a moonlighting college professor. Actually, Sully had been surprised when Peter appeared in the El Camino two weeks after returning to West Virginia. That period of time had been nearly sufficient for Sully to forget the offer of work he had extended to his son, work he'd since come to think of as his own and Rub's. Which meant that he'd either have to let Rub go back to work for his cousins or find additional work. So he told Cass not to worry about finding a breakfast fry cook, at least for the rest of the winter. That decision was easy once he made his mind up. More difficult was coaxing work out of Carl Roebuck, who was constantly bellyaching that Tip Top Construction was slowly going under and claiming it would go under fast if Clive Peoples fucked up and let the Ultimate Escape deal go south. Sully doubted whether this was any more than bellyaching, and while he was confident of Clive Jr.'s ability to fuck anything up, he doubted it would happen in this instance, because that could just conceivably ruin Carl Roebuck, whose good fortune, Sully believed, was one of the few constants in an otherwise mutable life. It was true enough that Carl never had much at this time of year. Worse, he was a wizard at sensing Sully's need and was not above paying him less than Sully would have accepted if his need hadn't been so great and then telling him he was a lot more likable when he was humble, to which Sully always responded that this was one of the differences between them—that Carl was never likable.

At six-thirty, when Cass unlocked the front door, a small cluster of men, Rub among them, had gathered outside and were stamping their feet in the cold, awaiting admittance into the warmth and light. Rub immediately slid onto the stool closest to where Sully was stationed at the grill, mixing eggs in a bowl with a metal whisk. This last week, since Peter's return to Bath, had been tough on Rub. He was used to having Sully all to himself, not having to share him with Peter and the little boy. Until a month ago Rub had been blissfully ignorant of the fact that Sully had a son, much less a grandson, and he didn't think it was quite fair for these two people to turn up now without warning and just assume they were welcome. He didn't like having to work with Peter, who was not a good listener like Sully. Plus, when Peter talked to Rub at all, which was not often, it was in a different kind of English than Rub was used to, an English that made him feel stupid. Old Lady Peoples had warned him when he was in the eighth grade that the world rewarded people who talked well enough to make other people feel stupid, and of course it was true, so he wasn't really that surprised. Even worse, Sully himself had started talking differently, at least to Peter. It was his son that Sully seemed to have things to say to now, not Rub, and there was also some evidence to suggest that Sully actually listened to what his son was saying in return. That Sully would listen and respond to Peter particularly annoyed Rub, who liked to think of Sully as his one true friend. After all, Rub told Sully things he never told anybody else, even Bootsie, his wife. With Sully he shared his deepest desires, which had nothing to do with Bootsie, holding nothing back. As soon as it occurred to Rub to desire something, he told Sully about it right away, so they could contemplate it together. To Rub's mind, Sully's one human flaw was that he didn't seem to want much more than he had, which seemed unaccountable. If you were standing outside in the cold and wet, it was only natural to wish you were inside where it was warm and dry, so Rub wished it, and not just selfishly for himself, but for Sully too. That was friendship. Maybe Peter was Sully's son, but Rub was pretty sure Peter had no such strong feelings for Sully. He wasn't really Sully's friend. And as Rub slid onto the stool, as close as he could get to Sully on the other side of the counter, he'd have liked to explain this whole friendship deal to him, so he'd know. Instead he said, "Could I borrow a dollar?"

Sully slipped his long spatula under a phalanx of sausage links and flipped them before turning to Rub, who immediately looked at the countertop and flushed. "No," Sully told him.

"Okay." Rub shrugged.

Sully sighed and shook his head. "You can borrow a couple eggs if you want."

"You can't borrow eggs," Rub said. "Once you eat them, they're gone."

"When I give you money, it's gone too," Sully pointed out. "I'd rather give you eggs."

Sully cracked two eggs onto the grill, where they sputtered in bacon grease. Since taking over the morning grill at Hattie's he'd made several small but significant changes by executive decision. One was that eggs got fried in bacon grease. They tasted better that way, in Sully's opinion, and the grease was already sitting there anyhow. He also gave people the kind of toast he had handy. White, whole wheat. Once it was toasted you could hardly tell the difference, and Sully liked to finish one loaf before starting another. His inflexibility at the grill was already the occasion of considerable joking from men who knew he was going to make their breakfasts his way. They ordered poached eggs over rye toast, fresh-squeezed orange juice, a croissant and orange marmalade and herbal tea, thereby ensuring that when their breakfast was set in front of them (juice from the carton, eggs scrambled, white toast with strawberry preserves, muddy coffee) it would contain not a single item they'd ordered.

Sully put the plate of eggs in front of Rub. "You know what I'm dreaming of?" he said.

Rub dug into his eggs hungrily.

"Hey," Sully said.

Rub looked up.

"I'm talking to you."

"What?" Rub said. It was just like Sully to ignore him until he gave him his food and then want to talk.

"What am I dreaming of?"

Rub looked at his friend's face, as if the answer might be written there.

"I'll give you one hint. It's the same thing I was dreaming of yesterday and the day before that. I've been dreaming of this one thing for the last two weeks, and every morning I've dreamed it right in front of you. I've sung this dream out loud."

Rub, forkful of bleeding eggs halfway to his open mouth, tried to remember yesterday. Cass and the two men at the counter who'd been listening in to this conversation began to hum "White Christmas" significantly. Then suddenly the answer was there. "A white fucking Christmas," Rub said and sucked the eggs into his mouth happily.

"That's what I'm dreaming of, all right," Sully said. "A white fucking Christmas."

The men at the counter began to sing it. "I'm dreaming of a white fucking Christmas." Old Hattie rocked in her booth, her eyes serene, contemplative. The song had always been one of her favorites.

The singing had just died down when Peter and Will came in, the little boy looking sleepy but happy, his father just sleepy. Peter helped Will onto the stool next to Rub, then slid onto the one next to his son. Will wrinkled his nose. "Something smells," he whispered.

Sully nodded. "Switch stools with your father," he suggested.

They switched.

"Better?" Sully said.

"A little," the boy said.

"It'll be much better in a minute," Sully said. Rub was mopping up the remainder of his egg yolk and unmindful of every other reality. Sully doubted he'd heard a word of the conversation.

"You had breakfast?" Sully asked the boy.

He nodded. "Grandma made me toast."

"Can't you make your own toast?"

"Not in Grandma's kitchen," Peter said.

"You want a hot chocolate?"

"Okay."

Sully made him hot chocolate from a packet, added a spurt of whipped cream from a can. "You going to be my helper again today?"

"Okay," the boy agreed, whipped cream on his nose.

Sully was studying Peter, who looked extra morose this morning. He was not used to getting up early and was usually silent until midmorning. "How about some coffee?" Sully said.

"Nope," Peter said sleepily. He was eyeing Rub, who pushed his plate away and noticed Peter there for the first time. "Morning, Sancho," Peter said.

"You got time for a cup," Sully said. "Rub's in no hurry, are you, Rub?"

Rub studied Sully, aware that this might be a trick question. Sometimes Sully said exactly this to indicate that it was time he got off his ass and went to work.

"What do you want us to do today?" Peter said.

Sully shrugged. "It's supposed to be nice. Up in the forties. I'd work outside. Chop those hedges back, rake up all the sticks and branches, haul it all off someplace. Give our employer the impression we're making progress in case he shows up, God forbid. We're going to have to remove that tree stump at some point."

"I was thinking that would be a good spring job." Peter ventured a half grin. "Sometime when I'm gone."

"I don't see what that stump's hurting," Rub said as he did each time the subject of the stump arose. "How come he don't just leave it alone?"

"Some people don't like tree stumps in their front yard," Sully said. "Be thankful. It'll probably take us a week to dig it out. That's a week's pay."

"Stumps don't hurt anything, is what I'm saying," Rub said. He was particularly inflexible on the subject of the stump. "Elm roots go halfway to China. Remember over at Carl's?"

"Don't get me started about that," Sully said.

"I wisht he'd pay us for that job," Rub said, his face clouding over.

"He will, eventually," Sully said. "I'll make sure of it."

"When?" Rub wondered.

"Eventually," Sully repeated. "Just like eventually you'll go to work today."

"You're the one just said there was no hurry," Rub said.

"That was half an hour ago."

Rub slid off his stool. "You coming over when you're done here?" Sully said he would.

When Rub and his father were gone, Will slurped the dregs of his hot chocolate from the bottom of his mug. He still had a spot of whipped cream on his nose. Sully removed it with a napkin. The boy smiled at his grandfather, then frowned in the direction of the front door his father and Rub had just disappeared out of, something clearly troubling him. Leaning toward Sully, he whispered, full of embarrassment, "Rub stinks."

There'd been several reasons Sully hadn't wanted to buy the truck he was now driving courtesy of Harold's Automotive World. One was he couldn't afford it, even without the snowplow apparatus. The other was that whoever had owned the truck previously had pampered it. There was no rust anywhere, and the upholstery in the cab was without meaningful incision. Even the exterior paint job had been maintained. True, the truck had nearly sixty thousand miles on it, but Sully could tell they weren't hard miles, and so he distrusted them. There was a distinct possibility that nobody had ever worked in this truck, and he was going to have to work in it. Trucks, to Sully's mind, were a lot like people. If you pampered them early, they got spoiled and then later became undependable. And so he'd set immediately about showing the truck that the good old days were over. The first day he owned it, he accidentally backed into a pole, splintering the red reflector of the taillight and denting the rear bumper. The following week he'd opened the driver's side door into a fire hydrant outside the OTB where he'd stopped to play his 1-2-3 triple, dinging the finish impressively. The previous owner had put a mat down in the bed to protect it, a pretty foolish thing to Sully's way of thinking. He liked to hear the sound his tools made when he tossed them into his truck at the end of the day. A crowbar bouncing off the bed of a pickup truck was a satisfying sound, and he refused to be cheated out of it. The first time he'd tossed a wrench onto the mat he'd heard nothing at all, leading him to believe he'd missed the bed of the truck altogether, and he'd gone around the other side to look for a wrench-shaped pattern in the snowbank. When there wasn't one, he looked in the bed of the pickup, and there sat the wrench in the middle of the rubber mat. The next day he'd sold the mat for twenty dollars to Ruth's son, Gregory, who needed cheering up. He'd dropped out of school after the Bath-Schuyler game, gone to work as a stockboy at the new supermarket by the interstate, bought himself a pickup truck so he could get there. He liked the pad. With the pad and an air mattress, you could get laid in the back of the truck. Theoretically.

And so when Sully and Will left Hattie's at midmorning and climbed into the truck, he noted with satisfaction that the vehicle was beginning to look and feel and even smell like a truck he might own, instead of one he couldn't afford. The windows were pleasantly dirty, and he'd begun to amass a collection of styrofoam coffee cups and sections of dirty, boot-printed newspaper on the floor. Will had apparently also concluded that it was beginning to look like a truck his grandfather might own, because he climbed in cautiously, testing his footing, as if the newspaper might conceal a hole in the floorboards.

When Sully turned the key in the ignition and started to back out from behind Hattie's, the boy said, "My seat belt, Grandpa," and so Sully braked and hooked the boy up.

"There," Sully said. "Your grandmother finds out I'm driving you around without a seat belt, I'm history, aren't I."

"Mom, too," the boy said, his face clouding over.

"You talk to her lately?" Sully ventured as he put the truck back into reverse and let off the brake.

"She called last night. They yelled at each other," Will confessed, ashamed.

"Mmmm," Sully said. "They love *you* just the same. Just 'cause they get mad at each other doesn't mean they don't love you."

The boy didn't say anything.

When Sully pulled out of the alley onto Main, he said, "You know what?"

When the boy didn't answer, Sully nudged him. "Grandpa loves you too."

Will frowned. "Grandpa Ralph?"

"No," Sully said. "Grandpa Me."

"I know," the boy said.

The damndest thing about what Sully'd said, he realized, was that it was true. He enjoyed having his grandson around. The first morning Peter had appeared for work with Will in tow, Sully'd let it be known that it wasn't such a great idea. "He won't get in the way," Peter had promised, his voice lowered.

"That's not the point," Sully'd responded, though it *was* the point, or a large part of the point. "What if he gets hurt?"

"How?"

"Suppose you whack a nail off center and it flies through the air and catches him in the eye. Your mother will have both our asses."

Peter shook his head. "Well, what do you know? My father is worried something might fly through the air and hit his grandson."

"Okay," Sully said. "You don't want me to worry about him, I won't."

"Worry all you want," Peter had said. "It's a little out of character, is all I'm saying."

"I never worried about you, is that what you're saying?"

"Hey," Peter said, shrugging his shoulders significantly.

And he was right, of course. Sully hadn't worried about Peter once during his entire childhood. Partly because he'd had his own worries. Partly because Vera could worry enough for ten people. Partly because he just hadn't. He'd neglected to, not feeling much need, even glad to be out of the picture, telling himself during moments of self-pity (self-knowledge?) that if he were involved in his son's life it would probably be to fuck things up.

That had been his attitude at the time, and in truth it had not felt as unnatural as this new attitude, this tightness of the heart he felt for his grandson, as if some natural, biological affection were coming to him late, after skipping a generation.

"Anyhow," Peter had remarked, "we don't have much choice."

The reason they didn't, Peter explained, was that Vera was working mornings at the stationer's, a job she'd taken after Ralph's first visit to the hospital.

"What about Ralph?" Sully said. "Don't tell me he's going back to work too."

"He offered to watch Will, but . . ."

"But?"

Peter had explained later, when the boy wasn't around, that Will hadn't wanted to stay alone in the house with Grandpa Ralph, who, the boy knew, had recently been in the hospital. He was afraid his grandfather would die while the others were away, that he'd be alone in the house with a dead man until everybody returned. Maybe that was part of Sully's strange affection for the boy, who seemed to Sully a quivering collection of terrible, unnecessary fears. Also, Ralph had a lot of running around to do. His work with the Lions, the Parks Commission.

Instead of joining Rub and Peter at the Miles Anderson house, Sully swung by Carl Roebuck's office. It had been a couple days since he'd seen Carl, who'd made an elliptical reference to the possibility of work. With an unpaid-for truck, Sully couldn't afford to ignore any elliptical references. He parked the truck in the street below and, with Will in tow, climbed the narrow stairs to the third floor, figuring that if Carl was not there—always a distinct possibility—maybe he'd be able to find out where he was from Ruby, who might be wearing her see-through blouse again, always a heartwarming spectacle, that. To his surprise, Ruby wasn't there. Toby Roebuck was, though she wasn't wearing anything see-through. What she had on was a bulky gray sweatshirt of the sort that usually said "property of" some college athletic department. What did it mean, Sully wondered, that he preferred the sight of Toby Roebuck in a bulky sweatshirt to Ruby, a young woman not without physical charms, in a see-through blouse? It meant, he suspected, that he was sixty. And a fool. And maybe other things too, none of them good. No matter what it meant, he was glad to see her there at Ruby's desk with the phone to her ear and apparently in good spirits, to judge from the grin she flashed him. She motioned to the two chairs behind the coffee table.

"I'll tell him, Clyde," she was saying. "No guarantees. You know how he is . . ."

Sully ignored the invitation to sit down but stuck his head inside Carl's inner office. No Carl.

Toby hung up the phone, stared at Sully. "I heard you'd made another career move," she said. "You smell like grease."

Sully had been all set to comment on her own apparent career move before being beaten to the punch. Also, it was disquieting to note how often women commented upon how he smelled right up front, before hello even.

"It's a terrible thing to have so many talents," he told her.

"Who's this?" she said, examining Will, whose existence Sully had momentarily forgotten under Toby Roebuck's influence.

"My grandson," he told her, then to Will, "Say hi to Mrs. Roebuck."

Will, shy as always, murmured something like a hello.

"I hadn't even gotten used to the idea that you had a son yet," Toby observed, "and here you are a grandfather. Hard to imagine."

"My son said almost the same thing this morning," he admitted. "What's the deal? Is Ruby sick?"

She made a face. "Alas, Ruby is no more, having tendered her resignation last Friday. I should have warned her that resignation would be the outcome."

"Where'd she go?"

She shrugged. "We could follow the trail of mascara . . ."

"Let's not," Sully suggested. "It's pretty discouraging to think about so many girls crying over your husband. I know since women's lib we're not supposed to say that women are stupid, but the way they all fall for Carl kind of suggests it."

"You think they should all fall for you?"

"Not all," Sully said. "But if Carl can fool them all, I ought to be able to fool one or two."

"You aren't fooling Ruth any more?"

Sully ignored the question behind the question. In fact, he had not seen Ruth in three weeks, since Janey's husband, Roy, shot up the wrong house and put Janey into the hospital with a broken jaw and a severe concussion. Somehow, Ruth had construed the entire series of events to be Sully's fault. That was the message she'd delivered bright and early the next morning, before he was completely awake even. It had not been one of their usual arguments, carried on in private, in some motel room or the front seat of Sully's pickup. She'd suddenly just materialized there at Hattie's before he'd even loaned Rub his first dollar of the day, before he'd taken a sip of his coffee, before he'd even gotten to square one in the business of figuring out what he was going to say to Ruth when he ran into her. He had only just finished hearing about the events in question from a still badly shaken Miss Beryl a few minutes before. In fact, the part of the problem he was working on there at Hattie's was whether to go looking for Ruth or let her find him. On general principle he hated to go looking for trouble, but he was also aware that trouble could get worse if you let it find you. And here it was before he could decide. He hadn't even been aware of Ruth at first, just that the lunch counter had gone silent, as if everyone were holding his breath.

And when he turned and saw who it was at his shoulder, it wasn't Ruth's sudden presence that concerned him so much as her appearance. She looked like a woman who'd lost what remained of her youth over night. She looked every day of her forty-eight-plus years, and there was something terrible about her expression, too, as if she herself realized that she'd lost, decisively, some great battle she'd been waging, and was glad, now that she'd thought about it, to have lost it.

Whatever battle she'd lost, Sully could tell she had no intention of losing the fight she was about to pick with him. She looked ready to make short work of him and anyone foolish enough to take his side. The only person in the diner who might remotely have been Sully's ally was Rub, who occupied the stool on Sully's other side and who was so scared when he saw Ruth coming that he was unable to find his voice to warn Sully. In fact, he couldn't have been more frightened if he'd just been informed that Carl Roebuck had found all those blocks they'd dumped behind the demonic clown, or even if Bootsie had come to whack his peenie.

And indeed Ruth had made short work of Sully, who'd boldly played the only card in his hand, having mistakenly concluded that it was trump. "I wasn't even there, Ruth," he said.

She'd let this statement hang there until the words themselves began to form, like skywriting, in the air between them. "I know you weren't, Sully," she told him, lowering her gruff voice like she always did when she was about to deliver a direct hit. "But then when was the last time you *were* there for anybody who needed you?"

Ruth always had a flair for exit lines. Sully watched her go without getting up from his stool, without calling to her, watched her through the diner's front window as she got into the car where Zack, to Sully's further astonishment, had been waiting for her. Then the diner was filled with mad cackling. For a moment he wondered if what he was hearing was interior, his own confusion made audible, but it turned out to be old Hattie behind him in her booth, the old woman reacting to dimly perceived tension with raucous hilarity. It had taken Cass the rest of the morning to calm her mother down.

"I never did fool Ruth," Sully told Toby Roebuck now. "She just happened to like me regardless."

"That's the way everybody likes you, Sully."

"Well, it's better than being disliked, I guess," Sully said.

Toby Roebuck didn't respond right away, which left the proceedings pretty empty. Had Sully been asked at that moment to name one thing he particularly disliked about women, even women he was most fond of, he'd have said it was the way they could get significantly quiet, as if to afford a man the opportunity to consider what he'd just said.

"I ran into her yesterday, actually," Toby said finally.

"Who?"

"Who?" she repeated. "Ruth, who. Who were we just talking about?"

"Oh, her," Sully said, forcing a grin.

"She had a tiny little girl with her."

This was probably a question, but Sully decided not to go into it. Janey had still not been released from the hospital. Sully himself had only a sketchy knowledge of what had transpired during the last two weeks. Vince had come into The Horse late one night after closing Jerry's Pizza and filled him in. According to Vince, Ruth had taken her two weeks' vacation from her day job at the IGA, as well as from her waitressing at the restaurant (for which Vince held Sully responsible) so she could look after Tina while Janey remained at the hospital. This loss of income from his wife's two jobs had forced Zack to contemplate finding a steady job himself. Janey's husband, Roy, having failed to make bond, was still in jail awaiting trial. Everyone seemed to agree that that was the best place for him, especially since he'd threatened, as soon as he got out, to get even with Sully for hiding his wife and kid.

"So," Toby Roebuck said.

"So," Sully agreed. To what, he had no idea.

"So, just like that, you and Ruth are finished."

"It's true I'm available, if that's what you're getting at."

"Sully, Sully, Sully."

"That's what your husband always says," Sully told her. Then, seeing a welcome opportunity to change the subject, "You didn't answer my question, though. Are you just filling in, or can I sneak up here and find you any time?"

"For a while, it looks like," she said. "He's out at the yard, in case you were wondering. He's a new man, he says. A man of many resolutions. You should ask him all about them. They're over an hour old, though, so he may not remember."

Sully nodded, getting to his feet. "I can't wait to hear all about it. If I miss him, tell him I was here." To Will: "What do you say, sport? You ready to go?"

Will, who had not uttered a word since his mumbled hello, got to his feet and preceded his grandfather into the hall.

"You're sure he's related to you?" Toby said.

"I know," Sully said. Then, since the boy was out of earshot, he said, "I don't want to say anything, but Ruby always wore see-through blouses. Of course, it's up to you . . ."

Sully wasn't sure what he expected the result of this teasing to be. Maybe that she'd pitch something at him in mock outrage. And so he was closing the door, even as he spoke, and the door was almost closed by the time he finished. Almost. Which meant that he almost didn't see when Toby Roebuck flashed him from where she sat behind the desk, her sweatshirt pulled up and then back down for a millisecond. Unsure he'd seen what he'd seen, he remained rooted to the spot in the hall outside the door. Exactly how long he stood there, he wasn't sure. A beat? Two beats? Three?

It was Will's voice coming from the head of the stairs that reestablished a time/space context. "What's the matter, Grandpa?" the boy said, his face a mask of urgent worry.

From inside, a peal of hilarity. "Yeah, Grandpa," Toby Roebuck called. "What's the matter?"

The night Sully and Peter had stolen the snowblower from Carl Roebuck's equipment yard there had been, unknown to them, a casualty, indeed a near fatality. Rasputin, Carl's Doberman, had suffered a stroke. Sully and Peter had seen the dog crumple, but they'd assumed it had simply gone to sleep on its feet and dropped. This was not the case. The dog's training, to attack savagely any unauthorized nocturnal visitors to the yard, had come into deep psychological conflict with drug-induced goodwill and drowsiness. Unable to resolve the urge to kill with the urge to sleep, Rasputin's circuitry had simply shut down.

Since that night the dog had regained only a small measure of its physical capabilities. He had a lopsided appearance now, one side of his body, corresponding to the opposite side of his brain, pretty much non-functional, his former ferocity vanished. As if the dog had learned the value of a good night's sleep, he now slept most of the time and even when awake wandered along the perimeter of the fence aimlessly, drooling out of one side of his mouth, as if in search of his lost aggression. Visitors he'd previously made nervous with deep-throated growls he now nuzzled affectionately with his long snout, then licked their fingers. All except Sully.

It is possible a dog will not forget his poisoner. When Sully pulled up and parked by the fence, Rasputin, who had been lying asleep in his favorite spot—the one where he'd collapsed the night Sully's hamburger changed his life—woke up, growled deep in his throat and tried to stand, an activity that always drew a crowd. Carl Roebuck and two of his men, just emerging from the Tip Top Construction trailer, stopped to watch this excellent entertainment. Once Rasputin was on his feet he could limp along well enough, but getting up from the cold ground after a long nap required, on the average, half a dozen attempts. The problem seemed to be that the animal's good side, which responded as it always had, was impatient with the defective side, which refused to function at high speed, causing the dog to circle itself, like a boat with only one oar in the water, until finally the animal collapsed and had to start over again. Only when the dog was sufficiently exhausted for the functioning side of his body to go slowly enough to meet the requirements of the stroke-damaged side could he stand. By then he was ready for another nap.

The men on the trailer steps watched several of these aborted attempts, shaking their heads in good-humored disbelief. Sully and Will watched for a moment also, the boy's eyes growing wide and round with wonder and fear.

"What's wrong with him, Grandpa?" the boy asked.

"He had a little accident a couple weeks ago," explained Sully, who had seen the dog a couple of times in the interim. "You want to ride on my shoulders?"

When Will nodded enthusiastically, Sully swung him aboard.

"Look who's here," Carl Roebuck said when he noticed Sully and the boy approaching. "You come to admire your handiwork?"

"It's not my fault you got a spastic Doberman," Sully said, setting Will down on the step. The boy was still warily watching Rasputin circle. Hearing Sully's voice, the dog was now emitting small howls of frustration.

"I think it *is* your fault," Carl said. "I just wish I could prove it." Then, to the two men who were watching the dog, "I know you guys'd love to stay here all afternoon and watch this dog have another stroke . . ."

"I would," one of the men said. "I admit it." But he and the other man headed for the gate, and Carl and Sully and the boy went inside the trailer.

Carl Roebuck went around behind the small metal desk and sat down, put his feet up and studied first the boy, then Sully. "Don Sullivan," he said knowingly. "Thief of Snowblowers, Poisoner of Dogs, Flipper of Pancakes. Secret Father and Grandfather. Jack-Off, All Trades. How they hangin'?"

Sully took a seat. "By a thread, as usual," he said. He motioned for Will to go ahead and sit on the sofa. "Don't ruin that," he warned.

Will looked at the sofa fearfully. It was torn to shreds, stuffing exploding from slits in the upholstery. Will climbed on carefully and found both men grinning at him.

"Your grandfather tell you how he poisons dogs?"

Will's eyes got big again.

"He steals people's snowblowers, too."

"Don't pay any attention to him," Sully said. "He just can't keep track of his possessions."

"You hid it pretty well, I'll give you that," Carl said.

Sully nodded. "I think you've lost it for good this time," he said. He'd told Miss Beryl to expect Carl Roebuck to come nosing around after the snowblower, and sure enough, Carl had. He'd told her to let him search the flat too, if he felt like it. But when she offered, Carl had declined, observing sadly that Sully wouldn't hide it anyplace so obvious and he didn't have anything up there to encourage collateral theft.

"It'll turn up eventually," Carl said. "When it snows, for sure."

"I'd like to see it snow," Sully admitted, thinking again about Harold Proxmire's snowplow blade and the money he could make with it. "A good blizzard or two, and I'd be free of you for good."

Carl grinned. "You'll never be free of me. If there were twenty blizzards and you had twenty plows, you'd still be desperate a week later."

"I never claimed to be lucky," Sully admitted. "In a town this size there's only room for one lucky man, and you're him. The rest of us just have to do the best we can."

Carl snorted. "You're the only man I know who believes in luck."

Sully nodded. "I believed in intelligence and hard work until I met you. Only luck explains you."

"That still leaves your own self with no good explanation."

"*Bad* luck explains me." Sully grinned.

Carl Roebuck grinned his infuriating grin. "You find a new place to live yet?"

"Don't remind me," Sully told him. He'd promised Miss Beryl to be out by the first of the year, which left about two weeks, but so far he hadn't made much progress in locating another flat. It had been Clive Jr., the day after the shooting incident, who'd tried to evict him first, but Sully had told him to go fuck himself. When Miss Beryl said she wanted him out, he'd go, but not before. Despite the fact that just about everybody wanted to blame him for just about everything, Sully wasn't buying. He hadn't been there at the time, and he'd never met the man who'd done the shooting. Maybe Janey *had* come to Miss Beryl's looking for him, for a place to hide, but that didn't make him responsible for what trailed in her wake. In fact, after he'd had a chance to let all the accusations leveled against him sift down, he'd come to the conclusion that there was a little too much loose blame flying in his direction. His ears were still ringing with Ruth's denunciation when Clive Jr. had started in. Screw him and the horse he rode in on, was the way Sully looked at it.

But later that night, when he sat zigging at The Horse with Wirf, he'd decided that maybe he'd move. Miss Beryl hadn't blamed him, and her refusal to do so made Sully think maybe he should return the kindness by making sure she wasn't in the line of fire any more. Maybe he hadn't caused the events in question, but they couldn't have happened without him. Maybe he was right and Janey wasn't his daughter, but Ruth persisted in believing she was, and maybe Janey believed it too. And maybe Zack. It was all pretty complicated, and it reminded Sully of one of those cockamamie theories his young philosophy professor had so enjoyed tossing out. According to him, everybody, all the people in the world, were linked by invisible strings, and when you moved you were really exerting influence on other people. Even if you couldn't see the strings pulling, they were there just the same. At the time Sully had considered the idea bullshit. After all, he'd been lurching through life for pretty close to sixty years without having any noticeable effect on anybody but himself, and maybe Rub. His wife had barely noticed his absence after the divorce and a new life had closed in around her. His son thought of another man as his father. Again, excepting Rub, he couldn't think of anybody who depended on him, which demonstrated, he had to admit, their good judgment.

But all this had been before Thanksgiving, before Peter showed up needing things and bringing his own needy little boy with him, before Janey had come looking for him when she needed a place to hide, before he learned of Ralph and Vera's troubles and that Wirf was sick. Maybe there were strings. Maybe you caused things even when you tried hard not to. If that was the case, he probably should find a new place to live. Miss Beryl was eighty and a hell of a good sport, but she deserved some peace and quiet in her old age. She didn't deserve to have dead deer turn up on her terrace and crazy, jealous husbands from the wrong side of the Schuyler Springs tracks shooting up her neighborhood, and with Sully gone, they wouldn't.

So the next morning he'd told his landlady he'd move out the first of the year, provided Clive Jr. stayed the hell out of his way and didn't badger him further. Though she'd appeared genuinely saddened by his decision, Miss Beryl hadn't objected, and it occurred to Sully, as it had off and on for forty years, that maybe he was the dangerous man people considered him to be.

"I'm not too worried," he told Carl Roebuck now. "Toby says I can stay with you until something turns up. 'It'd be nice to have a man around the house' were her exact words."

Outside the trailer door there was a low growl, then a scratching and sniffing at the door. Will edged closer to Sully on the sofa.

"Funny how that dog hates you," Carl observed.

"How do you know it's me?"

Another low growl from outside.

Carl Roebuck grinned. "His master's voice."

"Can he get in?" Will wanted to know.

"Watch this," Carl told the boy. "Go over to that window. Peek through the curtain."

Will looked more than a little dubious but did as instructed.

"Is he standing there?"

When Will nodded, Carl Roebuck kicked the door, hard. Outside, there was a muffled thud.

"He fell down," Will reported.

Carl shook his head at Sully. "Isn't that pitiful? A perfectly good Doberman, mean as hell. Ruined."

"Listen," Sully said. "I heard you had some work for me."

"That depends," Carl said, sitting back down and putting his feet up again. "You still own that piece of shit property on Bowdon?"

"Beats me."

"You don't know?"

"I don't care," Sully told him, though this response was more force of habit than literal truth. In the last few weeks he'd found himself thinking about the house almost every day. He'd even wandered down from the Anderson place and contemplated it one afternoon, wondered again if the property could be worth more than the taxes owed on it and, if so, how much more. Enough more to be a possible solution to his deepening financial woes, for instance. Or enough more to make a difference to Peter. His son's return to Bath had caused the resurgence of Sully's unaccountable desire to give him something. When Peter was a boy, Sully'd sent him presents for Christmas and, when he remembered, on his birthday, but he couldn't remember a single specific gift, which felt a lot to Sully like he hadn't given anything. Maybe if he gave Peter the house, or the money from selling the house, it'd be something.

"You remember if it had hardwood floors?"

Sully said it had. He could picture his mother cleaning them on her knees.

Carl picked up the phone and dialed it. "Hi," he said, not bothering to identify himself. "Do me a favor. Call City Hall and find out the status of Sully's place on Bowdon. He doesn't seem to know if it's his. Give little Rodrigo a kiss for me."

Before Sully could attempt to make sense of this conversation, Carl hung up and said, "You want to run by there and take a look?"

"We could," Sully said, feigning indifference. In fact, the idea of getting Carl's opinion of the place appealed to him. He'd even considered asking him for that opinion more than once and had been prevented only by the fact that by asking Carl's opinion he might appear to be wavering from his public view that Carl Roebuck's advice on any subject was not worth having.

"Let's," Carl suggested without getting up or even taking his feet off the desk. Will, taking their apparent agreement literally, stood up, then, seeing that neither man had moved, sat down again, confused.

Sully studied Carl carefully. Something about his attitude was different, and he recalled Toby Roebuck's remark that her husband was a changed man. "You're looking especially smug today," Sully observed, leaning forward and pulling a small end table covered with magazines around in front of the sofa so he could put his own feet up. To Sully's way of thinking, if there were two men in a room and one of them had his feet up on something, that man had a distinct advantage. Especially if the man was Carl Roebuck. Whenever possible, Sully liked to put his feet up around Carl, even if the maneuver hurt, and he did so now, especially pleased with the fact that his work shoes were wet and that a slushy puddle began immediately to form on the cover of the top magazine.

"It's true," Carl said. "I'm in such a good mood that even a visit from you hasn't dampened my spirits."

"I'm glad to hear it," Sully told him. "I'm glad to know that people like you are happy. Of course, I'd be happy too if I'd inherited a fortune, married the prettiest girl in the county and got to bang all the others besides."

Carl grinned and leaned even farther back in his swivel chair, hooking his fingers behind his neck. "You're right," he admitted, sadly it seemed to Sully. "She is the prettiest girl in the county."

"I've been telling you that for years, if you recall."

"Okay, you told me so, smart-ass," Carl conceded. "In which case you'll be pleased to know I've turned over a new leaf."

"That's what she just told me," Sully told him. "I didn't have the heart to remind her who she was talking about."

"Mock on, mock on, Voltaire, Rousseau," Carl said. Whatever it was that Carl was feeling so smug about, he was dying to tell somebody about it. Which meant that the only thing for Sully to do was feign absolute indifference.

"Mock on who?"

Carl ignored this. "You saw Toby over at the office?"

"I did indeed," Sully told him. And if he hadn't been taken by surprise, he'd have really seen what he saw. With Carl Roebuck sitting there looking so smug, Sully actually considered for a brief moment telling Carl about what had happened, just to see if maybe that good mood couldn't be ruined after all. What prevented him was the possibility, however remote, that Toby Roebuck's flashing him had been some sort of invitation to return when he didn't have his grandson with him. He'd been flirting with the woman for years, after all. She'd be foolish to take him seriously, but a woman capable of taking Carl Roebuck seriously just might.

"She didn't say anything to you?" Carl was still grinning maniacally. "Well, never mind," he continued. "She's probably only telling people she likes."

Suddenly Sully figured it out. "What?" he said. "Don't tell me she's pregnant?"

"Knocked up like a cheerleader," Carl said. His grin had taken over his face so completely now that Sully himself couldn't help grinning through the disappointment.

Neither man said anything for a long moment.

"So," Carl Roebuck said finally. "Now I suppose you'll want to be the godfather."

"I can't be both the father *and* the godfather," Sully said. "You're going to have to contribute *some* goddamn thing."

"Anyhow. No more messing around for the studmeister. I realize now," he explained, pulling on his heavy coat, gloves, tweed hat, "that I just wanted to be a father. Isn't it something the way the mind works?"

"It sure is," Sully agreed. "You had the rest of us fooled completely. We figured you were just a jerk. How long you figure you can keep this up?"

Carl took a deep breath. "Except for Toby I've been a monk for three days, and I'm not even horny. I've never felt better, in fact. You should have told me it was okay to have a limp dick. I'm giving up gambling and drinking and smoking and all of it. Everything but bad companions, which is why I'm still talking to you."

Outside, in front of the trailer, Carl let out a Tarzan yell, pounded his chest. "White hunter make baby!" he crowed. "Let's take two cars. I'll meet you there."

Sully said that was fine with him. He'd taken several steps toward the gate when he realized Will was not at his side. The boy was still on the trailer step, casting about nervously in search of Rasputin, who was not in evidence. "Where is he?" the boy said.

"Come here," Sully said. "Hold my hand."

Will did, warily. "There he is," he said, spying the dog.

Rasputin was leaning, cross-legged, against the chain-link fence near the gate, as if he were resting. Had he been a human being, his posture would have suggested that he was about to light a cigarette and take a relaxing five minutes to smoke it.

"Isn't this a pitiful fucking sight," Carl said, going over to his once faithful watchdog. Rasputin lurched feebly, unable to right himself. Clearly, he'd lost his equilibrium again and slumped against the fence, which was holding him up.

Carl went around behind the dog, lifted him off the fence, set him down again gently. "You know what he reminds me of?" he said. Before Sully could say no, Carl told him. "You," he said.

Sully nodded. "He is pretty well hung at that," he admitted. "I never noticed it before."

Noon found Miss Beryl in the kitchen, staring up into her cupboard and contemplating a bowl of soup as a solution not to hunger so much as to the duty to eat something. Normally possessed of an excellent appetite for a woman her age, she'd been off her feed for the last two weeks. The worst of it was that she knew why, and it wasn't, as Mrs. Gruber insisted, simple discombobulation, the residual effect of having a crazy man shoot up the neighborhood. Nor was it, as Clive Jr. had suggested, that she was feeling adrift as a result of not traveling this year. Late December was usually such a busy time, preparing for the holidays and for her travels to whatever foreign place she planned to sally forth. Clive Jr. still thought she should go. This year, the plan had been Africa, where Miss Beryl had hoped to find a mate for Driver Ed. If Ed were more content, maybe he'd quit whispering subversion into her ear. For a mate, she had in mind some tolerant she-mask whose demeanor suggested she wouldn't mind sharing a wall with a dour old shape shifter like Ed, who had grown more dour of late, now that she'd started listening to Clive Jr.'s advice.

Her decision not to travel this year meant, among other things, that Ed would have to remain without a mate. Over the weekend Miss Beryl, realizing that she was going to have time on her hands during the long Bath winter, had sallied forth with Mrs. Gruber to purchase the most difficult jigsaw puzzle she could find. They went to an overpriced hobby shop in Schuyler Springs, where Miss Beryl bought a puzzle and Mrs. Gruber purchased a Slinky, claiming never to have seen such a thing before. "It's alive almost," Mrs. Gruber kept saying when the Slinky, apparently of its own volition, descended the stairs set up for it.

On the way home Miss Beryl, who had driven to Schuyler Springs a thousand times, had somehow taken a wrong turn, realizing her mistake only when they passed beneath the interstate and heard the roar of semis on their way to Canada. Mrs. Gruber, who never observed anything out a car window, remained innocent of her friend's error, allowing Miss Beryl to seek a solution. She didn't want just to stop and make a three-point turn in the middle of the country road, a maneuver that might alert even Mrs. Gruber to her mistake. So she kept on going for another mile or two, turned right at a rural intersection and headed, she hoped, south, and then right again at the first opportunity, theoretically west, toward Bath. Which indeed it was. The road took them back beneath the interstate past the new supermarket and onto the four-lane spur. When they passed the demonic clown advertising the future site of The Ultimate Escape, Mrs. Gruber, who'd been by it half a dozen times before without noticing, exclaimed, "Oh look, dear! It's Clive Jr.!"

The jigsaw puzzle Miss Beryl purchased at the hobby shop in Schuyler Springs was a snowy winter scene that reminded her of the Robert Frost poem she taught to eighth-graders for so many years. The puzzle's woods were dark and deep, a tangle of black branches. "Why that one?" Mrs. Gruber had wanted to know. "It'd make me all nerves."

Miss Beryl now wished she had listened. Robert Frost aside, the puzzle had not been a good choice. The color of the snow was almost identical to that of the sky, and once Miss Beryl got the puzzle's edge constructed, she found the rest mighty slow going. The maze of blacks and whites (not to mention grays) made it difficult to know whether any given piece might belong to the background or the foreground of the scene, the left or right side of the puzzle. Miss Beryl averaged a piece or two an hour and even these successes were often due to blind luck. She found she was able to stare at the puzzle for only so long before she had to take a break, and she learned quickly not to go over to her front window, as was her habit, and stare up into the trees, for it invariably dawned on her when she did this that the scene outside her window was virtually the same as the puzzle. Better to go into her bright yellow kitchen.

But today, as Miss Beryl stared up into her soup cupboard, anxious to blame her offishness, her discombobulation, on puzzles and wrong turns and strangers with guns, she had to admit that these were not to blame. No, it was because she had done a bad thing, and her stomach had not been right since she did it.

She would not soon forget the look on Sully's face the morning he'd told her Clive Jr. was right, it would probably be best if he moved out come the first of the year. He'd stopped in on his way to work the second day after the terrible events outside her house and said, as he always did, "Well, I see you're still alive," the old joke taking on an extra dimension—even Sully seemed to realize this—when strangers started shooting rifles at the house next door, meaning, in fact, to shoot at your house. Sully was carrying his work boots and looking around for the Queen Anne to sit in. "What'd you do with my chair?"

"My son's fiancée sat in it and broke it," Miss Beryl told him. She'd taken the pieces to a man in Schuyler Springs named Mr. Blue, who'd claimed over the phone that he could repair anything.

Miss Beryl was still miffed with the Joyce woman, whose personality had not improved upon further acquaintance. She'd accompanied Clive Jr. the evening of the shooting incident, about which she voiced a great many entirely irrelevant opinions. In fact, the woman had opened her mouth and not shut it again for half an hour. The entire culture, she explained, was in rapid decline. The evidence was everywhere. Why, she herself could barely stand to watch the local news. There used to be a thing called neighborhoods, but not anymore. Why, even in her own neighborhood in Lake George things were happening that you associated with New York City or New Jersey. Animals, these people were, and nothing but. On and on she went, a juggernaut of personal opinion. By way of revenge Miss Beryl had gone into the kitchen and served the woman an extra-strong cup of "decaf."

Oddly enough, Sully, who was famous for refusing to assume the mantle of even the lightest responsibility, acknowledged this one. "The chair was probably my fault," he admitted sadly. "I noticed it felt wobbly the last couple times I sat in it. I should have said something."

He was still standing there in the middle of the room, work boots in hand, looking to Miss Beryl even more like a ghost than usual, his brows knit thoughtfully. "In fact," he added, "I should have fixed it. I meant to, actually."

Miss Beryl had almost interrupted him, told him forget it, as if that were necessary with Sully, but he seemed so deep in uncharacteristic thought that Miss Beryl had said nothing.

"Anyhow, listen," he said, snapping out of it. "If I left at the end of the month, do you think you could find another renter?"

"Where would you go?" Miss Beryl had wondered out loud, realizing even as she spoke that her question had contained an unintended insult by suggesting that there was no place else in the wide world prepared to welcome him.

Fortunately, Sully neither heard the insult nor shared her doubt. "I'll find a spot," he shrugged. "This town's always about half empty. I could use a smaller place anyhow. In fact, I could probably get away with a room and a bath. I never use the kitchen. I just don't want to leave you in the lurch, is all."

"I don't *need* a renter, Donald," she assured him. "I've enjoyed your company." Realizing that this was a foolish observation since he was there only to sleep and bathe, she added, "knowing you were around."

"I haven't *been* around that much," he admitted. "And I wasn't around Friday when I should have been . . . "

"He'd have just shot you dead," Miss Beryl told him. "Your presence would have just made things worse."

"Well, thanks for saying so, Mrs. Peoples." Sully grinned wryly. "But I have this idea my leaving will make things quieter. That's what your son thinks, and he could be right for once. Nobody can be wrong all the while. Not even The Bank."

This, in fact, had been Miss Beryl's own reasoning on the subject, so she didn't disagree. "If you change your mind, Donald—"

"I won't," Sully said. "Not once it's made up. Besides," he added, looking around, "you don't even have a place for me to sit down anymore."

All that had been two weeks ago, and in the interim Miss Beryl had not been herself. Since giving notice, Sully was even less in evidence than before. Part of it was that he'd started working mornings at Hattie's, and this required him to get up half an hour earlier. Instead of waiting outside for Hattie's to open, he now helped open it, which meant that he had to set the alarm that never woke him up half an hour earlier. Its buzzing in the bedroom above her own woke Miss Beryl, who now kept the broom she used to thump her ceiling right beside her bed. From the moment she heard Sully's heavy feet hit the floor, it was usually less than five minutes before he stumbled out the door and into the gray street. He put his work boots on at the foot of the stairs now and was quickly gone. Sometimes Miss Beryl saw him late in the afternoon when he came home from work to bathe before going out again, but she missed their morning repartee. She was thinking just how much she missed it, and was going to miss Sully when he was gone, when her doorbell rang.

Miss Beryl's first thought, fear really, was that it must be Mrs. Gruber, who'd called midmorning to find out whether Miss Beryl might want to sally forth for lunch and who had been greatly distressed to learn that, no, her friend was still not feeling any better. Winters were difficult for Mrs. Gruber, who liked to take walks but was forced to quit them after Thanksgiving when the weather got bitter and she feared she would catch her death. She did not dare resume them until the tulips bloomed along the side of her house in April. And so, except when she was able to talk Miss Beryl into driving them someplace in the Ford, she was housebound. Thus she had a vested interest in Miss Beryl's health. At first thrilled to learn that her friend would not be traveling this winter, Mrs. Gruber now realized— and how her spirits plummeted in this sad knowledge—that Miss Beryl not only intended to eschew international travel but also entertained no plans to sally forth locally. Convinced that Miss Beryl suffered more from simple discombobulation than anything else, Mrs. Gruber gave every indication of having formulated an ambitious plan to nurse her friend back to physical and emotional health and to nurse Miss Beryl's Ford back onto the interstate in time to take advantage of postholiday sales. Which was why Miss Beryl feared that it would be Mrs. Gruber at the door with a steaming pot of Campbell's chicken noodle soup, made the way Mrs. Gruber always made it, with too much water. On the way to answer the door Miss Beryl peeped through her lace curtain to see if she was right.

She was not. The woman waiting patiently on Miss Beryl's porch was a tall, lanky middle-aged woman dressed in cheap slacks and a man's canvas jacket and no hat. Miss Beryl recognized her in stages. The first of these stages was abstract. "I know you," she murmured to herself, studying the woman. Then, "How about it, Ed? Where do I know her from?" Ed could not be induced to contribute. The problem with having taught school in a small town for so long was that she "knew" just about everyone, or rather recognized in their adult visages some distant eighth-grader. It was Miss Beryl's theory that the idea of reincarnation had probably been invented by a small-town public school teacher gone slightly batty, the victim of a constant, vague impression that she'd known everyone she met on the street in some previous life. But it was this tall woman's adult self that she seemed to recognize, which deepened the mystery, since Miss Beryl's circle of acquaintance had had, this last decade, an ever shrinking radius. She appealed this time to her husband. "Don't just sit there, Clive," she said. "Help me out here." Why in her mind's eye did she see this woman in uniform?

Ask the right question, get an answer. Miss Beryl had no sooner asked it than she recognized the woman as one of the checkers at the IGA. "Now we're cooking with gas," she told her advisers, though all was still not clear. Why a checker from the IGA would be on her doorstep, for instance, was not evident. She wasn't holding a can, which meant she wasn't collecting for the heart fund. Miss Beryl supposed that in order to clear this mystery up, she'd have to answer the door and ask. She was about to let the curtain fall back into place when she noticed that behind the tall woman, almost out of view, stood the little girl with the wandering eye, which made the tall woman the child's grandmother and, according to local gossip, Sully's longtime paramour. Was it the little girl's bad eye or the good that fixed Miss Beryl before she could let go of the curtain?

The bell rang a second time as Miss Beryl opened the door. "Oh," the tall woman said, appearing startled. Her voice was as gruff and mannish as her clothes. "I was about to give up. . . . I mean, I thought you weren't home."

"No, I just check people out through the window before opening the door," Miss Beryl admitted. As she spoke, Miss Beryl was trying to peer around the tall woman at the little girl, but the child had gone into hiding behind the woman's legs. "I just let Mormons stand there. They do, too. Stand right there, like they're waiting for the Second Coming. Them and insurance salesmen."

"I'm Ruth. You remember this one?" the woman said.

"I sure do," Miss Beryl said. "You gave me the slip, didn't you? I looked up and you were gone."

It had been one of the worst moments of Miss Beryl's life. Such a simple task, so profoundly botched. She had failed to protect a child. After hitting the little girl's mother with his rifle, the father had simply collected his daughter, put her into the truck and driven away. The stupid policeman had stood right there and let him.

"She can move when she wants to, all right," Ruth said, her tone suggesting that the child didn't want to very often.

Miss Beryl remembered her manners. "Come in out of the cold," she said. "Little One wouldn't eat my cookies last time, but she might now that we're old friends."

The child was still in hiding behind Ruth, refusing, so far, to acknowledge Miss Beryl.

"We can only stay a minute," Ruth said. "We just dropped by to say thanks."

"What for?" Miss Beryl asked, genuinely curious.

"For calling the police. Who knows what would have happened if you hadn't? We're sorry for all the trouble, aren't we, Two Shoes? We would have stopped sooner except we've been spending most of our time at the hospital."

To Miss Beryl's surprise, the little girl spoke from her hiding place. "Tomorrow," she said.

Ruth turned and picked the child up. "That's right, darlin'. Tomorrow's the big day, isn't it. Mom gets out of the hospital tomorrow and Grandma gets to go back to work. At least for a while."

Miss Beryl took their coats and hung them up while Ruth and the child went into the living room. "Mommy was right," Miss Beryl heard Ruth say. "This is some place. Look at all the Christmas decorations!"

Miss Beryl couldn't help smiling, since she had not, thanks to her blue funk, felt up to the task of decorating for the holiday. All of her Christmas things were still in storage. Probably Ruth's eye had caught the small table that served as a stand for her nutcrackers. Maybe at first glance the rest of her exotica resembled Christmas to Ruth, who didn't look like a traveler. "And look. Mrs. Peoples is doing a puzzle. There isn't much we like more than puzzles, huh."

The child glanced at the puzzle and then back at Miss Beryl, causing the old woman to wonder if the little girl's grandmother might be expressing a wish—that the child would be interested in something. When Ruth took a seat on the sofa, the child turned her back to the puzzle, climbed onto the sofa next to her grandmother and, all the while never taking her eyes off Miss Beryl, found Ruth's earlobe with her thumb and forefinger. An expression like serenity came over the child's face then.

Ruth got off the sofa then and sat on the floor beneath the child. "There. Now you can reach it, huh," she said.

"Are you quitting the IGA?" Miss Beryl wondered in response to Ruth's remark "at least for a while."

"It's quitting us. They haven't said so in public, but they're going to close the store." Ruth explained that the new supermarket at the interstate had put the financially troubled little IGA out of its final misery, just as the IGA had killed the corner groceries two decades earlier.

"Will you go to work out there?" Miss Beryl wondered.

Ruth shook her head. "I don't think they've hired anybody over twenty-five. No, Grandma will have to find something else, right, Two Shoes?"

The little girl continued to stare at Miss Beryl.

"We don't know quite what yet, but some damn thing," Ruth continued. "You can't stand still in this life or you get run over. We'll have to figure out something when the time comes. If all else fails, maybe we could find Grandpa Zack a job. That'd be a kick, wouldn't it? Watch Grandpa Zack work for a change?"

Miss Beryl listened to the woman, fascinated by her vocal resemblance to her daughter. It was as if the younger woman had suddenly awakened thirty years older and wiser, the sharp edge of her anger and tongue having eroded while leaving the same bedrock personality.

"Maybe something will present itself," Miss Beryl said, trying to sound encouraging. "Clive Jr., star of my firmament, claims this is going to be the Gold Coast before long."

Ruth looked vaguely puzzled by this, though Miss Beryl couldn't be sure whether the source of her puzzlement was that she didn't know who Clive Jr. was, or whether she didn't know what a firmament was, or whether she shared Miss Beryl's own doubts about the existence of a Gold Coast anywhere near Bath. In any event, she didn't seem interested in contesting the point. "We could stand a little gold, couldn't we, Two Shoes? We'd know just what to do with it."

"How about that cookie?" Miss Beryl said, remembering her promise.

"We might eat one," Ruth answered for the child. "You never can tell."

Miss Beryl went into the kitchen to fetch cookies. When she returned, to her surprise the little girl had left her grandmother and was standing at the table where Miss Beryl had set up the jigsaw puzzle, her arms hanging straight down at her sides. Miss Beryl set the plate of cookies down on the coffee table and joined the little girl. "Find me that piece right there," she suggested, pointing at the small space in the upper right-hand corner. "I've been looking for that piece for three days, and I don't think it's here. It'd be just like the people who make these dern things to leave one piece out, just to torment old ladies."

"Check the floor," Ruth suggested. "That's where the pieces I need always are."

"I've checked everywhere," Miss Beryl said, returning to her seat opposite Ruth, who had taken and was chewing a cookie thoughtfully as she studied her granddaughter.

Miss Beryl was delighted to see that Ruth had been right, after all. The little girl did appear interested in the puzzle, which meant that the child's grandmother had a better understanding of her than the mother, who, Miss Beryl suspected, would have interrupted her daughter and tried to get her to eat a cookie. Indeed, Miss Beryl could almost hear the young woman. ("Come eat a cookie, Birdbrain. This old lady was nice enough to get it for you. The goddamn least you can do is eat one.")

"Did you say her mother gets out of the hospital tomorrow?"

"They're unwiring her jaw right now," Ruth explained. "Tomorrow she'll be ready to come home. We've been having a lot of trouble understanding why Mommy doesn't talk to us. Normally we can't get her to shut up, and now she won't talk. But the main thing is that she'll be home . . . and that other person won't be."

"What's wrong with him, anyway?" Miss Beryl wondered out loud.

There'd been something strange and military about the way the man had methodically and without visible emotion shot out the windows of the house next door, as if he were acting on orders that were being transmitted that moment through headphones.

"He's a moron," Ruth said. A simple explanation that fit the facts. "Comes from a long line of them. With him out of the way it'll be a second chance for my daughter. Who knows? She might even be smart enough to realize it."

"Maybe you and your mom can come visit me sometime," Miss Beryl said to the child, who continued staring at the puzzle without exhibiting any inclination to touch it. "I'm an old lady, and I don't get very many visitors, except that lady down the street I told you about."

Was it a smile that began to form on the child's lips? A smile, Miss Beryl realized, became an ambiguous thing when the eyes were not in harmony. "Snail," the little girl whispered.

"Right," Miss Beryl said, cheered by this response. "The one who ate the snail."

Ruth smiled. "So that's where the snail came from. Snails are all we've heard about for two weeks."

"Well, if you come back and visit me, we'll call up the lady who ate the snail and ask her to come over so you can meet her. She even looks like somebody who'd eat a snail," Miss Beryl said, then glanced at Ruth. "Grandma'd be welcome too if she felt like coming."

"Grandma will be back to work by then," Ruth said, leaning forward, running the backs of her fingers along her granddaughter's calf. "Besides. If I started coming over here regular, people would think I was visiting someone else."

At this reference to Sully, Miss Beryl felt guilt rise in her throat like illness. "Donald will be moving the first of the year," she said. "He didn't tell you?"

"We're on the outs at the moment," Ruth admitted. "I'd heard a rumor, though."

"I'm going to miss him. Clive Jr., star of my firmament, is convinced he's a dangerous man, but he's wrong. Donald is careless, but he's always been his own worst enemy."

"I know what you mean," Ruth said. "I've finally given up, though. I'm going to be fifty on my next birthday. Which means some damn thing, I'm not sure what. That I'm too old for all this foolishness, I guess. And I've got a feeling I'm going to inherit a responsibility soon"—she nodded almost imperceptibly at the little girl—"and responsibility is not our mutual friend's long suit."

"He might fool you," Miss Beryl said, regretting this observation immediately. In truth, Miss Beryl, who was simply inclined to think well of Sully, had long been waiting for him to redeem himself somehow, but it was beginning to look like his stubbornness was going to outlast her faith. It had always been her belief that people changed when life made them change, a belief Sully's dogged daily struggles—what he himself called "shoveling shit against the tide"—seemed designed to challenge.

"He might." Ruth smiled sadly. It was a wonderful open smile that transformed her appearance completely, softening it, making her almost beautiful, and Miss Beryl thought she saw what must have kept Sully interested all these years, because otherwise she was a very plain-looking woman. The mystery of affection, in particular Clive Sr.'s affection for her, was one of life's great mysteries. What, she had often wondered, had made her the center of his life? Miss Beryl had always been realistic about her odd physical appearance, and even as a young woman she'd concluded that Clive Sr. must have possessed the special gift of being able to see past that appearance. She remembered her mother's slender consolation to her unpopular child: "Don't you worry. You have what's called inner beauty, and the right man will see it." Ruth's remarkable smile offered a subtle variation on her mother's clichéd wisdom.

"It'd be just like him to surprise me, now that it's too late to make much difference," Ruth said.

"We wear the chains we forge in life," Miss Beryl said. "Donald said that to me one day not long ago. I almost dropped my teeth."

Ruth smiled, then frowned deeply. "He's going to end up alone, isn't he," she said, her eyes filling up.

"We all do," Miss Beryl almost said. Beneath the dark branches of its ancient elms, Upper Main was full of lonely widows, solitary watchers and waiters. Miss Beryl didn't worry about them. Didn't worry about herself, not really. Why then worry about Sully? What if he did appear a little more ghostlike every time she saw him, as if he were fading out of himself, as if, when people finally lost faith in him and quietly drifted away as she and Ruth were now doing, they were taking part of him with them? His life seemed governed by some cruel law of subtraction, and his sum total was already in single digits. When he left the upstairs flat for new lodgings, would there be enough left of him to require a place? Why worry about someone ending up alone when that someone did everything he could to ensure it? "With Donald," she explained, "I've always just left the door open."

Ruth smiled her sad smile again. "That's always been my strategy too," she admitted, looking up at the second story of Miss Beryl's house, as if she imagined Sully might be up there. "My problem is, I can't stop watching the doorway and being disappointed," she explained, then looked over at her granddaughter again.

Miss Beryl studied the child too, thinking, as she often had when she surveyed her eighth-grade classes, that maybe people did wear chains of their own forging, but often those chains were half complete before they'd added their own first heavy link. Maybe completing other people's work was the business of life.

"Let's go, squirt," Ruth said to the child, who did not respond until she was touched, and then she slid back onto the sofa and began to grope for Ruth's ear.

Ruth gently removed the little girl's hand. "We're going to see Mommy, and you can play with her ear all afternoon, okay? Give Grandma's ear a rest."

The child was staring at Miss Beryl again, almost smiling, it seemed.

"We know every bend in the road between here and the hospital, don't we, Tina?" Ruth said, taking the child's small hand. "We go back and forth to Schuyler once a day at least."

"I thought about paying a visit," Miss Beryl said, "but my driving isn't what it used to be. The last time I went there I got lost."

Miss Beryl walked grandmother and granddaughter to the door and watched them retreat down the steps and get into Ruth's old car, which started up noisily and got even noisier when she shifted into reverse, put her foot on the gas and backed slowly, with an apologetic shrug for the noise, into Main Street. Feeling distant from her extremities, her toes and fingertips tingling vaguely, Miss Beryl went into the bathroom and blew her nose hard, inspecting the tissue for blood. When there was none, she returned to her front room, where the telephone was ringing.

"Why don't I make us a big steaming pot of chicken noodle soup?" Mrs. Gruber said in lieu of hello. It would take her another minute or two of inconsequential small talk before she'd get around to mentioning that she'd noticed a strange car in her friend's driveway. Instead of dropping her voice, she'd let the sentence hang, to signify her desire for a thorough, detailed explanation. It would be amusing, Miss Beryl thought to herself, to withhold that explanation awhile, to watch her nosy friend suffer.

"Because I'm feeling better," she told Mrs. Gruber, which was true. For when she picked up the phone, Miss Beryl noticed the corner of the jigsaw puzzle and saw that the piece she'd been looking for was no longer missing. The child had found it, slipped it quietly into place, never said anything. "Let's go someplace for lunch."

"Goody," said Mrs. Gruber.

"This is vintage Sully," Carl Roebuck said.

The two men were standing on the back porch of the Bowdon Street house. Will, forgotten, stood off to one side. The weathered porch sloped furiously, the remnants of two-week-old snow having gathered in one corner where the sun didn't reach. Will looked past his grandfather at the gray, crooked house. He did not want to go inside. He was hoping his grandfather would not be able to get the door open. The house was all crooked and haunted-looking, and he knew that his mother, had she been there, would not have wanted him to go inside. Grandma Vera wouldn't have wanted it either, and when he thought of her he recalled a conversation he had overheard between her and Grandpa Ralph. In Grandma Vera's opinion it was dangerous for Will to accompany Grandpa Sully on his morning rounds. She didn't say why Grandpa Sully was dangerous, but Will, though his affection for the stranger of his two Bath grandfathers was growing daily, thought he understood why his grandmother was worried. Grandpa Sully took him up dark, smelly stairways in the back of buildings, and to places where there were wild dogs, and now to a house about to fall down. Some of Grandpa Sully's friends smelled bad, too. In his grandfather's company, Will found that he was often torn between opposing fears. He understood that getting too close to his grandfather was dangerous, especially if Grandpa Sully was wielding a hammer or, like now, a crowbar, or the long, sharp spatula he used in the restaurant to flip eggs. Even his father had warned him not to get too close to Grandpa Sully when he had any sort of tool in his hand, which was why Will had not even ventured up onto the porch when his grandfather started after the back door with his crowbar.

The problem was that Will knew he didn't dare let his grandfather get out of sight either, sensing that if this happened he'd lose his grandfather's protection in a hostile environment. He knew Grandpa Sully was forgetful, entirely capable of forgetting Will altogether. In fact, he'd done it once already. One day last week they'd gone to the lumberyard outside of town, and when they got inside, Grandpa Sully had stationed Will near the front door and told him to wait right there. Then he'd gone over and talked to the man behind the counter. After a few minutes the two men went out the side door and into the big yard where mountains of boards were stacked. Through the window Will had watched his grandfather and the man load a dozen or so boards onto the back of Grandpa Sully's truck and tie them in place with the rope. To the end of the boards the man had attached a red flag, which blew in the breeze. Will made a mental note to ask his grandfather what the flag was for. The two men outside shook hands then, and Grandpa Sully got back into the truck and drove off, the red flag waving good-bye around the corner. Will then watched the hands of the big clock inch around the dial, forever it had seemed, until Grandpa Sully returned, going, it seemed to Will, dangerously fast, even in the parking lot.

The truck came to a skidding halt, pebbles rattling against the window through which Will stood peering, his eyes liquid. He was not actually crying, though, and he was proud of that. In fact, since returning to North Bath with his father he hadn't cried once, having resolved not to. He'd decided now that Wacker was gone that he'd try to be brave. When Grandpa Sully got out of the truck and headed inside, he was moving faster than Will had ever seen him go. He looked scared too, which made Will feel better, knowing that a man as fierce as Grandpa Sully could worry.

"I bet you thought Grandpa'd forgotten all about you," he said.

Will nodded. That was exactly the conclusion he'd come to, there was no denying it.

"Only for a minute," Grandpa Sully had explained. Clearly, forgetting for such a short period of time didn't really count as forgetting to his grandfather, who was used to forgetting things, Will guessed, for a lot longer. "Don't tell your grandmother," he warned when they were back in the truck and barreling down the road. "And if your mother calls, don't tell her either."

Will had promised he wouldn't.

"In fact," Sully had continued upon further reflection, "don't even tell your father."

The boards loaded onto the back of Grandpa Sully's truck had come loose then and started tumbling off and bouncing along the blacktop, and Grandpa Sully had skidded over onto the shoulder and gotten out to retrieve them. Most of them fit onto the truck better now. From inside the cab, Will could hear his grandfather swearing at the boards and also at the drivers of the other cars on the road who had to swerve around both the lumber and Grandpa Sully. But by the time his grandfather had collected the last of the boards and dropped them into the bed of the truck, he had calmed down some, and after he took a deep breath and got back into the truck, he'd looked over at Will and continued the instructions he'd been giving before all the boards fell out of the truck. "In fact," he said "don't tell anybody."

Will had kept his promise and not told a soul, but this present circumstance already reminded him of what had happened at the lumberyard, and Will sensed that this would be the beginning of something else that Grandpa Sully'd be instructing him not to tell anyone about. His grandfather was mad again and banging things and cursing, and the old house he was kicking looked like it would fall down for sure if he didn't stop. Or maybe it would wait until they were all inside and then fall down on them. Or maybe they'd all go inside and he'd be told to wait someplace and Grandpa Sully and the other man would forget about him and drive off, and then it would fall down.

Sully, who hadn't, as far as he knew, a key, was trying to force the rear door with a crowbar. The gray wood, its paint long ago stripped away, had grown soft and porous, which meant the crowbar wasn't working very well. So far, Sully had managed only to mutilate the door, which held fast.

"Who but Don Sullivan would use a crowbar to enter his own house?" Carl wondered out loud, stamping his feet in the cold.

"Stand back a second," Sully said, putting his weight against the bar. Like everything else about the house, the door hung crooked, and Sully had managed to create a space between the door and its frame, a space large enough to insert the flat end of the crowbar. When he levered himself against the bar, however, the steel simply sank deeper into the rotten wood.

"Why I should be surprised is another question," Carl continued. "Your grandfather is a crowbar kind of guy, Will. He'd use a crowbar to remove the back of his wristwatch."

"I don't own a wristwatch," Sully reminded him. "And if you don't shut up, I'm going to use this crowbar to remove you entirely."

Carl leaned up against the porch railing, ignoring this threat like he did all of Sully's threats. "What worries me is that just about the time you succeed in breaking in, the cops are going to arrive, charge us with burglary and throw our asses in jail."

"Me, maybe," Sully stood upright for a moment to catch his breath. "I'm the one breaking and entering. As usual, you haven't done shit."

Carl lit a cigarette, peeked in the kitchen window. "Hey," he said. "I just had a hell of an idea. You could move in here." He inhaled deeply, then remembered he'd quit smoking and flicked the cigarette over the porch railing.

Sully was grinning at him. "You aren't going to make it, are you?"

"You want these?" Carl said, offering Sully the pack of cigarettes. "Take 'em."

Sully took them, put the pack into his pocket.

Carl looked surprised. Clearly, he'd intended the gesture to be symbolic and wouldn't have offered the cigarettes to Sully had he thought Sully might actually take them. It wasn't this actual pack of smokes he'd intended to give up but some future pack. He already missed this particular pack. "Those aren't even your brand," he pointed out.

"I'll smoke them anyhow," Sully said. "I've gotten something for nothing from you about twice in the twenty years I've known you."

"That's better than the nothing for something I always get when I hire you," Carl said. "Why don't you just break one of those small windowpanes and reach inside and unlock the door?"

"Because then I'd have to replace the glass," Sully said, stepping back and eyeing the door savagely. "Here."

Carl caught the crowbar. "Can this be?" he said in mock astonishment. "Has Don Sullivan, Jack-Off, All Trades conceded that his trusty crowbar is not the precise tool for the task at hand?"

Sully grinned at him, measured his distance to the door. "You're right for once in your life," he admitted. "And here's the precise tool I need."

Planting on his bad leg, he kicked the door as hard as he could with his good, just above the knob, to gunshot effect. The door held, but all four panes of glass came free and shattered at Sully's feet. "You prick," he said, addressing the door.

Carl, shaking his head, handed the crowbar back to Sully. "Allow me," he said, reaching inside and unlocking the door. Glass crackled underfoot.

At this point Sully remembered Will and was astonished to discover that the boy was crying. Sully went to his grandson then and sat down at the bottom of the steps so he'd be eye level. "Hey," he said. Finally Will looked at him. "What's up?"

Will looked away.

"Did Grandpa scare you?" Sully guessed.

The boy snuffed his nose.

"I didn't mean to."

Will looked at him again, his eyes red.

"We can go in now," Sully told him. "Don't you want to see the house where Grandpa grew up?"

"Grandpa Ralph?"

"No. Grandpa Me.

"There's nothing to be afraid of, you know," Sully told him.

Will snuffed his nose, continued to cry softly. It was always Grandpa Sully's kindness that made him want to cry the worst. It was as if his grandfather truly needed him to be brave, and that made being brave even harder.

"Grandpa wouldn't let anything happen to you," he said, and when Will looked at the ground, he added, "Hey . . . look at me a minute."

Will did.

"Quit that," Sully told him.

Will stifled a sob.

"Good boy," his grandfather told him. "Now. You decide. We can go inside for a minute and you can see where Grandpa grew up, or we can go over to the other house and see Dad."

"Okay," Will croaked.

"Okay which?"

"Go see Dad," Will managed, just as certain that this was the wrong answer as he was that it was the only answer he could give.

"Christ," his grandfather muttered. "Jesus H."

When Sully drove up, Rub and Peter were on a break, Rub seated on the steps of Miles Anderson's front porch, Peter sitting a few feet away, his back up against the front door. Whether they'd been sitting that way for five minutes or an hour was anybody's guess. Since it was anybody's, Sully guessed an hour. Also, it had probably been that long since either had spoken to the other. Rub continued to be resentful of Peter's presence, just as he resented all the other people—Miss Beryl, Wirf, Ruth, Carl Roebuck—who seemed to him competitors for his best friend's affection. The difference was that these other people didn't horn in on their workday and subtract from Rub's quality time. Peter had made a few halfhearted friendly overtures but apparently felt no great urgency about winning over Rub.

They'd gotten some work done, at least. The bare forsythia had been trimmed back and a huge pile of sticks and branches raked onto the terrace. Sully's ax stood upright, its blade embedded in the center of the tree trunk on the front lawn. A few wood chips littered the immediate vicinity of the stump, but otherwise there was little evidence they'd made much of an impression on it. Rub was right. Elm tree roots went halfway to China. It was okay with Sully that they hadn't gotten very far. Getting the elm stump out of the lawn was going to be a ballbuster of a job, but it was one he could do himself, come spring, when the ground softened. He could do it with an ax and a shovel, a chain saw if he felt like borrowing one, and he could do it standing more or less straight up. It was the kind of work he specialized in, that he'd spent his life doing, the kind of work that required no special skills beyond dogged determination and the belief that he'd still be there when the stump was gone. The kind of job it would have probably been better to do another way, with the right equipment, quicker and with less effort. It had always been Ruth's position that if Sully had put his bullheadedness to some constructive purpose when he was younger he could have been president.

Will scampered up the walk past Sully and joined his father, who studied the boy's face knowledgeably. The boy wasn't crying anymore, but Peter probably had enough of a father's eye to guess that he had been. Sully himself had always been dumbstruck by grief, even his own, and considered it one of life's wonders that other people had the ability to see grief coming from a long way off or to detect when it had recently passed. One of the things every woman he'd ever been associated with had held against him was his inability to see when they were grief-stricken. Even his own son seemed to possess this ability so conspicuously lacking in himself.

"I thought you said you was coming by after Hattie's," Rub said, sounding not a little like a child suffering a broken promise.

"And here I am," Sully pointed out.

"It's almost lunchtime," Rub observed. "You probably aren't even going to let us eat lunch today, are you?"

"Go ahead," Sully suggested. "If you're going to sit around all day, you might as well go eat."

"We was just waiting for the truck," Rub explained. "We'd have to make about ten trips in the Canimo."

"Camino," Sully corrected him. Rub was unable to pronounce this word. "El Camino."

"We needed the truck," Rub stated, too wise to try the word again, knowing the price of failure around Sully.

Sully handed him the keys. "Try not to wreck it," he suggested. "At least not until I make the first payment."

"I've never wrecked a single truck of yours," Rub pointed out.

"It's the reason we're still friends," Sully assured him.

Rub shrugged. "You're more *his* friend now," he remarked sadly, his voice lowered so Peter wouldn't hear.

"Peter's my son, Rub," Sully told him. "I'm sorry if you object, but I'm allowed to be friends with my son if I want to."

"He doesn't even like you," Rub said.

"True," Sully admitted, not minding if his voice was audible to Peter. "But I'm growing on him. He just needs a little more time to get over the fact that I ignored him for about thirty years. He hasn't quite figured out yet that I did it for his own good."

Rub's brow furrowed deeper. "How come he always calls me Sancho? It's like he thinks I'm stupid."

"Well," Sully said.

Rub surrendered a half grin. "How come I don't mind when *you* say I'm stupid?" he asked with genuine curiosity.

Sully was grinning too now. Nobody could cheer him up faster than Rub. "Because we're friends, Rub. Friends can tell each other the truth."

"How come I don't get to tell you you're stupid?"

"Because I'm smart," Sully told him.

Rub sighed. They'd had this conversation before, and it always came out the same way.

Peter had been talking to Will in hushed tones, the boy seated on his lap. Peter listened, nodded knowingly, glanced at Sully, then said something to his son that Sully couldn't quite make out. Then the boy scooted down the steps past them, down the walk and into the front seat of the El Camino, which was parked at the curb.

"I guess I'll take him back," Peter said to no one in particular. "Mom should be getting home about now."

"Okay," Sully said, meeting his son's accusing eye.

"You want to tell me what happened?"

Sully shrugged. "I wish I knew," he said truthfully. "I looked over and he was crying."

"He said you got angry."

"Not at him."

"Well, something sure scared him," Peter insisted.

"Just about everything seems to," Sully said and was immediately sorry. "If I scared him, I sure didn't mean to," he added lamely.

Peter snorted. "You forgot all about him, didn't you? You forgot he was even there."

Which made Sully wonder if Will had told him about the lumberyard.

He decided probably not. If Peter'd found out about that he'd have said something. Or he'd have said, "You forgot him *again*."

"I don't remember *you* being there," he said weakly. Nevertheless, Sully was stung by the accuracy of Peter's intuition.

"That's *my* line," Peter said by way of a parting shot. He fished in his pocket for the keys to the El Camino. "I'll be back in a few minutes."

Sully and Rub watched him depart. Starting the El Camino up, Peter did a U-turn and whipped the car back down Main. Sully caught just a glimpse of his grandson's white face in the front seat before it and the car disappeared, leaving Sully to contemplate the fact that his son had just echoed Ruth's refrain—that he was never around when needed. It had been one of Vera's principal complaints, too, Sully remembered, though it had gotten lost in all her other complaints. Other people also offered variations on this same theme. From his old football coach, Clive Peoples Sr., who'd become homicidal when Sully strayed from his assigned duties, to Carl Roebuck, who would send him someplace and come by later and find him gone, to Rub, who would have liked to know right where Sully was every minute. In fact, so many people seemed to agree that Sully was never where he was needed that he was greatly tempted to acknowledge the truth of the observation, except that this would in turn have led to the sort of specific regret that Sully was too wise to indulge.

"Well." Sully frowned at Rub. "You want to hear the good news?"

"I guess so," Rub said a little suspiciously. Sully's good news sometimes meant they'd been hired to dig up somebody's ruptured septic tank.

"I got us another job," Sully told him. "Working for your favorite person, too."

Rub's eyes narrowed. "Carl?"

Sully nodded. "He's waiting for us. Impatiently, would be my guess."

"Waiting where?"

"At the house," Sully nodded in the direction of his father's place.

"I thought you said you didn't want nothing to do with that place," Rub remembered.

It was one of the things about Rub that Sully couldn't get used to. Occasionally, out of the blue Rub would remember something, sometimes a thing he'd been told only once, or overheard. Usually the things Rub recalled at moments like these were things Sully'd just as soon he forgot.

"I guess I did say that, didn't I," Sully admitted. He wasn't sure how to explain to Rub or anyone else the attraction of ripping up the floors of his father's house, gutting the inside, furthering the house's destruction.

"You also said we weren't ever going to work for Carl Roebuck again," Rub added petulantly as they sauntered down the walk. When Rub started to get into the truck, Sully stopped him. "Let's walk," he suggested. "You can walk a whole block, can't you?"

Rub shut the door again. "I figured you'd want to drive."

"Why?"

" 'Cause of your knee."

"It's good of you to remember, Rub, but I'd rather walk."

"How come?"

"Because of my knee."

Rub thought about it. "How come when you're mad at Peter you're mean to me?"

"When my knee feels half decent, I like to walk. When it hurts, I like to ride," Sully explained. "Being mad at you takes my mind off it entirely. And I'm not mad at Peter. He's mad at me."

On the way, Sully told Rub about Carl Roebuck's plan to pull up the hardwood floors in the house on Bowdon, lay them again in the lakefront camp that he and Toby owned and seldom used.

"How come we have to tear up a floor when Carl could just buy new wood?"

"Hardwood is expensive."

"So?" Rub shrugged. "Carl's rich."

Rub had, Sully knew, an imperfect grasp of wealth, of what things cost. To Rub's way of thinking, some people—Carl Roebuck, for instance—had money, which meant they could afford things that other people—Rub, for instance—could not. What people like Carl Roebuck could afford was everything Rub couldn't. The central fact of Rub's existence was what he couldn't afford, and what he couldn't afford was nearly everything. Therefore, conversely, what Carl Roebuck *could* afford must be nearly everything. The idea that people who had money might have money problems was inconceivable to Rub, who saw no reason for them to economize.

"That's how people get rich," Sully explained. "Instead of doing things the expensive way, they save a few bucks here and there. They hire guys like us to make their lives nice."

Rub's face was a thundercloud so dark that only profound stupidity could be at its center. "And then they don't even pay us," he said, remembering the trench they'd dug at Carl's house.

The two men crossed the street in the middle of the block. Will was right, Sully thought as he looked at his father's house from the distance of about fifty yards. It did look like it might fall down. "Carl'll pay us."

"He didn't before."

"Once. He'll pay us this time. He paid us for moving all those blocks you broke, remember?"

Rub's anger was instantly replaced by fear, and he slowed down. "It was both of us broke those blocks, not just me."

"I know that, Rub," Sully said, grinning.

"You were the one hit that pothole, not me."

"True."

"I never even loaded those blocks."

"You're getting all worked up," Sully pointed out. In fact, fear had caused Rub's face to go bright red. "Carl's not such a bad guy, is all I'm saying. Even if he knew you broke all those blocks, I bet he'd forgive you."

"Shhhh," Rub said. "There he is."

Carl Roebuck had come out on the front porch and was watching the two of them approach him. Just as they arrived, Peter returned in the El Camino. When he got out, he refused to meet Sully's eye, which meant he'd gotten a clearer account of what had transpired from Will. But he fell into step behind Rub as they entered through the gate and proceeded up the walkway together, Carl Roebuck shaking his head at them the whole way. "Sullivan Enterprises," Carl snorted. "Moe, Larry and Curly." He held the screen door open. "I don't suppose any of you has ever laid a hardwood floor?"

"I was once laid *on* a hardwood floor," Sully said.

"How was it?" Carl wondered.

"I don't remember."

"It smells like about ten generations of dead Sullivans in here," Carl observed when they went inside.

"I don't smell anything," Rub said, his brow knit with concentration. Everyone looked at him and grinned.

"Well, I don't," Rub insisted angrily.

Carl squatted and ran his thumb along the floor, removing its thick skin of dust. Beneath, the wood still had some of its sheen.

"How many square feet would you say?"

"Up and down?"

Carl nodded. "We're going to lose one room upstairs to water damage. I don't suppose you knew there's a hole in the roof?"

Sully said he didn't.

"How about the furniture?"

"What furniture?" Sully said.

"There's a roomful of furniture, Schmucko," Carl Roebuck said. "There's a sofa that's in better condition than the piece of shit in your own living room. There's a bed and a dresser. All kinds of shit. You can hardly get the bedroom door open."

"Good," Sully said. He had, in fact, some vague recollection of all this. When his father died, somebody had told him he should have an auction, but he'd declined, at least for the present, and hired a couple boys to shove all the furniture into one of the upstairs bedrooms, telling himself that he'd deal with it all later, which he knew he wouldn't. And hadn't.

Carl Roebuck shook his head. "You could have saved this house," he said. "You could have rented it. You could have sold it and put the money in your pocket and let someone else take care of it."

"I didn't want the money."

Carl turned to Peter. "He didn't want the money."

Peter shrugged. It was clear that he would have liked to disavow any relationship.

"You know what, Rub?" Carl said.

Rub started. He was seldom acknowledged in Carl Roebuck's presence. "What," Rub said.

"You aren't the dumbest man in Bath. Don't let anybody tell you you are."

"Okay," Rub said.

"So what are you saying?" Sully said. "Do you want these floors or not?"

"That depends upon what extortionary amount you have in mind to charge me."

"I tell you what," Sully said. "You can have the wood for free. Just pay us for the labor."

"By the hour, I suppose."

"Why not?"

Carl snorted. "If I pay the three of you by the hour, the wood's not free. You'll still be working on it in May."

"You want me to give you an estimate on a job I haven't done before, right?" Sully said. "That strikes you as fair?"

To everyone's surprise, Peter, who had been examining the baseboards along one wall, spoke up. "A thousand dollars," he said.

All three men looked at him.

"It'll take three men about a week," he said. "A day or two to tear up the floors here. We'll lose about every fourth board even if we're careful because they splinter. Each board has a side groove that fits into a slot, and you can't always yank them up without breaking one or the other. Laying them again is slow going. Three days, probably. Then you have to sand and varnish. New wood alone would cost you more than a thousand, though."

Carl looked at Sully, and both men shrugged.

"Leaving only the issue of collateral damage," Carl said, "the unforeseen destruction sure to occur when somebody's stupid enough to allow Don Sullivan into his house with a crowbar." He shook his head wearily. "My camp is liable to end up looking like this before he's through."

"Eleven hundred," Sully said.

"What?" Carl said.

"That insult just cost you a hundred dollars," Sully said. "And I'll take six hundred up front, since I'm dealing with you."

"I'm going to regret this," Carl reached into his pants pocket. "I can tell already."

He counted out six hundred dollars from a large roll of bills.

"You're right," Sully said. "I am the dumbest man in Bath. If I had any sense I'd hit you over the head with this crowbar, take that wad of money, bury you beneath the floor and see if anybody'd miss you."

"*You'd* miss me, snookums," Carl Roebuck said confidently, giving Sully a pinch on the cheek.

To celebrate, lunch at The Horse.

As usual during the noon hour, the place was crowded with businessmen from up and down the length of Main Street, every table taken. There were three stools at the end of the bar, though, and Sully pointed Rub and Peter in their direction. Clive Jr. and a woman Sully'd never seen before were just getting up from a table near the window. When Clive Jr. saw Sully, his face clouded over and he looked at the woman he was with almost fearfully, Sully thought.

"I got to go talk to that prick," Carl said when Sully, Peter and Rub headed for the bar.

"Who? The Bank?"

"I'm hearing things I don't want to hear," Carl said. "That goddamn deal is heading south. I can feel it."

"The theme park?"

"What a putz," Carl said, eyeing Clive Jr. across the room. "If it'd been me I'd have had that Texas big shot laid and then blown and then back on a plane before the ink was dry on the contract. Dickhead over there is just like his old man. The square of all squares. Can you believe that woman he's going to marry?"

"She's not getting much of a bargain, either," Sully reminded him. "Go ahead. We'll send the check over when we're done."

"It'd be just like you," Carl Roebuck said.

"Slide down one," Sully told Rub, indicating the next stool.

Rub looked reluctant. "How come?"

"So I can be on the end."

"How come?"

"So you won't swing around on that stool and bang my knee, like you're so fond of doing."

Rub moved. "How come I'm always the one you boss?" he wondered, settling onto the middle stool.

Sully moved the stool Rub had vacated so he could stand next to it. "What? You want me to give Peter an order, is that it?"

Rub shrugged, embarrassed to have instigated open conflict.

"Well?" Sully said.

"I just don't see—"

Sully held up a hand and Rub stopped. "I just want to know what would make you happy, Rub. If it'll make you happy, I'll give Peter a direct order. And if he's smart he'll do as he's told, too."

Rub shrugged again, but clearly the idea appealed to him.

"Are you ready?" Sully said. "Are you paying attention?"

Rub said he was.

"Son."

"What?" said Peter, who seemed not to be in the mood for such games. He was still half angry about Will, was Sully's guess.

"I want you to stay right where you are," Sully told him. "Don't get off that fucking stool. That's an order."

Peter surrendered a reluctant grin. "Okay," he said.

Sully turned back to Rub. "There," he said. "You happy now?"

Rub was not happy, but he knew better than to say so. Blessedly, Birdie came over and was waiting to take their order. "We got a new item," she told them. "Hot buffalo wings."

"I didn't know buffalos *had* wings," said Peter, who for some reason was fond of Birdie, or of her flattery of himself.

Rub frowned, stared at Peter malevolently. "They don't," he said, then checked with Sully to make sure.

"You had two calls," Birdie said. "Your ex and Mrs. Roebuck."

"Okay," Sully said dubiously, fishing around in his pants pocket for change. "What's your mother want to talk to me about?"

"No clue," Peter said, insincerely, it seemed to Sully.

He located two dimes. "She probably wants to inform me I'm not much of a grandfather," he decided. "Okay if I tell her you already did?"

"You want to order, at least, before you run off?" Birdie said.

"A hamburger," Sully said.

"You don't want to try the wings?"

"All right, suit yourself," Sully said.

"Don't get huffy. I was just asking."

"Cheeseburger," Rub said when Birdie looked at him.

"Try the wings," Sully suggested.

"Okay," Rub said.

"How about you, handsome?" Birdie said to Peter.

"Hamburger. Fries."

"Make it easy on yourself," Sully told her on the way to the pay phone. "Bring us three orders of wings."

Since there was no way to guess how long these calls would take, Sully took his bar stool with him and set it up beneath the pay telephone. He had two calls to make. One to the prettiest girl in Bath, who just conceivably might have been calling to extend some invitation, and one from his ex-wife, who'd almost certainly called to read him the riot act about something. Who to call back first?

"Hi, dolly," Sully said when Toby Roebuck answered. "Your no-good husband's down here at The Horse." Clive Jr. and the woman he was with had left. Carl had joined a table of local businessmen and had begun to tell them what a putz Clive Jr. was, Sully could tell. "He just ordered lunch. I can be there in five minutes."

"You talk a good fight over the phone," she said. It was amazing how she never missed a beat calling his bluffs. In fact, it was probably this that convinced him that he *was* bluffing. "Besides," she said. "You couldn't be here in five minutes. It takes you that long just to climb the stairs."

"I bet I could cut my time in half for the right reason," Sully told her. It was true. He did talk a good fight over the phone. "What the hell's this I hear about you being knocked up?"

"Too true," Toby Roebuck admitted. "Is he still strutting and crowing?"

"Like the little bantam rooster he is."

"You gotta love him."

"Nope," Sully said. "*You* gotta love him."

"Anyway," Toby Roebuck said like a woman who'd enjoyed about as much banter as she could stand. "Here's the skinny on the house."

"What house?"

"Your house, Sully. Turn the page. We've moved on to a new subject."

Sully remembered now that Carl had asked her to check on the status of the Bowdon Street house, and he became aware of something like a hope regarding it, a hope that was there before he could banish it.

"Technically," she said, "you still own it."

"Technically," Sully repeated, not much caring for the sound of the word.

"You're in what's called a redemption period. You've been in it for over a month. You must have gotten a notice."

"I must've," Sully agreed.

Toby Roebuck let that go. "What it means is that somebody has contracted to purchase the house for back taxes. But if you come up with the same money by February first, the property reverts to you."

"Who bought it?"

"I don't know. The buyers are not required to disclose their identities."

Sully considered this. "Well," he said after a moment, "whoever bought it is in for a big surprise, because I just sold the floors to your husband."

"Hmmmm."

"Who would *want* it is what I'd like to know," Sully said, though even as he wondered, it occurred to him that the owners of the Sans Souci might want the tiny postage stamp of property that abutted their land. Maybe they just wanted everything on the north side of Bowdon to be theirs, neat and tidy. Which led to an obvious question. How much did they want it? "What are the back taxes?"

"Are you ready?"

"I think so," Sully said, guessing five thousand dollars.

"Just over ten thousand."

"You're kidding."

"Sorry."

Sully took a deep breath. That settled the matter, anyway. "That's a lot of money for a house with no floors," he said. "I don't suppose you'd like to loan it to me?"

That struck Toby Roebuck as pretty funny. "Oh, Sully," she sighed before hanging up. "You are a stitch."

Vera answered on the first ring.

"Hi," Sully said, not bothering to identify himself. With Vera, he always liked to go on the assumption that she'd recognize his voice, even if he hadn't spoken to her in a year. This much he took as his due, the result of their having been married long enough to have a son. The way he saw it, any woman you married owed you that much, especially if you weren't going to ask her for anything else. "What's up?"

"Who is this?"

In fact, Sully was tempted to fire the same question back. Unless he'd dialed the wrong number, this had to be Vera, but it didn't sound like her, the voice lower by several notes. Whoever it was sounded like she'd just awakened from a two-day sleep. "Vera?"

"Oh," she said.

"What do you mean, oh," he said, already annoyed. "I had a message you called."

"Just to say you win."

Sully considered this. He couldn't think of anything he'd won. Certainly not anything concerning Vera. "What the hell are you talking about?"

"I just wanted to tell you that you'd won."

"Won what, Vera?" he said, but she'd already hung up.

Sully stared at the phone for a second before hanging up and heading back to the bar where Rub and Peter were eating chicken wings. Since neither of them looked up, he went back to the phone and dialed Vera's number again. This time the phone rang twenty times before she answered. "What the hell's going on?" he said. "And don't hang up on me, either. It'd take me about two minutes to get over there. Don't think Ralph'll keep me out either, because he won't."

"I have no illusions about my husband ever standing up for me, Sully," she said, her voice full of self-pity. "At the moment, he isn't even here."

"I don't blame him," Sully told her. The words were out before he could call them back, not that he necessarily would have, had he been able to. When the other end was silent too long, he said, "What's the matter, Vera? You wouldn't have called if you didn't want to tell me."

When she spoke this time, he could hear the give in her voice. "It's just that . . . I've tried . . . so . . . hard," she finally sobbed.

Sully was suspicious of his ex-wife's grief, knowing from long experience Vera's inclination toward theater. With Vera the road to hysteria was short in all situations, large and small.

"You never tried at all," she continued, "and you end up with him."

"Is it Peter we're talking about?" Sully said, catching, he thought, a glimmer. He'd been so sure this would be about Will that he couldn't switch gears.

"You won," she said again, "but you didn't win much."

"The hell with you, Vera," he said, ready himself to hang up.

"Have him tell you about the foul-mouthed little tramp he's got in Morgantown."

"Peter doesn't tell me shit, Vera," Sully assured her.

"He will," she told him. "You're soul mates. I'm the one he despises."

"You're crazy, too."

Silence again. More theater, probably. Though perhaps something else. "You know when you've lost somebody, Sully. At least I do. Practice makes perfect. When something means the world to me, I know it's only a matter of time."

"You haven't lost Peter," he told her. "And I certainly haven't won him. I haven't even tried to win him."

"That's what attracts him," she said, sniffling now. "I've loved him until my heart broke right in two. You could care less, so you're the one he wants."

"Listen, Vera—"

"You should have heard the filth that little tramp said to me," she said. "It was like a terrible *smell* coming out of the phone, polluting my home."

"I wasn't there, Vera," Sully reminded her. "I didn't hear it."

"Like a foul stench," she went on. "I've made a clean home, Sully."

"You sure have."

"And this is what he trails into it," she said. "What's the use?"

"I don't know, Vera," he conceded, tired of the conversation. "I'm going to hang up now."

"Right," she said. "Run away."

"Screw yourself, Vera."

"Be thankful you can run away," she said. "Be thankful you're not the one with no place to go."

Back at the bar Rub and Peter were right where he'd left them, and before them a pretty amazing pile of chicken bones. Peter met Sully's eye, and his expression was that of a man who'd intuited at least portions of Sully's conversation with his mother. Just as mysterious and annoying, Rub, for some reason, was crying.

"What the hell's wrong with you?"

"They're spicy," Rub explained. He had the orange sauce all over him. His hands were orange to the wrist, as were his cheeks and the tip of his nose. There was orange in his crew cut.

"Messy, too, looks like," Sully observed. Even Peter, a fastidious eater, Vera's boy, had orange hands.

Rub examined his own as if for the first time, then began licking his fingers.

"I bet they were good," Sully said. "You know how I can tell?"

Rub looked genuinely curious, as he usually was concerning all forms of mental telepathy.

"Because you didn't save me a single one."

Rub looked down at the pile of bones in front of him, as if in search of any that had not been picked completely clean. Not finding any, his expression darkened. "He ate as many as me," he said, indicating Peter. "How come you never get mad at him?"

"I'm not mad at anybody, Rub," Sully said. "I was just making a simple observation. I noticed you ate all the wings."

"Him too," Rub insisted.

Sully couldn't help grinning at Rub's wonderful ability to restore other people's spirits at the cost of his own. "Don't get me wrong. I'm *glad* you had a good lunch. You might have saved me one wing, but if you were hungry, I'm glad you ate them all."

Rub's head hung even lower now. For such a short man, he had a large head, and when it was full of shame, he was unable to hold it erect. Peter, who'd been toweling off with napkins and was apparently disinclined to share Rub's burden of shame, leaned over and stage-whispered, "If he wants to talk about sharing, you might remind him that the six hundred Carl Roebuck paid us went right into his pocket and never came out again."

Since this was true, Sully gave them each two hundred. Rub folded his bills carefully with orange fingers and put them in his shirt pocket. "How come you're looking at me?" Rub said, since everybody seemed to be.

"What do you say we go back to work?"

"Okay," Rub said, sliding off his stool.

"Wait outside a minute," Sully told him. "I need to talk to my son."

Rub's face clouded over again.

"Next time save me a wing and I'll talk to you too," Sully said.

When he was gone, Peter said, "Jesus, you're mean to him."

"He knows I don't mean anything."

"You're sure?" Peter said skeptically.

"Pretty sure."

Peter didn't say anything.

"You better take a few minutes and go see your mother," Sully told him. "She's all upset."

Peter sighed, shook his head. "About Will?"

"About you."

"Me? What about me?"

"Who the hell knows? I never pretended to understand your mother. She did say you'd gotten a phone call from some woman in West Virginia."

Peter rolled his eyes. "Oh, Christ. Okay."

"Your mother thought you might want to tell me about it."

"I don't."

"I told her you wouldn't."

"You were right."

"Fine. Keep all the secrets. Keep every fucking one. I'll tell you one thing though. I don't think I'm going to eat too much more of your sullen shit," Sully told him. "I know you think I've got it coming, but that doesn't mean I'm going to take it."

Peter seemed to be on the verge of saying something further, but whatever it was, he let it slide.

"Go make sure your mother's okay. We'll start on the floors."

"Start upstairs on the boards that are already ruined," Peter advised. "It takes a while before you get the hang of not splintering them."

"How do you know?"

"This will be the third hardwood floor I've laid for a professor," Peter explained. "One when I was a graduate student, for my dissertation director. Another in West Virginia two summers ago. I should have been working on my book, but I needed the money. So I laid this full professor's floor, and three months later he voted no on my promotion and tenure committee. He said I didn't seem to have my priorities straight. But at least I've got a talent to fall back on, right?"

"You mean laying floors or feeling sorry for yourself?" Sully said, again letting the words escape, trailing regret.

"Thanks," Peter said. "I knew you'd understand."

When he was gone, Sully drained the rest of his draft beer. "Birdie," he said, since she was right there. "I don't know."

"That makes two of us," she commiserated. "And that's not the worst of it."

Sully frowned at her suspiciously. "What's the worst of it?"

"Somebody owes me for three orders of wings."

Sully looked around the bar, which had pretty much cleared out, all of Main Street's businessmen having returned to their afternoon's labors. Carl Roebuck, unfortunately, was also gone.

"I guess," Sully admitted, "that'd be me."

On their way back to the house on Bowdon, Sully and Rub were greeted by a strange sight. As they drove up Main, Rub, still stung at having been sent outside so Sully could talk to Peter privately, was staring morosely out the passenger side window when he noticed a car parked crazily in the middle of the Anderson lawn. Nearby, on the porch steps, sat a well-dressed middle-aged woman who appeared to be sobbing. It was a sight odd enough to cause Rub to forget his grievance. "Look over there," he said when Sully stopped at the intersection of Main and Bowdon. What really puzzled Rub wasn't so much the car sitting on the lawn or the strange, weeping woman on the steps as it was that something was missing. Ever since they'd taken on the job of fixing up the Anderson property, Rub had been dreading the day they'd have to attack the tree stump in the middle of the front lawn. "Somebody took the stump," he told Sully hopefully.

Sully backed from the intersection to the curb, parked and got out. The woman looked like the one who'd been with Clive Jr. at The Horse. She was talking to herself, apparently, in between sobs. She looked up at the sound of their doors closing and was apparently further chagrined to discover that they were not who she hoped they'd be. The look on her face suggested that Sully's and Rub's sudden appearance on the scene represented for her the final indignity of her situation, whatever her situation was.

"Ask her who took the stump," Rub suggested.

Sully looked at him, shook his head. "Nobody took the stump, dummy. It's under the car."

Rub squatted and looked. Sully was right, the stump *was* under the car. In fact, the car was *on* the stump, accounting for its crazy angle.

Sully saw Clive Jr. emerge from Alice Gruber's house down the street and head toward them on foot, looking small and incongruous beneath the rows of giant black elms. When he saw who was waiting for him, his gait altered imperceptibly, as if registering that a bad thing had just gotten worse. Which it had.

"Hi, dolly," Sully called to the woman. In point of fact, she looked a lot older than the women Sully usually called "dolly," but she also looked like she could use some cheering up.

"Are you the tow truck?" the woman asked so miserably that Sully sensed melodrama.

"Am I a tow truck? No. Do I look like one?"

"My fiancée called . . . a tow truck," she explained, her voice quavering.

Rub glared at her as he might have a mythical beast.

"Could you make that horrid man go away?" the woman begged, indicating Rub.

"Nope," Sully admitted. "I've never been able to. You're welcome to try your luck, though."

She looked away, up the street, hopelessly, in the direction of the Sans Souci.

"Hi, Clive," Sully grinned when Clive Jr. arrived on the scene.

"Sully," Clive Jr. acknowledged. The woman on the steps had gotten to her feet when she saw Clive Jr., but she stayed where she was by the porch.

"I don't want to say anything," Sully told Clive Jr., "but you appear to be up a stump."

Clive Jr. looked at the deep tire tracks that began at the curb and stopped where the car perched. He sighed. "It was an accident," he said.

"I figured you didn't park there on purpose," Sully said.

"It wasn't me," Clive Jr. said. "I was giving Joyce a driving lesson." Something like a sly smile played across Clive Jr.'s mouth. "I bet you were surprised to see her again."

"Who?" Sully wondered.

All three men turned to look at the grieving woman.

"Joyce," Clive Jr. explained.

"Joyce who?" Sully wanted to know.

The smile, if it had been a smile, was gone now. "My fiancée. You used to date her."

Sully took another, closer look at the woman on the porch steps. "I've never seen her before in my life," he assured Clive Jr. "She doesn't know me, either. She thought I was a tow truck, in fact."

"You went out with her in high school," Clive Jr. said.

Sully was delighted to see that Clive Jr. was angry. "Never," he said. "Not a chance."

"Her name was Joyce Freeman."

"Never heard of her."

"How come she keeps crying?" Rub wondered.

Clive Jr. glared at Rub homicidally until Rub stared at his shoes and nudged Sully in an attempt at confidentiality. "How come she keeps crying?" he asked Sully.

"She's probably thinking about her future," Sully told him. "She's marrying Junior here. Lighten up, Clive. That was a joke."

Clive Jr. looked grateful to hear it and to Sully's surprise did lighten up a little, reluctantly explaining how the whole thing had come about. According to Clive Jr., Joyce had never learned to drive. For the last few weeks he had been instructing her. Today, they'd been parallel parking along Upper Main, where there was plenty of room and almost no traffic. Joyce was not a natural. Despite his patient instruction, she kept cutting the wheel too much and hitting the curb when she backed in. When Clive Jr. saw that she was about to do the same thing again, he told her to start over again. She apparently had forgotten she was in reverse and was surprised when she let up on the brake and the car went backwards. She immediately leapt to the wrong conclusion, that she was rolling, and the solution that occurred to her at that moment was more gas. "I told her there was nothing wrong with her logic," Clive Jr. explained, "but she's inconsolable."

"You want me to try?" Sully offered. "Since she used to be my girlfriend?"

Clive Jr.'s eyes narrowed. "You were a senior. She was a junior."

"Whatever you say, Clive. You want us to lift you off that stump?" Sully offered.

"I told you," Clive Jr. said. "The tow truck's on its way."

"I don't think they'll be able to just pull you off," Sully said. "Look where the rear axle is."

"They'll know what to do," Clive Jr. maintained stubbornly, his face a storm cloud again. Sully's solemn refusal to recognize his fiancée was the reason, Sully could tell. "Don't feel you have to hang around."

At that moment the tow truck arrived, Harold Proxmire of Harold's Automotive World at the wheel, his red-haired teenager, Dwayne, seated beside him in the cab. Since Dwayne could not always be trusted to tow the correct vehicle, Harold was apparently along to supervise.

Harold, dressed in gray and looking gray as usual, parked the tow truck on the other side of the street and climbed out wearily, shaking his head when he saw Sully. "I might have known you'd be involved in this," he said, taking in the situation. "That a tree stump you're sitting on, Mr. Peoples?"

Clive Jr. admitted it was, explained again how events had come to pass. In Harold Proxmire, Clive Jr. found a more sympathetic listener than he'd had in Sully. Harold nodded soberly and when Clive Jr. was finished said, "Bad luck the stump had to be right there."

"Good luck, you mean," Sully said. "If it hadn't been for the stump, she'd have kept going right into the living room, probably."

"I told him he could leave anytime he wanted," Clive Jr. told Harold, who had gotten down on his knees to peer under the car.

"I'm glad he didn't," Harold said. "We're going to have to lift you off."

"You could hitch up to the car and pull the stump out too," Sully suggested. "Save us some work later."

"Quit picking your nose and go lift that car, Dwayne," Harold suggested.

The boy had been engaged in this surreptitious activity, and he blushed the color of his hair. He, Sully and Rub took up positions behind the car while Harold went around, opened the driver's side door and took hold of the steering wheel.

"Where do you want me?" Clive Jr. asked Harold, noticing he'd been ignored in the matter of his own car. Now there was no room at the rear bumper where Sully and Rub and the boy were preparing to lift.

"How about over there next to her?" Sully suggested.

"I think we got her covered, Mr. Peoples," Harold said. He counted three and they lifted. The car rolled forward with surprising ease. The only casualty was Dwayne, who, stationed in the middle between Sully and Rub, stumbled over the tree stump as they went forward, fell and bloodied his lower lip.

"There you go, Mr. Peoples," Harold said, putting the car into park. "You're a free man."

Clive Jr. did not look like a free man. He looked like a man wearing an invisible yoke, pulling something he alone was aware of. "What do I owe you?" he said.

"Just for the service call, I guess. We didn't have to hitch you up. If I was you I'd put it up on a rack someplace and let somebody have a good look. Make sure you didn't crack that axle."

Clive Jr. gave Harold a twenty, then turned to Sully.

"Don't be silly, Clive," Sully told him.

They were still standing around the newly freed car. Five men, none of whom seemed to possess the authority to adjourn the meeting. "Dwayne and I better get on back before the boss gets suspicious," Harold finally said. "Tell your lady friend these things happen, Mr. Peoples. She should see some of the fixes I pull people out of."

"And I'll have that stump out of there pretty soon," Sully said. "In case you want to start up your lessons again."

"I don't suppose you found a new flat yet," Clive Jr. said.

"Not yet," Sully grinned. "But thanks for asking."

Sully and Rub followed Harold and the boy over to where the tow truck was parked. Harold got in the passenger side, Dwayne the driver's. "Take this before I do something foolish with it," Sully said, handing Harold the two hundred dollars left from Carl Roebuck's six.

"You sure?" Harold said.

Sully said he was sure.

"You want a receipt?"

"Nope," Sully said. "I want it to snow, is what I want."

"Well," Harold said. "Don't worry about me. I'm not going to repossess you."

"I know you wouldn't," Sully said. "Esmerelda might, though."

"She *is* the meanest Christian woman in the county," Harold admitted. "Isn't she, Dwayne?"

Dwayne apparently didn't see much margin in responding to this query, because he just shrugged.

"Was that her I saw on the tube one night last week?" Sully thought to ask. He'd been in The Horse and glanced up at the TV just in time to catch the last second or two of a piece on a group protesting The Ultimate Escape Fun Park.

Harold sighed, nodded.

"I thought so," Sully said. "I was watching on a small screen, though, and it didn't get all of her hair, so I couldn't be sure."

Harold ignored this. "Our boy is in the cemetery out there," he explained to Sully, who'd half forgotten that the Proxmires had had a son killed in Vietnam. "She don't want to see him disturbed."

"I can understand that," Sully admitted, sorry now that he'd joked about Mrs. Harold.

"Funny time to protest," Harold said, his eyes filling. "She wouldn't during the war. Wouldn't let me either."

"We did fight ourselves, if I recall," Sully reminded Harold, who had also served.

Harold nodded. "We did indeed. I thought we'd never stop."

Neither man said anything for a moment.

"Did I hear your son's back in town?" Harold said.

Sully nodded, feeling strange. Not many people remembered he had a son, and not many of those who did would have thought of Peter as Sully's. Having Harold refer to him this way also reminded him of Vera's contention that Peter was his now, that he'd won their son. "He's helping me out for a week or two," he explained, almost adding, until he goes back to teaching at the college. That, it occurred to him, would have been an unkind thing to say to a man whose own son lay buried a mile outside of town. It also would have been a boast. My son the professor. A boast Sully didn't feel he had any right to.

Harold nodded in the direction of Clive Jr., who had finally coaxed his weeping fiancée off the porch steps and was leading her over to the car, which still sat in the middle of the lawn. He had her by the elbow and was leading her like a blind woman. "When I was a kid, I had an Irish setter like her. All nerves."

They watched Clive put the woman in the car on the passenger side, then go around and get in behind the wheel. The car started right up, and Clive drove off the lawn and gently over the curb. "He should get that axle checked," Harold said. "But I bet he won't."

"He'll be fine," Sully said. "Bad things don't happen to bankers." Though he thought about Carl Roebuck's misgivings concerning The Ultimate Escape and wondered if Clive Jr. might be in for trouble. For Miss Beryl's sake, he hoped not.

"I don't think I'd give any more driving lessons if I was him. That's how his old man got killed, wasn't it?"

"Some people never learn," he said. "Tell Esmerelda hello."

When the tow truck pulled away from the curb, Sully noticed that Rub was looking glum. "What's the matter with you?"

"I wisht you'd took it," Rub said.

"Took what?"

"He had a twenty-dollar bill out."

"Who?" Sully said.

"The bank guy," Rub said. "I could've used that twenty dollars."

"Ten, you mean."

"It was a twenty," Rub insisted. "I saw it."

"But only half would have been yours, right?"

Rub shrugged.

"Or did you want the whole twenty for yourself and leave me with nothing?"

"I didn't get either half," Rub pointed out. "Nothing was what I got."

"Well, that's what I got too," Sully said.

Rub sighed. This had all the earmarks of another argument with Sully that he wasn't going to win.

"Here comes Peter," Rub observed sadly when the El Camino came into view. "You probably would have shared it with him, and he wasn't even there."

"How's work?" Wirf wanted to know that evening when Sully came into The Horse and slid onto the stool next to him. Something about the lawyer's tone of voice suggested to Sully that this was not a casual question.

"Hard," Sully told him. "Dirty. Unrewarding." He nodded at the sweating bottle of beer in front of Wirf. Lately Wirf had been cutting back by drinking soda water until Sully joined him sometime after dinner. "I see you're zigging already."

"I've been contemplating," Wirf said. "Zigging helps me to contemplate. Would you like to know what I've been contemplating?"

"No," Sully told him.

"Stupidity," Wirf said.

Sully studied him, trying to gauge Wirf's level of intoxication, never an easy task. "You aren't in a very good mood, Wirf. I can tell."

Birdie came over, gave Sully the beer she knew he'd order. "He wouldn't even bet on *The People's Court*," she said sadly.

"I think I'll have one more, Birdie," Wirf said, "now that the subject of all my contemplation has arrived."

When Birdie bent over to fish a bottle of beer from the cooler, Sully made a theatrical point of standing up on the rungs of his bar stool and craning forward to look down her shirt. "What kind of bra is that?"

"A two-seater," she informed him. Then she set the beer in front of Wirf and made a face at the lawyer. "On the subject of stupidity."

"I'm not stupid," Wirf said. "Merely self-destructive."

"Where's Jeff?" Sully wondered out loud, noticing it was well past Birdie's usual time to go home.

"Tiny let him go," she said.

"How come?"

"You shouldn't steal when business is slow," Birdie said significantly before heading back down the bar to take care of Jocko, who had just come in, leaving Sully and Wirf alone in their corner.

"That was one of the original Ten Commandments, you'll recall," Wirf said. "Thou Shalt Not Steal When Business Is Slow. It came right after Thou Shalt Stay in School. Which was preceded by Thou Shalt Not Get Caught Working When Thou Art Collecting Disability from the State."

"Look," Sully said. "I have no idea what bug crawled up your ass tonight, but I happen to be in a good mood for once. I don't know how long it'll be before the next one rolls around, so I'm not going to let you ruin this one, if that's all right with you."

Wirf suddenly looked sober and determined. "I bet I can ruin it for you."

"I bet you can't," Sully said, sliding off his stool and taking his beer with him. Since he arrived at the other end of the bar at the same moment as Jocko's drink, and since Jocko's last vial of mystery pills had been a great improvement over the ones that had put him to sleep and given Carl Roebuck's Doberman a stroke, Sully paid for it.

"Don't tell me one-two-three ran today," Jocko said, peering over the tops of his thick glasses, "because I know it didn't."

"I just wanted to say thanks," Sully said, his voice low. "Those little blue jobs are the best yet."

Jocko nodded. "I thought you might like them. They're new. I wouldn't necessarily mix them with alcohol."

"I wouldn't either," Sully agreed, taking a swig of beer. "I take mine in the morning with my prune juice."

"I've got something for that, too," Jocko said.

Birdie was there again, this time with a note for Sully, written in Wirf's hand on a bar napkin. It said: "And then there's: Thou Shalt Not Be Videotaped Loading Concrete Blocks Onto a Truck When Thou Art Suing for Total Disability." Wirf was grinning at him. Sully could see that much all the way from the opposite end of the bar.

"I doubt it's the pills, actually," Jocko explained. "They say arthritis is better when you exercise. Which is not to say I recommend your working on that knee."

"I'm not hurting quite as much, for some reason," Sully said, wadding up Wirf's note into a ball and tossing it. The guy in the dark sedan, no doubt, Sully thought. The one he'd thought might be an investigator hired to document Carl Roebuck's myriad infidelities.

Wirf was scribbling on another napkin.

"Is our legal friend composing briefs?" Jocko wondered.

"I'd be surprised if he was even wearing briefs," Sully said.

Birdie brought the new note. "For Verily I Say unto Thee. If Thou Art Caught Working Whilst on Disability, Thou Art Truly and Forever Fucked in the Eyes of the State."

Sully wadded this one up too and strolled back down the bar. "Video-taped?"

"Verily."

"Hmmm," Sully said, running his fingers through his hair. "So that's who that guy was. I figured he was somebody's husband planning to assassinate Carl Roebuck. I thought he had binoculars."

"A video camera."

"No shit."

"Verily."

"So what can they do?"

"I don't know," Wirf admitted. "Depends on how nasty they want to get. They could sue to recover the partial disability payments. And the education benefit."

"Will they?"

"Probably not. I'd make them enter the tape into evidence, and my guess is a tape showing you at work would do us as much good as them. They'd be going to a lot of trouble for nothing. See, we got one of the original Ten Commandments on our side."

"Only one?"

"Thou Canst Not Get Blood from a Turnip."

Sully shrugged. "Then what are we worried about?"

Wirf was grinning at him now, as Sully slid back onto the bar stool. "Sully, Sully, Sully," he said, and together they settled pleasantly into what remained of the evening.

WEDNESDAY

S now.
   A snow not quite like any Miss Beryl could ever remember, and she watched it fall through the open blinds of her front room hypnotically. She'd awakened feeling woozy, as if she'd gotten out of bed too quickly, except that she'd gotten up slowly and then stood by the side of her bed wondering if she might need to sit back down. Flu, she thought, dern it. Miss Beryl hadn't had the flu in a long time, almost a decade, and so her recollection of how you were supposed to feel was vague. What she *did* feel, in addition to the wooziness, was an odd sensation of distance from her extremities, her feet and fingers miles away, as if they belonged to someone else, and to account for this, the word "flu" entered her consciousness whole, like a loaf of something fresh from the oven, warm and full of leavening explanation.

Flu. It explained her offishness of the past few days, even, perhaps, her persistent feelings of guilt about Sully. Miss Beryl was of the opinion that guilt grew like a culture in the atmosphere of illness and that an attack of guilt often augured the approach of a virus. This particular virus was probably a gift from the dreadful Joyce woman, Miss Beryl decided. Not that the Joyce woman had exhibited flu symptoms exactly. Rather, she had simply impressed Miss Beryl as someone who had a lot ailing her. (Miss Beryl had heard about yesterday's episode with the car from Mrs. Gruber, who'd let Clive Jr. use her phone to call the tow truck in return for a full account. And that account confirmed Miss Beryl's initial opinion, that the Joyce woman was a menace.) It certainly wouldn't surprise her to learn that Clive Jr.'s fiancée was a carrier of flu viruses.

Since her retirement from teaching Miss Beryl's health had in many respects greatly improved, despite her advancing years. An eighth-grade classroom was an excellent place to snag whatever was in the air in the way of illness. Also depression, which, Miss Beryl believed, in conjunction with guilt, opened the door to illness. Miss Beryl didn't know any teachers who weren't habitually guilty and depressed—guilty they hadn't accomplished more with their students, depressed that very little more was possible. Since retiring, Miss Beryl had far fewer occasions to indulge either guilt or depression. Except for reminding herself that she should feel more affection for Clive Jr., she had little to feel guilty about, and except for Friday afternoons when the *North Bath Weekly Journal* was published, she seldom felt depressed. So the portals to illness remained, for the most part, shut tight. No, Miss Beryl decided, it was the dreadful Joyce woman, wrecker of cars, destroyer of chairs, whose mouth was always open spewing noxious opinions and who knew what else into the atmosphere, who was the culprit. Miss Beryl felt a little better to have settled the issue to her own satisfaction. But not much.

The source of her wooziness established, Miss Beryl decided that the best way to proceed was to treat the virus the way you'd treat the person it came from. That is, ignore it the best she could and hope it'd go away. Make your morning tea, old woman, she told herself, and put on a pair of good warm socks. So she did, and this too made her feel a little better, even though the strange feeling of distance from her extremities seemed to increase as she navigated her bright kitchen, making her tea. Now, she thought, bouncing her teabag in the steaming water. There. That's done. You've made your tea, and you don't feel any worse. Take the tea into the front room and check the street for wandering old women and fallen tree limbs. See if God has lowered the boom on anyone while you were asleep, the sneaky booger.

It was when she got to the front window and opened the blinds that she noticed it was snowing and remarked the strange, glittery quality to the snow. It was as if it were snowing with the sun out, each flake igniting as it fell. The street was alive with dancing, firefly snowflakes, and Miss Beryl sat down to watch the performance with quiet wonder, perplexed too that the cup of hot tea in her hands did so little to warm her fingers. It seemed beyond her ability to wiggle her toes in her socks, and those toes seemed very far away. It made no sense. At scarcely five feet tall, Miss Beryl was not very far from her toes.

And this was the way Sully found her when he came downstairs, poked his head in for the first time in a week, saw that his landlady was indeed up and dressed and seated with her back to him, staring out the front window into the street. "All right, ignore me," he said when she didn't respond to his usual observation that she wasn't dead yet.

But she didn't respond to this either, and when he raised his voice to inquire if she was all right and Miss Beryl still did not respond, he went over to her and peered around at the old woman suspiciously, as he might have inspected a store mannequin he suspected of being a real person practicing mime.

Miss Beryl, who had not heard him come in or speak, was delighted to discover her tenant's face in her peripheral vision. It had been Sully, after all, who'd been praying for this snow, and Miss Beryl was pleased that his modest prayer had been answered. She just hoped that this strange snow, igniting as it did on its way to earth, would accumulate in sufficient quantity to require removal. She would have liked to tell Sully that she wished him well in this way, indeed in all ways, that having done him wrong, he retained a place in her affections, but her voice seemed as far off as her toes and fingers. "Look," she finally managed, her voice sounding as if it belonged to someone else, Mrs. Gruber maybe, "at all the lovely snow."

Sully would have liked nothing better than to see snow, but in fact the street outside Miss Beryl's front window was bathed in bright winter sunshine. His landlady's chin, her neck, the front of her robe and nightgown were bathed in blood.

"Which way?" Sully said.

"Up!" Hattie thundered. They were standing at the edge of the single stair, the old woman clutching onto Sully's arm for support and balance. She looked strangely like a child learning how to ice-skate, feet wide apart, knees almost touching. Her hands were swollen from pounding on the apartment door. Sully had been late getting to the diner, unwilling to leave Miss Beryl until he was sure she was all right. When she'd first spoken, the old woman had seemed to be in some kind of a trance, but then she'd snapped right out of it, maintaining that she'd simply had another "gusher" of a nosebleed. She insisted that he not worry about it and was particularly adamant that he not mention the matter to Clive Jr., which

Sully had reluctantly agreed not to do. In fact, she did seem fine, scurrying between the kitchen and the front room, cleaning up the mess she'd made. He promised to look in on her midmorning when he finished at Hattie's, and she had promised to get checked out by her doctor, but the sight of Miss Beryl, glistening with hemorrhaged blood, was still with him, especially with old Hattie teetering on him. If he lost her, she could end up in the same condition. How did the world get so full of old women, was what he wanted to know.

"Yeah?" Sully said. "Well, the stair goes down, so that's the direction we better go, unless you can fly."

"Down!" Hattie agreed, and together they took the step, teetering.

"There," Sully said when they had come to terms with down. "That's the most dangerous thing I do all day," he added as they made their way into the diner. "Someday you're going to try to go up, and we're both going to go down and stay down."

"Down is to hell," the old woman observed.

"I don't plan to follow you that far," Sully assured her.

Hattie did not strictly comprehend this discourse, Sully knew. Since Thanksgiving her hearing had failed, and you could tell the old woman no longer had the capacity to follow conversations whole. She'd catch a word or two and make do, which was why he took her through their morning "up" and "down" ritual. He suspected that she enjoyed the sound of these two words in her own mouth and that she appreciated being engaged in dialogue, even a monosyllabic one. The words exploded from the old woman's mouth with terrific energy and satisfaction.

"Make 'em pay," she muttered as they made their way between the lunch counter and the table along the wall. Cass, who had not given them so much as a glance as they made their slow way, now looked up at the old woman homicidally.

"What'd she say?"

Her daughter's voice registered with the old woman, who turned to face it. "Make 'em PAY!" she bellowed.

Cass looked like it might be her intention to vault the lunch counter and throttle the old woman. "Ma!" she shouted back. "Listen to me now. I'm not going to put up with that all day. You hear me? Not again today. If you don't behave, you're going back to your room. You'll be locked in, do you understand?"

Hattie turned away, resumed her course. "Make 'em pay," she muttered again.

"She'll be all right," Sully assured Cass, then said to Hattie, "Don't you worry, old girl. We'll make every one of 'em pay. We'll make 'em pay twice. How's that?"

"Pay," Hattie agreed.

"There you go," Sully said when he had the old woman situated in her booth. "Sit up straight, now. No slouching."

"No slouching," Hattie repeated. "Make 'em pay."

Sully grabbed an apron and joined Cass behind the counter. Cass was still glaring at her mother with what appeared to be genuine menace. Yesterday had not been good. For months the diner's monstrous cash register, which was nearly as old as Hattie herself and had been part of the establishment since the beginning, had been acting temperamental, its cash drawer often refusing to open. Finally it had fused shut and Cass had ordered a new register from a restaurant supplier in Schuyler Springs. Yesterday, it had been installed during the lull between the breakfast and lunch crowds.

The problem was that the old register had been full of noisy clangs and bangs, sounds that over the years had become part of old Hattie's world, increasingly so as her cataracts got worse. The loud, discordant music of the register penetrated her deafness, evidence that commerce was taking place. The new register offered no such reassuring sounds. If you happened to be standing next to it, you might detect some insectlike whispers, but the designers of the machine had apparently considered quiet a virtue. In the absence of the usual clanging and banging, Hattie watched the shapes and shadows of her customers file into and out of the diner and apparently concluded that her daughter was giving away free food, an idea that had enraged her completely. As the lunch customers continued to file past Hattie's booth near the door, she'd begun to screech, "Make 'em pay! Make 'em pay!" The old woman's fury had been comic at first, but the look on her face was so ferocious and her rage so consuming that even large men gave her wide berth on their way out, as they might a small, rabid dog on a thin leash.

Nor did her rage diminish. As the shadows of her customers continued to move past the old woman relentlessly, the door opening and closing just beyond her reach, Hattie had hurled first warnings, then obscenities. Her customers didn't mind so much being called fart blossoms, but the sight of an old woman so possessed was unnerving, and those who'd escaped were glad to be safely out in the street. When it became clear to Hattie that neither warnings nor insults stemmed the tide of her customers out the front door, she picked up and chucked a full salt shaker, hitting Otis Wilson behind the right ear, spinning him around on his seat at the lunch counter.

"Christmas," Cass said to Sully now, her voice low and threatening. Sully didn't usually notice such things, but he observed that Cass looked exhausted this morning, herself yet another old woman.

"She's all right," he said, hoping to strike a note of comfort and, of course, hitting something else entirely. "She'll quiet down."

They both studied the old woman then. Hattie's jaw was set in such a way that it was difficult for either of them to imagine that she'd changed her mind about anything recently. Or conceded anything.

"After Christmas is when she'll be all right," Cass said.

This morning Sully had noticed on the way in that there was a sign taped to the front door announcing that Hattie's would be closed the week between Christmas and New Year's, which, if true, would be a first. The diner was often shut on major holidays, but a whole week between Christmas and New Year's had never been done before, so far as Sully recollected. The hasty lettering on the sign, taken in conjunction with the fact that Cass had said nothing to Sully about the closing before, suggested to him that she'd arrived at the decision during the night. The deep lines etched beneath her eyes suggested early morning. "She's not going to go for that," Sully said, nodding at the sign and noticing as he did so that Rub was there on the other side of the door, shifting his weight from one foot to the other in the gray half light of early morning, his hands thrust deep into his coat pockets, clearly hoping to attract someone's attention inside, where it was light and warm. He was just tall enough to see over the top of the sign, and Sully could tell he was pleased to have attracted notice, though his face clouded over when nothing came of it. He consulted his wrist then, as if to check how long it would be before the diner officially opened. Since Rub never wore a watch, there was nothing on his wrist that was of the slightest use in this regard. Sully wondered where he could have possibly picked up such a gesture.

"She hasn't got any say in the matter," said Cass, who hadn't noticed Rub. The tone of this observation suggested a challenge. Sully could dispute the statement if he dared.

"Okay," said Sully, who didn't dare. "I just meant she wasn't going to like the idea, that's all."

"No," Cass said. "You meant more than that. You meant that I'd never make it stick and that I shouldn't even try. You meant that it would be simpler to let her have her way like always, since she's going to get it in the end anyway. That's what you meant by 'she won't go for it.' "

Well, it was true. That *was* pretty much what he'd meant. "I didn't mean that at all," he objected.

"Yesterday was the last straw," she told him, pointing a handful of knives, fresh from their rack on the drainboard, at him. "Yesterday tore it. She's going into professional care. She can abuse people who are paid to take it." She slung the knives into the plastic trough beneath the counter.

"Okay," Sully agreed. "Fine."

Somehow, by appearing to question her judgment or perhaps her will, he'd managed to get Cass angry at *him*. There were times when he wondered if this were a special skill he possessed, this ability to redirect almost any woman's anger to himself. They all seemed perfectly prepared to surrender their original object of scorn. Whenever Ruth was angry at Zack, Vera at Ralph, Toby Roebuck (and all the other women in Carl's life) at Carl—these women were all apparently satisfied to vent their fury on Sully if he happened to be handy, as if he embodied in concentrated form some male principle they considered to be the cause of their dissatisfaction with their own men. Which made him wonder if there might be a way to distract Cass before she got up a good head of steam. "You want to let Rub in?" he suggested.

Rub was dancing faster now in the entryway.

"He gets here earlier every morning," Cass said. "If I let him in, it'll look like we're open."

"He'll make you feel better," Sully predicted.

"How?"

"I don't know," Sully confessed. "He always does, though."

"You just like tormenting him."

"Wave to him," Sully suggested.

They waved. Rub scowled, did not wave back.

"All right, I can't stand it," Cass said, trying to suppress a smile. "Go let him in."

"See?" Sully said, moving past her.

"Before you do," she caught him.

"What?"

"I'm going to need some help next week. I don't know who else to ask."

"Okay," Sully said.

"Don't say you will unless you mean it."

"I'll make time."

"One morning should do it. There's two places I want to look at. One in Schuyler, one in Albany."

"Okay."

"Quit saying okay."

"Okay."

"Go let him in."

Sully did.

"You two were talking about me," Rub said as Sully closed the door behind him and relocked it. "I could tell."

"Make him pay," old Hattie said audibly at Rub's elbow.

Rub, who was frightened of all old women, stepped quickly aside to look at Hattie and determine, if possible, if she'd been addressing him. She never had, even once, during all the years he'd been coming there, though it appeared she was doing so now, and, even worse, demanding money he didn't have. Without taking his eyes off the old woman, he whispered, "Could I borrow a dollar?"

When Peter, sleepy-eyed but dressed for work, emerged from the room he and Will were sharing at his mother's, he caught Ralph poised and listening outside his wife's bedroom door. In times of trouble, their bedroom became her bedroom, and Ralph knew he was not allowed in without permission. Together the two men stood in the narrow hallway between bedrooms, listening for sounds on the other side of the door. But the only sounds in the whole house emanated from downstairs in the kitchen, Will's spoon scraping his cereal bowl. When Peter turned and headed down, Ralph followed him.

"You ready, sport?" Peter said.

Will was ready. He'd finished his cereal and was engaged in a scientific experiment with the few remaining Cheerios in his bowl. In the beginning, they floated. You could hold a Cheerio under the surface of milk for a long time, but as soon as you removed the spoon, it floated right to the top. You could break it in half, and then the two halves floated. Break the two halves in half and all four floated. But when you broke them into smaller pieces, they bloated up, lost their buoyancy, turned to brown muck in the bottom of the bowl. Without arriving at any conclusions as to what this phenomenon might mean, Will nevertheless found it interesting. It was nice to be able to think such thoughts in peace. Until recently, he'd get about halfway through such a complex thought and Wacker, who could sense other people thinking, would do one of his sneak attacks. Will rubbed the tender flesh along the inside of his right arm between the elbow and the armpit. The soreness was going away. He was beginning to heal. He smiled at his father and grandfather.

"How about putting that over on the sink," his father suggested. "Help Grandma out, okay?"

Will did as he was told. "Is Grandma sick?" he said. He knew something had his grandmother all upset, and he hoped that soon somebody would explain why. It had something to do with the telephone and somebody who kept calling his father and talking to Grandma Vera instead. And it had something to do with the fact that they weren't living with Mommy and Wacker and Andy anymore. And it had something to do with Daddy telling Grandma Vera last night that maybe he wouldn't go back to his teaching after Christmas. Maybe they'd stay and he'd work with Grandpa Sully. Grandma Vera had gotten maddest at that. She was still mad. Mad at Daddy and at Grandpa Sully and Grandpa Ralph for not being on her side. She was mad at Mommy for leaving. About the only person she wasn't mad at was Will himself, for which he was grateful, except she kept asking Daddy, "What's going to happen to this child? What's going to happen to your family?" Which made Will wonder if she could see some danger coming that he was unaware of.

When Will took his cereal bowl and placed it on the drainboard, Peter said to his stepfather, "Why don't you come along and grab a cup of coffee at the diner?"

"I better not," Ralph said.

Peter shook his head. "I'd sure get out of here for a while," he said. "You're going to bear the brunt of this if you're handy."

Ralph shrugged, followed them out to the back porch, where Peter and the boy donned their heavy coats and gloves. "I'm used to it," he said, his voice prudently low. Actually, it was more than prudence that caused Ralph not to say it too loudly. There was also guilt. Saying "I'm used to it" felt like an admission, as if to suggest that they both saw Vera in the same unflattering light, which wasn't true. Ralph wouldn't have gone so far as to say that his wife was wrong to be upset. He'd have been upset himself if it had been any of his business, which it wasn't, none of it. People *would* get themselves into fixes, was the way Ralph looked at it. Peter had gotten himself into one, and that was all there was to it. And since it was the kind of fix Ralph had no real experience with, he considered it morally imperative not to suggest a resolution. Probably he'd suggest exactly the wrong thing. Vera, on the other hand, seemed to know what Peter should do, which was typical. His wife's strong suit was providing other people a sense of direction, and this was what Ralph was really acknowledging when he said he was used to it. What he was used to was his wife knowing what to do next and making sure it got done.

"Your mother just wants what's best for you, is all," he said.

"I know," Peter said, zipping Will's jacket. The little boy, who had apparently had his throat zipped into his zipper at some point, always put his mittened hand beneath his chin to prevent it from happening again. Sully was right, of course, Peter reflected, the boy was scared of just about everything. "And that would be fine if she didn't always assume she *knew* what was best for me. Me and everybody else," he added, to indicate he understood that Ralph too suffered her certainty.

"Heck," Ralph shrugged. "It's only love, is all it is."

Peter shook his head. "No, Pop, you're wrong. It's love, all right, but it's not *only* love."

Ralph wasn't sure he followed Peter's distinction, but never mind. "Anyhow," he said. "Don't pay no attention to what she said. You know you're welcome to stay here as long as you need to. This house is part mine too, and as long as it is, you and yours . . ."

Ralph discovered he was unable to continue, his voice having suddenly constricted with complex and powerful affection for all concerned. Constricted with love. With only love.

Peter studied his stepfather. "How do you do it, Pop?" he wondered. "How do you put up with it?"

Ralph was grateful for the appreciation but had no idea how to respond to Peter's question without seeming to grant another admission. "I'll handle things here," he said. "She never stays like this long. By tonight . . ." He let the statement trail off when he remembered who he was talking to. He might have been able to convince a stranger that things would be better by evening. But Peter knew his mother, and therefore he knew better. In truth, Ralph himself had never seen Vera more down than she was now. "I just hope we don't get no more phone calls."

Peter looked down at the garage floor. "I have no idea how she got the number." Actually, this was not true. It had occurred to him late last night that he'd called Deirdre collect over Thanksgiving. The number had probably appeared on her phone bill. Concerned as he was by the phone calls, they weren't his worst fear, which was that Didi herself might show up, which she had in fact threatened to do.

"How'd you ever go and meet somebody like her?" Ralph asked. This was the question that had been puzzling him since the previous afternoon when he had taken the last of the calls and wished he hadn't. Ralph had no firsthand experience with academic people, but he imagined them to be like the people he saw on the Albany educational channel on the cable. Vera liked watching that channel and was always contemptuous of Ralph when he had to confess after watching one of those drama shows for a full hour that he wasn't too sure he understood what was going on. The way he figured it, everybody at Peter's university probably talked the way they did on educational TV, and so he was not prepared when the young woman on the telephone who kept calling and demanding to talk to Peter and who apparently refused to believe that he wasn't there said to Ralph, "Okay, but just ask when he gets home, okay? Just ask him. Do I, or do I not, give the best head on the East Coast."

"I met her at a poetry reading," Peter told him in answer to his question.

Ralph nodded soberly, feigning comprehension. "The women who go to those things all like her?"

Peter couldn't help but grin. "A surprising number."

Ralph shook his head. He'd never been to a poetry reading. The reason he'd never gone to one—that people would be reading poetry there—had always seemed sufficient, but now he had another reason if he ever needed one. Vera'd never asked him to attend a poetry reading, but it was the sort of thing she might do someday if she got annoyed at him and was searching for a punishment and was tired of the educational channel. The good news was that there weren't any poetry readings in Bath, but Schuyler Springs wasn't very far away and they probably had them there. Maybe Albany, for all he knew. It was a scary thought. A man could be surrounded by poetry readings and not know it.

Ralph had been too embarrassed to pass along to Peter the young woman's question about whether she did or did not give the best head on the East Coast. Ralph would no more have repeated what the young woman said to him than he would have confessed to having, when he was a young man, once been the recipient of a blow job. It had happened in South Carolina, where it had been against the law, and not just the fact that they'd paid for it, either. Like most horrible experiences, Ralph had not been able to forget it. What had he been thinking of, to go along? Now, at fifty-eight, he asked himself the same question he'd asked himself as an eighteen-year-old. And answered it the same way. That he hadn't known what it would be like until it was too late to back out. Ralph had imagined, for one thing, that they would *each* have a girl. And a room. A different girl and separate rooms. That was the way he'd thought it would go. Not the same girl for all of them and all of them crowded into a hot, dark little room. It was a private act he'd imagined, not a public performance. And pleasure, not some vague distant rumbling, like a churning stomach. He'd imagined two naked people, not a fully dressed girl servicing six men who dropped their trousers down around their ankles when it was their turn and pulled them up again as soon as they were finished. He had not imagined performing to a gallery, accepting advice, criticism and finally applause. How had he allowed himself to take part in something so sordid?

Well, he hadn't meant to, was about all he could say in his own defense. He honestly hadn't meant to. He hadn't known what he was getting into, and he felt certain that the same thing must be true of Peter, whom Ralph refused to think badly of. If Ralph blamed anyone, as the two men and the boy stood awkwardly at the back door, limited in what could be said by the presence of the boy, he blamed himself for not knowing what to advise. He hadn't even advised Peter about the existence of such women as this one he'd fallen in with, the kind who could make a man feel like something not quite a man and accomplish it in a way no other man, however jeering and contemptuous, could do. "You ain't quite up for this, are you, Mr. Limp?" the sneering girl they'd hired in South Carolina had said after she'd been working on young Ralph awhile, to little effect, and a couple of his friends had howled appreciatively at this insult. But a boy who hadn't had his turn yet and probably feared a similar difficulty had come to Ralph's defense and told the girl not to talk with her mouth full, and this act of friendship had allowed Ralph to relax and concentrate until the vague rumbling finally came and went, like a train into and then out of the station of the next town over. No, Ralph refused to think badly of his stepson. He would have liked to say something witty and comforting like the boy had done in South Carolina, something like Sully always came up with, but about the best he could do was tell Peter he and the boy were welcome to stay with them as long as they needed to. Hiding, Ralph suspected, was what Peter was doing, and Ralph didn't blame him a bit. Even forty years later, if that girl from South Carolina ever turned up in Bath, Ralph would have bolted, maybe up into the Adirondacks someplace into the deep woods, until he was sure she was gone again and it was safe to return. And Ralph didn't consider himself a coward either. A man had a right to be scared of such women. A moral duty to, probably.

"You ain't really going to quit your teaching, are you?" Ralph said. He'd been almost as surprised as Vera when Peter announced that maybe he'd just make a clean break—from Charlotte, a woman who hadn't cared for him much until she'd discovered there was someone else; from Deirdre, the woman from the poetry reading; from college teaching, which had turned out to be the worst kind of servitude, the most unrewarding work he'd ever done; from West Virginia, which was, well, West Virginia. Besides, Peter said, Sully could use his help if he decided to stick around, and maybe they could use some help too, meaning Vera and Ralph.

"I don't know, Pop," Peter said now. "I've only got the one more semester anyway. This way I have the pleasure of quitting."

"I guess I never did understand that whole tenure deal," Ralph said. Peter had explained, more than once, that he'd been turned down the previous spring and given one academic year to find another position, but that didn't make any sense to Ralph. How could you fire a man who'd done his job for five years? According to Peter, his boss (his department chairman, Peter had called him) admitted that Peter'd gotten a raw deal, that he'd been a good teacher and had high ratings or whatever you got when students liked you. But the college was going to let him go anyhow, because there'd been some way or other he hadn't measured up and they could use that way to hire some new young professor cheaper than they could keep Peter. Vera had been furious, but Peter had told her not to be. The truth was, he said, that he wasn't that great a teacher and he was no great scholar either, and they'd expected him to be both. That Peter would say such a thing had infuriated Vera—a woman who never granted a concession—almost as much as the tenure denial itself. And Peter's announcement last night that he'd decided not to go back for his final semester had been proof positive that he was giving up his life, conceding defeat. She couldn't believe he was any son of hers, she said. She couldn't believe he was Robert Halsey's grandson.

Peter had only smiled ruefully, said he wasn't surprised he hadn't measured up, in her eyes, to Robert Halsey, since no one ever had. And he told her the rest of what she'd said was off base too. He assured her he hadn't any bridges to burn; they'd already been burned for him. He wasn't turning away from teaching; he'd been terminated. He wasn't even ending his marriage; Charlotte had done that. As soon as she'd returned to Morgantown, she'd withdrawn what little money they had from their savings account, rented a small U-Haul truck and returned with Wacker and little Andy to Ohio and her parents. The only thing waiting for him in West Virginia now was his landlord and the first-of-the-month bills he didn't have the money to pay.

"I'm not giving up much by quitting now," Peter assured his stepfather. "Once you're denied tenure, you're a leper. About the best I could do is teach in some Baptist college in Oklahoma. A community college in South Carolina, maybe. I'd rather not."

Ralph shuddered at the mention of South Carolina. "At least that'd be something, wouldn't it?"

"Depends on your definition of 'something,' " Peter said.

Ralph nodded. "Well, I don't blame you if you don't want to. Your mother can't quite understand, is all. You know how proud she is. First doctorate in the family. All your honors. Seems to her they should count for something."

"I'm sorry to disappoint her," Peter said. "I'm a little disappointed myself."

"I would be too," Ralph sighed. "You worked awful hard. I couldn't sit and stare at books half as long as you did. Your mother's right, though. There isn't much opportunity around here."

Peter shrugged. "Maybe I'll teach a night class or two at Schuyler CC."

Ralph nodded, trying not to encourage Peter too much. Truth be told, he liked the idea of having his stepson around. "You'd be keeping your hand in, anyhow," he offered.

Peter was grinning now. "Dad says he knows a couple people there. That'd be a kick, wouldn't it? If I got a job teaching college on Don Sullivan's recommendation?"

Ralph didn't see why that was so strange. "People like Sully," he said. "I do myself. He's . . ." Ralph tried to think what Sully was.

"Right," Peter said. "He sure is."

Ralph, feeling his throat constrict again with only love, looked around the garage for some object to distract him from his feelings. There in the corner of the garage was the snowblower Sully'd given him. "You know, it hasn't snowed once since your dad give us that," he remarked.

"That's another thing Mom's right about," Peter acknowledged. "She always said if you needed something from Dad, it'd be the thing he didn't have. And what he did have would be of no use."

Together, Ralph and Peter regarded the snowblower, as if it contained significance worthy of such extended consideration. Outside, a car driving by backfired loudly, causing Will, stricken with fright, to squeal. "That ain't nothin,' " Ralph told the boy. "There's nothin' to be scared of."

"I know," Will lied.

■ ■ ■

It was nearly ten-thirty when Sully tossed his grease-stained apron into the linen barrel, nearly half an hour later than he was supposed to finish up at Hattie's, which had stayed busy longer than usual. The day before had been dramatic, and people wanted to see if old Hattie would still be on the warpath, hurling obscenities and salt shakers.

"What do you say, sport?" Sully called over to Will, who was bussing the last of the booths. "You ready to go see if we can get lucky?" Before joining Rub and Peter, they'd make a quick stop at the OTB.

"Okay," Will agreed, turning away from the task that had occupied him and causing Sully to smile. To keep the boy from getting bored, Sully had taught him how to bus the tables, how to clear the dirty dishes and glasses into plastic tubs, keeping things separate and orderly. In just two days Will had gotten pretty good at it, working proudly and, for the most part, efficiently, despite his natural tendency to become transfixed, hypnotized really, by an interesting egg yolk pattern on a dirty dish or a conversation going on at the next table. Sully'd had to teach him not to stare and eavesdrop.

Peter had been the same way as a kid, Sully remembered. Easily abstracted, prone to daydreaming. Of course, Sully himself had been a younger man then, and he'd found his son's introspection, his apparent inability to keep any task in focus, more than a little irritating. Just how impatient he'd been with his son he could not now remember. Pretty impatient, probably, though not violently so, like Big Jim Sullivan. And, of course, Sully'd not been around his son enough to do much damage, regardless. And Ralph's long suit, Sully knew for a fact, was patience. He'd stayed married to Vera, after all. Than which there was no truer litmus test. And it was thanks to their combined efforts that Peter had turned out well, even if at the moment his life happened to be pretty messed up. Maybe, given Vera's love (never mind its more bizarre manifestations) and Ralph's steadying influence, they could even keep their grandson from having a nervous breakdown before he reached puberty. Who knew? Maybe even Sully himself might help prevent that, if he could just keep his mind about him and not scare the boy like he'd done yesterday.

"Why don't you go ahead and take that tub over to the dishwasher?" he suggested to the boy. "Then you'd be done."

"Okay," Will said, picking up the big tub full of dirty dishes and glassware, his eyes wide with effort. Cass, down the counter, winced, but

Sully shook his head at her—the boy would be all right. Sully grabbed the rubber trash barrel and wheeled it along behind the boy. When Will managed to hoist the tub up onto the drainboard, Cass gave him two one-dollar bills from the silent new cash register. "You're getting to be a pretty good helper," she said. "What am I going to do when you go back to West Virginia?"

Will blushed with pride and pleasure. "We're staying here," he told her. That, at least, was his understanding from the last adult conversation he'd half overheard.

Cass raised her eyebrows questioningly at Sully.

"News to me," Sully admitted. "People never talk to me, of course."

"People talk to you all the time," Cass grinned. "You just never pay attention."

"That so?"

"Where are you going to be the day after Christmas?"

This had the feel of a trick question, so instead of announcing that he had no idea, he thought about it. Luckily, that did some good. "Helping you," he remembered.

"You had to think about it, didn't you?"

"I'm sorry," Sully said. "I thought I was allowed to."

Cass grew serious. "Come here," she said, and when he took a suspicious step toward her, Cass planted a grateful kiss on his forehead. "Thanks," she said, and they both glanced over at Hattie's booth, though from where they were standing, only a puff of the old woman's gray hair was visible from where she now sat behind the ancient cash register.

"God," Cass said, glancing back at Sully. "You're blushing. How old are you?"

"Who's blushing?"

"You are. Look at your grandfather," Cass encouraged Will. "Tell him he's blushing."

"You are, Grandpa."

Sully *was* blushing, and he knew it. "Let's you and me trade places tomorrow," he suggested to Cass. "You stand in front of that hot grill for about four hours, and we'll see if *you* blush."

"Go on and bet your triple," Cass told him, then, to the boy, "Don't let Grandpa make a gambler out of you."

"Let's go," Sully said, prodding his grandson into motion. "We've got just enough time. If we don't get to the house by eleven, Uncle Rub'll have kittens."

Will made a face.

"Don't worry," Sully told him. "You're not really related to Rub."

They stopped at Hattie's booth on their way out. "How you doing, old woman?" Sully said loudly. "You feeling better, now you got your register?"

Clearly, the old woman's spirits were restored. "You sound like that darn Sully," she grinned.

"That's who I am," Sully told her. "I'm the one who gave you the register. Can't you remember anything?" Actually, it had been his idea. It had required Peter and Rub to lug it over to her booth.

Hattie depressed one of the cash register's heavy bronze keys, which clanged reassuringly, forcing a small card that read .80 to jump up into the rectangular window. There were already several others of varying amounts nesting there.

"I don't know if I can afford all that," Sully told her. "Besides. I work here. You going to charge me to work here?"

Hattie cackled joyfully, depressed two more keys, forced two more cards to jump into the window. "Pay!" she bellowed.

"Pay," Sully repeated, glancing over his shoulder at Cass, whose expression as she watched all of this was the saddest imaginable. "Okay, here."

Sully handed the old woman a dollar, which she snatched.

"You see money fine, don't you?" he said. "How come you don't see anything else?"

The old woman was fumbling with the register, trying to get the cash drawer to open.

"That doesn't open anymore, remember?" Sully said. "What are we doing with all the money?"

She handed the bill back to him. "Right," Sully said. "We give the money to Cass. You ring it up, she takes the money."

This arrangement apparently satisfied the old woman, who'd been ringing wild amounts on the register all morning. The only problem was that unless she hit the total key by accident, the numbered cards she rang stacked up in the window, forming a thick clump. Sully punched the total key, which resulted in an even louder and more satisfying clanging. "Money!" she whispered.

"I know it," Sully said. "We're all getting rich now. I'll see you in the morning, old girl. Which way will we go?"

"Up!"

"Okay, up," he sighed. "I'm tired of arguing with you."

Officer Raymer was standing guard outside the OTB when Sully and Will pulled up in the El Camino, ignored a perfectly legal parking space and backed into the striped triangle clearly marked NO PARKING. The policeman sighed visibly. In the past couple weeks he'd written Sully half a dozen parking tickets even though the El Camino wasn't his car, even though the policeman knew it belonged to Carl Roebuck, who was in tight with the chief of police and could fix any tickets that Officer Raymer wrote. By ignoring the legal parking space, Sully was taunting him. And it was only the beginning.

"Let's have some fun," Sully said to Will as they got out of the El Camino. Then, louder, "Say hi to that big ugly fellow in the uniform."

Will smiled weakly, said hello.

The policeman did not look at the boy or acknowledge that he'd been spoken to. Instead he glared at Sully murderously. "Don't start in," he warned.

"Hey," Sully said, holding up his hands, as if in surrender. "I just want you to clarify something for me. There's one little thing that confuses me."

"Don't start."

"No, really. I just want to understand. Correct me if I get the details wrong, okay, because I wasn't there."

Officer Raymer turned away, looked up the street in the other direction. Two men on their way into the OTB stopped to listen.

"So," Sully went on. "You're asked to go see about a disturbance. You drive up, and what do you see? There's a man standing in the middle of the driveway with a deer rifle and he's shooting out windows on a residential street. Now correct me if I'm wrong, but . . . that'd be against the law, right?"

Officer Raymer turned back to study Sully, noticed that the two passersby had stopped to listen, said nothing.

"A good-looking girl comes up to the guy with the rifle, so he clubs her with the gun, breaks her jaw in about fifteen places, then kicks her once or twice for good measure. That'd be against the law, wouldn't it?"

"He done that before I got there," the policeman said. "I never saw him hit her."

Some more men on the way into the OTB also stopped now.

"Okay," Sully said agreeably. "That's what I mean. I just want to understand how it happened. So you pull up, and the guy with the gun is standing over the girl with the broken jaw who's lying on the ground. And he's pointing the rifle at her and saying what he ought to do is just blow her brains out. That'd be against the law, wouldn't it?"

"Definitely," said one of the two men who'd stopped first.

The policeman glared at the man who'd spoken for a moment before turning his attention back to Sully. "I'm going to give you about ten seconds to get the fuck away from me, Sully."

Sully consulted his watch. "So what do you do? You let the guy with the rifle take a little girl, get back in his truck and drive away."

"It was a domestic dispute. A judgment call. They picked him up ten minutes later, for Christ sake."

"A judgment call," Sully repeated.

Officer Raymer knew his mistake now. It was allowing himself to be drawn into this discussion. "You should try being a cop for about one day, Sully," he said weakly.

Sully was grinning, and so, slyly, were the men who'd gathered. "A judgment call," he repeated as he turned to head into the OTB. "You take care now, Officer."

"I hope you don't ever catch fire and have me standing nearby with a hose," the policeman said to Sully's retreating form.

"That's where you'd be, all right," Sully said over his shoulder. "Off at a safe distance, holding your hose."

Inside the OTB were clusters of the windbreaker men, though most of these were now wearing their post-Thanksgiving heavy outerwear, and Sully spotted Otis right away due to the white bandage behind his ear.

"Oh, God," Otis said when he became aware of Sully standing in the doorway and grinning at him maliciously. Instead of having to deal with Sully once, midmorning, at the OTB, now, since Sully'd started working mornings at Hattie's, he got a double dose. Sully'd warned him against breakfasting at the donut shop, too, threatening to go down there and bring him back by force if he had to. "Have mercy and stay away from me, will you? Can't you see I'm injured?"

Sully inspected the swelling behind Otis's ear. "I worry about you, Otis," Sully told him.

"Well, don't," Otis insisted. "Just stay away from me and I'll be fine."

"I worry about a man who comes out second best to a ninety-year-old blind woman and then insists on going down into alligator country without a guide."

"You couldn't guide me to Albany."

Sully threw up his hands. "You want to try it on your own, be my guest. When they send your remains back home, what should we do with them?"

"He won't go away," Otis wept.

"Okay, I'll have to use my own discretion," Sully said. "There probably won't be much to send back. All they usually find is a blood-stained shoe, maybe part of the foot still in it. Let me look at your shoes so I'll be able to make the identification."

"Dear God, take him." Otis looked up at the roof of the OTB. "Open the sky and just take him."

Sully spied Jocko leaning against the wall by the window. "If it's you, I'll just put it in a shoebox and put it on my mantel."

"This man gives me nightmares every night."

"I'm just trying to make you watchful, Otis. There's danger every-where."

"There's danger everywhere you are, is what you mean," Otis said.

"Let's go see this guy over here," Sully said to Will. "Maybe he'll be more appreciative."

Will was squinting at yesterday's results posted on the wall, but he followed along.

"If you won another triple, don't tell me about it," Sully warned Jocko, who looked up when they came over.

"Okay," he agreed. "If you lost another one, I don't want to hear about that either. Who's this?"

"Say hi to Jocko. He's our friendly neighborhood pharmacist."

Will was still squinting at the wall.

"Speaking of which. I don't suppose you got any more of those you gave me the last time?"

"Not on me," Jocko said. "I got some new samples in yesterday, though. I thought immediately of you."

"You're the boss."

"Come out to my office."

"Can you wait here a minute?" Sully asked Will, who was tugging on his sleeve. A look of panic immediately swept Will's face. "I'll only be a minute. Can you be brave that long? I'll be in that car. You can see it from here." He pointed out the window at Jocko's Marquis. "Go see what the triple was yesterday, and by the time you do that, I'll be back. Okay?"

Will took a deep breath. Okay.

Outside, Jocko rummaged through his candy store glovebox, holding up vials of pills to the light, glowering at them through his thick glasses. "Here," he said finally, "eat these."

Sully held them up, noted their color, pocketed them. "I wondered if you'd ever give me anything yellow. I've had just about every other color of the rainbow, I think. What are these?"

"Screaming yellow zonkers. One should do the trick."

"Okay."

"Let me know if they turn your pee yellow."

"My pee *is* yellow," Sully said.

"Oh-oh." Jocko grinned. "It may already be too late."

They got out of the car again. "What do I owe you?"

As usual, Jocko waved this off. "Nada. I told you. They're samples."

"That's what you always say."

"That's what they always are," Jocko said. "You're becoming a regular laboratory rat."

"I come from a long line of rats," Sully said. He could see his grandson at the window, watching anxiously, his courage nearly exhausted.

"Good-looking kid," Jocko remarked.

"He's a good boy," Sully said, feeling suddenly swollen with pride, just as he had in talking about Peter the day before with Harold Proxmire. "I like having him around. He's a little on the nervous side, like his father always was."

"They get that from Vera," Jocko said thoughtfully. "She and her husband have sure had their share lately."

"I don't know much about it," Sully admitted. "I know Ralph's been in the hospital."

"In and out," Jocko said. "They're about a gazillion bucks in debt. Got to be."

"I doubt it," Sully said. "Ralph worked for the post office all those years. He's got to be covered."

"Insurance usually gets the first eighty percent," Jocko admitted. "You ever tried to pay the other twenty after something major?"

"I'm not saying they don't have problems," Sully said.

"I shouldn't tell you this—" Jocko began.

"Then don't, for Christ sake," Sully said.

"Okay," Jocko said agreeably enough.

Sully studied him sadly. He waved at Will, who waved back. "What?" he said finally.

"Just be careful of Vera if you run into her," said Jocko, owl-eyed behind his thick glasses, unusually serious.

"I'm always careful around Vera," Sully told him. "I wear a cup, in fact."

"You miss my point. She's the one I worry about, not you."

Sully frowned. Jocko, a pharmacist, often knew medical information about people in town. "She isn't sick?"

"Not exactly," Jocko admitted, adjusting his glasses up the bridge of his nose significantly. "If this goes any farther, you're going to have to find a new source of pain pills."

Sully promised not to tell anyone.

"About a month ago, one of my clerks caught her shoplifting. I got back just in time to keep her from being arrested."

"You're kidding," Sully said, because Jocko so clearly was not kidding.

"I wish."

"I can't believe it."

"Neither could I. I took her back in the office and she came unglued. Un-fucking-glued, Sully. She scared the shit out of me. I thought she was going to have a breakdown right there. Sobbing about disgracing her father. Sixty years old, and she's worried about ruining her father's reputation."

"What'd you do?"

"Gave her a Valium and sent her home and told her to forget it. She hasn't been back since. She's shopping at the drugstore out by the interstate now."

Sully nodded. "No good deed ever goes unpunished."

"I'm grateful," Jocko said as though he meant it. "When I was a kid, one of my friends stole a toy truck of mine. I saw him take it, and I could never face him afterwards. I felt more guilty than if I stole *his* truck."

Will met them at the back door. He was holding a ticket. Sully had given the boy his triple ticket the day before to hold on to for luck. Sully couldn't quite read yesterday's results from where they were standing. "What was yesterday?" he asked Jocko.

"Four-five-seven."

Sully nodded, took the ticket from Will, glancing at it with disinterest.

"I haven't been off the schnide all week. You're supposed to be able to pick one of the three, aren't you?"

"Just as well you didn't hit yesterday," Jocko commiserated. "The payoff would have just pissed you off. Nice two-eight daily double, though, for the magician who could have picked it."

Sully blinked at the ticket Will had handed him. Two-eight, it said. "Here's the magician right here," he told Jocko. He'd completely forgotten he'd bought the boy a ticket, let him pick the numbers. In fact, he'd been about to tear the ticket up.

Jocko examined the ticket, then the board, then Will, who was beaming and blushing. "That's the genuine article. Hundred and eighty-seven fifty."

"How do you like that?" Sully said. "You're rich."

Jocko handed Will his racing form. "Who do you like today, kid?"

Sully and the boy had been sitting outside at the curb for nearly five minutes when Rub, who had all kinds of things to tell Sully, couldn't take it any longer. First Sully didn't come, and then he still didn't, and then he finally did come, and now he was finally here but still wouldn't get out of the car. A lot had happened since Rub and Peter had left Hattie's over three hours ago, and Rub didn't approve of any of it. It wasn't bad enough that Peter had just gone off like he was the boss and could give himself orders, leaving Rub to work all by himself and take messages for everybody in town who wanted to leave one. But now when Sully and the boy finally did come back, they had to just sit there by the curb while he was inside doing his work and everybody else's, full of longing and the morning's unspoken wishes and messages and information. To Rub's way of thinking, there were suddenly too many people in the world, and two of the extra unnecessary ones were Sully's son and his grandson who, together, had sort of made Rub himself disappear. So he went out to where they sat at the curb and reasserted his existence. He went around to the driver's side and knocked on the window.

Inside, Sully and the boy kept talking. Actually, Sully was talking, and Rub thought he had an idea what he was saying. He was telling the little boy to pretend he didn't see Rub, who was standing right there in plain sight. "Don't look at him," Sully was saying, the words barely audible outside the glass. The little boy tried not to, but he kept darting furtive glances at Rub, who understood that this was one of Sully's games. One of the ones designed to make himself feel like shit. Which was exactly how he did feel already. So he rapped harder on the window.

This time Sully noticed him, and he mouthed the words, "Hi, Rub," as if he and the boy were a long way off, too far for a human voice to carry. Then he whispered something to the boy and they waved at him together. For Rub there were a great many mysteries, but none was more perplexing than the way his best friend would team up with any human being on earth against himself. It was almost enough to make Rub doubt that they *were* best friends.

When Sully and the kid were through waving at him, Rub made a circular motion in the air to signify that Sully should roll down the window. That way, at least, Sully couldn't pretend not to hear. Not that Rub expected this ploy to work, and indeed he was not surprised when Sully feigned confusion and made the same motion back at him. Slowly, silently, Rub mouthed the words "ROLL DOWN THE WINDOW."

Sully rolled it down. "What?" he said.

"What are you doing?" Rub wanted to know.

"Who?"

"You. The both of you," Rub explained. "You're just sitting there."

Sully shrugged. "What do you want, Rub?"

What Rub wanted was in. In the car. In the conversation. Back in his friend's company. In. "Can I get in?" he said. "It's cold out here."

"In here too," Sully told him. "The heater doesn't work. We'll only be another minute. Then we'll get out and all be cold together." And then he rolled up the window, leaving Rub to stare at his own reflection. Even his reflection appeared to be inside the car, where it was warm, or warmer.

Rub was contemplating all of this, including the unfairness of his own reflection being inside the car while he was kept out, when the window rolled back down again a minute later. "What're you doing?" Sully wanted to know.

"Waiting," Rub explained.

"Well, do it over there," Sully told him. "Go sit on the porch."

"I ain't hurting anything here," said Rub, who knew his rights. This was a public street. "Couldn't I just tell you one thing?"

"In a minute you can tell me everything. Go over and sit down on the porch."

Sully said all of this as he was rolling the window up, and it closed completely just as the sentence ended. Leaving Rub alone once again with just his own reflection for company. The young man who stared back at

Rub looked like somebody full of need but fresh out of options. Reluctantly, Rub did what he was told.

Inside the car, Sully and Will watched a sullen Rub retreat up the walkway to the front porch steps, where he stubbornly took a cold seat. What they'd been talking about was fear. Will was still afraid to enter his grandfather's house. Sully had explained to him that when he was Will's age, he'd been afraid of things too. Will appeared to doubt this.

He eyed the ramshackle house fearfully. It looked even scarier than it had the day before, because now there was a mountain of boards stacked on the sloping front porch, which, to Will's way of thinking, meant that there was even less holding up the house than there had been. "You want to know what Grandpa used to do?" Sully said.

He wasn't sure he wanted to know what Grandpa Sully had done to combat fear, because he sensed that after his grandfather explained what had worked for him, he'd want Will to try it out, and Will already knew he didn't want to. He doubted sincerely that Grandpa Sully had ever been truly afraid of anything. He could no more imagine his grandfather afraid than he could imagine his brother Wacker merciful. Wacker was a boy without pity. Add pity and he'd no longer be Wacker. He'd be somebody else entirely who looked liked Wacker. They'd have to rename him. Grandpa Sully? Who wasn't even afraid of a policeman with a gun?

"I used to make a deal with myself," Grandpa Sully explained. "I'd tell myself I'd be brave for exactly a minute."

Will frowned, studied his grandfather.

"You could stand being brave for a minute, couldn't you? You were brave for more than a minute back at the betting place, and a good thing happened. You won money."

"What happened after the minute?"

"Then I'd let myself be scared again. But at least I could say I'd been brave for a minute. The next time I'd try to be brave for two minutes. That way I'd be getting braver and braver all the time."

Will continued to study his grandfather, who appeared to be telling the truth. "What were you scared of?"

His grandfather shrugged. "I don't remember. You won't either when you're my age."

Will looked out the window at his fear. He didn't believe he'd ever forget what he was afraid of. He didn't believe his grandfather had forgotten. Which meant he hadn't *been* afraid.

"Wait here a minute," Grandpa Sully said, getting out of the car and limping around to the open rear end of the El Camino. Throwing open the lid to the big toolbox he kept there, Sully rummaged around in it, making a racket. Eventually he must have found whatever he was looking for, because he let the heavy lid of the toolbox fall shut and slid back into the front seat next to Will. "Here," he said, tossing something heavy and metallic into Will's lap.

Will caught the thing between his knees, then picked it up and examined it, confused until he identified the object as a stopwatch.

"You can time yourself," his grandfather explained, showing Will how it worked. "That way you'll know exactly how long you were brave."

Will studied the watch dubiously for a minute, then the house more dubiously still, finally his grandfather. Then he took a deep breath. "Okay."

"Good boy."

They got out of the El Camino and made their way up the rippled walkway, Will watching the second hand make its slow sweep, as if to get straight in his own mind just how long the minute he'd agreed to would be in real time.

Somewhere close by a dog was barking. It sounded to Sully like the dog was right out back of the house, though that was unlikely.

Sully came to a halt where Rub was seated, still sulking, and looked up at the house. There were no sounds of boards being ripped asunder, or any kind of work being accomplished, for that matter. "Where's Peter?" it occurred to him to wonder.

Wherever the dog was, he barked louder and seemingly nearer now, a bark that had an angry, strangling quality to it.

"That's what I come out to tell you," Rub said angrily, "but all you wanted to do was pretend I wasn't even there. So now I'm not telling nothing." He looked away again, whether out of anger or because he had tears in his eyes Sully couldn't tell.

Will looked so worried by Rub's refusal that Sully gave him a quick wink and a grin. "Rub?" he said.

"What?"

"Where's Peter?"

"Over to the other house," Rub said, still pouting but apparently satisfied that he'd held out as long as he could under such fierce interrogation.

"What other house, Rub? There are about five hundred other houses right here in Bath. More if we include the whole state."

"The other house we're working on," Rub said, angrily again.

"Carl's camp?" Sully said. Had Peter taken a load of hardwood out to the lake?

"No, that one," Rub said, pointing up the street at the Miles Anderson house. They all turned to look then, just as Peter and another man came out the front door and stood on the porch talking. When they shook hands, Sully frowned and said, "Who's that with Peter, Rub? And don't tell me it's Miles Anderson either, because he said he wasn't coming up till the first of the year."

Rub started to open his mouth, then shut it again.

"Who is it, Rub?"

"It's Miles Fuckin' Anderson, just like you said. And don't blame me."

"Shit," Sully said. The person he blamed was Carl Roebuck for taking him off the big job to do a little one which would probably cost him the big one. Then again, maybe not. They heard laughter coming from up the block, and Peter and Miles Anderson sauntered down the steps together amiably enough. And when Anderson got into his little car, Peter leaned down and waved in the window. When Anderson did a U-turn and headed back up Main toward the village, Peter watched him go for a second, then crossed the street and started toward them.

Will darted down the steps and up the street toward his father, while Sully took a seat on the porch steps next to Rub, who continued morose. "I wouldn't sit here too long," Sully advised. "The tip of your dick'll freeze to the step."

Rub glanced down to see if this were possible.

"I forgot," Sully said. "Yours doesn't hang down quite that far, does it."

"Yours don't either," Rub said, grinning sheepishly now, too happy to have his friend back to hold a grudge much longer.

"That's true," Sully said, nudging Rub hard. "I fold it so it won't."

Rub slid away, out of easy nudging range.

"You want to know how many times I have to fold it?" Sully said, nudging Rub again, since he hadn't moved quite far enough to be out of nudging range completely.

"It would hurt if you folded it," Rub said, imagining.

"Not mine," Sully assured him. "You know what I like best?"

Rub blushed, wondered if it had to do with ole Toby Roebuck.

"Carnation Milk," Sully said. "You know why?"

Rub was frowning, trying to recall why. He felt like he knew the answer to this question, though it wouldn't come.

"No tits to pull, no shit to haul," Sully explained. "You get any work done in there?"

"Almost all of it. Are we going to stop for lunch?"

"Stop work or stop sitting here freezing our dicks?"

"Work."

"I suppose."

"Good," Rub said. Together they sat and listened to the barking dog.

Will had joined up with his father and they were slowly making their way up the street toward where Sully and Rub were sitting. The boy was talking excitedly, showing his father the money he'd won, the stopwatch Sully had given him. Even a block away, Peter looked less than thrilled.

"Where the hell's that damn dog I'm hearing?" Sully wondered. "He sounds like he's inside the house."

"He's in the kitchen," Rub said.

"Who?"

"The dog," Rub said. He could have sworn they'd been discussing the dog.

"What dog?"

"The one that's barking. Carl's," Rub explained. That had been the second thing he'd been trying to tell Sully when he'd gone out to the car and been sent away for his trouble. There'd been a third thing too, but now Rub couldn't remember what it was.

Sully opened the front door and stepped inside. From the doorway he could see Rasputin slumped against the kitchen cabinet Carl Roebuck had chained him to. The reason the dog's bark had a strangling quality to it was that the dog was apparently strangling. Carl had run the animal's chain through one of the upper kitchen cabinets, which was fine as long as the dog was standing up, because the chain was just long enough. But either the dog had lost his balance and slumped against the cabinets or had tried to lie down of his own volition, only to discover that the chain did not allow this. Spying Sully and Rub in the doorway, the dog tried valiantly to get to its feet, but the linoleum floor did not provide much traction and the stroke-deadened side of its body did not work in concert with the good side, and so the dog quickly gave up and slumped against the cabinets again, his head and neck suspended mere inches from the floor.

"Careful," Rub warned, and Sully at first thought he meant the dog before noticing that there was no floor between where they stood and the kitchen, just the lengthwise-running foundation beams and the darkness of the deep cellar below. To Sully's surprise, he felt vaguely embarrassed to see the house he'd grown up in flayed back for inspection, like a terminally ill patient, its pipes and wires and wood exposed. Certainly the sight was not as satisfying as he'd hoped.

Rub slid a sheet of plywood he'd apparently been using to stand on into position in front of them, stepped onto it, then danced nimbly onto a double floor beam and into the kitchen.

"Right," Sully said, stepping onto the plywood and recollecting as he did so that he'd just been encouraging his grandson to go on into a house with no floor. Also Otis's observation that there was danger everywhere Sully was.

Rub held out his hand. "I'll grab you," he said.

"Get away," Sully said. "You'll just make me bang my knee, is all you'll do."

Rub frowned, his feelings hurt yet again, but stepped back as he was told. Sully tested the double beam with his good leg, pushed off, and strode forward across the dark gap, landing on the kitchen's linoleum. He felt his bad knee start to give under the full weight, but he caught the door frame for support and quickly shifted his weight.

"You should have just gone around," Rub said.

"It's just like you to give me good advice after I've killed myself," Sully told him, wiping the cold sweat from his brow with his sleeve.

When the Doberman again tried to stand, Sully noticed there was an envelope taped to the animal's collar. Since the crowbar he'd used the day before to get into the house was still sitting on the counter, Sully picked it up and showed it to the dog. "If you bite me, I'm going to beat you to death right here in the kitchen," he said.

The dog seemed to understand this threat and quit growling and lay still while Sully removed the small envelope, which was addressed in Carl Roebuck's graceful, almost feminine, hand to Don Sullivan, Jack-Off, All Trades. The note inside said simply: YOU BROKE HIM. HE'S YOURS.

As if to confirm this, the dog strained forward as far as he could and licked Sully's knuckles.

When Peter and the boy arrived a minute later, having gone around back, Sully showed his son the note. Peter read it and chuckled unpleasantly. Will, who'd hesitated on the back porch, took a deep breath, engaged his stopwatch, eyed the dog warily and stepped inside.

■ ■ ■

"Did you feel light-headed at the time, Mrs. Peoples?" the young doctor wanted to know. He was pumping air into the black blood pressure sleeve, which tightened relentlessly around her upper arm. The unpleasant sensation seemed a natural extension of recent events. Since that first morning before Thanksgiving when she'd looked up into the trees and concluded that this might be her year, she'd suffered the sensation of things closing in. Deciding not to travel had aggravated it, no doubt. Clive Jr. had been right about that. She should have gone as planned. On the other hand, he'd been wrong about Sully, who had proven himself this morning to be the trustworthy soul she'd always known him to be. It was not Sully who was lowering the boom, but God Himself, the sneaky booger, and this doctor was going to explain how, and so Miss Beryl prepared herself to accept reality.

This was the second time in half an hour she'd had her blood pressure taken. The first time, the nurse had done it. During his examination of her, Miss Beryl had been studying the young doctor almost as closely as he'd been studying her, though without the benefit of intrusive, cold, probing instruments. The gene pool again, she told herself, though this was Schuyler Springs, not Bath, and she could easily be mistaken. The chances that she'd taught this particular young physician when he was in the eighth grade were only so-so, though he did look vaguely familiar, an older version of somebody—some Ur-eighth-grader, probably. One of the unfortunate side effects of teaching for forty years was that the task was so monumental, even in recollection, that it sometimes seemed you'd tried to teach everyone on the planet. What Miss Beryl looked for in each adult face was the evidence of some failed lesson in some distant yesterday that might predict incompetence today. In this young doctor, Miss Beryl was looking to justify in advance her decision not to follow any advice she didn't like. One surely was not required to follow the advice of one's own "C" students, if they could be identified.

"I did," she admitted, in answer to his prescient question about the light-headedness that had preceded her gusher. "Now that it's all over, I feel lighthearted," she added.

The young man surrendered a tolerant, professional half smile. "Lighthearted? Do you mean reinvigorated?"

Miss Beryl made a face. Like most young professionals of Miss Beryl's recent acquaintance, this young man had no sense of play about him, no love of language, probably no imagination. As a boy Clive Jr. had been the same way. Every time she'd tried to play with him, he'd just frowned at her, puzzled. This young doctor was too bright to have been a "C" student, probably, but she could see herself putting a B-minus at the top of one of his adolescent compositions twenty years ago and waiting for him to complain. What's wrong with it? he'd have wanted to know. Where had she taken off points? Where had he lost credit?

But, yes, reinvigorated was precisely how she'd felt after the nose-bleed. And so she raised his grade to a B-plus now, just as she probably had then, after a stern lecture that life wasn't a matter of simply avoiding mistakes, of losing credit, but rather of earning. She decided to confide in him. "I kept thinking it was snowing," she said, feeling a little foolish. "I could *see* it snowing."

The doctor nodded, apparently not at all surprised by what struck Miss Beryl as the most bizarre of her symptoms. He let the air out of the sleeve all at once then and pulled apart the Velcro seam. When she rubbed her flesh, he said, "Did that cause discomfort?"

"It hurt, if that's what you mean. Are we finished?"

"Just about. I think it would be wise to order some blood work done, though," he said.

Miss Beryl flapped her sore arm like a wing. "Am I correct in assuming you'll want to use *my* blood?"

Another trace of a smile. "Well, we could use mine, but then we'd know about me."

Miss Beryl stood, then sat back down again when the doctor, who was sitting across from her, did not get to his feet. "You fellows are like the police. You're never around when you're needed. If you'd been at my house at six o'clock this morning you could have had the blood you wanted, and you wouldn't have required a syringe to get it either. You could have used a salad bowl. Now you want more."

"Just a little," he assured her. "You aren't afraid of the needle, are you? It won't hurt."

"Will I feel any discomfort?"

"Maybe a smidgen," he conceded seriously, tossing the blood pressure sleeve carelessly onto the desk and crossing one knee over the other. He opened his mouth to speak, hesitated and closed it again.

"This is the part where we converse meaningfully, ain't it," Miss Beryl said.

"It is," he said. "You have a family physician in Bath?"

Miss Beryl said she did.

"Yet you didn't go to him about this?"

"He's a snitch," Miss Beryl explained. "Reports directly to my son. The only reason I'm here is that I promised Donald."

"Donald?"

"Sullivan," she said. "You probably don't know him." Indeed, she had promised Sully she'd go to the doctor. It had been the only way she could get him out of her flat so she could clean up the bloody mess she'd made. In fact, Sully had insisted on driving her to the doctor over the noon hour, had promised to drop by and pick her up. Probably he'd forget, but the way her luck was going this would be the time he'd remember, so she made an appointment at the clinic in Schuyler, called Mrs. Gruber for company, explaining that she'd been referred to the clinic for her annual checkup, and left Sully a note on the door, explaining that she'd gone to the doctor without mentioning which one or where, confident that Sully seldom required more information than people gave him. What she'd had in mind, though, was a doctor like her own in Bath, an older man, understanding but not too swift, but a stranger, someone who wouldn't snitch. She hadn't been prepared for this mere boy.

"You live alone?" asked the mere boy.

Miss Beryl said she did, adding that she had done so, pretty much without incident, since her husband's death nearly thirty years before.

"And you fear losing your independence?"

Miss Beryl raised his grade from a B-plus to an A-minus. "Such as it is," she admitted.

"Do you drive?"

"Seldom. To the store and back. I'm thinking of giving it up altogether. Frankly, I've never understood this nation's obsession with cars. It means something, and I hate to think what. I also hate to think I might do something foolish and harm someone. My husband, Clive—star of my firmament—was killed in a car, and my son's fiancée, who is a wrecker even when afoot, nearly killed him in one yesterday."

The young man was nodding at her, clearly pretending comprehension.

"I only use the Ford for grocery shopping," Miss Beryl repeated. "And when there's a grand opening in some store between here and Albany I get roped into taking Mrs. Gruber, my neighbor. She's a snitch too." In fact, Mrs. Gruber was waiting for her in the lobby of the clinic, happily contemplating lunch in the new hospital cafeteria she'd read about

in the *North Bath Weekly Journal* and had long hoped to visit. Miss Beryl
had told her friend nothing of the gusher, fearing that the information
would find its way back to Clive Jr. "So you see I wouldn't miss driving.
My independence is my routine, my way of doing things, which is not the
way others do them. I eat what I want and when I want. I read and talk
to myself and look out my window and contemplate the verities. I know
my neighbors and I like them, but I wouldn't want them any closer, and
I certainly wouldn't want to share living quarters with the best of them. I
have a boarder upstairs, and the best thing about him is that he's seldom
home. He drops in in the morning to find out if I'm still alive and then he
leaves, doesn't come home until the bars close. He's a free spirit. Donald
Sullivan. I may have mentioned him. Clive says I'd be happier if I had
companionship. He doesn't count his father and Ed."

The young man frowned. "I thought you said your husband was
killed in a car accident."

"He was," Miss Beryl said, delighted to discover that her listener had
been paying attention.

"And yet . . ."

"I keep his photograph on the television, and we continue many of
the discussions we had when he was alive. We never reached conclusions
then, and we still don't."

"Which leaves . . . Ed?"

"Ed's a Zamble."

"A which?"

"An African spirit mask. Part human, part animal, part bird. Like the
rest of us."

The young man smiled. "I think I see what you mean about talking
to yourself. Do you find yourself entertaining?"

"Mildly," Miss Beryl told him. "Compared to television. Clive thinks
I should get cable. That's what he means when he says I should have more
companionship."

The doctor was squinting now.

"Clive Jr.," Miss Beryl decided to help the young man out, since he
was trying. "Clive Sr. is dead. His son survives."

"*His* son?"

"Our son," Miss Beryl conceded. "There. I've admitted it. I hope
you're happy."

"You and your son don't see eye to eye, I take it?"

"He's a banker," Miss Beryl explained.

The doctor appeared to be waiting for her to continue.

"You don't think that's sufficient reason, I gather."

More confusion. "For what?"

"He's the one responsible for that new theme park they're going to build. He thinks Bath is the Gold Coast. He says money is creeping up the interstate."

"Hmmm," the young doctor said.

"Let's discuss something you may know about," Miss Beryl suggested. "What's wrong with me? In addition to my being eighty years old."

When the young physician opened his mouth to speak, Miss Beryl interrupted him.

"Don't pussyfoot. Pretend you're telling Clive."

"Which Clive?"

"Junior. This is just pretend. You won't actually tell him anything. Ever."

"Well, Mrs. Peoples—"

"This isn't going to be very convincing," she interrupted again, "if you call Clive by his mother's name."

The young man was grinning broadly now. "Well, Clive," he went on, "the best I can do right now is give you an educated guess."

"Ma's an educator," she said, imitating her son's voice. "She'll understand."

Her listener grew sober. "I think—I'm reasonably certain—that your mother suffered a stroke this morning. Call it a ministroke if you like. They're not at all uncommon among women of your mother's advanced age. A momentary disruption of oxygen to the brain, causing a feeling of light-headedness, the illusion that it was snowing. Cause? A small blood clot, likely, though we may never know. The causes may have been building up for weeks."

Miss Beryl took this in, wondering whether the causes the young fellow alluded to were strictly physical or whether there might be spiritual causes as well. Could betrayals cause clots? Miss Beryl was inclined to believe they could. "Should she expect more?"

The doctor hesitated, then nodded. "You—sorry—*she* might not have another for a year or longer. She could have another next month. The next one could be stronger or less strong. If she starts to have a series of them, they could presage a more damaging stroke down the road. If she has any more symptoms like she had today, she should see me immediately. You should impress that on her."

"Ma's pretty stubborn," Miss Beryl heard herself say in her son's voice. It was startling how easy it was to do Clive Jr.'s voice. And not just the more irritating aspects of his speech, like his referring to her as "Ma," but the more subtle tone and cadence of his words. It was as if she could call upon some complex genetic common denominator in their physical makeup (in the vocal cords themselves?) to reproduce Clive's sound exactly. This was the first time she'd ever done her son's voice for a stranger, and she felt the quick betrayal of it and wondered if she'd just formed another clot. "You could wallop her on the head with a stick, but you couldn't get her to change her mind once it's made up."

"That was my impression of her exactly," the doctor responded, grinning at her now to show how much he was enjoying the game. "She's a corker, in fact."

The doctor stepped out into the corridor then and flagged a nurse. "When I've had a look at your blood work, I may write you a prescription for a blood thinner," he said. "Until then, you take care, Mrs. Peoples . . . it is Mrs. Peoples I'm addressing?"

The nurse who came in to take her blood was the same one who'd taken her blood pressure earlier, and she slapped the flesh on Miss Beryl's arm with some annoyance, as if she'd have preferred it to assume some other shape. Miss Beryl knew just how the woman felt.

"I wisht these nails wouldn't all bend," Rub said when another one did. The flooring nails used to fasten the thin hardwood boards to the studs beneath were soft and triangular, and they bent easily when pounded from the bottom. Pulling them out of the wood, as Peter predicted, had turned into a time-consuming and frustrating job. They'd set up two sawhorses on plywood sheets in the middle of the living room, creating an island surrounded by holes large enough for a careless man to fall through all the way to the cellar floor, a dangerous situation given the fact that these were two of the more careless men in Bath. Below, in the darkness, they occasionally heard scurrying sounds. Sully had no intention of going down into the cellar to investigate. He'd heard earlier in the year that the men restoring the Sans Souci complained that there were rats everywhere in the lower reaches of the rambling structure and elsewhere on the grounds, stirred into restless activity, no doubt, by all the heavy machinery. Exterminators had apparently been hired, though for all Sully knew they could have hired a piper to lead the entire rat population of the Sans Souci into the small cellar of what had once been his home.

"I wisht you hadn't told me those were rats," Rub said, listening to the sounds like rustling paper below.

Anyone overhearing Rub's conversation during the long afternoon would have taken him for a malcontent, but Sully knew better. Despite the wish parade, Rub was the most content he'd been in two weeks, since Peter's return, to be precise. After lunch, Ralph had unexpectedly showed up and spoken to Peter in private, after which Peter had left with his stepfather without explanation. Something was clearly going on, but it apparently wasn't anything either man felt compelled to share with Sully, who suspected it was some sort of crisis with Vera. All afternoon, he hadn't been able to get the image of his ex-wife, caught shoplifting in Jocko's Rexall, out of his mind. He wondered if Peter knew. If Ralph knew.

Anyway, Rub was not sorry to see Peter depart, which meant he had Sully right where he wanted him. With the two sawhorses set up in the middle of the living room and surrounded by a mine field of dangerous holes in the flooring, they faced each other throughout the long afternoon, wrenching reluctant nails from boards so the hardwood could be reused. When they finished with the ones they'd piled along the west wall, Rub fetched the ones they'd piled out on the porch, hopping nimbly from stud to stud, his arms weighted down with lumber, while Sully remained on the more stable island of plywood, swearing at the soft nails.

All afternoon they'd faced each other in that charmed circle, close enough to touch, though Rub wouldn't have done that. He had a deep and abiding adolescent fear of being thought "queer," a fear that was always coming into conflict with his equally powerful need to keep his best friend in the whole world as close by as possible, so he could share with Sully his deepest wishes and needs, as they occurred to him, every single one. Rub's wishes didn't travel well. They came out best when he didn't have to raise his voice, when he was in a ditch, for instance, and Sully was there in the same ditch a few feet away and ready to receive them. He didn't like to expel wishes forcefully but rather to release them gently, allow them to locate Sully of their own impetus, on their own struggling wings. Like recently hatched birds, Rub's wishes were too new to the world and too clumsy to sustain extended flight. They liked the nest.

So far this afternoon Rub had wished that Peter would quit calling him Sancho, because he hated that name; that they could turn on the heat here in the house, which was almost as cold indoors as out, so they wouldn't have to wear gloves, which made the delicate task of pounding out the nails that much more difficult; that his wife, Bootsie, would quit stealing so much from the Woolworth's where she worked before she got caught and they both got sent to jail; that the Sans Souci, one wing of which was visible through the northeast window beyond the grove of naked trees, would hire him and Sully to be handymen at about twenty dollars an hour when the spa opened in the summer. That he could be invisible for a day, so he could sneak in and watch ole Toby Roebuck in the shower.

Sully only half listened. As always, he was amazed by the modesty of Rub's fantasies. How like him it was to bestow upon himself the gift of invisibility and then imagine it would be his for only a single day. Often there was a curious wisdom about Rub's imaginings, as if he'd learned about life that nothing ever comes to you clean but instead with caveats and provisos that could render the gifts worthless or leave you hungry for more. It was as if somewhere in the back of Rub's mind he knew that he was better off without whatever it was he wished for. Which was certainly true in the case of invisibility. In most social situations, Rub was closer to invisibility than he knew, and to disappear completely would not be in his best interest.

Though he only half listened, Sully was grateful for Rub's litany, if only to keep the Bowdon Street ghosts at arm's length. His father, full to the throat with cheap beer and moral indignation, the stench of both on his breath, seemed as if he might reel noisily through the front door once again, its frame barely wide enough to contain him in this condition. There too in the shadows Sully's mother quietly awaited him, just as she had for years awaited the religious miracle the priest kept assuring her would come if only her faith were strong enough, his advice deepening her despair even as it gave her strength to face one more homecoming. A large, content man this priest had been, almost as large as Big Jim, in fact. Large enough, Sully had thought at the time, to perhaps prevent his father's behavior if he chose to, but even more self-satisfied and inert than large. Even though Sully had been just a boy, he had understood that the priest would not help, that he was content that people's lives should be studies in hurt and fear. He seemed not in the least surprised by anything Sully's mother told him about her marriage, about what life was like in their home. The priest took none of it personally, nor did he seem at all discouraged by any sordidness. He himself had found a line of work he enjoyed, and offering spiritual counsel to the wretched was part of his job. And he seemed to understand that to wish people less wretched would be to put himself out of a job.

"It's a sin, Isobel," Sully recalled the priest telling his mother in hushed, holy tones. She had not wanted to bring Sully with her to the church, but he'd been too small to leave alone in the house. She'd placed him in a pew midway up the center aisle, then gone to meet the priest near the altar rail and the confessional. He had wanted her to enter the confessional, to make a confession, but his mother had refused, claiming she was not sorry, that she was not asking for forgiveness. She made regular confessions, but this time she was adamant.

What she had to say to the priest was not for Sully to hear, but their voices had carried in the cool, dark church, empty except for themselves. "It's a black sin to imagine that God hasn't the power to do good in His own world," the priest told her. "To God all things are possible. It is only to us that things seem difficult. Blacker sinners than your husband have been brought to Him in a moment. Remember St. Paul, struck from his horse on the road to Damascus, the road to faith."

"It's what I pray for," his mother, one eye swollen shut, had wept, and the priest had smiled down at her until she continued. "I pray that he'll be struck down," she explained. "Struck down so that he'll never get up again."

"Shush, Isobel," the priest told her. "When such terrible things leave your tongue, they fly directly to God's ear."

She had stood then and turned, peering into the darkness of the church for Sully, who had sunk down into his pew. "What difference?" she said. "God isn't listening."

His mother had never spoken to the priest again. Nor did she attend his funeral later that year. Not that her absence was missed. People came from all over the state to both the viewing and the Requiem Mass. Sully's father had gone and taken his sons with him. Sully could still remember how they'd dressed up for the occasion, his father and brother in dark, ill-fitting suits, himself in a white shirt that was too small for him, the collar so tight at the neck that his cheeks and forehead pulsed with warmth. The viewing was held not in a funeral home but rather at the rectory, and the line of the faithful come to pay respects extended down the steps and around the corner and up the street all the way to the church.

The priest had choked to death on a bone. Had anyone been with him, he might have been saved, but he dined alone in the huge rectory dining room which three days later held his coffin. By the time his housekeeper, in the next room, had heard him thrashing in his chair it was too late. By the time she came to his aid, his eyes had already bugged out in stark terror, as if he'd been forced to bear witness to something so ugly that his reason had come unhinged and he had stopped breathing. So, almost, had the housekeeper, so terrifying was the sight.

One must assume that the mortician, a member of the parish, had done his best, but the results were shockingly inadequate, for despite all efforts the dead priest's expression retained much of the horror present when he was first discovered by the housekeeper. And so many of the faithful were given quite a turn when they saw the priest for the final time in his rich casket. The mortician had worked feverishly on the bugged eyes and contorted features and had managed to mute the expression of abject terror, but the priest still looked anything but confident about meeting his maker, and those who had for years followed his spiritual guidance did not stay long in his presence. The line past the casket moved swiftly, a bottle-neck forming only once, when Sully's father held things up by kneeling to say a prayer, though something about his posture suggested he might be whispering advice to an old friend. For the rest of the mourners, a single stunned glance was sufficient to send them packing into the next room.

Only later, when those who had been at the front of the line compared nervous notes with those who had been nearer the rear, did it become clear that during the viewing, the dead man's mouth had gradually opened. At first his lips had been clamped tight, forming a white crease, but two hours later, when the last of the faithful had been led, like the blind, out of the dark rectory and into the afternoon sunlight, the mortician had had to go back to work, for the priest's mouth had opened wide and the last unnerved mourners recalled vividly that the dead man had appeared to be begging them to reach into his throat and remove the bone that had choked him to death two days before.

But what Sully recollected more vividly than the appearance of the dead priest was his own father. Even as a boy, Sully had understood about his father's ingratiating charm, even about the way it worked. His father was the sort of man people hated to see coming. If they noticed him before he saw them, they'd turn away and their heads would come together to plot escape. Perhaps they'd seen him drunk and belligerent the night before, or maybe he'd actually been in a fight and been thrown out of a bar and they'd tried to help him off the sidewalk, and maybe he'd looked up at them then, bloody-chinned and bleary-eyed, and told them right where they could stuff it. Or maybe they'd just heard a grim story about him. Big Jim had a reputation as a hard man in his own home, this being the euphemism for wife beaters at the time. At any rate, it was frequently within the social context of some prejudice against him that Sully's father deftly charmed his way into acceptance. Before he was finished, the very people who'd pretended not to see him when he entered the room were slapping him on the back, doubting the truth of the tale they'd heard about him or even the evidence of their own senses, the ones who'd seen his face turn black with rage and red with his own blood. Now they hated to see him go, he was such a good fellow, and their only reservations were that he was a trifle crude and laughed a little too loud.

The day of the viewing, Sully's father was the only one in the crowded rectory who appeared unfazed by the dead priest's ghastly appearance, as if, to Big Jim, the priest had always looked this way. After holding up the line so he could pretend to say a prayer and then making his sons do the same at the ornate kneeler, he'd introduced himself and the two boys to the bishop, who had come up from Albany to say tomorrow's high requiem Mass. Sully noticed that several of the parishioners had kissed the bishop's ring and was grateful when neither he nor his brother nor his father was required to do so. Indeed, the robed man appeared to take in Sully's father whole, in a single glance, and he stared a hole right through him.

Before leaving the rectory, Big Jim told Sully and his brother to wait where they were, he'd be back in a minute. In the hallway they saw him lean toward the old woman who had been the dead priest's housekeeper and ask her something. Flustered, she pointed down the hall. Sully and his brother watched their father start out in the direction the old woman pointed, then dart left unexpectedly and head up the big staircase that led to the rectory's upper rooms. Sully's brother grinned at him knowingly.

When their father did not return for what seemed a long time, Sully, nervous, told his brother he had to go. "Bad," he added, so there'd be no mistake. If it was okay for his father to pee in the dead priest's house, maybe it would be okay if he did too. He needed to do it, in any case.

Since there was no one to tell them they shouldn't—indeed, no one seemed to notice—they followed their father upstairs. The upper story of the rectory contained five rooms so lavishly furnished that Sully and his brother were stunned, having never seen anything like it.

They found their father in the priest's study, just standing in the middle of the book-lined room, taking it all in—the plush leather sofa, the silver-framed pictures hanging from pristine white walls, the huge oak rolltop desk with its brass lamp, the gigantic free-standing globe, the leather-bound books from floor to ceiling, and pervading the room the smells of tobacco and what Sully would later identify as cologne and liqueurs. On the desk's blotter there lay a gold pen and pencil set, along with a sleek gold letter opener.

Their father seemed neither surprised nor angry to see them, despite the fact that on other occasions he'd been known to strap them for not obeying his orders to stay put. "Not a bad racket, huh?" he said with a sweeping gesture that included not just the priest's study but the surrounding rooms upstairs and down. "Those nickels and dimes in the collection plate add up, don't they? All those collections, seven days a week, three on Sundays. You can do all right. See all this? This is what they call a vow of poverty. I bet the bastard was as chaste as he was poor too, what do you think?"

Sully didn't know what the word chaste meant, but he knew he had to go to the bathroom. "In there," his father pointed. "It don't look like one, but that's what it is just the same."

Truly, had it not been for the commode, Sully would not have recognized it for a bathroom. It was bigger than his and his brother's bedroom. There was a sofa along one wall, velvet drapes concealing the tub and shower. The atmosphere was foul though, thanks to Big Jim's visit. Sully himself finished his own business quickly and guiltily, washing his hands and drying them on his pants to avoid soiling the priest's thick purple towels. "Some shitter, huh?" his father said when Sully emerged, and then they waited for Sully's brother to go too, though the boy said he didn't have to. "Try," Sully's father insisted. "You'll be able to squeeze something out."

They stopped at a bar on the way home so Sully's father could describe the rectory for the bartender. He remembered all the details Sully'd missed, and the more beer his father drank, the more vivid and angry his memory became. "You should see the shitter," he told the man behind the bar, who, Sully could tell, was already tired of hearing about the rectory. "It's bigger than your goddamn house."

"You never even seen my house, Sully," the man said.

"Yeah?" Sully's father said. "Well, you never saw that shitter either, because you wouldn't believe it. Not only that. You shoulda seen the getup the bishop was wearing. Cost more than all your clothes put together, just that one robe. All your clothes and your wife's put together, I bet, and we're just talking about what he had on."

"I ain't even married, Sully," the man said.

"Lucky you," his father said. "This religion is some goddamn racket.

We should all drop what we're doing and start wearing gold crosses and passing collection plates."

The bartender had gone pale. "How about a little respect? It's a dead priest you're talking about. The guy just died. God's priest he was, Sully."

"You oughta see the casket he's gonna be buried in," Sully's father went on, undeterred. "I bet it cost more than this whole bar."

"Why don't you go home, Sully," the bartender said.

"Why don't you go fuck a rock, George, you dumb Pollack ass-kisser," Sully's father replied.

They'd walked the rest of the way home then, Sully's father getting angrier every step of the way, the beer churning in him, souring his vision. "You see the way that asshole bishop looked at me?" he nudged Sully's brother, Patrick.

"I don't think he liked you, Pop," Patrick admitted.

"You figure out why?"

Patrick wanted to know why.

" 'Cause I wouldn't kiss his ring, is why," their father explained proudly. "You see that big shiny ring he had on? You're supposed to kiss it, because he's the bishop and you're nobody. But he'd kiss my ass before I'd kiss his ring, and he knew it, too. All those bastards can go straight to hell, is what I say."

"Me too," Patrick agreed, and to prove he shared their father's contempt, he took from his jacket pocket the sleek gold letter opener he'd clipped from the priest's study.

Seeing this, their father's rage disappeared, and he howled appreciatively, slapping Patrick on the back. "Why the hell not?" he wanted to know. "He won't be needing it anymore, will he? The bastard's opened his last letter."

It was years later, long after his mother's death, that Sully remembered what she'd said to the priest that afternoon in the dark church, how she'd wept and confessed her secret shame, that she'd prayed every day for her own husband to be struck down. How old had he been when he realized that his mother's prayer had been answered, or half answered? She'd prayed for Sully's father to be struck down—emphatically, decisively, unambiguously—so there would be no question about the message. The priest who reminded her of Paul's conversion needn't have. A direct hit with a lightning bolt, preferably to the center of the forehead, was precisely the sort of message she'd hoped God would deliver. She knew her husband, and she knew, even if God didn't, that no glancing blow would suffice. But instead of sending a divine lightning bolt, God had sent an endless progression of ham-fisted bartenders and bouncers and cops to show her husband the way, as if, even in His infinite wisdom, He wasn't quite savvy enough to realize that Big Jim Sullivan had a head of pure stone and that, in the end, all those bartenders and bouncers and cops would do was scrape their knuckles on such a skull. It was only the man's intoxication that allowed them to do what little damage they did. They waited until he was stinking drunk before tossing him out into the rainy gutter, calling instructions after him. "Go home, Sully," they advised. Advice he always followed with fists clenched.

The night he and his sons went to the rectory, he'd finally delivered them back home in the early evening and then gone back out again, leaving the house quiet. In bed, in the dark of their room, the boys had discussed the day's events until Sully's brother, Patrick, fell asleep, still fingering the gold-plated letter opener he'd stolen from the rectory. Sully himself had lain awake, cruelly ashamed that he himself had stolen nothing, for of course he saw the wisdom of his father's logic. The rich priest wasn't going to need any of his wealth anymore, and what's more, he didn't have any children of his own to inherit his possessions. Sully thought he would have liked to have the big globe, the one that stood as tall as he was, with its vast blue oceans and tall mountains jutting out in relief, all contained inside the sickle of gleaming brass. He could see himself standing next to it, poring over the globe for hours, spinning it, even as the world it represented spun through space, and he would know that this world was his. He'd finally fallen asleep thinking about it, and somewhere in the middle of the night his father had come back home again, this time drunk beyond redemption, and he'd shaken Sully awake in his bed. Had the boy's last happy waking thought been etched there on his sleeping face for his father to read in the dark? Was that why Big Jim had awakened him? Impossible, but that was the impression Sully had when his father, his breath boozy and sour, issued him a warning. "Don't think you're going to grow up and be somebody, 'cause you're not. So you can get *that* shit right out of your head."

The next morning, the bright morning sun streaming in the bedroom window, Sully saw that his father was right. Swiping a slender, gold-plated letter opener from a dead priest was something a person could do. But you couldn't steal the whole world.

■ ■ ■

They finished late that afternoon, just about the time Peter returned. Rub didn't look too happy to see Peter until he saw the six-pack of Genesee. "Howdy, Sancho," Peter said, extending the beer. Rub frowned at the nickname but expertly twisted a can free of its plastic ring.

Sully took one too, opened the passenger side door and sat down, flexing his knee, flinching as he did so. "Your timing's getting better," he observed, taking a swig of beer. "We only finished up about thirty seconds ago."

"I know," Peter said, setting the other three beers on the hood of the El Camino. "I drove by and you weren't done yet, so I drove around the block."

Rub looked like he believed this.

"Besides," Peter said. "I already earned *my* money this morning."

"When?" Rub wanted to know. He remembered the morning clearly, and what he remembered was that he'd worked alone in the cold while Peter went off without permission and spent the morning in Miles Anderson's house, where it was warm. All he'd done over there was talk, too. He hadn't done any work at all.

"You'll have to tell me all about it," Sully said. "I take it we haven't been fired?"

"I assured him the house was getting our full attention. Not an easy point to demonstrate in your absence. I told him I'd see the job through to conclusion myself. He likes the idea of employing junior faculty."

Sully crushed his beer can, tossed it onto the floor of the truck. "You think we'll be done by the middle of January?"

Peter crushed his own, tossed it onto the floor of the El Camino. "I've pretty much made up my mind to stick around."

Sully nodded. "I'd heard a rumor you might. You told your mother yet?"

"Last night."

"Which is why she's all upset today?"

"Among other reasons."

"She get around to blaming me yet?"

Peter was grinning now. "She got around to it right away."

"Good. Maybe that'll give you some breathing room." When Peter had no response, Sully decided to ask, "Is she all right?"

"Who?" Peter frowned.

"Your mother. The person we're talking about."

Peter thought about it. "Well . . ." he said.

"Fine," Sully told him. "Be that way."

"All right," Peter agreed, maddeningly.

"I tell you what," Sully said to Peter, grateful, in truth, not to know more than Peter wanted to tell him. "You help me run this load of hardwood out to Carl's camp and I'll introduce you to the prettiest girl in Bath."

Rub perked up, recognizing the allusion to Toby Roebuck. "Can I go?"

"No," Sully said. "You're married. It wouldn't be good for you."

"He's married too," Rub pointed out, indicating Peter.

"Not happily though, like you," Sully pointed out.

Rub frowned. "I never said I was happy."

"I know," Sully conceded. "It was Bootsie who told me you were. You better had be, was what she actually said."

"If she looked like ole Toby, I'd be happy," he said.

"Well," Sully said. "Go on home before Bootsie notices you aren't there and blames me. I've got too many women mad at me already."

Rub balked at being dismissed in this fashion. The last thing he wanted to do was go home to Bootsie, especially when seeing her meant missing Carl's wife. Even more important, three Genesee's were still sitting on the hood of the El Camino. Rub had been doing the math in his head, and according to his calculations, one of the three remaining cans of beer would find its way into his hand if he could just keep from being sent away until either Peter or Sully reached for a second beer. It'd been a good afternoon with Sully, just the two of them again, like old times, before he had to start sharing his best friend. And now here he was, already having to share all over again. The unfairness of it was just about bearable if he didn't get cheated out of the can of beer too. "Could I have one more of those?" he said.

"What're you asking me for?" Sully said.

Because Rub didn't want to ask Peter, was the answer, of course, though he saw Peter pull a can from the plastic ring. "You're the one that's the boss, not him," Rub said, his purpose, as always, a simple indication of loyalty to Sully, which he would have liked, just once, to be returned.

"But I didn't buy the beer," Sully said. "And besides, you never do as I say anyhow. You won't even go home when I tell you."

"Here, Sancho," Peter said, tossing Rub the can of beer.

Rub caught the can at the same instant he caught the nickname he hated, and in that instant the unfairness and terrible disappointment of life was in his throat and making it so full that he couldn't imagine drinking the very beer he'd not wanted to be cheated out of just a few seconds before. Catching the can of beer cleanly with one hand, he turned and heaved it at Sully's house, where it found a second story window, which exploded upon impact. Inside, Rasputin barked, then was still. "I quit," Rub said, and those two words were all that he could have gotten out. If ole Toby Roebuck had been there and offered to sit on his face in return for a few words of elaboration, he'd have been unable to deliver. Not if she was naked and offering handfuls of hundred-dollar bills. The two words he'd gotten out—"I quit"—contained his soul, and having said them he turned his back on all that he'd quit and started for home, on foot.

"Hey," Sully called after him, half ashamed and half astonished that his customary ragging had produced these unexpected results. "Don't be that way."

Rub continued walking, a study in dejected defiance. At that moment, to Sully at least, he looked oddly like a little boy. The picture couldn't have been more complete had he been dragging a baseball bat behind him.

"Rub," Sully called. "Hey."

Peter crushed his empty beer can and tossed it into the El Camino's front seat.

"Shit," Sully said, finally glancing at his son and finding in Peter's expression the disapproval he might have predicted. "Now you're mad at me too, right?"

"Why do you have to be so mean to him?"

In fact, Sully didn't know. He wasn't even sure he *had* been mean. It had always been his impression that Rub enjoyed getting ragged. It had always been Sully's position that people who hung around with him knew they were going to get ragged.

"*You* stand about two feet away from him and listen to him talk nonstop for about five hours, we'll see if you feel mean or not," Sully said, aware, even as he offered this justification, that it was invalid. For one thing, Peter did stand next to and work with Rub every morning while Sully was at Hattie's. For another, Rub's chatter had nothing to do with what had just taken place. In truth, Sully'd always found Rub's chatter soothing, like a radio station playing the sort of music you didn't feel obliged to listen to. "Shit," he said again. "Give me one of those."

When Peter handed him one of the last two beers, Sully heaved it at the house also. Instead of finding the window he'd aimed at, Sully's beer can hit the eave and dropped noiselessly to the frozen ground below, where it ruptured and sprayed foam into the air like a lawn sprinkler.

Sully and Peter watched the can until it stopped. "See if I buy another six-pack of beer," Peter said.

They caught up to Rub at the Main Street intersection, in front of Miles Anderson's house. Rub was aware that they were creeping along behind him—he could hear hardwood bouncing in the bed of the truck, the sound of the tires on the pavement mere inches behind him—but he refused to look back or even to hurry across the intersection. They could run over him if they wanted to. Finish him off. He wisht they would, in fact. What he feared worse than death beneath the pickup's wheels was that Sully was going to get up real close and blow the horn.

When Rub got to the curb, he was relieved, assuming he'd be safe on the sidewalk, but right behind him he heard the truck bump up over the curb, still inching along at the pace he himself was setting. He didn't dare look around, afraid of what he'd find if he did and unwilling to surrender the last remnants of his dignity by exhibiting curiosity or alarm. Also, to turn and face the vehicle, it would be necessary for Rub to reveal, to both Sully and Peter, that he was crying, crying like the baby that Sully would surely accuse him of being. Either that or he'd ask Rub if he couldn't take a joke, and that would make him feel even worse, because maybe he wasn't sure exactly what he was feeling or why he was feeling it, but Rub was sure it was no joke.

And so the widows who lived along the two-block residential stretch of Upper Main Street and who happened to be looking out their front windows this late afternoon were treated to a strange sight. Mrs. Gruber, for instance, who spent a good deal of her lonely time gazing into the comforting, familiar street from between half-closed blinds, blinked twice to make sure she wasn't asleep or hallucinating. Across the street a pickup truck was driving on the sidewalk, two of its wheels on the concrete, the other two on her neighbors' terraces. A few short paces in front of the truck, a short, almost dwarflike man, looking maniacally determined, bent forward into the teeth of the wind which had been making the ancient elms moan all afternoon. Because he was leaning forward into this wind and appeared to take no notice of the pickup truck that was inching along behind him on the sidewalk, Mrs. Gruber concluded at first that the dwarflike man must be yoked to the truck with some sort of invisible tether, for he appeared to be pulling the truck up the street. Mrs. Gruber considered the logic of this and decided she must be mistaken. The truck could not be on the sidewalk. After all, why would a man pull a truck over a bumpy sidewalk when he could just pull it up the smooth blacktop street? The truck, therefore, was not on the sidewalk but merely appeared to be.

Mrs. Gruber blinked again and prepared to see something truer to reality. But the truck *was* on the sidewalk. She could tell by the fact that it passed behind, not in front of, the elms. So did the dwarflike man who was towing it. Since the telephone was right there, she picked it up and dialed Miss Beryl. In a minute both man and truck would pass directly in front of her friend's house, and Miss Beryl would have a better view.

"Dad," said Peter in the front seat of the truck. "Dad."

Sully paid him no attention. He was hunched forward over the steering wheel, concentrating on the delicate task of keeping the truck right behind Rub while at the same time avoiding obstacles. In places where hedges grew close to the sidewalk it was a very slender passage, and the truck brushed the hedges noisily on the left even as it climbed up and over the huge, spreading roots of the elms on the right. "Look at him," Sully said, indicating Rub, who still refused to acknowledge their presence. "Have you ever seen anybody that stubborn?"

"Yes," Peter said. "I have."

Sully ignored this. "Look at him," he repeated, his voice full of wonder. He tooted the horn. Rub jumped but did not turn around. "Amazing," Sully said.

"Here's a driveway," Peter pointed. "Get back on the street."

"Amazing," Sully said again. "What would you do if you were him?"

"Jesus," Peter said. Sully had driven past the driveway, had clearly not even considered ending this insanity.

"He can't figure it out," Sully marveled. "All he's got to do is step behind one of those trees and we're fucked."

"Oh, I'd have to say we're fucked anyhow," Peter observed. "You see what's coming up the street?"

"No, what?" Sully said, slowing down for another narrow passage. The right front wheel encountered the base of one of the street's oldest elms, its giant roots twisted obscenely above ground. The truck strained to climb, got partway, then rolled back. "Shit," Sully said, giving the engine a little more gas with his right foot, keeping the clutch engaged with his left, as he craned and peered past Peter. "I can't see. Am I going to make it?"

"I don't think so," Peter said, though he was not checking for clearance. What had his attention was the police cruiser he'd seen coming toward them.

"I think I can," Sully said calmly, as if the question were purely academic. He let up on the clutch and again the truck climbed and tilted.

Gaining the top of the gnarled root, the truck slid quickly over, scraping its underbelly before Sully could prevent it.

The police cruiser had pulled over to the curb, and Officer Raymer got out, looking confused and angry. "Hey!" he called. "You're on the sidewalk!"

Sully noticed the policeman for the first time and put his foot on the brake. "Roll your window down a second," he told Peter. When Peter did as he was told, Sully leaned across him and called over to the policeman, "Fuck off!"

Then he took his foot off the brake and the truck lurched forward again, its back wheel climbing the side of the elm and banging down again, its load of hardwood clattering fearfully.

Being told to fuck off by Sully seemed to clarify Officer Raymer's thinking, because he got back into the cruiser, did a screeching three-point turn, roared back in the direction he'd come and pulled into a driveway between Rub and the pickup. Sully saw this strategy too late to prevent it.

Had the policeman stayed in the car, he'd have been fine. But he made the mistake of getting out again and grinning triumphantly at Sully, who, when he saw this, saw too that he was not through with his stupid streak. I'm about to fuck up, he thought clearly, and his next thought was, but I don't have to. This was followed closely by a third thought, the last of this familiar sequence, which was, but I'm going to anyway. And, as always, this third thought was oddly liberating, though Sully knew from experience that the sensation, however pleasurable, would be short-lived. He was about to harm himself. There could be no doubt of this. But at such moments of liberation, the clear knowledge that he was about to do himself in coexisted with the exhilarating, if entirely false, sense that he was about to reshape, through the force of his own will, his reality. At this moment reality was a police cruiser in his way and a grinning cop with a grudge and the upper hand, but what Sully saw in his mind's eye was the ability to remove these. He wasn't sure he could remove the cruiser or the cop exactly, but he was certain he could remove the cop's grin, and that was a beginning. It was more than a beginning, in fact, for the moment he'd seen that grin, thought became secondary to some deeper instinct. If Ruth had seen him, she'd have seen what she termed "the old Sully," and in fact he half wished that Ruth were here to witness the old Sully's triumphant return. He also thought of his father with uncharacteristic fondness, understanding that this was the precise moment his father always drank toward, the exquisite moment when both the obstacle and the means of its removal came into clear focus. In his mind's eye Sully could see the exact spot where the pickup's massive bumper would encounter the side of the parked police cruiser, saw it jolt and shudder, saw the side of the car crumple and finally cave in as the pickup pushed it down the sidewalk until it slid off to one side on the terrace.

But first, it was only fair to issue a warning. Sully put the truck into park, rolled down the window and poked his head out. His voice, as always at such times, was calm. A smarter cop would have heard in it a warning, but there was no smarter cop around. "That's not a good place to park," Sully said. "I'd move if I were you."

"You get on out now, Sully," Officer Raymer said. "Fun's over. I'm going to have to put you under—"

Sully, having rolled up the window again, didn't hear the rest. "Wrong, asshole," he said. "The fun's just beginning."

"Dad—" Peter said. He, at least, had heard the warning.

In fact, Sully had nearly forgotten his son was present. "This is the point where people usually get out of the truck," he told Peter.

"Dad—" Peter began.

"Okay," Sully said, shifting back into drive. "Suit yourself."

When the policeman heard the truck go from park to drive and saw it grunt forward, his triumphant grin disappeared, just as Sully had seen it disappear in his mind's eye. Now it was his turn to grin. "Yeah, you prick," he said under his breath, nodding at the policeman through the windshield. "You just figured this out, didn't you."

"Dad—" Peter said, pushing both legs straight out in front of him, as if onto an imaginary passenger side brake. "Jesus."

For he'd seen Officer Raymer take the revolver out of its holster and point it, two handed, in their direction. Sully saw it too, though he didn't care. "He'll never shoot," he assured Peter, just a split second before the policeman fired.

A warning shot was what Officer Raymer had in mind when the truck kept coming. He fired over the cab so there could be no mistake. The explosion ripped through the quiet street, however, like thunder, reverberating so loudly that Officer Raymer was not sure whether or not he heard a distant tinkling of glass up the street. When the echoes died, he was still listening in the hope of hearing that tinkling sound again. Probably wind chimes, he told himself. Anyhow, the truck had stopped.

Inside, Sully looked over at his son, who was shielding his face with his elbow, as if against the glare of the sun. The concussion had been so loud that it had penetrated Sully's furious trance. "Did he actually shoot?" Sully asked Peter, wanting to be sure of his facts before proceeding.

"I believe that *was* a gunshot, yes," Peter said. "I vote we surrender. If I have a vote."

"That's goddamn irresponsible," Sully said, glaring at the policeman. He rolled down the window again. "You stupid prick," he called. Then, to Peter, "Do you believe that?"

"Dad—" Peter began again, but Sully had already gotten out of the truck and was limping over to the policeman, who was looking at the revolver in his hand as if he were surprised to discover it there. Or as if, now that he knew it would fire when he pulled the trigger, he'd discovered its uselessness. Holding it didn't even slow the advance of the man coming toward him. He might as well have been holding his dick, just as Sully always accused him of doing. Never, Peter thought, had a man looked so helpless. Peter rolled down his own window and called out to his father. "Dad—"

He said it just as his father delivered a short right that caught the policeman flush on the nose. Officer Raymer didn't even raise an arm to block the blow. His head went backward and returned red, his hat landing topside down on the roof of the cruiser. Then his knees gave and he slumped gracefully against the side of the car. Sully stood over the man for a second, then looked back at Peter, whose head was still out the window. "What?" Sully said.

Peter shook his head, rolled the window back up.

Sully opened the cruiser's door then and turned the key in the ignition to off. The car shuddered and was still. Then Sully returned to the truck and got back in. "There," he said. "Where'd Rub go?" he wondered, scanning the street. Rub was gone.

Peter was staring at his father.

"What?" Sully asked again.

Peter shook his head in disbelief. "Nothing," he said, throwing up his hands.

"Good," Sully said. "For a minute there, I thought you were going to be critical."

"You were right about one thing," Peter said as they passed the IGA and through the intersection, heading out of town toward the lake in pursuit of Toby Roebuck's Bronco. "She's the prettiest woman in Bath."

They'd pulled up in front of Tip Top Construction just as Toby was locking the street door. She hadn't the slightest idea where her husband was, but she was willing to show them where the camp was located so they could unload the wood. "Won't your husband be suspicious if you come home late?" Sully'd asked, flirtatious in such safe circumstances.

"I'll just tell him I was with you," she replied, "since that's always such a chaste experience. Who's this?"

Sully introduced Peter, who leaned across the front seat to shake her hand. Sully noticed the ease of his son's gesture, the way Peter was able to convey through it his admiration of Toby Roebuck's beauty without suggesting he was in awe of it, and Sully wondered where he'd learned such easy confidence. Not from Ralph, certainly. Nor even himself.

"Your son, huh?" Toby had observed. "I guess that means there was a time when you weren't such a chaste experience."

"I wouldn't be now if I had more energy," Sully assured her, adding, "Let's hit the road, dolly, before the cops find me by accident and my son has to do this whole job by himself."

She looked at him quizzically.

"You know an Officer Raymer?"

She made a face. "He's the one they're trying to fire, right?"

"He and I just had a little difference of opinion," Sully said. "He should be just about coming to."

Toby studied first Sully, then Peter, who nodded at her ruefully that this was true. "Sully, Sully, Sully," she observed.

And so now they were racing through the dusk toward the lake where the Roebucks' camp was located, their load of hardwood rattling so noisily in the back that they practically had to shout to be heard above the racket.

"She's one of the nicest, too," Sully observed in response to Peter's observation about Toby's being the prettiest woman in Bath. "Her husband treats her like shit, of course. He's given her the clap three times this year. Can you imagine doing that to a girl like her?"

Peter didn't answer the question right away, perhaps because he was trying to interpret it. After a moment Sully noticed his son was grinning at him in the near dark. "What?" he said.

"How long have you had this crush on her?"

Sully frowned at him. "She's a little young for me."

"That's not what I asked," Peter pointed out, still grinning at him slyly.

"I just hate to see such a nice girl treated like that, is all," he explained.

Again Peter delayed answering for a meaningful beat, then finally said, "Okay."

"You don't believe me, wise ass?"

"Whatever you say," Peter agreed, looking ahead at the Bronco's taillights. "You'd probably have better luck if you thought of her as a woman. Women don't like to be referred to as 'girls' anymore."

"They don't?"

"Nope."

"You learn that at the university?"

"Among other things."

"And now you know all the right things to say?"

"Nope," he said. "Just some of the wrong ones."

"What happened to the shy kid you used to be?"

"I don't know. Why?"

"I liked him."

"Really?" Peter said. "You should have said something."

The Roebucks' camp was located on the far end of the lake, accessible via a rutted, unpaved road that wound in and out of the trees along the water's edge. The water was a sheet of glass reflecting the quarter moon. They'd left all the other camps behind when Toby finally pulled off the road and down a steep embankment, parking on a narrow ledge just wide enough for one car. Sully pulled in behind her diagonally and turned off the engine, then the headlights, which illuminated the large roof of the camp still farther down the bank. When they got out, they could hear the waves lapping against the shore below.

"Nice hideout, sweetheart," Peter said, doing Humphrey Bogart. "The cops'll never find us here."

"They're not after *you*," Sully pointed out.

"With my luck I'll be nabbed as your accomplice."

"I'll tell them you were no help," Sully said. "As usual."

"Don Sullivan, the last of the tough guys," Toby Roebuck said, her voice near in the dark. Also her perfume, which mingled with the crisp air off the lake below, creating an intoxicating mixture of damp earth and leaves and water and girl. Not woman, in Sully's opinion. Girl. "I better have the goddamn key," she said. They could hear her rummaging through her purse.

"We could probably get in anyhow," Sully said, getting out.

"Right," Toby snorted. "I heard all about you and your crowbar. There!" she held up the key triumphantly, a glint of silver in the moonlight. "Watch the steps."

"Okay," Sully said. "What steps?"

She took his hand then, placing it on a railing he hadn't noticed. "Four, then level, then three more," she said, leading the way, her hand on his elbow now in much the same fashion, he noted, to his embarrassment, that he led old Hattie from the apartment into the diner each morning.

"Ouch," he said, finding a patch of unlevel ground where his ankle turned, shooting pain from his knee to his groin.

"Why don't you wait here," she suggested. "Let me go unlock and turn the kitchen light on."

As she said this, a light *came* on, not from below and ahead, but rather from above and behind. There was now enough light for Sully to see that Peter was no longer with them. His voice came to them from above, where they'd left the vehicles. "That help?"

"Hey," Toby said. "A Sullivan with a brain." In truth, the headlights helped only marginally, illuminating the trees and the camp's roof but not the path. "Wait, okay?" she whispered.

Sully decided he would. A moment later Peter joined him, watching dubiously as Sully flexed his knee.

"You okay?"

"Fine," Sully said. "Terrific."

"Listen," Peter said, his voice low and confidential. "Let me do the unloading."

"I'm fine," Sully insisted. "I'll go slow."

Several lights came on inside the camp and they could see Toby Roebuck moving swiftly from room to room, her hair bouncing.

"Why not just let me?" Peter said.

"Because."

"Oh," Peter said. "Well. As long as you have a reason."

"Look," Sully said. "When I can't work any more, I'll quit, okay. Is that all right with you?"

"Anything you say, boss."

Neither said anything for a moment then, and there was just the sound of the wind high in the trees and the tiny waves lapping against the shore and Toby Roebuck returning through the camp, all of its windows now streaming yellow and illuminating the treacherous footing between where they stood and the camp's back porch.

"Well, I guess it's true," Peter observed. "Life is full of surprises. Who'd have thought you and I would ever argue over a woman?"

Sully stared at his son, whose eyes gleamed in the darkness like a cat's. "Is *that* what you think we're doing?"

Toby bounced back out onto the porch then and peered up the embankment toward her two male companions, who remained invisible in the dark midground between the light from above and that from below. She could see neither of them, though when Peter spoke, his voice was close enough to touch. "That's what I think we're doing," she heard him say.

The job took about an hour, and in the end Sully let Peter and Toby Roebuck do most of the hauling up and down the bank. Even with the camp's back door light on, the slope remained dark, the footing treacherous, and so Sully stayed with the truck, pulling the now tangled boards free and leaning them against the tailgate so Toby and his son could grab a convenient armful. Watching them work together, he decided that Peter had been right. They *were* arguing about a woman. He also had to admit that he was jealous of his son's two good legs. Of course, Peter himself had to be a good ten years older than Toby Roebuck, and he too seemed slightly in awe of her energy going up and down the bank with an armful of hardwood. Peter went slower, carrying a far larger load over his shoulder.

They'd decided the best place to stack the wood was on the screened-in porch that wrapped around the camp, and once when Toby, who was making two bouncing trips to Peter's one, caught up with him there on the porch, they took a short break. Sully could hear their voices borne up from the lake on the frigid wind, and once he heard Toby Roebuck laugh, a sound that made him wish Rub had come along. Rub would have been full of angry wishes. He'd have wanted to know how come guys like Peter and Carl had all the luck with women while they never had any. He'd have wished all this running up and down the hill would make ole Toby hot and sweaty so she'd take off her jacket and let them watch her tits jiggle. When Sully pointed out it was December and about ten degrees above zero, Rub would just wish it was summer. Rub's wishes, when you totaled them up, meant simply that he'd have preferred a different sort of world, one where he got his share—of money, pussy, food, warmth, ease. Sully's job, as he perceived it, was to defend the world they were stuck with, a task made infinitely easier by Rub's presence.

In his absence, Sully, sitting on the tailgate of the pickup waiting for his son and the prettiest girl in Bath to climb the bank for the last few armloads of wood, found himself alone with a few wishes of his own. He didn't waste much time on the big ones—that he was younger, less stubborn, more flexible, less in debt, more careful. He concentrated instead on the more specific and immediate things that had at one time been within the sphere of his influence to effect, or, failing that, were statistically probable. He wished he hadn't tried to climb down the bank in the dark, causing his knee to scream at him now in protest. He wished that he and Ruth weren't on the outs, because he would have enjoyed her company tonight, just as he always did after he'd done something foolish, as if she possessed the power of absolution. She'd tell him there was a new Sully, not just the old one, and he'd be free to choose between believing and resenting her. He also wished that he hadn't been quite so mean to Rub, whom he'd now have to cajole into coming back to work, that he hadn't assaulted a policeman in broad daylight on Main Street, that it would start snowing so he could make some money, that the bitter wind would stop blowing long enough for him to light a cigarette. Since a couple of these were in the nature of specific regrets of the sort he disliked indulging, he decided he'd write them all off as bad debts if he could just get a cigarette lit. And this was what he was attempting to do when a set of headlights cut through the trees some distance away and he became aware of the sound of a small car engine whining closer, which could mean only one thing. In another minute Carl Roebuck's Camaro careened into view and skidded to a halt about a foot from where Sully sat on the tailgate.

"Don Sullivan," Carl said, getting out. Even in the dark Sully could see he was grinning. "Fugitive."

"I'm not running, I'm working," Sully explained, flicking the useless match away. "If you'd ever worked a day in your life you'd know the difference."

"How come every time I see you, you're sitting on that tailgate and claiming to be working?" Carl said, pulling out his lighter and cupping his hand around it.

Sully's cigarette caught just as the wind blew out the flame. "I'm too tired to explain."

"Well," Carl said, locating Sully's cigarettes in his shirt pocket and extracting one from the pack, "I have a feeling you're going to get a few days off at county expense."

"Nah." Sully exhaled through his nose. "I've got the best one-legged Jewish lawyer in Bath."

"That reminds me," Carl said, inhaling his own cigarette rapturously. "Wirf said to give you this."

"This" was a cocktail napkin. Sully unfolded and read the message Wirf had scrawled there by the light of Carl's left head lamp. "Verily," the note said, "this Time Thou Art Truly and Forever Fucked."

Sully wadded up the napkin and gave it a toss. "He puts up a smooth defense, doesn't he?"

"I'd like to see him on the Supreme Court. Legal opinions on cocktail napkins. What the hell ever possessed you to punch a cop?"

"It seemed like a hell of a fine idea at the time." Sully sighed, then provided a short version of what had happened.

Carl was skeptical. "He drew his gun on you?"

"Pointed it at me too, the prick."

"I don't think anybody'd believe that unless you had a witness."

"If there weren't any witnesses, then I didn't punch him," Sully said. "My son was there, though."

"That's something, I suppose," Carl said, "though it'd be better to have the sort of witness who wouldn't lie to save you."

"I don't think he would, actually," Sully admitted.

"An honorable man, huh?"

"I don't know about that," Sully said. "I just don't think he likes me well enough to lie for me."

Carl took a thoughtful drag on his cigarette. "You know why this is happening, don't you?"

It occurred to Sully when Carl said this that Carl was seriously pissed. Which meant they were on the verge of a real argument. After the last one, Sully hadn't spoken to him for four months. "Because I'm so lucky?"

"Bullshit," Carl said. "You know why these things keep happening to you. It's because you have to rag everybody twenty-four hours a day. It's because you never, *ever* fucking let up."

"Oh," Sully said. "That's why."

"Why were you driving up the sidewalk, Sully?" Carl persisted. "You ragged Rub until even he couldn't stand it any more, and you still couldn't let it alone. You had to make it worse. You had to completely humiliate that poor simple little fuck."

"I don't believe I'm hearing this from you," Sully said. "When have you ever done anything but insult him?"

"There's a difference, Sully," Carl said without the slightest hint of hypocrisy.

"What difference is that, Carl?" Sully said, flicking the remains of his cigarette. "Tell me why your ragging is okay and mine isn't, because I want to hear this."

"Because he's not in love with me," Carl said.

"Get the fuck away," Sully said, genuinely furious now, sliding off the tailgate. "He's no more queer than you."

"I know it," Carl said. "But he'd blow you on the four corners at high noon if you asked him to, and *you* know that, Sully."

In fact, Sully did know it, or knew the power of Rub's devotion. It was this knowledge, in fact, that had caused him to follow Rub up the sidewalk, hoping to joke him back into their friendship, something he'd always been able to do in the past. It had not been, as Carl had suggested, a desire to humiliate him further. Still, Sully had to admit, a simple apology would have done the trick. "I'll make it up to him," he heard himself say weakly.

"How?" Carl wanted to know. "You'll buy him a jelly donut, right?"

Sully had to snort at this. "Unless I'm mistaken, I'll end up buying him about ten thousand jelly donuts before I'm done."

"And you think you can pay your debts in jelly donuts?"

"I can't even get jelly donuts out of you half the time," Sully pointed out, relieved that they were not apparently going to argue that seriously after all. "I'd be happy if I could."

"See?" Carl said. "That's exactly what I mean. Always ragging. You rag that dumb cop outside the OTB every morning for a month, and then you're surprised when he wants to shoot you. Everybody who knows you wants to shoot you, Sully. The only thing that saves you is the rest of us aren't armed."

In the dark below they heard the camp door swing shut and low voices coming up the bank toward them. Carl quickly took one last drag of his cigarette, then ground it under his foot.

"Zip your fly too while you're at it," Sully advised.

Carl checked, found it zipped and Sully grinning at him. "That's *exactly* the sort of shit I'm talking about," he said, his voice lowered significantly.

"Tell me something," Sully said, sensing that with Toby's arrival he would gain the upper hand. "Do you know what a hypocrite is?"

"I can answer that one," Toby said, arriving on cue. "He doesn't."

"See the thanks I get?" Carl appealed to Sully. "My pregnant wife is hustled off into the woods by two shady characters, I race to her rescue, and what do I get? Heartache."

"One shady character," Peter corrected.

"Besides," Toby said. "It wasn't much of a rescue. You've been standing up here talking to Sully for ten minutes."

"Did that cop really pull his gun?" Carl asked Peter.

Peter nodded.

"You didn't believe me, right?" Sully said.

Carl Roebuck ignored him. "Come here, woman," he said, suddenly dropping to his knees.

"I will," Toby said. "But only because I want witnesses."

When she was within reach, Carl drew her to him, lifted her sweater and inserted his head underneath.

"Would you two like to be alone?" Sully said.

"Absolutely not," Toby said as Carl nuzzled her tummy.

"How's my little Rodrigo?" Carl's muffled voice came from beneath the sweater. "Was Mommy nice to you today?"

"Enough," Toby said, trying to back away. "Your nose is cold."

But Carl had linked his arms behind her thighs and she couldn't move. "Rodrigo, Rodrigo, it's your papa come to visit."

"I've warned him," Toby told them, "that I'll abort this child before I'll let him be christened Rodrigo Roebuck."

"Don't listen, Rodrigo," Carl begged. "Mommy's a meany, but your daddy loves you."

"Daddy's about to get a knee in the windpipe."

"Goodnight, my little one," said Carl, apparently taking this threat seriously and coming out from under his wife's sweater. "Who the hell's going to lay this floor with you in jail?" he wanted to know.

"Speak to my assistant," Sully said, indicating Peter. "He was going to do it anyhow."

"What about your dwarf?" Carl said. "Will he help?"

"Sure," Sully said, though he was not confident Rub would work with Peter if Sully wasn't there. "You could always lend a hand yourself if you got really desperate," he suggested.

"I've got a business to run," Carl said. "I was counting on you, and you fucked up."

"Don't start again," Sully warned him. "You aren't even going to use the camp again until June, right? This job doesn't have to be done tomorrow."

"Wrong," Carl said. "Wrong again. Wrong, still and forever fucking wrong. You're a compass that points due south, do you know that? Do you want to know why you're wrong this time, schmucko?"

"Not really."

"Then I'll tell you. I've got a buyer coming up to look at it during the holidays."

"This is the first I've heard about any buyer," Sully said.

Carl shook his head. "You are *so* shameless. Now you're telling me if you'd known we were selling the camp you wouldn't have gone and coldcocked a cop, is that it? Is that what you're telling me?"

"Son," Sully said, "be a good boy and take this asshole down to the lake and drown him. Put stones in his pockets."

"Maybe he won't have to go to jail," Toby suggested.

"He assaulted a police officer, for Christ sake," Carl said, exasperated. "Of course he's going to jail. It's two days before Christmas. We'll be lucky to get him arraigned before the first of the year."

"You're getting all upset, Carl," Sully said, since pointing this out was about the only pleasure to be derived from the situation. In fact, he'd been going over the whole situation in his mind and had come to pretty much the same conclusion about how things would go. He had indeed fucked up, and the earlier illusion of freedom, the euphoria of the moment, had dissipated in the cruel December wind.

"I'm going to visit you every day," Carl promised. "I want to see you suffer."

"A visit from you every day would do the trick," Sully conceded.

"Let's go home," Toby Roebuck suggested. "It's cold, and we aren't going to find out what's going to happen standing out here."

"The voice of reason at last," said Peter, who'd been observing these proceedings with his customary distant amusement.

"What use is reason when you're dealing with Don Sullivan?" Carl, still combative, wanted to know. "Jesus."

"He's all upset." Sully winked at Peter.

"You want some advice?" Carl said. "Turn yourself in. Don't wait for them to find you. Just drive over to City Hall, go in and ask which cell."

"That's your advice?"

"That's my advice."

"Okay," Sully said. "Then I won't do it."

Carl threw up his hands and turned to Peter. "Due fucking south," he said. "Every time."

■ ■ ■

Midnight. The Horse. Roll call.

Regulars present, all in a row, drunk: Wirf (completely), Peter (sleepily), Sully (aspiring).

Regulars present, sober: Birdie, seated at the end of the bar (benevolent, watchful), Tiny, behind the bar (malevolent, watchful).

Regulars absent, among others: Rub Squeers.

"Don't forget to get Rub to help you," Sully said for about the fifth time that hour.

"Okay," Peter agreed. It was pointless to argue, he knew. His father's giving all this advice, he understood, was in lieu of an apology. Do as I tell you and this will still work out fine, was another meaning. A warrant, they learned from Wirf, had indeed been issued for Sully's arrest. They'd parked the pickup out back of The Horse in the hope that they might be able to drink a beer in peace before he was arrested, but that had been many beers ago. The sense of their living (drinking) on borrowed time had at first contributed to a festive atmosphere which had only with this most recent round (Wirf's, like most of the others) begun to wind down.

"Try to get over to Hattie's by six," Sully advised. "You know how to fry an egg, don't you?"

"Better than you."

"There's not very much to breakfast," Sully assured him, though this was untrue. Short-order cooks were skilled jugglers and masters of timing. But Cass would keep an eye out and help him. Either that or she'd cook and let him work the register and the tables. Which reminded him of the promise he'd made to her and which he would now be unable to keep unless Wirf could spring him before New Year's. "Tell her I'll do that favor for her as soon as I get out," he added.

"Okay," Peter repeated.

"Let Miles Anderson go until you get the floor in at the camp."

"Oooo-kay."

"You know how to work a circular saw?"

Peter grinned drunkenly. "Better than you."

Sully nodded. Smart-ass kid. "How long do you figure it'll take you?"

"By myself, three days, maybe four."

"You won't be by yourself."

"Oh, yeah," Peter said, remembering his father's injunction: get Rub to help.

"He'll be fine by tomorrow," Sully insisted. "Buy him breakfast. Loan him a dollar to bet his double."

"Okay," Peter said.

Wirf, who had been taking in this conversation, shook his head. "You make me zig, you know that?"

Sully rotated on his stool. "I make you sick?"

"No," Wirf said. "You make me zig. I zig in response to the craziness of existence. If it weren't for you, I'd live a virtuous life."

"You should be thankful I'm around, then," Sully said, then turned back to his son. "You think you can figure out how to hitch that plow blade to the truck if it snows?"

"If you can do it, I can do it."

"Tell Harold to rig it for you," Sully decided on further reflection. "Tell him you're my son."

"Right," Wirf agreed. "You run into problems, drop your old man's name. Watch all the doors fly open."

Sully rotated on his stool again. "I can't believe it's going to take you a week to get me out," Sully said.

"I'm a Jew. These aren't my holidays," he said. "Besides. How can I start getting you out when you won't even go in?"

"You're the one who keeps buying beer," Sully pointed out. "How can I give myself up with you buying another round every time I get halfway through the beer I'm drinking?"

"That's Zen Buddhist philosophy," Wirf remarked. "If there were no beer there'd be no drunks. Or is it the other way around? If there were no drunks there'd be no beer. If I weren't so drunk I could tell you."

Sully shook his head. "A zillion lawyers in the state of New York, and I end up with a drunk, one-legged, Buddhist Jew."

"Hand me one of those eggs," Wirf said, pointing to the big jar on the bar in front of Peter.

"No," Sully said. "I don't think I could stand that."

Peter, who had been nearly asleep, unscrewed the top, reached into the brine and withdrew an egg.

"Toss it," Wirf said.

Peter flipped him the egg, which missed Wirf's hand, continued over his shoulder and onto the floor.

Wirf looked at his empty hand. "I'm going to need another egg."

Peter reached around his father with this one, placing the egg in Wirf's hand. "Ah," Wirf said.

"How much do you want to bet that prick charges you for both eggs?" Sully said softly, indicating, at the other end of the bar, Tiny, who'd been watching but so far had made no move to get off his stool and adjust Wirf's tab.

"Oh God, here we go," Wirf said. "You've never seen this, have you?" he asked Peter.

Sully took out all the money he had and put it onto the bar. "I got forty-two dollars says he puts two eggs on your tab."

Wirf sighed. "Why shouldn't he charge me for eggs?"

"How much money have you dropped in here tonight?" Sully wanted to know.

"Not a dime yet."

"What do you figure? What was your tab last night?"

"I don't remember."

"I do," Sully said. "It was over forty dollars. Tonight will be more."

"I've done more zigging," Wirf pointed out. "And had more company. This has been team zigging. Synchronized team zigging."

"Here he goes," Sully whispered, nudging Peter, who was again at sleep's door.

Tiny had slid off his stool, come halfway up the bar to where the tabs were kept next to the register, where he casually turned one over and made a notation.

"Hey!" Sully thundered, causing Tiny to leap.

"Goddamn you, Sully," the big man said guiltily. "What?"

"Bring that down here a minute," Sully said.

"What?" Tiny said, looking around.

"I want to see what you just wrote on that tab."

"It wasn't even your tab I was writing on," Tiny said. "So take a hike."

"I know it wasn't my tab. Bring it down here. I want to see what you wrote."

Tiny grabbed a tab and came down the bar with it. "You know what, Sully? You're an asshole. Your father was an asshole. Your brother was an asshole. And you're an asshole."

He slapped the tab on the bar in front of Sully. "Go to jail," he said. "Do us all a favor."

Sully turned the tab over, saw that it was his own, and flicked it back at the bartender. The tab caught an air current and dropped straight to the floor like a stone. "That's not the one you wrote on," Sully said.

Tiny grunted, bent at the knees and picked it up and put it back on the bar. "It's your tab, Sully. And that's the only one you got any business looking at."

"I want to know what you wrote on his," Sully said, then turned to Wirf. "Tell him you want to see your tab."

"But I *don't* want to see my tab," Wirf said. "Ever."

"Show him his tab," Sully said.

"Fuck off, Sully," Tiny said, turning and heading back down the bar.

Sully watched him go, vaguely aware that Wirf had taken out a pen and was scribbling on a cocktail napkin. "Why do you let him piss on your shoes?" Sully said.

Wirf grinned, handed him the napkin. Sully opened it. "Why do you let him piss on your shoes?" was what it said. "Tell me you aren't the most predictable man in Bath."

"Yeah, okay, so what," Sully said. "You still haven't answered the question."

"Let's go home," Wirf suggested. "Your kid's asleep."

They turned and studied Peter, whose head lay on the bar. When he exhaled from his nose, he made ripples in the puddle of condensation on the bar.

"Kids are cute when they're asleep, aren't they?" Wirf observed.

Sully nudged his son, who started awake and said, "Okay."

"It's your round," Sully said, "and don't pretend to be asleep either."

"God," Peter moaned. "Let's go home."

"Hey," Sully called down the bar to Tiny. "Let's settle up. Bring Wirf's tab."

"Here we go again," Wirf said.

Tiny brought Wirf's tab. Sully's was already in front of him. They had not allowed Peter to buy a round. When Sully reached for Wirf's tab, Tiny slapped a big paw on top of it. "That's your tab," he said, indicating Sully's.

"I tell you what," Sully said to Wirf, pushing all the money he had on the bar at Wirf. "I bet you all of it that this greedy cocksucker charged you for both eggs. The one you ate and the one on the floor."

Wirf took the tab from Tiny, glanced at it, handed the bartender three twenties. Tiny took them and the tab and retreated to the register. "Let's go home," Wirf said.

"No," Sully said. "Well, how about it? If he didn't charge you for both eggs, I'll not only give you the money, I'll eat the egg on the floor."

Tiny was on his way back with Wirf's change. When he got there, he slammed Wirf's tab down on the bar faceup in front of Sully. "Read it and weep, asshole," he said, pointing at the last entry. "One egg I charged him for." Then he pointed at the floor. "There's your dinner."

Sully studied the tab closely to make sure nothing had been erased. Then he gathered the money and stuffed it into Wirf's shirt pocket. "The perfect end to a perfect day," he said.

Wirf was shaking his head. "How come you never see anything headed your way until it runs over you?"

"I'd have bet everything he charged you for both eggs," Sully admitted.

"You *did* bet everything," Wirf pointed out.

All three men slid off their stools then, and Sully went over and picked up the egg off the floor. "Hey," he said to Tiny, who was grinning now. "I knew if I came in this place long enough I'd get something for free, you cheap prick." Then he ate the egg, washing it down with the last swallow of his beer.

"Go to jail, Sully," Tiny said. "It's where you belong."

Outside, the wind had died down, leaving the night sky full of stars. The three intersections of downtown Bath were strung with holiday lights.

"It doesn't feel like Christmas, somehow," Sully said.

Wirf looked at him a little cross-eyed and, finding Sully serious, exploded into laughter. Peter was chuckling too. When Birdie came out, Wirf made him repeat what he'd said, and when Sully did, Wirf laughed so hard again that he had to sit down on the curb. "It's for moments like these that I zig with you," he said.

Sully, who didn't see anything that funny about what he'd said, turned to Birdie. "You know it's customary to give a condemned man one last request. My truck's out back. What do you say we go get naked and see what happens."

Birdie thought about it. "Okay," she said without visible enthusiasm.

"Don't you have any pride at all?" Sully said, taken aback.

"All talk," she said. "Just as I suspected."

When they got Wirf onto his feet again and headed, under Birdie's guidance, toward his car, Sully and Peter ambled up the street toward the police station. When they got to the alley alongside Woolworth's, Sully said, "Wait here a minute," and disappeared into the darkness, from which Peter heard him retching. After a minute Sully returned, looking pale and unsteady. "You all set on tomorrow?"

"All set," Peter said, holding up a thumb to show he meant it. For the last two hours, Peter's mood had been strangely agreeable, his customary sarcasm and wry distance absent. Not at all his usual tight-assed self, in Sully's opinion. Maybe his son just needed to drink more. Or perhaps he was still under the spell of the prettiest girl in Bath.

They walked, slowly.

"Tiny was right about one thing," Sully said. "Your grandfather was some asshole."

"I don't really remember him," Peter admitted.

"Good," Sully told him. "I know you think I'm an asshole too, but I'm nothing compared to him. Not really."

"No, you're not," Peter agreed. "Not really."

"What're you planning to tell Will?" Sully asked, since that was what he'd been thinking about all night. Of all the regrets he refused to indulge, this was the biggest.

Peter was clearly surprised by the question. "What do you want me to tell him?"

In truth, Sully didn't know. "Tell him his grandfather's an asshole, I guess. Tell him it runs in the family."

"Thanks."

"I wasn't thinking about you," Sully said truthfully. He'd been thinking about his brother and how much like Big Jim Patrick had become before he'd been killed in the head-on collision.

"Thanks again," Peter said.

"You really planning on staying around here after the first of the year?"

"I don't know," Peter said. "I thought I might."

"Every day won't be like today," Sully promised.

"No?"

"Your mother's right, though. You'd be better off to go back to your college." When Peter didn't say anything to this, Sully said, "You want to hear something funny? I liked college," he confessed, for the first time, to anyone.

Peter studied him, surprised. "You quit, though."

Sully shrugged. "I didn't say I belonged there. I just said I liked it."

"Where *do* you belong, Dad?"

They'd arrived at City Hall, and Sully pointed up the stone steps at the lighted police department door. "Right here, I guess," he said. "For tonight, at least."

"I'll look after things the best I can," Peter promised seriously.

"Okay," Sully said. "Good."

"You want me to come in with you?"

"No, I don't."

"Good," Peter said.

To their mutual surprise, they shook hands then at the foot of the steps. "I'll see you before you know it," Sully said. "Pray for snow."

They both looked up at the cloudless sky, then Sully limped up the Town Hall steps. When Sully got to the top he went inside and let the door swing shut behind him, then came back out again. "Don't forget to feed the dog," he called.

Peter had forgotten all about Rasputin, who was presumably still chained to the kitchen cabinet in the Bowdon Street house. "It's not going to be easy being you, is it?" he called back.

Sully raised his hands out to his sides, shoulder level, as if he were about to burst into song. "Don't expect too much of yourself in the beginning," he advised. "I couldn't do everything at first either."

PART THREE

THURSDAY

Downtown Bath, first light. Both traffic signals blinking yellow. Caution.

Clive Jr., sitting in his Lincoln outside the North Bath Savings and Loan, three large suitcases safely stowed in the trunk, was in a contemplative mood. The way the parking space angled toward the curb, he was able to see both blinking yellows in the small rectangle of his rearview. Caution. And then again, in case anyone missed the first, caution. Funny how over a lifetime meanings changed. Caution was what he'd been taught in school, but experience had taught him other meanings and the blinking yellow had come to mean You Don't Have to Stop Here, or Do Not Accelerate. For years now he had gone through blinking yellows with his foot poised midway between brake and gas, vaguely thankful that these indulgent yellows were not reds. And every time he rolled beneath the signal, You Do Not Have to Stop Here fired somewhere in the back of his brain, where the deepest truths of human understanding lie untroubled, unquestioned. Mistaken.

The yellow traffic signals continued to blink caution relentlessly in Clive Jr.'s rearview, their original meaning fully restored now. Too late, naturally. The more he thought about it, life's truest meanings were all childhood meanings, childhood understandings of how things worked, what they *were*. Do we ever know as deeply as we know in childhood? Does adult life amount to anything more than a futile attempt to invalidate the deepest truths we know about ourselves and our world? Well, yes, perhaps, Clive Jr. conceded. No point getting carried away, epistemologywise. It did no good to lament the loss of innocence or to suspect that the child might indeed be father to the man. He was no longer the little boy he'd once been when he and his father had visited the Capitol and Clive Sr. had interpreted traffic signals for him as they waited to cross at a busy intersection. He was now the chief executive officer of the financial institution before him, an institution whose edifice, at least, was constructed of solid granite, stone strong enough to withstand ill winds, like the ones again tunneling up Main and making the deserted street feel lonesome and ghostly. And if he himself was not made of stone, well, neither was he made of paper to be blown about like a hamburger wrapper from the Dairy Queen on Lower Main.

Speaking of ill winds. The van that carried huge bales of the *Schuyler Springs Sentinel* pulled up behind him, did a three-point turn in the empty street and backed up to the curb in front of the Rexall. The driver got out then, opened the rear hatch and dropped a bale of *Sentinel*s into the darkened, recessed doorway. Clive Jr. already had a copy of the *Sentinel* on the front seat next to him, having driven from his golf course town home into Schuyler Springs at four-thirty in the morning to buy one. Not that anything in the paper was news to him. He'd gotten a call from Florida late yesterday afternoon, so he knew, of course, that Escape Enterprises was now, at the last minute, pulling out, refusing to exercise its option, having chosen instead to build their amusement park near Portland, Maine. The *Sentinel* had reported the reasons they'd given for this most recent decision. The tract of land between North Bath and the interstate that had seemed so huge to residents of the region had seemed to the developers only marginally adequate, and adequate only if they could content themselves not to expand at a later date. The fact that the land itself was swampy had not been the impediment, as many had feared. What was Disney World but a reclaimed swamp? But you couldn't invent more swamp to fill later on if you wanted to double the size of your park, and expansion was the name of the game. Plus the tax structure and regulations in Maine were more conducive to development, and given the fact that this resort was going to be basically a summer operation, the Maine demographics and climate also made more sense. There were *other* reasons for people to go to Maine, which had the ocean and L. L. Bean, whereas if they built in Bath they'd have to be *the* reason.

The *Sentinel* had run an editorial right on the front page attacking this stated rationale for the developer's eleventh-hour about-face. Normally, the

Schuyler Sentinel wouldn't have sympathized with the plight of its smaller neighbor, but this was different. The Ultimate Escape was to have been a boon for the entire region, not just Bath, and in a magnanimous gesture the editors of the newspaper had apparently decided that the whole region had been slighted, not just their neighbors. And for no good reason. The proposed site, they pointed out, had not become suddenly smaller than when negotiations began, nor had the tax structure and inadequate incentives the developers now complained of been raised as issues before. The location hadn't changed, and neither had the climate. There was a resort town just up the road with a racetrack and baths and a summer concert series. What were the *real* reasons for the pullout? the *Sentinel* editorial had asked significantly, even hinting that the state of Maine might have greased a few palms. It also suggested that the decision had nothing to do with the cemetery controversy the Schuyler paper had done so much to publicize. No, it had to be something else.

Clive Jr. knew the real reason, because he'd asked the same question of D. C. Collins of Escape Enterprises, who'd called him personally from Texas yesterday afternoon to apologize for the decision. "I know how hard you folks worked," Collins admitted. "You did everything we asked." Beyond which he hadn't wanted to explain, and he wouldn't have done so either if Clive Jr. hadn't pleaded with the man so abjectly, not even bothering to conceal his personal frustration. "Well, okay," Collins had finally agreed, "if you really want to know why, I'll tell you. This is between you and me, though, and I'll deny it later if I have to. But here's the deal. Straight scoop. I'm the one made this decision, and I'll tell you why. We're looking to invest, what, about ninety million dollars. That's a fair piece of change, Clive. It's more than that. It's an investment of time and material, and it doesn't stop there. When we finally get the son of a bitch built, we're going to hire a lot of people in the area. We have to do that, because we can't afford ill will. We need a supportive environment. Now this is where I don't want you to get me wrong. I know your people have all been cooperative. What I'm talking now has more to do with . . . what's the word? . . . ambience. Here's the deal. A lot of the people up in your neck of the woods behave funny. Hell, Clive, no offense, but they *look* funny."

Collins had paused to let this sink in. "You got yourself some real beautiful country up there, and I mean that. Nice trees especially. But you also got yourself some people who look like they live in trees, and that's the cruel goddamn truth. We need a different ambience entirely. We need people who look more like people look in southern Maine. Massachusetts, really." This is what it had come down to. People in Bath looked funny.

At that moment a noisy garbage truck marked SQUEERS WASTE RE-MOVAL roared around the corner onto Main from Division Street, having apparently interpreted the traffic signal, in conjunction with the time of day, as meaning You Do Not Have to Stop Here. Three small, powerfully built men in filthy jeans, navy blue hooded sweatshirts and heavy orange plaid outer coats clung to the sides of the truck like flies. One of these men, whom Clive Jr. recognized as the same fellow who frequently tagged along with Sully, lost his footing on the side of the truck (the other two men seemed to occupy safer positions along the rear bumper, which provided a wide, flat surface to stand on) and had to hang on with both hands to a metal loop, his booted feet frantically searching the side of the truck for a foothold. Before they were able to locate one, the truck skidded to an abrupt halt behind Clive Jr.'s Continental, and the morose-looking Rub Squeers let go and leapt to the pavement, where he hit an icy patch and ended up on his behind. His two companions dismounted more gracefully, grinning at each other as they did so. One signaled a thumbs-up to the driver, who was grinning into his big passenger side-view mirror. Rub picked himself up without comment, ignoring his companions, who wanted to know if he was okay, and went to fetch the metal garbage can that sat in the doorway of the Rexall next to the stack of newspapers. The other two men lumbered off in the direction of other cans.

Clive Jr. watched them, especially Sully's friend Rub. Well, he conceded, people in his "neck of the woods" *were* funny-looking. These garbage men, these Squeers, taken together, looked like some failed genetic experiment—round-shouldered, waistless, neckless, almost kneeless, to judge from the way they lumbered. When one of the two Squeers who had been riding on the back of the truck returned with a garbage can and paused to remove his cloth hood and scratch his dome, Clive Jr. noticed that the hair on top of his skull was exactly the same length as the stubble on his chin, and suddenly Clive Jr. was certain that D. C. Collins, who had twice visited Bath, had witnessed this same scene. Clive Jr. had tried to control what Collins saw during his visits to the region, introducing him to Bath's better-educated and more successful business people, then hustling him out of town and to dinner at one of Schuyler Springs' finer restaurants, using that city's proximity, as he always did, as a recruiting tool. But on one or two occasions Collins had been slippery, and one morning when Clive Jr. had gone to Collins' Schuyler Springs hotel, he'd learned that the man had headed into Bath in his rental car. Clive Jr. had found him at Hattie's, of all places. He now imagined Collins getting out of his rental car just in time to see the Squeers garbage truck careen around the corner, various and assorted stubbly Squeers clinging stubbornly to its sides like cockroaches. Lord.

Sully's Squeers, perhaps the funniest-looking of the lot, his face a thundercloud of resentment and grievance, grabbed the garbage can angrily from the doorway of the Rexall and started to return to the truck. He carried the heavy garbage can by its handles, balancing it against his hip so that the bottom of the can stuck out a good distance, and when he passed Clive Jr.'s car, Clive heard the bottom of the can graze the side of the Continental. The young man looked up then, surprised, as if the car had that moment materialized, magically, in his path. He looked even more surprised to discover that the vehicle had an occupant. Apparently the driver of the garbage truck had also witnessed the incident, because when Clive Jr. got out and shut his own door, he heard the truck's door slam angrily and saw a fourth Squeers, the shortest of the lot, come running over. In fact, all four Squeers convened at the Continental's tail end to examine the scratch Rub had put there. The Squeers boys, standing together like that, bore an eerie resemblance to four human thumbs. "Now you done it," said the driver, glaring at the angry scratch, a gash really, in Clive Jr.'s paint job.

Rub sighed. "I wisht I'd seen you there."

"The only car on the whole damn street, and you got to bang into it," the driver said. "Jesus Christ on a crutch!"

The other two Squeers were looking at Clive Jr. expectantly.

"I'm real sorry about this, Mr. Peoples," said the driver, surprising Clive, until he remembered having met the man once before, having turned him down, in fact, for a loan to purchase the very truck he was now driving. "We'll take care of it, I promise you that."

Suddenly Clive Jr. was sorry he hadn't loaned this Squeers the money, remembering how the man had gotten all dressed up in an ill-fitting suit to ask for it. "Well, hell," Clive Jr. said, risking a comradely profanity. "These things just happen, I guess."

"To some people more than others," the Squeers man said, eyeing Rub. "I sure appreciate you not getting all bent out of shape, Mr. Peoples. You get that fixed and send me the bill. If we could just handle the whole thing without involving the insurance people, I'd be grateful."

"We don't have no use a-tall for them fuckin' scumsuckers," ventured another Squeers, the one who'd removed his hat to scratch. He was apparently buoyed by the fact that they were all getting along so well.

"I'd like to shoot 'em all, just to watch 'em die," said the only one who hadn't spoken.

"Don't you guys have nothing to do?" said the head Squeers, who apparently saw himself as the management arm of the firm.

Well, it was true, there was plenty to do, and so off they went, cuffing Rub as they left, leaving the management Squeers and Clive Jr. alone, two struggling businessmen. Squeers knelt next to the Continental and ran his index finger along the scratch. "We'll make this good, Mr. Peoples," he said again. "You can trust me."

"I know I can," Clive Jr. said, feeling an odd, warming trust welling up in his chest. Also welling up, a little nausea, perhaps due to the proximity of the garbage truck.

"You just let me know the damages, and I'll be right there. You won't have to ask no second time."

"That'll be fine," Clive Jr. agreed.

And so there was nothing left to do but examine the scratch one last time, as if to acknowledge its seriousness and the resultant bond of faith between them. "How's your business going?" Clive Jr. decided to ask when the silence and goodwill between them became insupportable.

"Good," Squeers said, adding philosophically, "There's always trash, no matter what. People don't like to let it build up, except in New York City. I figured we wouldn't go broke, and we haven't."

"I'm glad," Clive Jr. said, sensing that the turned-down loan application was hovering there, tangible, in the brittle air between them. Both men seemed to be searching for a way to say there were no hard feelings.

"So I guess they aren't going to build that new park, huh?" Squeers observed after another long moment of silence. He seemed to be enjoying this opportunity to talk seriously with a banker, and he kept looking around the deserted street as if hoping there'd be a witness to him doing it.

"No," Clive Jr. agreed. "I guess not."

"Well, to hell with them, then," Squeers said. "We done without 'em before, I guess we can again."

"I guess we will," Clive agreed.

"Too bad, though," Squeers added. "I figure it would have just about tripled the trash around here."

They shook hands then, and Clive Jr. was surprised that Squeers' hand, once removed from the work glove, looked and felt clean.

When the Squeers were gone, Clive Jr. climbed back into the Lincoln, backed out of his space beneath the new banner that had been hung yesterday before the news broke. Its message was typical Bath boosterism of the sort that Clive Jr. himself had been guilty of fostering back when he still believed that caution lights meant "You don't have to stop here." The banner's meaning, however, seemed different today than it had yesterday. What it said was: 1985: THE FIRST YEAR OF THE REST OF OUR LIVES.

Clive Jr. headed south on Main past the doomed IGA and out of town via the new spur, where he would pick up the interstate and head north toward Schuyler Springs and luck. This route was the long way, but at least he wouldn't have to drive past his mother's house. It was one thing to face the collapse of The Ultimate Escape, a project huge in imagination and planning and execution. It was another to realize he'd been unable to effect even so small a personal design as to get Sully, finally, out of his mother's house. True, Sully'd promised to be out by the first of the year, but then he'd gotten himself thrown in jail, which meant the first would be impossible, and Clive Jr. realized now that Sully would never be gone, not really. He'd not only wanted Sully out of his mother's house, but out of her affection, outside the circle of her protection, so that Sully could at last complete the task of destroying himself, a task begun so long ago and drawn out far too long already. It was still beyond Clive Jr.'s understanding that Sully's destruction was taking so long. Sully, after all, was a man who ignored not only blinking yellows but strident reds. Maybe that was the point. If you were going to be reckless in this life, you needed total commitment to the principle.

This early in the morning Clive Jr. had the spur all to himself. Off to his left was the cemetery that had given rise to controversy, and beyond it the huge tract of land that was to have been The Ultimate Escape—both of them graveyards now. Clive Jr. tried to imagine the boggy land cleared, filled and paved, a huge roller coaster and double Ferris wheel, sky blue corkscrewing water slides in the distance. Brightly colored landscaping reminiscent of the Judy Garland Oz movie. The image had been the staple of his imagination a couple of days ago, but now the land looked defiantly swamplike. It not only looked like a swamp right this minute, it looked like the sort of swamp that would reassert its swamp nature. He'd been assured by engineers that it could be filled and built upon, but he was no longer sure it would be wise to try. In twenty years the concrete in the huge parking lot would begin to ripple and crack, emitting foul, pent-up swamp gases. Weeds would push up through the cracks faster than they could be poisoned. It would be discovered that the Ferris wheels had been sinking an inch a year. In fact, the whole park would be subsiding gradually. State inspectors would be called in, and they'd scratch their heads thoughtfully and inform county officials that this whole area had once been wetland, and deep down still was.

When Clive Jr. arrived at the small subdivision of the Farm Home subsidy housing Carl Roebuck was building on the edge of Ultimate Escape land, he pulled off onto the gravel road and studied the half-built, no-frills, three-bedroom ranch houses. Now here, he thought, was a Bath-size, small-potatoes, strictly fringe financial venture. Imaginationwise, it was one small step above Squeers Waste. A lot of area small businesses that had made plans contingent upon the existence of the theme park were going to be in serious trouble now. He'd heard a rumor that Carl Roebuck was building these houses not with an eye toward selling them but rather to be compensated for them when he sold the land. If true, they wouldn't even pass an honest inspection. Of course, for the right price, he could get the right inspection, just as Clive had managed to get a high appraisal on the tract of swampland that was to have been The Ultimate Escape and would now be worthless again, much to the astonishment of the investors. Clive Jr. couldn't help but smile. He had long wanted to be the most important man in Bath, a man who, like his father, everyone knew. Well, in another week—another few days, probably—he was going to be famous.

Clive Jr. sat with the engine running, visible exhaust billowing from the Continental's tailpipe. His mother had been right, as usual. There would always be bad locations. And, also in accordance with her prediction, he'd discovered this truth by investing in this one, personally and profes-sionally. Where had he gone wrong? In Texas and Arizona, he had learned about faith and land. D. C. Collins, years ago, had explained it to him, taken him out to the middle of the desert where there was nothing but stone and sand and cactus and sun. That and a promotional billboard announcing Silver Lake Estates. "See the lake?" Collins asked, pointing off at nothing. Clive Jr. had seen no lake and said so. "You're wrong, though," Collins had explained. "It's there because people believe it will be there. If enough people believe there's going to be a lake, there will be one. It'll get built somehow. Look at this land." He offered a sweeping gesture that took in the whole desert, from the ground they were standing on all the way to California. "What's the first thing you notice?" Before Clive Jr. could speak, Collins answered. "No water. Not a drop. So how come these cities keep growing? Dallas. Phoenix. Tucson. It's because people believe there will be water. And they're right. If people keep moving, they'll pipe water all the way from Antarctica if they have to. Trust me. You come back here in two years, and there'll be the prettiest little lake you ever saw, right out there, a fountain in the middle of it, shooting water fifty feet in the air. The only thing that can stop it from happening is if about half the people who have already invested their money get cold feet. If that happens, there won't be enough water out here to support a family of Gila monsters. We're talking faith here, Clive. Trust that billboard, because it's the future, sure as shootin', or if it isn't we're all fucked."

Clive Jr. had learned his lesson, trusted the billboard. The first thing he'd done was put up one of his own, announcing his faith in the future. It had seemed to him that Collins was right and that he himself, Clive Jr., was the man to bring the message home. Bath's problem, he saw, in light of this revelation, was a lack of faith, a timidity, a small-mindedness. Two hundred years ago the citizens of Bath had not believed in Jedediah Halsey's Sans Souci, his grand hotel in the wilderness, with its three hundred rooms. Imagine. Scoffing at a man's faith in the future. No wonder God had allowed their springs to run dry.

From where Clive Jr. sat alongside the road at the entrance to Carl Roebuck's development, he could see the demonic clown billboard in the distance on the other side of the highway. A couple of months ago he'd overheard two employees at the bank agree that the clown bore a striking resemblance to himself. No doubt they'd soon be referring to the failed project as Clive's Folly. He adjusted his rearview so that he could see his own reflection, examine his own features "after the fall" to see if he could spot the resemblance. Not much, he decided. Actually, he took after his father, a fact for which he'd often given profound thanks. And yet, it now occurred to him, imagining Clive Sr. the way he'd looked when Clive Jr. was a boy, his father had what could only be described as a pointed head, which was why he always wore a baseball cap, even in the house when Miss Beryl would let him. Clive Sr. had seemed to understand that when he took it off, with his virtuous, close-cropped hair and his large ears, he was, well, funny-looking.

Clive Jr. readjusted the rearview, regarded the gray exhaust escaping from the Continental's tailpipe and tried, as he'd been trying all morning, to stave off panic, the worst panic he could recall feeling since he was a boy fearful of a beating at the hands of a gang of neighborhood bullies. Were he sitting in a closed garage, it occurred to him, this very same behavior would be the death of him. But as it was the plumes of blue smoke dissipated harmlessly, or at least invisibly, into the wide world of air and earth and water.

Had Sully been the sort of man to indulge regret, he'd have regretted not having done his laundry before going to jail. Socks seemed to be the main problem. Or rather, the complete absence of clean socks. Dirty ones were his long suit. He thought of Carl Roebuck's bureau, so full of socks and underwear, a month's supply, and felt a stab of envy. "We gotta make a quick stop at the men's store," he called out to Wirf, who snorted awake on the sofa where he'd fallen asleep watching television while Sully was in the shower.

"What?"

Sully slipped into his dress shoes, barefoot. "I gotta get some socks."

Silence a moment for this to compute. "How does a man in jail run out of socks?"

"Easy," Sully explained from the doorway. "I was out of socks when I went in. This look okay?"

In addition to having no clean socks, he was also missing the pants that matched his suit jacket. Had he been a betting man, and he was, he'd have bet they were at the dry cleaner's and had been since the last time he wore his suit. Which would have been when? Things he took to the dry cleaner's usually stayed there until he needed them again.

"Spiffy," Wirf said without much interest. "I'm not sure I'd even bother with socks. You don't want to overdress."

"Spoken like a man with only one foot to freeze," Sully said. "Let's go."

Wirf stood, looked at the television all the way across the huge living room. "You need a remote control for this thing," he observed.

Sully looked around the room, did a quick inventory. He needed a lot of things. A remote control wouldn't even make the list. Still, he had the impression, indeed had felt it as soon as they'd entered, that there was something different about the flat. Nothing was missing, nothing misplaced so far as he could tell, yet it still felt different, somehow. An atmospheric shift, he decided, of the sort that always registered after one of Clive Jr.'s unauthorized visits, except that Clive's presence was easy to detect because of his aftershave. This was a more subtly sweet smell that he couldn't quite place. It smelled like something young, he finally decided.

Or maybe it was just his own absence he was smelling. A week of no rank work clothes piling up on the floor of his bedroom closet. Which reminded him that in two days, the first of the year, he was supposed to be permanently absent from this flat. "Where's this apartment I'm supposed to look at?" he asked Wirf.

"On Spruce," Wirf said. "Two fifty a month."

"One bedroom?"

"Two."

"I don't need two, really," Sully said, pulling on his parka over his suit coat. The bottom of the parka came about eight inches above the bottom of the suit jacket.

"Jesus Christ," Wirf said. "You don't own an overcoat?"

"What would I do with an overcoat?" Sully said. "Two-fifty a month is more than I pay here," Sully said.

"You could stay in jail," Wirf suggested. "That'd solve your housing problem. I could spring you for weddings and funerals."

"I make more money in there, actually," Sully said. During his six days of incarceration he'd won over two hundred dollars playing cribbage with three different cops.

Together the two men made their slow way down Sully's front stairs, Sully limping and groaning, Wirf stumping and puffing. "I hope all the others aren't cripples," Wirf said at the landing.

In point of fact, Hattie's bearers were not an able-bodied crew. In addition to Wirf and Sully, there were Carl Roebuck, who had a quadruple bypass on his recent medical résumé; Jocko, whose knees, ruined by high school football, had twice been replaced and sometimes clicked audibly; and Otis, who got red-faced getting into and out of cars. And Peter, thank God. On short notice they couldn't have done much better without recruiting women. Old Hattie's casket would have been in safer hands with Ruth and Toby Roebuck and Cass and Birdie at the handles. In fact, Sully could think of only two women in town who wouldn't have been a physical improvement. One was his landlady and the other was in the casket they were going to bear. But custom was custom, and custom, in this case, demanded six men, never mind in what condition.

Thinking of his landlady, Sully decided to look in on Miss Beryl, whom he hadn't seen since the morning he'd discovered her covered with blood. According to Peter, who'd looked in on her a couple times, she was doing fine. "You know my landlady?" he asked Wirf.

"I'm her attorney," Wirf said.

"No shit?"

"I need a few paying customers to offset my pro bono work."

"Meaning me?"

"No," Wirf said. "You're my pro bonehead work. You I do strictly for laughs."

Sully ignored this, knocked on Miss Beryl's door and opened it all in the same motion, calling, "You still alive in here, old woman?"

Miss Beryl was not only alive but dressed for the funeral. She had her hat on, in fact. "I thought you were still in the hoosegow," she said.

Sully entered, Wirf following reluctantly, unused to barging into the living quarters of elderly women without invitation.

"I've got a good lawyer," Sully explained. "He can spring me for funerals."

"Just the ones he's responsible for," Wirf corrected, this in reference to old Hattie's bizarre end. Sully still wasn't sure he believed it. He'd gotten the story separately from Peter, Wirf, and Carl Roebuck, and while their versions differed in tone according to their personalities (Peter maddeningly detached; Wirf sentimental and apologetic; Carl choking with hilarity), nevertheless the facts were consistent, and so Sully guessed they must be true, however improbable. Peter, as far as Sully could tell, hadn't the imagination to think up such a lie, Wirf was too kind, Carl too self-absorbed.

What had happened was this. After Sully's brainstorm to set up the old cash register at Hattie's booth, the old woman had been content, ringing crazy, random totals every time one of her customers passed her on the way out of the diner. Some of these customers, who had ignored her for years when she sat small and blind and nearly deaf, though still malicious-looking, in her booth by the door, now found it easy to stop on their way out and argue good-naturedly about the price that sprang into the cash register's window, into the clogged nest of previous numbers. One of these had been Otis Wilson, who may have wanted to convey to the old woman that he held no grudge against her for hitting him behind the ear with her salt shaker. On the fateful morning in question, old Hattie had gradually slumped down in her booth until she looked like she was in danger of slipping beneath the table and onto the floor. Other than her daughter, who was usually too busy, Sully was the only one who ever took the liberty of grabbing the old woman by the shoulders and righting her on his way out. Certainly Otis wouldn't have dared touch the old woman, whom he considered lethal, though he was inclined to play to the assembled crowd by loudly refusing to pay twenty-two fifty for a cup of coffee. "Pay!" the old woman had predictably cackled, leaning forward, squirming, struggling to lever herself up straighter just as Otis hit the total key of the old register, which usually had the effect of clearing the nest of numbers in the register's window. This time, for reasons still unexplained, the cash register's drawer, long frozen shut, shot forward with the force of long-repressed desire, nailing the poor old woman in the middle of her forehead. She had died, without protest, on impact, sitting straight up.

Miss Beryl went over to her drop-leaf table, picked up a legal-size envelope sitting there and handed it to Wirf. "Since you're here . . . you're authorized to pursue both matters we discussed."

Wirf took the envelope, a little reluctantly, Sully thought. "You're sure you feel okay about this, Mrs. Peoples?"

Sully frowned at them. Another riddle. Since getting out of jail, he'd been feeling increasingly disoriented. He wouldn't have dreamed he could fall so far behind on current events by spending a few days in the Bath jail. Had the whole town gone crazy in his absence?

"As to this house, it's time, Abraham," she said, not exactly answering his question. "Only a stubborn, selfish old nuisance of a woman would have put it off as long as I have." She looked at Sully now and nodded. "While old Harriet was alive and always trying to fly the coop I knew I wasn't the battiest old woman in town. With her gone I just might be the oddest creature around, so I decided to take care of things before I'm the one you all have to start chasing with a net."

Wirf put the envelope into his pocket. "You understand you may not be able to undo this next month if you change your mind."

Miss Beryl, who followed the envelope into her attorney's pocket with a wary eye, looked like she might have changed it already. "I won't," she assured him. "If I'm to be seeing Clive Sr., star of my firmament"—here she indicated her late husband's photograph on the mantle—"again in the near future, I need to put things in order. Lately he's been chiding me."

"Well," Sully said. "If you're hearing voices, it probably won't be long."

Miss Beryl, who usually enjoyed Sully's mordant humor, now stared at him with the expression she reserved for those occasions when he'd been an especially bad boy. "Donald," she said. "You and I have known each other for more years than I care to add up. Might I offer a personal observation?"

"You always do, Mrs. Peoples," Sully said. In fact, he'd been wondering when she'd get around to chastising him for his latest round of misdeeds. Doubtless his punching a policeman and getting thrown in jail for the holidays struck Miss Beryl as conduct unbecoming a man of his years, a man with a son and a grandson and a handful, at least, of adult responsibilities he'd not succeeded in dodging. When was he going to grow up? Since Miss Beryl was the only person he allowed to lecture him, he took a deep breath and prepared to take his medicine.

"It'd give me great pleasure to overlook the matter," she began ominously enough, fixing him with her stern gaze, "but I cannot. Try as I might to ignore your shortcomings, I feel compelled to mention that you are not wearing hose this morning and that you look positively ridiculous as a result."

Sully looked down at his shoes and bare ankles. "It's our next stop," he promised.

"Well, I should think so," she said. "I'll thank you to remember that when you leave this house, you reflect upon me as well as yourself. There are times, I suspect," she added significantly, "when you forget this."

This, Sully realized, was his lecture. "I'm sorry if I do, Mrs. Peoples," he said, because he genuinely was sorry. "I never mean to shame you."

"It's true," Wirf put in. "Most of the time he's content to shame himself."

"Well, no man is an island," Miss Beryl reminded them both. "Do you recall who said that?"

Sully nodded. "You did," he said, his standard response when his landlady began lobbing quotations at him. "All through eighth grade."

Miss Beryl turned to Wirf. "It frightens me to think, Abraham, that I helped to shape this life. What will God say?"

"Be just like Him to blame you," Sully agreed. In his experience, people usually got blamed for the very things they were most innocent of. It happened to himself so frequently that he'd come to think of the phenomenon as a facet of divine Providence. Its corollary was that the things a person really was guilty of were mostly ignored. His father, for instance. Big Jim had never even been charged in the matter of the boy who'd been impaled on the spike. The lifelong drunken cruelty he'd inflicted on his family had gone unpunished. He'd died well fed, untroubled by conscience, happily playing grab-ass with nurses who considered him full of spunk. As near as Sully could figure it, there was something in human nature that sought to ignore or absolve obvious guilt on the one hand even as it sought to establish connections and therefore responsibility in the most unrelated things.

Of course, these principles applied to himself as well as others. He'd made his share of mistakes, and there was plenty of legitimate blame that might be laid on his doorstep, but his sense of things was that other people mistook what they were. He had not been the best husband to Vera, who had legitimate gripes. But she had been uncanny in her ability to select, as the focus of her fury, something he hadn't done. Ruth was the same way, trying to make him feel responsible for Janey. For his worst blunders, on the other hand, he'd been consistently rewarded. After burning down Kenny Roebuck's house, he'd been thanked profusely. The result of ignoring his son was that Vera and Ralph had managed to make an educated man out of him. He was beginning to sense in all of this perversity the way his current situation would eventually shake down. Somehow, although he'd assaulted a police officer in front of witnesses, he was going to walk. He could feel it. In return for which it would generally be conceded that he was responsible for Hattie's death.

No, the world, in Sully's view, did little to inspire belief in justice. The conventional Christian wisdom seemed to be that all of this world's inequities would be rectified in the next, but Sully had his doubts. Wasn't the perversity of the world he knew more likely a true reflection of its source? What if Big Jim Sullivan was grinning down at him from heaven, seated comfortably at the right hand of the Father? That would surprise a lot of people, though not Sully.

"Listen. Tell The Bank I'll get out upstairs as soon as I can. My lawyer says I could get out as soon as tomorrow, though he's been known to be mistaken."

"I'll handle Clive," she said, then to Wirf, "Just don't let him punch the judge."

"You want to ride with us?"

"No, I'm going with Mrs. Gruber," Miss Beryl told him.

"Alice knew Hattie?"

"Not to my knowledge," she admitted. "She just hates to miss anything."

Outside on the porch, Sully noticed the corner of the envelope Miss Beryl had given him sticking out of the pocket of Wirf's overcoat. "She finally signing the house over to Clive?" he asked.

"None of your business," Wirf said, not unexpectedly, pushing the envelope out of sight.

"You sure are a secretive prick, you know that?"

Wirf shrugged. "You ever hear of confidentiality?"

"Here I've known you all these years and today I find out your name is Abraham."

"You didn't know that?" Wirf said. "It's on the door of my office."

"You have an office?"

"Sully, Sully, Sully."

Wirf put his gloves on and grabbed the porch railing, which wobbled at the base where Carl Roebuck, the rat, had removed the screws. Sully made a mental note to fix it as soon as he got out of jail, lest Miss Beryl kill herself and he find himself responsible for the death of two old women.

Organ music, vaguely religious, was being played throughout the funeral home at a volume designed, it seemed to Sully, to get just under the skin. It was slightly louder in the tiny bathroom he'd been shown to so he could change his pants and put on the socks he'd bought at the men's store. The cramped room was about the size of a closet, containing a commode, a tiny sink, a warped mirror. Above, in one corner, was a small speaker from which the organ music leaked. When Sully sat on the commode, his knees nearly touched the door he'd closed behind him when he entered. His knee, defying logic as usual, seemed to have gotten worse in jail, and changing his pants and putting on the new socks proved a slow, awkward, painful task. He'd worked up a full sweat when the door he'd forgotten to lock opened, catching him sitting on the commode in his undershorts, one sock on, one sock off.

"Jesus Christ," Jocko said, going scarlet and quickly closing the door again. Then, just his voice through the door, "Didn't anybody ever tell you that you don't have to take your pants completely off to relieve yourself?"

"Don't go away," Sully said to the door. "I want to talk to you."

Sully pulled on the second sock, then the suit pants that matched his jacket. The dry cleaner, one of two in Bath, was located right next door to the men's store where he'd bought his socks, so he had talked Wirf into stopping in on the off chance. "That's them, right there," Sully'd pointed when the pants came by, recognizing them among the first batch of items that creaked past them on the overhead chain.

"Unbelievable," Wirf had muttered.

The girl blinked when she read the date on the ticket. "Nineteen eighty-two?" she read. "You brought these in two years ago?"

"Don't tell me they're not done yet, either," Sully warned her. "I need them right now."

Jocko was still standing guard outside when Sully finally emerged, zipping his fly for emphasis. "I thought you were in jail," Jocko said.

"I was," Sully admitted. "I've been given a three-hour furlough. Since I'm a bearer."

Jocko snorted at this. "God, I love small towns," he said. "You even been arraigned?"

"Tomorrow," Sully told him.

"Didn't I tell you to watch out for that cop?" Jocko said.

"I don't know, did you?"

Jocko made a gurgling sound in his throat. "How are you going to plead?"

"Temporary insanity," Sully told him. "We're going to contend that those pills of yours made me crazy."

All the blood drained out of Jocko's face.

"Speaking of which"—Sully grinned at him—"I'm almost out again."

"You're a bad man, Sully."

"So people say," Sully conceded. "I don't really believe it, though."

"I looked all over for you yesterday," Jocko recollected. "I didn't know you were in jail."

"Then you were the only one who didn't," Sully said. His assault of Officer Raymer had achieved wide notoriety even before a detailed account had appeared in the *North Bath Weekly Journal,* accompanied by a strong editorial that decried what the writer perceived to be a new spirit of lawlessness threatening not just their community but the very foundations of civilization. Coming, as this most recent episode had, on the very heels of the last, when a crazed deer hunter, not content to precipitate carnage in nearby forests, had come into town and begun shooting out windows along Upper Main Street. The editorial suggested that a trend was emerging and warned against the temptation to discount the earlier incident because the perpetrator resided in Schuyler Springs, a community with many undesirables, where such atrocities might be expected. No, there was in reality a series of subtle connections linking these two events if anyone cared to look for them. Indeed, there were families right in their own communities that had a documented history of violent behavior (the Sullivans, father and two sons, were not named), perhaps even, it was hinted, a genetic predisposition toward violence. The editorial ended on this ominous scientific note.

"I was in Gettysburg, Pennsylvania, visiting my ex," Jocko explained apologetically. "We reenacted the famous battle all week. Anyway, your exploits were not carried there."

"Good," Sully said, then frowned at Jocko. "How come you were looking for me?"

"I saw your crazy-ass triple ran the day before, and I wanted to make sure you knew and didn't toss the ticket."

Sully just stared at him.

"Sorry," Jocko said. "I thought you knew."

"It ran when I was in jail?"

Jocko adjusted his thick bifocals, looking genuinely worried now. "You wouldn't strike a man with glasses?"

Sully would not have hit Jocko. Had God Himself been there (surely this was the same perverse deity he'd so long expected the existence of), however, he might have taken a swing.

"I thought you knew," Jocko repeated.

"Do me a favor," Sully said.

"Anything," Jocko said. "Just don't punch me."

"Don't tell me what it paid," Sully said. "Ever. No matter how I beg you."

"Hey," Jocko said, stepping into the bathroom Sully had just vacated. "You got it."

Sully heard the door lock. Some people, he reflected, were just careful. Generally, God did not toy with them.

The room where old Hattie lay in her casket was empty except for the other bearers and one or two employees of the funeral home. The old woman had outlived all of her contemporaries and was survived only by Cass. Which had made rounding up the requisite number of bearers difficult. Peter had been dragooned, and Sully, from jail, had recruited Carl Roebuck and Jocko and Wirf. Otis, who felt responsible, volunteered. Ralph, good-hearted as always, had offered too, until Vera unvolunteered him, claiming he shouldn't be lifting after his operation. Rub had been briefly considered, then rejected out of respect for the deceased. Carl and Wirf and Otis were now huddled in the far corner of the room, speaking softly below the organ music. Cass, dressed in black, stood near the casket, conversing quietly with one of the funeral home employees. Peter leaned against the opposite wall, looking stylish in a tweed jacket, button-down oxford shirt and narrow knit tie.

Sully joined him there. "What are you doing over here by yourself?"

Peter shrugged. "Waiting for you?"

"You don't like these other people?"

Peter shrugged again, infuriatingly.

"Do you believe in luck?" Sully asked him.

"Not really," Peter said.

Sully nodded, suspecting as much. "You know what? I do."

Peter smiled, also apparently suspecting as much.

"You know that triple I've been betting for the last two years?" Sully asked. "It ran while I was in jail."

"When?"

"Yesterday. The day before yesterday," Sully said, trying to recall what Jocko said.

"Really."

"That doesn't strike you as bad luck?" Sully said.

"Luck didn't have much to do with you being in jail," Peter pointed out.

"How about you?" Sully asked him. "Have you ever been unlucky?"

"Never," Peter said, grinning. "Not once."

"Not even in your choice of fathers?"

"Ralph's been a terrific father."

"Smart-ass."

Neither man said anything more for a few moments. It was Peter who finally broke the silence. "I've got to go to West Virginia tomorrow, settle things there. Get the stuff from my office, whatever's left at the apartment. I'm going to leave as soon as we're done here."

"Can you handle that by yourself?"

Peter surrendered his maddening half smile. "I have a friend that's going to help."

"If you can wait till I get out, I'll help. Wirf says it won't be more than another day or two."

"I better do it now," Peter said, without, apparently, feeling any need to explain why.

"Suit yourself," Sully said.

"Okay."

"How come you didn't bring Will?"

"Grandma wouldn't allow it," Peter said. "It's probably just as well."

"I guess," Sully conceded, though he realized he'd been hoping to see his grandson. "Is she any better?" Peter had been to see him twice in jail, and while he was his usual reticent self, he didn't bother to deny that Vera was making life miserable for everyone. There had been more phone calls from Peter's woman in West Virginia, and Robert Halsey's health had taken another turn for the worse.

Peter nodded in the direction of the casket. "I think they're going to close that," he said.

In fact, the casket's lid had been lowered by the time Sully managed to limp up the aisle. When the funeral home employees noticed Sully, they managed to convey that raising it again might be a violation of the rules. "Everybody's waiting," they said.

"She's my mother," Sully told them.

"No, she's not," one of the young men said.

"Well," Sully conceded, "not by blood."

"Half a minute." The young man raised the lid. "We'll be late at the church."

Old Hattie stared up at him with the same expression of grim, unfocused willfulness that she'd borne in life. If anything, she looked even more determined now. Sully, still reeling from the knowledge that his triple had finally run, albeit without him aboard, contemplated whether he'd swap places with the dead woman if he were offered the opportunity. It was tempting. "She doesn't look finished even now, does she," Cass said at his elbow.

"She is, though," Sully said. "I guess it wasn't such a great idea to move the cash register after all. How're you feeling?"

"Hypocritical," Cass admitted. "I wished her dead a dozen times a day, Sully."

Together they stared down at the old woman, Cass weeping quietly.

"With her alive and making everything impossible, all I could think of was all the places I could go, all the things I could do if only she'd die. Now I'm not so sure it was her."

"Give yourself time," Sully said for something to say. Actually, he shared her doubts. He'd imagined the world would be a better place when it was rid of Big Jim Sullivan, but it had remained pretty much the same place, with just one less person to blame things on. Though Sully had solemnly pledged to keep blaming things on him anyway. "Did I hear you sold the restaurant?"

"Shhh—" Cass whispered, nodding at her mother, who, to judge from her fierce, frozen expression, might well have been not only listening but plotting intricate retribution. "To a friend of yours, actually."

"I heard a rumor," Sully said. It had been more than a rumor, actually. It was Wirf who was handling the details of the sale, and he'd told

Sully that Vince and Ruth would be partners, Vince putting up the money with the understanding that Ruth would buy him out when she could.

"She'll make a go of it if anybody can. Ruth knows restaurants. And she's a hard worker. Now she'll be working for herself. She promised she'd keep the name, which should please the dead."

They both looked again at Hattie, who, if she was pleased, didn't show it.

"I hope you didn't sell too soon," Sully said. "What if the theme park opens and the place becomes a gold mine?"

"If the theme park opens, so will a dozen new restaurants. Besides, did you see today's paper?"

Sully nodded. "Still, who knows?"

"We both know," Cass said. "This town will never change."

Sully would have been pleased to agree. Actually, what he'd been thinking was how many things had changed just during the week he'd been the guest of the county. Losing Hattie and having Cass move away would be plenty big changes for a town like Bath.

"Peter do a good job for you?" Sully decided to ask.

"He was fine," Cass said, without, it seemed to Sully, much enthusiasm.

Sully was oddly grateful on both counts. He'd wanted Peter to do a good job for Cass's sake, but he was beginning to wonder if Peter's joking claim that he could do anything better than Sully might be true. He and Cass both stole a glance at Peter, who'd taken a seat now on one of the folding chairs near the back of the room and appeared to be going through his wallet, probably seeing if he had enough money to make it to West Virginia and back. Sully made a mental note to offer him his poker winnings.

"He did that job like he's doing this one," Cass commented.

"He's tough that way," Sully conceded. "Too much education, probably. Either that or too much of his mother."

"Or there's a zucchini up his tailpipe," Cass offered, surprising Sully. It hadn't occurred to him that she might actively dislike Peter, and he wondered why she would.

"I'm glad he's here this morning," Sully admitted, again reflecting that his son was the only able-bodied man among the bearers. But for him, the others might go down like so many bowling pins on the icy sidewalk.

"Don't get me wrong," Cass said. "I was grateful to have an experienced short-order cook."

Sully frowned. Another surprise. "I didn't know he had any experience."

"Hell, yes," Cass said. "He can make an egg, even if he can't make conversation."

Sully nodded. "It's surprising how many things he *can* do." Apparently he'd laid the hardwood floor at Carl's camp all by himself.

Cass offered him a knowing grin. "I didn't mean to suggest you shouldn't be a proud papa." Somewhere along the line she'd stopped crying, though her cheeks were dry-streaked now. "He just doesn't have his old man's ability to make people feel better, that's all."

Sully decided to take this compliment in the spirit it was offered, though he doubted making people feel good was much of a talent. More tellingly, he understood that the mechanism behind making people feel good was providing them with an object lesson that things could be worse. That was the principal benefit in having Rub around, for instance.

Cass caught the attention of one of the anxious funeral home employees and indicated that they could come close the casket again, and together she and Sully turned away. They heard Carl Roebuck say to Wirf and the others, "Okay, girls, we're on," and Peter rose from his chair in the rear of the room. "I can see why all the women go for him, I guess," Cass admitted. "He's handsome enough."

All what women? Sully wondered. "Just like his father," Sully offered.

"Right," Cass agreed. "Only handsome, like I said."

Sully joined the other men at the casket.

"Is the professor going to help, or what?" Carl Roebuck wondered. Actually, Peter was making his way leisurely toward them. When he arrived, he took the place left for him at the head of Hattie's casket. "Let's put the one-legged lawyer and Sullivan Senior in the middle so we don't lose them," Carl Roebuck suggested.

Otis was the only one who didn't crack a smile at this. In fact, as he was staring at old Hattie's closed casket his lip began to quiver and he began to squeak.

"Damn, Otis," Carl Roebuck said. "Quit that."

"I can't help it," Otis blubbered.

"Hey, buck up," Sully said, putting his arm around Otis's shoulder and giving him a comforting pat. Only Jocko seemed to notice through his thick glasses that when Sully took his arm away he slipped the rubber alligator he'd bought at Harold's Automotive World into Otis's overcoat pocket.

"You're *such* a bad man, Sully," Jocko said as they took their positions alongside Hattie's casket.

"Okay, everybody," Carl Roebuck said as they grabbed hold of the silver handles. "On three."

From the kitchen window Janey saw her father emerge from the trailer, breathing steam through his nostrils like a bull. Built as he was, low and wide, with the big head sitting on his narrow shoulders without the benefit of a neck, he looked rather like a bull in other respects as well. And about as smart, Janey thought. No, that wasn't true. Further, it was unkind. Zack was smarter than your average bull, which was so dumb it imagined it could win against that great crowd of people, one of which, in addition to the red cape, was holding a sword. Your average bull saw the red and nothing more. Her father was more like that cartoon bull that was always smelling flowers. What was his name? Ferdinand.

Halfway along the frozen path that led from the trailer to the big garage, Zack saw his daughter at the window of the trailer, stopped and gave a tentative wave, which caused him to lose his balance on the ice, regaining it again at the expense of his dignity, both arms whirling, windmill fashion, in the air. To return his greeting, Janey made her own frantic windmill motion at the kitchen window.

Ruth, who was seated with her granddaughter on the sofa in the living room where they were examining pictures in magazines, looked up when she saw Jancy's flurry in her peripheral vision and studied her daughter with relief. At last Janey was beginning to recover, Ruth thought. For the longest time—her entire stay at the hospital—Janey had been unlike herself, and Ruth had worried that maybe her injuries were more than physical, more than a concussion and a multiply fractured jaw. It wasn't until her jaw was unwired that Ruth realized how much of her daughter's personality resided in her smile, which the wiring had prevented or rather modified to look sad. A world-weary smile had not been in Janey's normal repertoire of expressions.

Like Ruth herself, Janey most naturally reflected emotional extremes. Their faces eagerly registered anger and joy, and these emotions often lingered in their facial expressions long after they ceased to be felt. Sully was always accusing Ruth of getting mad at him without warning, an accusation that always made her madder, but she realized that even though she'd been *getting* angry at him for the last hour, her face was still registering joy at something he'd done earlier that delighted her. With Zack it was even worse. To be around Zack was to be angry, at least as far as Ruth was concerned, and the more-or-less constant residual anger she felt in response to her husband remained etched on her face even during those rare moments when by mistake he'd do something that pleased her. In this way, after thirty years of marriage, Zack still had no idea when he'd done something right so he could do it again. Now Janey had inherited Ruth's lack of subtlety with regard to expressing her emotions, residual joy and anger lingering deceptively, dangerously, on her features when inside her emotional tide had turned.

"Don't encourage your father," Ruth said, taking in at a glance what was happening at the kitchen window.

Janey wrung out her dishtowel in the sudsy water thoughtfully. "I can't help it," she said as her father disappeared into the garage. "He looks so lost."

"Of course he looks lost," Ruth said, turning a page in the magazine angrily, causing Tina to turn it back again. One of the many things Ruth didn't quite comprehend about her granddaughter was precisely what she was examining so closely when they looked at pictures, one of the little girl's favorite pastimes. Every other kid Ruth had ever known wanted to go fast. Janey, as a little girl, couldn't wait for her mother to finish the text of her storybooks so the page could be turned. She had waited impatiently for Ruth to catch up, her own imagination and curiosity racing forward needfully, so that sometimes pages got torn when Ruth was holding them down with a thumb and Janey was tugging with her little fingers. With Tina, you couldn't go slowly enough. The child seemed not to look at pictures so much as absorb them, and Ruth wondered, as she so often did, whether Tina was slow or deep. Slow seemed to be the conventional wisdom, though the jury was still out and probably would be for a while, but Ruth noticed that Tina was observant and retained most of what she saw. Two Christmases ago Ruth had bought her a book called *Find the Bunny,* which asked the child to locate a variety of animals concealed in busy, complicated drawings. Sometimes the animal was a minute detail hidden, for instance, in the high, dense branches of a tree; other times the animal was made up of a series of disparate objects which seen together formed the outline of the animal in question. Tina had located each animal so swiftly—long before Ruth was able to—that Ruth had concluded that she must have seen the book before and was working not from observation but from memory, but Janey swore this was not the case. Roy, she said, hadn't gone over it with her either, doubted in fact that Roy could find the bunny himself.

"Why shouldn't your father look lost?" Ruth continued. "He's *been* lost every day of his life."

"Yeah, I know," Janey said sadly, "but he's always had you, so it didn't matter. You should at least let him come visit us."

With Janey's husband in jail, Ruth had insisted they repossess the trailer their daughter and son-in-law had been living in. They'd hauled it from Schuyler back to Bath, setting it up in the yard alongside the garage, right where it had been before. They themselves had inherited it furnished when Zack's brother drove his four-wheeler out onto a frozen lake during a thaw. Their first thought had been to sell it until they discovered how little the trailer would bring, with its rusted skirting and brown snow marks halfway up the sides. Inside, the trailer was drafty, and Ruth suspected the utility bill was going to be obscene. But if ever there was a man who deserved to live in a dilapidated trailer, that man was her husband.

"You're just unhappy 'cause you lost Sully, and now you're taking it out on Daddy," Janey suggested without turning around.

"I didn't lose anybody," Ruth corrected her daughter. She'd seen Sully this morning at the funeral, and he'd looked so needy that she'd suffered a moment's misgiving before redoubling her resolve. "I quit the both of them. Life can't be that much worse without men in it. At least the men I seem to attract."

"If it wasn't for bad taste you wouldn't have any at all," Janey cheerfully admitted.

"I liked you better with your mouth wired shut," Ruth said, adding, "and you're a fine one to talk about taste in men."

"Yeah, well . . ." Janey said in that irritating manner she had of not letting her voice drop. What it was supposed to mean, Ruth had discovered, was that in Janey's considered opinion, whoever was talking was full of shit.

"Don't 'Yeah, well' me," Ruth said. "You know how I hate that."

"Yeah, well . . ."

"And I don't want you taking food over to your father, either," Ruth said, voicing another of her suspicions.

"I haven't taken him anything," Janey insisted. As she spoke, Zack emerged from the garage and made his slippery way back to the trailer. Under one arm he was carrying a package the size and shape of a football wrapped in aluminum foil. This time he didn't wave or even glance in the direction of the house. "What's that disease you get if you don't eat any vegetables?"

Ruth thought for a minute. "Rickets," she said, remembering.

"Yeah, that's it," Janey said. "You want to see Daddy with rickets?"

"I'd like to see him with boils," Ruth replied. She knew what her daughter was talking about. Since Ruth had banished her husband to the trailer nearly two weeks before, Zack had been subsisting, exclusively she suspected, on fried venison steaks.

In truth, it was the deer that had caused her to give him the boot. Even before the deer she'd been furious with her husband, of course. Zack had stubbornly refused to admit that he was the one who'd sent Roy over to Sully's to look for Janey, but he'd looked guilty as hell and it was just the sort of gutless thing he'd do, especially if Roy had threatened him.

But when he'd claimed the deer that Roy had shot and left lying with its tongue lolling out on Upper Main Street, that was too much. She could just see Zack arguing for the deer, explaining how he'd cart it off for free, how it was by rights his daughter's anyhow since her husband, who'd shot the deer, would be going off to jail. He'd probably explained how he had a freezer out in the garage, how he'd have the animal butchered and stored there. How it had been killed legally. Otherwise, what? It'd be a crime to waste two hundred pounds of meat. This last was the argument he'd used with Ruth: "It'd be a crime to waste it." He'd shrugged his narrow shoulders, the dumbest and most pitiful gesture Zack had in his impressive arsenal of dumb, pitiful gestures.

Yes, it had been the deer that Ruth had been unable to face. They'd eaten another deer one winter several years before, and she'd made up her mind then that she'd never eat another. This earlier deer Zack had bagged himself with his Dodge pickup, knocking the animal right back into the woods from which it had darted in front of him, as inescapable as rare good fortune. Even before he'd skidded to a stop, Zack had concluded that they were going to need a freezer, and he knew a guy who had a good used one for sale. He bought it on the way home, put it into the bed of the truck with the dead deer. Then he'd driven over to the IGA, parked in the lot and gone to fetch Ruth from her cash register. "Free meat for the winter," he said. Ruth had examined first the dead deer and then her live husband. It was the pleased look on Zack's face that got to her. Clearly, he couldn't have been more proud of his deer had he shot it with a bow and arrow at a distance of a hundred and fifty yards. "Hell, I can pound that out," he said when she went around to examine the stove-in, bloody grille of the Dodge. But she'd already turned and headed back into the IGA and her register, preferring to say nothing than to give voice to the clearest sentiment she was at that moment feeling—that she'd married a man whose idea of luck was a road kill. They'd eaten venison that entire winter, and with every forkful she'd had to swallow his reminder that the meat was free.

When Zack claimed this second deer, something in Ruth that had been stretched thin and taut for a long time had snapped. She was married to a hyena. Their house was full of junk he scavenged from the dump, trash he'd brought home and insisted she inspect. Often the things he brought home were not even complete things but rather the insides of things— copper coils and rotors and sections of fiberglass and electromagnets, all of which he insisted were "perfectly good," by which he meant perfectly free. There were a great many mysteries in Zack's life, but the one he kept returning to, the one that caused him to scratch his furrowed brow in slack-jawed disbelief, was that so many people just up and threw away things that were "perfectly good"—tires with enough tread to be re-capped, appliances with motors and pumps that still worked, heavy hunks of metal that could be sold for scrap. It was amazing how much of it there was out there, and Zack brought it all home. What he couldn't seem to grasp was that his wife's objection was to his practice of scavenging, not his selections. He kept thinking that once he explained an item's value, she'd understand. He didn't grasp that the only thing she hated worse than being married to a scavenger was having to listen to the reasoning of one. Her idea of hell was having to listen to Zack explain, throughout eternity, all the things that people thought were worthless that you could actually get two cents a pound for if you knew where to go.

Janey was drying her hands now, and Ruth studied her daughter, fighting back unexpected tears as she did so. How different Janey's life would have been, Ruth thought, if she had been pretty. With that body, had Janey been pretty, the boys would have been scared and given her room. It wasn't that Janey was ugly, just plain, like Ruth herself, and it was that plainness that always gave boys courage. And of course they couldn't keep their hands off her. At thirteen she'd had the bust development of a twenty-year-old, and at fourteen Ruth had come home late one afternoon to find a boy groping her on the living room sofa, both hands caught underneath Janey's bra by Ruth's sudden appearance. To Ruth, her daughter was still that vulnerable teenager whose body was well out ahead of her brain. She wasn't innocent, exactly. Janey enjoyed the groping, had been enjoying it even that afternoon when Ruth had interrupted. Her problem was that she couldn't seem to put the groping into perspective. Ruth sympathized. Her daughter came by her limitations rightly.

"I don't suppose I could get you to watch Birdbrain while I go out for a couple hours?" Janey said from the doorway.

"Out where?" Ruth inquired before she could stop herself.

"Out of here," Janey explained. "Don't be nosy. I'm grown up."

"You just got out of the hospital."

"And you're afraid I might have some fun. You decide to swear off men, so I'm supposed to do the same thing."

There was enough truth to this to bring Ruth up short. Having decided to try celibacy, she'd have preferred company. Lots of it. Rather than admit this, she reminded her daughter, "I've got an early morning tomorrow. I could use some help."

"I thought Cass was going to be there."

"She is," Ruth admitted. Cass had promised to guide her through the rest of the week to ease the transition with customers and deliverymen, both of who seemed anxious for the diner, which had been closed for almost a week since Hattie's death, to open again.

"Then you won't need me," Janey said, throwing on her coat.

"You think you'll take my old job?"

"Hard to say," Janey responded, as if this too were an unwarranted intrusion into her private affairs.

"Vince will need to hire somebody. He won't hold it open for you forever."

"Yes, he will." Janey grinned. "He's got the world's fattest crush on me."

Ruth considered this. It might, she decided, be true. "You could do worse. Vince is a sweet man. He'd be good to you."

"He's an old man, Mama."

"He's younger than I am."

"Yeah, well . . ." she came over to the sofa and lifted Tina, rubbed noses with the little girl. "Mommy's going out for a while, Birdbrain. Be a good girl for Grandma."

"She'll be fine," Ruth said. "*You* be a good girl for Grandma."

"Grandma was never a good girl," Janey pointed out. "I don't know why I should be."

"So you won't end up like Grandma?" Ruth offered.

Janey grew suddenly serious, though the glow of anticipated groping lingered on her features maddeningly. "I don't know what I'd do without Grandma."

When her daughter was gone, Ruth let the tears come. She wept quietly so Tina wouldn't know. The little girl, who was studying a picture in the magazine intently, as if she expected to be tested on its contents later in the day, hadn't even looked up when her mother left. When she finally allowed Ruth to turn the page, Tina broke into a big grin, and her small hand reached up and found her grandmother's earlobe.

Pointing to the picture, she said, "Snail."

The clock in the Lincoln said three-thirty A.M., and Clive Jr. couldn't remember the last time he was awake at such an hour. And not just awake. Wide awake. Full of wakefulness. Alert down to his pores. Trees were flying by, big ones, raked by his headlights. He imagined his brights as laser beams slicing through bark and wood effortlessly, imagined the giant trees, severed, crashing into the road behind him, cutting off pursuit.

Not that there would be any actual pursuit for a while. Maybe never, in the conventional sense. Perhaps his trail of credit card purchases might be tracked through a computer, but not Clive Jr. himself and not the Lincoln. Still, he was enjoying the sensation of flight and pursuit. As a boy he had run from bullies, but then he'd been humiliated and it had never occurred to him that running could be fun, exhilarating, a challenge—that flight needn't be blind panic but rather liberating, like knowledge, like the taste of one's own blood. Clive Jr. ran his tongue over his busted lip and smiled. Who could have guessed that the taste of blood could *dispel* fear? This was what Sully must have known even as a teenager. It was what had given him the courage to pick himself up off the turf, his nose bloodied, and go right back into battle. Perhaps it was even what Clive Jr.'s own father had been trying to teach him—that blood and pain were manageable things.

When the right front wheel of the Lincoln located the soft shoulder, Clive Jr. yanked the big car back into the center of the two-lane blacktop, where he straddled the solid yellow line, noting again the strange absence of fear that had accompanied his departure almost from the beginning. He was now in the twenty-first hour of his flight, which had begun that morning where the spur intersected the interstate, where he'd been faced with a choice he hadn't anticipated. North lay Schuyler Springs and Lake George, where Joyce, suitcases packed, awaited him and their planned long weekend in the Bahamas. Instead he had headed south and punched the accelerator, sensing immediately the power of his decision just to leave her behind with the rest of it. Something about meeting the Squeers boys that morning had allowed him to see everything in a new light, and one of the things he saw differently was Joyce, who, it occurred to him for the first time, was neurotic, self-centered, used up. Marrying her, he saw with stunning clarity, would guarantee a life of misery.

He was somewhere in western Pennsylvania, he wasn't sure where. Half an hour ago he'd flown by a sign that said Pittsburgh was seventy-five miles, but he'd come upon two forks in the road since then and he was now seeing signs for places he'd never heard of. In the glove compartment he had three speeding tickets, one from New York, the other two from here in Pennsylvania, both issued by the same patrolman. In New York he'd been clocked at eighty-five, the two Pennsylvania citations had him doing exactly ninety. This was not a coincidence, since Clive Jr. had set the cruise control for this speed. He'd accepted the first Pennsylvania ticket and put it into the glove compartment without a word, refusing the young cop the satisfaction of visible regret. Another liberating experience. All his life, Clive Jr. had sweet-talked cops. Caught speeding, he always started off by admitting his guilt. ("I guess I was lead-footing it a little, right, Officer?") Admitting guilt took away a trooper's opening questions ("Do you know the speed limit here, Mr. Peoples? Do you know how fast you were going?") and forced him to script the rest of the conversation on the spot. A fair number of cops, faced with this dilemma, concluded it was easier to let this one off with a warning. And Clive Jr. had sensed that this young trooper might have been susceptible to just such a tactic, but one of the things he had sworn off when he headed south out of Bath instead of north toward Lake George and his fiancée, was genuflecting for cops.

In fact, Clive Jr. had pretty much decided to give up genuflecting altogether. So he'd silently accepted the citation, stuffed it into the glove box and, after being instructed by the young trooper to have a good evening, pulled the Lincoln back onto the interstate and punched it back up to cruise control ninety. When the same trooper pulled him over again ten miles farther west on the interstate, he seemed genuinely perplexed. "You're a slow learner, Mr. Peoples," he observed, and this time he had Clive Jr. assume the position alongside the Lincoln. It was snowy there on the shoulder, and when the patrolman helped him spread his legs, Clive Jr. had lost his footing and slumped to his knees in the snow, banging his mouth on the roof of the Lincoln on the way. The patrolman allowed him to climb back to his feet then and shined his flashlight into Clive Jr.'s face, revealing the busted, bloody lip. "Tell me what you're grinning at, Mr. Peoples. I'd like to know." But Clive Jr. had again said nothing. Instead, he'd turned away from the question and spat red into the snow, one of the more satisfying gestures of his life, he now thought.

The patrolman had detained him there in the cold for nearly half an hour, talking on the radio, while Clive Jr. first stood in the frigid wind, then finally sat in the Lincoln. Eventually, the cop let him go again, this time with a stern warning. "I think I may just follow you a ways, Mr. Peoples. Do ninety again, and we'll see who grins."

And so Clive Jr. had gotten off at the next exit, headed south along the deserted two-lane blacktops of the western Alleghenies, flying through at two in the morning a series of tiny, dying villages with little more than a dark, run-down gas station/garage/convenience store to offer. America, it occurred to him now, was still full of bad locations.

Feeling the shoulder again, Clive Jr. pulled the Lincoln back onto the blacktop, surprised by the fact that the car did not react immediately to his command. There seemed to be a split-second delay between his turning the wheel and the car's responding, which caused Clive Jr. to wonder if he had been in a rut. But when he hit a straightaway, the car felt fine again. The sensation was strange but also familiar, though he had to travel back more than fifty years to locate it. How old had he been at that amusement park when he was placed in one of the brightly painted kiddie cars that slowly circled an oval track? He couldn't remember, but what he did recall was his sense of disappointment to discover that the little car's steering wheel was a fraud, that his spinning it left or right, fast or slow, had no effect upon the car's direction, anymore than the two fake pedals—supposedly accelerator and brake—on the floor had. And he remembered trying to conceal his disappointment from his father and mother, even, perhaps, from himself.

In a wide spot in the road called Hatch, Clive Jr. flew out of the woods, took the blinking yellow caution light at sixty-five and was just as quickly back in the woods again, tall trees forming a cathedral arch above. Then the three-quarter moon came out from behind some clouds and sat on the Lincoln's hood ornament, on what Clive Jr. imagined must be the western horizon, lighting his way. He wondered how fast he'd have to go to keep the moon right there, to keep the sun from rising behind him. It would have been nice to prevent another sunrise. Speed, enough of it, could do that. He checked his rearview to make sure that nothing, not even the dawn, was gaining on him, and was gratified to see that the small rectangle of mirror was perfectly black.

Even had he not been looking at the rearview, it was unlikely that he would have seen the pothole or, having seen it, would have been able to avoid it. The Lincoln's right front tire hit the hole dead center, the right rear wheel a quickened heartbeat later, sending a shiver throughout the Lincoln and a buzz through the steering wheel and into Clive Jr.'s soft hands. "Ouch," he said out loud and, hearing his voice, considered it might be wise to slow down. He couldn't, after all, outrun the dawn. Then he felt the Lincoln on the shoulder again, and felt that too when he turned the steering wheel, the Lincoln did not respond.

Before him, a two-hundred-yard straightaway and, at sixty-five miles an hour, not much time. Enough, though, to recall Harold Proxmire's warning to get the Lincoln's axle checked after Joyce parked it on the tree stump, enough time to imagine what lay ahead at the end of the straightaway, enough time to imagine what it would feel like to leave the road, to be briefly airborne, headlights straining to locate the other side of the ravine, with only darkness and silence below, time to reflect that his own father had been killed going thirty miles an hour on a quiet residential street without the car hitting anything, time to calculate his own slim odds.

When to Clive Jr.'s surprise the Lincoln's steering responded again and he took the curve at sixty, sending pebbles screaming off into the dark ravine, he was curiously devoid of emotion, and when he ran his tongue over his swollen lower lip, he was disappointed to discover that very little of the salty blood taste lingered there. By applying pressure on the swelling with his teeth, however, he was able to burst the ruptured skin like a grape, after which his tongue was again rich with the sweet taste of blood.

Ahead a vista opened in the trees, and far below Clive Jr. saw a major highway running straight toward a glow in the west. It looked like a scene viewed from the window of an airplane. The Pennsylvania Turnpike, he guessed, and Pittsburgh.

He felt again, without fear, the play in the wheel, that he was neither in nor out of control. So this, he reflected, was what it felt like to be Sully.

FRIDAY

Judge Barton Flatt was not a well man. His jowls were loose and jaundiced, and except for a single tuft of hair on his forehead, his hair had fallen out, thanks to the chemotherapy. He was ensconced in a leather chair behind his huge oak desk in chambers, but he was still visibly uncomfortable, as his incessant squirming testified. He had the look of a man in a titanic struggle against imminent flatulence, and the other men in chambers eyed him nervously. In addition to the sick judge there were in attendance Satch Henry, the county prosecutor, Police Chief Ollie Quinn, Officer Doug Raymer in civies and sunglasses, a red-eyed Wirf, who looked as if someone had dressed him while he lay in bed, and of course Sully, in whose honor this meeting had been called. "Okay, boys and girls," said Judge Flatt, closing the cover of the manila folder on the police report in front of him. "Let's see if we can't dispense some small-town justice right here, right now."

"Your Honor, could we all sit down, at least?" Chief Quinn requested. Five folding chairs had been set up in a semicircle around the judge's desk, and all five were occupied except Sully's. Sully was limping along the back, book-lined wall. His knee was throbbing to the beat of a brass band, and he'd decided it was best to march.

"Mr. Sullivan," said Judge Flatt, "would you be more comfortable seated or standing?"

"Standing, right now," Sully said, adding, after a moment, "your Honor."

"He's not standing, he's pacing," the police chief observed.

Judge Flatt shifted in his chair, causing the other men to lean back in theirs, as if from a jab. "I may join him before we're through."

"He's making me nervous, is all," the chief explained, looking over his shoulder at Sully warily.

"Everybody who isn't in jail makes you nervous, Ollie," the judge observed. "You're perpetuating a fascist stereotype." Then to Sully, "Go pace over on that side of the room, Mr. Sullivan. Our police chief fears a sneak attack."

"Your Honor," said Satch Henry, his hand raised like an obedient student in an elementary school. "If you aren't feeling well, we could postpone—"

"No, we're going to do this now," Judge Flatt said. "Mr. Sullivan here's already spent one holiday in jail, and I'm not going to feel any more like doing this next week than I do now. Unless you were suggesting this be postponed until next month after I'm retired and you can bring this case before someone more to your liking."

"That's *not* what I meant at all, your Honor," Henry said quickly.

"Good," said the judge. "Then let's proceed."

Wirf, who had not said a word since entering chambers, examined his fingernails, a trace of a smile on his lips. He and Sully had conferred briefly a half hour before, and Wirf had explained what he thought was likely to happen. "If things go like I think they will, I'm not going to say much ("You never do," Sully had reminded him), and I don't want you to open your mouth unless you're asked a direct question. Just remember, no matter what happens in there, the fact that we're in chambers to begin with is the good news. Satch Henry knows that, and he's ready to bust a gut. This thing's going to go our way unless we mess it up."

Sully was less certain. During the last two years, he and Wirf had been involved in a lot of judicial proceedings together, and they'd never yet gone Sully's way. Still, he had to admit, this was, so far, an auspicious beginning. According to Wirf there was a lot of bad blood between the judge and the district attorney's office, and it appeared to Sully that this might be true, though Judge Flatt's tongue was legendary, its targets democratic. Still, Wirf might be right for once. He guessed right on *People's Court* every now and then, so why not in a real-life judicial proceeding?

Judge Flatt slid the manila folder containing the police report across his desk with his index finger in Satch Henry's direction. "Okay, Satch, I want you to tell me the truth, the whole truth, and nothing but the truth.

Do you really want to arraign Mr. Sullivan on these charges, put this whole thing into court, spend a lot of taxpayers' money?"

Satch Henry went purple. "Your Honor, I believe there is some precedent for indicting and convicting people who assault police officers. Mr. Sullivan has a history of violent behavior. He broke Officer Raymer's nose and gave him a concussion. Take off those dark glasses, Doug."

Officer Raymer took off his sunglasses. He had two black eyes. Green eyes, really, the puffy skin on both sides of his swollen nose having gone from purple to motel green.

Judge Flatt studied the policeman. "They still call those shiners?" he inquired. "That's what they called 'em when I was boy."

Officer Raymer looked confused by this unexpected question. "I guess so," he said. "That and 'black eye.' "

"You ever been in a fistfight before, Officer Raymer?"

"Sure," the policeman said. "Lots of times."

"What do you usually do when somebody throws a punch at you?"

Officer Raymer cocked his head and thought about this. "Duck?" he guessed.

"Why didn't you duck this time?"

"Your Honor—" Satch Henry began.

"Don't interrupt me, Satch. Can't you see I'm talking to this man?"

Satch Henry opened his mouth to say something else, then closed it again. Wirf allowed himself another trace of a smile.

"Why didn't you duck this time?" the judge repeated.

"I guess I never thought he'd do it," the policeman sulked.

"Why not?" Judge Flatt wanted to know. "As Satch here says, Mr. Sullivan has a history of violence. Comes from a long line of amateur barroom pugilists. Why didn't you think he'd pop you one?"

"Well, hell, Judge," Officer Raymer exploded, exasperated. "I was holding my goddamn gun on him. The son of a bitch is crazy."

Judge Flatt turned his attention to the prosecutor now. "You say you want this man on the stand, do you? He's just admitted to aiming his weapon at an unarmed sixty-year-old cripple."

"I don't think I'd describe Sully as a cripple," Satch Henry said weakly, though the point had clearly struck home.

"Come over here a minute, Mr. Sullivan," the judge said. "Pull up your pant leg for these gentlemen."

"I'd rather not," Sully said, feeling rather like a little boy who's been ordered to drop his trousers in a game of doctor.

"Do it anyway, Mr. Sullivan," the judge said. "Come over here where we can all see."

Sully did as he was told, putting his boot up on the chair that had been reserved for him, then gingerly pulling his pant leg up until his knee was exposed. He himself looked at the knee for the first time in a while. It looked like an exotic fruit ready to rupture.

The sight of it affected everyone in the room. Wirf had to look away, and even Officer Raymer winced. Satch Henry was the first to recover. "May it be stated for the record, your Honor, that Officer Raymer is not responsible for the condition of Sully's knee, whereas Sully is responsible for this police officer's contusions and concussion?"

"No, it may not be stated for the record, Satch," Judge Flatt said, pausing rhetorically. "It may not. Because there *is* no record here in chambers."

"Can I let my pant leg down?" Sully said.

"Yes, you may," the judge said. "In fact, I insist."

All the other men watched him lower his pant leg.

"That hurt as bad as it looks, Mr. Sullivan?"

"I take pain pills," Sully said, aware of where the judge was heading. "Some days are pretty good. I get through the others somehow."

"What effect do the pills have?"

"They make me sleepy."

"Nervous? Edgy?"

"Not really, no."

"You wouldn't blame the fact that you punched this policeman on the medication you're taking?"

"No, not really."

"The smart answer to that question would have been yes," the judge pointed out. "Okay, if it wasn't the pills, why'd you coldcock this policeman?"

In truth, the answer to that was so complicated that Sully despaired of ever understanding it himself, much less of being able to explain it to an impatient, sick judge. "I don't know," he heard himself say. "I was tired, I guess. It'd been a long day."

Judge Flatt paused, and Sully wondered if he was expected to go on. When he didn't, the judge said, "Okay, Mr. Sullivan," and turned back to Satch Henry and Ollie Quinn. "I can understand tired. I'm tired myself. Sick and tired. That's why I'm retiring next month. Because I'm sick and tired and unfit for human companionship. Half the time I feel like shooting somebody myself, which means it's time for me to step down and leave small-town justice to somebody else, and may God have mercy on his soul. Anyhow, I'm going to make a prediction and then a recommendation and then I'm going to leave it to you to decide what you want to do, Satch. If you insist on going to trial, go, but you'll go before me, and I'll tell you right now that you'll wish you hadn't."

"Your Honor—" Satch Henry began.

"Pipe down, Satch, I got the floor here."

Satch Henry piped down.

"Here's what we got," Barton Flatt said. "We got Mr. Sullivan here, who did a dumb thing and did it in front of witnesses. There's a good chance you could get a conviction, Satch. But Lord love a duck, what a show Mr. Wirfly here could put on. If Mr. Sullivan's got a history of pugilism, your officer here's got a history of his own. Just in the last six months he's terrorized an old woman over a pizza and let a lunatic with a deer rifle shoot out windows on Main Street, assault a young woman and then walk away from the scene. On that occasion he saw fit to leave his weapon in his holster, but later, with Mr. Sullivan here, he not only takes out his firearm, he actually discharges it and the bullet hits a house a block away. You claim Mr. Sullivan here is a menace, but Mr. Wirfly here's going to prove there's two menaces at least. Before this is done, you're going to look like God's own fool, Satch, and Ollie's going to look like a fool, and your police officer, who *is* a fool, is going to look like one too. And unless Mr. Wirfly's a fool, he's going to file a countersuit against the police department and city that will make headlines for months in the Schuyler paper, maybe even Albany, not that it will matter to you, Satch, because you'll be out of office come next November. Don't set this thing in motion, that's my recommendation. Settle it here and now and in this room, not that one out there."

"Your Honor—" Satch Henry tried again, the judge's voice having fallen.

"Nope," the judge shook his head, holding up one hand. "I still got the floor. It's still mine. And you're going to listen another minute yet. I've told you what's going to happen, and now I'm going to tell you how to avoid it. I've got a half-dozen sensible recommendations, and the first is that we now send Mr. Sullivan and Officer Raymer out, because I don't think their presence is necessary from this point forward. In fact, Mr. Sullivan's pacing is getting to me too, and I've never much liked the look of policemen in sunglasses." He turned now to Sully and Officer Raymer, looking back and forth between them dubiously. "If we ask you to step outside, gentlemen, do you think you'd be capable of refraining from further hostilities? I want you to be honest about this, because I can provide you a chaperon if you have any doubts."

"I think I can guarantee my client's behavior," Wirf said, shooting Sully a warning glance.

The judge regarded Wirf as he might a naughty child. "Don't insult my intelligence, Mr. Wirfly. I know you and I know your client, and I know you can guarantee no such thing."

Wirf, chastened, conceded that this was true.

"How about it, Mr. Sullivan?" the judge wanted to know. "You aren't feeling tired, are you? Like you were when you thought it might be a good idea to sucker-punch a police officer? You think you can behave like an adult for about ten minutes?"

"I'll try, your Honor," Sully promised.

"Don't try," the judge advised. "Just do it. And how about you, Officer?"

Officer Raymer's brow had clouded. He wasn't sure, but it was his impression that the judge had called him a fool a moment before, and in his opinion that was uncalled for. "I'd just like to say what's this country coming to, that's all I'd like to know. I can't believe this whole thing, and I just want to say that for the record."

"Well, you can't," Judge Flatt told him. "Go out in the hall and sit and think about it for a while and it'll come to you why you can't say anything for the record, because I've already explained it once."

Both Satch Henry and the chief of police were trying to suppress grins now, and Officer Raymer, noticing this and intuiting that his support was eroding, bolted angrily from the room. Sully followed at a more leisurely pace, still arriving at the door to the judge's chambers in time to prevent it from slamming and to see Officer Raymer disappear into the men's room across the hall. From inside the rest room came the sound of a trash canister being kicked hard.

There was a lounge at the far end of the hall, so Sully made for this in the hope that there might be a coffee machine. He had a pocketful of change from the nickel-dime-quarter poker game he'd gotten into the night before when Wirf and Carl Roebuck stopped by to see him. Carl seemed to be monumentally pissed off at him, but he refused to say why in jail. During the course of the evening, Carl Roebuck had called him every name he could think of. He smoked and drank all night long, and didn't seem to want to be reminded of his recent resolutions. Sully had attributed his mood to the reported collapse of the Ultimate Escape deal. When the game grew too large for his cell, they'd had to move it down to the conference room next door to Booking. Sully had won all night long, with the result that he now had enough change in his pocket to set off a metal detector.

His luck from the night before seemed to be holding today, because there was indeed a coffee machine, and when he fed it two quarters and got in return a half cup of tar-black coffee, he still could not shake the overall feeling of good fortune, his sense that perhaps he had played out his stupid streak, that things just might conceivably work out after all. He was sitting with his leg up on a plastic chair and contemplating the still long odds when Officer Raymer entered, his fly at half staff. When he saw Sully, he considered turning on his heel and leaving again, Sully could tell.

Sully pushed a plastic chair out from underneath the table. "Sit down," he suggested. "Take a load off."

"No thanks," Officer Raymer said, staring at Sully from behind his dark glasses. "You know, there's no such fucking thing as justice. That's what gripes me."

"Of course there isn't," Sully conceded. "How old are you?"

"Well, it sucks," Officer Raymer said.

Sully nodded. "It absolutely does. How about a cup of coffee? I'll buy."

"I can buy my own coffee," the policeman said, fishing in his pocket as he headed for the coffee machine.

From where he was seated, Sully could see that Officer Raymer was mistaken. The coins in his palm appeared to total about forty-five cents. A few machines down the wall was a dollar-bill changer with a handwritten OUT OF ORDER sign affixed to it. Officer Raymer did not observe this until after he'd inserted a dollar bill and had it rejected. Sully grabbed a handful of change and spread it out on the plastic tabletop. The policeman, seething, made change and tossed the dollar bill on top of the pile of Sully's coins. When, for fifty cents, Officer Raymer received the same half cup of muddy liquid Sully'd received, Sully, who had a lifetime of experience with what the policeman was feeling, saw what was coming and said, "Hold on a minute" and moved to another table. When he judged himself safe from ricochet, he said, "Okay, go ahead," and Officer Raymer, who had grabbed the machine with his hands, began to heave and rock it until the top of the machine slammed against the wall and rebounded, only to be slammed again and again. This the policeman continued to do until something ruptured inside the machine and coffee gushed out onto the floor. Officer Raymer stepped back then and watched, with unalloyed satisfaction, as the puddle became a lake. "There," he said.

Ollie Quinn burst in just as Officer Raymer pulled up a chair at Sully's table. "Jesus," the chief said, surveying the damage. "I thought it was gunfire." Then he disappeared again.

Officer Raymer took a sip of his coffee and allowed the color to drain from his cheeks. He'd gone from enraged to sheepish in the time it took to destroy a coffee machine, and Sully understood this too. The policeman sighed. "It all just gets to you sometimes, don't it?" he said.

Sully was about to share with Officer Raymer that this was precisely the feeling that had caused Sully to punch him, that it hadn't been anything personal, when he looked up and noticed Peter and his grandson standing in the entryway just vacated by the chief of police. Peter took in the scene with that detached, ironic expression that had so annoyed Cass, as if to suggest that other people's lunacy was to be expected. Sully doubted the little boy, on the other hand, would ever master such detachment. As always, Will looked strangely adult in the way he approached his grandfather, climbed onto his good leg, gave him a hug around the neck. Another kid would have run. Another kid would have forgotten which leg was the bad one. Another kid would have forgotten that there *was* a bad one.

"What do you say, sport?"

"Wacker's in the hospital," he reported.

Peter pulled up a chair, nodding a greeting at the morose policeman. If he was surprised to find Officer Raymer and his father sitting peacefully together at the same table, he didn't say so.

"You met my son?" Sully asked.

Officer Raymer frowned. "You were in the truck, right?"

Peter acknowledged that this was true as they shook hands.

"What's this about Wacker?" Sully asked.

"Had his tonsils out," Peter said.

"Everything go okay?"

Peter shrugged. "So I'm told. The only reason I was notified was so I could expect the hospital bill."

Sully nodded. "I didn't figure you'd be back so soon," he said. Peter had taken the truck after the funeral and driven to Morgantown to settle his remaining business there—gather his things from the house he and Charlotte had been renting, close their bank accounts, gather his books from his office at the university, see about extending his insurance benefits since Sullivan Enterprises did not offer Blue Cross–Blue Shield.

"I just got back," Peter said.

"You must have driven all night."

"There wasn't much to do," Peter explained. "Charlotte took most of it. I had more stuff at the office than the house."

"What'd they think about you leaving at the college?" Sully wondered.

Peter smiled his infuriating, self-pitying smile. "They weren't nearly as sad to see me go as my landlord, who expressed his disappointment by refusing to refund our security deposit."

Sully nodded. "I'd buy you a cup of coffee," Sully offered, "but our friend here just totaled the machine."

Officer Raymer, who had lapsed back into morose contemplation of his now empty cup, looked up at this reference to himself. "Piece of shit was already broke," he said angrily.

"How about a soda?" Sully suggested to Will.

"Okay."

Sully indicated the pile of coins, and Will fished for the ones he'd need.

"Great," Peter said when his son made a wide loop around the coffee lake on the way to the soda machine. "Get him drinking soda at eleven o'clock in the morning."

Sully hadn't even thought about the time. "Sorry," he said. "I just wanted to get him something."

"I know," Peter said, with some kindness, perhaps to suggest that whatever his father had to offer was never the right thing.

"How much you want to bet they make me pay for it anyhow?" Officer Raymer said.

"Anybody see you break it?" Sully said.

"You."

"Not me," Sully said. "It was like that when I came in."

Will came back with a small plastic glass half full of soda. "They don't give you very much," he said apologetically. He had two coins, a dime and a nickel left over, and he returned them to Sully's pile.

"Tell this guy," Sully indicated the policeman. "He'll fix it. He works here."

"Wacker gets to eat nothing but ice cream and soda for two days," Will said, half expecting some reply. Instead, his father, grandfather and the man who worked there fixing the machines all just looked at him, making him feel strange and nervous, the way it always did when adults acknowledged his existence too directly. He stared at his soda until they quit, then took a sip, paying special attention to the way the cold felt along the back of his throat, and he thought of his little brother in the hospital, surrounded by doctors, one of whom had reached into Wacker's throat with scissors, and he imagined his brother plotting complicated revenge against them.

Down the hall, small-town justice was done.

The apartment Wirf had located was off South Main in a neighborhood of large, shabby houses and sidewalks that were cracked and weed-infested roller coasters bordering lawns that were patchworks of brown grass and browner bare earth. There were houses on only one side of the street, and these faced the rear parking lot and Dumpsters of the IGA, whose sign now read CLOSING JAN 15. When Wirf pulled up at the curb and all four—Wirf and Sully in front, Peter and Will in back—got out, they were greeted by a chorus of barking dogs, one of which strained against a leash anchored to the railing of the porch next door. Which reminded Sully of two things—that he still needed to fix Miss Beryl's railing and that he still owned a dog. According to Peter, Rasputin was still canine-in-residence at the house on Bowdon, sleeping in the kitchen at night, enjoying the run of the back porch during the day.

"Second floor?" Sully said, staring up at the dark vacant windows.

Wirf admitted it was.

"Good thing it doesn't have four floors, or you'd want me to live on the fourth," Sully said.

"Ever the ingrate," Wirf said as they made their way up the front porch steps.

The flat had its own entrance, which had been left unlocked so they could inspect the premises. The landlord was at work. The stairs were steep and narrow, and Sully noticed Will regarding them warily. "Take Grandpa's hand," Sully suggested. "You still got your stopwatch?"

Will took it out of his pocket, showed his grandfather.

The apartment was a good deal smaller than Sully's current flat, though the kitchen was bigger. There would be room for his dinette and chairs and enough room left over for him to get by without constantly banging into them. The appliances and fixtures were old, which was okay too, since he wouldn't be using them. The living room had a fireplace complete with a charred log and two years' worth of gray ash. The fireplace was surrounded by built-in bookcases. "What the hell am I going to do with that?" Sully said.

"God, you're a pain in the ass," Wirf said. "Go back to jail, why don't you?"

Will's eyes widened at this apparently serious suggestion.

The embarrassing truth was that Sully did not need a lot more space than he had in his cell. He needed a place to go to sleep at night. A place to shower. A commode. A closet for his clothes. His real homes were The Horse, Hattie's, the OTB, Carl Roebuck's office. And this flat was at the wrong end of Main Street, a lot farther from these homes than his place above Miss Beryl. Thinking of Hattie's reminded him of another duty he had today. Hattie's wasn't really Hattie's anymore, it was Ruth's, and today was the Grand Reopening. He'd driven by that morning and saw the banner out front, then driven to the donut shop for his coffee. Sooner or later, though, he'd have to go in, find out where he stood with Ruth, whom he'd seen in the congregation at Hattie's funeral yesterday, find out whether Hattie's, perhaps the most comfortable place in Bath, was still a place he'd be comfortable in.

"It's more than I need, Wirf," he confided when Peter disappeared into one of the two bedrooms, taking Will with him. "Also more than I can afford."

"Where are you going to find anything for less than two-fifty a month?" Wirf said. "You want to live in a trailer?"

"I'm only paying two hundred a month now," Sully pointed out.

"That's because your landlady's carrying you," Wirf said. "She could get four hundred a month for that flat, easy."

Sully shrugged. "Okay, if you think I should take it, I'll take it."

Wirf threw up his hands.

"What?" Sully said. "What do you want from me?"

"Why do I bother?"

"No clue," Sully admitted.

Wirf waved him away with both hands. They were grinning at each other now. "What'd Barton want with you?"

After the judge and Wirf and the county prosecutor and the police chief had hammered out their settlement, Judge Flatt had sent for Sully. Wirf, afraid Sully would do something stupid to queer the deal, had wanted to stay, but Flatt had sternly banished him to the corridor outside. To Sully's astonishment, what the judge wanted to ask him about was what had really happened all those years ago when the boy had been impaled on the spiked fence. The judge, himself a young man then, had been one of those who'd gathered on the sidewalk to await the ambulance. Like Sully, he'd apparently never forgotten the scene. Sully explained that he hadn't been there to see it happen, hadn't witnessed any more than the other gawkers. And he thought about telling the judge what his brother had told him, that the reason the boy had been impaled was that his father had shaken the iron fence, shaken it in a paroxysm of rage until the boy fell. That was what the boy had later said happened, but it had been his word against Sully's father's, and anyway, the boy had been where he wasn't supposed to be. Sully had started to tell the judge what he knew, then, without knowing why, decided not to.

"Nothing important," Sully told Wirf now, feeling the same odd reticence. He'd never made any attempt to conceal his contempt for his father, but he'd never shared with anyone what his brother had told him that day.

"Okay, fine," Wirf said. "Don't confide in your own lawyer. See if I care."

"Okay," Sully agreed.

"Goddamn you."

"What?" Sully said.

"You've hurt my feelings."

"You just said 'See if I care.' "

"I'm your lawyer. We zig together. And this is the thanks I get." Wirf pouted. "Piss on you."

Sully sat on one of the radiators and flexed his knee.

"What the hell's the matter with you today?" Wirf wanted to know. "I get you out of jail, and you act like somebody died."

It was true. An hour or so ago, sitting alone in the drab coffee room at City Hall, before he even knew for sure that he was going to be released, that the assault charges would be dropped, he'd felt his spirits soar. There were indications that his stupid streak had run its tortured course, that luck was back on his side. He still felt this to be true. Why then the sudden sense that this shift of fortune wouldn't mean much? That all the luck in the world might not be enough? Probably he was just feeling a little overwhelmed. Jail had been an odd, unexpected release from anxiety and expectation. If he wasn't making any progress toward resolving his various financial and personal headaches, neither was he making them worse, and nobody could justifiably expect much of him, at least until he got out again.

Now that he was a free man, he saw that he had a mountain to move. There was the truck to pay for and Miles Anderson's house to transform. He owed Harold Proxmire and Wirf, and in order to pay them he was going to have to work, and in order to work he was going to have to make things up with Rub. Most of this, with effort, could be done. There was still the outside possibility of selling the Bowdon Street property, though he knew he was very near the end of the so-called redemption period.

Even more disturbing was that Sully could trace his plummeting spirits to the precise moment when he looked up and saw his son and grandson standing in the doorway of the lounge area of City Hall moments after Officer Raymer's demolition of the coffee machine. Every time he laid eyes on Peter he felt in the pit of his stomach the vague, monstrous debt a man owes, a debt more difficult to make good on than money you don't have. A grandson simply extended the debt, let you know that you still owed it, that the interest is compounded. The more he thought about what he owed Peter, the more he despaired of identifying the debt, even as the need to give his son something became more real and urgent. His having thoughtlessly bought his grandson a Coke at eleven in the morning had stayed with him, as had Peter's observation that whatever Sully had to give, you could be sure that this was not what was needed at the moment.

To make matters worse, Peter seemed intent on enlarging the debt. He'd turned out to be a first-rate worker, managing to keep Sully's various irons in their various fires while Sully himself was out of commission. True, every job Peter did he managed to convey, without exactly saying so, that he was doing it under protest, but he did get things done and he did them more quickly and efficiently than Sully could have managed. Peter, Sully had to admit, was part of the reason his luck had changed. If he was able to climb out of the hole he was in, it would be largely due to his son, while Sully seemed largely incompetent to help Peter with his own myriad difficulties—a suddenly disintegrating marriage, the loss of not only his job but his profession, his hopes for a solvent future. And by allowing Peter to help him out, he was putting himself at odds with Vera, who was counseling their son to look for a new job teaching college, steer clear of that wreck waiting to happen that was Don Sullivan. And who could blame her?

More to the point, Sully wasn't sure his pride would allow Peter—the son whose existence he'd often allowed himself to forget for many months at a stretch—to be his savior. It might have been different, maybe, if he were more fond of the man his son had become. There were times when he thought he could learn to be fond of him, and other times when it seemed he already did love his son. But it wasn't the kind of constant affection he felt for Wirf and Ruth and Miss Beryl and even Rub. It wasn't even as powerful as the affection mixed with aggravation that he felt toward Carl Roebuck. Strangely, it was closer to his feeling for Carl's wife, Toby, a feeling he couldn't articulate that resided in the pit of his stomach and made him feel foolish, warning him away—perhaps for the same reason, the deep-down knowledge that these were things he couldn't have, that would not be granted him, a beautiful young woman he had no right to expect, a son he didn't deserve. It didn't bother him much that Peter seemed unable to surrender his grudges. Grudges were understandable enough. Sully had no intention of surrendering his far more numerous grudges against his own father, and so he didn't expect Peter to forgive. What *did* he expect, then?

Possibly, he just wished Peter were a little more like himself. True, he was a hard worker, and, Sully had to admit, a more talented worker as well, slower to become impatient, quicker to understand, more steady of temperament. What negated so many of these qualities was his son's apparent expectation that hard work would be rewarded, a childish attitude that Vera had instilled in him. Because he'd worked hard in school and made good grades, he expected a good job and good pay and security. Because he'd been a competent teacher, he apparently expected promotions and respect. When these hadn't followed, he'd felt self-pity, another of his mother's gifts. Moral outrage and self-pity had always been Vera's strong suits.

As contemptuous as Sully felt toward his own father, at least the two had always conceded, though the concession was unspoken, that Sully was Big Jim's son, that the apple hadn't fallen so very far from the tree. The old man understood and accepted his son's contempt, realizing too its measure of self-loathing. During the last twenty years of Big Jim's life, Sully hadn't even seen him more than half a dozen times, but on each of those occasions something had taken place between them that Sully couldn't deny. He'd catch the old man looking at him as if to say, "I *know* you, buddy boy, know you better than you know your own self." And Sully would always have to look away from the smirk that followed, away from the truth it contained. Maybe that's what Sully wanted from Peter, a firmer sense that the boy *was* his son, that the apple hadn't fallen so far from the tree. Except for rare moments, like the night he'd gone to jail and he and Peter and Wirf had spent the evening drinking at The Horse, it seemed to him that the apple had rolled all the way down the hill and into the next county, which made it hard for Sully to feel much more affection for Peter than he did for the ex-wife, who'd made him, single-handedly.

From where Sully was seated on the radiator, he could hear Peter talking quietly to Will in one of the two bedrooms, their voices echoing in the hollowness, the words not quite audible. It was one of the things that irritated Sully most, he realized, that his son always spoke to Will in whispers, as if Sully were not to be trusted with the contents of even the most casual conversations, or as if he hadn't earned the right to share them. Wirf was also listening to the low murmur of voices and seemed to understand some of what Sully was feeling. "Black thoughts," he grinned. "You're full of black thoughts today."

There didn't seem to be any point in denying this, so Sully didn't.

"Well," Peter said, when he and the boy rejoined them. "You going to take it?"

"My lawyer thinks I should," Sully said.

"Which means he won't," Wirf said. "He's never taken my advice yet."

"If you don't take it, I will," Peter offered.

Sully took this in, part of him pleased. "Good," he said, wondering if this gesture would ease his need to give his son something. "Take it. It'd work better for you anyhow."

"Okay," Peter agreed. "Thanks."

"I guess this means you're going to stick around awhile," Sully ventured.

Peter nodded. "I picked up a couple night courses at Schuyler CC," he said.

"Good," Sully said, impressed that his son could go out to the college and come back home with work. "It's not such a bad place."

"That's what the chair of the department said. 'Not as bad as you might imagine' were his exact words."

"You have to start somewhere." Sully shrugged, hoping to cheer his son up.

"I started at a university," Peter said. "This is where I'm ending, not starting."

Sully decided to give up. "You got enough money for first and last months' rent?" he wondered, trying to think how much he could contribute.

Peter nodded, surprising him.

"I could let you have a hundred or two if you need it," Sully offered.

"I don't," Peter said. "But thanks."

Sully nodded, winking at Wirf. "I'm glad somebody in my family's got money."

"You've got more than you know," Peter said, taking out his wallet and handing Sully a parimutuel racing ticket. A 1-2-3 trifecta, to be exact. Sully checked the date. Two days previous.

"You were on this?"

"No," Peter said. "*You* were. You don't even remember, do you?"

Suddenly he did. Sometime during that drunken night before he'd gone to jail, among all the other instructions he'd had for Peter—what to do first at the Miles Anderson house, how to cook eggs at Hattie's, how to get Rub to help him lay the floor at the Roebuck camp, to look in on Miss Beryl when he thought about it, to feed Rasputin—somewhere among these myriad instructions he vaguely remembered instructing Peter to bet his triple, explaining that it would be just his luck for the son of a bitch to run while he was in jail, further evidence of the evil deity whose existence Sully had long suspected, the god who was probably listening to the whispered instructions of Sully's own father, whose life on earth would have earned him a place in such a deity's inner circle, a chosen advisor, confidant, secretary of war. Miraculously, through drunken inspiration, Sully had apparently thwarted divine intention.

"I would have given it to you at the funeral," Peter said, "but I didn't know there'd been a winner until you told me, and you didn't know which day. I forgot to bet it a couple days."

Before Sully could fully absorb the fact that the ticket in his hand was worth over three thousand dollars, he was assailed by a doubt. "Did I give you the money?"

"What money?"

"To bet the triple."

"Who knows?" Peter said. "Who cares?"

Sully could tell he hadn't given his son the money. "Because if you bet your money, then what you won is yours. That's the way it works."

"I wouldn't even have gone into the OTB except on your instructions," Peter pointed out.

"That's not the issue."

"This'll be rich," Wirf broke in. "I always love it when your father explains the moral significance of things. Follow the logic and win a prize."

"How did *you* get into this conversation?" Sully wondered.

"I don't know," Wirf admitted. "I think I'll go downstairs and stand in the cold."

"Good," Sully said. "Go."

Father, son and grandson listened to him lumber down the stairs.

Sully studied his son and felt even more powerfully than before that he couldn't let Peter be his deliverer.

"Listen, you take this," he said. "You got Will, and you got Wacker's doctor bills now. You're going to need it."

"Not as bad as you," Peter said. "I don't owe anybody."

Sully considered these words. For most of his life he'd been able to say the same thing. Now, suddenly, he was awash in debt. "I tell you what," Sully said, arriving at a compromise. "Why don't we call it a loan?"

From the back stairs came a peal of laughter from Wirf, who had stopped to wait on the landing, still in listening range. "That's your old man," he called up to Peter. "He'd rather owe it to you than cheat you out of it."

They left it that Sully and Peter would meet back at the flat in an hour to unload Peter's things, which were still sitting in a small U-Haul trailer in the driveway at Ralph and Vera's house. Peter would pack the rest of his and Will's clothes into their suitcases, leave Will with Ralph while Peter and Sully effected the move. Vera, blessedly, would not be there, having driven to Schuyler Springs VA hospital, to which Robert Halsey had been admitted during the night. Sully would use the hour to locate Rub, whose assistance they would need to cart the furniture up the narrow stairs to the flat. "Good luck," said Peter, who was convinced that Rub would have nothing more to do with them.

"He'll do what I ask him," Sully assured his son, though he himself was far from certain. In fact, he was not looking forward to what was almost certain to be a humbling experience. Sully wasn't the sort of man to offer direct apology, and he had a feeling that the indirect ones he usually used on Rub—offering to buy him a big ole cheeseburger at The Horse, for instance—might not work this time. He might actually have to say he was sorry for the way he'd acted. Which he was. It wasn't that he denied that he owed Rub an apology. He just hated to establish an ugly precedent of public apology, which could conceivably open the floodgates to other forms of regret.

A good place to start looking for Rub, he decided, was the OTB. Not because Rub would be there so much as that he could cash his triple and bet another. This was no time to come off 1-2-3. In a perverse world it was liable to pop twice in the same week, especially if he wasn't on it.

The windbreaker men had all left, but Jocko was there, peering at the racing form through his thick glasses. When Sully's shadow fell across it, he peered up over the top of his glasses, which had slid down his nose. "Free at lass, free at lass," he said. "Thank God a'mighty."

"It's a great country," Sully agreed.

"Somebody said you'd walked," Jocko folded his racing form and slipped it under his arm. "I found that difficult to credit."

"It's true, though," Sully said. "I punched out the right cop, as it turned out."

"How did Barton look?"

"The judge? Half dead. At least half."

"You're lucky. He used to be a terror. He must be preparing to meet his maker."

"You haven't seen Rub around?" Sully inquired.

"Not once since you went in. Is his wife's name Elizabeth?"

Sully shook his head. "Bootsie," though now that he thought about it, Bootsie could conceivably derive from Elizabeth.

"Big fat girl? Worked at the dime store?"

"Right."

"She was arrested this morning."

"Good God," Sully said. "What for?"

"Theft. She had half the dime store out at their house."

Sully nodded. "She did have a habit of taking a little something home with her every day."

"Turns out they been watching her do it for about a month."

"I hope they have bigger jail cells than the one I was in. Bootsie wouldn't be able to turn around in that one," Sully said, then showed Jocko his ticket. "By the way. Turns out I was on this after all."

Buoyed by the security of his windfall, Sully decided now might be the best time to stop into the diner. It was after one o'clock, and the small lunch crowd would be gone.

Indeed, when he arrived the diner was empty except for Cass, who was sponging down the lunch counter and, to Sully's surprise, Roof, who'd been gone for a month. Ruth was not in evidence, and the combination of her absence and Roof's unexplained presence was disorienting. It was as if Sully'd stepped back in time, and he checked Hattie's booth to make sure she wasn't there, that he hadn't dreamed the events of the last several days. That he'd dreamed the last month of his life seemed a distinct possibility, given the fact that the dream ended with his winning a triple. But Roof was there, all right, wordlessly scrubbing the grill two-handed with the charcoal brick, and Sully selected a stool nearby, in case he needed an ally.

"You're back, Rufus," he ventured.

Roof did not turn around. Nor did he ever. When the diner was busy and the door opened, everyone up and down the lunch counter leaned forward or backward to see who it was, except Roof, who preferred to face his work than the cause of it. "Town this size need a colored man," he observed.

"We realized that when you left," Sully said, grinning at Cass, who'd watched him come in with knowing amusement and had as yet made no move in his direction. "Can I get a cup of coffee, or are you on strike?"

"I should be on strike where you're concerned," she told him, grabbing the pot. "Anybody ever tell you that funerals aren't the place for practical jokes?"

Yesterday, halfway through the service, Otis had discovered the rubber alligator in his pocket and let out a bleat that had caused everyone in the church but Hattie to jump.

"He was supposed to find it when he got home," Sully admitted.

There was enough thick coffee in the bottom of the pot to give Sully about three quarters of a cup. "There," Cass told him. "That's all you get, and more than you deserve."

"Don't make another pot," Sully told her.

"I won't," she assured him. "Starting next week, other people make the coffee."

"Speaking of other people . . ."

"She's out back, taking a delivery," Cass explained. "We had a bet. She said you wouldn't have the nerve to come in today. Nerve is my word, not hers."

"I wish people would quit wagering on my behavior," Sully admitted, recalling that someone (who?) had won a pool when he dropped out of the college.

"You make things up with Rub yet?" Cass said.

"I'm on my way over there as soon as I leave here," Sully told her.

"Good," Cass said. "You two were a popular quinella."

They were grinning at each other now, two old friends. "You going to stay around awhile, or what?"

She shook her head. "The movers come Monday. Wirf's going to mail me a check when the sale goes through."

"Mail it where?"

"Boulder, Colorado."

"Why, for Christ sake?"

"Why not?"

Sully shrugged. "All right, be that way."

"I will."

Her certainty made Sully nervous.

"Roof came back, didn't you, Rufus," Sully observed. "You didn't like North Carolina?"

Finished, Roof tossed his brick aside. "Full of lazy kids," he said with surprising vehemence. "My grandkids. They think you stupid if you work. Make damn near as much not working. Do a little scammin' on the side. They say, what the matter with yo' brain? Workin' like a nigger. I told 'em, I don't know what you are, but I'm a nigger. A workin' nigger."

Sully looked at Cass, who was also stunned. This was more than Roof had said in twenty years. It sounded like twenty years of need might be behind it.

"Ain't nothin' wrong with work but the pay," he said, pouring vinegar on the grill, causing a toxic cloud.

Sully leaned back from the powerful fumes. "That and the conditions."

"And the time wasted," Cass added.

"And the aches and pains," Sully said.

"Ain't nothin' wrong with work," Roof repeated. Perhaps a man who's waited twenty years to say something is not easily joked out of it. Finished with the grill, he filled his water glass, drained it, then ambled out from behind the counter, tossing his apron into the linen hamper. "Y'all be good in Colorado," he told Cass without looking at her. And then, setting his empty glass on the counter, he left.

"You don't suppose Rufus has flipped, do you?" Sully said when the door swung shut behind him.

"No, I don't," Cass told him.

From the back room, Sully heard Ruth's voice and turned on his stool, expecting to see her come in. "Who's going to live in the apartment out back?" it occurred to him to ask.

"Probably Ruth," she said.

Sully frowned at this intelligence.

"She's thinking about putting the house on the market."

"What about Zack?"

"At the moment he's living in the trailer out back."

This was the first Sully had heard of any of these arrangements. They increased his feeling of disorientation. "What trailer?"

"The one the daughter had been living in. You should talk her into renting the apartment to you," she suggested.

"I don't think so." Sully grinned, though the possibility had momentarily crossed his mind. "I'd be better off going to Colorado with you. Safer."

"You'll be plenty safe right here," Cass said significantly.

"Meaning?"

"Meaning Ruth's through with you. Meaning you've finally managed to lose one of the few women in this town worth wanting."

"Who are the others?"

"Good." Cass threw up her hands. "Make a joke."

"You think Ruth would have been better off if she'd divorced Zack and married me?"

Ruth came in from out back right then, saving Cass from having to answer. Ruth studied Sully a moment, then consulted her watch.

"You owe me a dollar," Cass told her.

"Put it on my tab," Sully suggested.

Ruth went to the register, lifted the bottom of the cash drawer, slid a folded invoice underneath. "Your days of running tabs are over, friend."

Sully shrugged, took out a dollar and slid it next to his empty cup. "Maybe if I start paying I can get a full cup of coffee now and then."

The two women exchanged glances. "You okay to close by yourself?" Cass said.

"Yup," Ruth assured her. "You're a free woman."

"My philosophy professor says there's no such thing as freedom," Sully offered.

"He said this before or after he met you?" Ruth wondered.

Cass was looking around the place with what were clearly mixed emotions.

Sully, for some reason, squirmed. "What time are you off Monday?"

"Early."

"How early?"

"Six," she said. "Maybe seven."

"You need help packing?"

"The movers are doing it all," she said. "I'm not lifting a finger."

Sully shrugged. "I'll come by."

"Don't," Cass said, sounding like she meant it, and he saw that her eyes were full.

"Send me a postcard," he suggested.

"Addressed where?"

"To The Horse, with the rest of my mail. Piss Tiny off."

She came around the counter then and they hugged, and Cass whispered a thanks in his ear. "What for?" he said.

"No clue," she admitted.

"Don't look at *me* like that," Ruth warned when Cass was gone.

"Like what?"

"Like I just won her restaurant in a crooked poker game."

"I didn't mean to," Sully said, realizing that this was precisely the way he must have looked. "In fact, I was about to ask how business was."

"Too early to tell," she said. "Some of the regulars are going down to the donut shop for their morning coffee, or so I hear."

Sully nodded, ashamed. "They'll be back."

"If not, to hell with them," Ruth said jauntily, meeting his eye directly.

"You get a good deal on this place?" Sully said, deciding a subtle change of emphasis couldn't hurt.

"The best," Ruth said. "I got a good price and used Vince's money."

"Can't beat that," Sully conceded.

"Nope," Ruth agreed. "It reminded me a lot of the deal Kenny Roebuck offered you twenty years ago."

Sully nodded, not so much acknowledging the truth of her observation as her apparent decision that they would quarrel. "I hope you'll be as content with your decision as I've always been with mine," he told her.

Ruth couldn't help but smile. "Your head must be made of solid granite."

"It's a good thing, too," Sully said, "since everybody keeps kicking it."

"*You*'re the one that keeps kicking it," she assured him. "You're double-jointed, and you don't know it."

The front door opened then, and Janey, in a white waitress uniform identical to the one Ruth used to wear waiting tables at Jerry's Pizza, came in, impatiently towing her daughter. Janey took in the situation at a glance, let the door swing shut behind them. Then she deposited the child and a small stuffed dog she was carrying into the small booth where Hattie used to sit. It seemed to Sully that he'd seen the animal the little girl was carrying somewhere before, but he couldn't think where. The child was studying it with strange intensity, as if she suspected there might be a real live dog underneath the fabric. "You sit right here, okay?" Janey told her daughter.

"Mommy's just going over there, and Grandma's here too, okay? You can see us both. Nobody's going to leave you. You just sit right here for a minute."

Then she came over to where Ruth had begun to ring out the register. "Is she getting up?" she whispered.

"No, she's sitting right where you put her."

"I can't believe it. She's getting better." Janey slipped by her mother and around the counter, where she drew herself a soda from the machine. "Consider the baton officially passed."

"Make yourself at home," Ruth told her.

"I will," Janey said. "And since you're so nice, I'll tell you I saw Daddy pulling in to the alley. He'll be coming in the back any second." She looked at Sully significantly here. "How you doing, Mr. Sullivan?"

"Wonderful," Sully assured her. "Things just keep getting better and better."

"You're out of jail, at least," Janey said, apparently unaware that this bordered on a personal observation. "Next they'll be letting my husband out."

"They better not," Ruth said, glancing over to where the child sat. Sully followed her gaze. With the afternoon light behind her making a halo of her blond hair, the little girl looked unnervingly like old Hattie, who in the last few months had shrunken to near child size. "Not when we're just starting to make progress."

"She just did about half that old lady's jigsaw puzzle yesterday," Janey said, confusing Sully, who was still thinking about Hattie.

"What old lady?"

"Your landlady," she said, causing Sully to remember where he'd seen the stuffed dog before. Then, to her mother, "Does he get up to speed?"

"Not anymore." Ruth grinned.

Janey seemed to accept this as truer than true. "Hey, Birdbrain. Mama's going to work now. You're going to stay with Grandma, okay? Grandpa'll be here in a minute, too. You gonna be okay?"

"She'll be fine," Ruth assured her.

"Better, you mean," Janey said. "Better off with you than me."

"You're late for work," Ruth said, glancing at the clock.

"It's okay. The boss is in love with me."

All three heard the back door open then, and all three waited for Zack to appear, although Sully didn't turn around. "We're in here, dumbbell," Sully called, grateful actually for the arrival of someone he might be able to hold his own against. He often did poorly against women individually, and when they ganged up on him, like Janey and Ruth were doing, he knew it was time to fold the tent. "Just follow the light."

Zack came in, slid onto the stool one down from Sully. In lieu of saying hello to anyone, he asked Ruth, "What're you going to do with that old cash register?"

"It's broke," Ruth told him. "And it killed an old woman."

This latter piece of information either did not impress Zack as germane to his inquiry, or else he'd heard how Hattie died. "I know a guy in Schuyler'd probably give you five hundred for it. They don't make keys like them no more."

Ruth studied her husband malevolently. "Do me a favor," she told him.

"Okay," Zack shrugged.

"From now on, come in the front door," Ruth told him.

"I don't know why you bother, Daddy," his daughter said. "Can't you see she just wants to be mean to somebody? Before you came in she was being mean to Sully. She'd be mean to me too if I'd let her."

Zack shrugged again. "He might even go seven hundred," he told his wife. "This guy, he collects cash registers. All kinds."

"Fuck me," Janey murmured, rolling her eyes at the ceiling.

Ruth studied the two of them, first her husband, then her daughter, then sighed in Sully's direction. "Genetics," she said, and then she surrendered the generous smile that had made him love her so long ago and kept her rooted so deep in his affection now. Cass had been right, of course, Ruth was worth wanting. He just hadn't wanted her bad enough, and in truth he still didn't. He could be ashamed of that, but he couldn't change it. He also realized two other things: first, that Ruth's remark was an act of generosity, the first time she'd ever acknowledged that Janey was not theirs, and second, ironically, that they were indeed through, this time for good, except possibly as friends.

"All right, I'll go," Zack was saying, though he made no move to get up off his stool. "I just come by to see how you made out, if there was anything you needed."

"There isn't," Ruth said. She had finished counting money out of the drawer and was binding wads of ones, fives and tens together with rubber bands.

Zack seemed to understand the sad truth of the situation, that his wife didn't need him, didn't need the other man sitting one stool down the counter either.

"Well," Sully said, sliding gingerly off his stool. "I better go find Rub."

"You like deer meat?" Zack asked suddenly, throwing Sully off guard.

"Who, me?" he said. "No, I don't."

"I got a freezer full, is why I asked," Zack admitted sheepishly. "There's some real nice steaks. I wouldn't charge you nothin' if you wanted to take a couple."

"I haven't cooked anything for myself in twenty years, Zachary," Sully admitted. "Thanks, though."

Janey was chuckling unpleasantly now.

"What's so funny?" Ruth said, shutting the drawer to the cash register in a way that suggested her daughter's explanation had better be good.

"I was just thinking I'm the only one here who's got anything anybody else wants." She adjusted her breasts for emphasis.

"Enjoy it while you can," her mother advised.

"You know what this kind of dog says?" Sully asked the little girl on the way out, wondering if Miss Beryl had told her.

It was Tina's bad eye that found him, her good one still examining the dog, and once again Sully had the strange feeling that he was addressing old Hattie reincarnated. Just when he concluded the child wouldn't answer, she said, almost inaudibly, "Foo on you."

"Right," Sully agreed. "Foo on me."

The front door to Rub and Bootsie's flat was unlocked, so Sully went in, knocking loudly as he did. For a moment he thought he'd made a mistake and walked into the wrong house. Rub and Bootsie's had always been crowded with end tables, lamps, the big aquarium, the zillion knickknacks Bootsie had lifted from the dime store. The walls had been covered with huge paintings of waterfalls, sad clowns, puppies and Elvis. Now the flat resembled Sully's. The walls were bare, and about the only things that remained were the Squeers' ratty sofa and their old console television.

Rub was sitting on the floor in the front room, motionless, his back against the wall. For a fleeting moment Sully thought he was dead. He had his overcoat on and his work boots, his wool cap pulled down over his ears. Next to him was a jug of Thunderbird wine. He glanced up at Sully, dazed, then went back to studying his own booted feet.

"Hello, dumbbell," Sully said.

"Hi," Rub said, as if it was all he could do to choke out this single syllable.

Sully cuffed him gently, knocking off his filthy wool cap. "Take your hat off. You're indoors."

Rub picked the cap up off the rug and fingered it. "I wisht we was still friends," he said.

"We still are, Rub," Sully assured him.

Rub looked up at him again, dubiously.

"You know what *I* wish?" Sully said.

"What?" Rub seemed genuinely curious.

"I wish you'd get up off your ass. We got a lot of work to do, and I can't do it all by myself."

Rub stood unsteadily, kicking over the empty bottle of Thunderbird. "Bootsie got herself arrested."

Sully nodded. "So I heard."

"Did you see her in jail?"

"They don't put the men and women in the same place."

"They took back all the stuff she stole," he added, looking around the empty flat.

"Now you got some room to breathe in here," Sully said, though breathing wasn't something he'd have recommended. The place still smelled like ten pounds of dead dime-store fish. "Let's go to work."

"Okay," Rub agreed.

They went outside. "How come you got the Canimo?" Rub said, climbing in.

"Camino, you dope," Sully corrected him. "How many times do I have to tell you that?"

Rub thought about this and rephrased the question. "Where's the truck?"

"Peter's got it."

"He's still here?" Rub said, clearly disappointed to hear it.

Sully turned the key in the ignition, then turned it off again. "Hey," he said.

Rub studied his knees.

"Look at me," Sully insisted. "He's my son. You're my best friend. That okay with you?"

Rub nodded, snuffed his nose.

"Don't cry either," Sully warned him, intuiting this possibility too late. "You hear me?"

"I won't," Rub said, though it was a promise he couldn't keep.

Sully watched him, shook his head in disbelief, and sighed. He'd gotten away without apologizing, but this was worse. "I should have stayed in jail," he said, turning the key in the ignition again. Then he put the radio on to drown out the sound of his best friend's sniffles.

Since it hadn't taken nearly as long to locate Rub as Sully had anticipated, he decided to swing by Silver Street, where Vera and Ralph lived, in case Peter was still there. Apparently he was, because the U-Haul trailer was still in the drive. For some reason, it was unhitched from the ball of Sully's truck and resting off to the side. The back door to the house, the one that opened into the garage, had been propped open. Since Vera's car wasn't in evidence, Sully backed the El Camino next to the curb and turned the ignition off.

Rub opened the passenger side door and threw up into the gutter, practically the same spot where Sully had upchucked on Thanksgiving. Rub had more to offer. A whole jug of Thunderbird, apparently. When he finished, he said, "I feel better."

"I bet," said Sully, who sympathized, though he had declined to watch.

They were halfway up the drive when Peter backed out the kitchen door holding on to one end of a box spring. "You got a step coming, Pop," he warned.

Then Ralph appeared on the other end. "I know it," he said. "Set it down a minute."

They noticed Sully and Rub then, and Ralph looked relieved. "Just lean it up against the door," he suggested.

"You know Rub Squeers?" Sully asked.

"I don't think so," Ralph said, extending his hand. Rub, who was surprised by Sully's introduction, missed two full beats before realizing what had happened, a look of pure astonishment on his face. Also, he was embarrassed by the condition of his shirtfront.

"He's my best friend," Sully explained, "but he's a little slow on the uptake."

"You never introduced me before," Rub said.

"Sure I have," Sully said. "You just forgot."

"Well, I don't remember it," Rub explained.

"That's what I just said," Sully pointed out.

"I'd remember," Rub insisted.

Sully nodded, grinning at him. "Say the Carnation Milk jingle."

"I like tits best of all," Rub began confidently, only to discover he was lost.

"Aren't you going to say hi to Peter?" Sully suggested.

"Howdy, Sancho," Peter said.

"Hi." Rub scowled.

"Why don't you grab the other end of that mattress?" Sully suggested. "Ralph here looks pooped."

"I am too," Ralph admitted. "I don't have to do nothing to *get* pooped, either."

"That's because you're old," Sully explained.

"I'm not as old as you, and you work all day."

"Actually, he watches us work," Peter observed over his shoulder as he and Rub, who'd begun to look a little pale again, carted the mattress past them toward the U-Haul.

"You want a cup of coffee, Sully?" Ralph offered. "I got some made."

"Good," Sully said. "Let's go inside and sit down and watch them work. It's cold out here."

Ralph led the way. Will was in the kitchen drinking from a coffee cup, so Sully pulled up a chair next to his grandson. "What's that?"

"Hot chocolate."

"I can make you that if you want," Ralph offered.

"Coffee's fine," Sully assured him.

"No trouble," Ralph said. "The cocoa's right here."

"Coffee's fine."

"Take me two minutes to heat the water, is all."

"No wonder Vera's annoyed with you all the while," Sully said. "Bring me a cup of coffee."

Ralph poured a cup from the coffee maker on the drain board. "You want cream and sugar?"

"No, I want coffee."

"They're right here," Ralph said, indicating them and that it was no trouble.

Sully nudged Will. "I still don't have my coffee," he said. "I could have drunk three cups by now."

"Here," Ralph said, setting the cup in front of Sully and pulling up a chair. "I'm glad you and your friend showed up. Now maybe it'll all be done before Vera gets back from Schuyler. That's the bed from the guest room they're loading, and she's going to have a kitten."

"They could take my bed," Sully suggested.

"Then where would you sleep?"

"On the couch. I don't sleep enough to bother anymore anyhow."

"Me neither," Ralph said sadly. "I bet I'm up twenty times a night."

"Vera finds out you let Peter take that bed, and you're going to be the one with no place to sleep."

"I wish I hadn't been asleep last night," he said. "We were burglarized."

"You're kidding."

Ralph looked guilty. "Just the garage. You'll never guess what they took."

"Yes, I will," Sully warned him. "They took the snowblower."

"Was it you who did it?" Ralph said, slack-jawed with amazement.

"No, but I know who did."

"Who?"

"The guy I stole it from. Don't worry. I'll steal it back."

Ralph shook his head, studied Will, who was taking all this in. "Your grandpa Sully's one of a kind, ain't he?"

Will looked back and forth between the two men, clearly unprepared to voice an opinion.

"You want some more hot chocolate?" Ralph said.

Will shook his head.

"You want a poke in the eye with a sharp stick?" Sully offered.

"You don't have a stick," Will pointed out.

"You going to let your two grandpas visit you in your new apartment?"

"And Grandma Vera."

"Right," Sully said.

Peter and Rub came back through then. "Just the top mattress, and we're set," Peter said. "Step down, Sancho," he reminded Rub.

"I know it," Rub responded, though he sounded content to be warned. Sully could almost see Rub's slow brain working, adjusting to this new reality that Sully had taught him—that Peter was Sully's son, Rub his best friend. It'd take him a while to master the intricacies. Sully understood how Rub felt.

Ralph was cocking his head and listening. "Uh-oh," he said.

"What?"

Ralph got up and went to the window. "I was afraid of this."

"You want me to talk to her?" Sully offered.

Ralph gave careful thought to what he clearly considered to be a brave and generous offer, but he finally shook his head. "No, you fellows best go on. Will and I'll be fine, won't we, Willer?"

"Okay." Sully got to his feet and peered out the kitchen window. "I think they're all loaded anyhow."

In fact, Peter and Rub were tugging at the U-Haul, trying to get the hitch to slip back onto the ball joint on Sully's rear bumper.

At first Sully thought his ex-wife was going to simply walk past all of it as if nothing taking place in her driveway were real. She looked like she hadn't the slightest intention of acknowledging her son. Her face was set in stony denial until she caught a glimpse of Rub in her peripheral vision, but she stopped dead then, turning and staring at him. She wore at that moment the expression of a woman who has just picked the cold-blooded murderer of her own parents out of a police lineup.

"Uh-oh," Ralph said again. Sully had already started for the door, skipping on his good leg, the bad one refusing to bear so much weight so soon after he'd been sitting down.

By the time he got outside, Peter had come around the U-Haul and taken ahold of his mother, who was straining against him like a dog on a leash. "Get him away!" she howled. "Get him away!"

"Mom," Peter said, trying to get her attention by getting his face up close to hers so she couldn't see past him. She'd broken one arm free and was pointing at Rub, as if there might be some confusion about whose presence she objected to.

"Get that foul thing away!" she screamed, still pointing. Every time Peter grabbed ahold of her arm and forced it to her side, she yanked the other one free and pointed again. "Why is he still standing there?" she cried. "Get him away! Get him off my property!"

Indeed, Rub was too stunned and confused by this turn of events to move. There could be no doubt who she was pointing at, but he couldn't shake the notion that it must be somebody else. He couldn't ever remember seeing the woman before. And to his way of thinking he'd been invited here. Perhaps not by this crazy woman herself, but by other people who apparently lived there. True, he'd been wrong before about other places where he'd assumed he'd been welcome, and there were times he'd been asked to leave. But this was different. This woman looked like she wanted to exterminate him. He hadn't said a word to her, even, and here she was furious at him, pointing and screaming. A woman he'd never seen before.

Vera never saw Sully until he too came between herself and Rub Squeers. "Vera," he said calmly. "Quit this. Right now."

"You're responsible for this," she sobbed. "*You* brought this to my home. Why must you"—here she searched for the right word—"*contaminate* everything? Why can't you *leave us alone?*"

"Dad," Peter pleaded, "go. I'll take care of this."

"Okay," Sully said, having witnessed enough. "You're nuts, Vera," he said by way of good-bye. "You always were, and now you *really* are."

Ralph was there now too, extending, ineffectually, his hand to his wife, who slapped it away. "Don't touch me!" she wailed. "Don't any of you *touch* me!"

"I never done nothing to her," Rub said when Sully yanked the El Camino away from the curb. Rub was staring back over his shoulder at the scene still unfolding in the driveway as Peter and Ralph tried to get Sully's ex-wife to go inside. Several neighbors had come outside to watch. "I never even seen her before."

"Forget it," Sully told him. "None of that had anything to do with you."

Rub was glad to hear it, glad to have Sully to tell him what to remember, what to forget. "She looked like she wanted to kill me," he said.

"It's me she wants to kill," Sully assured him, "not you."

Rub frowned. "I wisht she'd yell at you, then. I never done nothing to her. I never even seen her before."

"I know that, Rub, goddamn it," Sully said. "I told you to forget about it. Don't tell me you can't forget things, because I know better."

"I don't feel too good," Rub said, leaning his head against the cool pane of glass.

Instead of returning to the new apartment, Sully drove back to Rub's, depositing him there at the curb. "Take a nap," he said. "I'll come back for you later."

"When?"

"Later." He saw Rub's doubt, though. "I promise."

Then, against orders and his own better judgment, Sully drove back to Silver Street.

He had no intention of actually making another appearance. Peter was right. Things had a better chance of quieting down without Sully in the picture. His plan was just to drive by and make sure that Peter and Ralph had succeeded in getting her inside and off the street. Somehow he wasn't sure they'd be able to. He'd always considered Vera to be mildly crazy, but this was a new madness he'd seen in her eyes, and it had frightened him. He fully expected to see police cars and a crowd when he turned the corner onto Silver.

But there were no police cars, and all was quiet in front of his ex-wife's house. The U-Haul still sat in the driveway, still unhitched, which meant Peter might need help getting the trailer's hitch up onto the ball. He pulled over to the curb to consider this but did not get out. If Peter emerged in the next few minutes, Sully'd offer a hand. Otherwise, he'd head back to the flat, out of harm's way.

Farther up the street Sully noticed that a small crowd had gathered. Something was going on, and Sully was thankful that whatever it was, it had nothing to do with him. At least he was thankful until he remembered that Robert Halsey's house, where Vera'd grown up, had been on that block, right about where everybody was gathered. He was trying to muddle his way through what this might mean when he noticed that his grandson Will was standing shyly at the front door of Vera's house, between the outer glass door and the inner one, which stood open behind him. When Sully waved, the boy pointed up the street.

Sully had not been by Robert Halsey's old property in—what?— thirty years? He almost didn't recognize it. Once one of the most meticulous houses on the street, it was now the most neglected. Its weathered gray wood showed through to such an extent that it was impossible to tell what color it had last been painted, and its rotting porch sloped hazardously. Sully remembered its having had a side porch at one time, but somebody had apparently wrenched it away, and the back door now opened onto thin air. The place was in just slightly better condition than his own father's house on Bowdon Street.

When he got out of the El Camino, he was immediately recognized by a man who was a regular at Hattie's. "What's going on, Buster?" Sully said, trying to maintain rhetorical distance from what promised to be an ugly circumstance.

"It's your wife, Sully," Buster said, apparently unwilling to grant him distance, rhetorical or other.

"Can't be," Sully said, moving past the man. "I'm not married."

"Sully to the rescue!" somebody called as he climbed the slanting front porch steps with the aid of a wobbly railing. "Go, Sully," called somebody else, and then a chant started up, "Go, go, go, go." In the distance, a siren.

Ralph stood just inside the doorway, looking plain scared. Vera stood in the center of the room, still wild-eyed, frantically tearing pages from a glossy magazine. Peter, his back to this scene, was on the telephone. "No," he was saying. "No one's been hurt."

"Let's go home, Vera," Ralph said, extending his hand to her as he'd done back in their driveway. Vera ignored him, continued tearing out pages, flinging them at a stupefied fat man seated on a ratty sofa. "She don't have no right to tear up my *Playboy*s," the man said to Sully, though his statement contained an implied question ("Does she?"), as if to suggest that perhaps this berserk woman had a moral right but not a legal one.

Vera flung another fistful of pages at him. "Filth!" she raged. "You brought filth into my father's house. *You're* filth."

At this moment a woman with two frightened children appeared from the back of the house. They were all bundled up in winter coats and hats and gloves, apparently prepared to vacate the premises, though clearly under protest. She steered the children around Vera, keeping them as far away as she could. Sully waited until they were out the front door, then said, "Vera."

His ex-wife refused to acknowledge his presence, but Peter did, turning around with the telephone still cradled to his ear, apparently on hold. The look on his face said, terrific, what else could go wrong?

"Vera," Sully said again, and this time she looked up.

"This is all your fault," she said.

"Yeah, I know it," he said agreeably. "We're going to have to leave now, though, old girl. The cops are coming, and you don't want to get arrested."

She seemed actually to consider the wisdom of this for a moment, until she noticed the *Playboy* in her hands and commenced tearing again. When she finished that issue, she grabbed another. Either this was one of the fat man's favorites or he'd simply drawn the line, because he lunged for the magazine and there was a brief tug-of-war, which Vera won, causing the man to throw up his hands. "There she goes again," he said when she resumed ripping out the pages.

"Vera," Sully said, stepping forward.

Peter said something and hung up the phone. "Dad," he warned, "you'll only make it worse."

"Like hell," Sully said. The only way he could see to make things worse was to let them continue. "Vera," he said again.

His ex-wife continued to struggle with the pages.

"Vera, you're either going to stop this shit and go home or I'm going to knock you right on your ass," he said, adding, "You know I will."

Vera's problem appeared to be that she had ahold of a swatch of pages too thick to tear clean, though she refused to give up and tugged at them furiously, her face bloodred with effort.

Sully made good on his promise then, slapping her harder than he meant to, so hard that the partial plate he didn't know she wore shot from her mouth like a boxer's mouthpiece and skittered under a chair. He stepped back then, as if he was the one who'd been hit, stunned at the sight of his ex-wife without her upper teeth. For her part, Vera seemed not to notice their absence. Everything else about her situation seemed to come home to her in that moment, however, and she sank to her knees and began to sob so hard her shoulders shook. "Ook ut ey've done, 'ully," she wept, looking up at him from where she knelt on the floor.

Peter, looking pale and shaken, moved the chair and located his mother's partial plate. Ralph, Sully noticed, had turned away.

"Jesus Christ," said the fat man on the sofa, "you didn't have to knock her teeth out."

When Sully held his hand out to Peter, he handed over her plate, and Sully went down on his good knee, the bad one throbbing so horribly that he thought he might faint. Vera, still on her own knees, had buried her face in her hands now, and so he had to say her name twice before she'd look at him. "Here," he said, handing his ex-wife her teeth.

She took them, puzzled for a moment, then slipped them into her mouth.

"We're going to stand up now," he told her, and when she seemed incapable, he helped her and she allowed Sully to draw her to him. She buried her head in his shoulder and sobbed. "I hate you *so* much, Sully," she told him.

"I know, darlin'," he assured her, steering her toward the door. Peter moved to meet them there, and Sully turned her over to him and Ralph. Outside, the siren, which had been getting ever closer, Sully now realized, burped once and was silent. Sully peered out the window and saw that it was an ambulance, and right behind it was a police cruiser. Sully decided to stay where he was for a minute lest the cops see him and jump to the wrong conclusion. He was pretty sure that the two young fellows who jumped out of the ambulance were the same two who'd come to Vera's house on Thanksgiving when they'd all thought he was dead.

So he stayed inside for the moment in the fat man's living room. The man still hadn't moved from the sofa, still looked stupefied. Sully found a twenty-dollar bill in his pocket and handed it to the man. "For your magazines," he said.

The man studied the twenty unhappily. "She tore up the Vanna White one," he said. "That's a collector's item."

"Who's Vanna White?" Sully said.

"*Wheel of Fortune?*" the man explained.

Sully placed her now. It was the show that came on after *The People's Court* at The Horse. "Sorry," he said.

"They didn't show that much," the fat man conceded. "No snatch."

To Sully's surprise, he felt some of Vera's own righteous anger welling up. And he was glad she wasn't there to hear such a word uttered in her father's house. "I wouldn't press charges if I were you," he said.

"Okay," the man agreed. "We don't want no trouble with the neighbors."

Sully went to the window and peeked outside. Vera was being helped into the ambulance like an invalid. The crowd was beginning to scatter. After a few minutes he went outside.

Ralph was seated on the top step of the porch, holding on to the railing for support. When Sully sat down next to him, Ralph showed him his free hand, which was shaking uncontrollably. "I ain't nothing but nerves anymore, Sully," he said. "Look at that."

"Well," Sully said, "it's all over now."

"I don't see why people can't get along," Ralph said sadly, returning to his familiar refrain. "That's what I can't understand."

Sully couldn't help smiling.

"Her father did keep this house nice," Ralph said, examining the rotting wood of the porch floor. "I guess it breaks her heart to see it let go like this."

"I know," Sully said, though his own experience had been different. Watching his own father's house decay and fall apart had been deeply satisfying. He was willing to concede that neither Vera's view nor his own was particularly healthy. "You done the right thing," Ralph said, probably in reference to Sully's having slapped her.

Sully was happy to hear it, having come to the opposite conclusion himself. "You want to go out to the hospital," he said. "I'll give you a lift."

"Peter's with her. I'd just be in the way," Ralph said, studying his jittery hands. "I'm no good like this."

Sully fished in his pocket for the most recent vial of Jocko's pills, taking out two of them. "Take one of these."

"What is it?"

"No clue," Sully admitted. "Guaranteed to calm you down, though."

Ralph put it into his shirt pocket while Sully swallowed his dry.

"How do you do that?" Ralph said.

"I don't know," Sully said. "I just do."

"I better get back to the house," Ralph said, struggling to his feet with the help of the railing. "Will's probably staring at that stopwatch you gave him and wondering if we all abandoned him."

In the commotion, Sully had forgotten about the boy. He thought about him alone in the house, trying not to panic. Maybe he'd already panicked. Sully felt a small measure of the boy's fear in his own stomach and considered the implications of the fact that he'd forgotten his grandson again. It was one of the things that Vera and Ruth both held against him, his ability to lose sight of important things. "How can you do that?" they'd both asked him at various times during their relationship. "How can you just forget people?" It was a rhetorical question, he understood, and so he'd never answered. Had he been required to answer, he'd have given the same response he'd just given Ralph when he'd wondered how Sully could swallow a pill dry. He didn't know how. He just could.

Another fifteen minutes found Sully seated by himself at the end of the bar at The Horse, halfway through the first of what would almost certainly be many bottles of beer, waiting for Jocko's pill to kick in and considering a second pill just to make sure (one strategy) and a shot of Jack Daniel's to jump start the first pill (another strategy) and relying on faith (a third) that he had positioned himself correctly at the end of the bar to encounter a distraction or two. The sight of his ex-wife gone over the edge, her heartfelt expression of contempt for himself, seeing her packed into an ambulance and taken to the hospital to be sedated, had penetrated Sully's durable, time-tested defenses, and the blood that was now pounding in his knee hammered so incessantly that the pain was threatening to reach some new crescendo of rhythmic musical agony, the whole orchestra strumming and thrumming and blowing and whacking away at their instruments, awaiting only the crash of cymbals that would, Sully felt sure, allow him to pass out. He could feel the son of a bitch of a cymbal player getting to his feet in the back row, cymbal in each hand, grinning, ready to unload. It was his father, naturally, that one-note musician, percussive and vengeful, who had a cymbal in each hand and was grinning at him, get ready you bastard, 'cause here it comes. Big Jim raised them high above his head for maximum torque. You call this music? That's what Sully would like to ask him.

"Do I call *what* music?" Wirf said, sliding onto the bar stool next to him.

"I wasn't talking to you," Sully told him.

Wirf studied him a moment. "You look like you're about to cash in."

"I just took a pill," Sully told him. "As soon as it kicks in, I'll be fine."

Wirf slid off his stool. "I gotta pee. Order me a club soda with a squeeze of lime," he said.

"Okay."

"And when it arrives, pay for it."

"Okay."

"And an egg. I haven't eaten today. I see the loyal opposition's here," Wirf observed, indicating the large table in the corner, a party of eight that included Satch Henry and Ollie Quinn.

Sully had barely noticed.

"I haven't been invited to join them," Sully said.

"Me, either," Wirf conceded. "I bet they're afraid we'd snub them."

Sully nodded. "One of us might."

"Look who else is back," Wirf said, indicating Jeff, who was tending bar again.

Sully nodded. "He's already bought my first beer."

"I'll hurry back," Wirf said.

On the way to the men's room Wirf passed Carl Roebuck, who was on the way in. On Carl's arm was a young woman who looked to be in her late twenties. Beautywise, she wasn't in Toby Roebuck's league, but she wasn't Texas league either. She wore her hair long, and when Carl Roebuck offered to hang her coat on the rack near the door with the others, she said no, she was cold. Something about the way she hugged the coat to her chest suggested to Sully that she might have nothing on underneath. Or maybe it was just that she was with Carl Roebuck.

"Here's somebody you'll want to steer clear of," Carl told her when they joined Sully at the end of the bar. "Didi, meet Sully. Sully, the lovely Deirdre."

The girl looked Sully over with what seemed to him genuine interest. "I've heard all about you," she said, which seemed to surprise Carl Roebuck until he thought about it. "Oh, right," he said.

Jocko's pill was kicking in, Sully concluded. The conversation seemed just beyond his grasp.

Still examining Sully, the girl nuzzled into Carl's shoulder, whispering something sweet into his ear.

"Right by where we came in," Carl directed her.

"Come with?"

Carl snorted and returned her nuzzling. He was drunk, Sully realized. "You want me to come with you to the girl's room?"

"Women's room, you pig," she said without a trace of seriousness. "You might enjoy yourself."

"I need to talk to this man," Carl told her. "He's my confessor."

"Okay," she said, little-girl voice, then to Sully, "He's got a lot to confess."

They watched her head in the direction of the rest rooms. When she disappeared into the one labeled "Setters," Carl Roebuck swung on his bar stool to face Sully. "You know that I have some experience in these matters," he confided, bleary-eyed.

"What matters?"

"Sexual matters," Carl explained. "You might say I have considerable experience."

"You might," Sully agreed.

"And that I'm not prone to hyperbole," Carl continued.

"I might say that if I knew what hyperbole meant," Sully said.

"Exaggeration," Carl explained. "Overstatement. Didn't you ever go to school?"

"Blow me," Sully suggested.

Carl rapped the bar enthusiastically. "That's my *point*!" he said gleefully. "This girl gives the best head on the East Coast. She could suck the cork out of a champagne bottle. She could suck the lug nuts off a tractor. She could probably bring you to climax, Sully."

Sully ignored the insult. "You want to know what I find hard to believe?"

"What? Tell me. Ask me any fucking thing. I'm the answer man."

"Okay," Sully said. "We'll start with an easy one. Why are you drunk at"—he consulted the clock on the wall—"one o'clock in the afternoon?"

"Because I'm in pain," Carl said, apparently serious. "You're right. That was easy. Next question."

Sully shook his head. "*You're* in pain?"

"I'm . . . in . . . pain," Carl repeated. "What? You think you've got a lock on pain? You think you've got the pain market cornered in this burg?"

Sully took out his vial of pills and set them on the bar between them. "Eat one of these," he suggested. In fact, the throbbing in his own knee had begun to level off, though he could not be sure that this was because of the pill or because the distraction he'd hoped for had arrived.

Carl waved the pills off. "Do they cure heartache?"

"Do blow jobs?"

"For their duration, they do indeed," Carl said. "That was another easy question. Ask me a hard one."

"Okay," Sully said. "What became of all that happy horseshit you were feeding everybody last week? About how you were turning over a new leaf? About how you weren't even horny any more now that you were going to be a father?"

Carl Roebuck was grinning at him now and pretending astonishment, index fingers of both hands pointing at his temples, as if he were receiving telepathic messages. "I *knew* you were going to ask that!" he exclaimed. "In fact, that's the question you were thinking when I walked in here with the queen of the headers. Admit it. *That's* your idea of a tough question, isn't it?"

Sully took an apprehensive swig of beer. He'd seen Carl Roebuck behave like this before. It meant he was about to drop some sort of bombshell. Or what he considered to be a bombshell. Sully studied Carl warily before answering. "Well, I don't know how hard the question is," he said, "but I notice you haven't answered it."

"Then I will," Carl said. "All that happy horseshit? You want to know where all the happy horseshit went? I'll tell you. All that happy horseshit was before somebody named Sullivan managed to fuck up my marriage, before somebody named Sullivan started fucking up my life."

Sully blinked at him, speechless, feeling vaguely guilty. True, he'd had a crush on Toby Roebuck for a long time and probably would have fucked up their marriage if he had the opportunity. But he hadn't had the opportunity. Was somebody spreading rumors? "You know what?" Sully said, when he located his voice.

"No, what?" Carl said, still grinning.

"There are too many people saying things like that to me today. My ex-wife just got done telling me I'm to blame for everything wrong in her life. I expect to hear that shit from her, because she's nuts. But not you.

If you think I've fucked up *your* life, then you're even crazier than she is."

"Sully," Jeff called from down the bar. He made a motion with his hand for Sully to keep his voice down. Several people at the table of eight that contained Ollie Quinn and Satch Henry were looking in his direction.

"Sully, Sully, Sully," Carl Roebuck shook his head sadly. "Who said anything about you?"

Again Sully had the feeling that he was on the fringes of the conversation. "You did. About two seconds ago."

"No I didn't, schmucko," Carl held up one finger, as if to call a point of order. "Scroll back. What did Carl say?"

"You said I fucked up your marriage and your life," Sully said, getting more and more exasperated.

Carl Roebuck made a loud honking noise. "Wrong-o! That was Beulah the buzzer, and *you* don't win a prize. Tell schmucko here what Carl said, Don Pardo!" Then, in a TV game show announcer's voice, he continued, "What Mr. Roebuck actually said was that *somebody named Sullivan* had fucked up his life and marriage. Those were his exact words."

The young woman named Didi returned then, sliding onto the stool next to Carl's and running her hand along the inside of his thigh.

"Watch this," Carl told her excitedly, pointing at Sully. "This is always exciting. He's about to grasp something. There! See it? Truth is beginning to dawn! By Jove, I think he's got it! We've struck brain!"

Both of them were grinning at him now, the girl rather lewdly, Sully thought, Carl Roebuck maddeningly, and then suddenly Carl was on his back on the floor, the bar stool across his legs. Wirf, who had that moment returned, helped Carl to his feet and stood the bar stool back upright. "I can't leave you alone for a minute, can I?" Wirf said, wedging his big, soft body in between Sully's and Carl Roebuck's stools.

Carl Roebuck, feeling the back of his head where he had landed, climbed tentatively back onto his bar stool. "You've hurt me, Sully," he said. "I'm wounded. You've busted my lip, and you've hurt my feelings. I try to be your friend, and what do I get? Heartache."

"I didn't bust your lip," Sully said. "I hit you in the jaw. You bit your own lip."

Carl tasted the blood with his tongue. "Oh," he said. "Then I guess it's my own fault."

Ollie Quinn came up to the bar with a fistful of bills to pay for lunch. From the register he studied the knot of people at the end of the bar—Carl Roebuck fingering his lip, the girl Didi examining Carl's scalp, Wirf standing, Sully still seated, just as he had been when he delivered the blow, flexing his right hand incriminatingly. "You're still pretty quick for an old fart, Sully," Ollie Quinn offered. He took a toothpick from the shot glass next to the register, lodged it between his front teeth with his tongue and made a sucking noise. "You should've seen his old man, though. Now *there* was a brawler."

"A legend," Satch Henry agreed from across the room. "Quick hands," he remembered. "Smarter too. He would've waited till the chief of police left the room."

"Don't say a fuckin' word," Wirf advised under his breath.

"You want to press charges, Mr. Roebuck?" Ollie Quinn said.

"I sure do," Carl said. "But not against him."

The chief of police nodded at Sully. "This is your lucky day," he said.

At noon Miss Beryl fired up the Ford, backed out of the garage, pointed the car in the direction of Schuyler Springs and drove up Main Street past Mrs. Gruber's house, where her heartbroken friend stood at the window, waving at her pathetically. This was the first time in recent memory that Miss Beryl had gone anywhere in the Ford and not taken Mrs. Gruber, who never cared where they were going as long as they went. And so Miss Beryl was not surprised when her friend was unable to understand this act of treachery. She wouldn't have called Mrs. Gruber in the first place except she was afraid her friend would spy the Ford backing out of the driveway and bolt from her house and hurt herself when Miss Beryl drove by.

"I'm all ready," Mrs. Gruber had pleaded. "I'll just throw on my coat and kerchief."

But Miss Beryl had said no. "I'm not fit for human companionship today," she'd explained as patiently as she could, hoping that under the circumstances this explanation would suffice and knowing it wouldn't.

"You're fit for me," Mrs. Gruber had assured her stubbornly.

"If I'm not back by five, send out a search party," Miss Beryl told her friend, half wondering if this might indeed prove necessary if she became lost again or, worse, if she had one of her spells in the car.

"You're all discombobulated," Mrs. Gruber said. "I can tell."

"I'll be fine," Miss Beryl assured her, adding cruelly, "And if I'm not fine, that's fine too."

Which was the way she felt. The phone had been ringing off the hook all morning, people wanting to know where Clive Jr. might be. Actually, the phone calls had begun yesterday, a series of them from the dreadful Joyce woman who'd been waiting, her suitcases packed, for Clive Jr. to pick her up for their long-planned weekend in the Bahamas. The calls had gone from anxious ("I wonder where he could be? Something awful must have happened!") to vengeful ("He may think he can get away with this, but he can't. He's made promises!"). Vengeful was the result of Miss Beryl, who had taken pity on the woman and told her the most likely scenario—that Clive Jr. had simply run away. A story had appeared that morning in the *Schuyler Springs Sentinel* hinting at the possibility of an investigation into the North Bath Savings and Loan, particularly its connection to several other savings institutions in Florida and Texas. The story also suggested that some of the Bath institution's considerable assets might have been inflated through a scheme of buying and selling tracts of land and other properties, transactions that existed on paper without any actual money ever changing hands. This story had prompted a call from a reporter in Albany and even an inquiry from the often inebriated, always scooped editor of the *North Bath Weekly Journal,* a longtime acquaintance of Miss Beryl's who'd started to ask her the same questions as his colleagues, then said to hell with it, apologized for intruding and advised her, "Don't give the bloodsuckers so much as a syllable." In addition to calls from the newspapers, there'd also been several agitated calls from the junior vice president of the savings and loan, wanting to know if Clive Jr. had been in touch with her. He had not taken his flight to the Bahamas, the woman said. He was not at home. She wanted to impress upon Miss Beryl that she needed to speak to Clive Jr. immediately, as in yesterday, if not before. "ASAP," the woman said. Miss Beryl, who understood none of this, nevertheless had a pretty good idea of what it all added up to. Her son was a ruined man.

Miss Beryl had been about to take the phone off the hook when Mr. Blue called to tell her that the Queen Anne had been repaired and was ready to be picked up. "I'd deliver it myself," he explained, "except I had an accident and broke my ankle."

Miss Beryl, grateful for a legitimate reason to leave the house and the phone, had agreed to drive to Schuyler Springs.

"My grandson'll be here to help you put it in the car," Mr. Blue told her, adding sadly, "I'd do it myself if I could."

He gave her directions to his shop, which was located on an avenue that intersected the main street of Schuyler's business district. Without Mrs. Gruber's incessant chatter to distract her, Miss Beryl found the shop without difficulty. In winter, Schuyler Springs looked nearly as unlucky and deserted as Bath, and there was a parking space right in front of the store. Mr. Blue, a man in his late sixties, awaited her on crutches in the doorway, his right ankle so heavily wrapped in a tan bandage that it reminded Miss Beryl of a wasp's nest. "I feel awful making you come out here, Mrs. Peoples," he said, ushering her into the shop where a boy with coffee-colored skin and kinky hair with reddish highlights sat on the counter next to the register, banging his heels and staring at both Miss Beryl and his grandfather contemptuously. He looked to be about twelve or thirteen, an age Miss Beryl knew well.

"Down off there," Mr. Blue told the boy, adding, "Stand up straight" when his grandson settled into a sullen slouch.

"This is my grandson, Leon. He comes up here on vacations to help me out," Mr. Blue told Miss Beryl. Something about the way he said it suggested a different truth entirely—that this was a troubled boy, sent away at every opportunity into a less volatile environment. The boy gave his grandfather the kind of look that said, who are you kidding?

Mr. Blue had done a wonderful job on the Queen Anne. No one who didn't know it had been demolished could tell by looking at it. "Don't be afraid to sit in it," he said, clearly proud of his work.

"Really?"

"It's fixed," he assured her. "People don't believe things can be fixed anymore. They break something and throw it away first thing. That's what I'm trying to teach the boy here. Things can be fixed. Better than new sometimes."

"New's better," the boy said stubbornly. "New's new."

"Yeah?" his grandfather said. "Well put this old chair out in this fine lady's old car, and do it careful."

"I ain't broke nothin' yet," the boy reminded Mr. Blue.

"Broke my heart is what he broke," he said when his grandson was out the door. "Him and his mother and her nigger boyfriend."

Given this ugly sentiment, Miss Beryl couldn't decide whether it was appropriate to sympathize with Mr. Blue, but she did anyway. An imperfect human heart, perfectly shattered, was her conclusion. A condition so common as to be virtually universal, rendering issues of right and wrong almost incidental.

Outside, Miss Beryl found the boy standing next to the locked Ford, looking cosmically annoyed at having been assigned an impossible task. In another year or two, he'd view all tasks in this same light.

"Let's try putting it in the backseat," she told him with as much good cheer as she could muster. Short as she was, getting anything heavy or awkward out of the Ford's trunk was a struggle.

When she opened the back door for Mr. Blue's grandson, he surveyed the space, then the chair, then the gnomelike old woman who wanted him to put the chair where there wasn't room. "Muthafucka ain't gon' fit," he said.

"Try," Miss Beryl told him.

The chair fit. Not by much, but it slid along the backseat with a slender inch to spare. Clearly, having been wrong had no effect on the boy, who looked no less put upon. He was at an emotional age where he was right by definition, because other people were stupid. There existed no proof to the contrary.

Miss Beryl got in the Ford and sat for a moment, thinking about her son and wondering how far he would run. As a boy he'd shamed Clive Sr., who'd tried, without much success, to teach his son to defend himself. But even sparring with Clive Sr. had frightened the boy. His father had taught him how to keep his hands up, to protect his face, but as soon as Clive Sr. aimed a feather punch at the boy's soft tummy, the hands came down, and when his father cuffed him lightly on the ear to illustrate his mistake, Clive Jr. flat quit. He hadn't wanted any lessons in self-defense. He'd wanted his father to protect him, to be on his side, to follow the bullies home from school and beat them up.

No doubt it was what he'd wanted from her too. To take his side in things. To see things his way. To trust him. To be the star of her firmament. Love, probably, was not too strong a word for what Clive Jr. wanted.

There were two naked people sitting at the table, though it took Sully's grandson Will a moment to realize this because, in the center of the table, in addition to a pile of crumpled money, was a mound of clothing and a revolver and, most startling to Will, the lower half of a leg, standing up straight. The leg wore a shoe, a brown wing tip, and a sock, argyle, and above the sock the leg was pink, the color of Will's own skin when his mother or Grandma Vera drew his bathwater too hot and he'd stayed in it too long. Near the top of the limb was what looked like some sort of complex harness. Because he was busy trying to account for this leg, he didn't immediately notice the two naked people.

"Oh, look!" squealed the girl, who was wearing a green visor and no shirt. "A little boy!" It was then that Will noticed her nakedness and was embarrassed. Her chest looked unnatural, limp, as if some invisible bone had been broken. Will had seen his mother bare-chested before and remembered feeling the same way at that sight, as if these breasts that women had were the result of some terrible injury, a bad fall perhaps. He stayed where he was when the girl in the green visor beckoned to him, her arms extended. "Isn't he handsome?"

"You stay away from my grandson," Sully, mildly drunk, advised her, rotating in his chair to acknowledge Ralph, who, when he saw a bare-chested woman seated at the poker table, had also taken an involuntary step backward, followed by several more voluntary ones, so that he was now almost back out through the door and into the bar again. "We're almost done here," Sully said, gathering his grandson to him. "This is the last hand. These people have already lost their shirts."

"How about closing that door?" Carl Roebuck said, indicating the one Ralph and the boy had just entered through. "I'm feeling a little naked here."

"This is the asshole that stole your snowblower," Sully explained by way of introducing Carl Roebuck, whose jaw had swollen monstrously in the hours since Sully had punched him off his bar stool.

Carl, as it became apparent when he stood, was not only feeling a little naked, he was literally naked except for his socks. When he stood and went over to shake Ralph's hand, the latter looked for a moment like he might bolt. "I'll give it back to you," Carl promised, "as soon as your son returns my wife."

"He's my son," Sully reminded Carl when he returned to the table. "No son of Ralph's would do such a thing, would he, Ralph?"

Ralph did not understand any of this. Not the naked people. Not the pile of clothes in the center of the table. Not the revolver. Not the prosthetic limb. Certainly not the apparent reference to Peter. It was as if he'd stumbled into a poetry reading. He'd been on the lookout for poetry readings since Peter had described the way they worked, and he half expected someone to start reciting a rhyme or two now. Either all of this was crazy or all these people were drunk or that pill that Sully had given him during the noon hour, which had made him feel like a visitor from another planet, was releasing another spurt of medication.

"Don't worry about the snowblower," Sully said, returning his attention to his hole cards. "I've got a pretty good idea where he's hid it."

Ollie Quinn, who'd been sleeping with his head back and mouth open, snorted awake when Carl sat back down at the table. The chief of police rubbed his eyes. "How come she's naked?" he said, noticing the girl. Sully had tossed her Carl Roebuck's shirt when Ralph and his grandson entered, and she was slipping it on over her head.

"What do you mean, how come *she's* naked?" Carl Roebuck said.

Ollie started. "Jesus," he said. "So are you."

"Why the hell not?" Carl said. "Why not let this be the day I lose everything, right down to my shorts?"

This was in reference to the Ultimate Escape deal having gone south, as Carl had known it would, and to Clive Jr., the putz, the man everybody in Bath wanted answers from, having gone off on vacation to the Bahamas. Some people were whispering that he hadn't gone to the Bahamas, he'd just gone.

"You fell asleep during my horse story," Carl told the police chief. "Now that you're awake again, I can finish it."

"Go back to sleep," Sully suggested to Ollie Quinn. "Nobody wants to hear him tell hard luck stories."

"Ten lengths," Carl Roebuck said, starting in where he'd left off. "He had a lead of ten fucking lengths coming into the far turn."

Ollie Quinn seemed immediately engrossed in the story.

"Guess what happened," Carl insisted.

"He was shot by a sniper in the grandstand," Sully guessed.

Carl, who had been about to continue, glared at Sully.

"Let me make this long story short," Sully said. "Carl's horse was outrun down the stretch, and he doesn't think things like that should happen to him. They usually don't either."

Carl turned back to Ollie Quinn with the air of a reporter who's just learned he's been scooped. "*Ten lengths* he gave up in the last two hundred yards," he told the police chief.

Ollie Quinn looked disappointed, like he was still waiting for the end of the story or as if he'd preferred Sully's version with the sniper.

"Wouldn't you swear he'd never seen a horse race before," Sully said. "He can't stand it when his luck doesn't hold, even for a minute."

"It's not enough I've got to lose all my money," Carl continued, going back to his cards now. "I have to lose the last of it to the dumbest man in Bath."

"I *said* this was Sully's lucky day," Ollie Quinn reminded them. He stared dully at the collection of items at the center of the table, including Wirf's prosthesis. "Whose gun is that?"

"Yours," said Carl, who had disarmed the police chief in his sleep just before Ralph and the boy entered. "It's your ante."

Ollie Quinn checked his empty holster and saw that this was true. "I should have busted this game two hours ago," he observed.

"If we could ever finish this fucking hand, there'd be no need," Carl pointed out, then, to Sully, "Tell your lawyer to shit or get off the pot."

Wirf, who looked half asleep himself, tossed his cards into the center of the table. "I play better poker drunk," he said, taking a sip of his club soda.

"Not much better," Sully told him, raising the bet.

"We just come to tell you Peter's over at the flat," Ralph said. "He said he was going to start unloading."

"Okay, I'll go over," Sully said. "Hang around for a minute, why don't you. I'll be done here real quick."

"We'll wait outside," Ralph said, motioning for Will to join him. "Don't take too long."

Out in the bar, Ralph, wishing he could escape with Will out into the street and its clean cold air, helped Will up onto a stool and ordered sodas. "Can't let the boy sit at the bar," the fat bartender told him. "Sorry. It's the law."

"That's okay," Ralph said guiltily. Vera, who was staying the night in the hospital for further observation, would have wanted to know what was wrong with him for putting the boy on a bar stool to begin with, and he would have had to say he wasn't thinking. He was glad that at least Vera had been spared the sight of the goings-on in the next room. She'd have had a week's worth of opinions on such degradation, and she'd be right. Ralph made a mental note to warn the boy not to tell her what he'd seen. "You stand down there," he told Will, "until the man brings us our sodas."

A roar went up in the next room and there was the sound of scraping chairs. Ollie Quinn, returning his revolver to his holster, was first to emerge from the room, then Sully, who had a wad of money in one hand and Wirf's leg in the other. He planted the leg upright on the bar, stuffed the money into his front pants pockets and helped Will back up onto a bar stool just as Tiny returned with the sodas. "He can't sit at the bar, Sully."

Sully frowned. "Why not?"

"It's against the law."

"Bullshit."

"It's against the goddamn law, Sully."

"So's poker," Sully said. "You saying you didn't know there was a poker game going on back there?"

"Don't start with me, Sully," Tiny warned. "You're on thin ice tonight. You've already punched one of my customers. Jeff should have run your ass then. This is thin fucking ice you're skating on here."

Sully nodded at him, "Well," he said to Ralph, who had already gotten off his stool and had the boy under the arms, "maybe we *better* go over there to one of those tables. Because if this is thin ice we're on, we don't want this fat fuck anywhere near us."

Carl Roebuck and the girl Didi, both fully clothed again, emerged from the room. "Let me take another one of those magic pills," Carl Roebuck said. "I think you broke my jaw."

Sully handed him the vial of Jocko's pills. "I hate to say it," he said, studying Carl's face. The jaw had gradually ballooned all afternoon until now it looked as though it had grown a tumor. "But you may be right."

Carl swallowed the pill with the last of his Jack Daniel's and set the glass in the center of the table Sully and Ralph and the boy had selected. Then Carl collapsed into a chair, pulling the girl onto his knee. "What a day," he said. In fact, he said it with such conviction that Sully was on the verge of feeling sorry for him, when he turned the girl toward him, buried his face between her breasts and commenced to make blubbering noises.

"Don't let him drive, dolly," Sully warned the girl. "The second one is really magic."

"I won't," she said, her eyes meeting Sully's seriously and soberly, as they had done several times during the afternoon. She'd been drinking as heavily as the men, but she looked to be in a lot better condition for it. So this was the girl who had wrecked Peter's marriage and talked dirty to Vera on the telephone, Sully thought. No wonder his ex-wife had gone into a tizzy. Vera was, and always had been, a close-your-eyes, missionary-position sort of woman. She probably hadn't done much to prepare Peter for the likes of Didi. Apparently even Carl Roebuck hadn't been prepared. "If you see Peter, tell him I said hi," she said.

"I will," Sully promised.

"You will not," Carl Roebuck said, his voice muffled in the girl's sweater. "He can't have both these women."

"Carl's used to having all the girls in Bath to himself," Sully explained to her.

Didi looked down at him. "His heart's broken," she said. "It's kind of sweet, don't you think?"

"Kind of," Sully said.

"I bet no girl ever broke your heart," she said, her eyes meeting his again.

"He's in love with my wife too," Carl said. "Everybody loves Toby. Nobody loves me."

Wirf appeared in the doorway, using an inverted push broom as a crutch, his empty pant leg dangling. "You'd keep my leg, wouldn't you?" he said to Sully.

"You don't need a leg," Carl Roebuck turned and studied him. "You need a parrot."

"Should we give him back his leg?" Sully asked Will.

Will nodded eagerly.

Sully slid Wirf's prosthesis in front of the boy. "Go ahead."

The boy's eyes got wide, and he shook his head, leaning away from it.

"It's not alive," Sully said, rapping it. "See?"

"He don't want to, Sully," said Ralph, who looked like he didn't want to either.

"You could tell your brother," Sully said. "You think he'd believe you?"

Will stared at the limb with fear and longing. The idea clearly appealed to him. The limb clearly did not.

"Sully—" Ralph began, but Sully held up his hand, and after a long moment the boy reached out and took Wirf's leg with both hands, as if he suspected that it contained the man's liquid life and the spilling of a drop would mean less of him. They all watched the boy as he carried the limb to Wirf where he leaned against the door frame. When Didi snuffed her nose, Sully looked and saw that she was crying, tears rolling silently down her cheeks.

Wirf drew up a chair and accepted the prosthesis from Sully's grandson. "Thanks," he said, pulling up his pant cuff. No one, not even Will, looked away as he fastened his leg. "Your rotten grandfather would have kept it. Now I'm a whole man again."

For a moment, as Sully watched, it wasn't Will standing there but Peter, the Peter he remembered as a boy. Or maybe even himself, the boy he remembered himself to have been so long ago, the boy who had a heart capable of being broken.

"Jesus Christ," Carl Roebuck said softly. "What a day."

■ ■ ■

By the time Sully arrived at the flat the U-Haul was nearly unloaded. The only things left inside were an oak desk and a tall file cabinet. Peter had backed the trailer up over the curb to the base of the front porch and laid a ramp that angled from the inside of the U-Haul to the top of the steps. Sully was inside tugging the desk from the rear of the U-Haul toward the front when Peter appeared on the porch. "Grab the other end," Sully suggested. Thankfully, Peter had taken the drawers out.

Peter moved past him to the other end of the desk but declined to lift just yet. "Where's Rub?"

"Home," Sully said. "I thought I'd give him the night off." Actually, he'd thought about fetching Rub, but it was late and Rub was probably still sick. Also, he'd heard that Bootsie had been released, and Sully couldn't face Rub's wife, not after the kind of day this had been. "You going to pick up that end, or what?"

"You're drunk," Peter guessed. Either that or he could smell the beer in the confined space of the U-Haul trailer.

"A little," Sully admitted.

"This is heavy," Peter said.

"I can lift my end," Sully assured him. "Just worry about your own."

Peter studied him a moment. "I get this feeling we're fighting over a woman again."

"I get the feeling you expect this desk to walk upstairs on its own if you wait long enough," Sully said. "Come on."

"Fine," Peter said. "Kill yourself."

When they got up the ramp and onto the porch, Peter set his end down. "Let me back up, at least," he suggested.

"No."

"Fine."

They lifted then and moved through the door to the foot of the stairs, Sully backing, Peter inching forward.

"Slow now," Sully said, feeling the first step at his heel. The problem, he knew, was how to use the bad leg—to step with it or plant with it. Plant, he decided, since the good leg would bend at the knee and he'd have to thrust off it. They began going up the stairs a step at a time. He lifted from a ridge underneath the rim, and after each step he allowed the legs of the desk to rest a moment on the step below. They'd only gone four or five steps before he could see, even through his beery fog, that this was foolishness. Peter and Rub could walk the bastard of a desk right up in the morning. It would take them thirty seconds, and they wouldn't have to stop once, much less at every step. A year ago Sully himself would not have had to stop. Worse, their slow progress was making the job twice as hard on Peter, who had to bear the weight of the desk between lifts. Sully could see his son sweating profusely in the frigid air. "You enjoying yourself?" Peter wanted to know when they were about halfway.

"Yes, I am," Sully said, hoisting another step.

"Have you decided what it is you're trying to prove?"

"We're arguing over a woman, I thought."

"That's right."

Sully heaved again, and they went up another step. "Well, pray for me then," he suggested. "Because if I lose my end of this desk, we won't have a dick between us."

The living room that had seemed so spacious that morning was now crowded with boxes that Peter had stacked in rows in front of the fireplace and the built-in bookshelves and along the walls. The two men guided the desk between them and to the far corner, where Peter had reserved a space for it.

"I thought you said Charlotte took everything," Sully said, looking around the room at all the cardboard boxes.

"She did," Peter said. "These are mostly my books."

Sully tried to take this in. There had to be seventy boxes. In the next room, the shower thunked off. Sully hadn't been aware of the sound, or its significance, until it stopped. He studied Peter, who leaned against the desk. "Didi says hi," he told his son.

If Peter was surprised, he didn't show it. "I was afraid she'd turn up. She jump you yet?"

"No. She jumped Carl, though."

"She will," he said, adding, "Just to get at me."

"I should probably let her," Sully said. "Just to get at you."

More sounds from the next room. "I better say you're here."

They heard the bathroom door open then, and Sully purposely turned away. He was tempted to leave, and when Peter followed Toby Roebuck into the bedroom, he nearly did. Behind the door he could hear urgent, confidential voices. From the front window he saw the big IGA sign across the street flicker and go dark, but just before it did he caught a flicker of shiny red metal in the street below.

Sitting on the big oak desk, he leaned back against the wall and closed his eyes for a second, enjoying the dark, even though the solitude turned up the volume on the song his knee was singing. That afternoon and evening, once Jocko's pill took effect and he'd found a few decent distractions (beer, bourbon, poker, a pretty half-naked young woman), he'd almost been able to forget about Vera and his knee, its singing reduced to background vocals, the orchestration to soft violins. Now the marching band was back again, but just tuning up, not stomping to the rhythm of the bass drums. For which he was thankful, being far too worn out to march.

And indeed there were other things to be thankful for. His luck had finally turned. He still had his triple winnings and another five hundred or so from the afternoon's poker game. He wasn't out of the woods, but tomorrow he'd be able to go see Harold Proxmire and give him fifteen hundred on the truck, which would hold him for another couple months. And he'd have his first and last months' rent on the new apartment he hadn't found yet. If his luck held, Miles Anderson wouldn't return for a while and see how far behind he was on the house. It shouldn't take more than a couple weeks to get more or less caught up now that Rub was back in the fold. Peter had managed to convince Anderson that everything would get done. Probably the smart thing would be to turn the whole Anderson project over to Peter. If it snowed, he could afford to do that. Maybe he could afford to anyway. Sully felt the big wad of bills bulging comfortably in his pants pocket. He hadn't even counted it yet. Maybe he was even better off than he knew.

When he awoke with a start, he saw that over half the boxes in the living room were now unpacked and the floor-to-ceiling bookcases were now full of books. Toby Roebuck, barefoot, her hair still damp, dressed in jeans and a sweatshirt, was standing on a chair and filling up the top shelf with volumes Peter was handing to her. The empty boxes they had used to form a wall between themselves and him. It was Toby Roebuck who first noticed he was awake. "Sully," she said. "How can you sleep sitting up like that?"

In fact, he wished he hadn't, at least not for so long. He'd slept slumped against the wall, and his neck was stiff. "Hello, Mrs. Roebuck," he said, trying to stretch some of the kinks out.

She gave him a look. "Don't Mrs. Roebuck me, Sully," she said cheerfully. "You're a documented sinner."

"That was a long time ago," he said, standing up and testing his knee. "Anymore I'm too tired to sin."

"My point exactly. Don't criticize people who have the energy." She cast a glance at Peter, who didn't look like he had any great wealth of energy himself. He must have, though, Sully reflected. There were at least two women who thought so.

"I don't recall saying anything except hello," Sully told her. "If you decide to get married, let me know. I'll give away the bride."

"Don't pretend you approve, either," Toby Roebuck said. "That's even worse."

Sully flexed tentatively at the knee. "Let me see if I understand. I'm not supposed to approve and I'm not supposed to disapprove. What the hell *am* I supposed to do?"

"Break down some of these boxes," Peter suggested. "There's a pair of scissors right behind you on the desk."

"Just don't throw them all away," Sully told him, picking up the scissors. "I'm moving myself in a couple days."

"I'll save a couple," Peter agreed. "You think two will do it?"

"I wish I'd known you were attracted to smart-asses," Sully told Toby Roebuck.

"He has other qualities," she said. "If it were just being a smart-ass, I'd be attracted to you."

They finished about half an hour later. With all the books on the shelves and the boxes broken down and in a single tall pile, the flat again looked bare. "You're going to need a few things, aren't you," Sully said.

Toby's voice came in from the kitchen. "Pots and pans and plates and glasses and silverware, for instance."

"I've got all that stuff," Sully said. "We can bring it over tomorrow."

"Then what would you use?" Peter asked.

"I haven't eaten a meal at home in five years," Sully told him truthfully, pulling on his coat and gloves to leave.

"That's sad," Toby said from the kitchen doorway.

"Not really, dolly," Sully said, going over to the window. The street was dark, but he could make out the shape of Carl Roebuck's sports car at the curb below.

Peter put on his coat too. "I'll walk you down. I've got to close up the trailer anyhow."

Sully glanced around the room again. Even empty it looked good. The fireplace, surrounded by books. He hadn't seen that in his mind's eye when they'd looked at the flat this morning, hadn't imagined how it might look. "The place is going to be all right," he admitted. "Bring your mother over tomorrow. It'll make her feel better."

Peter nodded. "Nothing reassures her like books."

"She'll love it here, then. It's a regular library," Toby said, pronouncing it "lie-berry," and Sully thought he saw Peter smile.

Sully led the way down the dark stairway, holding on to the railing and taking the stairs one at a time, both feet on each step before proceeding to the next. What had possessed him, he wondered, a few hours ago, to back up these same stairs with a heavy oak desk? On the other hand, what had possessed him to punch a policeman last week or Carl Roebuck this afternoon? As always, to Sully, the deepest of life's mysteries were the mysteries of his own behavior.

At the foot of the stairs, Peter flicked a wall switch to no purpose. "One more thing to do tomorrow," he said, staring up into the dark of the vaulted ceiling. "Thanks for the help with the desk."

Sully nodded, didn't say anything for a minute. Peter, he was coming to understand, was capable of generosity. Sully hadn't been a help with the desk, he knew. He'd made more of a job of it, not less. His son was simply being kind. Maybe this was one of the other qualities Toby Roebuck was referring to. "I'd lock up down here if she stays the night," Sully warned. "That's her husband parked across the street in the red car."

"He followed us as far as Albany," Peter said. "When we went to Morgantown."

"She went with you?"

Peter didn't say anything.

"How did all of this come about?" Sully wondered, genuinely curious.

"Quickly," Peter said, as if this explanation might suffice. It did not. Sully had never fallen in with any woman quickly.

"Well," Sully said. "Look out for Carl. This is all new to him." It was odd talking to Peter in such a confined, dark space. Easier, in some ways. Often it was the expression on his son's face that made talking to him difficult, the wry, detached smugness. His voice, on the other hand, was pleasant enough. "He's the one that's always playing around," Sully explained. "He's got to get used to the shoe being on the other foot."

Sully could see just well enough to see his son shrug. "The shoe's been on the other foot before," Peter said. "At least according to Toby."

Sully considered this for a moment. "I doubt it," he said.

"Okay," Peter agreed. "Have it your way."

"She's a pretty nice girl."

Peter chuckled. "She's a pretty nice woman. And you've put her on a pretty tall pedestal."

"Well," Sully said and let his voice trail off, glad that Peter apparently had no interest in confiding to him Toby Roebuck's past transgressions, if indeed he knew of any. "Swing by the house on Bowdon in the morning before you return the trailer. There's some furniture in the spare room. If there's anything you want, take it."

Peter said he would.

"There might not be anything you can use," Sully admitted. "Who knows?" He put his hand on the doorknob. "I'll have a word with our friend on the way out. He'll listen to me."

"Do me a favor and don't," Peter told him. "You'll just make things worse. Again."

This, Sully realized, was a reference to his earlier refusal to wait for the ambulance when he'd slapped Vera. The horror of the scene had been running through his mind all afternoon, despite the excellent diversions— beer and poker and bare-breasted girls—with which he'd been surrounded. "You think your mother's going to be okay?"

"I don't know," Peter admitted. "They're going to keep her at Schuyler overnight. You know how she is. She's not any different, really, just worse."

"You could probably help her out more," Sully ventured.

"Not really," Peter said. "The world doesn't do what she wants it to, and she gets frustrated."

This was the same conclusion Sully had come to thirty-five years ago, of course, and Peter couldn't make his mother happy or content anymore than Sully had been able to all those years ago. Still, it now seemed cowardly that Sully had not tried harder, endured more. It was one thing to realize you were shoveling shit against the tide, another to give up the enterprise before you got soiled. Especially when, in other respects, you intended to keep shoveling different shit against other tides. "It sure doesn't take much to get her started anymore," Sully reflected, recalling that the mere sight of Rub in her driveway had set her off. Or maybe it had been the knowledge that he himself had been inside, that he had invaded her home. Contaminate it, was what she'd said.

"There was more to it than you know," Peter said. "Grandpa went into the hospital this morning. He couldn't breathe, even with the oxygen."

Sully thought about Robert Halsey, the way he'd looked at Thanksgiving, and made a mental note to shoot himself before he ever got like that. "When he dies, you'll be all your mother's got."

"She's got Ralph."

"She doesn't count Ralph. You know that."

"I do," Peter said. "Ralph's the one I worry about."

"He doesn't look too good, does he," Sully admitted.

"He's a wreck," Peter said. "If I ever get my shit together, it'll be for him, not her. He's been a good father."

"And there's Will," Sully ventured.

"Kids are resilient," Peter said. "Look at me."

"I *am* looking at you," Sully said to the darkness.

"Well," he said. "If it'll ease your mind, this isn't anything serious upstairs."

Sully nodded. He'd gathered that much. Seen it when Peter had smiled at Toby Roebuck's pronunciation of the word "library." Peter had too much of Vera in him, too much educational reinforcement ever to fall in love with someone who said "lie-berry."

"I'm glad to hear it," Sully said, because he was.

"I bet you are," Peter said. Even in the dark, Sully could tell his son was grinning. Maybe that was all Toby Roebuck meant to him. They'd argued over a woman, and he'd won the argument.

"I was thinking of her husband," Sully said, surprised to discover that this was true. "I'm not sure he'll be able to spare her."

"He's not out of the woods yet," Peter said. "There's some woman in Schuyler."

Sully snorted. "Carl's got women everywhere, not just Schuyler."

"It's not Carl I was talking about."

It took Sully a moment, but somehow this knowledge was easier to process in the dark. The possibility wouldn't have occurred to him in a hundred years, but now that the words had been spoken in the intimate dark, he saw they must be true "Why, then?" he finally said.

"Why what?"

"Why are you doing what you're doing?"

"I have no idea," his son said, and for once it sounded like simple, unadorned truth. No irony, no sarcasm, no anger.

"Well," Sully sighed, opening the door onto the porch. "It's time I went home."

He was on the top step when Peter said, "You going by Bowdon Street tonight?"

"I hadn't planned to. Why?"

"That dog needs to be fed."

"Shit. I forgot all about him," Sully admitted.

"Hold that thought."

"He's not really my dog," Sully said in his own defense.

"Right," Peter said, his usual sarcasm back again. "Not really your dog. And the house he's locked up in isn't really your house. You're a free man."

"You're damn right, son," Sully said. "Don't forget. Lock the door."

Sully waited to hear the bolt fall into place behind him before he crossed the street to where Carl Roebuck's car idled, a plume of white exhaust trailing off down the street. When he got close, Carl rolled down the driver's side window halfway and said, "Hello, schmucko."

"You follow me over here?" Sully wondered.

"I did," Carl admitted. "I forgot my cigarettes, too. Let me take one."

Sully shook a cigarette up through the opening in the pack. Carl took it. "Let me have the whole pack. I'm going to stick around for a while," he said, studying Sully in the pale light of the street lamp. He tossed the pack of cigarettes onto the dash. There was just enough light for Sully to see that Carl's jaw was a balloon, his grin hideous. "You look like a man who's just discovered the cruel truth of life," Carl ventured.

Something stirred inside the dark car, and Carl looked down at his lap. "It's okay, darlin'. Go back to sleep," he said. "I'll roll up the window in a second."

From inside, a murmur and then silence.

"You gotta see this," Carl whispered after a moment, reaching behind him to flip on the dome light. He left it on for only a second, but that was long enough. At first Sully thought the girl Didi had simply fallen asleep with her head in Carl's lap, but then saw that she had his flaccid penis in her mouth like a pacifier. "Isn't that sweet?" Carl said.

"Adorable," Sully said. "I hope she doesn't have a nightmare."

"*You* hope."

"I'm going home," Sully said. "I'm tired, and you're too fucked up to talk to, even."

"Ain't it the truth," Carl said.

"Don't go upstairs," Sully told him.

"Okay," Carl said.

"I mean it," Sully warned him.

"I know you mean it."

"Then don't."

Didi sat up and rubbed her eyes. "It's cold," she said sleepily, shivering. "Hi, Sully."

"Now look what you did," Carl said, rolling up the window.

Sully would have liked to warn Carl one more time, but he was too exhausted to make him roll down the window again.

On the way to Rub's an odd thing happened. The day's bizarre events unreeling through his mind, Sully missed his turn, went one block too far and turned there, not realizing his mistake and suffering a stunning loss of orientation as a result. This dark street was clearly one he knew, a street in the town he'd lived his entire life, yet despite its familiarity he suddenly had no idea where he was. How had these houses come to be on Rub's street? Where had the house that Rub and Bootsie rented disappeared to? He squinted in the dark at each house he passed, certain that theirs would appear any moment and his sense of equilibrium would be restored. When it didn't he stopped in the middle of the street and just sat, thankful that it was late, that there was no one around to witness this, that he'd be spared the humiliation of rolling down his window and asking someone for directions. In the end there was nothing to do but back up, and so he did, understanding his mistake only when he'd backed all the way to the intersection and saw the street sign. A minute later when he pulled into the driveway next to the small two-family house where Rub and Bootsie lived, he gave the horn three short, light taps, his signal for Rub to come out and get instructions for tomorrow. Bootsie had made bail by calling her sister in Schuyler, and rumor had it she'd left the courthouse on the warpath. Sully had no intention of encountering her tonight if he could help it.

Blessedly, it was Rub's round head that appeared at the window, and a moment later he came out in his undershirt, boot laces flapping, and climbed into the El Camino, where it was warm. He faced away, though, until the dome light went off. Sully opened his door so it would come back on and he saw Rub's swollen eye.

"Jesus, Rub," he said, closing the door again.

Rub shrugged. "What am I supposed to do? Guys aren't supposed to hit girls."

"You aren't supposed to let them hit you, either," Sully pointed out for argument's sake.

"I didn't let her," Rub explained. "She just did it."

"You're supposed to duck," Sully explained.

"I did," Rub explained. "She done this with her knee when I did duck."

"Well," Sully sighed. "I guess you did all you could, then."

Rub shrugged.

"Meet me at Hattie's in the morning. Early. Six-thirty. We're going to move some shit out of the house on Bowdon first thing. I wish we'd thought to do it before we took the floor up."

Rub said he wisht they had too.

"What are you going to do tomorrow? Say it back to me."

"Meet you at Hattie's at six-thirty."

He'd be there, too, Sully knew, one of the few things he could count on. "I'll buy your breakfast," he promised.

"Good," Rub said. "I don't have any money."

"I've got a hammer in back," Sully suggested. "We could go in and whack her on the noggin and bury her in the woods under all those blocks you broke. They'd probably never find her."

"I wisht we could," Rub said, getting out of the El Camino again. "She's fat and ugly and mean."

When Rub closed the door, Sully started to back out, only to hear Rub rap on the door as if he'd suddenly remembered something. He opened the door again. "And stingy," he said.

Sully, unwilling to get involved for long, checked out The Horse through the beer sign in the front window before entering. It looked like Tiny had only two customers. Wirf, predictably, and, less predictably, Jocko. Both men rotated on their stools when Sully entered and ducked into the men's room.

A moment later Jocko was standing at Sully's side, unzipping before the second of the two wall urinals, making Sully glad that he'd decided, despite his exhaustion, to stand to pee.

"Somebody told me this was your lucky day," Jocko offered, awaiting his urine while Sully dripped toward unsatisfactory conclusion.

Sully considered this, supposed it was true, after a fashion.

"It figures your luck would turn around just as the town's went south," Jocko offered.

"The town's luck went south about two hundred years ago, pretty near," Sully observed.

"True," Jocko admitted, still awaiting his water. "But this'll finish it. A good strong wind'll blow us all away now. I bet half of Main Street will be boarded up within a year."

Sully shrugged, zipped up, flushed. He usually felt at ease talking to Jocko, but this was a strange conversation. Jocko's very presence in the men's room felt not quite right in a way Sully couldn't exactly put his finger on. They'd peed side by side into these same urinals on other occasions. Maybe it was that Jocko wasn't peeing, he decided.

Since he had company, Sully washed his hands, then dried them on a paper towel.

"Should be plenty of work for you if you want it," Jocko offered mysteriously.

"How's that?"

"I know a guy right now who'd pay you a couple grand to torch his store."

Sully let this offer sink in a moment, studying his longtime acquaintance, who seemed less embarrassed by what he'd just proposed than by the fact that he couldn't seem to squeeze even a drop from his dick.

"Where'd this guy get the idea I'm in the arson business?" Sully finally said.

"Well," Jocko said, giving up the pretense and zipping himself back into his pants.

"No, really," Sully insisted.

Jocko shrugged, met Sully's eyes for a moment before looking away. "He must have heard it somewhere."

"Must've," Sully agreed. "I'm afraid I'm going to have to disappoint him."

"He'll get over it," Jocko said quietly. "He'll be sorry he misjudged you, probably."

"Let's find a new place to drink," Sully said, sliding onto the stool next to Wirf, who was chatting pleasantly with Tiny at the end of the bar. There was a full bottle of beer in front of the stool where Jocko had been sitting. Wirf, Sully noticed, had switched from club soda to beer.

"What's wrong with this one?" Wirf said. Tiny had stiffened when Sully approached. In fact, he was glowering at Sully and not bothering to conceal the fact that personally he liked his bar better when Sully wasn't in it.

Sully, still unsettled by his conversation with Jocko, studied Tiny before responding. "Nothing," he said finally. "This place is perfect. It's so friendly, is what I like best."

"How about one of these?" Wirf said, tinking his beer bottle, their regular brand, with his glass.

"Are they good?"

"I like them."

"Will they make this day end peacefully?"

"Let's find out."

"Let's."

Tiny went to the other end of the bar where the cooler was and returned with a beer. "You want a glass, Sully?"

"Am I entitled to one?"

Tiny gave him a glass. Also a piece of mail. Sully said thanks and swallowed a second of Jocko's pills, chasing it with a swig of beer from the bottle. The second pill was probably not a good idea, but he figured he was close to home. The mail bore the logo of Schuyler Springs Community College. The address Sully had given at registration had been care of the White Horse Tavern, just to piss Tiny off. The envelope contained his grades for the fall semester. F's except in philosophy, for which his young professor had awarded him an incomplete. "Good news," Sully said, wadding up the letter and tossing it in the direction of the garbage bucket Tiny kept behind the bar. "I made the dean's list."

Wirf was still eyeing the unused glass, anxious as always to head off hostilities. "You hear Tiny's hired a band for tomorrow night?"

"What's the occasion?"

"New Year's Eve," Tiny said, coming back over to pick up the wad of paper from the floor. "Some people like to go out and celebrate that night."

In truth, Sully had lost track of what day it was. "Will I need reservations?"

"A free buffet, too," Wirf interrupted. "For all the regular customers."

"Seventy-five pounds of chicken wings I ordered," Tiny grumbled proudly.

"Those fucking things," Sully said. "The whole town will be shitting razor blades sideways for a week."

"Then don't eat them," Tiny said, instantly angry, as Sully had hoped. "Who cares what you want, Sully?"

"Nobody," Sully admitted. "For twenty years I've wanted somebody to open another bar on Main Street and put your ugly ass out of business."

"*Twenty* years?" Tiny said. "Try forty. Forty years I been right here. There were four bars right on Main Street back when your old man was around being the same kind of asshole you are now. Now I'm the only one left."

"The only asshole?" Sully said.

"The only bar."

"Survival of the dumbest," Sully offered, by way of explanation.

"Twenty minutes to closing," Tiny said, heading off down the bar toward the bar stool he kept on his side.

"There," Sully grinned at Wirf. "Thank God he's gone."

Going through his pockets, he put all the money he was carrying on the bar in front of them and started to make sense of the random denominations. It made an impressive sight, though Sully knew it wasn't nearly enough to square his debts. When the money was arranged, he counted out five hundred dollars and slid the money in front of Wirf.

Wirf studied it. "You sure?" he said. "I know you've got other problems."

"Take it," Tiny advised from down the bar. "When's he going to have that kind of money again?"

"I wish somebody would offer me a hundred to shoot you in the head," Sully returned. "In fact, I'd do it for free if I thought it would kill you."

"You hear the weather forecast for tomorrow?" Wirf said.

Sully admitted he hadn't.

"Supposed to snow like hell."

Sully sighed, ran his fingers through his hair.

"Hell, I thought that would cheer you up. You've been pissing and moaning about no snow for a month."

This was true, and yet Sully couldn't help thinking of all the other things he had to do tomorrow. Going out to Harold's and getting the plow rigged onto his pickup was one more thing. On the other hand, he was going to have to go see Harold tomorrow anyway and give him some of the money he was carrying around before it leaked away.

"He was in here earlier," Wirf said at the mention of Harold's name.

"He must have heard about my triple," Sully surmised. He'd never seen Harold at The Horse or any other bar.

Wirf shook his head. "He sat right where you're sitting, drank a Jack Daniel's."

"Next you'll be telling me his wife was with him drinking Singapore Slings."

"You know that kid Dwayne they hired? Red hair? Always picking his nose?"

Sully said he knew Dwayne.

"He emptied the cash register on them and took off," Wirf said.

"Harold was supposed to be out looking for him, but he didn't have the heart."

"This is about the fifth time it's happened," Sully observed.

Wirf nodded. "Have you ever noticed how people do the same things over and over?"

"You don't mean us?"

"No. I was referring to other people," Wirf explained. "Hell, we're full of surprises."

In fact, the conclusion Sully'd come to today was that just about everybody was full of surprises. A month ago he'd have agreed with Wirf that both people and events were predictable to the point of boredom. But since getting out of jail this morning, Sully had been pursued by the strange sensation that everything had changed, that the rules of existence had been subverted somehow while he was away. Even the fact that his luck had changed contributed to this somewhat otherworldly feeling, as if he'd returned to a place he no longer knew. It looked the same, but it felt deep down different. How else to explain the fact that he'd gotten lost going to Bootsie and Rub's flat? How else to explain the strange conversation he'd just had with Jocko, who'd not even returned to the bar but rather slunk out the door? Exhausted as he was, the only reason he'd come into The Horse at all was in the hopes of ending the day with some degree of normalcy, some zigging with Wirf and quarreling with Tiny to restore his equilibrium, dispel the sense of disorientation that had him reeling.

And now here was Wirf, for all his bleary-eyed normality, the most predictable of humans, studying him with an odd seriousness, Sully's five hundred dollars still sitting in front of him. Wirf looked for all the world like a man about to zag in the face of a man who'd joined him in the hopes of zigging.

"What?" Sully said finally. "You're not going to start in on me, are you?"

"No," Wirf promised. "But I am going to ask you a favor."

"Okay," Sully said. "As long as you don't want me to do it tonight."

Wirf consulted his watch. "It probably won't be tonight," he said seriously. "But whenever it is, I want you to do it."

"Ask, then," Sully said. "How can I do it or not do it if you won't tell me what it is?"

"I just want you to know I'm serious," Wirf went on. "I know you think I wouldn't say shit if I had a mouthful, and that's true most of the time, but right now I want you to promise me this, and if you don't, we're through."

Sully studied his friend warily. "I'm not quitting work," he said. "And I'm not going back to college, not even for you. My son's going to start teaching out there next term, and with my luck they'll make me take his course."

Wirf grinned broadly at the idea. "That's not the favor. The favor is your landlady."

Sully was enormously relieved to hear it. After all the buildup, maybe this would be easy after all. "Anything I can do for Beryl, I'll do. I'll be more than happy to, in fact."

Wirf was looking at him with the same almost cross-eyed seriousness. "She feels the same way about you. Which is why she did something for you, with my help."

"What?" Sully said, though he had an idea.

"You own the house on Bowdon again," Wirf said.

"She paid the back taxes?"

"Just over ten grand."

"And you let her."

"I encouraged her," Wirf said emphatically.

"Knowing I wanted no fucking part of the place, knowing that it wasn't worth selling for scrap, you let her."

"It's worth twenty thousand at least, maybe more," Wirf said.

"You're full of shit."

Wirf shook his head. "I already have an offer of twenty from the people who own the Sans Souci. They'll go higher, too."

"Why?"

"To avoid litigation. That dirt road they carved runs right across the corner of your property. I checked. And they don't have an easement. We could sue their asses. They might give twice what they've offered so far. Three times." He stopped, let Sully digest this. "At the very least, at twenty thousand, you could pay her back, square away your truck, start new."

Sully thought about it. Starting new was an attractive concept. Why didn't he believe in it? Big Jim Sullivan again, no doubt. This would be his father's money, a windfall from the one direction he couldn't accept it.

"That's the favor," Wirf said. "When she tells you, be grateful. Thanks to that son of hers, she's going to have a rough time for a while. Make her feel good."

"It's not that—" Sully started to explain.

"I don't give a shit what it is, Sully," Wirf said. "You're going to do this, or we're through."

Neither man said anything for a moment. Sully could feel Jocko's second pill kicking in, could feel himself going fuzzy about the edges. There was no place on the planet where he felt more comfortable than The Horse, than this particular stool, next to this particular man, and yet how strange it all seemed right then. The Christmas lights strung along the back wall, half of them flickering or dead out, Tiny seated on his invisible stool at the other end of the bar, magically supported on a cushion of air, even Wirf glaring at him so seriously. Even The Horse had taken on the quality of strangeness, and he felt the same panic that had come over him half an hour earlier when he'd gotten lost on a street he knew. He heard himself say okay, but it was almost another person speaking, someone far away. Then, just as suddenly, he was back again.

"Good," Wirf said, apparently satisfied. "Now tell me. What'd Barton want with you this morning?"

Sully snorted. "He wanted to know about the day my old man spiked that kid on the fence."

Wirf nodded thoughtfully. "He must be preparing to die," he said finally, as if he knew. "Tying up loose ends. What'd you tell him?"

"Nothing," Sully said. "That it was an accident."

Wirf nodded.

"Which was a lie. He shook the fence until the kid lost his grip and fell."

"You saw him?"

"My brother did," Sully grinned. "All I saw was the kid hanging there by his jaw with the spike sticking out his mouth."

Wirf took off his glasses and rubbed his eyes. "It's a wonder we aren't all insane," he said.

"We are," Sully said, getting up from his stool. His conviction surprised him. "I believe that."

Sully glanced at the clock above the bar. In less than five hours he was going to have to meet Rub at the house on Bowdon. Which reminded him. "I'm going to feed my dog and then go home."

"When did you get a dog?"

"I don't know," Sully said. "But I'm told I have one. By the way, did you know about my son and Carl's wife?"

"Sure," Wirf said.

"How come you never said anything?"

"Because I'm the only one in this town who doesn't repeat gossip. Actually, I was surprised. I'd been hearing she had a girlfriend in Schuyler."

"I guess I'm the last to know about that too," he said. "You think Carl is going to be okay?" Sully wondered, not even sure exactly what he meant by the question.

"No, I don't," Wirf said.

"He's parked out front of Peter's right now," Sully said. "Toby's up there with him."

"That girl with the tits still with Carl?"

Sully said she was.

"As long as she's with him, he'll be okay," Wirf said.

"That was my thought, too," Sully told him. "I just don't want to be wrong."

"It's none of your business anyhow," Wirf said.

Words to live by, Sully had to admit. But he kept hearing Peter's mockery. Not really his dog. Not really his house. Not really his business. And there were other not reallys as well. There was Vera, who was not really his wife anymore, gone round the bend today. And Ruth, who had broken things off with him, for good this time, he knew, and was not really his lover anymore. And there was Big Jim Sullivan, who was long dead, deader than a doornail, deader than a mackerel, deader than Kelsey's nuts, dead as dead could be. Except, somehow, not really. It was Big Jim Sullivan, full of rage and pain and fear, who had lashed out at Carl Roebuck earlier in the afternoon before Sully could control him, just as it had been Big Jim who'd wiped the smirk off Officer Raymer's face.

At the door, as Sully struggled into his heavy coat, he became aware that something stank, and this time it wasn't either a clam or the proximity of the men's room. What it smelled like was destiny.

One-thirty A.M., New Year's Eve morning.

On Silver Street, Ralph stood before the toilet, awaiting his urine. He didn't really have to go. He just didn't want to retire without checking, as if what he feared would use the night and his negligence to do its work if he wasn't vigilant. And the events of the day were still very much with him. Ralph was not a jealous man, but he couldn't forget the way his wife had fallen into Sully's arms today, whispering intimate expressions of profound contempt, promising to hate Sully always. How natural they had looked in their embrace, how well fitted to each other. It had made Ralph feel like an interloper in his own marriage. It made him weak in the knees, and he'd had to go out on the porch for air.

When Ralph's urine finally came, hot and painfully slow, Ralph studied both the stream and the darkening pool in the commode for the blood he still feared, despite the oncologist's assurances. But there was none.

With Vera in the hospital overnight and Peter over at his new flat, Ralph had full responsibility for his grandson, and so, when he left the bathroom, he checked on Will one more time. He liked to think of the boy as his grandson, even though he knew he really wasn't. One of the things that had come home to him today was that he'd have to share this boy with his real grandfather. It wouldn't be like Peter, whom Sully hadn't been interested in. No, Ralph had seen the love in Sully's eyes when the boy climbed onto his lap at the White Horse Tavern. But Ralph also knew that Sully would share, that he wouldn't be greedy. And of course Ralph also continued to believe that people could get along.

The boy was sleeping, peacefully for a change, the stopwatch Sully had given him ticking reassuringly a few inches away on the bed stand. Ralph had more than once heard the boy whimper fearfully in his sleep, but Will's respiration was rhythmic now, unlabored. Ralph could smell his grandson's sweet breath in the air above the bed, and he felt his throat constrict with only love. All evening, since returning home from the bar downtown, Will had talked of nothing but the leg, and Ralph knew that touching it, bringing the limb to the crippled lawyer, was the bravest thing his grandson had ever done and that the boy was full of pride. In the awful white flesh of Mr. Wirfly's stump, Will had found—what?—comfort. How could this be? Ralph wondered.

In his own room, the room he had shared with Vera for so many years, Ralph undressed unself-consciously for once and resisted the impulse to check himself one last time before turning in. Vera had always been, and was now, a difficult woman, but he couldn't imagine life without her, couldn't imagine the big bed to himself, couldn't imagine Sully's life, his having chosen it. Ralph made up his mind to go to the hospital first thing in the morning and bring his wife back to their home. He would try even harder to make her happy. She was not a bad woman.

Sully pointed the El Camino up Main toward Bowdon and the house where he'd spent so many long nights as a child, waiting for his father, part-time caretaker and full-time barroom brawler, to come home with a snootful, limping, face swollen, tossed forcefully from the society of tough men and left with no alternative but to return, still full of rage, to the bosom of his family, to a wife who didn't know enough to run, or perhaps did not know where, or even how; to an older son who was biding his time, dreaming of cars and motorcycles, anything with wheels that would roll and roll and carry him away to freedom; to a younger son who was not old enough yet to dream of escape but old enough to make a solemn oath, and who made that oath and reaffirmed it every night, a single binding oath forged in the depths of that boy's blood: never forgive.

This was the oath Sully had faithfully kept, and when he parked the El Camino at the curb and limped up the walk toward what could be only, in this too quiet night, an ambush, he felt the oath strengthen under the influence of beer and pain and painkillers and fear, and though he understood it was probably unwise to be so faithful to any oath, yet as always he was unwilling to indulge regret. According to Ruth, it was wrong of him not to forgive, but in truth the only time he'd even been tempted was at his brother's funeral. There, in church, his parents had both surprised him. His mother, dry-eyed and dressed in somber black, had borne a look closer to triumph than to grief. This is *his* doing, she seemed to be saying of the big man who stood, hunched over the wooden pew, sobbing next to her.

Big Jim had worn an ill-fitting suit of mismatched plaid so outrageously inappropriate for a funeral that Sully, himself dressed in his brother's old sport coat, a dark color at least, had noticed and felt terrible shame on top of his sorrow. Still, his father's wracking sobs in the front pew of the church seemed so genuine that Sully had wavered in his oath until he remembered the way his father had behaved at the funeral home, the way he'd greeted each visitor to his son's casket in a voice clear and rich with whiskey, "Come look what they've done to my boy," as if he himself were the victim of this accident, as if Patrick were just a prop, a visible proof of Big Jim's loss. It was the same way he'd behaved the day he impaled the boy on the fence. Before the boy even could be taken down, Big Jim had convinced the crowd to feel sorry for himself. And self, in the end, was the source of Big Jim's sorrow at the loss of his eldest son, Sully realized. For months, maybe years, Sully had watched his brother's transformation, watched Patrick become more and more like his father—more cruel, more careless, more angry, more of a bully. Though only seventeen, he was often drunk, and he'd been drunk when he hit the other driver head on. Big Jim was, in a sense, mourning his own death, and Sully decided not to, not then when Patrick died, not many years later when Big Jim himself finally died peacefully in his untroubled sleep.

Halfway up the walk, Sully paused, stared at the house of his child-hood, listening in the stillness to what sounded like freeway traffic, though it could not be. The interstate was miles away, and Sully couldn't remember ever hearing the sound of it, even on the stillest nights. For the umpteenth time today Sully felt disoriented, as if the geography of his life were suddenly subject to new rules, as if his young philosophy professor had gone right on disproving things during the long weeks since Sully dropped out of school and as if now, as things disappeared, the spaces between them were shrinking. Somebody had apparently disproved The Ultimate Escape, and maybe the huge tract of marshland the park was to sit on had disap-peared along with Carl Roebuck's housing development. Perhaps the disappearance of all these things had drawn the once distant interstate closer, everything shrinking to fill up the void occasioned by rampant philosophy. That would explain the traffic sounds, which grew louder as Sully halted on the top step, listening to them.

To Ruth's way of thinking, Sully's unwillingness to forgive was the source of his own stubborn failures, and in the past she'd been capable of being very persuasive on this subject, would in fact have persuaded just about anyone but Sully. Her failure to convince him was probably the best single explanation for why things never worked out between them. She made it clear that he could not have them both—herself and his stubborn, fixed determination. For a while he'd allowed her to undermine it in subtle ways. Once they'd even visited Big Jim in his nursing home. But Sully could only surrender so much, and he understood that if he and Ruth married, she'd eventually have him visiting Big Jim's grave with fresh flowers. She'd go with him and make sure he left them. And where was the justice in that? It would mean that in the end Big Jim had fooled them all and beat the rap, walked out of court on some flimsy Christian loophole called forgive-ness. No. Fuck him. Eternally.

"Fuck you," Sully said out loud at the front door to the house on Bowdon Street, pushing it open angrily as the second of Jocko's screaming yellow zonkers finally ripped wide open the portal to the past, setting his brain, his heart, his soul churning. "Fuck you, old man," the words he'd wanted to say as a boy, words that sounded fine, even now, in the empty house.

Big Jim Sullivan, at the base of the stairs and about to head up with fists clenched, turned drunkenly to face Sully in the doorway, nothing but darkness between them. His face was bloody and unnatural, its skin pulled tightly in conflicting directions by the clumsy stitches of old wounds. His nose, broken half a dozen times in brawls, was no longer plumb, his respiration audible. He grinned at his son across what separated them, the same grin Sully remembered from the day he missed the next rung of the ladder and fell off. That day, a tall chain-link fence had separated them. Now, nothing.

"It's about time you decided to stand up and testify," Big Jim said.

"I'm right here, old man," Sully assured him, feeling solid for the first time in days. If this was destiny, so be it. "Let's go a few rounds, you and me. We'll see who quits first."

His father's grin broadened. "Come take your medicine," he said.

Still sensing ambush, Sully let the door swing shut behind him so there could be no retreat. Unless his father had made friends in Hell, it was just the two of them.

At two o'clock Miss Beryl was awakened by what sounded like someone dragging a heavy chain across some distant floor. "We wear the chains we forge in life," she thought, half expecting Clive Jr., gotten up as a ghost in Dickensian garb, to appear at her bedroom door. She wondered if what all this meant was that she was about to have another gusher. She sat up in bed and swung her feet over the side in search of her slippers. Before standing up, she wiggled her toes and flexed her fingers questioningly. In the past her spells had been preceded by a tingling at the extremities, though she felt no such sensation now. Nor, when she stood, did she feel woozy or distant.

Maybe it was just that the long day—so lacking in pity—was still not finished with her. She found her robe and made her way into the kitchen, where she turned on the bright overhead, confident that if there was a chain-rattling ghost on the premises, it wouldn't possess the temerity to pursue her into this cheerful, bright, hundred-watt realm. Tea, at this hour, was probably not a good idea, but she put the kettle on anyway and stood watching it, half expecting the phone in the next room to ring.

It had been ringing when she returned from Schuyler Springs, and she took several calls before unplugging the phone. There'd been two more from reporters, who were now referring to Clive Jr.'s unavailability for comment as his disappearance. There had also been another call from the woman at the savings and loan, who sounded suspicious when Miss Beryl insisted that, no, Clive Jr. had not contacted her, had not left her any instructions, no hint of a destination or intentions.

In her mailbox when she returned from Schuyler Springs there'd been the manila envelope she'd given to Abraham Wirfly the day before. Its contents, for which she should have been relieved and grateful, had done little to cheer her up. Inside, she found a handwritten note: "Unable to reach you, I've taken the rather large liberty of rescuing the enclosed from the county clerk's office, where it had not been fully processed. We can, of course, refile any time you wish, but given recent events I must strongly advise you against transferring any property to your son at this time. The second matter we discussed has been dealt with as per your instructions."

This, then, was what had come of her poor compromise, her attempt to do right, to separate the conflicting dictates of head and heart, to assuage conscience, which was, as Mark Twain had shrewdly observed, "no better than an old yeller dog." For fairness and loyalty, however important to the head, were issues that could seldom be squared in the human heart, at the deepest depths of which lay the mystery of affection, of love, which you either felt or you didn't, pure as instinct, which seized you, not the other way around, making a mockery of words like "should" and "ought." The human heart, where compromise could not be struck, not ever. Where transgressions exacted a terrible price. Where tangled black limbs fell. Where the boom got lowered.

When Miss Beryl again heard the sound of a distant chain being dragged across a floor, she went to investigate, turning on lights as she moved from one room to the next. She traced the sound to the hallway she shared with Sully, and she contemplated the wisdom of opening her door to see what manner of thing was on the other side. Still, God hates a coward, she thought, and opened the door a crack.

The hall light was on, and there, just outside her door by the stairway that led up to Sully's flat, stood a Doberman with a lopsided grin. One end of the chain she'd been hearing was attached to the dog's rhinestone collar. The other end was attached to nothing at all. As far as she could tell, the dog was the only occupant of the hallway, though she was unwilling to open the door any wider to be sure. "Who are you?" she asked the Doberman, which started at the sound of her voice, suffered some kind of spasm and slumped against the banister as if shot. Before Miss Beryl could process this, the outside door opened and Sully materialized, screwdriver in hand.

"I tightened that railing back down for you," he told Miss Beryl when she opened the door to survey the strange scene in full. Sully seemed not to be surprised by the fact that there was a Doberman slumped against the stairs, which might or might not have meant that the dog was with him.

Neither did Sully seem surprised that his landlady was awake at two in the morning.

In fact, her tenant looked to Miss Beryl like a man for whom there were no more surprises. He was paler and thinner and more ghostlike than ever, though not exactly Dickensian. "You mind if I come in and take my boots off, Mrs. Peoples?"

"Of course not, Donald," she said, stepping back from the door.

At this the dog let out a huge sigh and slumped all the way to the floor. Both Sully and Miss Beryl studied the animal. Sully shook his head. "What's your policy on pets?"

"Does he bark?" Miss Beryl wondered.

"He did a few minutes ago," Sully told her, his voice, for some reason, shaky. "Just in time, too. I was about to step into thin air."

Miss Beryl waited for him to elaborate, but he didn't. So pale and thin, Sully looked like air might well be his natural element.

"I can only stay a minute," he told her, collapsing into the newly repaired Queen Anne, which protested audibly but held together. Mr. Blue had been right. It was fixed.

"I'm making tea," she said. "Can I interest you in a cup?"

"No, you can't," he said, grinning at her now. "How many times do I have to tell you?"

"Other people change their minds occasionally," she told him. "I keep thinking you might."

Sully lit a cigarette and seemed to consider this. "You do?"

His question seemed less mocking than wistful, as if he was grateful for her refusal to accept his bullheadedness at face value. Outside in the hall the dog's chain rattled.

Sully glanced around her flat as if for the first time, taking things in. "I guess it's just you and me, old girl," Sully said, no doubt in reference to Clive Jr.

At this, Miss Beryl herself sat down. "I've been discussing Clive Jr. with his father all afternoon," she admitted. "We failed him, I guess. It pains me to admit, but somehow we managed to raise a son with no . . ." She let her sentence die, unable to locate a word for what her son lacked, at least a word that would not represent a further betrayal.

"Well," Sully said. "At least you raised him. You did your best."

"He was never the star of my firmament, somehow," Miss Beryl confessed, sharing this sad truth for the first time with another living human. It was what Clive Sr. had accused her of one afternoon not long before Audrey Peach had sent him through the windshield. By then Sully had gone off to join the war, and Miss Beryl had already resigned herself to the certainty that he'd be killed. She was so sure he would be that she'd already begun to apportion blame. Most of it, of course, rested squarely on the shoulders of the brutal, stupid man who was the boy's father and part of what was left on Sully's mother, who'd found such grateful solace in her own victimization. But there was some blame left over, and Miss Beryl had located what remained in her own home. She wasn't supposed to know that her husband and son had gone over to Bowdon Street to put an end to Sully's tenure at their dinner table, to expel him from their family, but she did know it. She also knew that her husband and son had done this out of jealousy and fear.

What a terrible thing it had been for her to realize—that part of her husband's devotion to her was predicated on the understanding that no one else shared this devotion, that his love was a gift contingent upon her receiving no other gifts. This was what Miss Beryl had still been trying to forgive him for when Audrey Peach stole from her the opportunity to explain why forgiveness was necessary.

In their worst argument—the one Miss Beryl, during the long years of her widowhood, refused to remember and yet could not forget—Clive Sr. had accused her of being unnatural, of inviting "strangeness" into their home. This was apparently as close as Clive Sr. could get to articulating what was troubling him. He'd stood in the middle of their living room and offered the room itself as evidence. African masks and Etruscan spirit boats and two-headed Foo dogs everywhere. "It's like living in a jungle," he complained so seriously that Miss Beryl did not smile, as was her habit when her husband became serious. What it all meant, she realized, was that he was unhappy with her, that he regretted his choice, that he blamed her for the son who could neither dribble a ball nor defend himself, and that in addition to all this he also blamed her for not loving this boy more, for instead being so fond of another boy who could have no legitimate claim to their affections, for welcoming the world's strangeness into their home to subvert them all. She could still see the look on his face, and Miss Beryl realized that it was this expression—this stubborn, injured disapproval that she'd witnessed in her husband only on this single occasion—that Clive Jr. had grown into, that made it so difficult for her to feel for him what she knew she ought to feel for a son. It was as if Clive Jr. had been sent to remind her of the terrible moment of his father's unspoken regret at having loved her. "I don't think you know what love means," Clive Sr. had told her petulantly, as if to suggest that his affection for her was unrequited. Which, until that moment, it had not been.

But part of what he had said was true—she *didn't* understand love. This was what Miss Beryl had been coming back to, all day, all her life probably, to the mystery of affection, of the heart inclining in one direction and not another, of its unexpected, unwished-for pirouettes, its ability to make a fool, a villain, of its owner, if indeed any human can be said to own his heart. "I know this," she'd told Clive Sr. that long-ago afternoon. "Love is a stupid thing."

It was, then and now, her final wisdom on the subject. No doubt, in his own way Clive Sr. already knew this to be true, had realized it when he found himself to be in love with her, a thing nobody would ever be able to understand.

If Sully was horrified by her admission that Clive Jr. was not the star of Miss Beryl's firmament, he gave no sign. With one hand he was holding his cigarette vertically now, its ash having lengthened dangerously, while he leaned forward to untie the laces of his work boots with the other. This effort seemed to sap his last ounce of strength.

Miss Beryl's tea kettle began to sing in the kitchen. When she stood, Sully said, "I heard a rumor you did a good deed."

Miss Beryl understood that this must be a reference to the house on Bowdon, understood too that it was the subject that would not wait until morning. He was looking at her now with an expression she'd never witnessed in him before, the expression of a man much harder and more dangerous than she had believed Sully to be.

"You stuck your nose where it didn't belong," he said.

"I know it," Miss Beryl conceded. "I'm an old woman, though. I'm entitled."

He didn't reply for a long moment, the hardness remaining in his black eyes until his more familiar sheepish grin released it. "Anyhow," he said. "I forgive you."

"Thank you, Donald," she told him, and then neither of them spoke for some time, the urgent whistle of the tea kettle the only sound in the flat. "You're certain you wouldn't like a cup of tea?"

Again he didn't answer, though she couldn't tell whether it was because she already had her answer or because he'd been overtaken finally by exhaustion or because it had occurred to him that he had no idea what he wanted.

When she returned with her own cup of tea, he was asleep, his head back, mouth open, snoring. It was a thunderous sound, the first time she'd heard it so close, without the ceiling between them. He'd fallen asleep in the act of removing one boot with the toe of the other.

Miss Beryl located the ashtray she kept for Sully in the end table and put it under his cigarette just as the tall ash toppled. When she removed the cigarette itself from between his stained thumb and forefinger, she noticed that Sully slept with his eyes open, the knowledge of which caused her to smile. Old houses surrendered a great many secrets, and in the twenty-some years she'd listened to Sully living above her, she'd concluded that she knew just about everything there was to know about her tenant. But here was a new thing.

Outside in the cold hall, the dog's chain rattled again, and when Miss Beryl opened the door, the Doberman scrambled with great, spastic effort to its feet, circling itself in the process several times, stepping on its own chain, until it finally located its fragile equilibrium. Then it stood looking at her expectantly, as if to suggest the hope that it hadn't gone to so much trouble for nothing.

"You might as well come in too," she told the animal.

The dog apparently understood, because it loped past her, collapsing again with another massive sigh at the foot of the Queen Anne, its nub of a tail twitching in what—who could know?—just might be contentment.

BOOKS BY RICHARD RUSSO

MOHAWK

Mohawk, New York, is one of those small towns that lie almost entirely on the wrong side of the tracks. Dallas Younger, a star athlete in high school, now drifts from tavern to poker game, while his ex-wife, Anne, is stuck in a losing battle with her mother over the care of her sick father. Out of derailed ambitions and old loves, secret hatreds and communal myths, Russo creates a novel that captures every nuance of America's backyard.

Fiction/Literature/0-679-75382-6

NOBODY'S FOOL

This slyly funny novel follows the unexpected operation of grace in a deadbeat town in upstate New York—and in the life of one of its unluckiest citizens, Sully. Divorced from his own wife and carrying on halfheartedly with another man's and saddled with a bum knee, Sully now has one new problem to cope with: an estranged son in danger of following in his father's footsteps.

Fiction/0-679-75333-8

THE RISK POOL

Ned Hall is doing his best to grow up, even though neither of his estranged parents can properly be called adult. As Ned veers between allegiances, his father, Sam, cultivates bad habits, and his mother, Jenny, is slowly going crazy from resentment at a husband who refuses to either stay or go away.

Fiction/Literature/0-679-75383-4

STRAIGHT MAN

Russo's "straight man" is William Henry Devereaux, Jr., a once-promising novelist who, as he approaches fifty, finds himself the reluctant chairman of the English department of a badly underfunded college. In one week, Devereaux will have his nose mangled by an angry colleague, suspect his wife of betraying him with the dean, and deal with the ominous failure of certain bodily functions.

Fiction/Literature/0-375-70190-7

VINTAGE CONTEMPORARIES
Available at your local bookstore, or call toll-free to order:
1-800-793-2665 (credit cards only).